# THE
# CARDINAL'S
# NIECE

# THE
# CARDINAL'S
# NIECE

## AN EROTIC OBSESSION

PHILIP RAWORTH

# THE CARDINAL'S NIECE
## AN EROTIC OBSESSION

iUniverse books may be ordered through booksellers or by contacting:

iUniverse
1663 Liberty Drive
Bloomington, IN 47403
www.iuniverse.com
844-349-9409

ISBN: 978-1-6632-4066-8 (sc)
ISBN: 978-1-6632-4067-5 (e)

Library of Congress Control Number: 2022910355

Print information available on the last page.

iUniverse rev. date: 07/12/2022

For my late wife, Marie-Gabrielle, whose beauty
and sensuality inspired this novel

# PROLOGUE

T HE FALL OF 1959 was beautiful in Vienna, and the two young men were in a merry mood. The Augustinerkeller was known for its excellent grilled chicken, and the beer that had accompanied--and followed--it contributed to their good spirits. They were both students at the University of Vienna. The taller of the two, Count Giovanni Palmieri, was a handsome Italian with fine features and dark, sleek black hair that betrayed his Neapolitan and Spanish ancestry. His close friend, Philip Markham, whose rugged features and shock of unruly hair had captivated more than one lady in the city of music, was from England. He was the grandson of the Marquis of Derwent, whose title he would one day inherit.

In addition to their aristocratic birth and rather tepid Catholicism, the two friends had one other thing in common. Both were in love with women below their class whom their parents disapproved of. In Philip's case, it was a pretty, blond English girl called Jane, whom he'd met in his final year at Cambridge University. He corresponded with her daily and refused to be drawn into any adventures in Vienna despite many opportunities.

These opportunities were less now that Giovanni had renounced his unending pursuit of female conquests after meeting Luisa. She was German and worked for Lufthansa at Schwechet airport in Vienna. She was fair, very pretty, and had a wonderful disposition. She was no great intellect and had a limited taste for the cultural delights of the Austrian capital, but she had ignited a passion in Giovanni. His eyes glistened when he talked of her candid smile, the softness of her long, blond hair, and her unsuccessful attempts to imitate the German of the Viennese. But, as he sadly confided to his friend, there was no way his father, a typically bigoted and class-conscious Palmieri, would ever consent to the marriage.

"I'll marry her anyway," Giovanni insisted, banging rather too hard on the table to the annoyance of a Viennese family nearby.

"Well, I intend to marry Jane too," Philip replied.

Giovanni looked hard at his friend. "You know, Philip, we've been friends now for two years, and we've had a lot of fun together. Why don't we swear an oath to marry a child from your family to one of mine? That way, we can unite the two families."

It was a quite irrational proposition; even in the late fifty's marriages were no longer arranged between parents. But the beer--or the schnaps that was following it--swept away any objection, and Philip agreed enthusiastically. He picked up a knife and pricked his finger. Giovanni did likewise, and the oath was sealed in blood. It occurred to neither of them in their euphoric state that there was something, if not blasphemous, at least profane about their proceeding.

Philip did indeed marry Jane, and they had four children: two girls, Louise and Marie, and two sons, Charles and James. Of the four it was James who most resembled his father. He had the same unruly locks and the same nonchalant good looks. He had his father's charm, but he was more serious and could be very stubborn and unwilling to compromise. He was generally of good humor like his father but prone to occasional outbursts of irritable anger. He'd also inherited his father's fluency in languages, speaking fluent French, Spanish and Italian. Philip had always thought that if any member of his family was to fulfill the oath sworn in Vienna, it would be James, but he was now married, albeit, it seemed to his father, unhappily.

Giovanni did not marry Luisa. On November 1, 1961 he and Luisa went off on a motorcycle trip in the hills around Florence. They stopped for lunch at a little restaurant, where Giovanni drank too much. He was driving his motorcycle very fast, with Luisa perched on the back, when he collided with a car that had failed to respect a stop sign. Luisa was killed on the spot, and Giovanni was taken with severe injuries to the Careggi hospital in Florence. As he lay there for months grieving over his loss, he was beset by remorse for the irresponsible conduct that had caused Luisa's death. This was Giovanni's Garden of Gethsemane, but out of this mental agony/came a spiritual awakening. A priest visited him almost every day, and their discussions helped Giovanni regain his serenity. With Luisa dead, his former life held no attraction for him, and gradually the resolution to become a priest took shape within his mind. In July 1963 he entered the Athenaeum Pontificium Regina Apostolorum in Rome to study for the priesthood and renounced his title. Thanks to his aristocratic connections and his own administrative skills, he rose swiftly in the Church hierarchy. Today he was the Cardinal Archbishop of Florence.

～✹～

Philip and Giovanni had their annual get-together a month before the events took place that are related in this novel. With regret the two friends had to acknowledge that their families would not be joined. Philip's children were all married, and Giovanni had none.

～✹～

The two friends failed to take into consideration that Giovanni was not the only Palmieri. He had a sister, Caterina, who was married to Count Paolo dell Chiesa of the black Roman nobility*. She too had four children. Her younger son, Giovanni, had made a suitable aristocratic marriage, but the elder son, Paolo, was, to his mother's horror, living with an American employee of the family bank, of which he'd just been made vice-president. There were also two daughters. The younger daughter, Carla, was an attractive girl, but she'd inherited the same angular features as her mother from her Spanish ancestry and had as well her mother's proud, aristocratic attitudes. The elder daughter was quite different. She was vivacious, volatile, passionate, and impatient with the social etiquette of the Italian nobility. She was a picture of sultry and dazzling beauty. Her finely chiseled features exuded sensuality. Her eyes were a deep black and would shimmer with passion or anger. She had high cheek bones, a pleasantly oval face and a rounded nose of perfect composition. Her mouth was exquisite, prettily seductive, her lips soft and enticing, her teeth a radiant whiteness. Her lustrous dark hair fell unfettered around her shoulders or was swept to one side across her full and shapely bosom. Her name was Antonietta, and she was the Cardinal's niece.

## Chapter 1

# Sunday June 24, 2001

A NTONIETTA WALKED, NAKED, TOWARDS the door of the bedroom. She could feel Giacomo's eyes following her and sensed his desire for her. Before, this would have been enough to send her back to bed, whatever her other plans for the day, but she'd been with Giacomo for eight months, and the relationship now palled on her. Soon, very soon, she would end it as she was leaving Italy to study in Canada. She apprehended this moment for she knew that Giacomo, whatever he might pretend, was deeply in love with her. Antonietta had never been in love with him, and now she no longer really desired him. It was a typical end to her relationships with men, and it disturbed her.

Antonietta stared at herself in the bathroom mirror. She saw Giacomo enter the bathroom and watched him place his hands on her breasts and fondle them. She felt him hard against her buttocks and let him take her. Gazing at herself in the mirror having sex, she became aroused as well. There was little emotion in her physical pleasure. When it was over, she coolly returned to the bedroom to dress.

She put on a bra that barely covered her nipples, as if offering up her perfectly rounded breasts like fruit to be enjoyed. Her minuscule string seemed to emphasize the lure of her sex and left her buttocks bare, as Giacomo could see when she turned to fetch her sweater and jeans. The sweater fitted tightly and exhibited the opulence of her bosom. The jeans showed off the rounded form of her firm buttocks.

"You're going to Mass, I suppose"? Giacomo hated Antonietta going to Mass.

"Yes, Giacomo. I'm a practicing Catholic, and I go to Mass. Whether you like it or not."

"I suppose that Fascist uncle of your's is doing the honors."

Antonietta didn't rise to the bait. She just shook her head. "You're an idiot, Giacomo.

You don't even know what Fascism is. My uncle's a Monarchist, not a Fascist."

"Same thing," Giacomo retorted.

"Oh really! I'm sure the Queen of England would be surprised to know she's a Fascist."

Giacomo was preparing his riposte, but Antonietta had no wish to continue the conversation. Ever since the left-wing coalition known as the *Ulivo* had lost the election in May to the *Casa delle Liberte*, a right-wing grouping, Giacomo was very bitter and never lost an opportunity to criticize the political views of Antonietta and her family. She made to leave. Seeing the mournful look on Giacomo's face, she returned to give him a kiss.

"See you this afternoon at the *Calcio*\* tournament," she said. "Don't be late." She smiled at him and left the apartment.

Giacomo watched her go. He knew the end of their relationship was near and was angry with himself for the grief this caused him. He'd told himself from the start that there was no possibility of a common future for the Communist son of a poor cobbler and a Catholic countess with predictably reactionary views. He would, however, miss her splendid body and effervescent sexuality.

Antonietta shut the door of the apartment building behind her. She walked along the Via del Ponte dell' Asse where Giacomo lived down to the Piazza San Jacopino and then along the Via Cimarosa until she came to the Via Benedetto Marcello. In the distance over the railway tracks rose the imposing Fortezza di Basso. It was a monumental complex that had been constructed in the sixteenth century to protect the city, but it had never been attacked. Many thought that its real purpose had been to protect the ruling Medici family against their own subjects. The fortress was now the main exhibition center in Florence, and a modem pavilion, which Antonietta detested, had been built in the center of the great square inside it.

Antonietta admired the Medici for their love of beauty and art. Moreover, it was with Medici money that the della Chiesa's had founded the family bank. Its initial purpose had been to fund aspiring artisans, but it had soon become enmeshed in the convoluted politics of Renaissance Italy and had lent money to Giovanni de' Medici to help him acquire the Papacy. Antonietta had a soft spot for Pope Leo X*. As an individual he was a rather endearing rogue and is perhaps best known to posterity for this remark to his brother, the Ruler of Florence: "God has given us the Papacy, let us enjoy it"! He was a disaster as Pope, precipitating the Reformation by his reckless use of indulgences to finance the rebuilding of St. Peter's and by his excommunication of Luther. However, the della Chiesa family had reason to be grateful to him, for it was Leo who had raised them to the dignity of counts in 1515.

As she crossed the Via Marcello to take the Via della Carra, Antonietta reflected on her love of Florence. It was grandiose but intimate at the same time, unlike Rome. Her journey also recalled her pride in being Italian. Both Cimarosa and Benedetto Marcello were famous baroque composers, at least in Antonietta's view.

It was a beautiful day, and she had a full schedule ahead of her. After Mass there would be lunch with her family and an afternoon with Giacomo watching their team from Santa Maria Novella play Santo Spirito in the final of the *Calcio* competition. Around six o'clock she would attend the reception at her uncle's palace, and in the evening she would meet friends to watch the traditional firework display from the Piazzale Michelangelo on the other side of the Arno.

Antonietta was not entirely happy. She was ashamed that she hadn't found the courage to end her relationship with Giacomo. It was easy to tell herself that she didn't want to spoil the day's festivities, or that she didn't want to hurt him. In truth, her inaction came from more selfish reasons. She no longer felt the strong physical attraction for Giacomo she'd experienced at the start of their relationship, but he still satisfied her sexual needs. More or less. This was important for Antonietta.

By now she'd reached the Piazzale di Porta al Prato and straight before her lay the Via Il Prato and then the Borgo Ognissanti, where she had her apartment between the Hotel Goldoni and the Piazza of the same name. The streets were beginning to fill up. As she passed a café, she noticed that it was full of men drinking coffee and talking. Antonietta felt a flash of indignation. What were these men doing there while their wives were toiling to prepare the festive dinner for the Feast of San Giovanni? "What a macho lot Italian men are," she thought.

As she neared her apartment, she made the firm resolution to break with Giacomo the following Wednesday. There was no point in ruining today's celebrations, and she was busy at the Crusca Academy* on Monday and Tuesday helping to put the finishing touches to the Academy's new multilingual dictionary. This would give her time to decide how to do it. What could she say to him? He no longer attracted her. She'd never loved him, and it was time to search for a more meaningful relationship? Or simply that she was going to study in Canada? She would probably settle on the last alternative. It would be up to Giacomo to draw whatever conclusions he wanted. If only he knew how much she wished it'd been different, but it never was. Each relationship would leave her with a yearning for the unattainable. It was hardly surprising that her favorite poet was Leopardi*, whose poems expressed so well her sense of desolation.

She reached her apartment and noticed two men, older but still attractive, in a Mercedes convertible staring at her, her voluptuous forms accentuated by the tight sweater and jeans. "Yes, I'm beautiful," she thought, "and I can have any man I want. But what's the use when it always ends like this"?

Once in her apartment she turned on the answering machine. There were several calls, including one from her mother. She would have to think of a story to justify her absence from the apartment that night. Her mother didn't approve of her sleeping around, particularly not with an anti-clerical, Communist labor lawyer like Giacomo. If he were a member of the black nobility, she might have gotten away with it. Antonietta had great difficulty with her mother's class consciousness and intransigent Catholicism, which were so very Spanish. She pitied her father, of whom she was very fond. He was totally unlike her mother.

4

She was proud of his achievements, which had nothing to do with his noble birth. A respected surgeon, he was now Professor of Surgery at the University of Florence and head of surgery at the Policlinico de Careggi, the largest in Tuscany.

She began to feel regret at agreeing to meet the family, but it was a family custom to attend High Mass together on the feast of San Giovanni. She would be glad to see her father, and he would make up for the others.

Although she didn't share her mother's attitudes, Antonietta had to admit that she was not entirely wrong in her criticisms of her daughter's lifestyle. Her life was aimless. There seemed to be no meaning to anything she did. She'd taken a joint degree in Italian and Economics at the University of Florence, but she didn't really know why. Luckily, it had enabled her to find a job at the prestigious Crusca Academy, where her knowledge of the English and Italian languages combined with her economics background was put to good use on the multilingual dictionary they were preparing. It was almost finished, but Antonietta had no desire to continue at the Academy. She'd be twenty-four in three week's time and had no idea what she wanted to do. That's why she'd followed a girlfriend's advice to try something different. The result was her decision to study for a master's degree in international relations at the National Institute of International Studies in Quebec. Perhaps this would help her to a diplomatic career. Ironically, the Duke of Messina, a family friend and Antonietta's godfather, had just been appointed Italian Ambassador to Canada. The stay in Quebec would also enable her to improve her French without having to go to France. Antonietta disliked the French. They looked down on Italians even though, as Antonietta fiercely contended, Italian wine and Italian cuisine, not to mention Italian music, were superior to anything the French could offer.

It was in her personal life that Antonietta most felt the lack of meaning. Only once had she thought herself to be in love, and she'd been betrayed. She'd met Mario, two years her senior, in November 1995 shortly after starting her studies at the university. It was her first sexual experience with a man, and although it was disappointing, she'd fallen in love with the dark, tall law student. The following April her friends had told her than Mario was boasting to all and sundry that he'd bedded a countess. Antonietta was revolted and immediately ended the relationship, resolving never to mix out of her class again. The result was her affair with Alessandro Ottoreschi, the eldest son of the Marquis Ottoreschi.

For nearly a year the young aristocrats roamed the nightclubs, roared around Tuscany in a Lamborghini, and made love amid bottles of champagne. Then, one rainy day in March 1997, Antonietta realized that Alessandro with his rich, aristocratic lifestyle didn't fulfill her. She was bored, and she left him. After that she'd flitted from man to man, searching only for physical satisfaction. Giacomo was the latest of these flings, but at the beginning he'd seemed to promise more. Antonietta had even tolerated his left-wing anti-clericalism, but now it and Giacomo both irritated her.

She felt herself between two worlds. She couldn't forget she belonged to the aristocracy, and she had seen nothing in the other strata of society to suggest, as Giacomo kept telling her, that they were in any way superior. There were individuals just as acquisitive, as snobbish, as crass in the "people" as among the nobility. Class, contrary to what Giacomo might like to believe, played little if any role in the determination of human nature. For Antonietta it was essentially a question of personality, of finding a man, from whatever world he came, who could satisfy the complex yearning within her. Up until now no man had been able to do so. Worse still, none had bestowed on her the same exquisite sexual pleasure that she'd experienced at school with Dana.

She undressed and stood, naked, looking at herself in the mirror. She imagined Dana caressing her breasts and licking and sucking her nipples. She remembered the violent pleasure that her intrusive fingers and tongue had procured for her in the most intimate parts of her body. With men sex was so prosaic. All they were really interested in was their own pleasure, which they quickly took after some perfunctory and often frustrating foreplay. But she wanted a man not a woman, a man who could fulfill her sexually and emotionally. Was there such a man?

Beset by these depressing thoughts, Antonietta finished dressing for Mass. She replaced the string and deeply cut bra with more decent lingerie and the tight jeans and T-shirt with an elegant blouse and skirt.. She wore a skirt rather than pants, which she felt were too masculine.

Antonietta didn't like women who wore pant suits. She wore a dress rather than pants, which she felt were too masculine. She didn't like women who wore pant suits.

⤰

Many thousands of kilometers away in Quebec, the Markham family was preparing to go to Mass at the church in the nearby town of Saint-Sauveur.

"Mommy, I'm hungry," said Peter, the Markham's eight-year-old son.

"So am I," his six-year-old sister chimed in.

Their mother was unmoved. "You can eat after Mass. You know we fast before taking communion."

The children sighed and looked to their father for support.

"I don't see the point, Veronica, of making Susanna fast. She's not even going to take communion."

"It's good for her to prepare herself for when she does take communion," was his wife's stern reply.

James let the matter drop. He found his wife's insistence on fasting before taking communion quite absurd as the Church no longer required it. It was just another of her religious excesses, which were becoming ever more frequent and tiresome since she'd become a Benedictine oblate* attached to the convent in England where her widowed mother was a nun. He went upstairs to shave and dress.

"James, hurry up, or we'll be late." There was plenty of time, but Veronica lived in constant fear of being late for Mass. "Anyone would think you went to hell if you missed a single minute of the Holy Office," James muttered to himself. Irritated, he decided to have a little revenge.

"Did I ever tell you the joke about Marie-Chantal and Gérard"? he asked.

Veronica frowned. "I hope it's not one Bill Leaman told you. If so, I don't want to hear it."

"No. I heard it years ago from my French grandmother." This was a lie, but it was the only way to get Veronica to listen to the joke. "It's French."

Veronica put on a long-suffering look, and James embarked on his joke.

"Marie-Chantal and Gérard are getting ready to go to Mass, like us, and he asks her to give him a little treat, or a *pipe* as the French call it. Marie-Chantal looks at him in horror and exclaims: 'But Gérard, you know I always fast before taking communion'."

Veronica was predictably outraged. "That's absolutely disgusting, James, and typically French."

James sighed. Veronica's taste for sex and for any but the most conventional practices had waned immediately she'd achieved her objective of marrying him. In a way it was understandable. After the premature death of her father from cancer in 1980 she'd been brought up by her deeply religious mother, who'd found solace for her widowhood in an ever-increasing devotion to the Catholic religion. She'd become a Benedictine oblate in 1987 and seven years later had entered a convent as a postulant. Since last year she was a nun under the name of Sister Benedicta. Veronica's spiritual development since their marriage in 1992 had been heavily influenced by that of her mother, and last February she'd confessed to him that the previous summer she too had become an oblate. Their sexual relations, which in any case were very occasional, had ceased from that time. If James had insisted, no doubt Veronica would have accommodated him, but the idea of making love to a reluctant woman was repugnant to him. He didn't hold Veronica's distaste for sex against her, but he resented the masquerade she'd played before their marriage. If he'd known her true attitude, he would never have married her. Now he was married and, as a Catholic, divorce was not an option. So he contented himself with extra-marital flings with willing South American girls on his frequent trips to the southern hemisphere in his capacity as Assistant Dean of International Relations.

The family set off and was soon ensconced in the church. It was a typical Quebec small-town church: large and imposing but almost empty. Religious practice in Quebec had declined dramatically since the Quiet Revolution\*. Paying scant attention to the liturgy, James reflected on his life. There was not really much substance left to his marriage. He and Veronica had grown apart and merely tolerated each other. He escaped whenever he could from the cloying religiosity of his home to the company of his three closest colleagues at the National Institute for International Studies: Bill Leaman, a brash American; Danny, a divorced Irish Catholic, who was Dean of Administration; and Piotr, a very serious Pole. James had been a professor at the Institute for the last nine years.

On the whole James was satisfied with his choice of career. Initially he'd intended to join the family bank, but after finishing his doctorate in European Union law at the European University in Florence, he'd decided to give academia a try. He enjoyed the freedom it gave him, and although he didn't particularly enjoy the teaching, he found legal research stimulating. He'd acquired an international reputation as an expert on the institutional law of the European Union.

His decision to come to Canada had been vigorously opposed by his mother, the Marchioness of Derwent. Although from a middle-class background, Lady Derwent had quickly adapted to an aristocratic lifestyle and become an inveterate snob. "You won't even be able to use your title in Canada," she'd told her son. "They'll just call you Mister Markham." This was irrelevant for James as the only time he used his title was to get into fully booked restaurants. Most restaurateurs in England couldn't resist having a lord at one of their tables. His father had approved his choice or at least had not raised any objections.

James's thoughts returned to the Institute. His rise there had been swift, and last year he'd been made a full professor as well as acting Head of the Law and International Relations Section (LIR). He was worried about the new Rector. Harold Winstone had come from DEFAIT* a year ago to take over from the colorful but erratic Guy Lafarge. In James's view, it was a bad appointment. Winstone had pursued a very undistinguished academic career at the Carleton School of International Relations, the Institute's Ontario rival, before joining DEFAIT in 1998. He was a far cry from Tom Buchanan, a gregarious American, who, as Rector a few years back, had turned a failing institution into a world-class school.

Apart from Danny, there were two other Deans. Tom Buchanan was now the Dean of International Relations. Ilse Bromhoeffer was the Dean in charge of Admissions and Student Affairs. She was a hard-working and meticulous fifty-year old spinster from Germany, whom

Bill had rather unkindly nicknamed "The She-Wolf". James had a good relationship with both.

James had had little to do with the Senior Dean-to-be, Roy Arbuthnot, a dour Presbyterian Scot from Glasgow, but they would cross swords the following Friday when James intended to oppose a full professorship for one of Arbuthnot's protégés, Len Flint. James distrusted Arbuthnot, or "HB" as he was popularly called. He was unscrupulous, manipulative, and he made no secret of his ambition to dominate the Institute. He had started his rise within the Institute under Guy Lafarge, whom he had persuaded to appoint him Head of the powerful Ethics Committee. This committee dealt with cases of sexual harassment and other unbecoming conduct on the part of the faculty. More serious, in James's view, was his influence over the new Rector, who had appointed him Senior Dean. This was a new position, which would take effect on July I. The Senior Dean was the Rector's deputy, and he was going to take over the responsibilities for external affairs from Danny Redfern and course development and evaluation from Ilse Bromhoeffer. Arbuthnot would also usurp the Dean of Administration's traditional position as senior Dean as well as his office. Danny was furious, and rumor had it that Ilse was none too happy either.

James did not regret that his appointment as acting Head of the Law and International Relations Section would soon be over. Apart from the time it involved, dealing with Harold Winstone had been difficult. He had a deliberately loosy-goosy style of management that left you wondering what he really wanted and allowed him to back out of any commitments you thought he'd made. James suspected that this untrustworthy and devious façade hid a lack of confidence in his ability to lead the Institute, and this was probably why he'd come to rely so heavily on HB.

As far as the other Section Heads were concerned, James got on well with Pierre Forget, an honest, well-meaning, but not over-bright francophone from Saskatchewan who headed the Section on Languages and Culture (LAC). Pierre was nearing fifty and kept out of Institute politics, refusing to be drawn when James talked to him of his misgivings about Winstone and HB. Hamid Khan, the Head of the Section of Finance, Economics and Business Studies (FEB), was fifty-eight and no longer felt capable of conducting a full research program. He was grateful to Arbuthnot for securing his appointment as Section Head and in return was a loyal supporter. A pleasant and kind man, he was generally liked in the Institute, and James hadn't experienced any problems with him.

James was wrenched from his reverie by a fierce whisper from his wife.

"James, you're not paying attention to Mass. That's a dreadful example for the children."

James looked up at the altar and saw to his surprise that the priest had finished his homily and was starting on the prayer that led to the sanctus and the consecration. Sheepishly he knelt to follow the prayers, but his daughter tugging at his arm disturbed his adopted piety. He turned and saw her conniving grin.

"Behave yourself, you little heathen," he whispered.

"Mommy thinks you're the heathen," she whispered back.

Veronica gave both a baleful look, and they returned to their devotions.

"Thank God for the children," James thought. He was very fond of them and infinitely relieved that neither showed any inclination to emulate their mother's religious excesses. They, rather than his rather tepid Catholicism, were the real reason why he stayed in such an unfulfilling marriage.

# Sunday June 24, 2001

A NTONIETTA LEFT HER APARTMENT and walked slowly along the Via della
Vigna Nuova and the Via dei Tornabuoni, looking at the shops and
their elegant wares. Some were open and fleecing unsuspecting tourists.
Few Florentines would be shopping on the feast day of San Giovanni.
She reached the Piazza Antinori and took the Via degli Agli and the
Via de' Pecori to reach the Piazza San Giovanni, which housed the
Archbishop's Palace, and then the adjoining Piazza del Duomo, where
she met her family before the steps of the Basilica of Santa Maria del
Fiore.

Antonietta greeted them cautiously. Her mother asked her where
she'd been the previous evening. Antonietta lied and said she'd gone to
the cinema. Renata, her sister-in-law of two months, asked her which
film she'd seen. Antonietta hesitated, trying desperately to remember
which films were playing in Florence. She was rescued by her father,
who ushered them all up the steps into the Cathedral.

"She was with that Communist last night," Renata whispered to
Giovanni.

Antonietta genuflected before the altar and knelt in her pew to say a
prayer. The rest of her family did the same, but her mother and Renata
quickly crossed themselves and started looking around to see whom they
knew in the congregation. Antonietta remained an unusually long time
on her knees. She desperately needed some direction, some meaning
to her life, and she prayed for help to find it. She made the sign of the

cross and sat down. Her father, who was seated next to her, gave her a look of concern.

"Are you alright, Antonietta"? he asked. Antonietta was amused. "You're not used to seeing me pray"? "Well, not quite so long," he admitted. "I was praying for my knight in shining armor," she told him. Her father looked relieved. "Not Giacomo, then"? "No, father, not Giacomo."

The organ started up, and Antonietta's uncle, decked out in his episcopal vestments and accompanied by the auxiliary bishop, two priests and two deacons. walked down the aisle. He stopped and kissed the small altar that had been placed at the front of the chancel to accommodate the New Order of Mass and continued to the high altar with its monumental crucifix designed by Benedetto da Maiano. When the Cardinal celebrated a High Tridentine Mass, he always did so in the traditional way at the high altar with his back to the congregation.

After genuflecting before the high altar the Cardinal took the aspergillum from the hands of one of the deacons and proceeded slowly down the aisle. As he sprinkled the congregation with holy water, the choir sang the *Asperges me* in Gregorian chant. Antonietta crossed herself when she felt the drops of water on her face. The Cardinal returned to the high altar.

"*Introibo ad altare Dei*," he intoned, and the choir replied in similar fashion, "*Ad Deum qui laetificat juventutem meam.*" The Cardinal then sat down in the bishop's seat, and the choir sang Palestrina's setting of the Forty-Second Psalm. Antonietta, at first transported by the celestial purity of the music, was soon lost in her own thoughts. Despite her sexually indulgent lifestyle, Antonietta was genuinely pious, but today she paid little attention to the liturgy. She recollected her uncle's sermon in which he had stressed the importance of attending Mass, not just because the Church required such attendance but also because it was at the center of Catholic life. "At least I should get some brownie points for that," she'd thought. "Perhaps it'll make up for the rest." Then her mind wandered to her disappointments with men, her upcoming move to Canada, her fears and hopes.

She took communion from her uncle and returned to her pew to pray. The Cardinal recited the Last Gospel in Latin and then led the procession of celebrants and assistants down the aisle to a Gregorian chant that Antonietta didn't recognize. Mass was over. She left with her family who all, as it was a public occasion, kissed Giovanni's ring on leaving the Basilica.

Once the family was reunited outside the Cathedral, they made their way down the Via del Proconsolo to the Via Ghibellina and a restaurant called La Baraonda. It served Tuscan fare and was Paolo's favorite in the historic city. After they'd finished ordering, Giovanni complained that they always went to Italian restaurants.

"What do you expect," Antonietta observed drily, "We're in Italy."

Renata came to her husband's aid. "There are other types of restaurants in Florence as well, Antonietta. There's a lovely French restaurant in the Via Romana."

"I prefer Italian food," Antonietta replied. "It's lighter and more natural than all those heavy French sauces. I also prefer Italian wines."

"How can you talk such nonsense"! Giovanni protested. "Nothing compares with a good Bordeaux or a good Burgundy."

"Just because we don't classify our vineyards or list our 'grand crus' like the French doesn't mean our wines are inferior," Antonietta retorted

Paolo came to his daughter's aid. "Giovanni, it is certainly true that French wines are among the finest wines in the world, but we have fine wines that are their equal."

"Which ones"? Renata asked curtly. Even Caterina, who admired her well-born daughter-in-law, was taken aback by her aggressive tone. Antonietta glared at her angrily.

"Let's see," Paolo replied, ignoring his daughter-in-law's rudeness, "Among the reds, I would choose a Barolo, a Chianti Riserva, an Amarone or a Brunello di Montalcino. As for the whites, I don't believe the French whites can ever rival a Verdicchio dei Castelli di Jesi or a good Soave."

Renata was silent, and Giovanni pouted. Paolo changed the subject.

"Does anyone know what's on at the opera next season"? he asked.

Unfortunately, the subject was ill chosen. Caterina was upset because there was no Rossini, who was her particular favorite, and she was horrified that they were doing *Adriana Lecouvreur.* "It only has one tune, and the plot's quite unseemly. Imagine a royal duke wanting to marry an immoral woman"!

"My dear Caterina," Paolo placed his arm around his wife. "there may be only one tune, but it carries the action with haunting beauty. Anyway, Maurice is not a royal duke but a philandering adventurer who happens to be the illegitimate son of a king."

"The heroine's still immoral," Caterina insisted, slightly mollified by Paolo's gesture of affection.

"She was also one of the most famous actresses of her day and no more immoral than her rival, the Princess. Besides, if we took all the immoral women out of opera, there wouldn't be many left. It's full of what you'd term immoral women: Tosca, Manon Lescaut, La Gioconda, Mimi, to name but a few. Even poor old Santuzza in *Cavalleria Rusticana* is a sinner."

The conversation stagnated after this as everyone strived to avoid any more subjects of discord. Once he'd finished his expresso, Paolo left for the hospital to visit his patients. He never operated after taking lunch because he insisted that eating without wine was at best vulgar but more likely a mortal sin. He was always horrified on his occasional visits to the United States to witness people drinking watery coffee with their meals. Even worse, he'd even seen grown-up persons swilling down milk as they ate. Mind you, he'd once remarked, the food served in some American restaurants probably didn't merit being accompanied by a bottle of wine.

Giovanni and Renata left shortly after Paolo. They kissed Caterina warmly and Antonietta somewhat frostily. Antonietta was preparing to leave as well when her mother said that she wanted to talk to her.

"*Mamma*, do we have to have this discussion yet again"? Antonietta sighed and tried to hide her irritation. "I'm old enough to decide how to lead my life."

"Antonietta, I know you think it's none of my business, but the way you live your life affects the way people think of our whole family. When they see you always with a different man, and, apart from Alessandro Ottoreschi, none from our class, they judge all of us badly. Remember that you are a Countess della Chiesa."

"I'm not always with a different man," Antonietta protested. "I've been with Giacomo since last October."

Far from conciliating her mother, this fact served only to increase Caterina's ire.

"Do you think that helps"? Caterina's voice trembled with sarcasm. "Why can't you be more like Carla? At least she knows what's expected of her."

"What's that, *mamma*"? Antonietta tried not to sound too insolent.

"She keeps to her own class and married young instead of meandering promiscuously through life without any purpose like you're doing at present, and in poor company at that. Do you realize how scandalized people were that she married first even though she's the younger daughter"?

"I don't see anything commendable in giving up university to marry on your nineteenth birthday."

"You may not, but that's what well brought-up aristocratic girls should do. Look at Renata. She was only twenty when she married Giovanni."

Antonietta was tempted to make an unflattering comment about her sister-in-law but stopped herself. Silence was the best way to deal with her mother when she was in one of these moods. Any riposte would only infuriate her even more.

"If only you'd gone to the Sacred Heart in Rome, like Carla and Renata, instead of that convent in England. It was your uncle's silly idea. Ever since he was Papal Nuncio there, he's been besotted by the English. Goodness knows why. It's all very well for Giovanni to go on about his English Catholic friend, Philip Something or Other, but it's still a Protestant country. They think differently from us. They don't have the same moral sense."

This was the first time Antonietta had heard mention of Giovanni's English Catholic friend. She wondered who he was but suppressed her curiosity. It was better to let her mother finish her jeremiad, or she would be late for the *Calcio*.

"I was against the idea from the start, and now look at the result. You're twenty-four next month, still unmarried, working for a living, and going around with a Communist cobbler."

"His father's the cobbler, he's a lawyer," interposed Antonietta. Her mother ignored her.

"Look at the way you dress. I mean, today you're respectable, but otherwise those tight jeans and blouses you wear are indecent. They're provocative, and vulgar too. Mind you, I blame your father with his ridiculous idea of moving to Florence when you were seven. It cut us off from Roman society and disoriented you. Goodness knows why he did it. He had a brilliant career ahead of him at the Gemelli clinic. He'd probably be the Holy Father's doctor by now if we'd stayed in Rome."

Antonietta pointed out that her father was a surgeon, and apart from serious occurrences like the attempted assassination of the Pope in 1981, he was unlikely to have had much contact with the Holy Father.

"Perhaps not," Caterina admitted, "but the Pope would certainly have chosen him as his surgeon." She then launched into one her favorite tirades.

"There's just no comparison between Rome and Florence. It's so provincial here. It has none of the grandeur of Rome."

"You can't compare the two," Antonietta replied. She was tired of her mother's constant carping about the city she loved. "Florence is smaller and more intimate than Rome, and it has its own treasures - the medieval streets, the Renaissance palaces, the Cathedral."

"Rome has St. Peter's, and there's nothing here to compare with the Forum or the Pantheon or even what's left of the Colosseum except the Fortezza da Basso, which is an eyesore."

Caterina finished her coffee and stood up to go.

"I want you to talk to your uncle Giovanni," she told Antonietta. "Hopefully, you'll listen to him."

"As you wish." Antonietta liked her uncle, and she wasn't averse to seeking his counsel. Her mother was not entirely wrong. Her life indeed lacked purpose, and Antonietta was tired of the void she never managed to fill.

"Good. He'll see you after the reception at the Archbishop's Palace. Around eight."

They parted, and Antoniette hurried off to meet Giacomo and watch the final game of the *Calcio* between Santa Croce and Santa Maria Novella

Antonietta arrived late and somewhat out of breath at her uncle's reception. The Calcio game hadn't finished until quite late in the afternoon, and afterwards she and Giacomo had joined their friends for a celebratory drink. Their team, Santa Maria Novella, had won the tournament. She was a little tipsy and desperately hoped it didn't show. Her uncle greeted her at the foot of the imposing circular staircase that led up to the large, ornate reception room on the first floor. Portraits of earlier Archbishops of Florence lined the wall as you mounted the stairs.

"I want a talk with you after the reception, young lady," her uncle told her with mock severity. As it was a public occasion, she kissed his episcopal ring.

"Yes, *mamma* told me." She gave her uncle a radiant smile and whispered, "I'm afraid I'm a little tipsy."

Her uncle chuckled. "Does that mean Santa Maria Novella won"?

Antonietta nodded a reply and made her way upstairs to the reception. Her parents were already there, and she joined them. Her father offered to fetch her a glass of champagne. Antonietta refused. She didn't particularly like champagne, and she'd drunk enough with her friends.

"Look, Antonietta." Her mother pointed towards a group of young men talking and laughing in the middle of the room, "There's Count Guardini's son and the nephew of the Marchese di Lescia. Why don't you go and talk to them"?

"Are you trying to marry me off again, *mamma*"?

"No, not at all. I just like to see you mixing with young people of your own class."

Antonietta decided to be cooperative. She was not ready for another sterile confrontation with her mother, so she wandered off and joined the young men. Rodolfo Guardini greeted her with a broad smile.

"Your team won, I hear. Why aren't you celebrating"?

"I've already celebrated enough," Antonietta replied. "If I have another drink, I'll probably disgrace myself."

"I'd like to see that," remarked Fabio di Lescia, and the assembled group of young nobles laughed uproariously. Antonietta walked away in disgust and stumbled upon her brother, Giovanni, and his wife. "Things are going from bad to worse," she thought.

"How was the tournament"? her brother asked.

Antonietta knew Giovanni had no interest in *Calcio* and replied simply that her team had won. The conversation dragged on for a few more minutes before Giovanni and Renata moved on to mingle with other guests. Her sister-in-law hadn't said a single word to her. "At least she could pretend not to dislike me," Antonietta thought sadly. If it weren't for the meeting with her uncle, she would have left the reception.

The guests began to leave. Cardinal Palmieri came up to his niece and invited her into his private apartments on the second floor.

"This is your mother's idea," he told her, motioning Antonietta to sit down, "I don't like playing the family priest, as you well know." He walked over to a small fridge and took out a bottle of Soave Bolla. He poured a glass for each of them. The sight of her uncle in his cardinal's robes acting as barman caused Antonietta to burst out laughing. He didn't share her amusement.

"Even Princes of the Church have the right to enjoy the good things of life," he told her, "and that includes drinking a glass of chilled Italian white wine."

"I agree, uncle, but you must admit that it's an unusual sight to see a cardinal pouring out drinks."

They toasted each other and chatted idly for a while. Giovanni was in no hurry to bring up the subject of Antonietta's lifestyle, but, after two glasses of Soave Bolla, Antonietta protested that if they didn't have their serious talk soon, she wouldn't be in a fit state. Reluctantly her uncle agreed. He asked her if there was a reason why she couldn't find a lasting relationship with a man. Antonietta blushed deeply.

"No, I'm not referring to that episode at the boarding school in England," he assured her. "I'm sure that has nothing to do with it."

Antonietta was thoroughly disquieted by her uncle's allusion to her seduction by an older girl at school as she was by no means sure that this episode was not at least partially responsible for her predicament. Realizing his niece's disarray, Giovanni put his arm around her.

"Have you never felt real passion"?

"What is real passion"?

"An overwhelming attraction to another person that is at once physical and emotional and which impels you to surrender yourself completely to that person."

"And love"?

"The more serene happiness of wanting to be with someone and care for that person."

"Does one lead to the other"? There was a plaintive note in Antonietta's voice.

"Ideally, yes," her uncle replied, "although in *Romeo and Juliet* Shakespeare tells us that the greater the passion, the more likely it is to exhaust itself. 'Love moderately' was the priest's advice to the young couple."

"Do you agree with him, uncle"?

"There's some truth in what he says, but you don't really have a choice. If you're smitten by a real passion, it's almost impossible to resist."

Antonietta was surprised by her uncle's candor. She couldn't resist teasing him.

"Those are hardly the words one expects to hear from the Archbishop of Florence. *Mamma* would be shocked"!

Giovanni laughed. "Don't forget that before I became a priest, I was a young man who enjoyed life to the full."

Antonietta looked at him questioningly, but the Cardinal was not prepared to divulge more. "We're not here to discuss my youthful ways, but yours's," he reminded her, adding "That is, if you want to discuss them with me."

Antonietta thought for a moment. She was reluctant to talk about her personal life, even with an uncle whom she adored, but she felt a need to tell someone about the emptiness within her.

"You asked me whether I've ever felt real passion. The answer is not in the way you describe it. I feel attraction for a man, but it's purely physical. Every time I hope the relationship will lead to some emotional involvement, but it never does. The physical attraction eventually exhausts itself, and there's nothing left but a terrible void. It's very depressing, and it worries me."

"You've never been in love"?

"Once I thought I was in love, but I was betrayed. That's another problem." Antonietta smiled sadly. "What am I to do, uncle"?

"There's no need for you to feel depressed. You know, you can't force emotional attachment, and if you haven't experienced it, it's because you haven't met the right man."

"It's taking a long time," Antonietta objected.

"There's a reason for that. Many people fool themselves that they have an emotional attachment to another person when in reality it's just physical infatuation. Look at all those Hollywood film stars. They divorce, remarry, divorce again with depressing regularity, and each time they fool themselves into believing they've found true love. Your character is too forthright to deceive yourself in this way, and you should be grateful for that. It will save you from making a serious mistake that, as a Catholic, you wouldn't be able to remedy. Anyway, you're still young. There's plenty of time for you to meet a man to whom you're both physically and emotionally attracted."

"*Mamma* doesn't think so. She thinks I should have married at nineteen like Carla."

"Rushing into marriage is hardly a solution for you. Carla's a different person. She finds her fulfillment in being a Roman aristocrat. I doubt whether there's real passion between her and Filiberto, or between Giovanni and Renata. You have a passionate nature, and an aristocratic marriage by itself wouldn't fulfill you."

Antonietta took comfort from her uncle's words, but she still wanted his advice on her immediate plans.

"You've made a good decision to leave Italy for a while, and Canada is a good choice. You'll meet a different kind of person, encounter different attitudes. It'll be a refreshing change that will do you a lot of good. How long are you going for"?

"Two years. One year to do the courses and one year to complete the master's thesis."

"Whatever you do, keep your background a secret. No one needs to know you're a countess. The Canadians probably wouldn't care one way or another, but don't take chances. Who knows, perhaps there you'll find the passion that's eluded you in Italy."

"You insist on me finding passion"? Antonietta asked with amusement.

"Why not.? You're a young woman of outstanding beauty with a lot of spirit, and for you not to experience real passion would be a sin against nature."

"To experience it would be a sin against the precepts of the Church," she countered with a smile.

The Cardinal sighed. "I know the Church takes a takes a very dim view of premarital sex, but compared to murder, oppressing the poor, greed and envy, I don't rate it that high on the scale of sin."

"However," he added, "take care not to fall into promiscuity. I may not entirely agree with the Church's strict attitude toward sex, but sex that is divorced completely from real passion cheapens the wonderful gift God has given us. Promiscuity renders sex mundane and bereft of spirituality.

"You excuse sex out of marriage"? Antonietta asked in surprise.

"I didn't say that," Giovanni hurried to reply, fearing he'd gone too far in divulging his unorthodox views on sexuality, "It *is* a sin, but where there's true passion, it's perhaps the most excusable of sins. As long as no one else is hurt. That's why adultery is so wrong, and why it always leads to unhappiness."

The Cardinal stood up and led Antonietta to the door.

"Now, young lady, you must leave me to my devotions. It's time for vespers." Antonietta kissed her uncle.

"Are you going to watch the firework display"? he asked her.

"Yes, but it's not until eleven. I've got plenty of time." She turned to leave, but her uncle called her back.

"Don't tell your mother about our conversation. I don't think it's quite what she had in mind."

Antonietta laughed, "Don't worry, I won't."

She made her way down the baroque stairway and, gazing upon the austere faces of her uncle's predecessors, she realized how different he was, and why he was considered in the higher ranks of the Church to be a dangerous liberal.

$\mathcal{E}$

*Chapter 3*

# Wednesday June 27, 2001

J AMES MARKHAM WAS FOND of the Irish, but at this very moment he could cheerfully have wrung their collective necks. He'd spent the best part of two weeks in May revising his class notes for the course on European Law and Politics to take into account the changes brought about by the Treaty of Nice, only to have the Irish reject the Treaty in a referendum on June 7. As the Treaty needed to be ratified by all the Member States of the European Union, this meant that it couldn't enter into effect. This put James in a quandary. Contrary to its obsession with democracy, human rights, and the rule of law, the European Union took a dim view of people voting against its projects. They were supposed to follow their leaders in endorsing whatever the latter had drawn up in secret conclaves usually dominated by the lowest common denominator. It was probable, therefore, that the Irish would be summoned to vote again, and, having been appropriately brainwashed, they would obediently do the decent thing and vote yes. This is what had happened to the Danes, who, after rejecting the Treaty of Maastricht in June 1992, had been persuaded to change their mind in another referendum in May 1993. Democracy for the European Union meant not taking no for an answer.

James decided to stick to his revised notes. He was sure the Treaty of Nice would eventually come into force, and there was little point in teaching his students law that would change within the next two years. He was about to turn his attention to administrative matters affecting the Section when Bill Leaman burst into his office. His face was ashen.

"Good Lord! Whatever's the matter, Bill"?

"It's bad, Jimmy, very bad."

James ignored Bill's irritating habit of disfiguring his name.

"What's happened? Someone stolen your Harley-Davidson"?

Bill's motorbike was his most treasured possession, but he ignored James's facetious allusion. "I'm in shit, deep shit," he groaned, slumping into the chair opposite James like a naughty student. "It's about Lisa."

James had met Bill and his attractive Vietnamese research assistant the day before in the campus bar. He'd drunk a beer with them and then left.

"After we left the bar, we went up to my office." Bill paused and gave a long sigh. "I think I screwed her."

"You *think* you screwed her"! James exclaimed. "Screwing your research assistant is bad enough, but not remembering whether you did is quite appalling, even by your lamentable standards of decency."

"I know I kissed her, and I think I took her bra off, but that's about all I can remember. I was pissed."

"When did you leave the bar"?

"Around eight."

"Jesus, Bill. I left you at three, and you two had already been drinking for three hours. No wonder you were pissed."

"This is going to get me kicked out of the Institute. Hard Balls will see to that."

"No, he won't. If you screw a student, you get kicked out. If you screw your research assistant, you get a reprimand and probably a fine. But you can kiss goodbye to your chances of getting early tenure this year."

Bill stared disconsolately at his feet. Then he looked up at James, his face suddenly alive with hope. He'd found the solution. "I'm going to phone Lisa and apologize."

"Are you mad"? James looked at his friend incredulously. "That's the worst thing you could do."

"Why"?

"For two reasons. If you were plastered, she must've been in even worse shape. I doubt whether she's used to drinking as much beer as you. She might well not remember any better than you what happened.

Though, I must say, it takes someone like you to forget something like that."

Bill was unconvinced. "What's the second reason"?

"Well," James replied, "Hasn't it occurred to you that she might have welcomed your advances. In that case to apologize for them would seem to her an insult."

"You think so"?

"Your hair's getting thinner, you smoke too much, and you have no dress sense, but apart from that you're a reasonably attractive man."

"What should I do"?

"Let sleeping dogs lie."

"She's not a dog. She's a damn good-looking girl."

James sighed. "It's a saying, Bill. I suppose you wouldn't know that, coming from Texas."

Bill was used to James poking fun at his native State. He was about to deliver a riposte, but James interrupted him.

"Why doesn't that wife of your's get a job with an airline based in Montreal? It's ridiculous for her to live in Vancouver when you're here. She could probably get a job with Air Canada."

"No, she couldn't. She's not ugly, old or unpleasant."

They both laughed, and Bill began to recover his normal pinkish complexion.

"Talking of Hard Balls, I was talking to Hunt. You know, the new guy they hired last year in FEB. He just rubbished Arbuthnot. Said his research was mundane, and as for his and Flint's strategy courses, he maintained they were mickey-mouse, and there were too many of them."

"He should be careful. He's not got tenure, and he's in HB's Section. That vindictive bugger will get him if he creates too many waves."

"He can't. Hunt got his Ph.D. at Cornell, and he's already published two top-tier articles. Hard Balls can't touch him."

"I'm not so sure. Arbuthnot and Winstone are as thick as thieves, and there's nothing mediocrities fear more than people who are intelligent, particularly if you're a megalomaniac like HB."

"I sometimes wonder why I stay here. What with that asshole and the She-Wolf, this place is worse than boot camp."

James laughed. "I take it you've had another run-in with Ilse"?

Bill nodded. "She's a goddam ball-breaker," he complained. "She was mad because I was late with my book lists."

"She's not that bad. She just takes her job a little too seriously. She *is* German."

"It's alright for you. You don't need balls with a wife like yours's." Bill checked himself. "I'm sorry, James, that was a bit out of line." He looked quizzically at his friend. "Tell me, why the hell did you marry Veronica"?

"I had my reasons," James replied cautiously. "I had a very bad experience at university in Cambridge. I fell for a girl and went out with her for over a year. Then, quite by chance, I discovered a postcard she'd written to a friend in France somewhere telling her that I was rather boring, but she couldn't pass up on being Lady Markham. Veronica was an aristocrat, so at least I knew there was no social climbing involved."

"Very convincing. Can't you dream up a better reason than that she has blue blood"?

James paused. He didn't particularly like calling up unpleasant memories, but he hadn't told Bill the whole truth.

"I had this Spanish girlfriend in Florence. She was a model. God, was she beautiful! Unfortunately, she was also a first-class bitch and bisexual as well. Eventually she left me for one of her lesbian lovers, and Veronica made sure she was around to pick up the pieces. I married her on what you might call the rebound."

"Well, you were a goddam fool. Tell me, if it weren't for that weird religion of yours's, would you dump her"?

"No. There's the kids, and my weird religion, as you call it, is a family tradition I respect."

"Well, I hope you get a bit on the side when you travel to Latin America."

"That's none of your damn business."

"Ha"! Bill cried, "That means you do. A little hooky on the side, a visit to the confessional, and all's back to normal, eh? Fucking Catholic hypocrite you are, James Lordy Markham."

"It's no more hypocritical than doing it, which I never said I did, and asking God's forgiveness without a confession and doing it again.

Anyway, no one makes personal confessions anymore, except for Veronica. God knows what she finds to confess."

"By the way, James, talking of fucking one's way around Latin America, what about our trip"?

"We leave on August 15 for Santiago in Chile. We'll stay there until Saturday morning and have talks with the Pontificia and the University of Chile. Then we'll go to Buenos Aires, do some sightseeing, and meet with the people from the University of Buenos Aires on Monday. We fly back the next day."

"Let's hope we have time for some fun."

"I'm told, Bill, that Buenos Aires has excellent brothels, if that's what you mean. Don't kid yourself, I'm not joining you."

Bill looked at his friend with a certain skepticism, but he didn't pursue the subject.

The conversation with Giacomo was even more painful than Antonietta had feared. She'd known it would be difficult because Giacomo was deeply in love with her. He was hurt and bitter.

"1 hope you enjoyed your little fling with someone from the working class."

Antonietta turned to leave. Looking back at him, she said, "However unrealistic, 1 wanted it to work out, Giacomo. That's the truth, even if you don't believe me. It's not your fault it didn't. I'm just incapable of sustaining a relationship, no matter which world the man comes from. Please forgive me."

Giacomo made no reply, and Antonietta left. It was a dreary day. The beautiful weather that had blessed the Feast of San Giovanni had turned to rain, and it was unseasonably cold. Antonietta had left work early for her unhappy meeting with Giacomo, and now she wondered what she would do with the rest of the afternoon. She wandered dejectedly back to her apartment along the route she'd always taken during the eight months of her relationship with him. When she reached the Via Benedetto Marcello, she looked up at the Fortezza di Basso looming before her. Perhaps it was the gloomy weather, but for the first time she agreed with her mother that it was an eyesore. Even the streets that she took--Via della Carra, Via del Ponte, Borgo Ognissanti--seemed dank and devoid of life. She felt glad to be leaving Florence. The city's intimacy now oppressed her.

Antonietta reached her apartment, but the prospect of sitting alone with only her regrets for company was too depressing. She decided to cheer herself up by going on a spending spree among the boutiques of Santa Maria Novella. In any case, she needed new clothes for Canada. She walked down to the Piazza Goldoni and along the Via della Vigna Nuova, but nothing caught her fancy. She looked at the clothes in Versace on the Via de' Tornabuoni, but they weren't sexy enough. "Modern women really don't like showing off their bodies," she thought. "It's a pity." She went to Armani on the same street and found more or less the same classic but dull style. A saleswoman approached her and offered help in gilded tones. She insisted on Antonietta inspecting the whole new collection, but there was nothing she liked.

"Perhaps something a little less expensive," the woman suggested.

Antonietta caught the insinuation and was about to put the woman in her place when the manageress came over. She was acquainted with Antonietta's mother and recognized her daughter.

"Can I be of assistance"? she asked

"I was suggesting to the young lady that perhaps she might like to see our less expensive offerings," the saleswoman interjected in the same insolent tone.

The manageress gave her employee a dismissive look. "I don't think money is a problem for the countess," she remarked. The saleswoman turned white, realizing her blunder and fearing for her employment.

"If you want something more trendy, countess, you should try Gianni Versace or the Emporium Armani," the manageress told Antonietta. She followed this advice, but the clothes in Gianni Versace were too modern. Baggy and extravagant. Disconsolately she made her way along the Via Strozzi to the square of the same name and entered the Emporium. There she found a classic but low-cut evening gown with slits up the side that exposed the thighs. She took it a young salesclerk and asked to try it on. The girl indicated the changing room and, to Antonietta's discomfiture, followed her in. Rather self-consciously

Antonietta stripped down to her extremely skimpy underwear. The young girl gasped.

*"Che c'è"?* Antonietta was irritated but also troubled by the girl's reaction.

*"Mi dispiace, signora,"* the girl stammered. *"È che...È che Lei è tanto bella."*

Antonietta looked at the girl suspiciously, but she saw only innocent admiration. Quickly she changed her tone. *"Grazie, signorina,"* she said with a smile. She put on the dress and looked at herself in the mirror. It was perfect: classic and provocatively sexy.

"There's a longer mirror outside," the girl said, her eyes fixed on Antonietta in wonder. Antonietta followed her out of the changing room. A middle-aged man, who was with his young mistress, stared at her. The woman noticed and looked at Antonietta with venom. *"Guardami, Giorgio,"* she told her lover crossly. With noticeable reluctance the man took his eyes off Antonietta.

"Why don't you try the red one," the salesgirl suggested.

Antonietta laughed. "Isn't that a bit too much? I'd look like a whore."

The very idea appealed to her. She returned to the changing room, this time alone, and put on the red dress. The effect was electric, but Antonietta was not completely satisfied. She needed a new bra that would lift up her breasts and flaunt them as befitted such a dress. She changed back, took the two dresses, and paid for them. The young girl, overcome by Antonietta's beauty, made a mess of wrapping them. She apologized profusely.

*"Non fa niente."* Antonietta gave the girl a five thousand lira tip.

The girl watched her leave the store and sighed. *"Che bella donna,"* she murmured.

Antonietta walked back to the Via Strozzi and along to the Piazza della Repubblica. She purchased a newspaper, *La Repubblica*, from a kiosk and sat down in a cafe to read it. The waiter came and offered a cup of coffee. Antonietta didn't share the Italian mania for drinking coffee at all times of the day and ordered a glass of red wine. A Chianti Classico. The waiter brought it with an air of disapproval.

Antonietta left the cafe and made her way to the Via dei Calzaiuoli and her favorite shop for lingerie, Intissimi. She picked out two bra's that would lift up her breasts and barely cover her nipples, a couple of thongs and variously colored strings. She preferred a string to a thong as the feel of it on her bare skin was more sensual, but it was also less comfortable. She took this collection of erotic lingerie to the nearest salesclerk, who was in early middle age and remarkably attractive. The woman gave Antonietta a sultry look and undressed her shamelessly with her eyes.

"Why don't you try on the bra's"? she asked, staring impenitently at Antonietta's comely bosom, "I think they may be too small."

There was no mistaking the real intention behind the woman's honeyed words, but they caught Antonietta off-guard. Despite herself, there was a moment of temptation and then revulsion at the way the woman was leering at her.

"No, thank you," she replied. "I like them a size too small."

The woman shrugged and took an inordinate time to process the bill. Antonietta was desperate to leave the shop and nearly departed without her purchases. It took a considerable effort to wait patiently while her libidinous admirer placed the lingerie in a box.

"Enjoy your purchase," she said, handing over the box. Without replying Antonietta grasped it and fled from the store.

She'd intended to go on to the Piazza del Duomo to buy some shoes at Marco Candido, but the scene with the lesbian shop assistant was too disturbing. The fact that she had momentarily been tempted by the woman's veiled invitation raised all her fears about her sexuality. It was all the worse now that she'd just registered another failure in her relations with men. So she cut through to the Via delle Belle Donne, which led to the Piazza Santa Maria Novella and the Dominican Basilica of the same name. The Basilica was the first of the great Florentine churches, and where Antonietta mostly went to hear Mass. She admired, as always, the elaborate façade of inlaid black and white marble and the works of Giotto, Orcagna, Brunelleschi and others that graced the interior of the Basilica. She walked along the cloisters that bore the frescoes of Paolo Uccello and other artists of the Florentine schools of the later Middle Ages and the Renaissance.

The awesome beauty of the Basilica inspired her to prayer. She lit a candle, knelt in a side chapel dedicated to Our Lady, and recited the *Memorare**. She prayed that she would meet a man who could fill the void in her life and still her fears.

*Chapter 4*

# Friday, June 29, 2001 to
# Sunday July 1, 2001

J AMES HERDED HIS TWO children into the Maserati station wagon and
stowed their equipment in the back. It was the last day of school, and
both were going to play soccer. They waved goodbye to Veronica and
proceeded down to highway 117 towards St. Jérôme and the children's
school. It was a beautiful day, but during the southward drive the
scenery was not particularly impressive. Prévost was the real beginning
of the Laurentians, and from there northwards up highway 117 or
motorway 15 to Saint-Sauveur, where the Institute was based, Ste-
Adèle, Ste-Agathe, and beyond, the colorful forests and towering hills
always inspired James with their imperious beauty. Unfortunately, the
weather was often cloudy in this part of Canada, but in the summer that
didn't seem to matter so much. In the winter, on the other hand, the
Laurentians were a most depressing place for James. James was a man for
southern climes, and he was constantly beset by nostalgia for southern
France where he'd spent so much of his youth at his grandmother's villa
in Bandol. He missed the warm sunny days, the Mediterranean, which,
despite all the pollution, still enchanted him, like a fading mistress
whose body conserves the erotic memories of earlier times, and he
longed to sit in the terraces of the many cafes along the ports of Bandol
or Sanary or Cassis, watching the sensuous dark-haired women of the
South stroll by.

They arrived at the school. It was a francophone state school, which shocked James's mother. He was never quite sure what disturbed her more: the fact that the children were educated in French, or the fact that they were not enrolled in some posh private school. Immediately the car stopped, Peter raced off to talk to his friends, leaving his father to extricate the soccer equipment from the car with a little help from Susanna.

Having settled his two children, James drove northwards to Saint-Sauveur and the Institute. It was an important day as there was a meeting of the Faculty Promotion Committee (FPC) to consider Len Flint's application to become a full professor. In the normal course of events this should have been a routine meeting. Section Heads didn't usually propose a candidate for a full professorship unless they were sure it would be granted. This applied even more in this case as Flint's application was being made earlier than five years since he obtained tenure. A refusal to grant the application under these circumstances meant that the candidate couldn't apply again before three more academic years had elapsed. This meant Flint would have to wait another four years.

This was not, however, just another routine meeting of FPC. As part of his new duties as Senior Dean, Arbuthnot had been given the right by Winstone to sit on FPC together with the Rector, the Heads of Section, one member at large appointed by the Rector and one elected by the faculty. It was a decision of questionable validity as Arbuthnot's appointment didn't take effect until July 1. That in itself was not particularly worrisome, and James hadn't bothered to protest; what was worrisome was the reason for Arbuthnot's premature appearance on FPC.

Len Flint was an amiable but thoroughly mediocre academic, whom Arbuthnot had taken under his wing. He taught business strategy like HB and, before obtaining a tenure-track position in the Institute, had worked for ten years as a sessional instructor. James suspected it was Arbuthnot's influence over the former Rector, Guy Lafarge, that had gained Len his tenure in 1998. At that time there had been questions asked in the Institute about granting tenure on the basis of two co-authored articles with HB. Now Flint was up for an early full professorship based on two more co-authored articles with HB and two ostensibly written by himself as sole author. James had many problems with this application.

In the first place, no faculty member had ever been granted a full professorship on the basis of such meager scholarship. James himself had submitted three books and eight articles in support of his own application for a full professorship. This was perhaps above the norm, but in James's view Flint was well below. James had studied the five most recent cases where a full professorship had been granted, and they all supported his contention.

Moreover, the two articles Flint had supposedly written himself appeared in second-rate journals, and even the co-authored articles were in journals that only the FEB Section considered first-tier. However, the outside references that Flint had submitted were all unanimous in their positive evaluation of these papers, and it was clear to James that Arbuthnot hoped to push through his protégé's promotion by relying on them. Unfortunately for HB, a colleague from FEB had furnished James with the names of leading academics in the field of business strategy, and he now had in his possession two references from world-renowned professors at the Harvard School of Business demolishing Flint's submissions. As Head of Section, he had the right to appeal to outside referees to complete a submission although this was rarely done. He'd deliberately circulated the supplementary references at the last moment so that Arbuthnot would not have time to react.

James's third problem was the veracity of the application. He'd compared both the co-authored articles and the supposedly sole-authored papers with some of Arbuthnot's work, and he'd observed that the turn of phrase in all of them was identical. James suspected that Flint had written little by himself. This type of academic fraud was becoming quite widespread, and one British law journal, the *European Law Observer*, now employed a stylistic expert to vet submissions for this vice. James had sent Flint's and a couple of Arbuthnot's papers to the expert, whom he knew, and he had confirmed James's suspicions.

However, Flint's promotion was a sideshow compared to the real issue at stake. HB was determined to assert his power, and what better way than to demonstrate to all and sundry that he could obtain promotion to full professor when and for whom he wished. Academia consists, although few outsiders would suspect it, of tender and frightened egos and, if HB were successful in obtaining promotion for such an inadequate applicant as Len Flint, he stood a chance of garnering the support he needed to rule the roost. James was determined to prevent this.

It wouldn't be easy. His best tack was to emphasize the inadequacy of the submission. This way he could avoid criticizing a colleague's work. James doubted this approach would suffice as a majority on the committee were likely to look favorably on the application. Arbuthnot would obviously support it, Hamid Khan was obliged to do so as the Section Head who was sponsoring the application, and the member appointed by Winstone, Georges Campeau from the LAC Section, was a friend of Flint's. Pierre Forget, the Head of LAC, might be persuaded, and the member elected by the faculty, Saleema Nadjani, was a brilliant, young accounting professor from Tunisia who had little time for mediocrity. The best scenario was three votes against, including his own, and three for. This left Winstone as chair with a casting vote, and it was customary for the Rector to support the Section Head.

James could go one step further and attack the quality of the submissions on the basis of the two references from Harvard, but this strategy could backfire. Winstone, and even Forget, might resent James introducing exogenous material to support his case. Moreover, implicit in the two references was a disparagement of Arbuthnot's work for they criticized the co-authored papers with the same severity as Flint's ostensibly own publications. Whatever James thought of HB's academic worth, it was risky to belittle the Senior Dean in front of a faculty committee. Winstone, and perhaps Pierre as well, would feel obliged to defend him by approving the application.

This left the most perilous course of action: the charge of academic fraud. How much would the opinion of an expert working for a British law journal count against the protestations of innocence from a senior member of the faculty? Even to suggest such fraud in open committee might seem outrageous and earn James the censure of many of his colleagues and HB their sympathy. The result would be exactly the opposite of what James intended. At the same time, he was convinced that only fear of an academic scandal would move Winstone to abandon

Arbuthnot's protégé. James thought for a few minutes and made an appointment to see the Rector alone before the meeting. If he could frighten him into at least abstaining, the application could be denied on a three-to-three split.

Winstone was not pleased to see him.

"Isn't this a little irregular? Canvassing the chair of a meeting just before it starts."

James met and held the Rector's cold stare. It was essential to convey a sense of confidence and resolve.

"I think not, under the circumstances," he replied as firmly as he could. "I believe that a decision in favor of Len could lead to an academic scandal."

The only possibility for mediocre people who are in positions that exceed their capabilities is to give the appearance of good management. They are incapable of any real achievements. Nothing, therefore, must be allowed to disturb the tranquil flow of events. That's why they fear scandal above all else for it undermines their whole *raison d'être*. James was banking on the fact that this was the case with Winstone.

"What do you mean"? The Rector's tone told James that he hadn't miscalculated.

"I don't believe that Len had any significant part in writing the papers he's submitted in support of his application."

James continued to look fixedly at Winstone, whose nervousness was now compounded by a growing sense of anxiety. But there was also anger beneath the surface.

"Whatever makes you say something so preposterous"?

"I've compared the co-authored papers, the papers Flint supposedly wrote himself, and some of Roy's own work, and it's clear that they're all written by the same person. You can be sure it's not Flint."

"Listen, James, I think you're overreaching yourself. How dare you presume to cast doubts on a colleague's honesty." Winstone's anger was by now submerging his nervousness.

"It's not just my opinion," James replied. He maintained a look of steely resolve, but inwardly he was dismayed by Winstone's apparent resilience. "I have a report from a stylistic expert who works for a top law journal."

James handed the report to Winstone, who perused it briefly. His reaction was not encouraging.

"You have the audacity to send work done by your colleagues to some British so-called expert and expect me to join in your little war against Roy Arbuthnot." Winstone's eyes were now blazing with anger. "I want you out of my office immediately."

This was the crucial moment. James had gone too far to back down but not far enough to attain his goal. He made his last play.

"You're the Rector and responsible for what goes on here. If you read the papers, you'll see that I'm right. If you refuse to do your duty, I'll have no alternative, *if Flint is promoted*, but to send the papers in question and the expert's report to the Quebec Ministry of Education."

Winstone's anger evaporated. "You wouldn't do that," he gasped.

James knew he'd won. "I'll see you in the meeting," he replied and left the Rector's office.

Winstone called the meeting of FPC to order, and the deliberations began. James's father had once told him that the secret of winning over a committee was to let the opposition have the first say. No matter how convincing they were, he told him, if you can come up with a cogent argument after they've shot their bolt, you'll win. Most people have short memories and tend to rally behind the last reasonable idea they've heard. Academics were no different, James reflected, so he let Hamid extol the collegial virtues of Len Flint, his devoted service to the Section, and almost as an afterthought his academic record. He was followed by Arbuthnot, who placed particular emphasis on Flint's scholarship and the excellent references it had obtained. "It's hardly surprising," James thought, "you wrote the damned stuff yourself"! Neither Khan nor HB mentioned the negative reports from Harvard. This was a clever strategy as it made it more difficult for James to bring them up. Happily for James, the third speaker, Georges Campeau, attacked him over the reports.

"Just because you have a few friends in Harvard doesn't mean we have to swallow what they say," he said, wagging his finger at James.

Campeau's stupidity ruined Arbuthnot's carefully laid strategy. It gave James the perfect opportunity to introduce the reports, and, even more importantly, the crass attack on a colleague earned James the sympathy of the two committee members he had to win over, Pierre Forget and Saleema Nadjani. He seized the moment.

"Firstly, Georges," he replied, "these people are not my friends. I don't know them, but as they're widely recognized experts in the field of business strategy, I assume Roy does." James looked questioningly at Arbuthnot, who was forced to nod his unwilling assent.

"Secondly, I'm not asking you to swallow anything. It merely seemed to me that the referees chosen by Len were, how shall I put it, a little inadequate. One of them isn't even a full professor, and two of the others haven't published anything for ages. So, I believed that this committee should have the benefit of opinions from other referees who cannot be impugned in this way. It's up to you to decide what weight to give them."

"Perhaps, James," Hamid said, looking very uncomfortable, "but it's not very collegial to question a Section Head's list of referees."

"It was absolutely necessary," Saleema Nadjani interjected, "The referees in the submission were second-rate. We should be grateful to Professor Markham for providing us with more reliable references."

Saleema's aggressive tone took everyone by surprise, including James, but her own excellent academic reputation gave her opinion weight and prompted Pierre Forget to come on side, albeit more diplomatically.

"I agree that the supplementary references are important," he said, "and certainly they're very categorical. Even without doubting the credibility of Len's own references, which Hamid accepted." Pierre turned towards Hamid. "And I don't doubt them, Hamid, but these additional references raise enough doubts to warrant refusing the application."

Winstone, who had been silent until now, in fact almost comatose after the scene with James, asked if there were any more comments to be made. Now that the tone of the meeting suggested a three-way split, he was anxious to conclude before anyone changed Forget's mind. The specter of scandal terrified him. Khan was smart enough to realize that Arbuthnot had sold him a false bill of goods and said nothing. Arbuthnot was confident that Winstone would cast his vote in favor of the application and had no wish to prolong a discussion that was proving embarrassing.

As expected, the committee split with James, Saleema and Pierre voting to reject and Hamid, HB and Campeau voting to accept the application. Arbuthnot looked expectantly at Winstone, who was squirming in his chair.

"You have the casting vote, Harold," HB purred.

James gave Winstone a warning look. "Don't you dare play me false, you bastard," it said. There was a short silence. Looking as if he were about to throw up, Winstone gave his reluctant verdict.

"I think there are enough doubts, as Pierre has said, surrounding this application to warrant me abstaining," he said.

"This means the application's refused"! Arbuthnot shouted in disbelief. "How can you do that, Harold"? HB was beside himself. Winstone, looking more ill by the moment, muttered something inaudible and rushed from the room. Arbuthnot glared at James.

"Markham, this is your doing. But it's not the end of the matter."

"Yes, it is." Saleema put in. "At least for three years."

James appreciated her support. "I wish she'd take off that damn scarf around her head," he thought inappropriately. "It'd be nice to see what she really looks like."

"Thank you for your support, Saleema," he told her after Arbuthnot had stalked off to give his protégé the bad news.

"It's not a question of supporting you," she replied. "It's a question of maintaining standards."

"Quite so, Saleema," James agreed, "but thanks anyway." He gave her a charming smile, and Saleema blushed. James chased away an even more inappropriate thought and left the room to return to his office. He passed Len Flint, who gave him a hurt look, and HB, who didn't bother to hide his venom.

"A good day's work, eh, Markham," he hissed in a Scottish brogue that James found as disagreeable as the man who uttered it.

On the way back to his office James was accosted by Nathan Goldberg. Nathan had been hired into the LIR Section two years ago by the former Section Head, Al Guarini, at Guy Lafarge's insistence. As a mark of his disapproval, Guarini had hired him at the lowest possible starting salary on the grounds that sociologists were two a penny. James had been impressed, however, by Nathan's article on the love-hate relationship, at times mutual hostility, between the French and the British and had succeeded in almost doubling Nathan's salary. Nathan was falling over himself with gratitude.

"Thank you, James," he said. "I really appreciate it." He went on to heap fulsome praise on James for his stewardship of the Section. This embarrassed James, who brought the conversation to an abrupt end.

"You deserved it, Nathan," he told the young academic, "You don't have to thank me."

James continued his way, leaving Nathan feeling unappreciated.

James was searching in his cellar for a bottle of scotch.

"Jesus"! he exclaimed in annoyance when he realized his search was in vain. He emerged from the cellar in high dudgeon. Veronica, who'd overheard him, asked what the matter was.

"There's no blended scotch," he replied.

"You wouldn't need any scotch at all if you stayed at home and prayed the rosary with us. Think what an awful example you set for the children by going off drinking."

"Look, Veronica, I go to Mass every Sunday and every Holy Day of Obligation, I fast before taking communion, I don't eat meat on Fridays, I don't use birth control, but I'm not, I repeat not, going to pray the rosary as well. You may be an oblate, but I'm not. Good Lord, woman, 1 don't even break any of the commandments."

"Except one," Veronica observed.

James had a moment of panic. Did she know about his Latin American frolics?

"Which one"?

"The fourth one, which, in case you don't know, is "Thou shalt not take the Name of the Lord thy God in vain."

James was immensely relieved. "Oh, that one. I've never thought it was that important, and anyway I'm sure the Lord knows I don't really mean to be rude."

"Don't add your normal facetiousness to blasphemy, James." Veronica glared at him, but he was saved from her righteous ire by Susanna, who entered the room at that moment.

"You're not staying for the rosary"? she asked him.

"No, Susanna, you must excuse me, but I don't like praying the rosary. Besides, it's Canada Day, and I have to celebrate."

"I know, Daddy," she replied, "but today it's the Glorious Mysteries*."

James felt a stab of remorse. He adored his daughter, but he was damned if he was going to give in to Veronica on yet another matter. She'd known when she married him that he was a tepid Catholic. His religion was more loyalty to a family tradition than real faith. He gave both his daughter and wife a perfunctory kiss, waved at Peter, who was clearly dreading the Glorious Mysteries, and quickly disappeared out of the front door.

As usual Bill was on his own, and so the evening would be spent at his place in Ste. Adèle. The house was situated in the higher, western part of the town and overlooked the Laurentians. In winter the snow and the bright lights of the ski runs gave them a fairytale appearance. In the summer the luscious growth on the trees created a carpet of colors. James preferred Bill's to his own house, which was surrounded by tall trees that seemed to die at an alarming rate. Their dwindling numbers were inexorably robbing the house of the privacy that was its only real attraction. James entered Bill's house without knocking to be greeted by a raucous but unmusical rendering of "See, the conquering hero comes"!

"I'm impressed," he told them. "That must've been Piotr's idea. You two," James pointed at Danny and Bill, "wouldn't know Handel from Paul McCartney."

"Markham," Bill riposted, "you're a goddam cultural snob, and if it hadn't been for your stirring victory over the forces of evil, I would've poured this bottle of scotch over your head. But tell me," he added with a grin, "Who the fuck is Handel anyway"?

Danny and Bill laughed uproariously, which was due more to their incipient drunkenness than the wittiness of the remark. Piotr wore the slightly bemused look he reserved for Bill's vulgarities. James remained pensive.

"What's the matter, my boy"? Danny asked. "You should be very pleased with yourself."

James poured himself a scotch. "I fear it may be a pyrrhic victory. I've now made two dangerous enemies, the Rector and the Senior Dean." He recounted how he had in effect blackmailed Winstone into abstaining. "Once HB gets to hear of that, he'll be after revenge, and Winstone must also have it in for me now."

"Well, you can't have everything, can you now"? Danny's Irish accent was becoming stronger as his sobriety declined. "You at least prevented HB from getting his own way, and what better man to suffer for all of us than you, James. A real Catholic saint striking at the heart of Calvinism."

"Thanks, Danny, that really makes me feel better." James gave the Irishman a sardonic smile. Danny laughed and slapped him on the back. "We're proud of you," he said.

"How did Saleema vote"? asked Bill.

"Against the application," James replied.

"She must want you to get into her pants."

"I don't think so, Bill. She thinks of me as an infidel." In fact, it was he who'd harbored lustful feelings for Saleema rather than the inverse, but he was damned well not going to admit that to his three friends. He could imagine their ribald comments.

"I think Hard Balls is a homosexual," Bill announced out of the blue. The other three looked at him in surprise.

"Why do you say that"? asked Piotr.

"Because his breath smells," Bill replied.

"Bad breath doesn't necessarily mean you're a homosexual," Piotr objected, "In fact, it's irrelevant."

"Nonsense," Bill retorted in the same self-assured tone, "Because he has bad breath, he's got to assfuck."

Danny and James both burst out laughing, but Piotr continued earnestly.

"You can do that with your wife."

With some impatience James put an end to this prurient conversation.

"It's not HB's alleged perversions that worry me, it's his megalomania. Our next fight, Danny, is on Wednesday. If Arbuthnot gets his proposal through the Governing Council, he'll effectively control research in the Institute. We know what that means."

"What exactly is his proposal," Piotr asked. He was even more worried about HB's rise than the others as he had neither Danny's seniority nor James's and Bill's research record.

"He wants the Senior Dean to have overall responsibility for research. This means that he will draw up and evaluate the various journals and give an evaluation of every professor's yearly research program in addition to the Section Heads. Knowing Winstone, HB's opinion will be the one that counts."

"How the hell can he evaluate my research or yours's"? Bill asked James in amazement. "Come to that, how could he evaluate anyone? He's a fucking zero."

"It's not his abilities that count, it's his power and in particular his power over Winstone."

"Will the proposal get through"? Piotr was clearly apprehensive.

"There's a chance. Hamid, Arbuthnot and that nonentity Tocheniuk from FEB Winstone appointed to the Council will vote in favor. Danny and I will vote against. Probably the faculty representative, Klaus Berger, as well. I'm not sure about Pierre and Ilse. Unfortunately Tom Buchanan doesn't have a vote. One thing's for sure. If it's a tie vote, Winstone will vote in favor of HB, particularly since he had to cross him over the Flint application."

A momentary gloom settled over the gang, but a few more scotches and some obscene jokes from Bill lightened the mood. But not for long.

"You're applying for early tenure this year, Bill"? Danny asked.

"You bet. I goddam well deserve it. I've published five articles in good journals and a book."

James shook his head. "I think it's chancy, Bill. It's not an open and shut case. You're above the average, but you only have one top journal, and you can be sure that Arbuthnot and Winstone will do everything they can to deny you as a way of paying me back for Flint."

"Fucking hell, James, I'm streets ahead of other people who've been granted tenure."

"Yes, but there are two assholes on FPC who are out to get you. Plus the additional asshole Winstone will doubtless appoint. Remember, Bill, if you're denied, that's it. You have to leave the Institute."

There was an ominous silence that was broken by a telephone call from Piotr's wife, Ela, ordering him home.

"I'd be better off divorced," he complained as he prepared to leave

"She's not being unreasonable." James told him. "She's looked after the kids all day."

"You're a fine one to talk," Piotr replied. "Your wife lets you out at nights."

"Well, at least Ela fucks Piotr," Danny remarked once Piotr had left. "I wouldn't mind having a beautiful woman like Ela ordering me home."

Bill gave James a knowing look. It was a sure sign that Danny was getting drunk when he became maudlin. Soon he'd begin reminiscing tearfully about his ex-wife, and Bill couldn't take that.

"Time to end," he declared. "I think we've drunk enough for one night."

The other two grudgingly agreed and left.

*Chapter 5*

# Saturday August 4, 2001 to Thursday August 9, 2001

ANTONIETTA LET THE SUN fill her body with its summer warmth. She was seated in the tree-lined Piazza Santo Spirito opposite the eponymous church designed by Brunelleschi with her childhood friend, Roberto della Rovere, his gay, Antonio, and two of her friends from university, Alessa and Paulina. The three girls were convulsed with laughter at Roberto's description of Antonio's attempts at renovating their apartment.

"We bought it for three hundred million lira," Roberto told them, "and now Antonio's renovated it, it's worth about a hundred million less."

Antonietta looked fondly at Roberto's smiling face. An aristocrat like her, he had nothing of the empty snobbery of their class. "It's a pity he's gay," she thought.

"That's unfair, Roberto," Antonio protested, sipping his expresso. "It's only worth fifty million less."

The laughter continued. Alessa and Paulina finished their white wine and stood up to go. They lived on the Via Roccetini, which was on Antonietta's way to her parents, where she was already expected for her farewell lunch. Her mother had decreed that today would be a full family occasion. In addition to Giovanni and Renata from Florence, Paolo and Monica, Carla and Filiberto and her uncle Andrea della Chiesa and his wife Maria Luisa would be coming from Rome. Thankfully, her Spanish grandmother, Maria Assunta, was not well enough to travel, and Uncle Andrea Palmieri and his wife, Laura Maria, were away on holiday.

"I'll give you a lift," she told the two girls. They left the men, who were ordering yet another expresso.

"No wonder the EU has too much wine," Alessa remarked. "Italians are addicted to coffee."

After dropping off her two friends, Antonietta pursued her drive towards Fiesole, her feelings of aimlessness soothed by the beautiful summer weather. She thought with some apprehension of the upcoming lunch. She hoped her uncle Giovanni would be present even though Saturday was normally a busy day for the Archbishop of Florence. Her Fiat climbed up the Via Vecchia Fiesolana, and, just before the ancient Etruscan town of Fiesole, she turned right into the Badia Fiesolana where her parents lived. As she descended from the car, she observed the breathtaking vista of Florence displayed beneath the villa. She could make out the Vecchio Palazzo and the Loggia dei Lanzi and the magnificent Cathedral soaring high over the city. In the distance the Arno glinted from the sun.

Antonietta was late and the last to arrive, which didn't make for an auspicious beginning to the celebration. Happily, her mother's glacial kiss and Renata's snide comments were overshadowed by Paolo's obvious pleasure at seeing his sister again. Monica too was delighted to see her. Carla and Filiberto were more circumspect, and Antonietta was happy to be rescued by her father from the beginning of a stilted conversation with them.

"It's lovely to see you. You're looking even more beautiful than normal." He gazed in admiration at his lovely daughter.

"It's the suntan," Antonietta replied with false modesty.

"I hear you're going to Canada," her aunt said. "That's a good idea. You'll see something different from our old Italy. It's good for young people to travel away from home."

Antonietta looked at her aunt with gratitude, wishing that her own mother were more like the easy-going Maria Luisa. Her uncle Giovanni also kissed her and wished her well for her trip to Canada. Antonietta was relieved to see him. Her mother was in awe of her older brother and less likely to indulge her aristocratic obsessions when he was present.

They all sat down for lunch. The cook, who was from Milan, had prepared a Milanese meal. It started with antipasto assortito, followed by risotto alla milanese and ossobuco milanese. After the main course there was a tomato and bocconcini salad and a tiramisu. It was an agreeable but, in Antonietta's view, rather pedestrian menu. She sought solace in the wines that her father had thoughtfully chosen with her in mind: an excellent white Vernaccia di San Gimignano and two reds, her favorite Barolo and a Brunello di Montalcino. She was feeling a little tipsy by the time the champagne came to be served with the dessert. It was an Extra Dry Veuve Cliquot, her father's only concession to the French.

As the meal was ending, her father rose to give a toast.

"On Tuesday Antonietta will be starting out on her adventure in the New World. We shall miss her, but I'm sure it will be an enriching experience, and we wish her well. He turned with a grin to his daughter. "Knowing your views, you will be happy to live for two years in a country with a Queen."

Monica looked at Paolo with astonishment. "Canada has a Queen"? she exclaimed, betraying the usual American ignorance of anything to do with their northern neighbor.

"Yes. Elizabeth the Second, to be precise."

"That's crazy. Monarchy is totally anachronistic and useless. All they do is smile, shake hands, open buildings, and cost a lot of money. I can't understand why people still tolerate them."

Fearing the shimmer in Antonietta's eyes presaged an explosion, the Cardinal intervened.

"I understand Monica's point of view," he said. "Today's monarchs, at least in Europe, don't appear to have any power, but that overlooks other important factors. There are many residual powers in a country that shouldn't be placed at the sole discretion of the majority that's temporarily in power. I'm thinking, for example, of the power to nominate the head of government, to appoint judges, to arbitrate where necessary between the parties, to dissolve the legislature, to act as head of the armed forces. You can either have a neutral head of state who exercises these powers, as in most European countries, or you have an executive head of state like the Americans. In the latter case you need so many checks and balances that either you end up with a cumbersome and inefficient system like the Americans, or you ignore the checks and balances and end up with authoritarian government, as happens so often in South America. I prefer the European system, and a hereditary monarch provides a more genuinely neutral arbiter than a president from a particular political party. A monarch is also an important link with a country's past, and like it or not, Monica, they inspire more respect than some superannuated politician as head of state."

The arrival of coffee and grappa ended the discussion. Caterina took cognac as she considered grappa beneath her. Sipping her liqueur, she remarked that Antonietta was not yet a lost cause.

"There's still time to stay in Italy," she told her daughter. "You could go to Rome."

"No thank you, *mamma*. I'm too young to bury myself in Roman society."

Carla was angry with her, and Antonietta was forced to apologize.

"I'm different from you, Carla," she explained. "A lot of people talk about Canada. It's an interesting country, and it's not going to do me any harm to go there."

"You're quite right," said her uncle Giovanni.

"You're too soft on her, Giovanni," Caterina complained

The Cardinal changed the conversation by asking Paolo how his new job as vice-president of the family bank was going.

"Lots of work," Paolo replied. "I'm glad you've brought the subject up. I was talking with Uncle Andrea." He turned towards his other uncle for support, "We both agree that the bank's name should be changed. Banco della Santissima Madre is a ridiculous name for a bank."

Andrea nodded in agreement, but Caterina disagreed forcefully.

"I agree with you too" said Paolo senior, ignoring his wife. "In any case, everyone refers to it as BSSM, which is hardly very proper."

The Cardinal agreed. "I've always thought there was something vaguely blasphemous about calling a bank after the Mother of God, even to show support for the Papacy."

"In that case, why not call it Banco del Popolo to show support for the democratic principle," joked Giovanni.

"You may be joking," replied his brother, "but that would bring us back to the roots of the bank. The only problem is that there would be confusion with the Banco Popolare."

Aware of the tension between the two brothers, their father steered the conversation to a less controversial topic.

"Has anyone been to the *Estate Fiesolana*\*," he asked.

It was Giovanni who replied. "No, but Renata and I are going to the *Marriage of Figaro* in two weeks."

Roy Arbuthnot was pleased with himself. He looked round his new office and savored his victory. Not only had he persuaded Winstone to appoint him Senior Dean, but he'd also succeeded in humiliating that Irish drunkard, Redfern, by taking over both his seniority and his office. All this was just the beginning. Winstone was a weak, vacillating fool, and Arbuthnot intended to control the Institute through him. However, the Rector's failure to support him over the Flint application was worrying. Did this mean that he had an independent streak or, as Arbuthnot suspected, had Markham got to him?

Markham! Arbuthnot's mouth twisted in hatred and disgust. That man represented everything he despised. He was English, a snotty aristocrat born with a golden spoon in his mouth, and a Papist into the bargain. Arbuthnot was convinced that under his airs of social correctness, Markham was a womanizer and a drunk. Why else would he hang out with that dissolute Leaman and Redfem? A right little Papist gang they were: Markham, Redfem and that dozy Polack, Leszek. Arbuthnot thanked God that his friend, Tom McGrath, another God-fearing Presbyterian like himself and of good Scottish blood, would soon replace Markham as head of LIR. Together, with help from Winstone, they'd deal with Markham and his friends. If necessary, he'd use his position as Chair of the Ethics Committee. The immediate task, however, was to reassert his dominance over the Rector.

There was a knock on the door. "Come" he shouted in the imperious manner he deemed fitting for his new position. A tall, handsome student entered the office.

"My name is Brett Doefman, I have a complaint to make about Professor Hunt."

Arbuthnot pricked up his ears. Hunt was a troublemaker. He might think of himself as a brilliant academic, but he had no appreciation for Arbuthnot's work or the strategy courses that he and Flint had developed. Arbuthnot was aware that Hunt was rubbishing both of them and their courses to other faculty members, and he'd vowed to get him despite all his scholarly credentials. Here was what seemed like a heaven-sent opportunity. If it was a question of ethics, he would drag Hunt before his Ethics Committee and destroy him. He asked the student for details in a conniving way that he knew would encourage him to tell all.

Doefman explained that Hunt had seduced his girlfriend. He'd managed to do this by making Doefman seem like an idiot. He'd put him down in class and given him low marks. His girlfriend, of course, had gotten good marks.

"When did your girlfriend end your relationship"? Arbuthnot asked.

"About two-thirds the way through the course," Doefman replied.

"When did her relationship start with Hunt? I mean, Professor Hunt."

"The same time."

Arbuthnot could hardly contain his jubilation. Sexual relations with a student in your class meant instant dismissal for a faculty member.

"Can you prove this"?

Doefman was not duped by Arbuthnot's non-committal manner. He knew from student gossip that the Senior Dean hated Hunt, and he would use this odium to have his revenge on the arrogant bastard who'd stolen his girlfriend. He'd waited for the marks to be published before assembling a group of students: three who had failed the course, and one who had received a conditional pass, like himself. He'd exploited their resentment in order to convince them that Hunt was a rotten individual who had it in for them. It'd been a small step to persuade them that they'd seen Hunt and Annya together or at least say this was the case. He would be careful not to tell Arbuthnot that Annya categorically denied that she and Hunt had started their relationship before the final marks were handed in.

"I have four other students who will testify that they saw Annya and Professor Hunt together."

"Why are you bringing this complaint to me rather than to Professor Khan, who is Professor Hunt's Section Head"? Arbuthnot could see through Doefman, but he needed to know how plausible a liar he could be.

"Because you're Chair of the Ethics Committee." There was a hint of a smirk on his face.

"He'll do," thought Arbuthnot. "Give me your telephone number. I'll be in contact."

Doefman wrote his cell number on the piece of paper Arbuthnot offered him. He also wrote down the names of the four students. He handed the paper back to Arbuthnot, and their eyes met. They understood each other perfectly.

Once Doefman left, Arbuthnot made his way to Ilse Bromhoeffer's office. He knew that he would have to tread carefully. Ilse was no fool and would immediately see through any clumsy attempt to get at Hunt. The animosity between them was too well known.

"Hello, Ilse, I hope I'm not disturbing you." His urbane greeting startled Ilse, who was more used to his normal gruff manner.

"I have much to do," she replied, "but if it's important..." She beckoned Arbuthnot to sit down without bothering to finish her sentence. It was not an auspicious beginning.

"I think it is, but before I come to that, I wanted to tell you I thoroughly support your new guidelines for marking." The truth was that he hadn't bothered to read them. Ilse was forever sending memos on marking, deadlines, office hours, and a myriad of other matters affecting students and their evaluation. The tactic of appealing to Ilse's self-importance worked as she immediately loosened up.

"Thank you. Does that mean you agree to reducing the number of grades"?

"Yes."

Ilse had been waging a campaign for the last two years to replace the 9-point scale with a scale ranging from A to D. Most of the faculty were opposed as it meant they had to change the way they marked, which they felt was an unnecessary waste of their time. Arbuthnot agreed with them, but at this precise moment he needed Ilse's cooperation.

Ilse beamed contentedly. "Well, Roy, what can 1 do for you"?

"I need to check some marks," he replied. "I've had a complaint from a student called Doefman in Elliot's class." He deliberately used Hunt's first name to give an appearance of collegiality.

Ilse looked at Arbuthnot skeptically, her distrust of him gaining the upper hand over her momentary feeling of gratitude.

"Why was the complaint made to you and not Hamid"?

"It involves a relationship between Elliot and Doefman's girlfriend. So it's a matter for the Ethics Committee."

Ilse was not so easily fooled. "Even ethical matters should first be brought before the Section Head," she insisted.

"Ilse, I can only think that Doefman was not aware of our normal procedure."

Arbuthnot was always at his most disarming when he lied, but Ilse was not convinced.

"I'm not sure, Roy. I don't like giving out marks without proper authorization."

"Listen, Ilse." Arbuthnot's voice suddenly became less affable. "I'm Chair of the Ethics Committee and Senior Dean. I think that's all the authorization you need."

The carrot wasn't working, so it was time for the stick.

Ilse hesitated. "Perhaps, but Doefman is a manipulator. He's always complaining about something. I wouldn't place too much confidence in his allegations."

"However, it's a fact that Hunt and Annya are seeing each other." Arbuthnot was categorical although he had no idea whether this was true. It was a gamble, but from the look of disapproval on Ilse's face, it had clearly paid off.

"That's true, but it doesn't mean they started while she was still in his class. Elliot has always seemed a very decent person. Now, if it were Bill Leaman, I would have less doubts about Doefman' accusation."

Unwittingly, Ilse had provided Arbuthnot with his opportunity.

"Hunt and Leaman are friends. You know the saying: birds of a feather flock together." This was probably a lie, but it was to a good end.

Ilse was still hesitating, but Arbuthnot was confident now he'd won. She went to a filing cabinet and took out a folder. She extracted from it the list of marks for Hunt's class.

"You can't take it away. You have to consult it here."

The Senior Dean nodded, not caring where he had to look at the list as long as he got what he wanted. He noted down the names of all the students who had failed the course or received conditional passes. There were eight in all, including Doefman and the four names he'd written down. He also noted Annya Nowak's mark of 8 out of 9. "He could have given her a 9," he thought derisively.

"I should like to have Doefman's paper," he told Ilse, who was watching him warily.

"I need his consent for that."

"Fine." Arbuthnot voice had recovered its earlier smoothness. He returned to his office and called Doefman.

"Mr. Doefman, I need your consent to get hold of your paper. I want to send it to a colleague of mine. He may find it has more merit than Professor Hunt did."

Doefman understood exactly what Arbuthnot had in mind. He readily gave his consent.

Twenty hours after saying goodbye to her father at the airport in Florence, Antonietta finally landed in Montreal. It was four-thirty in the afternoon on a Wednesday. She was tired and a little dispirited. Apart from her four years in England at St. Mary's Convent, Antonietta had rarely traveled outside Italy. She'd made the obligatory visits to her relatives in Spain, and she'd spent a week in Paris when she was eighteen, but that was all. Now here she was on another continent in a country where people spoke English like Americans and French in a way Antonietta had some difficulty understanding.

She presented her Italian passport and study permit to the immigration official, who, taken aback by Antonietta's beauty, just stared at her.

"*Est-ce un problème*"? she asked in faltering French. The immigration officer collected himself and beamed at her. "*Non, mademoiselle. Bienvenue au Québec.*" Antonietta was intrigued. She'd heard about Quebec separatism and assumed this was an example of it. "*Et au Canada, n'est-ce pas*"? "*Naturellement,*" he replied without much enthusiasm. It was a strange introduction to the country.

She took a taxi to rue Sherbrooke and the Hotel Versailles. She unpacked as she would probably be staying for at least a week until she found an apartment and furnished it. It was well after eight when she wandered outside into the humid heat of a Montreal summer evening. The Duke of Messina had recommended her to walk along the rue Ste. Catherine with its bistros and outdoor cafés. She was very hungry as the food on Air Canada had been barely fit for human consumption. She stopped at a terrace bar, ordered a glass of wine, and asked for the menu.

She was soon aware of the stares of the men around her. She dreaded the moment when one of them would accost her. She cursed her beauty, which seemed to bring her only problems and scant happiness. Soon enough, a young man with ridiculous rings in his ears sat down opposite her. He addressed her in a French that bore only the slightest local accent. At least she could understand him.

"*Tu as l'air d'une étrangère. D'où viens-tu*"?

"*Fichez-moi la paix, s'il vous plaît,*" Antonietta was surprised by her own rudeness. The young man shrugged and went back to his friends.

Afterwards Antonietta asked herself why she'd been so rude. Was it the stupid rings, the use of the familiar "tu", or simply the tiredness and irritation of a long and tedious journey? She left the terrace-bar without waiting for the wine. She returned to the hotel and sat alone and depressed in her room. What on earth had possessed her to come to this God-forsaken country? She thought of calling her parents, but it was the early morning hours in Italy, and a conversation with her mother was about the last thing she needed. Tears welled up in her eyes, and it was only with much effort that she fought them back.

Antonietta awoke in the same despondent mood as the evening before. She called her parents, but unfortunately only her mother was at home. The conversation was difficult. Her mother didn't understand what on earth she was doing in Canada and was not all sympathetic. This lack of comprehension compounded Antonietta's own doubts and unhappiness. After lying disconsolately in bed for a while, Antonietta decided it was time to pull herself together. She showered, made herself up, put on a fashionable but not too sexy summer dress she'd bought in the Via Borgognona on one of her rare visits to her sister in Rome, and left to find a café for her morning coffee.

She wandered down Sherbrooke and took University down to Ste. Cathérine. It was a beautiful sunny day, and, although it was early, there were already many people either bustling about or seated in the terraces having breakfast. It felt almost like Italy, and Antonietta's spirits began to revive. She quickly came upon a café called Chez Luigi and entered. Immediately she felt at home listening to the Italian chatter of four older men sitting at one of the tables. She sat down near an open window to watch the people go by. One of the men got up and came over to her.

"What would you like"? he asked gruffly in English. He was short and grey-haired with a swarthy complexion. Antonietta guessed he was from Sicily or Calabria.

"*Voglio un espresso macchiato.*" The man beamed at her, and his manner changed. "*Súbito, signorina.*"

The coffee arrived, and the man, who turned out to be Luigi, asked Antonietta how long she'd been in Montreal. She explained that she'd arrived the day before and was still getting used to being away from home.

"Don't worry, signorina," he told her. "A beautiful woman like you will soon have lots of friends." Seeing that she was not convinced, he went on to extol the glories of living in Canada. "It's an easy place to live. Easier than Italy. People are nice here; they let you do what you want. They don't interfere. The Frenchies are a pain trying to force us to speak French, but we play the game, and everyone's happy."

She stayed over an hour talking to Luigi, who explained the rudiments of living in Quebec and how to get around Montreal. She told him that she was going to study at an institute in Saint-Sauveur.

"My son lives near there. He's a Volkswagen dealer in St. Jérôme and lives in Ste. Anne des Lacs." He must have noticed a look of distrust enter Antonietta's expressive eyes for he added, "With his wife and five children."

Reassured, Antonietta let Luigi arrange for his son, Carlo, to come and pick her up at the hotel on Monday and drive her to St. Jérôme to choose a car. "You should visit Ste. Anne des Lacs too," he told her. "It's near Saint-Sauveur and very pretty. I'm sure you'd like living there."

After three coffees and several Italian pastries, all of which Luigi insisted on paying for, Antonietta decided to walk to Old Montreal. It would be a long haul, but after all the pastries she needed some exercise. She wanted to visit the Notre Dame Basilica, which was supposed to be a marvel of neo-gothic architecture with an interior modeled on the luminous Sainte-Chapelle in Paris. She was not disappointed, although it was more the ornamentation of the Basilica that was neo-gothic; the structure and form were more classical.

On entering the church she admired the beautiful sculptured baptismal font and made her way past the richly adorned chapels of the two Saint Margarets and the Chapel of the Holy Sacrament. The main altar was impressive, but the overall effect of the resplendent paintings and statues was spoiled by the new altar they'd been forced to place in front to accommodate the requirement of the Second Vatican Council that the priest face the congregation when saying Mass. "Why couldn't they have left things alone"? Antonietta asked herself. "That Council destroyed more things of beauty than all the wars of Europe put together."

She was surprised by the sanctuary, which was inspired by the mosaic found in the Basilica Santa Maria Maggiore in Rome, which she knew well. The beautiful and more modern Notre Dame Chapel behind the sanctuary offered an intimacy lacking in the grandeur of the rest of the Basilica. Antonietta knelt and prayed. As she walked back through the Basilica, she was struck by the contrast between the soaring lightness and color wrought by the richly hued stained-glass windows and the somberness of the base and buttresses of the Basilica. She now understood the comparison with the Sainte-Chapelle.

Antonietta came out of the Basilica into the bright sunshine. It was past noon and extremely hot. Across the street was a small restaurant that tempted her, but Luigi had told her to eat at one of the open-air cafes in the Place Jacques Cartier. So she made her way along St. Paul Street until she came to the square. The east and west sides of the square were lined with restaurants. They were all teeming with people, but she managed to find an empty table at one of them. The food was disappointing, the wine acceptable, and the price astronomical. It was a typical tourist trap, but Antonietta didn't mind. The waiter was friendly without being all over her, and no young men with rings in their ears accosted her. She was allowed to eat her lunch in peace, observe the people walking past, and gaze at the impressive St. Lawrence River in the distance to the south of the square. The price didn't bother her, although, when she came to pay the bill, she couldn't help thinking that it was a good thing her family owned a bank. "At least I can be rich even if I can't be fulfilled," she consoled herself.

After lunch she walked along the quays bordering the river. They were rather uninteresting, and she turned back toward Old Montreal and the Bonsecours Market. It was equally uninteresting. She ambled through the streets of the old city. It was quaint but compared poorly with the streets of Florence with their boutiques and cafes. The shops were quite dreary. They seemed to be stocked exclusively with jerseys, baseball caps, and touristic mementoes. After an hour or so she was bored and hailed a taxi. She was too tired to contemplate walking back to the hotel.

Antonietta went back to Luigi's for supper and spent the evening chattering with some of the regulars in Italian. It was well after midnight before she sank down into her bed. She had difficulty falling asleep. Her naked body tossed and turned in the bed. "I could use Giacomo at this moment," she confessed to herself.

*Chapter 6*

# Friday August 10, 2001 to
# Tuesday August 14, 2001

JAMES WAS SURVEYING HIS colleagues on the Governing Council. Hamid Khan and HB were seated together and looking very confidant. Pierre Forget as always looked a little confused and out of place. Tocheniuk was lolling in his chair with an air of self-importance. "Winstone really knows how to choose them," James thought. Klaus Berger, his colleague from LIR, was engaged in a conversation with Tom Buchanan about the fall in the value of the American dollar. Ilse came in and took a seat next to James. She looked very serious as usual but managed to give James a slight smile. "I think she might even like me," he mused. Now all they needed was the Rector.

Winstone arrived with his normal five-minute delay. Unlike King Louis XVIII of France, he obviously didn't believe in the politeness of punctuality*. His face had its habitual bland and expressionless look. If you can't tell what a person's thinking, James's father had once told him, it could be because he's not thinking. This was probably the case with Winstone. He left the thinking to HB.

The procedure on the Governing Council differed from that for FPC. Although it was customary here too for the Rector to vote only in the event of a tie, he nevertheless either introduced his own proposals or stated the Rectorate's position on proposals brought by others on the Council. He also had the final say before the vote was taken.

"Well, colleagues," he intoned, gazing loftily at his flock, "today we have an excellent proposal from Roy Arbuthnot. I'll leave it up to him to present, but I will tell you that I think it'll do much to raise the level of research in the Institute as well as ensuring fairness all round."

He turned to HB, who was sat next to him, and motioned him to start his presentation.

Arbuthnot was at his most ingratiating. First he stressed the importance of research in a university institution. "We're not just here to teach but to advance learning," he declared. He emphasized the necessity of a uniform approach across the Sections. "There's nothing worse in an institution than a feeling that some are being rewarded more than others for the same work," he stated.

James glanced at Danny. They were both thinking the same. If HB had his way, it would be his friends who would be more rewarded.

"What I'm proposing will in no way undermine the authority of the Section Heads. The Senior Dean will only play a coordinating role. He'll be responsible for publicizing grant opportunities and joint research possibilities with other institutions and encouraging professors to take full advantage of them. He would vet all grant proposals. This way he or she can help stimulate and increase our research output."

Arbuthnot paused. He was now coming to the real substance of his proposal, the mechanism that would permit him to gain a stranglehold on research activity in the Institute and promote his own work and that of his acolytes. He knew he had to tread carefully.

"Then, there's the question of equity. I believe the Senior Dean can play a subsidiary but key role here." He emphasized the word "subsidiary", looking directly at Forget. "God, he's really playing him for a fool," was James's reaction, "and he might get away with it." He watched Pierre carefully as Arbuthnot outlined his plan to draw up a common list of journals, each ranked according to its importance and prestige, that would apply across the Sections. Each year he would review a professor's research output on the basis of this list and add his report to the Section Head's annual report on the faculty member. "The Section Head's report takes precedence," he added in a reassuring tone, "and the Senior Dean's input is only to help ensure a more uniform approach towards evaluating research."

It was a virtuoso performance. By constantly referring to the Senior Dean, Arbuthnot avoided giving the impression of seeking power for himself. His emphasis on the subsidiary nature of his role cleverly masked its true importance.

Winstone had the first word as Rector. He lauded HB's research record, his many grants, and his cooperative research with other scholars both at the Institute and elsewhere. "We need to increase our research output and take a cross-section approach to evaluation, and Roy's proposal does both," he concluded.

The next speaker was Hamid Khan. Essentially he just repeated what Winstone had said, and no one seemed to take much notice. He ended by saying that he'd worked closely with Roy for the last three years, and he'd always found him fair and impartial. Danny and James exchanged looks, and James caught a hint of a smile on Ilse's face. That was encouraging.

James's optimism dissipated with Forget's intervention. He was not opposed in principle to Roy's proposal, he said, particularly if it increased research output and ensured a more uniform evaluation, but he wanted it made clear that the primary responsibility for evaluating a faculty member still lay with the Section Head. Winstone asked Arbuthnot to comment.

"I agree entirely, Pierre. The Senior Dean's role is supplementary. The Section Head's report remains the main basis for FPC decisions."

To James's dismay, Forget seemed convinced. It was time to go on the attack if they were going to get his vote. He and Danny had planned a two-pronged strategy, and Danny would go first. James nodded at him, but Tocheniuk's high-pitched voice was already in full flight

"Roy has immense standing in our Section and throughout the Institute. He's exactly the right person to oversee research. I've talked to many of my colleagues. They feel we don't apply a uniform standard, and this is causing dissension."

"That's not my reading," Klaus Berger interjected, "On the contrary, the colleagues seem quite content with the present system of evaluation by the Section Head."

"You must have talked to different people from me," Tocheniuk snapped.

To end the spat, Winstone hurriedly called on Danny. "I oppose the proposal," he said. "It duplicates what we're already doing satisfactorily. We don't need to reinvent the wheel, which is what Roy's proposal does. My office already provides all the information available on grant opportunities, and there's no need to vet the applications. Last year we got twice as much in grant monies as Carleton."

For the first time, Arbuthnot began to look discomfited. Danny noticed this and went on with even more force.

"It's all very well to talk of a uniform approach. To me it seems more like a straitjacket. It's not only journals that count in evaluating research; there are books, work in progress, conference papers, and other factors. That's what Section Heads look at, and for me it's a more balanced approach. Roy's proposal places too much emphasis on journals."

If Danny had stopped there, his contribution would have been perfect. Unfortunately, he let his bitterness over Hard Ball's humiliation of him get the upper hand.

"It seems to me, Roy, that not content with taking over some of the other Deans' responsibilities, you now want to start on the Section Heads."

James was aghast. Danny's attack on HB gave the impression they were out to get Arbuthnot, and James knew Pierre would never join in what he perceived as an anti-Arbuthnot campaign. Luckily, and unexpectedly, Ilse came to the rescue.

"I'm not worried about Section Heads losing authority, Danny, but I do agree with you that the present system works well, and I see no reason to change or duplicate it. There's simply no need for this proposal." She turned towards Tocheniuk and gave him a stern look. "I've never heard any complaints from colleagues about the present system."

Tocheniuk visibly wilted. James was relieved and also intrigued by the She-Wolf's intervention. He was glad they had her vote, but there was something else behind Ilse's words. It seemed like distrust of HB.

It was now his turn to speak. "I agree with Ilse and Danny," he began, deliberately giving the priority to Ilse in the hope that her intervention had overshadowed Danny's indiscretion. "but there's another aspect of the proposal that I find troublesome. I cannot see how Roy, or any person after him who acts in the same capacity, can evaluate journals that are not in his field. Under the present system it's the Section Head who ranks a particular journal after consulting with colleagues in the Section. The whole process is also more complex than Roy's intended approach. Generally speaking, junior faculty find it difficult to publish in top journals, particularly for their first papers. So, Section Heads may on occasion ask colleagues to comment on their papers. It even happens with more senior faculty. It's not at all unusual to have a very good paper that doesn't make it to a top journal for reasons other than its inadequacy."

James paused and waited for Arbuthnot's reply. It was important to give the impression of reasoned doubt rather than a categorical rejection that could be seen as a personal rejection of Arbuthnot.

"As I emphasized earlier," Arbuthnot replied, "I'm only suggesting a supplementary role for the Senior Dean. The Section Heads will carry on as you describe, but there will be the Senior Dean's report to correct any inequities across Sections." His tone was ingratiating, but James could sense HB' loathing for him. If only he could bring it to the surface, he might get Pierre Forget to change his mind

"Tell me, Roy, how do you intend to rank journals outside your area"?

HB now made his first mistake. "I shall ask colleagues from other institutions."

James didn't miss his chance. "Does this mean you don't trust your colleagues here in the Institute"?

"I didn't say that," Arbuthnot protested.

"Surely that's what you're implying by imposing a ranking of journals on the Institute that has in effect been drawn up by outsiders."

Hamid Khan attempted to come HB's rescue. "James, Section Heads sometimes go outside themselves."

"That's true, but only if there's no one internally who's suitable. It's never done instead of seeking the advice of colleagues, which is what this proposal intends."

James was looking at Pierre during these exchanges and was discouraged to note that they didn't appear to be convincing him. Then, on the brink of defeat, Arbuthnot suddenly handed him victory.

Irritated by James's remarks, detesting his clipped English accent, and still smarting from their previous duel, he let his feelings boil over.

"You're just being obstructive, Markham"! he shouted, "You shouldn't even be here. McGrath is now Section Head."

Controlling his jubilation at provoking HB into this disastrous attack on him, James remained calm. "My appointment lasts until Tom arrives, and that's not until July 23rd."

"That's true, Roy," Winstone was forced to concede.

Arbuthnot retreated into a sullen silence. Forget gave him a look of disgust that was balm to James and Danny. Berger and Tom Buchanan drove the nails into the coffin of HB's ambitious plans by forcefully rejecting the proposal.

"To go outside the Institute after all the work we've put in to make it the top faculty in our area makes absolutely no sense," Tom declared flatly.

It was now up to Winstone to give his closing assessment. It was a poor performance for he merely repeated what he'd said at the beginning. There was no attempt to counter the objections raised against the proposal. When the vote was taken, Arbuthnot, Khan and Tocheniuk voted in favor, and Danny, Berger, Ilse and James voted against. Forget abstained. This meant that even if Winstone ignored custom and voted for the proposal, it would result in a tie vote. To be adopted, a proposal needed a majority in favor. Winstone didn't bother to vote and looking severely at James left the room. Arbuthnot glared at James, got up, and marched out as well.

"I don't think you're very popular, James, my boy," Danny remarked, nodding after Winstone and Arbuthnot.

"They can go to hell," was James's reply.

"They will, my boy, they will indeed. Like all heretics."

They both laughed, perhaps more out of relief for their victory than at the not unpleasant image of Winstone and Arbuthnot in hellfire.

"Why are you two so pleased with yourselves"? Tom Buchanan had joined them. "You nearly blew it, Danny, and if Arbuthnot hadn't lost his temper, Pierre would've voted with him."

Danny looked crestfallen, but James was having none of it. "True, Tom, but it was I who drove him to lose his temper."

"That's true," Tom admitted, "but, to quote Wellington, it was a damn near run thing."*

"I need a drink," Danny announced once Tom had left. "Let's go to my place and get pissed. We deserve it, even if Tom doesn't think so."

"Good idea. I'll round up Bill and Piotr."

꧁

While the four friends were enjoying their sybaritic libations to the accompaniment of much laughter, a more sober and baleful drink was taking place in the Faculty Club.

"It's partly your fault, Roy," Winstone was saying. "If you hadn't lost your temper, Forget would have voted for you, and I could have given the casting vote in your favor."

Arbuthnot furrowed his brows. Winstone was right, and he was concerned that this second defeat would undermine his influence over the Rector. He went on to the attack.

"They're bad academics," he declared, ignoring Winstone's criticism. "The fact that they opposed my proposal shows that. They want to have things all their own way without any control. They don't want a higher standard of research because they can't meet it."

"But Markham has an excellent record."

"How do you know? Al Guarini would've swallowed anything Markham told him."

The Rector winced. Arbuthnot might be right, but somehow it was shocking to hear someone talk ill of a man who after eight years as Head of LIR had suddenly and inexplicably taken his own life.

"They're morally frivolous," Arbuthnot went on, "all that gang: Markham, Leaman, Leszek, Redfern. Three of them are Papists to boot. No wonder they drink so much. Leaman's always sniffing around the female students. Probably Markham too."

Winstone wanted to believe Arbuthnot. He couldn't forget how Markham had humiliated him, but he had difficulty believing in his moral turpitude. He looked unconvinced.

"Markham's too big for his boots," the Senior Dean declared, changing his approach. "He prevented Len from getting his professorship by going behind our backs, and now he's sabotaged my proposal to

63

improve our research record. He needs to be taken down a peg or two. And we must get rid of Leaman."

"How"? It wasn't the moral turpitude in his opponents that worried Winstone but how to deal with them.

"I'm opening a file on Elliot Hunt. A student came to see me to complain that Hunt had seduced his girlfriend during their class."

"How does this concern Markham or Leaman"?

"I'm going to see whether there is enough evidence to warrant bringing Hunt before the Ethics Committee, and if we do, we'll have Markham defend him."

Winstone was out of his depth. "Granted we appoint the faculty member to defend Hunt, but how does appointing Markham cut him down to size"? he asked, quite mystified.

Arbuthnot smiled with infinite malice. "If Markham wins, he'll be seen by the more decent elements of the Institute for what he is, a libertine. If he loses, he'll forfeit that aura of invincibility he's built up around the more seditious elements. Either way he'll lose."

Winstone lifted up his glass of white wine to Arbuthnot. "A stroke of genius," he exclaimed in admiration. "What about Leaman? Rumor has it he wants to come up this year for early tenure."

"All the better. Leave it to me. I'll fix Leaman."

Winstone finished his wine contentedly. It really did help having someone to deal with the unpleasant details. HB sipped the remaining drops of his tonic water. He was reassured; he had reestablished his ascendancy over the weak fool of a Rector.

Antonietta had harbored serious misgivings about agreeing to go with a complete stranger. She wondered whether she'd end up in some Middle Eastern harem. However, when Carlo arrived to collect her at the hotel, her fears dissipated for he could only be a car salesman. He was balding, overweight, and voluble.

They had some difficult communicating at first. Unlike his father, Carlo spoke pure Calabrian as he'd lived there for ten years with his grandparents after the premature death of his mother. Worse still, when Antonietta didn't understand his Italian, he would switch into the rustic Quebecois French he'd picked up from his wife, which she could understand even less. Eventually, they agreed to speak English, which worked for both even though at times Carlo had trouble with Antonietta's British version.

Antonietta was not impressed by the drive to St. Jérôme. She'd heard a lot about "La belle Province", but she found the scenery on this stretch of road far from beautiful. She was not particularly enamored of St. Jérôme either. Carlo's dealership was north of the city on the way to Prévost where the Laurentians really begin. It was a sunny day, and the tree-covered hills were magnificent in their summer splendor.

She'd been wrong about Carlo. He might look like a shyster, but he seemed genuine enough. There was no point in spending a lot of money on a new car, he told her, when she was only staying for two years. A used car that was still under warranty carried no more risk than a new one, and it was much less expensive. Alternatively, he could offer her a brand-new Jetta that had been used as a demonstration model. The price was very reasonable, and Antonietta decided to buy it.

Carlo took her to Saint-Sauveur to open a bank account. For the first time Antonietta was enthusiastic about her new abode. "It's so pretty, and there are so many restaurants." When Carlo agreed to let her have the car right away upon payment of a small deposit while she waited for funds to arrive from Italy, she seized upon the opportunity to invite him to lunch at one of the Italian restaurants in Saint-Sauveur.

After lunch Carlo took Antonietta to visit Ste. Anne des Lacs, which she found quite attractive. It was difficult to find accommodation in Saint-Sauveur, he told her, and Ste Anne was right close by. He introduced her to his wife, who suggested that Antonietta inspect a furnished cottage near the entrance to the village. It belonged to a friend of her's who was looking for a new tenant. They met the lady, who was from Montreal and spoke a French that Antonietta could easily understand.

The cottage was set back from the road and surrounded by trees. It was a little isolated, but there were two other houses at some distance on either side. Inside there were two rooms that could serve as a bedroom and a study, respectively, a small living room, and a large kitchen in which you could eat. The bathroom was small but modern. There was even a laundry room with a washer and dryer. The cottage was furnished simply but adequately. Antonietta was charmed by the place. There were a few pieces of furniture she would have to buy, but that was all. She agreed on the spot to rent the cottage, wrote a check on her new account for two months' rent, and arranged to move in the following Monday.

It was quite late when she arrived back at the hotel in her newly purchased Jetta, which she had some difficulty parking. She showered, changed her clothes, and went off to Luigi's to eat and recount her day. Luigi beamed when she told him that she hadn't only bought a car from his son, but also rented a cottage in Ste. Anne des Lacs as well.

"You'll love it there," he told her.

~*~

James was loading some heavy boxes and his computer on to a dolly and preparing to leave the Section Head's office, which he had occupied for over a year. At the door he came face to face with Tim McGrath, the new head of the Section

"Still here"? McGrath asked.

James's shackles rose at McGrath's manner, but he maintained his self-control.

"I couldn't get the dolly until today," he explained. "Otherwise I'd be long gone."

McGrath grunted and sat down behind what was now his desk.

"What are these papers"? he asked, pointing to a row of files that were arranged neatly on the desk.

"They're for you," James replied, trying to stay polite. "Some information on the Section and my comments on the faculty members to help you draw up their annual reports."

"Thank you, but I'll make up my own mind."

James was tempted by a tart reply but decided to leave before the conversation turned openly hostile. But McGrath was not finished with him.

"Roy told me about your opposition to his research proposal. I would've preferred you to ask my opinion first because I thoroughly support the proposal."

All James's suspicions about McGrath and his friendship with HB as well as his natural antipathy towards Scottish Presbyterians now came to the fore. He looked at McGrath with ill-disguised loathing.

"Until you arrived, I had full authority to act as Section Head, which is what I did. I didn't need your opinion."

"Well, now I'm here, and I intend to run the Section as I see fit."

"That's your prerogative," James commented and left the office without another word. "What an asshole," he said to himself. "Between him and HB, we're in for a rough time."

*Chapter 7*

# Wednesday August 15, 2001 to
# Sunday August 19, 2001

L AN FLIGHT 5531 TAXIED to its allotted bay at Arturo Merino Benitez airport in Santiago de Chile. "Thank God," Bill Leaman muttered. It had been a long journey from Miami, ten hours in all with a stopover in Lima, and before that there had been the flight from Montreal. He stood up and gathered his and James's briefcases from the overhead bin and prepared himself to endure the long wait that airlines normally inflict on their passengers before allowing them to disembark. To his surprise, the plane emptied very quickly.

"Chilean efficiency," James commented, aware of his friend's low opinion of Latin Americans.

The immigration and customs formalities were dispatched with equal efficiency, and James and Bill were soon standing outside the airport in line for a taxi to take them to the Hotel Bristol in downtown Santiago. It was twelve-thirty in the afternoon on a sunny but cool day.

"God damn, it's cold for August," Bill complained. He was wearing only the light jacket with which he'd left summery Montreal.

"Of course it is, it's winter." James replied. Bill grinned. James could always be relied upon to fall for his "ignorant American" routine.

Their taxi arrived. The international airport in Santiago lies to the east of the city, but the driver proceeded first southwards along the Vespucci ring road. At the junction with route 65, which to the left leads to the coast, he turned right towards Santiago's main street, Avenida Bernardo O'Higgins. It was early afternoon, but there were few cars on the road.

"They must all be having lunch," Bill remarked.

"It's a public holiday," James informed him. "The Feast of the Assumption."

"What the hell's that"?

Aware of his friend's religious skepticism, James answered Bill's question with as non-committal an explanation as possible of the assumption of the Virgin into heaven. Even so, Bill was incredulous.

"You mean to say the old bird just floated up, like a balloon"?

James couldn't help laughing despite the blasphemy. "That's not exactly the way I learned it at catechism, but you've got the essential idea."

"Amazing. Tell me, do you believe in that crap"?

"I believe in its symbolic importance."

Bill was really none the wiser with this enigmatic response, but he didn't persist. Although James was his closest friend, he never felt he knew the man completely. James kept much to himself. Just how religious was he, and was there a secret life that enabled him to support his arid marriage? These were questions Bill often asked himself. Even in his political discussions James conserved a certain ambiguity. At times he seemed as right-wing as Bill himself, at other times he would indulge in frankly vituperative remarks about George Bush Junior, the new President, and the American Right in general. This trip to South America, which was not a place Bill liked to visit, would perhaps allow him to penetrate the enigma. It was one of the reasons he'd decided to accompany James.

They arrived at the hotel. After a shower and shave the two met in the bar for a couple of scotches before a late lunch. The restaurant in the Hotel Bristol had five stars and boasted an excellent array of Chilean and international dishes. Bill gazed disconsolately at the first page of the menu.

"Do they have anything edible"?

"The international dishes are on the next page. You can probably find a steak."

James himself ordered Antarctic krill as an entrée and golden king klip filet with sea algae for the main course. "I'm not sure I even want to watch you eat that stuff," Bill complained. He ordered a steak for himself with a Caesar salad as his entrée. James asked for a bottle of Carmenere*, which was so enjoyable that they had a second bottle for their dessert, after which they both slept until evening.

~

The next day they walked to Avenida Diagonal Paraguay, which was just behind the hotel, to meet James's friend, Eduardo Valdes, who was head of the Economics Department of the University of Chile. A genial man in his middle forties, he welcomed them with open arms and was enthusiastic about the planned exchanges with NIIS. They were joined by Ricardo Moncada, who was in charge of international relations for the University of Chile, and Enrico Muñoz, who was the Dean of the Business School. The five of them spent an industrious morning discussing the various problems associated with student exchanges: the language barrier, student financing, course evaluation and equivalencies, insurance etc. James knew that, unless these issues were dealt with satisfactorily, any agreement between the two institutions was pointless. They agreed on special language courses--both prior and during the exchange--financial subsidies, and a general acceptance of equivalency for courses of equal length and covering substantially the same matter. Both sides agreed to take up with their respective health authorities the question of medical coverage for foreign guest students.

After the discussion Bill went off with Ricardo to meet his opposite number in charge of receiving foreign students--who turned out to be a very beautiful woman--while James went for a drink with Eduardo. He invited the two friends to dinner that evening at Coco's, Santiago's most famous restaurant. Bill eventually joined them and waited impatiently for Eduardo to leave so he could regale James with his impressions of Angelina Navarro.

"My God, I'd like to roger her."

"Her and a hundred other women. What you need is a good walk."

"I didn't come here for exercise," Bill protested, "I came here to get laid."

"I thought we came on academic business."

"That too, but the one doesn't exclude the other."

They took a taxi to the hotel, had a light lunch, and at James's insistence walked down the Avenida Bernardo O'Higgins. As they proceeded, Bill pointed out the extraordinary number of photo shops. There was one almost every hundred yards. "They sure like taking photos, these Chileans," he remarked. Eventually they reached the Moneda Palace, which is the residence of the Chilean President. Staring at it, Bill started imitating planes bombing the place.

"Just think, that's where we got that Commie Allende"! he exclaimed. "Without Pinochet, he would've turned Chile into another Cuba." He turned triumphantly towards James. "And who helped bring it about. We did. The good old US of A."

"Yes, you must've been very pleased with yourselves. You murdered a democratically elected President and replaced him with a thug who tortured and killed thousands of his own people. Well done"!

"Come on, Jimmy, don't be so fucking pinko. Allende was subverting the constitution, and after only three years in power there was nothing left in the shops."

"That's the official story, but I'm skeptical. Two days after the coup, the shops were full again. I think it was just another of your infamous regime changes."

"You can't deny that Pinochet did a lot for Chile," Bill insisted. "God damn it, he reduced poverty to below the US level. That's a hell of an achievement."

James was silent a moment. "Yes, I admit Pinochet did a good job with the Chilean economy, and I'm sure Allende would have ended up ruining the country in typical left-wing fashion. But that's not why you Americans overthrew him. You did it to put a thug in power who would safeguard your own geopolitical and economic interests. Don't try and make me believe you cared a fig for the wellbeing of the Chilean people. It was just happy chance that the thug ran the country well. Even so, that doesn't excuse his atrocities." James was going to add "which you Americans condoned and even participated in", but he knew this would make Bill really angry. As it was, he was upset.

"Come on, let's try and find a café to have a drink." James put his arm around Bill and led him away from the palace of discord. They reached the hotel without finding a single café. "They must be too busy taking photos to stop for a drink," Bill concluded. "There's a café on Vicuña Mackenna," James replied. Bill groaned. "Remind me to bring my running shoes next time I go anywhere with you." After a brisk walk they reached the café and sat there on an uncommonly warm winter's afternoon restoring their spirits with pisco*. They were more than a little merry when Eduardo arrived to take them to Coco's.

Coco's is a fish restaurant where you eat surrounded by sea motifs. Two large aquarians stand at each side of the entry filled with exotic fish of various colors. Behind the table where they were seated was an artificial waterfall, and they ate to the sound of flowing water. The waterfall was partially covered by bunches of rushes into which a myriad of little lights had been placed. On the sides were little ponds containing water lilies of bright red, blue, and yellow.

James ordered fresh king crab as an entrée and deep-fried conger eel for the main course. Bill, who considered fish to be food fit only for cats and sissies, scrutinized the menu in the hope of finding a beef dish. He was lucky and was able to order a Caesar Salad followed by baked spareribs.

"One of these days, you'll wake up speaking Latin," James quipped. Eduardo laughed uproariously, but Bill looked blank.

"Caesar, you see"? James explained.

Bill was not amused. "Very droll," he muttered.

"Well, it does lose something in the explanation," James admitted, but he refused to accommodate Bill's bad humor. The hilarity of his two companions proved infectious, and Bill joined in the laughter.

"Tell me, Eduardo, my friend James here thinks that the overthrow of Allende was illegal and another infamous example of American-engineered regime change. Do you agree"?

Eduardo raised his eyebrows in surprise. "I never took you for a left-winger, James," he said with more than a hint of deprecation in his voice.

"I'm *not*," James retorted. "I just don't approve of encouraging another country's Armed Forces to overthrow a democratically elected government."

"James, that's just left-wing propaganda to believe that Allende was the innocent victim of a military putsch. The truth is very different. Remember that in the 1970 election Allende received merely 36% of the vote, and Congress only agreed to appoint him President once he'd signed what was called a 'Statute of Constitutional Guarantees'. He didn't respect that Statute and started to rule illegally by decree. He interfered with the enforcement of judicial sentences, he imposed workers' committees on companies without the approval of Congress, he encouraged violent land takeovers, and he imported Cuban militia and Cuban arms into Chile. First the Constitutional Court and then the Chamber of Deputies declared that, because of its violation of the Statute, the Allende government had lost its legitimacy. It was the democratically elected Congress that called upon the Armed Forces to remove Allende and restore the rule of law. Even then the Armed Forces didn't act. Military takeovers are not in our tradition. It was only after Allende and his supporters fomented mutinies in the navy, and the country was on the brink of civil war, that the Armed Forces overthrew Allende. They were acting on behalf of the lawful Congress against an illegal regime"

There was silence while James digested Eduardo's presentation. Bill was beaming. "There was still American interference," was all James could manage as a riposte.

"A good thing too," Eduardo replied. "During the cold war it would have been criminal negligence to let a country like Chile slide into the Communist orbit. Once the Cubans and North Koreans started interfering, the Americans were not only justified but obliged to do likewise."

James could see that Eduardo was becoming worked up. He put his hand on the Chilean's shoulder. "You've convinced me, Eduardo."

James's capitulation and the arrival of the food restored Eduardo's normal good humor. The rest of the meal passed most agreeably, as did the numerous scotches with which Bill and James finished the evening at the Hotel Bristol.

⌒⪨⌒

The next day both were a little under the weather when they arrived at the Directorate for Academic Exchanges of the prestigious Pontificia

Universidad Católica de Chile. The Pontificia takes itself very seriously as one of the leading South American universities and is very choosy about its academic partners. Founded in 1881, it clearly looked with some disdain upon the upstart NISS, and the young Director received James and Bill with corresponding coolness. Any suggestion of a double degree at the master's or Ph.D. level was out of the question, he told them. The Pontificia was only prepared to look into a limited exchange at the undergraduate level. They would evaluate the courses in the various disciplines offered at NIIS, and there could be a more meaningful discussion next time James and Bill were in Santiago.

Barely concealing his anger, James glared at the Director. "That's a good idea," he said, "but before we go any further, I would like to know how many of your faculty members have doctorates."

"Enough," the Director replied, clearly taken aback by James's question.

"I'm afraid that's not an adequate answer. You see, all our faculty are required to have doctorates, except in law where an LL.M. is considered to be a final degree. I didn't realize this was not the case with the Pontificia." James knew full well this was not the case either with the Pontificia or the University of Chile, but his objective was to humiliate the Director.

"We only hire the most qualified and prestigious academics." The Director was clearly ruffled.

"I'm sure that's true." James's tone appeared more conciliatory, but it served only to render his final comment all the more incisive. "Nonetheless, we'll wait to make contact again until we have the exact figures on the doctorates."

The Director gasped at such impertinence. James stood up and pointed to their visiting cards, which the Director had thrown carelessly on his desk. "Please contact us at your convenience. I'm Dr. Markham and this is Dr. Leaman." He placed particular emphasis on their doctoral titles. Thereupon he nodded curtly and left the office without further ado, followed by an admiring and highly amused Bill Leaman.

"You can be a real bastard when you put your mind to it."

"Arrogant asshole. He deserved it."

They went back to the hotel, picked up their luggage, and left for the airport. They checked in at the LAN desk for their flight to Buenos Aires and had a long lunch. It hadn't been an entirely satisfactory visit to Santiago, but at least the arrangements with the University of Chile looked promising.

⌇

James bought a voucher for a taxi from the central stand at Ezeiza international airport, and soon he and Bill were headed eastwards towards the city of Buenos Aires. The taxi reached the city limits and proceeded down the Avenida 9 de Julio, the widest in the world, turning right onto the Avenida Santa Fe to take them to the Hotel Plaza San Martín. They made their way to the reception desk and stood in line. The receptionist, who was busy with another couple, was an extremely pretty blond.

"Shit, I'd like to roger that one," Bill whispered loudly to James, who looked at him aghast. "If you insist on being a vulgar American, couldn't you at least be a quiet vulgar American." Bill laughed. "She probably doesn't speak English." he said with assurance.

The girl was certainly very attractive. The women of Buenos Aires were known for their beauty, but it tended to be a diaphanous beauty. They were too slim for James's taste and lacked voluptuousness. This girl was different. Her figure was trim but full, and her bosom was barely contained by her blouse. She was a picture of lubricity.

The girl handed her clients their room key and turned towards Bill, who addressed her in the execrable Spanish he'd picked up in Texas.

"What is your name, Sir," she asked in perfect English. Bill reddened slightly and replied "Leaman." "Roger Leaman"? she asked. James could barely contain his mirth, but Bill was not amused." No, *Bill* Leaman," he replied surlily. The girl checked him in, took an imprint of his credit card, and handed him the room key. "Have an enjoyable stay," she said with a slight smirk. Bill slunk away without even waiting for James.

The girl turned towards James. "*Me llamo* Markham, James Markham," he told her. The girl looked up him with her clear blue eyes. "Do you have a reservation"? she asked in Spanish. "Yes, it was made from Canada at the same time as Dr. Leaman's," he replied in the same language, feeling that he owed it to Bill to raise his profile by emphasizing the doctoral title. The girl was too intrigued by James's faultless Spanish to pay any attention to Bill's academic credentials.

"*Como se hace que habla si bien el castellano*\*"? she asked, pronouncing "castellano" with the typical *porteño*\* slur.

"*Pasé mucho tiempo en España,*\*" James explained, aware of the growing attraction between the two of them. "*Pero soy inglés.*" He handed over his British passport.

The girl's attitude changed immediately. The blue eyes showed no emotion, but the tone became curt, even hostile.

"I believe you let the British into Argentina."

"Unlike you. Argentineans are not welcome in the Malvinas."

James was annoyed. "Good God," he thought, "the war's been over for years, and they're still sore about it."

"Well, we didn't invade you. That's the difference," he snapped and took back his passport with a gesture indicating that for him the conversation was over.

"You did, twice," the girl countered, turning the full force of her beautiful eyes upon James.

"We did"? This was the first time he'd heard of these invasions, and he didn't know whether to believe her. "What happened"? he asked nevertheless.

"We beat you both times," was the proud answer.\*

"Then it was about time you let us win one."

For the first time the blue eyes lost their serenity. "War is not a game. Many people died."

James's irritation vanished. There was a sadness in the girl's comment that made him suspect she was not a stranger to one of these deaths. He wanted to apologize but couldn't think of suitable words. The girl handed him back his credit card and told him the number of his room.

He was about to enter the elevator when he heard the girl call his name. He turned round and found her standing before him, the keycard to his room in her hand.

"I forgot to give you this," she said but made no effort to hand it to him. For a brief moment they just gazed at each other. Finally James found the words he wanted.

"I'm sorry for what I said. You're right, war is not a game."

"No, it's I who should apologize," the girl replied. She smiled at him. "It's not very professional to insult the guests."

God, those eyes! James couldn't resist them any longer. "When do you finish work"? he asked.

"At eleven," she replied. She had clearly been expecting the question.

"I thought I might have a drink in La Barra. Why don't you join me after work"?

"Perhaps."

"Well, perhaps you'll give me my keycard." Now it was James's turn to smile. "And tell me your name."

"Carolina."

She gave him the keycard.

*"Entonces, hasta luego, Carolina."*

The girl didn't answer but simply turned and walked back to the reception desk. It was no matter. James already knew the response.

⟶

After unpacking and taking a quick shower, James and Bill met in the lobby and set out for a small restaurant that James knew on Suipacha street. Bill looked in wonder at the menu, which consisted entirely of beef dishes. At last this was real food. He ordered beef empanadas as an entrée and *Churrasco*\* as a main course. James followed suit but had a tussle with the waiter, who insisted on bringing them the house wine. James sent it back and made the waiter go down to the cellar and find a bottle of Susana Balbo. Bill, for whom the quantity of wine was considerably more important than the quality, teased him.

"You're a wine snob."

"It's not snobbery. The main grape they use in Argentina is Malbec, and unless it's mixed with another grape, preferably Cabernet Sauvignon, it's tannic and unpleasant. I've had their house wine, and even you wouldn't like it. The Susana Balbo is excellent. It has about fifteen percent Cabernet."

The waiter arrived with the bottle, and Bill was forced to admit that it was a good-tasting wine. "I hope they've got a few more bottles," he remarked.

"I'm too tired to drink much," said James, thinking of the luscious blond that probably awaited him in La Barra.

"Hopefully not too tired for a visit to the bar across the road. It's full of women."

"They're hookers, Bill," James told him, but this didn't daunt Bill.

"So what? They can't be that expensive, and I brought some condoms with me."

James sighed. He knew Bill had been looking forward to his first night in Buenos Aires, but it was already ten-thirty, and by the time they'd paid and got back to the hotel, it would be past eleven. "Tomorrow, Bill, I promise, but tonight I'm too tired."

They returned to the hotel, and Bill retreated in bad humor to his room. Once he was sure that his friend was out of the way, James left the hotel and walked to La Barra. A few minutes later Carolina arrived.

Bill awoke early on Saturday morning after his disappointing evening. He took a shower and tried to call James, but he couldn't make head nor tail of the phone system. He walked down to James's room and knocked on the door. After an interval James emerged, swathed in a bath towel.

"What about breakfast"? Bill asked

"Go on ahead. I've still got to shower and deal with a few things."

It was clear to Bill that James didn't particularly want to come down for breakfast, although he had no idea why. If that meant he was going to spend the morning alone, he might as well visit the city. Brushing past James before he could be stopped, he went to pick up the book on Buenos Aires that was lying on the table. Carolina gasped and didn't have enough time to cover herself before Bill caught sight of her in the bed. He bowed slightly and excused himself. He took the book and made for the door.

"Too tired to go a whorehouse. You lying bastard."

"I'll see you around noon in the bar," James replied and hurried Bill out of the room.

He returned to the bed and lifted up the sheet to reveal Carolina's voluptuous and nude body.

"He wanted to go to a whorehouse"? she asked. "You too"?

James kissed her and caressed her breasts. "No. I had no need of a whorehouse."

"Tell your friend that the girls in the Recoleta are better looking than those on Suipacha."

"How do you know"?

"When I need some extra money, I go to the Recoleta."

"You're a hooker"? James was astonished at the girl's candor. Carolina laughed, her blue eyes serene and clear. "Only occasionally, and certainly not at this moment."

She kissed him and ran her tongue down his body. She took his sex between her pert breasts, excited him and then took it into her mouth and pleasured him. Afterwards she lay down with her legs wide open. He licked and sucked her breasts and sex before penetrating her.

⌒❧⌒

Antonietta enjoyed her new car, and on Friday she set out for Quebec City. Next week she would be arranging her cottage and buying whatever bits and pieces she needed, and the week after that she would have to register for her courses, buy materials, and attend an orientation course. So she'd decided to spoil herself and stay this weekend at the Chateau Frontenac in Quebec City. It stood majestically on a buff overlooking the St. Lawrence River in the heart of the city. She arrived around eight o' clock in the evening and dined alone in Le Bistro. She went to bed quite early, but it was quite a while before she fell asleep. "This can't go on," she told herself. "I need some sex."

The following day, Saturday, Antonietta toured Quebec City on foot. She wandered through the narrow and quaint streets down to the old port. The St. Lawrence River was so immense that it seemed like the ocean. Only the smell was missing. She walked around the market and then along the Rue St. André to a restaurant she'd been recommended, the Laurie Raphaël. She ate a hearty bistro-type meal, which she washed down with an excellent Chianti Classico. The waiter was obviously intrigued by this beautiful woman who ordered a whole bottle for herself. He asked where she came from, and they chatted happily for a few minutes. Antonietta's French was improving.

A little tipsy, Antonietta took a taxi back to the Chateau Frontenac. She was bored with her own company. However interesting Quebec City may be, she had no more stomach for wandering around alone. She stripped off her clothes and lay down on the bed, naked. She would have given anything to have an attractive man next to her. As there was no point in dwelling on her sexual frustration, she took a shower and settled down to read some poems by Leopardi. She admired his purity of style and classic forms, and his poetry encapsulated a romantic nostalgia for the unobtainable that so often gripped her. By the time she'd finished reading, she was thoroughly depressed. She slipped into a troubled sleep and awoke around seven thirty. She showered again, put on her make-up, chose the sexy black dress and bra she'd bought in Florence, and went down to have an evening meal in the sumptuous Le Champlain restaurant. It was part of the hotel and overlooked the St. Lawrence River. The staff were dressed in seventeenth century costumes and looked faintly comical.

A young waiter showed her to a table by the window. *"Vous avez une belle vue d'ici, mademoiselle,"* he told her. Antonietta sat down and looked across at the next table. A man, she guessed in his mid-forties, was also dining alone. He was very handsome and elegant. From his brief exchange with the unctuous waiter, Antonietta concluded that he was French.

She ate self-consciously and drank sparingly. She desperately wanted the man to talk to her. In fact, she wanted to be in his bed. The meal seemed to last an eternity, but still the man, who had long since finished his meal and was nursing a cognac, didn't say anything to her. "The one time I want to be irresistible," Antonietta said to herself, "I come across this man. He must be gay." But he didn't look gay. Antonietta finished her expresso and was on the point of leaving the table to go back to the cold solitude of her room when the man finally addressed her.

*"Mademoiselle, est-ce que vous voudriez prendre un digestif avec moi"*?

Desperately trying to hide her relief and enthusiasm, Antonietta acquiesced. The man introduced himself as "Philippe", and Antonietta also used only her first name. This suited her as what she wanted was a night of anonymous sex, not a relationship. They talked about Quebec City, Canada, France and Italy. Philippe showed a surprising familiarity with Italy. As he charmed her, Antonietta's prejudices against the French began to evaporate, and her desire for him became almost unbearable.

"What are you doing in Quebec City"? she asked, ordering her third cognac.

"I'm attending a conference of surgeons," he replied. Antonietta gave an involuntary gasp. "Did this man know her father"?

Philippe noticed her reaction and gave a short laugh. "You don't like surgeons"? Antonietta searched frantically for a convenient lie. "You don't look like a surgeon," she managed eventually. It was clear that Philippe didn't believe the answer, but he said nothing. They talked about her plans for a diplomatic career and the Institute in Saint-Sauveur. Antonietta motioned to the waiter.

"Please don't have another cognac." Philippe placed his hand on Antonietta's, which made her shiver. "I want to seduce you, but not after another cognac."

Antonietta felt insulted. "You don't want to make love to a drunk woman."

"I don't think there's a man on earth who would pass up the chance to make love to you, drunk or not," Philippe replied with a smile that completely disarmed Antonietta. "No, it's an old-fashioned question of honor. I like to think of myself as a gentleman, and I want you to go to bed with me *en pleine connaissance de cause*\*."

Antonietta waved the waiter away. She leaned over the table towards Philippe in such a way as to expose her breasts to his view. They were already hardening with the anticipation of pleasure.

"Finish your drink. A gentleman shouldn't keep a lady waiting."

Antonietta stretched as she awoke. After a night of sex she was spared her recent feeling of frustration, but she was still not completely satisfied. Philippe had proved to be a very conventional lover, and Antonietta craved more dissolute satisfaction. She looked over at the firm, nude body next to her and resolved to indulge herself. She stroked Philippe's face and kissed him until he stirred. Once he was awake, she ran her tongue down his torso towards his sex. She brushed her erect nipples along the shaft and took it into her mouth, applying herself until

Philippe came. She moved her damp lips up over his belly and stomach until she reached his face. She dangled her fulsome breasts before him, mounted him and obliged him to perform oral sex on her. "Suck me," she ordered and, arching her back, reached her climax. She remained on Philippe's mouth to enjoy the soft after-spasms of her remaining lust.

Sated at last, Antonietta regained her own room. She showered, did her hair, put on some make-up, and prepared to walk down to breakfast, a little embarrassed at the prospect of meeting the stranger upon whom she had forced herself with such lack of modesty.

Meanwhile Philippe de Pothiers had sat down at the table to which he'd been shown by the unctuous waiter from the previous evening. He was tired. This was certainly not the first time he'd spent the night with a woman other than his wife, but none of his lovers had been as uninhibited and demanding as this ravishing Italian from Florence. Her face radiated a wholesome beauty, but it belied a highly charged sensuality and an appetite for sex that was as dissolute as it was insatiable. For the first time in his life, Philippe felt inadequate and wondered whether he'd completely satisfied the young woman. "I'm getting old," he thought.

"Shall I set a place for Miss della Chiesa"? the waiter asked. Philippe looked at him in astonishment.

"*Who* did you say"?

"Miss della Chiesa."

There was a certain insolence in his voice. He clearly didn't believe Philippe's apparent ignorance about the name of his nighttime companion. Normally Philippe would have put the young man firmly in his place, but he was too taken aback. He just nodded and strove to gather his thoughts. Unfortunately, it was only too obvious. The name, the city she came from, her strange reaction when she found out he was a surgeon. "Oh, my God"! he realized with dismay. "I've just bedded the daughter of an eminent colleague, and the niece of a cardinal into the bargain."

At that moment Antonietta arrived. Philippe could not help wondering at her luminous beauty. He wondered too at the stark contrast between the elegant and poised young woman walking towards his table and the disheveled and shameless lover in his bed. She sat down and smiled at him. Philippe, knowing now who she was, felt embarrassed.

"I think I should introduce myself properly," he said.

Antonietta laughed, her eyes twinkling with malicious amusement. "You think it's more important to introduce yourself before breakfast than before spending the night with me"?

Philippe ignored her derision. "My full name is Philippe de Pothiers," he announced as casually as he could, adding, "To be exact, it's Count Philippe de Pothiers." Antonietta's eyes widened in surprise, but, before she could react, the Count switched into Italian.

*"E se non mi sbaglio, Lei è la contessa Antonietta della Chiesa."*

Antonietta was dumbstruck. She wasn't sure what astounded her more: the fact he knew who she was or his faultless Italian.

"How did you find out"? she stammered in Italian.

"Our rather over-observant waiter asked me if he should lay a place for Miss della Chiesa. After that it was simple deduction. You come from Florence, and you reacted strangely when I told you I was a surgeon. You had to be Paolo della Chiesa's daughter."

"And the Italian"?

"My mother's Italian. She's the sister of Angelina Farnese."

Antonietta gasped. Princess Angelina Farnese was the scion of an old Italian family that had ruled Parma for almost two hundred years and furnished the wife of King Philip V of Spain. She was an imposing fixture in Florentine society and a close friend of her uncle, the Cardinal. *And this man was her nephew!*

"We might have met," Antonietta said once she'd recovered her composure.

"I don't think so," Philippe replied, "You're not easy to forget." He looked at her intently, "If we ever do meet…"

Antonietta interrupted him before he could finish the sentence, "My lips are sealed," she told him with a grin. Philippe looked very relieved.

"What are your plans for the day, countess"? he asked, the intimacy of the night put aside.

Now it was Antonietta's turn to look embarrassed. "I know you'll think I'm a hypocrite, but I was intending to go to Mass."

Philippe laughed. "I would expect no less from a cardinal's niece. In any case you'd only be committing another sin if you didn't go."

They went to Mass together. Afterwards they lunched on the terrace of one of the restaurants opposite the Chateau Frontenac. They ate lightly, and Antonietta, contrary to her custom, drank only mineral water. She had to drive back to Ste. Anne des Lacs that afternoon. As they were parting after lunch, Philippe put his arms on Antonietta's shoulders in a fatherly way.

"Don't take it amiss, but there's something I must say to you, Antonietta. You shouldn't be here like this, having an adventure with a married man. You should be with your husband or your boyfriend. It's against nature for a woman of your rare beauty to be gallivanting around aimlessly on your own."

On the way back to Ste. Anne Antonietta reflected on her experience with Philippe de Pothiers. He was charming, good-looking, but a rather pedestrian lover. He'd accommodated her sexual needs, but she was aware that she'd shocked him. Nevertheless, she would gladly have consented to become his mistress. There were frequent direct flights between Montreal and Paris. Then she recalled his last words to her. He was right. Her life was aimless, and becoming the mistress of a married man who lived thousands of kilometers away was hardly a solution. The euphoria of her night of sex and the pleasant feelings evoked in her by Philippe's presence evaporated, and the old demons came back.

## Chapter 8

# Tuesday August 21, 2001, to
# Saturday August 25th, 2002

B ILL AND JAMES WERE seated in the Cumaná restaurant in the Recoleta waiting for their *churrascos*. It had been a frustrating day at the University of Buenos Aires, and they were in a mood to forget it with a good meal and plenty of Susana Balbo.

"They may be charming at UBA, but once you've cleared up one obstacle, the buggers come up with another, "James complained.

"Look on the bright side, Jimmy. It gives you a reason to come back and roger Carolina."

"Which reminds me, Bill," James said, anticipating his friend's displeasure, "I must be back at the hotel by midnight."

Bill had had his fill of Buenos Aires's nightlife, and he was more envious than anything else. "It's not right. It's me, the horny Yank, who gets to sleep alone and you, Mister perfect Catholic husband, who gets to roger. And to top it off, after goddam invading the girl's country"!

They tucked into the *churrascos* and ordered a couple of bottles of Susana Balbo. Bill wanted to order a third bottle, but James demurred.

"It's not just because of Carolina," he explained, noting his friend's disappointment. "We've got a helluva journey in front of us tomorrow. We leave Buenos Aires at eleven forty and have to spend seven hours in the airport at São Paolo. We won't be back in Montreal until Thursday morning."

"Well, don't overexert yourself tonight."

They left the restaurant and returned to the Hotel Bristol where Carolina was already awaiting James in his room.

"You're late," she said without reproach. "It was lucky I had a master key. Otherwise someone might have wondered what I was doing on this floor."

James took her into his arms and gazed into the bright blue eyes. He was always surprised by their serenity.

"I'll make up for it," he promised, deciding on the spot to take a hotel room at the airport in São Paolo in order to recover from what would doubtless be an exhausting night.

With an air of satisfaction Roy Arbuthnot placed the report in the file he'd opened on Elliot Hunt. His friend Graeme Hill from NUC days had done him proud. The report totally repudiated Hunt's appraisal of Doefman's paper, gave it 65%, and concluded with the comment that only bad faith on the part of the professor could explain the low mark attributed to it. It was a little too categorical, coming from an associate professor who still hadn't managed to achieve promotion. However, together with the testimony of the students against Hunt that Arbuthnot had obtained, it should do the job.

It hadn't been difficult to acquire the students' testimony. The four Doefman had rounded up needed no encouragement to assert that Hunt and Annya Nowak had started their affair before the end of class. Doefman concurred, but his testimony carried little weight because of his personal involvement in the case. It had taken a little more effort with the other four students. Arbuthnot had flattered them, sympathizing with their unfortunate experience in Hunt's class and assuring them that they would certainly do better if they took one of his classes next term. He was sure he could make room for them even though the deadline for enrolment had passed. Three of them had signed up.

Only one student had remained obdurate. Petra Markovic maintained she'd never seen Hunt and Annya together and doubted that they'd become intimate before the end of term. "Just because they were attracted to each other doesn't mean they didn't have the sense to wait," she insisted. Arbuthnot pointed out that she'd failed the course, but, unlike the others, Petra felt no animosity towards Hunt. "I assume I deserved to," she replied. Arbuthnot felt the girl's dislike of him, even contempt.

"This is an intimate faculty," he told her with the voice of authority, "and we expect students to show a spirit of solidarity. It's something we take into consideration when granting our degrees."

Beautiful, tall, with cold, grayish blue eyes full of disdain, Petra looked icily into Arbuthnot's pale and wrinkled face. "I hope you're not threatening me, Dr. Arbuthnot."

Doefman was venal, Winstone was weak and vain, Markham, Arbuthnot was convinced, hid a life a vice beneath an upright exterior, but this statuesque blond girl was impressive. Instinctively, he recoiled.

"I'm sorry if I expressed myself clumsily." Arbuthnot was very good at beating a retreat when necessary. "I never had the slightest intention of threatening you."

He could do without Petra Markovic, but he'd have his revenge on her. If the bitch thought she could intimidate the Senior Dean, she'd find out how wrong she was. "She's probably screwing Markham or Leaman," he told himself, not without a hint of envy.

The file was now complete. Arbuthnot picked up the phone and called the Rector's secretary, Eleanor Leatherbarrow.

"Eleanor, it's the Senior Dean. I'd like to see the Rector."

Eleanor was in her late fifties. She'd been the Rector's secretary from the very beginning of the Institute, and she remembered Arbuthnot as a young recruit. She was not at all intimidated by his new airs and graces.

"He's away today in Ottawa, Roy," she answered, "but he can see you first thing tomorrow."

Arbuthnot stifled his annoyance. He could sense the pleasure in Eleanor's voice at his discomfiture, but there was little he could do. Sooner or later, he promised himself, he'd get rid of Eleanor Leatherbarrow. Like Markham, she was an English Catholic and thus a potential fifth column in the Rector's office. "How come," he grumbled to himself, "all these English Papists wind up in *my* institute"?

James wondered why the Rector wanted to see him. It was unlikely to hear about his trip to South America. Winstone was not interested in the international program, and it would probably be axed if ever he had his way. That would also get rid of Tom Buchanan, who was a constant reminder to Winstone, and others, of the Rector's inadequacy. The message from Eleanor to Veronica announcing the meeting on Thursday had given no clues as to its purpose.

After an exhausting journey home, James had been greeted by a display of discreet affection from his wife, who hastened to tell him that she and the children were going to England for ten days at the end of October. They would spend the first few days with James's parents in Derwent and then go for a retreat at her mother's convent. James was not at all dismayed at the prospect, but he felt sorry for the children. A week in a religious retreat was hardly the way they would want to spend their fall break.

He arrived at the Rectorate and was greeted warmly by Eleanor Leatherbarrow.

"What's this all about, Eleanor"? he asked.

"I don't know," she replied and, dropping her voice to a whisper, added. "I think Arbuthnot has something to do with it. The Rector asked me to call your home after his meeting with Roy. So be careful."

After waiting a few minutes--Winstone always made people wait, doubtless it made him feel important--James was called into Rector's office.

"James, a nasty affair has blown up," he said, adopting a collegial tone, "I need your help to deal with it."

James was suspicious. It was most unlike Winstone to want his help, particularly after the business with Len Flint.

"It appears," the Rector went on, "that a member of faculty may have had an affair with a student while she was in his class. As you know, this is a dismissible offence. He is to be brought before the Ethics Committee, and I want you to defend him."

James immediately saw the trap to discredit him and remove him as a possible threat to Winstone and Arbuthnot. If he won, some people would think he was just protecting a colleague from his just deserts, and if he lost, he would forfeit some of his credibility among those faculty members who saw him as an alternative to the present regime.

"Who's the professor"?

"Elliot Hunt."

Now he understood. Arbuthnot wanted to get rid of Hunt, and James was sure that these were trumped-up charges to that effect. Winstone might be too stupid to see it, but James wasn't. No matter what the risk, he would take the case. He knew little about Hunt, but there was truth in the saying that your enemy's enemy is your friend. He accepted.

"The hearing's scheduled for Friday November 9," Winstone told him with an air of relief that didn't escape James. "That will give you time to prepare the defense." Then he added, "If there is one."

"Even in the Ethics Committee a person is presumed innocent, I believe, until proven guilty," James observed icily, taking the file from Winstone. He left the office without any further words being exchanged between them.

On the way back to his office James called in on Danny, who was with Bill Leaman. He recounted what had transpired in Winstone's office.

"I'm sure it's a machination to get rid of Hunt and discredit me."

"You can't be sure, James," Danny objected. "Hunt's a bit of a tearaway. There's no knowing what a hot-blooded Yank may get up to. You can't cry conspiracy just because Arbuthnot's involved."

"It's too neat," Bill opined, ignoring Danny's comment about Americans. "Hunt and James are both thorns in HB's side."

"Why would Winstone ask me to 'help' him, as he puts it? He hates my guts."

Danny pondered for a moment. "Before you jump to any conclusions, go through the file, James, and then get Hunt's version. That'll give you a better idea of what's going on."

James agreed and returned to his office to read the file. He noted the names of all the students who had testified against Hunt and went to see Ilse Bromhoeffer. He wasn't sure exactly how much he should tell the She-Wolf, so he just asked to see the marks for Hunt's class.

"You're the second person to ask me that. Why do you want to see them"?

James ignored Ilse's question. "Was the other person Roy Arbuthnot"?

Ilse nodded. "Did he tell you why"? Ilse nodded again.

"Well, I've been asked to defend Hunt, that's why I need to see the marks."

"Of course," Ilse managed a smile. "Thank God she likes me," James thought. "You'll have to consult them here," she told him.

It took James little time to confirm his suspicions. All seven students, including Doefman, had either failed Hunt's course or received a conditional pass. He pointed this out to Ilse. She agreed that it seemed more than just a coincidence. "Do you think it's a put-up job"?

James was taken aback by Ilse's frankness. But there was still the re-evaluation of Doefman's paper from Professor Hill. It didn't prove that Hunt had bedded Annya before the end of term, but it cast doubts on his integrity.

"I don't know, Ilse, but I'm damn well going to find out. I need the phone numbers of all the students in the class, including Annya's."

Ilse gave them to him without any vacillation. "Be careful of Doefman. He's a nasty piece of work.

"So is HB," James thought. He went back to his office and arranged to meet with Elliot Hunt on Friday afternoon.

Elliot Hunt seemed surprised by James's visit.

"Have you any idea why I might be here"? James asked, scrutinizing the man's reaction. Hunt's face was untroubled. He certainly didn't seem like someone with a guilty conscience. "I haven't a clue," he replied.

James explained about the complaint and the decision to bring the matter before the Ethics Committee. Hunt was extremely angry.

"What the fuck's going on? I never had any relationship with Annya before the end of term, not even a platonic one. And how come I wasn't informed that I'm to be brought before the Ethics Committee? That would seem to be the least I could expect."

"I'm informing you now, but I agree it's a cockeyed way of doing things."

"So you're one of the hatchet men"? The hostility in Hunt's voice was unmistakable.

"No, quite the opposite. I've been appointed to defend you."

"Appointed to defend me"! Hunt roared, "You mean I don't get to choose my own advocate."

"The policy in the Institute is to choose the defender; that way he has more credibility. It prevents people getting their friends to defend them, which normally backfires. If there is an appeal to a court of law, you will obviously have a right to your choice of defense counsel. The Ethics Committee is an internal procedure, and the Institute thinks it's not subject to the rules of due process."

Hunt was silent. He just glared at James, who added, "You have the right to refuse the Institute's choice of defender."

James could see that Hunt was of two minds. He had no reason to distrust James, who was in any case a lawyer. On the other hand, the arbitrary nature of the procedure clearly offended his American sense of civic rights.

"Why don't we discuss the case, and then you can make your mind up."

Hunt agreed and proceeded to tell his side of the story. Yes, Annya had been in his class and, from the moment he'd first seen her, he'd fallen head over heels in love with her. He'd never told her. Their only conversations had been strictly about the course.

"Did you know she was in love with you too"?

"There are ways of showing what you feel without saying it. We both knew we were attracted to each other. Unfortunately for us, so did Doefman, who was jealous and kept pestering her about me."

"How do you know that"?

Hunt looked at James disparagingly. "We talked afterwards, you know."

"Yes, of course," said James, feeling a little foolish. "Go on."

Hunt explained how Annya had become so exasperated with Doefman that she dumped him three quarters the way through class.

"Looking back on it, it was a dumb thing to do. Doefman thought it was because of me, so that's why he's concocted this whole story."

"The problem is that it was indeed because of her feelings for you. This became clear once she started going out with you. Tell me about Doefman and his record in class."

"He's an example of the worst type of student. Not as bright as he thinks and a lot to say in class. Most of it was useless babble to impress the others, particularly Annya. When he gets poor marks, he can't understand it and always contests them. Thinks it's the professor's fault."

"There's a lot of students like that," said James. "What about his final term paper"?

"It was not one of the worst, but lousy nevertheless. I gave him 40%, which is a conditional pass, but really he deserved to fail."

"Why didn't you fail him"?

"The guy's an asshole, but he'd just lost his girlfriend. I didn't like rubbing salt into the wound."

"You also knew that he'd soon find out that you two were together." James looked hard at Hunt, hoping he would give an honest answer.

"Yes," he admitted. "I hadn't talked to Annya yet, but I was pretty sure how things were going to turn out."

James was pleased with the answer. Hunt's version was plausible, and everything he knew about Doefman told in Hunt's favor. Except for the re-evaluation of the term paper. He showed Hunt Professor Hill's report.

"Graeme Hill"! Hunt exclaimed without bothering to read the report, "He's useless. He hasn't published a thing since he got tenure, and what he did before that was pretty awful. Arbuthnot picked him because they were both students at NUC."

Hunt's words removed the last doubts in James's mind. Arbuthnot had pulled the same trick in the Len Flint case, seeking references from his former classmates at NUC.

"Well, Elliot, it's up to you whether you want me to defend you, but I'm prepared to do it. Unless you're a very good actor, I believe you're telling the truth."

"Thanks, James." Hunt stood up and shook James by the hand. "I'd be honored to have you defend me."

"In that case, come to Danny Redfern's on Saturday evening, around eight. We'll get thoroughly pissed and plot strategy."

"I'm a Baptist. I don't drink, but I'll come anyway."

"Good God," thought James, "that's almost as bad as a Scottish Presbyterian." He made to leave Hunt's office when a final question suddenly occurred to him.

"It's just idle curiosity, but how did you and Annya hook up"?

"I wandered around the campus until I bumped into her."

⌣ℳ⌐

It was difficult to enjoy getting drunk in the presence of a Protestant teetotaler, so the four friends were still quite lucid even though it was quite late in the evening. They had discussed with Elliott their impressions of the faculty. Arbuthnot, all agreed, was the quintessence of mediocrity and wickedness. Winstone was weak and useless and HB's tool, as was Khan. Forget was a nice guy but none too bright.

"What about McGrath"? Hunt asked. James was about to answer with his normal Catholic prejudice, but Piotr, diplomatic as ever, intervened.

"We don't know yet, but he's another of HB's chums from NUC."

Hunt groaned. "That about says it all," he said. "And Ilse"?

Before anyone could stop him, Bill jumped into the fray. "We call her the She-Wolf. She's a lesbian."

Hunt was shocked to his Baptist roots. He just gaped. James moved hurriedly to placate him.

"That's Bill's theory, but there's nothing to substantiate it."

"Yes, there is,' Bill retorted, "She's not married, and it's obvious. Just like Hard Balls, he's gay."

"Knock it off, Bill," James ordered, aware that Hunt was beginning to ask himself into what den of iniquity he'd fallen. "Ilse's a good person, and HB is loathsome but married with three kids and is without any doubt heterosexual."

While Bill comforted himself by emptying the whisky bottle, the others turned to plotting strategy for Hunt's defense. It was agreed that, once term began on September 10, James would interview those students who hadn't received poor marks in the class and try to intimidate Doefman into retracting. His allies would certainly be forced to follow suit. He would also contact another professor with good academic credentials to review Doefman's final paper on labor regulation in Europe. Hunt suggested Ted Burstein from the University of Chicago. He was a leading expert in the field of labor regulation, he explained.

"Fine, I'll contact him," James agreed. "I'll see Annya as well next week."

Hunt looked embarrassed. "I'm afraid she won't be here. We're going to Hawaii for the week."

Bill chortled in the background. "Not very battist of you, Elliot," he slurred, "but it's nice to know you're not gay like Hard Balls."

James looked at Bill as if he could slaughter him, but Hunt saw the humor of the situation. To everyone's relief, he laughed.

"To the pure, all is pure," he told Bill.

## Chapter 9

# Sunday, September 2, 2001

LATER WHEN THEY WERE lovers, Antonietta and James would wonder that no premonitory signs had forewarned them of what was to happen this day. For it was so inexplicable, so overwhelming that nature could not have remained indifferent. Yet, that Sunday dawned like any other day. It was perhaps unseasonably warm, and the sun created a luminosity unusual for the time of year, but this was hardly enough to prepare them for the onslaught of a passion so powerful that it would overwhelm them and bring chaos into their lives.

For James it had been a very boring week. Bill was off in Vancouver visiting his errant wife, Piotr was in Poland, and Danny was tied up with preparations for the beginning of the new academic year. He'd wanted to spend the week by the ocean somewhere, but Veronica, who disliked traveling except to visit her mother's convent, had refused. To top it off, today was very much the normal dismal Sunday routine. The children were complaining of hunger because their mother insisted on them fasting before Mass, and Veronica was fretting that they would be late and suffer eternal damnation. James bore the whole recurring scenario with a resignation born of the prospect of a game of tennis with Danny that afternoon.

They arrived in Saint-Sauveur from Prévost in good time for the eleven o'clock Mass. James parked the car in the little car park just north of the church, and the family walked down to the Rue Principale. They turned right towards the church. As they entered, James noticed a young woman walking down the aisle ahead of them, her long dark hair falling loosely around her shoulders. "She must be a foreigner," he thought as the fashion in Quebec at that time was either for short hair or long hair done up in a ponytail. James liked neither style. He hoped the woman wouldn't turn round. So often a woman attractive from the back would spoil everything by turning round and exhibiting a plain or ugly face. He watched the woman genuflect before the altar and take her seat to the side in front of them.

He forgot the long dark hair once Mass started. It was not because of his devotions. His thoughts were on the upcoming tussle with HB over Elliot Hunt. He chased them away with recollections of his pleasant moments in Buenos Aires with Carolina. As always, Veronica noticed his lack of attention to Mass and chastised him. He made a half-hearted attempt to follow the priest's sermon, which was something about the fall being a time to cogitate on one's conduct during the preceding year. "Why the fall"? he wondered.

The priest took a mercifully short time to go through the remaining liturgy, and James was soon in line to take communion. Further on was the woman with the long, dark hair. She took the bread but refused the wine. "Good for you," thought James. He considered that communion under both species was another Protestant innovation introduced by the Second Vatican Council. As she turned to walk away, James caught a glimpse of her soft features. "She must be very pretty," he thought. It's a pity she hadn't turned round.

She already captivated him. She turned into the aisle that led to her pew and had no reason to glance back at the altar. But she did and looked straight at James. A shock went through his entire body, and his eyes locked on to her's. He had never in his whole life beheld such incandescent beauty, but it was not wonder, even less lust, that gripped him. It was an overpowering desire to run across and take her into his arms. Out of the blue he found himself submerged by an uncontrollable passion that made him tremble. The lady alongside looked at him in concern and asked if he was alright. James managed to mumble some answer without taking his eyes off the young woman. A slight push from behind told him that he was holding up the line. With an enormous effort he wrenched his eyes away from her wondrous beauty and arrived to receive communion from the priest. He was so distraught that, instead of holding out his hand, he opened his mouth to receive communion in the old way.

James was thoroughly shaken and knelt to collect himself. This was senseless, incredible. How could he feel such passion for a woman he'd only seen for a few seconds? This could only happen in books. It happened to poor old Tristan*, but at least he could blame it on a love potion. "You're crazy," he told himself roundly, you're a married man, you've two children, and you're in church. And she's a perfect stranger"! But he couldn't resist glancing over at her. Luckily, Veronica was deep in her prayers and she didn't notice. The woman--she must be in her early twenties, he decided--turned to look at him again. Their eyes met once more, and James knew that the passion was mutual. Afraid he would lose control, he averted his gaze.

"I want to go," Susanna complained, "Why does Mommy pray so much"?

His daughter's complaint brought him back to reality, and he realized that most people had left the church. The young woman was still there, and he was drawn ever more irresistibly to her. He knew he had to leave quickly before he did something irrevocable. He needed to get away and reason with himself.

"Come on, Veronica. I think you've said enough to God. Don't be too greedy. Let other people have a chat with Him too." Susanna giggled, and Veronica threw her husband one of her Victorian looks. She was not amused.

While Veronica was preparing to leave, the young woman walked hurriedly past them. Veronica commented on James staring at her. Before he could stop himself, he admitted that she fascinated him. Veronica was aghast at such thoughts in church. "Thank God for your excessive piety," James thought. "Any other wife would have been jealous."

For Antonietta it had been a busy week. She'd moved into the cottage on Monday and spent the week buying some extra furniture and other little things, such as a casserole for cooking pasta, a spiked saucer for crushing garlic, and a hooked serving spoon. She'd bought too much, but shopping gave her an excuse to go to Montreal and enjoy the warm familiarity of Luigi's café.

On Saturday she'd been alone arranging the cottage, and she was glad to go out to Mass this Sunday. She arrived early at Saint-Sauveur and took an expresso on the terrace of the Brûlerie des Monts just over from the church. It was a warm, sunny day, and Antonietta was determined to take advantage of it. Next week there would be registration, book buying, an orientation seminar, and a party for the new students. She'd been through it all before.

It was time for Mass, and she walked to the church. She dipped her finger into the font at the entrance of the church, crossed herself, and walked down the aisle. She was early, and, to save herself from having to let countless people through, she sat at the end of a row of pews to the left of the aisle. She knelt and murmured a quick prayer. The church filled up, and Mass started. She had difficulty following the priest who spoke very quickly with a thick Quebec accent. She understood even less of the sermon, which had something to do with fall and one's conduct throughout the year. "Why the fall"? she wondered.

Soon it was time to take communion. She was used to men staring at her, and this had given her a sixth sense. When she turned away from the altar, she was aware of James's gaze upon her. Normally this would have irritated her, but, still adrift in a new country, it was a comfort. She reached the left aisle that led to her pew and couldn't resist looking back at the queue of communicants in search of her admirer. That's when she saw James. Their eyes met, and in that instant her life changed.

Antonietta was electrified by the feelings evoked in her by this unknown man, and she caught her breath in shock. She realized immediately that this was the passion of which her uncle had talked, and she stared in wonder at James, devouring him with her shimmering dark eyes. She was possessed by an overpowering desire to run over and throw herself into his arms. She wanted desperately to give herself to him, body and soul. Suddenly to her dismay he turned away. A discreet cough from the lady behind made her realize that like herself he'd been holding up the people in his line. Comforted, she returned to her pew and rested her bowed head on her hands as if in prayer, pondering the enormity of what was happening to her. She felt elation at finding at last the man to fill her longing and emptiness and relief that she was a normal woman.

Unlike James who, with what Antonietta would later call his cold English reason, could not accept what had happened to him, Antonietta found it quite natural that the passion she had longed and prayed for would descend upon her like this, unannounced, unexpected, with a total stranger in the most unlikely of venues. Instinctively she knew that passion was irrational, that it could never be cultivated out of a friendship or even with a lover. If it was not there when you saw or met the person for the first time, however briefly, it would never be. And it could happen anywhere. Why not with a total stranger in church?

Who was he? He was taller than most French Canadians. He looked British, but in that case what was he doing at Mass? Although she had spent four years at a convent school in England, Antonietta persisted in regarding the British as a Protestant race. Intrigued and impelled by a desire to set her eyes upon him again, she turned round and sought him out. She found him; their eyes met and betrayed their passion for each other. Then she saw the two handsome young children on either side of him and the blond woman next to the boy, deep in prayer. The horrid truth hit her. The man was married!

Antonietta's world of a few delicious moments collapsed. She felt incomprehension, followed by despondency, and then by anger. "*E così che me ne remuneri?* she muttered, looking accusingly at the crucifix above the altar. The woman next to her gave her an odd look. Private prayer was not encouraged in the New Order of the Mass, particularly not in Latin, which is what she took Antonietta's Italian to be. Once everyone had taken communion, and the priest had read out notices for the parishioners, the woman left quickly. "That young lady is far too beautiful for her own good," she thought.

Antonietta was incapable of sorting out the powerful emotions that were in conflict within her. She stood up in a daze and, hardly aware of what she was doing, walked down the center aisle towards the man and his family. She couldn't bring herself to look at them and hurried past. Fighting back tears of distress and anger, she made for her car. She opened the door, threw herself down in the driver's seat, and put her head in her hands. It was all too cruel. How, after all her prayers, could God have played such a trick on her? She knew, in the depths of her being, that this was the only man for her But he was married! Antonietta was too Catholic, too attached to her family, to contemplate a marriage outside the Church. Nor could she ever just become his mistress. With him it would always be all or nothing, and once she surrendered to this passion, she knew that she would forever be its prisoner.

She looked up and saw that the family was out of the church. The wife was walking on ahead. She was a handsome, blond woman who held herself very erect, but there was a cheerlessness about her. She reminded Antonietta of the mothers of some of her English classmates. The boy was chatting animatedly with his father, and the young daughter, who was a much a prettier version of her mother, was tugging at his arm. Antonietta noted with unhappy satisfaction that he was adrift in his own thoughts and paying scant attention to his children. "I only hope he's going through what I am," she thought.

Antonietta gasped and tried to make herself as inconspicuous as possible, for the man had crossed the road with his daughter and was coming straight at her, followed by his son and wife. They were obviously going for brunch at the Brûlerie. Her heart pounded, and, in an instinctive but quite irrational gesture, she opened the back passenger window. "Daddy, I want pancakes," she heard the girl say in English with a Canadian accent. "What are you going to have"? "A treble scotch," her father replied. The girl giggled.

Antonietta lay back in her seat with her eyes closed. She couldn't bear to have the man in her sight anymore. The longing was too painful, but the three words she'd overheard, and the way he'd said them, told her all she wanted to know. He was indeed British, and he had their dry, self-ironical sense of humor that Antonietta had never quite understood. She knew she was the reason for the treble scotch. Mind you, he was out of luck as the Brûlerie didn't serve alcohol, but he was certainly aware of that. For Antonietta, his reply was an admission of the turmoil she was causing him, and this fed her passion. Reluctantly she drove off to her lonely cottage.

James was desperately trying to behave normally. The family had ordered their various dishes, and now there would be the long wait for them to arrive. The slowness of the service always irritated James, but today it was excruciating. All he wanted was to be alone.

"When we've finished breakfast, I must go and do some work at the office," he told his wife.

"I thought you were playing tennis with Danny," Veronica replied, persuaded now that the tennis game had been just another pretext for a drinking bout.

He'd forgotten about the game, and he didn't feel capable of playing. All he could think about was that vision of beauty in the church, the soft perfection of her features, her free flowing long black hair, the sexual promise beneath the modest summer dress, and the dark expressive eyes. She married sensuality and refined elegance in a way that set her apart from other women. He was sure she was European, possibly French or more likely Italian. Suddenly it occurred to him that she could be one of the Institute's foreign students. He groaned inwardly. A fling with girls like Carolina far from home was one thing, but this woman was something else. She was dangerous.

"Daddy, aren't you going to eat"? Susanna asked with her normal wide-eyed innocence. James realized that he hadn't even noticed the food arriving. He ate without pleasure, and eventually Veronica commented on his strange mood.

"The beginning of term always depresses me," he explained. The answer seemed to satisfy Veronica.

The family got up from the table, James paid, and he drove them to Prévost where he phoned Danny to cancel the game. James suspected Danny was relieved for he sounded a little the worse for wear. Around three o' clock James was at last alone in his office. It was then he grasped the full extent of the passion that had burst upon him. He'd felt lust for Leonora, in the first days affection for Veronica, and he'd enjoyed Carolina more than he would like to admit, but nothing in his previous experience with women had prepared him for the devastating force of his feelings for this unknown beauty. It was not her beauty alone, there was something indefinable about her that possessed him. He'd come to collect himself, to find a way back to sanity and reason, but most of the two hours in the office was spent bewitched by a vision of this incandescent beauty. Nevertheless, on leaving the office he resolved to do his best to put this madness behind him.

He was still thinking about her when he lay in bed next to Veronica. "I want you," he whispered unwittingly to the image that haunted him.

"Yes, but it's time to sleep," Veronica said, taking the words for herself.

James grimaced, partly because he'd nearly betrayed himself and partly out of irritation with his wife. "You're going to be a lot of help," he said to himself, "Let's just hope I never see that woman again".

Antonietta spent the rest of that Sunday between heaven and hell. In an ever-recurring cycle she would immerse herself in her passion, imagining their first meeting, the first words, the first kiss, until reality tugged her back to the horrible truth that her romantic imaginings were a chimera. The man was married with two children, and he was a Catholic as well. Idly she wondered whether he could get his marriage annulled. That was the only way they could be together, but with two children it was impossible. "It's a pity I'm not a Grimaldi*, "she reflected. Yet, no sooner had she set herself against the seductive fantasy of her passion than it seized control of her again, and she was soon lost once more in blissful daydreams.

After sitting around in the cottage for a few hours, alternately moping and indulging herself in the thrill of being in love at last, Antonietta realized she was extremely hungry. She thought of driving to Montreal to eat at Luigi's place, but she'd drunk too much wine, and she had a vague recollection of Luigi telling her that he closed on Sundays after summer's end. So, rather absently she set out to make a pasta sauce. Despite the conflict that was tearing her apart, she couldn't help laughing when she realized that inadvertently she'd cooked a *putanesca* sauce*. Perhaps someone up there was trying to tell her something!

She felt better after a good meal. She was also quite tipsy, which normally made her see life in more positive colors. She comforted herself with the knowledge that she was quite normal. She wasn't incapable of passion, and she wasn't a suppressed lesbian either.

As she lay in bed late that evening, half asleep, with her arms wrapped around a pillow, she murmured to her unknown love words that for the first time had real meaning for her: *Ti amo.*

*Chapter 10*

# Monday September 3, 2001
# to Friday September 7

ANTONIETTA SLAMMED ON THE brakes to avoid rear-ending a car that was halted at the stop sign at the entry to Saint-Sauveur. Her thoughts had been elsewhere. Ever since she'd got up that morning, they had constantly dwelled on the man she'd seen in Church. A good night's sleep had not calmed the storm of feelings he'd released within her. As she made her way through the town and up into the hills where the Institute was located, she wondered idly whether he was a professor there. He certainly had an intelligent face, but she decided he was too well-dressed to be a university professor. On the whole academics tended to be rather scruffy. "They must think it makes them appear more intellectual," Antonietta reflected with irony.

Upon arriving at the Institute, Antonietta saw with dismay the lines of students outside the Lecture Hall building registering for their courses. Once in line, she let herself sink into reveries of amorous bliss. After all, she told herself, unless she fell prey to the temptation of returning for Mass at Saint-Sauveur, she was unlikely to see the man again, and so what was the harm in indulging herself in a little bittersweet happiness.

She made the end of one line and registered for international economics from a professor called Leaman, then another line to register for North American history from Forget, and eventually she joined what seemed an even longer line for her course on the European Union from a Professor Markham. By now she'd tired of torturing herself with dreams of the impossible and tried to stifle the passion that was gnawing at her. She looked around and noticed behind her in the queue a tall, blond girl. She was very attractive, but her manner was cold and unresponsive. She caught her eyes briefly and was struck by their icy, grayish blue color. She stood out from the other students by her elegance and self-composure. The others were dressed in the normal drab student uniform of blue jeans and *t-shirts* with silly inscriptions on them and were constantly laughing and giggling at nothing in particular. The girl was wearing a skirt and a well-tailored and obviously very expensive jacket over a white silk blouse, which was unbuttoned low enough to afford a glimpse of the swell of her breasts. She wore her blond hair down to the nape of her neck in a stylish cut. Her apparent frostiness did not prevent Antonietta being drawn to her.

James was seated in his office trying to put the finishing touches to his notes for the class on the EU. It was his only class this term, and his plan this day had been to start preparing next term's lectures on international trade and perhaps make some progress on his latest article. It was a trenchant criticism of the Treaty of Nice, which he was writing in the forlorn hope that it would encourage the decision-makers in the EU to heed the Irish veto and come up with a better treaty. As it was, the plan was going completely awry. He was too obsessed by yesterday's sublime vision to concentrate on his work. Who was she? Would he ever see her again? Worse than these recurring questions was the longing for her that consumed him. "It's madness, downright madness," he told himself repeatedly, but to absolutely no effect. He couldn't wrench the image of her flawless beauty from his mind.

James was startled out of his trance by the telephone ringing. It was Carlos Guarnieri from the University of Buenos Aires with some questions on course equivalencies for exchange students. James was astonished as there was normally total silence from Latin American universities after you'd visited them. That Guarnieri had taken the initiative to call him was most gratifying, although in his present state of disarray he would've preferred an excuse to fly to Buenos Aires. Perhaps Carolina's charms would've restored him to sanity. He noted Carlos's suggestions and agreed to take part in a conference on the European Union some time in December at the University of Buenos Aires. Afterwards he walked through the quadrangle to the Administration building to discuss the matter of equivalencies with Ilse, relieved to be shut of his own company.

⟡

Antonietta was happy to be leaving Saint-Sauveur behind as she sped down the motorway to Montreal. Every step she took in that town was filled with the apprehension and hope of coming across that man. She felt emotionally drained and looked forward to the comforting ambiance of Luigi's café. First, she had to buy the books she needed for her courses at the bookstore across from McGill University.

It was late afternoon when she arrived at Luigi's. Scorning the obligatory expresso, she drank wine. By the time she'd finished her supper around eight, she was more than a little tipsy and nursed a grappa for the remainder of the evening. Fearing the inner turmoil that would invade her once she was on her own again in the solitude of the cottage, she gladly accepted Luigi's invitation to stay the night in his apartment. "You're not in a fit state to drive," he told her sternly.

'What's happening, Antonietta"? Luigi asked once they were settled in his living room. He looked at her with paternal disapproval as she poured herself another grappa. "Getting drunk isn't going to solve your problem."

Whether it was the alcohol, or the exhaustion of the roller coaster of emotions gripping her, or just the kindly presence of the older man, Antonietta burst out crying. Luigi put his arm round her. *"Parla, parla,"* he said. And out it all came. The aimlessness of her life in Italy, the yearning for fulfillment, and the man at Mass who seemed to be her salvation. "Then what are crying about, you silly girl"?

Antonietta turned her dark expressive eyes on Luigi, and he could feel her distress through them. "He's married," she replied glumly.

Luigi looked at her thoughtfully for a moment and asked whether the man was happily married.

Antonietta was perplexed by the question. "I haven't a clue. Why is that important? If he's married, he's married, whether he's happy with his wife or not."

Luigi, who'd lost his faith when his wife died young, had forgotten that Antonietta was a practicing Catholic. He apologized and went on to explain the reasoning behind his odd question. "It's one thing to ruin an unhappy marriage but quite another to ruin a happy marriage, particularly when there are two children involved."

Now it was Antonietta's turn to be thoughtful. She conjured up the picture of the family walking to the Brûlerie, the man walking ahead with his daughter and his wife, the cheerless blond, following with the son.

"No, I don't think he's happily married." For a brief instant, she found this reflection strangely consoling as if it excused her sinful dreams of adulterous bliss. But she knew this was not so. "I don't intend to return to the church in Saint-Sauveur. That way I won't see him again, so I won't be tempted. After all," she added, "I *am* a cardinal's niece."

When Antonietta was lying in bed, she realized that her head was spinning. She resolved to cut down on her drinking, and, as if to reward herself for this virtuous decision, she allowed herself to sink into rapturous dreams where she was making love to the stranger who had taken possession of her soul.

James was having another horrible day and was becoming ever angrier with himself. Furiously he threw the third attempt to write up a simple memorandum of understanding on course equivalency for the exchanges with Buenos Aires into the wastepaper bin.

"Damn you," he muttered, making a supreme effort to chase away thoughts of his ravishing nemesis. The fourth attempt at least produced a readable if not particularly lucid statement of the Institute's policy. It would have to do. He'd give it to Ilse, and she could clean it up.

By now it was nearly eleven-thirty. It was too late to work on his article, and it was pointless to do so in his present state. He left his office and marched to the Administration Building to haul Danny off for a liquid lunch. Unfortunately, Danny was tied up with the registration process and a myriad of other administrative matters that attend the beginning of term. Glumly James made his way back across the quadrangle towards the LIR building. Bill was still in Vancouver with his wife, so that left Piotr. James changed direction and made for the LAC building. Piotr was just leaving his office when James arrived. He explained that he was going to Montreal to buy a new recording of Szymanovski's Second Symphony in B Flat Major. Instead of mooning around the Institute or even worse returning to the religious austerity of his home, James decided to accompany Piotr.

"Please wait till you get home before playing it." The drive from Montreal was bad enough without the mournful dissonance of Szymanovski.

After spending a few unsuccessful hours in record stores, James persuaded Piotr to call off his search and have a drink. On the way to the bar, they passed a café Where, unbeknownst to them, a very beautiful dark-haired Italian girl was ordering her first glass of wine.

Bill introduced himself to the small gathering of foreign students. It was taking place in one of the large rooms in the Lecture Hall building. There were about twenty of them, and Bill had memorized the list. There were several earnest-looking Chinese, who would spend the next few years immured in the library, a rather solemn German, two scruffy Brits, some Latin Americans, and an Italian girl, who was hidden behind the German student.

"Well, guys, welcome to North America's most prestigious school for international studies." This wasn't entirely true, but it was a good line and made them feel it was worth coming to the Institute. "I'm going to bore you with academic matters, then Petra Markovic, the Vice-President of the Students Union, will make sure you know all you need to know in order to enjoy yourselves here, and finally Brett Taylor, the captain of the Institute's football team, will talk about our sports programs."

Antonietta liked Bill Leaman. He had a freshness and a down-to earth approach that set him apart from the pompous professors she'd known in Italy. He was still a good-looking man, but his lifestyle was clearly beginning to take its toll. She liked that too. People who insisted on doing everything in moderation were so tedious. After he'd finished explaining about the structure of the degree programs, the form of the lectures, marking, and appeals, he was followed by the tall blond girl Antonietta had noticed when registering.

Antonietta was struck again by the girl's attractiveness as well as her coldness. She listened to the mellifluous voice detailing in an almost detached way the campus facilities and nearby bars and restaurants. "One other important matter," she added. "The Students Union puts out a survey of the professors with a brief biography and a student evaluation." To Antonietta's surprise the girl gave Professor Leaman a puckish grin, and the coldness about her seemed to evaporate.

"It's all lies, that book," Bill interjected with a broad grin and everyone except the Chinese students and the solemn German laughed.

Petra was followed by Brett Taylor. Antonietta was not at all interested in sport, and when she'd come across American football on the television in her hotel room in Montreal, she'd found it rather comical. She paid scant attention to Brett, noticing instead how the tall blond girl was staring fondly at him. He must be her boyfriend, she concluded.

After the seminar Bill stood at the door to shake hands with every student and exchange a few words. When Antonietta arrived at the door, he was so awestruck by her beauty that he became tongue-tied. It was Antonietta who, embarrassed by his silence, took the initiative of introducing herself. "Pleased to meet you, Antonetta," he managed eventually, mangling her name. She gave him a dazzling smile that left him quite stunned.

Petra, who had witnessed the whole scene, couldn't resist teasing Bill, whom she had come to know quite well. She grinned mischievously at him.

"This is the first time I've seen you at a loss for words, Professor Leaman."

"That'll do from you, Markovic," Bill growled, still quite nonplussed.

Once the last student had left, he raced all the way to James's office where his friend was still trying desperately to write something for his article that made sense.

"Jimmy," Bill exclaimed breathlessly, "I've just seen the most beautiful girl I've ever seen. She's absolutely spectacular, fucking incredible." He stared at James with a look of wonder on his face. James waited for the rogering routine, but nothing came.

James was taken aback both by Bill's enthusiasm and his uncommon lack of vulgarity, apart from the obligatory expletive. "I suppose you'd like to roger her"?

"She's out of my league, man," was Bill's reply.

James's increasing astonishment at Bill's reaction to the girl began to give way to a nagging suspicion, for he too had seen a woman of incomparable beauty. Could it just be a coincidence? He felt a shiver go through his body. "What's she like"? he asked nervously.

"Long dark hair, soft features, a sensuous mouth, great tits, and unbelievable eyes." It was not perhaps the most eloquent of descriptions, but James needed no more. Half in horror and half in exhilaration, he now realized that the unknown beauty from *Mass was* a student in the Institute. He tried desperately to hide his agitation from Bill, but his friend was far too obsessed by what he'd seen to notice James's reaction.

"What's more, she's in my class. Why don't you look at your class list to see if she's in yours's."

"What's her name"?

"Something woppish. Della something."

James looked through his class list and found the name Antonietta della Chiesa.

"Is that the name"?

"Yes, that's her."

Fortunately he had to go to a meeting, and so the distraught James was left alone with his swirling emotions as it dawned on him that he would be seeing this woman every Tuesday and Thursday in class. He hadn't the slightest idea how he would cope.

He pushed away the article. There was no, absolutely no hope now for any meaningful progress, so he might as well indulge himself. He still remembered the password for accessing student records on the computer and looked up Antonietta. He felt a hollow feeling in his stomach as he put a personality to what until then had just been an image of sensual perfection. *Della Chiesa, Antonietta Maria Assunta, he read, born July 14, 1977 in Rome, Italy. Joint degree in Italian and Economics, University of Florence, 234 rue des Lacs, Ste Anne des Lacs, Québec.* There was no telephone number, but she had given her religion, *Roman Catholic.* This was unusual as it was not obligatory to state one's religion, and few students did so "It must mean she's a practicing Catholic," he thought. "So at least she's aware that ours's would be a forbidden love."

James stared at the screen. So this was her, *la beltade ignota.* He was no longer capable of stemming images of her from flooding his mind. He saw her in front of them as the family entered the church, in line to take communion, the glimpse of her lovely features as she turned away from the altar, the first sight of her matchless beauty, and the look she'd given him after turning round furtively in her pew in search of him. He suddenly realized that she must know he was married, and he wondered, no, hoped that she was suffering the same torment as himself. One thing was certain. He wouldn't go to Mass at Saint-Sauveur next Sunday.

"How about that drink, my good fellow"? James looked up, startled, and saw Danny beaming at him from the doorway.

"Right away," he replied, immensely grateful for the distraction.

Antonietta was bored and somewhat dismayed. She was at the reception for new students to the Institute sponsored by the Students Union. It was taking place in the same gloomy lecture hall as the seminar the previous Wednesday. Most of the students were first-year undergraduates, and they ignored her. Even the new graduate students seemed to give her a wide berth. She was not used to such treatment. Then the German exchange student, Wilhelm, came up and engaged her in a laborious conversation. They were both in Markham's and Leaman's classes, and Wilhelm had already read some of the textbooks for the two courses. Antonietta, who was too emotionally overwrought to settle down to reading about international economics or the European

Union, listened politely but took nothing in. Fortunately, she was rescued by the tall blond girl, whose name she didn't remember.

The girl introduced herself. "I'm Petra Markovic," she told Antonietta, interrupting Wilhelm, who went off sulkily to find another victim. "I believe we're both registered in Professor Markham's course."

Antonietta was taken aback by Petra's friendliness, but she remembered the incident at the seminar that had revealed a sense of fun beneath the icy exterior. She was glad to talk to her.

"Yes. Tell me, what's he like"?

"I had him for international trade last year. He's well-organized, fair but distant. Typically British."

"British"! The man at Mass was also British! Petra laughed at her response, and the cold blue eyes suddenly softened and sparkled with amusement.

"What's wrong with the British"?

Antonietta sought desperately for an adequate response. "Nothing. You just don't expect to find British people in Quebec." It was a sorry answer, and she quickly changed the subject. "By the way, my name's Antonietta, Antonietta della Chiesa." The two young women shook hands.

"You certainly made quite an impression on Bill Leaman," Petra remarked. "I bet he went straight to Professor Markham to tell him about the raven-haired beauty from Italy."

Antonietta was unusually pleased by the indirect compliment, but it was curiosity about this British professor that dominated her.

"Why would he go to see Professor Markham"?

Petra smirked knowingly, "They're good friends. Rumor has it that Markham, Leaman, Leszek and Redfern are drinking buddies."

Antonietta immediately thought of the triple scotch the man had wanted after seeing her at Mass. Could he possibly be this Markham? The thought set off again the longing within her, and she was aware that she was flushing.

"Are you alright"? Petra asked. There was no more trace of her coldness. It was clear she'd taken a liking to Antonietta.

'I'm a little upset," Antonietta replied. "Until you came up to talk me, everyone except that awful boring German ignored me." It was not the reason, but it was not a complete lie either. The indifference of her fellow students had indeed hurt her.

"It's because you're too beautiful. You intimidate the men, and the women are jealous of you. In any case, they're mostly undergraduates and younger than you. It's not much of a loss. The men are all jocks and the women mostly airheads."

Antonietta was amused by Petra's dismissive comments, but she doubted that she was being entirely truthful. "Even him"? she said, pointing to the football captain. Petra blushed, and Antonietta was surprised at her vulnerability.

"I hate myself for it, but I'm crazy about him. His name's Brett Taylor. Unfortunately he's going out with that vulgar Quebecoise." She motioned to the dark-haired girl standing next to him. She was wearing too much makeup, skintight jeans, and a halter-top.

"What about him"? Antonietta was referring to the young man next to Brett Taylor.

"That's Brett Doefman. He's a nasty piece of work, and Taylor's under his influence."

"And him"? Antonietta pointed to a short, rotund man with sparse reddish hair growing unevenly on his head.

"Another nasty piece of work. He's Arbuthnot, the Senior Dean. Everyone calls him HB, but no one really knows why. Some say it stands for Hard Balls." They both laughed. "He's powerful and vindictive. Once he tried to threaten me into testifying against a professor who's being accused of having sex with a student in his class."

Briefly she explained to Antonietta what she knew about the Hunt case. "I still think it's a put-up job orchestrated by that shit Doefman and HB. Naturally Markham's defending him."

"Why naturally"? Everything about Professor Markham now seemed important to Antonietta.

"Because he and HB are sworn enemies." For some reason, this piece of information pleased Antonietta.

They moved over to the table where the cheese and wine were laid out. The cheese was Dutch and German and the wine Australian and Chilean. Antonietta wrinkled up her nose in disgust. She hated Dutch cheese, which she found soapy, and she thoroughly disliked the sweet aftertaste of Australian and Chilean wine.

"Do you want to go to a good restaurant"? she asked Petra, who was laughing at the expression on Antonietta's face.

It was only five in the afternoon, but Quebeckers eat supper very early, and the many restaurants in Saint Sauveur were probably already open. In any case, it would take them some time to drive down into town. Petra was enthusiastic, and within half an hour they were ensconced in Gio's, where Antonietta had treated Carlo to lunch.

"I'm in my fourth year, I'm twenty-one, and I come from Edmonton, Alberta," Petra told Antonietta in answer to her questions. "I was born in Serbia, and I came to Canada when I was four. And I'm not going out with anyone."

"Nor am I," said Antonietta. She briefly recounted where she was born and where she'd lived before coming to Canada and then changed the subject. There was so much she didn't want to reveal, in particular the passion that was tearing her apart.

"Which courses are you taking"? she asked Petra. Petra replied and repeated the question to Antonietta. In response to Antonietta's answer, she pulled out of her briefcase the survey on the professors.

"Here. Look up your professors."

Antonietta read in alphabetical order, firstly Forget, then Leaman and finally Markham. Leaman was rated an excellent professor, Forget fair but boring. A strange nervousness gripped her when she turned to the entry on Markham.

*Markham, James. Educated at Ampleforth College, Cambridge University and...* Antonietta nearly choked and stopped reading. After four years at a convent school in England, she knew that Ampleforth was a Catholic school. So he was British and Catholic! Just like the man in Church, and how many of those could there be? Now she was certain that this Professor Markham, in whose class she would be every Tuesday and Thursday, was the object of her consuming passion. She was shaken by a thrill mixed with dread. When she saw him, how would she resist him? But she had to.

"Are you okay"? Antonietta's agitation was obvious to Petra.

"Yes," Antonietta replied. "It's just that some good friends of mine went to the same school as Professor Markham."

Petra looked at her skeptically but didn't press the point. "Everyone's entitled to their secrets," she thought, but this one promised to be more remarkable than most.

They left the restaurant, and Antonietta drove Petra back to the student residence just below the Institute. They agreed to go to Mont Tremblant together the next day. Once Antonietta was back at the cottage, she threw herself on to the bed. She was sure that the man in the church was James Markham, and she knew that her existence from now on in Quebec would be a torment. To see the man you long for twice every week and not be able to throw yourself into his arms and to have instead to take notes from him about the European Union, how more cruel could fate be? How would he react? Did he already know she was in his class?

One thing was certain. She wouldn't go to Mass at Saint-Sauveur on Sunday, and she would make sure that he suffered as much she was undoubtedly going to.

*Chapter 11*

# Sunday September 9, 2001 to
# Thursday September 13, 2001

AFTER MUCH DISCUSSION THE Markham family set out for Notre Dame Basilica in the old city of Montreal. At the same time and with the same intention Antonietta was leaving Ste. Anne des Lacs. She arrived first at the Basilica, which was already quite full. She found a seat at the back, which enabled her to take in all the magnificence of the building's interior. She said a brief prayer and settled back to contemplate the beautiful stained-glass windows. Something made her turn her gaze towards the entrance of the Basilica. Thunderstruck, she saw James and his family walk down the aisle, genuflect and sit a few rows in front of her.

Antonietta's immediate reaction was to get up and leave, but she couldn't. Her eyes riveted on James, the power of her passion prevented her from moving. She imagined herself in his arms, kissing him, and an irresistible force drew her towards him. Before she knew what she was doing, she found herself standing up, about to walk to where he was seated. Horrified, she stopped herself and sat down.

Once she was seated again, Antonietta silently prayed the *Memorare* and implored the Virgin to help her control herself. Her prayer was answered for she managed to stay for the whole Mass, but the yearning for the man she strongly suspected was her professor never left her. The worst moment was when he turned round, and their eyes met. Her only consolation was that it was clear from the man's expression that their feelings for each other were mutual, although this was hardly any help to either of them. She didn't take communion but remained seated, her head bowed in prayer, so as not to see James. After an atrocious hour, Mass ended, and Antonietta left quickly, emotionally exhausted.

❦

James felt ill at ease when the family took their seats in the Basilica. He put it down to the dreadful time he'd been through since last Sunday's fateful Mass. Nevertheless, it disturbed him, and he began to look around at the congregation to distract himself. In disbelief he found himself looking straight at Antonietta. He gasped involuntarily and quickly turned back. He was white, and even Veronica, who normally had eyes only for the crucified Christ above the altar, asked him whether he was feeling ill. For a brief moment he was tempted to tell Veronica the truth and go and fetch this Antonietta della Chiesa, but with a supreme effort he mastered the violence of his desires.

"Well"? his wife asked again.

"No, I'm fine, Veronica. Must've been Bill's scotch. He always buys this cheap stuff."

Veronica gave him a look of scornful disapproval and returned to her devotions without further comment. Peter, who had seen the look between his father and Antonietta, glanced at him inquisitively but said nothing.

James steeled himself not to turn round again and masked his inner turmoil by appearing to pray. But it was the vision of unparalleled beauty behind him that filled his thoughts, not the Lord or anyone else from the celestial host. He dreaded the walk back from taking communion when he couldn't fail to see her. Luckily, he couldn't see her face as she was praying, but the sight of her lovely long, black hair flowing past her shoulders was almost as unsettling. Usually James was ready to leave immediately Mass ended, but this time he stayed put, ostensibly praying, in order to have Antonietta leave first. He felt sick to his stomach from this effort at self-control. As the family left the Basilica, Veronica commented approvingly on his newly found religious fervor. In the distance he saw Antonietta opening the door of her car.

She looked up, and their eyes met again. Unhappily they went their separate ways.

⌒♫⌒

James was in his office thinking as always of Antonietta. It was worse now that he knew who she was, and seeing her at the Basilica had brought him almost to the point of surrender to the passion he felt for her. He longed to see her again, yet at the same time dreaded tomorrow's class. It would take a supreme act of will to behave normally, but somehow he had to find the strength to do so.

The telephone rang. It was Elliot Hunt informing him that he and Annya were back from their trip, and that Annya was at home awaiting his phone call. James realized he'd put the Hunt case completely out of his mind, so bedazzled had he been by his obsession with Antonietta.

"I'll call her straight away," he promised, which he did. It was arranged that Annya would come to his office at eleven-thirty on Wednesday morning.

⌒♫⌒

Antonietta had also come near to surrendering herself to James at the Basilica and entered Bill Leaman's class in a daze. Hard as she tried, she couldn't keep her attention fixed on what the professor was saying. More important to her was the fact that Leaman was a good friend of James Markham. She imagined the two of them drinking and laughing together, then she added herself to the imagined scene with James--he'd become James now in her reveries--putting his arm around her when they left the party together. She imagined them kissing before getting into the car and returning home, *their* home.

"Miss della Chiesa"! It was Professor Leaman who was calling her. She looked up, startled. "That's the second time I've called your name. You were daydreaming, I believe. Lucky fellow"!

The class burst out laughing, and Antonietta reddened with embarrassment. As she left the class, Bill took her aside and apologized. "I'm sorry if I embarrassed you." Antonietta gave him a lovely smile. "It's true that I was daydreaming. I should apologize too."

Bill went immediately to James's office to recount the incident to him. "She's even more gorgeous when she smiles. Try to make her smile in your class tomorrow, and you'll see for yourself." This was both the first and last thing James wanted to see. He rapidly changed the subject.

"I'm seeing Annya Nowak tomorrow, and I'll have to interview the students who've testified against Hunt and a sample of other students. After all that we must have a council of war with Hunt."

Bill was not interested in Hunt. He was still under the impact of Antonietta's beauty.

"She's just ravishing, I tell you," he said, adding with a malicious grin, "A fitting mistress for a British lord." James caught his breath, but fortunately Bill misinterpreted his reaction. "Don't be so goddam Catholic, Jimmy."

Before Bill left, James managed to summon up the presence of mind to admonish him to continuing silence on his title of nobility. "You know I don't want anyone to know about that if it can be helped. Arbuthnot already knows, and it's one of the reasons he hates my guts."

Bill could not resist teasing his friend. "And were a certain student to fall in love with you, you wouldn't want to think she's after your title, would you"?

"Get out of my office, Satan," James growled.

James drove his children to school and took the same road back to Prévost and on to Saint-Sauveur. It always irritated him that Veronica wouldn't take on this chore, but she insisted that driving the children interfered with her morning prayers, which had to be said at nine o'clock. James nursed his irritation. At least it distracted him from that infernal longing for Antonietta della Chiesa.

Once in his office James looked over his notes for the day's lecture. He might as well not have bothered, for his mind was locked firmly on the prospect, both exhilarating and alarming, of seeing and, God forbid, even meeting Antonietta. That was all he could think about, at least until a devastated Bill Leaman burst into his office with news of the attacks on the Twin Towers. James looked vacantly at his friend, who was practically in tears.

"You mean, they just flew two planes into them"? Bill, unable to speak anymore, just nodded.

They went down to the Faculty Lounge in the Administration building to watch the television. For some time, as the horror unfolded in New York, James didn't think of Antonietta. Winstone arrived and announced portentously that, in view of the national tragedy in the United States, classes would be canceled that day. James's immediate reaction was relief at the postponement of his ordeal, but beneath the relief was a disappointment that bordered on despair. He had to see Antonietta again. While his colleagues continued to watch with perverse fascination the scenes of destruction and death on the television, James found himself repeating wordlessly that name, Antonietta, which he found as enchanting as the irresistible woman who bore it.

Antonietta was in the Students' Union with Petra looking in horror at the dreadful images from New York.

"It's horrible," she cried, her eyes full of tears.

"It serves them right," said Petra coldly.

Antonietta was thoroughly shocked. "How can you say such a thing"?

Petra's eyes were icy blue. "They bombed my country. Now someone has bombed them. We're quits."

Antonietta remembered that Petra was from Serbia, but she couldn't accept her vengeful view.

"Serbia was bombed during an international crisis, but this is not a bombing campaign. It's terrorism on a large scale. Imagine flying a plane into a building and killing God knows how many innocent people just because you don't agree with American policy."

Petra didn't flinch. "You know how many innocent Serbs died because America decided we should get out of Kosovo, which is historically part of our country? Many, many." Her tone was hostile, but she didn't look at Antonietta when she was speaking. It was as if she were addressing an imaginary audience.

"We Italians were part of the Kosovo campaign. Does that mean you would like to see me killed"?

Petra trembled slightly and still staring into space answered with more feeling than Antonietta would have expected--or liked. "No, Antonietta, never, never."

"Actually, I understand your sentiments." Antonietta put her arm around Petra. "There was always something about the bombing campaign against Serbia that disturbed me. But, Petra, a war that's waged after every chance for peace has been given, even if the cause may be mistaken, is not the same as cold-blooded and unprovoked murder on a scale such as this," She waved her hand towards the television in a gesture of hopelessness.

"I don't agree," Petra replied.

Antonietta could take no more and was about to stalk off when Brett Taylor entered the room and announced that classes had been canceled for the day. Immediately the events in New York were relegated from her mind. One thought alone now dominated her. She wouldn't see him!

Forgetting her argument with Petra, indeed forgetting even her presence, Antonietta stood up. She'd apprehended the class with James to the point of considering withdrawal from the course, but now it had been canceled she felt the same emptiness that had plagued her at home in Italy. She fought back her tears and was about to rush off when Petra stopped her.

"Antonietta, I apologize. What I said was insane. It was a momentary reaction." The grayish blue eyes were misted over, and there was a pleading tone to her voice.

Impetuously Antonietta took Petra into her arms. "I'm not upset with you, Petra. It's something else."

Once back in the cottage Antonietta sat down with a much too large glass of scotch to take stock of her situation. So far in Quebec she'd slept with one married man and fallen desperately in love with another. To top it off, her relationship with her new friend, Petra, was not entirely free of sexual undertones. The obvious conclusion was to pack up and return home before she did something she would really regret.

It was by now eighth-thirty in the evening in Florence, and she called her parents. By a miracle her mother was out, and it was her father who answered. The mere sound of his warm voice strengthened

Antonietta's resolve to return home, but when her father asked her in jest whether she was returning, she said no.

"That's a very forceful no, Antonietta. You wouldn't have fallen in love, would you"?

Yes, she'd fallen in love, and at that moment she knew she couldn't leave. It was beyond her power to envisage an existence where she wouldn't see him.

"I hope you'll be back at Christmas in time for our wedding anniversary on December 17.

Antonietta grimaced. It was a family tradition to gather for her parents' wedding anniversary, but family gatherings were not always a joyous occasion for Antonietta. Nonetheless, she promised her father that she would come.

Piotr and Bill were engaged in an acrimonious argument about the attack on the Twin Towers.

"Our neighbors are Arabs, and they're great people," Piotr was saying.

"I don't care about your fucking neighbors," Bill retorted. "I care about the thousands murdered by a group of Arab terrorists."

The conversation was suddenly interrupted by a knock on the door. It was Annya Nowak. She was an extremely pretty blond, and at the sight of her Bill's humor improved considerably.

"Can't blame, Hunt, can you"? he commented to Piotr as they walked away. "She's a real dish."

"And a good Catholic Pole," Piotr added.

Annya was blushing, and James realized she'd heard the whole conversation. "Don't worry about Professor Leaman. He's incorrigible but quite harmless." He motioned her to sit down.

"I'd offer you a coffee, but my machine's broken down. How about a scotch"?

Annya looked at James in astonishment. "A scotch"?

"Yes, why not"? he replied, not thinking for one moment that she'd accept. It was just a ploy to make her feel at ease.

"As you say, Professor Markham, why not"?

Annya pushed back her blond hair with delightful nonchalance, and the joke was now on James. It was highly irregular to feed alcohol to students in your office, but he was hoisted by his own petard. "Not a very suitable wife for a Baptist," he thought as he poured out the two scotches.

"I might've known, seeing you're Polish."

"That's unfair," she protested, "Not all Poles drink."

"Not the Pope perhaps, but I'm not too sure about him either."

Annya grinned. She was now completely at ease. James could start his examination-in-chief.

"Okay, you know what's going on. I'm sure they're out to get Elliott, but I need to hear from you directly that your relationship didn't start before the marks were handed in."

"No. We both knew that we'd fallen for each other, but we didn't even speak of it before the end of term. We did nothing wrong." Annya seemed almost in tears at the injustice of the accusations against them.

"I believe you, Annya, but when did you finish with Doefman"?

"About two-thirds of the way through the class."

"Was it because of Elliott"?

Annya hesitated.

"Tell the truth. It won't hurt."

"At first I was attracted to Brett because he was good-looking, assertive, and popular. Later I realized he was a total jerk. He treated me like his property. It would never have lasted anyway, but once he realized I'd fallen for Elliott, he made my life a misery. I couldn't stand him anymore, so I dumped him."

James was satisfied with the explanation. "How did you and Elliott get together"?

"I wandered around the Institute until I bumped into him."

For some reason he couldn't fathom, this answer troubled James. He put his unease aside and asked the final question, somewhat embarrassed.

"When did you become....intimate"?

"That afternoon."

"Good Lord"! was all the reply James could muster. Annya's eyes showed amusement at James's reaction as well as something else that he didn't grasp at the time. She was still laughing when she left the office. Once she was gone, James called Doefman.

"I don't have much time. It's the beginning of term in case you hadn't noticed," he told James.

James's reply to this arrogance was scathing. "At four on Thursday, you have no class," he snapped. "You will be in my office if you wish to pursue your case. I will not be at your beck and call, young man."

He hung up without waiting for a response.

⚜

After her class with Professor Forget ended at noon, Antonietta intended to go straight to the library, but she went in the opposite direction and found herself in the LIR building near James's office, where she caught a glimpse of Annya leaving. She was laughing. A sting of jealousy whipped right through her. How dare he flirt with other girls! She made for his office, impelled by an irrational impulse to fling his supposed infidelity in his face. Fortunately, she bumped into Bill Leaman. He was surprised to see her.

"Miss della Chiesa! Are you on your way to see Professor Markham"?

Antonietta was thoroughly disconcerted. "No," she stammered, blushing. "I'm on my way to the library."

"Ah, I see." Bill eyed her doubtfully. "Well, you'd better go in the opposite direction."

By this time Antonietta could have wished herself anywhere, even her grandmother's villa in Rome. "Thank you," she murmured and turned round. Bill watched her walk away. "What was all that about"? he wondered.

Antonietta never went to the library. She was sick with jealousy and longing. She intended to go home but went instead to the church where her ordeal had started. Gazing upon the statue of the Virgin she prayed for strength to resist her adulterous passion.

⚜

Thursday dawned. For both Antonietta and James this was the day that they had both desired and feared. It would no longer be at a distance, sanctified in some way by the holy place in which it took place, that their eyes would meet, but close up in the relative intimacy of a classroom. Neither knew how they would cope, and both were full of apprehension, but neither would have forgone the moment.

James was pacing around his office.

"What the hell's the matter with you, Markham"? Bill had been watching James's performance from the open door. "You've been behaving like a fart in a frying pan for the last week."

"It's the beginning of term. It always makes me nervous."

"Bullshit. There's something else the matter, and nothing you say will convince me otherwise."

James stopped dead in his tracks. "There's nothing the matter. I tell you, I hate the beginning of term."

"Okay, I believe you, but if you continue to go round in circles, you're going to be late for class and the delectable Antonietta della Chiesa." He emphasized the last words, which merited a venomous glare from James.

Bill sighed as James marched off to his class. "What the hell's wrong with him"?

James entered the classroom. He always avoided looking at the students in a way that would enable him to identify individuals. He preferred them as a blur of anonymity. Today, however, he was on tenterhooks, and his eyes danced around the class seeking Antonietta. He saw her, and his mind became a complete daze. A slight murmur from the students awakened him to their expectation that he would say something. He introduced himself almost inaudibly and announced that he would go through the class list.

Antonietta was in no better shape. Before James arrived, she'd felt sick to her stomach. Petra, seated next to her, had commented on how white she was.

"It must be nerves," Antonietta told her.

"You don't need to be nervous. He's a good teacher and a very decent guy."

At that moment James entered the classroom and confirmed Antonietta's worst fears and fondest hopes. He was the man from Mass. She trembled and grasped the ridge of her desk.

James was going through the class list. "Anderson". "Present." Aworski." "Present" and so on. All by the surname. Then "Antonietta". Antonietta couldn't answer, overcome by the emotion of hearing him call her by name. Petra dug her in the ribs, and she managed to respond, "Present."

"How come he called you by your first name"? Petra whispered.

"Perhaps he can't pronounce my last name," Antonietta suggested.

"That can't be it. In my first year I had him for Italian literature."

Antonietta looked at Petra in amazement. "James knows Italian literature! That must mean he speaks Italian! God in Heaven, everything's conspiring against me. The next thing I'll find out is that he's an aristocrat"!

James was aware he was making a complete mess of his introductory class. Normally he used it to put the students at ease, make a few jokes, and set out the main tenets of his approach to the course. As it was, he was under the spell of hearing Antonietta's voice for the first time, of having his first conversation with her, as it were. He was quite unaware that he'd singled her out by using her first name. Eventually his professionalism imposed itself, and he went through the syllabus, the fact that there would be two examinations, and that he would not use any a priori making system.

Once the class was over, James quickly disappeared. Antonietta, at her wits' end, followed Petra aimlessly out of the room. Petra's face lit up when she saw Brett Taylor waiting for them with one of his friends.

"Do you two want to come for lunch"? he enquired.

All Antonietta wanted was to go home to the solitude of her own thoughts, but she could see that Petra was desperate for them to accept the invitation. She agreed all the more reluctantly as Wilhelm had ingratiated himself into the group. They made their way in glorious sunshine across the quadrangle past an incongruous fountain and between the FEB and Administration buildings to the Students Union. To Antonietta's dismay, the group made for the cafeteria where the food was of the sugar-laden, fat-sodden North American variety, and no alcohol was served. She picked up a wilted salad and a small bottle of Pellegrino water.

Meanwhile, James had regained his office. He was furious. He'd made a fool of himself in class because of that damned girl, but his irritation soon gave way to reminiscences of her in class: her beauty, the sound of her voice, her very name. All enchanted and captivated him. "God, I want her," he admitted to himself and then came a sobering reflection. He was a fine person to be defending Hunt. If he didn't pull himself together, he'd end up before the Ethics Committee himself.

The vision of a triumphant and vindictive HB lording it over him strengthened his determination to fight the foolish passion that was threatening to destroy both his marriage and his career. He called Claudio Pettroni for a game of squash. He didn't particularly like the game, but at least it would take his mind off Antonietta.

*⸜⸝*

Lunch was as excruciating as Antonietta had feared. Brett and his friend kept talking about James's weird behavior in class. Wilhelm remarked that he'd found him "disappointing", which infuriated Antonietta. Pompous ass, she felt like telling him. "It was probably just a hangover," concluded Brett with a chuckle. "He and his friends are big drinkers. He'll be okay the next class."

During the whole conversation, Petra observed how much it troubled Antonietta. She couldn't resist asking the question that had plagued her ever since James had called Antonietta by her first name.

"Have you met Professor Markham somewhere before, Antonietta"?

"No, never," Antonietta assured her.

There was no doubting the honesty is her expressive eyes, but Petra was perspicacious enough to catch the longing in them as well. She couldn't understand how it had come about, but her new friend seemed to have fallen desperately in love with James Markham.

A group of other students from their class with James arrived at the next table. They immediately began to talk about his strange behavior as well. Antonietta could bear it no longer and left. Once she arrived home, she collapsed on the sofa, overwrought, in tears. She wanted him, she wanted him so badly that it was physically painful. She had trouble breathing. More out of despair than a desire for a drink, she opened a bottle of wine and poured herself a glass. She picked up the registration package from the Institute and flipped through the notes on the professors until she came to the only one that mattered to her.

Now for the first time she read that James had done his doctorate at the European University Institute in Florence between 1989 and 1992. For three years they had lived in the same city, walked the same streets, perhaps even attended Mass in the same church.

It was incredible, she could hardly believe it. What would have happened if he'd seen her? Antonietta was suddenly beset by the dreadful idea that James might have glanced at the young teenager she was then without interest. He must have frequented women of his own age. She was overcome by a jealousy as powerful as it was irrational. She finished the bottle of wine listlessly and fell asleep on the sofa.

## *Chapter 12*

# Thursday September 13, 2001 to Wednesday September 19, 2001

DOEFMAN ENTERED JAMES'S OFFICE with an arrogant swagger and sat down without being invited. James looked at him searchingly and said nothing. After a few moments Doefman's confidence seemed to wane. He crossed his legs nervously.

"You have made a very serious allegation against Professor Hunt, Mr. Doefman," James said after the silence. There was a hint of menace in his voice when he added. "You'd better be able to back it up."

Doefman might have been nervous, but he was not intimidated by James's approach. "Hunt deserves to be fired," he spat out. "He did everything he could to make me seem like an idiot in class just so he could steal my girlfriend. I'm a good student, and that son of a bitch kept putting me down just to impress Annya."

"I think we can do without the bad language, Mr. Doefman," James interjected forcefully. He went on in the same vein. "I understand from Miss Nowak that she ended her relationship with you quite simply because she couldn't, as she put it, stand you anymore."

Doefman blanched but refused to budge. "That's not true. If it hadn't been for Hunt, she'd never have left me."

James realized that his attempts to intimidate Doefman were failing. So he changed tactics. "I notice that the students who, apart from yourself, testify to having seen Professor Hunt and Miss Nowak together are either friends of yours's or students who received a poor mark in the course."

"So"?

Despite the haughty tone, James sensed that for the first time Doefman was on the defensive. He pressed home the advantage. "It could be argued that they are no more impartial observers of what happened than yourself, and no more credible." Doefman was clearly taken aback by James's tack and remained silent. "I should also like to point out that seeing two people together doesn't necessarily mean they're having an intimate relationship, does it"?

"I have witnesses who saw them kissing," Doefman retorted. "The reason why these witnesses are my friends or students who got poor marks is because that's what motivated them to help me. The others didn't want to make waves."

Doefman was regaining his confidence, and James saw no further possibility of shaking his story. Perhaps he would have better luck with the other so-called witnesses. All he needed was for one to break down and confess that he or she had lied, and this should discredit the whole case against Hunt. James had a nasty feeling, however, that he was grasping at straws for so much depended on the make-up of the Ethics Committee. One member would be appointed by the Rector, one by Hamid Khan as Hunt's Head of Section and one chosen by the faculty at large. HB and Ilse were the two ex officio members. He could well end up with an overall hostile committee.

James had finished giving Ilse the names of the students he wanted to see in connection with the Hunt case. She'd agreed to have her secretary set up the meetings, which was a great relief. This also meant that he was back in his office with nothing else to do but work on his article. Try as he might to interest himself in the intricacies of the Treaty of Nice, Antonietta constantly returned to haunt him. He found himself imagining that he was kissing her, telling her he loved her, listening to her own protestations of love. "God, you're a soppy sentimentalist," he told himself crossly, putting an abrupt end to his seductive fantasies.

"James, don't forget the reception for the foreign students at three this afternoon." It was Bill Leaman. Realizing that Antonietta would doubtless be present, James demurred, pretexting the article he was writing.

"You must come. You're the Assistant Dean of International Affairs, and Tom can't make it."

James reluctantly agreed, but it was a reluctance tinged with barely suppressed excitement.

⸙

"Why don't you want to come"? Petra was asking Antonietta. "It should be enjoyable. You can even teach Professor Markham how to pronounce your family name."

"That's the whole point," Antonietta wanted to cry out, "*he'll* be there"! Although she longed to see and talk to him, she dreaded not being able to control herself and creating a scene that would be irremediable. However, maintaining her composure with great effort she went along with her friend's banter. "Do come," Petra insisted, and Antonietta finally agreed. It would give her a chance to see whether James was going through the same anguish as herself, although exactly how that was going to help was not at all clear. Nothing was any longer clear for Antonietta, buffeted unmercifully between her passion and her resolve to resist it.

⸙

James made his way to the Lecture Hall building. Halfway across the quadrangle he stopped. He was desperate to see Antonietta, but he felt he was putting his head into the lion's mouth. Nevertheless, he carried on as he knew he would to the lecture hall where Bill had arranged to hold the reception. "Why does he always choose this lugubrious place"? he wondered irritably. "Surely he could get permission to use the reception room on the top floor of the Administration building." Comforted by his manufactured displeasure, James entered the room.

He saw her immediately. She was thankfully at the other end of the large room, talking with Petra Markovic, who seemed to have become her friend. They made a stunning couple: the dark-haired Antonietta

131

with her incomparable beauty that smoldered with sensuality, and the blond Petra, whose classic, blond looks hinted at an innate eroticism underneath their chilliness. Entranced by the pair, a bizarre comparison occurred to James. Antonietta recalled for him Napoleon's younger sister, Pauline Borghese, and Petra, the hapless Queen of France.

Suddenly he was accosted by Wilhelm, who asked him about the chances of the Treaty of Nice being ratified. Not only was this a topic that held absolutely no interest for James at that very moment, but Wilhelm had also interposed his substantial frame between him and his view of Antonietta.

"The EU doesn't take no for an answer," James answered shortly, but Wilhelm was not to be so easily put off. "Will the Irish be prepared to vote again"? he insisted. James's only thought was to get this intrusive young man out of his path of vision. He wanted to watch Antonietta's reaction when she saw him. But Wilhelm was not budging. "Probably," he replied and moved to the right to look past him. He was met by the sight of Antonietta being literally marched towards him by Bill Leaman. He blanched.

It was Petra who'd seen James arrive in the room. "Look," she whispered to Antonietta, "Professor Markham has arrived."

Antonietta willed herself to keep calm and refused to turn round. "He had to come, didn't he? He's Assistant Dean of International Relations."

"Oh, my God," Petra exclaimed. "He's been nabbed by Wilhelm." Petra giggled, and Antonietta, despite the conflicting emotions of dread and longing that swirled within her, couldn't help emulating her.

"Miss della Chiesa, please come with me." It was Professor Leaman. Before Antonietta could object, he took her by the arm and led her towards James. "It's time you met Professor Markham."

Antonietta's stomach gave way, and she arrived before James and the ubiquitous Wilhelm trembling like a leaf.

"James, may I introduce the lovely Antonetta della Chiesa," Bill announced, still mangling Antonietta's name.

James and Antonietta were forced to look straight at each other.

James felt his resistance drain away with every second he gazed into Antonietta's dark, shimmering eyes. There was no mistaking the passion they expressed.

"Pleased to meet you," he said and brusquely left the room.

Bill stared after him, shocked by his apparent rudeness. "I apologize," he told Antonietta. "He's not normally such an asshole."

He couldn't know that Antonietta, who had with difficulty restrained herself from throwing herself into James's arms, was both relieved and elated by his departure. It had averted a potential scandal and at the same time shown her that he was undergoing the same ordeal as herself. Life would be agony for Antonietta at the Institute, but so would it be for the man she loved. That was a sort of consolation. More than that; in the midst of her anguish it brought her a measure of contentment.

"It's not important," she assured Bill. She stayed a little longer at the reception, but with James's departure and Petra flirting outrageously with Brett Taylor there was nothing to keep her there. She left.

⌘

Bill was highly indignant. "Markham, you're an asshole. I introduce you to the most divine girl we've ever had in this Institute, and you're rude to her. Do you have some explanation"?

James had been expecting Bill to come to his office and remonstrate with him over the episode at the reception, but he hadn't been able to decide whether to tell him the truth or not. It would be a relief to share his torment with a close friend, but he was afraid to appear a lovesick fool.

"Well, are you going to tell me"?

James sighed and looked warily across his desk at Bill. He caressed the afternoon stubble on his chin. He sighed again. It was time to confess.

"I'll tell you only if you promise not to make fun of me. It's bad enough as it is without me becoming a laughingstock for my friends."

Bill agreed, and James began his tale. He told Bill about the first time he'd seen Antonietta at Mass, the intensity of the feelings she'd evoked in him, his irresistible longing for her, the second sight of her in the Basilica, the mess he'd made of his introductory class because of her, and the fateful meeting that afternoon when he'd nearly lost control of himself.

"I'm at my wits' end, Bill. You can't imagine how desperately I want her. This whole business is just crazy."

There was a short silence while Bill reflected upon what James had told him. He had no desire to mock his friend.

"It's not that crazy, James. She's unbelievably beautiful and sexy as a goddess, but there's also something else, something deeper about her. If I wasn't so besotted by that errant wife of mine, I'd probably have fallen in love with her as well." James was silent, lost in his own thoughts. "Your problem's worse than you think," Bill went on. "She's nuts about you too."

"I know, but how come you do"?

"Our delightful Antonetta has been in a complete daze since the beginning of term. Once you left, she didn't even bother to stay at the reception. What's more, I caught her this week on her way to your office. When I challenged her, she turned all red and told me she was going to the library. She's not a very good liar."

"When did you see her"?

"Wednesday, the day you interviewed Annya."

This news took James completely by surprise. So Antonietta had already known who he was even before their class. But why was she coming to see him? Surely, it wasn't...?

"What are you going to do"? Bill asked with a trace of impatience, interrupting his friend's train of thought.

"What can I do? If ever I give in to this..." James hesitated a moment and then went on, "this passion, it'll be forever, and it'll destroy both my marriage and my career. After all, Bill, I *am* married, and she *is* a student in my class."

Bill was unimpressed. "That's not it at all, James, and you know it. Your marriage is a sham, and if you're very discreet, you can get away with sleeping with her. No, you're just afraid of losing control of your life. To put it bluntly, Jimmy, she scares the shit out of you."

Bill was partly right. James knew that once he surrendered to his passion for Antonietta, it would possess him completely.

"I'm going to say a few rosaries with Veronica. Perhaps the Lord will help me."

"Jimmy, you can say all the mumbo-jumbo Papist prayers you like, but you two are going to end up together." Bill stood up and made to leave the office. "Mark my words," was his parting shot.

James reflected on Bill's words. It was true that his marriage was an empty shell, but there were the children and the distress that a divorce would cause Veronica. Was it possible to have Antonietta as his mistress? Despite Bill's sanguinity, James was sure that sooner or later there would be a scandal, and this would cost him both his marriage and his career. In any case, his passion for Antonietta was like an alcoholic's craving for booze. Once he gave into it, he would be its slave. No, it was divorce and re-marriage or nothing at all, and he didn't want the emotional chaos such a scenario would provoke.

A foreboding descended upon James. He was resolved to combat the passion that threatened such havoc in his life, but where would he find the strength to deal with the constant presence of the woman he desired with such unyielding force?

⟡

It was Sunday evening, and James was driving with a feeling of immense relief to an evening with his friends. He expected to be the butt of much ribbing, but anything was better than trying to keep up appearances with his family. The constant effort was terribly wearing, and even Veronica had remarked on his tiredness. Her concern added guilt to his longing for Antonietta and made him feel even worse. At Mass he'd looked around surreptitiously in the hope of seeing her, but to no avail.

He arrived at Bill's. Danny and Bill were already well into their cups. but as always it was impossible to tell how much Piotr had drunk.

"Come in, Romeo," Danny cried from the living room as James let himself into the house. "Where's your gorgeous Italian"?

"Very funny," James called back. He went straight to the fridge, filled up a tumbler with ice cubes and made for the liquor cabinet. "God, I need this," he said with feeling.

He sat down on the couch and surveyed the expectant faces of his friends. "How much has Bill told you"?

"Not much, Jimmy. I thought it was better coming from the horse's mouth."

James recounted his saga again. He expected some ribald comments or at least some unmerciful teasing, but the emotional intensity of his account left his friends silent and reflective.

It was Piotr who first reacted in his normal earnest way. "You can't let a momentary passion ruin your whole life, James. You've got to beat this."

It was Danny who replied. "It's not as easy as that, Piotr. The way James tells it, it's much more than a momentary passion." He paused before addressing his question to James. "Are you sure it's not just lust? She's spectacularly beautiful and sexy as hell. Are you sure you don't just want to screw her"?

"Of course I want to screw her. Probably any man alive would want to screw her. But I want more than that. I want to possess her completely. To put it bluntly, I want her and no one else in my life. I want to marry her."

"You can't, James"! Piotr cried in horror. "You're already married."

"Oh, shit, Piotr," Bill interjected, "Can't you Papists ever see farther than your Pope's nose. Jimmy's marriage is a total sham, and he'd be a helluva lot better off out of it."

"Yes, but perhaps not with a student in his class," Danny observed. "That way he'll not only lose a wife, he'll lose his career as well. There are also the kids to think about." His voice became a little unsteady, and the others realized that he was thinking of his own daughter.

James finished his scotch and poured himself another, even larger one. It was time to end this conversation before Danny got maudlin. It was going nowhere.

"I'm not going to marry her, so let's drop it," he said and changed the topic.

The conversation turned to the Hunt case. James explained that he was going to interview all seven students who supported Doefman's accusation against Hunt and at least ten others.

"The problem is that even if all the others say they saw nothing, it doesn't repudiate the testimony of Doefman's witnesses. My only hope is that I can get someone to admit that they were put up to it by Doefman, and perhaps even by HB."

By this time Bill had had enough. "Oh, come on, you guys, what with Jimmy's lovesickness and Hunt's problems, this is turning out to be a pretty dreary evening."

Bill filled everyone's glass up, and the evening ended in raucous but somewhat artificial merriment.

On Monday James met two of the students who had testified against Hunt and two others who had not. It was a disappointing experience. The two hostile witnesses stuck firmly to their story that they'd seen Hunt and Annya kissing, although the number of times varied between once and four times. It was clear to James that they were lying, but he couldn't shake them. The other two students, who'd received good marks in the course, said they'd seen nothing, which, apart from adding some weight to James's contention that Hunt was a victim of students out for revenge, didn't prove anything tangible.

And so Tuesday came and the second class together for James and Antonietta. That morning Antonietta rose early to wash her hair and prepare herself. She wore a tight blouse that accentuated her bosom and which she wore unbuttoned low enough to afford a glimpse of her sumptuous breasts under the tiny bra that barely contained them. The blouse was tucked into a short, tight skirt that showed off her shapely, sunburned legs to perfection. Her long dark hair flowed down to her shoulders over the elegant Versace jacket that she left undone so that the view afforded by her blouse was not obstructed. She put on a tasteful but tantalizing amount of glossy lipstick and mascara. She would make James suffer as much she would from their class together.

Petra looked at her in amazement when she walked into class.

"You look incredible. Is this for Professor Markham"?

Antonietta was saved from having to reply by James's entry into the classroom. She could feel herself tense up as she waited for him to see her. Their eyes met briefly, and she was gratified by James's grimace. This time she would make sure to walk right past him at the end of class before he could rush off.

The effect on James of Antonietta's appearance was more devastating than she realized. Try as he might, he couldn't prevent his eyes constantly straying in her direction and devouring her brazen lubricity, which eclipsed all thoughts of the European Union. The lecture was a disaster. When it ended, several students came up with questions in order to make some sense out of the chaos of James's presentation. One of them, an arrogant young man by the name of Ken Wrangel, was extremely argumentative. Just at that moment Antonietta walked right past, and James forgot completely what Wrangel had asked him. He gave some evasive answer, and Wrangel stalked off in disgust.

Immediately after the class James drove to Ste Agathe des Monts and sat by the lake. What was he going to do? What did Antonietta's appearance mean? Was it just her way of dressing? After all, she was Italian. It was known that French women bought clothes that were one size too small for them. Italian women must buy them two sizes too small. James couldn't suppress the impression that she was flaunting herself at him. He would not give in, and in the next class, by God, he'd control himself. He was British, he told himself, well, at least three quarters British. He put his momentary weakness down to the genes he'd inherited from his French grandmother, Marie-Louise de Rougefort-Cabenas.

James's new-found determination to put the emotional turmoil of the last weeks behind him brought a certain peace of mind that enabled him to pursue his task as Hunt's defender with more success than heretofore. On the Wednesday after the second catastrophic class with Antonietta, he interviewed the remaining five students who were testifying against Hunt. One of these was Brett Taylor, and James had heard from Bill that he was a nice lad who had unfortunately fallen under Doefman's influence. James interviewed him alone.

"If I'm not mistaken, Mr. Taylor, Professor Hunt's course was the first you failed. Is that so"? Brett Taylor agreed.

"Do you think that's sufficient reason for wanting to destroy his career"? The change in tone was brutal, and Taylor turned white.

"That's not it at all, Professor Markham," he stammered.

"Then what is it"? James asked. He was impressed by Taylor's politeness, which contrasted sharply with the brittle arrogance of Doefman and his other cronies. Bill was right. Here was the weak point.

"He stole Brett Doefman's girlfriend," Taylor replied. It sounded just like the pat answer it was.

"Not according to her, and don't you think that she's in a better position to know than you"?

Taylor was silent for a few moments. He spoke very quietly and with little conviction. "I saw them walking hand in hand in the quadrangle."

"Oh. come on, Brett. Even if they were lovers, do you honestly expect me to believe they would hold hands in the middle of the bloody Institute"?

"It's the truth," Taylor insisted, but he was red in the face and clearly ill at ease.

"It's not, and you know it." He then added in a friendlier tone, "You're a nice kid, Brett, but you've let yourself be talked into participating in a very nasty and immoral machination to destroy an innocent man's career. Think about it and call me any time you feel like it."

Brett Taylor said nothing more and walked slowly out of James's office.

James began to feel a little more optimistic about Hunt's chances. It was possible that Brett would crack, and two of the other students seemed less dogmatic than their written testimony suggested. If the captain of the football team deserted Doefman, these two might well follow.

The phone rang. It was Ilse wanting to see him.

## Chapter 13

# Wednesday September 19. 2001
# to Friday September, 2001

J AMES ARRIVED AT ILSE'S office in response to her message. "What's up. Ilse"?

"Sit down, James." Ilse's manner was collegial, but it was clear she was embarrassed.

"James, you've always been one of our best professors, and the students have fought to get into your classes. However, today I've had three students who want to withdraw from it. Whatever is going on"?

James didn't answer immediately. He respected Ilse, and so he replied truthfully but vaguely. "I've a little problem, Ilse, but I think I'm dealing with it. I hope the lectures will improve."

Ilse looked at him keenly. "It wouldn't be because of a certain young woman in that class, would it"?

"How in God's name do you know"?

"It's very strange," she replied, "When I recommended your course to her, I had a premonition. I hope I wasn't right."

"Well, Ilse, she does have a nasty habit of putting me off my stroke."

Ilse smiled faintly. "Do you think that's an appropriate analogy, James"?

Ilse's comment took James completely by surprise, She was the last person he would have expected to make such an allusion. She laughed quietly at his stupefaction. "I know I'm German and a Lutheran, James, but I'm also a human being."

"So I see, Ilse, so I see." James turned to go.

"Don't put your career in danger, James. That would be a criminal waste, however beautiful she is. Remember Tristan and Isolde. They both died."

"That's very comforting, Ilse. Thanks for the warning. I'll make sure to heed it."

～

Unwisely Antonietta pursued her provocative way of dressing in the next class on Thursday. The weather had suddenly turned colder, and she was wearing a tight sweater over bare breasts and equally tight jeans without a string or thong. Petra shook her head on seeing her.

"Isn't that a bit much"?

"I'm Italian, and that's how we dress," Antonietta replied tartly. Nonetheless, Petra's comment made her feel ashamed, but she couldn't resist the temptation to enflame James. Though she wouldn't have been capable of saying to what end.

The class went off much better for James. He noticed Antonietta's sultry appearance, but he told himself that it was in poor taste and irresponsible. This enabled him to summon up sufficient self-control to concentrate on his lecture and make some sense. Even Ken Wrangel, who came up after class to pester him with questions that were more self-important than useful, seemed satisfied. Antonietta was plunged into despair by James's apparent indifference.

Brett Taylor was again waiting for Petra after the class. "If he's so keen on her, why the hell doesn't he do something"? Antonietta asked herself irritably. He was with his friend, Malcolm, and they wanted to go for lunch. Despite her anguish, Antonietta agreed to go for lunch on condition they went to the student bar. There was no way she was going to eat the awful food in the cafeteria and wash it down with water or the sickly coffee Canadians seemed to like. They started off in the company of the omnipresent Wilhelm, who appeared happier with the day's class. They were joined by the other scruffy British student, Simon.

Antonietta soon regretted her decision. Brett, Malcolm, and

Simon went on about James again; his first chaotic lecture, his alleged drinking habits, and his reputation as a decent guy. There was obviously something about him that fascinated the students.

"Mind you," Brett added, "it's not much fun being cross-examined by him."

Petra shot him an icy glare. "Is that to do with the Hunt case?'

Brett was clearly embarrassed and muttered something incomprehensible. Sensing the awkwardness of the situation, Simon brought the conversation back to James.

"What's his wife like"? he asked.

Petra glanced at Antonietta and answered quickly. "Insipid." Her attempt to shield Antonietta from a topic she knew would upset her was torpedoed by Brett.

"It shouldn't bother him. Rumor has it that he's got a mistress in Argentina."

Antonietta was looking down at the time, and no one saw the tears well up in her eyes. She quickly got up and, mumbling an apology, rushed to the washroom where she promptly threw up. She was beginning to hate James Markham. He was nothing but a selfish brute who enjoyed tormenting women. She didn't return to the bar, and Petra was left to explain her flight as best she could.

Antonietta drove back to the cottage, her view of the road almost obscured by the tears that filled her eyes and ran down her cheeks. Immediately she arrived, she ripped off her provocative clothing and changed into a pair of jeans and a blouse that she buttoned up to the very top. She felt betrayed, and an excruciating misery came upon her.

What exactly had she expected? That James would stop the lecture and sweep her off her feet and take her to his office? Is that what she really wanted, to be enslaved in a passion that meant a rupture with her family and excommunication from the Church? She threw herself down on the bed, feeling cheap and immoral. It still hurt terribly, that mistress in Argentina, but it was better than surrender to a passion that menaced everything she held dear. If only she didn't want him so badly.

There was a knock on the door. Intrigued, Antonietta wiped the tears from her face and went to open the door. It was Petra.

"How did you get here"? Antonietta asked in surprise. Petra had no car.

"I took a taxi. We need to talk."

"What about"?

"James Markham."

Antonietta gave a start. "How did you guess"?

Petra sat down on the sofa, where Antonietta joined her.

"It didn't take genius, Antonietta. I became suspicious when you overreacted to his biography. I hadn't a clue why, but it was strange. In class you're constantly on tenterhooks, and you spend all your time trying to catch his eye and then avoiding it. The notes you take don't make any sense. The last two times you've gone out of your way to dress for the class in the most outrageously sexy and provocative fashion."

"Did I look like a whore"?

"No, Antonietta." Petra put her arm around her friend's shoulders. "You were magnificent. He must be really British not to have cracked."

"Petra, I don't want him to crack. I'm Catholic, and he's married. We can only ever be lovers."

"What's wrong with that"?

"Petra," replied Antonietta, her eyes gleaming with intense emotion, "if ever I kissed him, let him into my bed, I would be his forever. That would be no better than him divorcing his wife and marrying me."

"Then why did you dress as you did"?

"To make him suffer like I'm suffering. But it didn't work. He didn't even notice me today. He was probably thinking of his Argentinean mistress."

Antonietta could no longer control her sobs. Petra comforted her, took her face, and wiped away the tears.

"Antonietta, there is no Argentinean mistress."

The grief in Antonietta's eyes vanished. "But Brett…"

"Brett was exaggerating. Bill Leaman told me that he and James Markham had a good time in Buenos Aires. I told Brett, and because of Leaman's reputation he made a mountain out of a molehill."

Tears of relief streamed down Antonietta's cheeks.

"What are you going to do? It's quite clear to me that James Markham's as crazy about you as you are about him."

Antonietta's momentary feeling of relief was swamped anew by the anguish of her predicament. "What I want is him, forever. I want to be his wife, bear his children, spend my life with him, that's what I want," she said, the emotion choking her voice. "But I can't. So I'm going to do nothing. Nothing, nothing..." Her voice trailed off.

"I don't believe you." Petra gave Antonietta a long, hard look. "If it's real passion you feel for him, and I think it is, you can't beat it. Eventually you'll succumb."

Petra's words echoed those of her uncle, and Antonietta found a strange comfort in them They did nothing to solve her dilemma, but they restored her spirits. She invited Petra to eat at the little French restaurant in Prévost on the road to Saint-Sauveur. They had an excellent meal, albeit preposterously expensive, and Antonietta was happy to forget her own troubles by listening to Petra's tale of amorous woe.

"I know Brett likes me, but he seems incapable of shaking off that Françoise. Who knows? She and Doefman are off to Ottawa for a debate next Wednesday and Thursday. I'm hoping something will happen then."

Antonietta paid for the meal and drove Petra to the student residence.

"Your family is wealthy, isn't it"? Petra remarked as she made to get out of the car. Antonietta nodded reluctantly. They were straying into dangerous territory

"Please, Petra, let's not go there." Antonietta looked imploringly at her friend, who made no answer but kissed her softly on the lips.

"Dress more modestly for class, Antonietta. If you feel you can't go through with it, it's unfair to tempt him." Whereupon she vanished quickly into the residence.

The pleasure of Petra's kiss lent another layer to Antonietta's problems.

*~*

On Monday James spent the day interviewing eight students who were not part of the case against Hunt. Five of them merely said that they had seen nothing untoward, which was not particularly helpful, but two of them were more vociferous. According to them, Doefman was an arrogant egoist, and Annya had told them both she was going to dump him. She hadn't mentioned Elliot, and both maintained she was not the sort of girl to latch on to a professor in the middle of a course.

"She's got class," said one of them, "It's not something she'd do."

The testimony was not a definitive exoneration of Elliot Hunt, but it might serve as corroborating evidence for James's contention that Hunt was the victim of a vendetta. Now he just had to await the re-evaluation of Doefman's paper from Ted Burstein. Hopefully, he would either agree with Hunt's assessment or even better assign a lower mark.

❦

It was Tuesday again and the ordeal of their class together. Following Petra's instructions, Antonietta dressed classically in her Versace jacket, a blouse demurely buttoned and a stylish skirt of modest length. "The perfect Italian aristocrat," she thought, looking at herself in the mirror before she left the cottage. Her mother would be proud of her.

"That's just right," Petra told her. "Mind you, I heard some of the other students in this class complaining that we both dressed like snobs."

Antonietta tossed her head in a dismissive gesture. "Snobs? Well, they're just slobs."

Petra laughed. "In any case, all the men think about is beer, sports, and who they're going to fuck tonight."

"And the girls"? Antonietta asked, amused as always by Petra's contempt for her fellow students. How she'd managed to be elected Vice-President with such an attitude surpassed her understanding.

"They're wondering who's going to fuck them."

James arrived. Petra looked at Antonietta and whispered in French courage. The connivance of her friend strengthened Antonietta, and she was able to deal with James's presence with greater equanimity. Her heart still jumped within her when he walked in, and her eyes sought his with the same desperation for reassurance, but she was no longer so tense. Now it was James's turn to notice Antonietta's composure as well her reticent attire, and to fall prey to doubts about her feelings for

145

him. With great difficulty he stuck to his lecture notes, but the delivery was flat and his points at times inconsistent with each other. It was not an impressive performance, and at the lunch that now traditionally followed the lecture, Brett and the others commented on this.

"It's not a bloody hangover, you know," mused Simon. "It's almost as if he's in love."

Antonietta could have kissed him.

It was black Wednesday for James and Elliot. The Rector's office had sent them both a formal notification of the composition of the Ethics Committee that would consider the accusations against Hunt. Apart from HB and Ilse Bromhoeffer, who were *ex officio* members, there was Fred Gowling from FEB, a protégé of HB's, who was appointed by Hamid Khan, Ed Williams from James's own Section, who was appointed by the Rector, and Claudio Pettroni from LAC, who had been elected by the faculty at large. Apart from Pettroni and Ilse, who would be fair, Gowling was closely linked to Arbuthnot and would doubtless follow his lead, and Williams' association with Winstone augured badly.

"We've got two definitely against us, but probably three," James told Elliot. "Unless we have what we're looking for from Burstein and hopefully a breakthrough with the students testifying against you, it doesn't look good."

Hunt left James's office decidedly shaken.

"Shit, shit and shit again." James looked in disbelief at Burstein's reassessment of Doefman's paper, which had arrived that Friday morning. Hunt had given him 40% and James had hoped to see an even lower mark from Burstein, but he'd given the paper 55%. This was lower than the 65% given by Graeme Hill, but it would not serve to exonerate Hunt. He couldn't use it. He had little difficulty imagining the hay that HB and his friends would make of it. They were stuck with Hill's reassessment.

James put his head in his hands. His whole defense of Hunt had been based on two key points: that the students who testified against him had received low marks and were out for revenge, and that Hunt had been fair in his marking of Doefman's paper. The second line of defense was now blown apart, and it was open to HB and his acolytes to use Hill's reassessment as evidence of bias in Hunt's evaluation of Doefman's paper. This would probably enable them to persuade a majority on the committee to accept the testimonies that Hunt had infringed the ethics code of the Institute. It was not entirely logical, but it was enough to cost Hunt his career.

James looked more closely at Burstein's evaluation of Doefman's paper. At one point Doefman had written that the time limitations on the working week imposed by the European Union applied to all countries of the Union. This was not true. The United Kingdom had obtained a derogation from this requirement. In another place Doefman had written that all employment contracts in France guaranteed security of employment. This also was false. Burstein appeared to have overlooked the errors.

James called Hunt to come and review Burstein's reassessment. His colleague was clearly shocked by the mark assigned to the paper and very quickly found a number of points that Burstein had tacitly approved but which he maintained were wrong.

"I believe you," said James, "I've already found two mistakes myself. But we can't use this reassessment. We're stuck with Hill's evaluation. Why the hell did you choose Burstein"?

"He's the authority in the US on labor relations, but I didn't realize how parochial he is. I guess he just knows about the US, not Europe."

"Why didn't he tell us that"?

Hunt gave a wry smile, "He's an academic. He thinks he knows it all."

James put his arm round Hunt. "Elliot, we're now stuck with Hill's reassessment, which means that we're probably fucked. As you're a religious man, I advise you to pray. I'll say a few Papist prayers for you as well. My dear Elliot, we need a miracle."

Once Hunt had left, James picked out an article he'd written on occupational health law in the European Union. It was part of a series edited by a Professor Ewart van Wezel of the Erasmus University in Rotterdam. He looked up the university on the Internet and noted van Wezel's email address. He wrote him a short email merely asking him to comment on Doefman's paper, which he scanned and enclosed as an attachment. European professors were an arrogant bunch, and he probably wouldn't reply, but it was worth a try.

⌇

With one suffering from unrequited love and the other fighting a passion that was devouring her, Petra and Antonietta decided to go shopping for clothes in Montreal.

"Ugly women cry," Petra told her friend. "Pretty women spend money."

So here they were buying clothes that Petra could ill afford and Antonietta didn't need. But it was a lot of fun and certainly helped take their minds off their unhappy love lives.

"Come with me. I'm going to try on those jeans. They're really sexy," Petra exclaimed.

"You'll never get in them," Antonietta replied. Petra was insistent, and once in the cubicle she stripped off the jeans she was wearing and the string underneath. Antonietta was fascinated by her sexual nudity.

"Do you shave there"?

Petra laughed. "No, it's just been used a lot."

"Petra"! Antonietta was shocked but couldn't help laughing.

"No, I have it waxed. They call it "un bikini intégral" in Quebec. You don't do that"?

Antonietta didn't really want to answer, but Petra pressed her. "No, in Italy women don't do that," she admitted.

"Well, you should. It improves the sensations."

Reluctantly, Antonietta let herself be dragged to a beauty salon. It was a very intimate and embarrassing experience, but the feel of the string afterwards on her naked flesh was highly erotic.

They arrived back at Antonietta's cottage, strangely exhilarated. They opened a bottle of wine and drank it and then another.

"I'm going to cook a *putanesca* sauce," said Antonietta. "It means a whore's sauce."

They both burst out laughing.

"I'd like to be a whore," said Petra quite seriously. "That way I'd get screwed as much as I wanted without any emotional attachment." She lifted up her glass, noticed it was half empty, filled it up to the brim, and lifted it up again. "Here's to one-night stands."

Antonietta looked at her open-mouthed. She'd never had a bawdy conversation like this with her friends in Italy.

"How many one-night stands have you had"?

Petra waved her hands airily. "Enough. How about you"?

"None. I specialize in meaningless relationships."

"They can't be worse than one-night stands. Normally the guy's drunk, gets off quickly, and you're left wondering what to do for the rest of the night."

"Sit down," Antonietta ordered, somewhat uncomfortable with Petra' frankness. She could hardly believe this was the same standoffish young woman she'd seen in the line-up for James's course. "The meal's ready." She served some fettucini and poured the Putanesca sauce over them. "Do you want some parmesan"? Without waiting for an answer she spooned some cheese over Petra's meal. She served herself and sat down to eat.

"Do you masturbate"? Petra asked out of the blue. Antonietta nearly choked on her pasta. All she could do was shake her head.

"I don't a lot," Petra went on, quite unperturbed by Antonietta's stunned reaction, "Except at one-night stands. There's not much else to do."

Antonietta laid down her fork and spoon as she was laughing too hard to eat. She'd never heard anyone say anything so outrageous in such a matter-of-fact way. "Petra, you're impossible. You're obsessed with sex."

"Yes, but it's been a few weeks since I had any, and I'm as horny as hell. What about you"?

"It's been too long, that's for sure."

They talked and drank into the early hours, mostly about their unhappy personal situations. Petra was particularly upset because she'd hoped against hope that Brett would profit from Françoise's absence in Ottawa to make a move. It hadn't happened. By the time they'd finished the last bottle of wine, which was an excellent Chianti Classico that neither was in a fit state to appreciate, they were both very drunk.

"I can't drive you back home," Antonietta slurred, "Why don't you stay here. I'll sleep on the couch."

Petra walked unsteadily to the bedroom and looked in. "Nonsense. This bed's big enough for two," she said.

They undressed down to their bra and strings and climbed into bed. Antonietta lay down, but she normally slept naked, and her bra bothered her. Without thinking she sat up and took it off. Petra stared at her bare breasts and very gently began to caress them. It took Antonietta a few seconds to realize what was happening, but this was time enough for her to become so aroused by Petra's delicate touch that she didn't protest when Petra began to use her tongue on her nipples.

Petra undid her own bra. Her breasts were smaller than Antonietta's, but they were shapely and inviting. Images of Dana came back to Antonietta and memories of the pleasure that the older girl had given her. She didn't resist when Petra pushed her down on the bed. Exhausted and frustrated by the heartache and yearning of the past weeks, Antonietta abandoned herself to her friend's lust.

Antonietta's body tensed as Petra slowly pulled down her string. Involuntarily she opened her thighs to receive Petra's tongue on her newly denuded sex and gasped when she felt it. Petra caressed and played lasciviously with her, and when she began to suck her clitoris, Antonietta was aware of nothing but her mounting desire. She let herself be turned over on her stomach and moaned blissfully as Petra opened her buttocks and ran her tongue along the crack between them. When Petra's stiff breasts brushed against Antonietta's buttocks and her tongue entered her anus, Antonietta cried out and begged for release. Petra obliged by sodomizing her with her tongue and using her fingers to penetrate and masturbate her sex. With tantalizing slowness she brought Antonietta to a violent and ejaculating climax. Still not finished, Petra turned her over and drained with her mouth the last remnants of Antonietta's sexual desire.

"Now it's my turn," Petra announced.

She lay down beside Antonietta, her lips glistening with her friend's wetness and her nude body eager for sex. Antonietta came on top of her and kissed and fondled her tight breasts, luxuriating in the softness of the skin and the hardness of the nipples on the palms of her hands. She licked and sucked them while pressing and gyrating her sex against Petra's. She ran her tongue down the golden smoothness of Petra's body until she reached her sex, where she quickly, almost impatiently, slipped off the string that barely covered it. She marveled at the discrepancy between the cold splendor of the young woman she'd first glimpsed at registration and the twisting, naked girl lying with her thighs wide open, avid for sexual pleasure.

"I want it like you," Petro whispered.

Antonietta turned Petra over onto her stomach and ran her nipples, still taut with lust, over her friend's buttocks and into her anus. She administered the same dissolute pleasure with her tongue and fingers that she'd enjoyed and brought Petra to a paroxysm of release that convulsed her whole body and inundated the sheets anew.

Antonietta moved her damp lips up Petra's body, paused to pass them over her breasts, and kissed her. Petra returned the kiss with ardor.

"You've done this before, haven't you"?

"Yes. So have you."

They both fell asleep, their naked and sated bodies intertwined

*Chapter 14*

# Saturday September 29, 2001 to Thursday, October 18, 2001

ANTONIETTA AWOKE FIRST, AND one glance at the naked Petra lying on her stomach next to her in bed recalled their erotic night. She jumped out of bed and rushed to put on a bathrobe.

"Oh, my God"! she exclaimed out loud.

She could hardly believe what she'd done, but, notwithstanding the drunkenness, the recollection was vivid. How after all these years could she have allowed herself to do this again with a girl? She felt dirty and above all guilty. She had sullied the passion that bound her to James. Worst of all, she had to admit to the intense sexual satisfaction that Petra had given her. It was better than any man she'd been with up to now. She persuaded herself that it was because of the waxing.

In a daze Antonietta wandered into the kitchen. Mechanically she ground some coffee and prepared two expressos. Embarrassed and repelled by her own perverted promiscuity, she woke Petra up.

"Petra, have some coffee."

Petra opened her eyes and smiled prettily at Antonietta. "Do you realize we're lovers," she said, turning over and exhibiting her breasts and sex quite barefacedly to her distraught friend.

"No, we're *not*. We were drunk, and it just happened."

"We were also very horny," Petra observed with a wanton smile.

"We both enjoyed it, so don't pretend otherwise. Why don't you come back to bed? I wouldn't mind doing it again now we're sober."

"Petra"! Antonietta stood up and walked away from the bed in horror. "Don't you realize what we did"?

"Don't be so dramatic, Antonietta. It's not that unusual for two women to be attracted to each other. Normally nothing comes of it, but sometimes it happens, like last night. That doesn't mean we're lesbians or even bisexual."

She could see Antonietta was not convinced. "Look, I've done this three times now, and each time it was when I was without a man. It's just letting off steam. Mind you," she added with the same puckish grin she'd given Bill Leaman at the introductory seminar, "this time was particularly spectacular."

Antonietta sat down and put her head in her hands. Petra came over and sat next to her.

"For God's sake, put some clothes on, Petra." Antonietta moved away.

"Afraid of being tempted again"?

"Petra, we're going to get dressed, and we're going to have breakfast at the Brûlerie."

Petra laughed. "Can I shower first"?

Antonietta bundled her into the bathroom and sat down to wait.

The problem was that she *was* tempted by Petra. She looked particularly sexy this morning in her erogenous, golden nudity with her normally impeccable hair completely disheveled from the sexual activity of the previous night. Petra stuck her head round the bathroom door.

"Admit you didn't think of James Markham while we were having sex."

It was true, but Antonietta didn't answer. She dressed quickly to put herself out of temptation's way.

It was an unusually warm day for the end of September, and the town was full of people sitting in the cafes or just strolling along the Rue Principale. Antonietta looked across at the church. It stood there as a monument of reproach for her immorality and her faithlessness. It was the place where she'd first seen James. The longing for him suddenly returned with a vengeance. Antonietta was glad of it. It made her feel like a normal woman again

After breakfast at the Brûlerie Antonietta drove Petra to the student residence.

"I've got two papers to write, so we'll see each other on Tuesday," she told Antonietta. "By that time our hormones should have settled down."

Antonietta's eyes clouded over. "I hope we'll still be friends, Petra. You're the only friend I have here."

Petra lent over and kissed her on the cheek. "Don't worry, Antonietta. We're still be friends." She got out of the car but poked her head back in. "You were a great lay. Best I've ever had." She grinned mischievously and walked off, leaving Antonietta completely mortified.

Antonietta returned to the cottage. She was still in a state of shock over her lapse, and Petra's crude comment made it seem even more blameworthy. It brought back all her old demons, but she was comforted by the ache she felt when she thought of James. She sought for some excuse for the unnatural delights of the previous night. It was possible that Petra was right; this sort of thing did happen occasionally between women. "In any case," she told herself, "I deserve some respite from the agony I'm going through." She managed to convince herself that it was all James's fault. If she didn't love him so much, she'd have found some man to relieve her sexual frustrations.

Danny lived in St. Jérôme in the more up-market area to the west of the Cathedral. The weather had suddenly turned quite cold again, and the town was shrouded in a misty rain. It was still fall, but winter was in the air, and as every year the dreariness of the season dulled the senses. "Decidedly," James thought as he drove towards Danny's house, "the Laurentians are not a place to be in winter." His despondency was accentuated by the seeming hopelessness of Hunt's case and the omnipresent longing for Antonietta.

Moreover, it was not their normal Sunday night booze-up. Hunt was also present, and it was difficult to over-indulge in alcohol beneath the baleful gaze of one of God's Elect. Even Bill was eyeing his whisky dispiritedly.

"Our problem is that we have no clear evidence to refute the accusations against Elliot," James repeated for the umpteenth time, clearly feeling the need to exculpate himself for the impasse in which they found themselves. "I can get the whole of the rest of the class to say that they saw no evidence of intimacy before the end of term, but so what? The fact they didn't see it may raise a reasonable doubt, particularly since the students accusing Elliott all failed or got low marks, but we'll have to wait until we're before a court of law before we can use that argument. I doubt if Arbuthnot even understands the meaning of the phrase 'beyond a reasonable doubt'. What really kills us is Burstein's fucking re-appraisal."

Hunt looked reproachfully at James. He didn't approve of bad language, but at this moment James really didn't give a fig about Hunt's sensitivities. Why the hell had he picked Burstein?

"The committee kills you too," Danny remarked. "I saw Williams and McGrath in the faculty lounge the other day. Thick of thieves, they were. So, with Williams and Gowling HB's got the committee stacked his way. He doesn't even need the votes of Pettroni and Ilse. Mind you, Elliot, it doesn't help either that you and Annya have moved in together."

"That's none of your business nor anyone else's," Hunt retorted. He picked up his coat. "I must be going. Annya's waiting for me," He nodded a curt goodbye and left.

"What do you think she sees in him"? James asked, shaking his head.

"Most women prefer assholes," Danny declared flatly, pouring all of them an extra-large scotch to make up for their earlier forced moderation.

"Or husbands they can torture," said Piot.

"Talking of the fair sex." Danny looked at James. "How's your luscious Italian, James"?

"I don't know, and I don't want to know."

"A good Catholic shouldn't lie, James."

"Nor should he have affairs with his students."

James finished his glass and poured himself another scotch.

⌒𝓂⌒

It was time again for James's class, but this time Antonietta was more apprehensive about finding Petra after their intimacies of Friday night. She'd passed Saturday afternoon and evening in Montreal at Luigi's restaurant in order to take her mind off the chaos in her personal life. She'd spent the night at Luigi's apartment, but she hadn't found the courage to confess her lesbian encounter with Petra. Sunday morning she'd attended Mass at the Basilica in the old city and prayed earnestly for forgiveness. There was an element of revolt in her penitence. "Send me a man who isn't married," she told the Lord, "or forgive me the consequences."

As it happened, Petra was all smiles and serenity when they met in class. "Oh boy," she told Antonietta breathlessly, "have I got some news for you." Antonietta was relieved but also irritated by Petra's welcome. They'd been lovers only a few days ago, but suddenly that seemed to count for nothing. Nonetheless, curiosity about what Petra had to tell her was a distraction from her obsession with James.

Brett was not waiting for them after class. Antonietta remarked on it, and Petra informed her that they were having lunch, just the two of them. "It's my turn to invite you to Gio's."

Once they were ensconced in the restaurant, Petra took a deep breath and began her tale of joy.

"You know that Doefman and Françoise were at that debate in Ottawa"? Antonietta nodded. "Well, they went to bed together"!

Antonietta looked at Petra in disbelief. "But Brett's supposed to be Doefman's best friend."

"No longer." Petra replied. "On Friday Françoise told Brett what had happened. Apparently, he and Doefman had a slanging match in the student bar. Doefman wanted a fight, and do you know what Brett said"? Antonietta shook her head. "I don't fight over a worthless woman! That night he called me."

"What's happened since"?

"We've spent all the time in bed."

Antonietta felt a stab of jealousy, but she quickly recovered herself. "I'm so glad for you, Petra. At least one of us has found happiness."

Petra fixed Antonietta with a penetrating look. "I want three things to be clear, Antonietta. Firstly, I want you to know that with you I had more pleasure than with Brett, but I want a man, not a woman. Secondly, you're my dearest friend here, and Brett's not going to change that. Thirdly, unless you snap out of this obsession with James Markham, I'll do my darndest to get you guys together." "Tonight," she went on, "Brett, me, and Simon, and probably Wilhelm, are meeting Bill Leaman for a drink in the students' bar. You must come."

Antonietta had no real desire to be a witness to Petra's and Brett's newly found happiness, It was partly jealousy, but above all their happiness highlighted her own misery. However, Bill Leaman would be there, and he was, if student gossip was to be believed, James's closest friend. So desperate was her longing for him that even a surrogate was better than a night alone with her sad fantasies in the cottage. She accepted.

Antonietta had no idea how to dress. She wanted Bill to go back to James with a tale of her sexy appearance, but she didn't want to appear a whore. You could never be sure with Anglo-Saxons. Her Latin temperament revolted. To hell with it. They can think what they like! It was cold and wet, so she put on the same clinging sweater and skintight jeans that had met with Petra's disapproval in class.

She was the last to arrive. Professor Leaman was already in an expansive mood. Petra and Brett were interlaced together, and Simon and Wilhelm were engaged in an acrimonious dispute about the 1966 World Cup Final*. Bill Leaman gleamed with delight at seeing her. He made a few totally inappropriate comments, which amused Antonietta. She hated people who weighed every word and always said the right thing. Suddenly he became serious and bent over to whisper in Antonietta's ear.

"Are they together"? he asked, pointing to Petra and Brett Taylor.

Antonietta nodded. "Françoise cheated on him with Doefman, so he's jumped on the occasion to leave her for Petra." Bill looked thoughtful and, after a few more mouthfuls of beer, was about to leave when Brett leaned over the table with a question.

"Tell me, Professor Leaman, is it true that Professor Markham has a mistress in Buenos Aires"?

Petra shot him a poisonous look, but Brett was too far into his cups to notice. Bill blinked drunkenly. Forgetting Antonietta's presence, he answered the question.

"I wouldn't say a mistress, but I think he and Carolina had a good time together."

"That happened a long time ago," Petra quickly interjected, aware of Antonietta's acute distress. Her hostile manner made Bill realize his lack of tact.

"Yes," he replied, anxious to make amends, "It was in August. We've never been back since." Upset by his indiscretion, he left hurriedly and once in his car called James.

⸙

"Hello, Jimmy. I've just spent the evening with Antonetta." There was silence at the other end of the phone,

"Is that all you're calling me about."

"No, you ungrateful son of a bitch, I'm calling to tell you that you may have a break in the Hunt case." Bill could hear James catch his breath. "Petra Markovic, you know who she is"?

"Yes. She's Vice-President of the Students Union."

"Well, she's now going out with Brett Taylor."

"So"?

"So, there's been a big bust-up between Doefman and Taylor. It seems Doefman fucked Taylor's girlfriend, and that's why he's now with Markovic."

"Will he testify against Doefman"?

"Leave it to me. I'll go through Markovic."

James put the phone down. At last there was a glimmer of hope for Elliot Hunt. He felt immensely relieved. He didn't like the man and couldn't help feeling that this antipathy accounted in some measure for his lack of success in making any headway against Hunt's accusers. He was also very envious. While he was grounded in the austerity of his house, Bill was talking and laughing no doubt with the woman he loved.

*⌇*

Antonietta didn't remain very long after Bill's departure. The sight of Petra and Brett evoked the hopelessness of her own passion, and now her jealousy had a name to feed on, Carolina. Her mind dulled by pain, she returned to the cottage.

*⌇*

Life was becoming unbearable for Antonietta. At the beginning the novelty of being in love had given a bitter sweetness to her sufferings, and there had been the excitement of seeing James in class and the malevolent joy of stoking his passion for her. Now these consolations had palled, and there was only hopeless longing and jealousy. What was more, Petra was completely caught up in her new love affair and, despite her promise, had little time to spare for Antonietta. Anyway, she didn't really want to be with them. Although she was genuinely happy for Petra, the contrast between her own misery and Petra's happiness was too painful.

Unable to concentrate on any work, Antonietta passed her lonely days drinking too much and listening to Laura Pausini*. As she played *In assenza di te* for the umpteenth time, she went listlessly through her notes from Professor Forget's class. She threw them down in despair. The paper on Canadian confederation due on Friday was beyond her present capabilities.

The next week on Monday she was summoned to Dr. Bromhoeffer's office.

"It appears you haven't handed in a paper for Professor Forget. Is there a reason for that"?

There was a reason, but she could hardly tell Dr. Bromhoeffer that she was prey to a hopeless passion for James Markham that completely paralyzed her. She turned red.

"I haven't done Professor Leaman's paper either."

Ilse looked searchingly at the young woman, whose anguish was only too obvious to her. "Antonietta, I'm not blind. I'm quite aware of what's distressing you. May I make a suggestion"?

Antonietta nodded apprehensively.

"Why don't you return to Italy? Your time here is doing you absolutely no good."

"I can't"! Antonietta almost shouted.

Ilse looked at her sympathetically. "You can't, or you don't want to"?

Antonietta was silent. What could she say? She didn't want to admit the truth to a colleague of James, but to lie was pointless.

"Do you think you could finish the paper for Professor Forget by next Wednesday"? Ilse asked, changing the subject. Glad of the chance to end this embarrassing interview, Antonietta nodded. "Good," said Ilse, "I'll think up some excuse for your lateness. And Professor Leaman's by the end of next week"?

Antonietta nodded again, stammered out her thanks, and fled from the office. For once Ilse appreciated Bill's laxness. The poor girl could hardly be expected to finish two papers by next Wednesday.

James was faring no better than Antonietta. He was unable to get a grip on himself, and the feeling of powerlessness made him very irritable. Even Veronica was beginning to notice his strange behavior, and he had reduced poor Susanna to tears by shouting at her for some peccadillo. Try as he might, he was quite unable to concentrate on his lectures with Antonietta present in his class, and he felt humiliated and angry at the resulting lack of respect this earned him from the students. The fact that today was Sunday, which he would have to spend with the family, added to his misery.

He called the children to prepare for Mass. Peter arrived.

"Daddy, I feel awful."

James looked at Peter hopefully. A sick child meant he could stay at home, as Veronica wouldn't miss Mass even if her offspring were about to expire. James felt Peter's forehead. It was a little warm.

"Veronica," he called, "Peter's ill. He's got a temperature."

Veronica came downstairs and eyed her son suspiciously. "Are you sure you're not just making this up, Peter"?

James came to his son's rescue with a thermometer. "Thirty-nine point six," he pronounced with satisfaction. "I'm afraid he's got to stay home."

"Well, you'll have to stay with him. I'm not missing Mass because of a little fever."

"Was it really so high, my temperature, Dad"? Peter asked once Veronica and Susanna were safely out of the house.

"Shame on you, Peter. As if I would lie to your mother"! His father's broad grin confirmed Peter's suspicion that this was exactly what he'd done.

⟶

The evening at Luigi's conversing with him and his Italian friends had alleviated Antonietta's misery without curing it. Now, on a dull Sunday morning, she was driving back to Saint-Sauveur. Originally, she'd intended to attend Mass at the Basilica in old Montreal, but she was drawn against her will to the church where it had all started. She knew that it would solve nothing, indeed it would make everything worse, but she had an overwhelming desire to set her eyes on James.

She arrived at the church just as Mass was starting. It was only partly full, and she had no difficulty finding a seat. She searched in vain for James. Then, to the right near the front she recognized James's daughter. She was turning round to survey the congregation, obviously bored with the liturgy, until her mother muttered something to her, and the young girl returned with noticeable reluctance to her devotions. Antonietta realized with dismay that James was not there. She moved down the church to a pew across from the two Markhams. She fastened Veronica in her sight. She was not unattractive with her golden blond hair, but her features had acquired a pinched aspect. She was, as Antonietta had noticed when she'd first seen her, cheerless. Yet this was the woman James slept with, made love to, had children with, lived with.

A furious jealousy seized hold of Antonietta. Why did this insipid, cold English woman have a right to the joys that were denied to her? What merit had she to enjoy the man who was her's by right of love? Watching Veronica cross herself and gaze in wonder at the altar, Antonietta rebelled against all she believed in. Life was unfair, God was deaf, the Virgin a hypocrite. She felt more and more nauseous as the jealous anger built up inside her. She rushed out of the church and threw up on the porch. A few passers-by below on the Rue Principale gave her strange looks. Overcome by embarrassment, Antonietta quickly made for the Jetta and returned home.

As she sat down in the cottage with another glass of wine, it was clear to Antonietta that this could not go on. What was the point of staying to suffer this torture? At least in Italy she had her friends; here she had only Petra and that friendship had a perverse side. She resolved to return to Italy at the end of the semester without asking herself why not immediately. For, like a smoker who believes that in a month's time he will find the strength to give up the vice he cannot give up today, or the alcoholic who vows to give up drinking on a morrow that never comes, Antonietta could only envisage leaving at a time that had not yet arrived. She skipped her classes on Monday and traveled to Montreal to book her flight for December 15, telling herself that this way she fulfilled the promise to her father to attend her parents' wedding anniversary on the seventeenth.

The next day Petra arrived on time at Bill's office looking her normal immaculate self. While they were waiting for James, Bill asked Petra if she'd seen Antonietta.

"She wasn't in my class," he told her. "What's more, her term paper is overdue."

He noticed the look of concern on Petra's face and guessed that Antonietta had confided in her. "How's she bearing up"?

"What do you mean"?

"Come on, Markovic, you know damn well what I mean."

"Badly," Petra admitted.

"So is Markham. He's crazy about her."

The conversation ended abruptly with James's arrival. It was the first time Petra had met James out of a classroom setting. She was intrigued. She had no difficulty understanding how he had stolen Antonietta's heart. He was tall, handsome and elegant. It was much more difficult for her to penetrate his reserved manner and picture him as lovesick as

Antonietta. She was torn from her musings by James's clipped British accent.

"Miss Markovic," he began. James felt ill at ease. Having to ask a favor from a student and particularly one as delicate as this one was embarrassing. It had to be done if Hunt's career was to be salvaged. "As you may possibly know, I'm representing Professor Hunt before the Ethics Committee. He is accused of..." James sought for the appropriate euphemism, "having a too close relationship with a female student in his class."

"I know about it," Petra said.

James found her poise unsettling and wasn't quite sure how to go on. Bill came to the rescue.

"The point is, Petra, James thinks that the students testifying against Hunt have been put up to it by Doefman, including your boyfriend, Brett Taylor. Brett's captain of the football team, and if we can get him to confess the truth, we're sure some of the others will follow suit."

"You want me to persuade him to confess"? Bill and James nodded. Petra was silent for a few seconds. "I'd like to help as I don't believe it either, but there's a problem. If Brett confesses that he lied, he's likely to be thrown out of the Institute."

"I understand your concern, Miss Markovic," James replied, his formality contrasting sharply with Bill's casual manner. "What I should like is for Brett to swear an affidavit, which I could use to persuade some of the others to retract and do likewise. I promise not to make the affidavits public without their consent."

"Then what use are they"? Petra asked, fixing James with her cool, grayish-blue eyes. "God, she's intimidating," he thought. "I'd rather not say," he replied, "I'm afraid you'll just have to trust me."

Petra wavered. James Markham was held in high esteem by the students, except perhaps those who were suffering through his present class, and this was due in no small measure to his reputation for being fair and straightforward. She decided to trust him.

"Okay, I'll do it."

"Thank you, Miss Markovic." James could barely suppress his amusement. Any other girl would have said she would try, but this one clearly intended to be obeyed. She might be very attractive, but James didn't envy Brett Taylor.

"Here is my home number." He handed Petra a card. "Call me there if I'm not at the Institute."

"Or at my place or Danny Redfern's more likely," Bill commented. Petra laughed. James glared at him.

Petra was worried. Antonietta had not shown up for Markham's class, and yesterday she had cut both her classes. Petra decided that she must go and find out what was going on. Brett offered to drive her to Antonietta's cottage, but Petra preferred to take a taxi. She was not ready to let Brett into Antonietta's confidence. She arrived at the cottage and was relieved to see Antonietta's Jetta parked outside. She knocked, and after a few moments Antonietta opened the door. Petra stared at her in horror. She was hardly recognizable. Her face was puffy, her normally shimmering eyes were dull and expressionless, and the lovely long dark hair lay lank and unkempt around her shoulders. She stood unsteadily in the doorway, dressed only in a bathrobe despite the advanced hour.

Petra threw her arms around her friend. "Good God, Antonietta. You look awful"! She led her to the sofa, and they sat down together.

"I *feel* awful. But I'm glad to see you."

Petra surveyed the scene of desolation around her. Books and papers littered the table, empty bottles of wine and whisky were strewn around, CDs and their boxes, as well as empty and half-empty glasses, were all over the place, an elegant jacket and skirt lay untidily on the floor, but there were no dirty dishes.

"When did you last eat"?

Antonietta answered with a shrug. Petra noticed an airline ticket on the coffee table. She picked it up.

"Are you going home for Christmas"?

"I'm going home for good," Antonietta replied, her voice choking with emotion.

"Then why did you buy a return ticket"?

"Because here I don't have the courage to buy a single ticket, but once I'm back in Italy away from him, I'll find the strength not to come back."

Petra looked skeptically at Antonietta. She pointed to the table. "Is that Leaman's overdue paper"?

"No, it's Forget's, but I don't care. I'm leaving the Institute anyway."

Antonietta's face was a picture of misery. It was difficult to visualize this dejected and broken young woman as the glowing beauty Petra had noticed at registration. She was shocked and saddened, but she was also immensely glad to have come. Antonietta desperately needed help, or she would crack completely.

"You go and take a shower, put on some make-up, and dress as sexily as only you know how," Petra ordered. "I'll clear up this mess."

Antonietta went off obediently into the bathroom.

"God, how much has she drunk"? Petra asked herself in dismay as she collected the bottles and empty glasses. While she was bringing some semblance of order to the cottage, she made her plans for Antonietta. They would have breakfast at the little café in Prevost, the Café des Artisans, then she would help Antonietta finish her essay for Professor Forget. It would probably take most of the day. Tomorrow she'd see Bill Leaman. He owed her a favor.

They had breakfast, and Petra told Antonietta of her talk with Bill Leaman. She didn't mention that she'd also met with James, but she did tell Antonietta what Bill Leaman had said about his sorry state. Antonietta's eyes glittered with content. After breakfast they spent the day working on the essay, interspersed with pasta cooked by Antonietta. Petra forbade her any wine until the essay was finished, and Antonietta submitted herself humbly to Petra's discipline. Once the term paper was finished, they celebrated with some wine. It was late, but Petra refused Antonietta's offer to drive her home.

"You're tired, and I'm not leaving you on your own. I want to make sure that you're in class tomorrow. By the way, what's the subject of Leaman's term paper"?

"It's on the Bretton Woods system. Why it failed, and what replaced it."

Petra laughed. "That's exactly the same topic as last year. I'll get my term paper. We'll make a few changes, and you'll have it done in time for Friday's class."

"What if he sees that I've used your paper."

Petra made a dismissive gesture. "He won't remember what I wrote, and even if he does, he won't do anything. He's James's best friend, and he's not going to rat on the love of James's life."

Antonietta laid her head on Petra's shoulder. "You've saved my life, Petra. I was in complete despair." She recounted to Petra the scene in the church, her return home, the drinking binge, the purchase of the ticket to Italy, her feelings of sheer hopelessness, and the drinking again.

Petra's face was solemn. "Promise me you'll pull yourself together, Antonietta. I don't want anything bad to happen to you." She was near to tears, and Antonietta couldn't resist kissing her.

"This time I'm sleeping on the sofa," Petra told her. "I don't trust myself in bed with you, and now I've Brett to think about."

Antonietta stood up and eyed Petra lustfully.

"That's a pity," she said and went off alone into the bedroom.

## Chapter 15

# Friday October 19, 2001 to
# Friday, October 26, 2001

P ETRA ESCORTED ANTONIETTA TO Dr. Bromhoeffer's office where they
handed in her paper for Professor Forget.

"She's been ill," Petra explained. "That's why it's late."

Ilse didn't ask any questions. She just took the paper and asked
Antonietta if she was feeling better.

"Yes, Dr. Bromhoeffer," Antonietta replied. "I'm going to hand in
Professor Leaman's paper at Wednesday's class."

Ilse looked relieved. "Take care of her," she told Petra.

Petra accompanied Antonietta to Professor Forget's class. Afterwards
she went to Bill Leaman's office.

"Professor Leaman"? she said, putting her head around the door.

"Why all the formality, Markovic"? Bill gazed at her appreciatively.

"Bill, I've agreed to do you a favor. Now I want one in return."

"You want me to go to bed with you, no doubt."

"Certainly not. Actually it's a favor for Antonietta, not me. I want
you to get her and James Markham together. She's near breaking point,
and I can't stand watching her suffer any more."

"She's in his class, and he's married." This was the party line after all.

"I don't give a fuck if he's married or if he's her professor," Petra
retorted, "I want this favor."

There was a moment's silence while Bill considered her request.

"Okay. I agree that this situation cannot go on. But how the hell are we going to persuade those two obstinate buggers to meet"?

"Well, we don't have to tell them. It's got to happen without them knowing beforehand."

Bill sighed.

"Please, Bill, try and think of something,"

"Give me some time. When I've thought of something, I'll tell you."

Petra left the office and was on her way to the cafeteria when Bill called her back.

"I've got it! You know the party for the foreign students at my place a week next Friday. We'll switch it to Jimmy's place."

Petra looked at him aghast. "How will that help? He's not going to do anything in front of his wife and kids."

"Ah, my dear Petra, the saintly Veronica and her two children will be in England. They're leaving on the previous Thursday for ten whole days."

Petra was radiant. "Oh, thank you, Bill," she said. "You make sure James agrees, and I'll deal with Antonietta." It was strange to be talking about Professor Markham as if she were familiar with him.

"Will she come"?

"She'll refuse at first, but I'll tell her that Annya Nowak will be there. For some unknown reason, she's very jealous of her."

Bill thought of the strange meeting with Antonietta near James's office a few weeks back. Now he understood.

"She saw her come out of James's office laughing. She must have thought he was flirting with her.

⌣ℳ⌣

Bill went immediately to talk to James, who was very pleased to see him.

"Time for a liquid lunch, Bill"?

"A good idea," Bill replied. He'd get James feeling nice and mellow with a few scotches inside him, and then he'd spring his request, get James to agree, and quickly inform everyone so that he couldn't change his mind. Bill had even worked out how to get James and Antonietta alone together at the end of the party. It required some help from Danny and Piotr, which was another hurdle to cross, and they had to make sure not only that Antonietta came to the party but that she stayed to the end. He asked James about changing the venue of the party.

"Good God, Bill, you must be crazy. I'm not having that woman in my house."

"Look, Jimmy," Bill was all sweet reasonableness. "There are more foreign students this year, and your house is bigger than mine. What's more, the weather's so cold that it'll probably snow, and unless they've cleared the road, it's a difficult drive up to my place. In any case, you know she won't come."

A couple of whiskies later James had agreed. Bill rushed off to make the necessary arrangements as quickly as possible. James returned morosely to his office. What had he done to deserve this? His life hadn't been a barrel of laughs before he saw Antonietta, but at least he'd come to terms with it, and it had its compensations: the guys, the trips abroad, uncomplicated girls like Carolina. "And now"? James groaned inwardly as he sat down in a vain attempt to advance his article. A single thought kept disturbing him.

"What if she did come"?

꙳

Piotr was the first to arrive at Bill's house that Sunday evening, glad of the excuse to flee his family obligations. He complained bitterly about Ela's insistence on taking the two girls with them next weekend to Mont Tremblant.

"It's not that abnormal to take your small children on vacation with you." Bill remarked, "I'm told lots of people do it."

Piotr sulkily poured himself another scotch. "I should have bought two more bottles," Bill thought, "God knows how much he'll go through when he's in this mood."

Danny's arrival dispelled the somber atmosphere. "Well, my boys, where's James"? he enquired.

"He's not coming," Bill replied.

"What! Saying the rosary with his wife? Poor fellow"! Danny chortled as he started on the bottle of scotch that Piotr had already nearly emptied.

"I didn't invite him because I want you two to help me get him and Antonietta together. She's going to pieces according to Petra Markovic, and I'm fed up with that mournful look James wears most of the time these days."

"You can't do that," Piotr protested. "James is married, and she's in his class. Just because she's very beautiful, and he thinks he's in love with her, doesn't change anything. He can't break up a family and ruin his career for a whim."

"Ah, Piotr, my boy." Danny had obviously been drinking before he arrived as his Irish accent was thicker than normal. "It's unfortunately not a whim, that it's not. It's the real thing, and I've been watching both of them. So, I ask myself, I do, what's worse. Letting her go to pieces and him ruin his reputation because he can't concentrate on anything, or bringing them together. If Bill's to be believed, it's not the first time he's had some spare stuff."

"You're contradicting yourself," Piotr replied. "Either it's the real thing or it's spare stuff. It can't be both. It's one thing to have some spare stuff as you call it far away in South America and some right here in his own class. And if it's not spare stuff, where will it lead"?

Bill decided it was time to intervene. "Listen, I can tell you now that it's not spare stuff. I know James, and this is serious. It's very serious for both of them. Now, are we going to stand back and let them destroy themselves for the sake of saving a sham marriage and some silly ethics rules"?

"Ah, rules," mused Danny. "rules are for the guidance of wise men and the obedience of fools."

"You're exaggerating, Bill. They're hardly destroying themselves," countered Piotr.

"Piotr, listen." Bill stared fixedly at his friend. "Antonietta failed to hand in two papers, and when Petra Markovic went round to see her, she said Antonietta was unrecognizable. She'd been drinking, she hadn't eaten, and the place was like a hovel. She managed to sort her out and helped her finish Forget's term paper. Unless we do something, this is going to happen again, if not something worse. I call that destroying yourself."

"And James"? Piotr was visibly shaken by Bill's forceful peroration.

"The She-Wolf has a third of the class complaining about his course, and, apart from drinking too much and playing squash with Claudio, which by the way is a game he hates, he just moons around all day. He even shouted at his daughter, and you know how potty he is about her. At this rate he'll ruin his chances of becoming Rector once they get rid of that idiot Winstone, and we'll be lumbered with HB."

"Yes, lads, we have to do something," Danny concluded.

Bill could see Piotr's opposition weakening. He wasn't sure whether it was his dramatic portrayal of Antonietta' plight or the prospect of HB as Dean. Finally, Piotr sighed and nodded. "Okay, what do you want us to do"?

"James has agreed to hold the party for the foreign students at his place." There was a murmur of surprise from the other two. "I lied. I told him Antonietta wouldn't come, but Markovic is making sure she does. Our job is to see that she stays on after everyone's left. That way she'll be alone with James."

"How do we do that"? Piotr enquired.

Bill divulged his plan.

⌒ɲⵊ⌒

After James's class on Tuesday, Petra forced Antonietta to go for lunch with her, Brett, Simon, and the inevitable Wilhelm, who was wailing about the course being a waste of time. Antonietta could have strangled him. Worse still, they were eating in the cafeteria. "We've got to do Leaman's paper this afternoon, Antonietta," Petra reminded her.

After lunch Antonietta accompanied Petra to the Students Union, where Petra knew she would find information on the change of venue for the foreign students' party.

"Oh, they've moved the party to Professor Markham's house," she told Antonietta, feigning innocent surprise.

Antonietta turned white and clutched Petra to steady herself. "I'm not going then. I couldn't bear to see him with his wife in his own home. That's too much."

Petra put her arm around her friend. "Don't worry. Bill told me that James's wife and children will be away in England."

Antonietta felt a sudden thrill go through her at the thought of James alone in his house. It was only momentary. "That doesn't change anything. I'm not going."

Petra knew Antonietta's weak point was her irrational jealousy. "A little white lie, and Antonietta will be there," she was thinking.

"I understand, Antonietta," she purred. "At least Annya Nowak will be pleased you're not going. Rumor has it things aren't working out with Elliot Hunt."

Antonietta looked at her in dismay. "She's after James"? she stammered.

"Wouldn't you be"? Petra replied without any shame. All's fair in love and war was her present motto, and if she had to lie to save Antonietta from herself, she'd damn well do so.

They returned to the cottage and worked on the term paper by brazenly plagiarized Petra's paper. In any case, Antonietta was in no fit state to produce thoughts of her own. She was dominated by the horrid image of the blond Annya laughing as she left James's office.

Petra resolved to keep Antonietta on a tight rein until the party when hopefully the drama would find its proper *dénouement*. Fortunately, the football team was training for the university final against the Ottawa GGs, and Brett was completely taken up with his role as captain. So Petra devoted her time to Antonietta. They met for lunch and often spent the afternoons together. On Thursday Antonietta took Petra to meet Luigi, and they had lunch at his café. To prepare the unsuspecting Antonietta for her night with James Markham, Petra persuaded her to return to the esthetician for another "bikini intégral". Antonietta was reluctant as the intimate intrusiveness of the waxing troubled her. She accused Petra of ulterior motives.

"Last time it was *you* who wanted to go to bed with *me*," her friend pointed out.

Antonietta blushed deeply. "I was upset."

Having agreed to hold the foreign students' party at his house, James was kept busy by Bill with the arrangements. He didn't object as it took his mind off Antonietta. On Saturday there was a concert at

Susanna's school, and she was playing the cello. She was remarkably gifted, and the joy of watching his pretty daughter proudly displaying her talent afforded him some respite from the constant struggle against his forbidden passion.

The next week was more morose, beginning with the normal torture of his Tuesday class with an Antonietta, who managed, it seemed to him, to become lovelier with every passing day. Then, on Wednesday morning, Klaus Berger erupted into his office with news that eclipsed thoughts even of Antonietta.

"Have you seen the agenda for the Section meeting next Wednesday"?

Since his term as Acting Head of the Section had come to an end, James had kept a low profile. This way the new man could establish himself. Tom had behaved like this with his successor, Guy Forget, and James had found it appropriate. In James's case it was also clear that McGrath wanted him on the sidelines. Then had come that fateful moment in the church at Saint-Sauveur, and ever since James had taken even less interest in Section affairs. He didn't even know what he'd done with the agenda.

"No, Klaus. What's up"?

Klaus handed James the agenda to read. He was aghast. McGrath was proposing that the Section agree to the three Section Heads and the Senior Dean drawing up a common list of journals for evaluating professors' research. It was nothing short of the proposal that had been rejected by the Governing Council, and all the Section Heads had apparently agreed to it.

"They can't do this"! James exclaimed. "It's up to the Governing Council to set policy for evaluating professors, not the Section Heads, or the Senior Dean."

"Well, what's to stop them getting the Governing Council to agree to this policy? It's clear that McGrath and Hamid have cooked this up with Arbuthnot. With you gone and Forget on side, they have the majority."

"They can't do that either," James reminded Klaus. "A proposal that is rejected by the Governing Council cannot be presented again until a year has elapsed unless the General Council of all professors agrees.

That's precisely why they're doing it this way. And that idiot Forget is going along with it."

"You must go and talk to him, James."

"I have no status to talk to him. I'm just a normal faculty member. You're the one who's on the Governing Council."

"He's prickly, and you can speak to him in French. It goes down better."

James reluctantly agreed, but the meeting was unsuccessful. Forget maintained he had never been against the principle of a uniform system of evaluation, just Arbuthnot's control of it. Under the new proposal the Section Heads had the dominant role in drawing up the list of journals. For this reason he also disagreed that it was a repetition of the proposal rejected by the Governing Council.

James and Klaus spent the rest of the week canvassing for support from the members of LIR. By the time James left on Friday for the party at his house, they seemed to have secured a majority against the proposal. It was agreed that Klaus would take the lead in opposing it with James as back-up.

*Chapter 16*

# Friday October 26, 2001001

NOTWITHSTANDING WHAT PETRA HAD told her about Annya Nowak, Antonietta was resolved not to go to the party at James Markham's house. This at any rate was her firm intention when she arose that Friday morning. After Forget's class she went to the library and attempted to immerse herself in Canadian history in order to chase away thoughts of James, Annya, and the temptation of the party. After a dispiriting hour or two leafing aimlessly though the textbook, she returned to the cottage and treated herself to *vitello alla marsala*. She was determined to spend the rest of the day and the evening on her own, but quite unusually, particularly for these days, she drank only one small glass of white wine at lunch.

At six-thirty she found herself in the shower, and half-an-hour later she was putting on lingerie that was blatantly erotic. Dressed in a bra that lifted up but barely contained her breasts and a tiny string that left her buttocks completely nude, she went to the bathroom where the light was brighter in order to make herself up. In the full-length mirror on the bathroom door she observed that the "bikini intégral" she'd repeated at Petra's insistence accorded well with the rampant lubricity of her underwear. She put her hair into a chignon, which emphasized her statuesque bearing. She slid on the provocative red dress she'd bought at the Emporium in the Via Strozzi. It exposed not only the enticing cleft between her breasts but also the smooth skin of her sunburned thighs.

Despite the cold weather, she kept her legs bare. Her high heels came from Marco Candido.

It was only when she was on the way out of the door of the cottage that Antonietta fully realized what she was doing. She wasn't going to the party, she reminded herself and hesitated. By now she was all dressed up, and it seemed silly to stay at home. Besides, she rationalized, it would be rude not to go. Already the other students thought she was stuck up. She wouldn't stay long.

Petra had insisted on giving Antonietta directions to James's house despite her repeated assertions that she wouldn't attend the party, and she was now following them with her stomach churning over. When she reached the small commercial center at the entrance to Prévost, she was trembling so hard that she had to pull in. "It's madness to go to James's house," she told herself. How would she react to being in the place where he lived with his wife and children? Would he speak to her, and if so would she be able to control herself? The only sensible thing was to turn back. It was too painful, and it would cost too much effort to enter the house of the man she ached for and behave as if it were a normal occurrence. She was on the point of returning to Ste. Anne des Lacs when the image of a laughing Annya Nowak suddenly flashed into her mind. Desperately trying to control the emotions that threatened to submerge her, Antonietta drove on to James's house.

She descended from the car and walked unsteadily to the front door. She tried to lift her arm to ring the bell, but she was paralyzed by a mixture of apprehension and excitement. Bill had been looking out for her, and he opened the door.

"Ah, Antonetta, I'm so glad you could make it." It was a heartfelt greeting as he'd been worried right up until this moment that she wouldn't come. "Let me take your coat."

He had to suppress a gasp when he saw how Antonietta was dressed. He had never seen a more voluptuous apparition. With some difficulty he stopped himself from staring at the sight of the uplifted and barely covered bosom offered by Antonietta's deep décolleté. The delicate outline of mascara accentuated her dark expressive eyes, and her sensuous lips glistened with glossy, pale-pink lipstick. The hair was done in a chignon, and the classic elegance of her provocative red dress complemented a ravishing ensemble of tasteful but overpowering sensuality. If James managed to resist her tonight, he was a hopeless case in Bill's opinion.

"Let me introduce you to our host. Hopefully, this time he'll be more polite."

"Please don't disturb him on my account," Antonietta replied, trying to head off the moment she dreaded but desired with all the force of her passion. Bill Leaman escorted her over to James, who was talking to Wilhelm and Petra. Petra broke off from the conversation and came towards Antonietta to embrace her.

"You came after all. I'm so glad." Petra and Bill exchanged a knowing glance that didn't escape Antonietta.

"What are you two up to"?

It was Bill who replied. "Nothing at all. Come on."

Sandwiched between Petra and Bill, Antonietta waited tremulously for James to finish his interminable conversation with Wilhelm. Bill interrupted the earnest German.

"James, you've met Antonietta della Chiesa before," he said, pronouncing her name correctly for the first time.

"Oh God, so she has come"! James was hit by an empty feeling in his stomach. Praying for strength he turned round to face Antonietta. What he saw was a woman even more captivating than the image he'd gleaned from his stolen glances at her. Awkward, nervous, trying to avoid her eyes, he was nonetheless forced to talk to her.

"Professor Leaman tells me I was very rude to you, Miss della Chiesa," he said so quickly that the words tumbled over each other. "I assure you that it wasn't meant that way. I hope, err, I hope you're enjoying yourself here." Bill looked at James incredulously. He'd never heard him so incoherent. Shit! If his lectures were like that, no wonder the students were pissed off.

Prodded by Petra, Antonietta replied in a quavering voice. "I never thought anything of it," she stammered. "Thank you."

No one, including Antonietta, had the slightest idea why she was thanking James. She lifted up her face, and they looked longingly at each other. Realizing the danger of the moment, Bill acted quickly to prevent a premature explosion of passion from ruining his carefully laid plans for the end of the evening.

"Come on Antonietta, let's get you something to drink."

Antonietta followed Bill to the bar in a state of shock. Petra had been detained by Wilhelm, and she was deprived of her friend's support. Thankfully, the two other professors, who were reputed to be close friends of James, were there to entertain her.

"Tell us about Florence, young lady. They say it's a lovely place, that they do."

Antonietta was amused by Danny's thick Irish accent, which she suspected was exaggerated for her benefit. She was glad to play the game. After a while they were joined by Petra, and, their job done, Danny and Piotr mingled with the other students.

"I don't see Annya," Antonietta observed. "She's not coming, is she"? Petra shook her head. "It was just a ploy to get me here, wasn't it"? Antonietta tried to sound cross.

"Yes, and it worked."

"No it didn't because I'm leaving soon."

Antonietta sounded very firm but let herself be led over to a group of students that included Simon, the British student. They were joined by Brett. The wine flowed, and there was much laughter, but Antonietta had the sensation of being a spectator of her physical self among this circle of students in James's living room. She listened to her words as if they were being spoken by another person. She kept hearing herself say that she was leaving soon, but she never made any move to go.

It was ten o'clock, and people were beginning to leave. Antonietta looked around for Petra, but she'd disappeared with Brett. Simon and the two other students in their group were also making for the hallway. She had no excuse to stay any longer. She was about to put down her wineglass when Professors Leaman and Redfern arrived with a full bottle of wine.

"I was just leaving," she protested, but she let Bill fill up her glass.

"Nonsense, the night is but young," Danny told her.

"The best time at a party is the end when all the boring people have left," Bill added.

Bill and Danny inveigled Antonietta into a long conversation about

Italy. Suddenly she realized that they were the only persons left. She could hear James taking leave of the last students. She was between dread and anticipation.

"Come on Danny, let's go and put some music on." Bill pulled at Danny's elbow. They both disappeared, and moments later Antonietta heard the voice of Umberto Tozzi. She waited for the two men to return, but it was James who entered the room. He looked at Antonietta in blank amazement.

"You're still here"! he exclaimed and immediately corrected himself. "Sorry, that sounds awful. It's just that everyone else has left."

"I'm waiting for Professor Leaman and Professor Redfern. They just went to put on some music."

James realized what was happening. His friends, with Bill no doubt in charge, had engineered this moment of intimacy between himself and Antonietta. He looked at the luscious young woman standing with her wineglass in *his* living room and wondered what on earth he was going to do.

"Bill and Danny have left."

"Well, I'd better leave too."

He could have said yes, bundled her out of the house, and spent the next few hours between relief and regret, but he couldn't bring himself to do it.

"No, you're not," he said, restraining himself from taking the trembling Antonietta into his arms, "I'll join you with a scotch while you finish your wine."

He walked over to the impromptu bar and swore. "Those blackguards have drunk all my scotch."

Antonietta was struck by the incongruity of the situation. Surely James knew as well as she that this was the decisive moment for them, and here he was complaining about an empty whisky bottle!

"I think there's another bottle in the kitchen," she murmured.

"In that case, let's go into the kitchen," James proposed, still avoiding the dark expressive eyes that would be his downfall.

Antonietta stood watching James pour out a glass of whisky, or rather she listened to him as he had his back to her. She waited for him to turn round. Surely he would put an end to this awful charade. Surely now he would take her into his arms.

James still had some will to resist. For weeks he'd fought this passion, this irrational, overwhelming passion. He'd wanted to protect his marriage and his integrity. Now he was alone with Antonietta and one word, one gesture would suffice to bring her into his arms and into his bed. If he turned round, he was lost.

He turned round.

They looked at each other, not furtively like all the times before but unabashedly without averting their gaze. James saw before him a young woman of incomparable beauty, elegantly erotic, her eyes shimmering with passion for him. He was speechless. As for Antonietta, she felt faint. How many times had she conjured up this scene only to deny to herself that it could ever happen. And now it was happening! She was so lost in the wonder of the moment that she let slip her wineglass. It crashed to the floor. Instinctively she bent to pick up the pieces of broken glass.

"No, Antonietta, don't"! James yelled, but it was too late. She had cut herself, and blood was oozing from the small wound on her finger. James took her hand and led her to the sink. He put the bleeding finger under the cold-water tap.

"I'll get something to bandage it."

Antonietta stared absently at her finger. She felt no pain and saw no blood. All she was aware of was that James had called out her name, touched her, taken her hand. She waited in a daze for him to return. He came back with a band-aid and gently wrapped it around the finger. When he'd finished, he continued to hold her hand. Antonietta could bear it no longer. She looked up at him with eyes full of longing and passion.

*"Non ne posso più."* She laid her head on James's shoulder.

He lifted her face and tenderly wiped away the tears that were beginning to trickle down her cheeks.

*"Neanch'io,"* he whispered, as if afraid of the words.

Their mouths moved slowly and irresistibly together. It was a long, intense kiss that for both seemed to last an eternity and into which they poured all the yearning and heartache of the past two months. James took Antonietta by the hand.

"*Vieni,*" he said and led her upstairs.

When they reached the top of the stairs, James felt Antonietta squeeze his hand. He turned round, and she drew him close to her. "*Stringimi, stringimi forte,*" she beseeched. James held her close and felt her body trembling.

"*Che cos' hai*"?

She lifted up her head and James saw tears in her beautiful eyes.

"*Ho paura, ho terribilemente paura,*" she answered.

James's eyes widened with surprise. "But why"?

"I'm afraid tomorrow you'll have regrets and send me away." Antonietta gave James a look of utter desolation. "I couldn't bear that."

Antonietta had seen into the faces of many men. She had seen lust, hope, despair, anger, even love, but never had she seen the infinite tenderness that James now showed. She was reassured even before he spoke, but his words brought her a transport of joy.

"I love you. I mean it. *È incancellàbile questo mio amore. Non potrò mai più vivere senza di te\*.*" He gave a questioning look. "*E tu*"?

Before responding, Antonietta kissed James rapturously. "*Ti amo con una passione insensata. Nell'istante che ti vidi la primera volta nella chiesa, come Isotta, mi perdei in te.\**"

James led Antonietta to the conjugal bedroom, but she shook her head. "No, not in there. Not where you make love to your wife."

"That was a very long time ago," he assured her, ushering her into the guest bedroom, which was bathed in moonlight.

Antonietta moved towards the window and stood in the light. The anguish, the tears, and the trembling were gone, and the self-assured young lady who deftly undid her chignon and let her long black hair flow down and partly cover her décolleté was unrecognizable from the despairing and emotionally distraught woman of less than an hour ago. She kicked off her shoes with a happy frivolity and slipped down the straps of her dress. It fell to the floor, and she stood there, dressed only in the skimpiest of bras and a tiny string. It was a sight of such rampant sensuality that James caught his breath in awe. With a slight smile on her face that recalled the Mona Lisa, Antonietta picked up her dress and turned to walk towards the armchair where she was going to place it. James stared in admiration at her firm and perfectly rounded buttocks, left completely nude by the string.

"Good God," he murmured.

Antonietta was facing him again now, and her hands moved behind her back to undo her bra.

"No, stay like that." He gazed at her as she stood, practically naked, in the moonlight and walked slowly over to her.

"*Le piace, signore*"?

"*Donna non vidi mai simile a questa\**," he replied, taking her into his arms. His hands moved down the smooth skin of her back to her buttocks. He felt her tense up as he caressed them.

Antonietta took off her bra and threw it carelessly to one side of the room. James hardened with lust before the overpowering lubricity of Antonietta's bare breasts. They were full but firm and perfectly shaped like ripe fruit. Hesitantly, scarcely aware of what he was doing, he passed his hands over the smooth, taut skin. He felt Antonietta shudder, and her nipples became erect under his touch. She pushed his arms aside and pressed her body against his, offering her mouth for a long and ardent kiss. Her flesh was hot with desire.

"*Fammi l'amore*," she whispered, "*Sùbito*."

She began to unbutton James's shirt.

"Such haste," he teased her.

"You've tortured me long enough, Professor Markham. It's time for you to make amends."

Antonietta pulled out the shirt from James's pants and made him take it off. They walked over to the bed, and James sat on it. Antonietta knelt in front of him. She took off his shoes and his socks. The spectacle of this woman he'd wanted for so long almost naked before him, undressing him, inflamed James. She undid his belt and slid off his pants. James could hardly believe what was happening when she took down his briefs and began to fondle him. She placed his shaft between her lush breasts and stroked it softly. Taking it into her hand, she ran her erect nipples along it. James was already at the height of sexual excitement when she took him into her mouth, her long dark hair falling over James's belly. She fellated him to an ejaculation of a violence he'd never experienced before.

Antonietta looked up, her lips wet from his effluent, and it was a vision of such perfect erotic splendor that James felt his virility stir anew. She moved her lips up his body and kissed him.

He placed her on the bed beside him and enjoyed her sumptuous breasts, kneading them and licking and sucking them before moving slowly down to her string. She opened her legs, and he ran his hands between her damp thighs. He could feel her impatience, but first he caressed the golden tanned skin of her long legs. "*Per favore,*" she pleaded, and at last he drew down the string to expose her bare sex.

He pleasured her with an intrusive expertise that had her twisting and moaning in rapture. Never had she tasted such sexual delight with a man. Aroused by the odor of Antonietta's sexuality, James hardened. Once he knew that her climax was near, he penetrated her. When Antonietta felt him enter, her body exploded, and she could hear herself scream. The climax was so brutal that she dug her nails into James's back. She squeezed her lover within her to bring him to his culmination, and when she felt James's warmth inundate her, she was submerged by a feeling of utter bliss. Their mouths met, and their tongues furrowed deep into the caverns that had given them so much pleasure.

"I hurt you," she exclaimed when James turned away, and she noticed his back. "I've never done that before. I'm sorry."

James turned back and kissed her. "Don't be sorry. I'm no masochist, but to know the pain came from you..."

He stopped, not knowing quite how to continue. Antonietta came on top of him, and as their kisses gained in intensity they made love again. This time, after descending to use her mouth, Antonietta mounted James, and they took their pleasure with the alluring sight of Antonietta's breasts heaving before James's eyes, inviting him to enjoy them. Still their lust was not stilled, and it was the early hours before their pent-up passion for each other was sated. Momentarily satisfied, they lay together intertwined.

"James, tell me again you love me."

"Say that again."

"Tell me again..."

"No, say my name again." Antonietta threw herself on James and repeated his name amidst countless kisses.

"Do you remember the first time I said your name"?

"Oh, that awful first class. I nearly died when you came in. When you called me Antonietta, I almost fainted."

"And now"?

"I can survive any class with you now, Professor Markham, because I'm your mistress."

James gave her a quizzical look. "You're a practicing Catholic. Being the mistress of a married man doesn't bother you"?

"Do I have a choice. Did I ever have a choice"?

There was a brief silence.

"No, no more than me. It was always inevitable although we fooled ourselves otherwise." He kissed her upturned mouth, but this didn't still his concern. "But are you happy"?

Antonietta smiled at his disquietude and brushed her lips against his chest. "Ecstatically happy, James, and after all I've been through, I deserve it." Antonietta stifled a yawn.

"Do you want to sleep"?

Antonietta propped herself up like an inquisitor. "Yes, but first, James, I want a truthful answer from you."

James was taken aback by the sudden change of mood. "Of course," he said with a trace of nervousness.

"Actually there are two questions. Firstly, why was Annya Nowak laughing when she came out of your office? Secondly, do you have an Argentinean mistress called Carolina. And," she added for good measure, "is she blond with blue eyes"?

James burst out laughing and tried to kiss Antonietta. "No," she told him. "Kisses are fine, but first I want the truth."

"Which fantasy shall we begin with"?

"Annya, and she's not a fantasy. She's here, and she left your office laughing, so you must have enjoyed your time together."

James was completely at a loss for he'd forgotten the whole incident with Annya. "I saw her because I'm defending a professor against allegations of sexual impropriety, and she's the girl in question. I have no idea why she was laughing." Unfortunately, he added, "Perhaps it was the whisky I gave her."

"Whisky"! Antonietta's eyes blazed with jealous anger. "You gave her *whisky*"!

"I didn't have any coffee," James replied, uncomfortably aware of the inadequacy of his response. But he wasn't prepared for the ferocity of Antonietta's reaction. She picked up a pillow and rained blows down on his head.

"I hate you," she cried, "*Spergiurato*"!

After the surprise at being attacked out of the blue by a pillow, James began to enjoy the sight of Antonietta's gorgeous breasts swaying in front of his eyes and her mouth pursed in indignant wrath. She was the perfect and irresistible image of sexual jealousy. After warding off several blows, he took hold of her hands and forced her down on the bed. He pressed his mouth against her's, and her resistance quickly crumbled. She pleaded with him to enter her. As they both reached their climax, James felt the sharp pain of Antonietta scratching the wound on his back.

"You little vixen."

"That was for the whisky."

James stroked Antonietta's hair and played with his tongue on her nipples. "How did you know she was coming out of my office? You didn't know who I was at that time." Aroused anew by James's sexual dalliance, Antonietta began to slide her lips down James's body, but he stopped her. "Tell me first how you knew." She moved back up and leaned on him, her breasts dangling provocatively before him.

"After I saw you the first time, I went back to the car. I realized you were married, and I was in despair. I saw you walking with your daughter towards me. I don't know why, but I lowered the back window, and I heard you tell your daughter that you wanted a treble scotch."

"You heard that? You were right there near us"?

Antonietta nodded and went on with her narrative. "So I knew you were British from your accent, Catholic because you'd taken communion, and you liked to drink. The day of the foreign students' seminar I met Petra. She told me you were British and that you drank a lot with your friends."

"Bloody cheek."

Antonietta grinned at him and gave him a kiss. "The truth often hurts," she said, ducking under his threatening arm. "At lunch she gave me that thing on the professors to read. I saw you went to Ampleforth, and so you were British, you liked drinking, and you were Catholic. It had to be you."

"How did you know Ampeforth was a Catholic school"?

"I spent four years at a convent school in England." Antonietta sensed danger. She remembered her uncle's advice not to divulge her background. She reverted quickly to the topic of Annya Nowak. "When I saw Annya coming out of your office, I was going to march in and tax you with inconstancy. But I bumped into Professor Leaman."

"Yes, he told me. I wish he hadn't stopped you. It would have saved us weeks of torment."

"No, James." Antonietta's expressive eyes became suddenly very serious. "I know that what we're doing is a sin. Now at least I can tell myself that I resisted the temptation until it was beyond my power to resist any longer. It makes the guilt easier to bear."

"Yes," James agreed after a few moments' reflection, "you're right. But why this jealousy about Annya? She's happily shacked up with her bloody Baptist."

"Petra told me they were having problems, and that she would be after you at the party."

"She told you that, and it made you jealous"? Antonietta nodded. "That's why you came to the party, because you were jealous of Annya"? Antonietta nodded again. James took her warm, nude body in his arms.

"Antonietta, we are the innocent victims of a Machiavellian plot hatched by your friend Petra and my friend Bill. He got me to host the party, and she made sure you would come. And here we are, irrevocably together."

"Do you regret it"? Antonietta asked, her eyes misting over. James gazed upon her exquisite face, put his hands around it, and drew it towards him.

"From the first instant I saw you in church, I've loved you in a way I never conceived possible. I tried to deny it to myself, to fight it, but in the end I no longer had the strength or the will. I never will have. *Como te l'ho già detto, non posso più vivere senza di te*\*."

Antonietta avoided James's embrace. "Did you say the same to your Argentinean mistress"? Her eyes all at once were burning with suspicion. Without waiting for her to take hold of her favorite weapon, James pinned Antonietta down on the bed.

"What's this nonsense about an Argentinean mistress"?

"I believe her name is Carolina."

"Did Bill tell you about her"? Antonietta nodded.

"God, he annoys me so much when he blabs to the students." James's words infuriated Antonietta, who wriggled out from his grasp and sat up glaring at him. "Oh, now I'm just another student, am I? Well, go back to your Carolina"!

Antonietta was about to get off the bed, but James pulled her back. "You're not going anywhere, Antonietta, and you're going to listen to me." Antonietta let herself be pushed back down on the bed, a trifle too easily in her mind, but she was relieved that James had stopped her leaving. "I met Carolina in August before I first saw you. She was the receptionist at the hotel Bill and I stayed at in Buenos Aires."

"Did you go to bed with her"?

James saw the resentment in Antonietta's in her eyes, but there was little point in lying.

"Yes."

"Was she blond"?

"Yes."

"With blue eyes"?

"Yes."

Antonietta looked at James dolefully. "You prefer blue-eyed blonds, don't you? Admit it. Like Annya, and your wife, and this Carolina." Tears welled up in eyes that gazed in sorrow at him.

James shook his head in disbelief. How could this woman, this flawless beauty for whom he would gladly sacrifice his marriage and his career, how could she be reduced to tears of jealousy over a young girl he hardly knew, a wife he'd never loved and a woman of passing pleasure in a far-away land? What could he say to chase away those tears and restore the shine of happiness to those lovely dark eyes? A comparison with Floria Tosca* occurred to him, and he resorted to the words Cavaradossi had used to pacify Tosca's jealousy of the blond, blue-eyed Marchesa Attavanti.

*"Qual occhio al mondo può star di paro all'ardente occhio tuo nero? È che l'esser mio s'affissa intero, occhio all'amor soave, all'ira fiero. Qual altro al mondo può star de paro all'occhio tuo nero\*"*?

It worked. The sorrow disappeared in an instant from Antonietta's eyes, and she replied with a radiant smile, using the same words Tosca had spoken to her lover. *"Come lo sai bene, l'arte de farti amare\*"*!

Antonietta let James kiss her, but between kisses she made him promise never to go to Argentina or indeed anywhere without her.

James agreed readily. "I long for an opportunity to take you with me away from here. Somewhere we can love openly and freely without fear of betrayal."

Antonietta rolled James over on to his back and resumed her lips' progress past his chest and abdomen. She pleasured him with her mouth and demanded he do the same to her.

⌒*∦*⌒

"Good God, it's past three o' clock" James exclaimed to Antonietta, who was nestling in his arms in the afterglow of sexual fulfillment. "Aren't you tired"?

"I'm exhausted, but I can't sleep until you've answered all the questions that torment me."

James caressed the strands of hair that were falling over her breasts. "I'll tell you whatever you want on condition that there's no more jealousy. You have nothing, nobody to be jealous of."

"I promise."

"Now," she went on, "How long were you in Florence"?

"Three years. 1989 until 1992."

"Who were you with"?

"Leonora Morrico was her name. She was Spanish."

Antonietta almost blurted out her own Spanish connections before remembering her uncle's admonition about her background. Instead, she asked whether she was blond. James laughed, but Antonietta remained deadly serious. "Well"?

"Yes, she was," he admitted. James could feel the tension mount.

"Did you love her"?

James wondered how long it would be before Antonietta attacked him. He eyed the pillows warily. "I thought I did at the time, but now I know it wasn't true. She was very beautiful but a real bitch."

"With blue eyes"?

James nodded. Antonietta moved to get hold of the pillow, but James stopped her. "And your promise"?

"It doesn't cover blue-eyed blonds."

"Antonietta." James was almost despairing. "You have no reason to be jealous. What I felt for other women is insignificant, absolutely nothing, in comparison to the passion I feel for you."

"How many other women were there"?

James felt a momentary relief. At least the answer to this particular question shouldn't call forth another bout of Antonietta's unruly jealousy. "Not that many. A few adolescent flirts, then Mary and Veronica at university, Leonora in Florence, and then Veronica again."

"Why did you marry Veronica"?

"I did it on the rebound." James put his hand up. "No more questions, Antonietta. For me life is quite simple. There is before and after I saw you the first time, and the before is of no consequence."

Antonietta was mollified, but she couldn't resist a final jab. "To think you were in Florence where I was living, and you were with another woman."

James shook his head in disbelief. "Antonietta, you were only twelve at the time"!

"I was fifteen when you left Florence, and men already used to turn and stare at me in the street." She pouted and looked so delightful that James felt himself wilt.

"You know, Antonietta, when you're angry or indignant or when you pout like you're doing now, you're even lovelier."

Antonietta flung herself at James and smothered him in passionate kisses. "Swear that there's been no one since you saw me."

"I've no need to swear. You know there's been no one. And you"?

Antonietta immediately thought of Petra. She could feel herself blush, but luckily James couldn't see it in the dark. "No man could ever have interested me since I saw you," she replied ingenuously. She climbed on him, and he marveled at the sight of her tight and enticing buttocks. They took their pleasure together.

Exhausted, Antonietta cradled herself in James's arms. Within seconds she was fast asleep.

*Chapter 17*

# Saturday October 27, 2001

JAMES AWOKE TO FIND his face covered by a woman's long, black hair. At first he was puzzled, and then he remembered. It wasn't a dream; it had really happened; that scene in the kitchen when the last shreds of his resistance had crumbled before the longing in Antonietta's eyes; their first kiss; Antonietta's fears and their passionate declarations of love; the indelible scenes in this very bedroom with Antonietta revealing the erotic perfection of her nude body; their unbridled lovemaking; Antonietta's fierce jealousy. James recalled with amusement her attacks on him with the pillow. "A woman could hardly be more Italian than Antonietta," he reflected.

He disengaged himself and contemplated her beauty. She looked even lovelier this morning, sleeping with a contented look on her face. He touched her breasts and ran his fingers lightly down the soft skin to her sex, which was still damp from the night's pleasures. He felt a fierce desire but stopped himself from waking her. He suspected she'd slept badly these last weeks, and he let her rest and made do with admiring the lubricious attractions of her naked body. It was at that moment he resolved to marry her. After a few minutes he went quietly downstairs to make two expressos.

Antonietta awoke after James left. She felt strange. The pain of longing that usually accompanied every awakening was absent, and where was she? She looked around the room and remembered. Relief and happiness flooded her senses. She'd surrendered at last, and the torment was over. She turned over and saw with horror the empty place next to her. In a panic she called out James's name.

"I'm here," he replied, entering the bedroom with two small cups of expresso coffee. He noticed the alarm in Antonietta's eyes. "What's the matter"? He quickly put down the two cups and took her in his arms. She pushed him away.

"*Never, never, never* get up without waking me first. I thought you'd left me"!

James shook his head. "What am I going to do with you. After all the times last night I told you that I loved you, that I couldn't live without you, you persist in believing I would leave you"?

"Promise you'll wake me first next time," Antonietta insisted. Forgetting the coffees, James laid her down on the bed, took off his dressing gown, and made love to her.

"No regrets"? James asked, stroking Antonietta's moist and satisfied body.

"Regrets"? she replied. There was a slight touch of irony, even bitterness in her voice. "Regret at not waking up every day aching for you, at not going to the Institute with that horrible mix of dread and hope that I might meet you, regret at suffering through the torture of your classes, regret at the loneliness and despair of sitting in the cottage drinking too much and listening endlessly to Laura Pausini. No, I've no regrets, none."

James was taken aback by Antonietta's forcefulness. "*Hai sofferto tanto*"?

"*Orribilemente.*" she replied and shuddered at the memory of it. "The worst time was the last three weeks." She told him about seeing Veronica in church and her near breakdown afterwards. "Without Petra I'm not sure what I would've done." She looked at James with anguish. He absorbed the tears that were beginning to flow with his tongue.

"All that is over. There'll be no more despair and loneliness, and at last I can start to do some work and give some decent lectures."

"Did I stop you"?

"You know damn well you did. All I could do was think of you, want you, and tell myself constantly that I couldn't have you. It was a lot of fun."

"Fun"! Antonietta exclaimed, making a move for the pillow. James stopped her. "Listen, my darling, you're going to have to get used to my British sense of humor, or we'll go through a helluva lot of pillows."

The phone rang. James picked it up. Antonietta draped herself over his shoulders and gave him kisses on the cheek. With some difficulty he managed to place the phone to his ear. It was Bill.

"Well, is she still there"?

"Who"?

"Very funny, Jimmy. Our Italian bombshell, who else"?

"A gentleman doesn't tell. But one thing I will tell you is that I'm bringing Antonietta to our get-togethers from now on."

"You can't bring her, it's only men."

"Listen, Bill, you're the one who, with Petra's help, got Antonietta and me together, and now you're going to have to put up with the consequences. The only reason we were only men was because your wife lives in Vancouver, Danny's has left, mine is a religious nut, and Piotr's has to look after the kids."

"Well, she'll have to put up with us as we are. We're not going to turn into a bunch of sissies just for a woman." He hung up in disgust.

"Are you really going to take me to your get-togethers," Antonietta asked after James had put the phone down.

"Yes, every time," he replied, testing the coffee. "It's cold. I'll go downstairs and make two fresh cups."

"I'm coming with you. I'm not letting you out of my sight."

James handed her a dressing gown, but she refused it and wrapped herself in a large towel. James stared at her. She was gorgeous with her hair disheveled, her lips slightly swollen from their various acts of love, and a soft, languorous look in her eyes. He resisted the temptation to take her right back to bed, and they made their way downstairs hand in hand.

James ground some fresh coffee and made two expressos. Antonietta drank her coffee and eyed James timidly.

"What's the matter, Antonietta"?

Tentatively Antonietta asked about his marriage with Veronica. "I know it's indelicate, but I think I have a right to know."

James drew her to him, undid the towel, kissed her, and laid her across his thighs. He caressed her breasts and belly lightly while he explained his relationship with his wife.

"She was always there, and in the end I married her. *Faute de mieux.* It was the summer after my last year in Florence, in 1992. Earlier that year I'd broken up with Leonor. Immediately we were married, Veronica lost interest in sex. Two years later her mother entered a convent as a postulant, and Veronica became more and more religious. After Susanna was born a year later, our sex life ended. I didn't find any pleasure in making love to a reluctant woman, and I didn't want any more children. Veronica refused to use contraception; it was against the Church's teaching, she would tell me. The summer before last, she became an oblate attached to her mother's convent. Since then she's become a religious fanatic. I feel sorry for the kids."

"Promise me you'll never make love to her again. I couldn't bear the thought of you with another woman." James bent down and kissed her. "I promise." Antonietta put her arm around his head so that his face remained close to her's. Her eyes had a melancholy look about them.

"What happens when she comes back"?

James stroked her hair in a comforting gesture. "We shall be together more often than you would imagine, and I'll arrange as many trips for us as I can. Unfortunately, you'll have to move your things back to the cottage when Veronica returns."

"Back to the cottage"?

James laughed at Antonietta's surprise. "Yes. While Veronica's away, you're going to live here." Antonietta sat up, turned herself round, threw her arms around James, and kissed him in a torrent of passion.

"Does that arrangement suit you, *signorina*"?

"It's the most wonderful present you could give me." In her excitement Antonietta had wrenched open James's dressing gown, and the sensation of her soft breasts against his chest inflamed his desire for her.

"Let's go back to bed."

"Yes, but first, James, you must shave or my thighs are going to be very sore."

"That sounds like an indecent invitation."

"Nothing's indecent between us, James."

They made their way up the stairs, James still in his bathrobe, Antonietta completely naked.

⌒ⁿ⌒

It was nearly three in the afternoon before they arrived at Antonietta's cottage to fetch her things. There was a message on the answering machine. It was Petra.

"Antonietta, I've been calling you all day. I guess things worked out with James Markham. I'm so glad for you. Tell him that I need to see him as I've got Brett to admit he lied about Hunt and Annya. Bye."

If Antonietta had turned the machine off at that moment, she would have spared herself a dreadful moment. Unfortunately, she left it on long enough to catch Petra's final comment.

"By the way, I hope he satisfied you in bed as well as I did."

Antonietta felt the blood rush to her head and her stomach give way. "Oh, Petra, how could you," she thought. For a brief instant she stood there, convinced that her happiness was in ruins. Shame and despair wracked her, and tears welled up her eyes. She was beginning to tremble when she felt James's arms engulfing her and his kiss on her neck. She dared not turn round to look him in the face.

"*Vieni.*"

"*Dove*"?

"*Nella camera. Dove altro*"?

James led a blushing Antonietta into the bedroom. "Undress," he told her. Obediently, her eyes avoiding his, Antonietta slipped off the long, red dress she'd donned for the party, unhooked her bra, which fell to the ground exposing her breasts, and removed her string. She stood there quite naked, her face bowed. She was acutely embarrassed, but her nudity before James, who still fully dressed, aroused her.

"Turn round."

"James, you're humiliating me," she protested but obeyed again.

James came up behind her. He passed his hands over her breasts, which were taut with desire, kissed her in the neck, and traced a line with his fingers down her back to her buttocks. He fondled them and ran his fingers along the moist flesh between them. Antonietta gasped.

"I'm not humiliating you," he said with the trace of a smirk that Antonietta couldn't see. "I'm appreciating what must have excited my rival."

"James"! Antonietta whirled around with a look of horror on her face. "How could…."

James stopped her protest with a kiss. "Lie down on the bed." Too ashamed and too sexually excited to argue, she lay down on the bed.

James undressed with agonizing slowness. Antonietta pleaded with him to hurry, but he took no notice. "You're torturing me," she moaned, "You're horrible." Her eyes glinted with a ferocious desire for him. At last he was naked, and he came on top of her. He fondled her breasts and licked and sucked on her nipples, making her groan with delight. Looking up at her with a sly grin he said, "I'll not be bested by Petra Markovic."

Once more Antonietta started to protest, but James cut her off with a fierce kiss that left her breathless. He ran his tongue with tantalizing slowness down her body, lingering at her navel and driving her to distraction. By the time he reached her thighs, they were glistening with moisture. Ignoring Antonietta's desperate calls for immediate satisfaction James played with her, using his tongue and fingers until she cried out with frustrated desire. Just when she thought deliverance was near, James made her turn over, forsaking her sex to enjoy her in other ways. Overwhelmed by an almost hysterical craving for the climax he was denying her, Antonietta lay helpless, twisting and moaning as James fondled and kissed her buttocks. Suddenly she felt his tongue where no man had ever touched her before and his fingers caressing her intimately. Disbelief mingled with a violent sense of pleasure. Soon Antonietta was no longer aware of anything but the sexual frenzy gripping her whole body. After what seemed an eternity, her body could take no more and convulsed in spasms of such intense pleasure that at first it was painful. She felt herself drowning in a sea of ecstasy and didn't even hear the screams that James was wrenching from her. After her orgasm had subsided, she was barely aware of James taking her in a way she had always refused to allow.

After her volcanic climax Antonietta remained on her stomach. James kissed her in the neck and whispered.

"Why don't you turn over"?

"Because I'm ashamed." When she did turn over, James could see she was blushing.

"How did you know what Petra did to me"? She looked away in embarrassment. James turned her face towards him and kissed her.

"Leonora was bisexual. She liked nothing better than regaling me with her lesbian infidelities."

Antonietta pulled herself away from their embrace and glared at James, her dark expressive eyes flashing with indignation.

"Is that how you think of me"? she cried. She picked up a pillow and rained down blows on James's head. Before he could react, Antonietta had him pinned him down on the bed.

"I'm not a lesbian, and I'm not bisexual. I'm a normal woman who was seduced by an older girl at school, which, by the way, happens to a lot of girls, and I've only had that one drunken episode with Petra ever since." "Besides," she added, "that was your fault."

"My fault? How do you work that one out"?

Her indignation passed, Antonietta grinned impishly at James. She knew that her explanation was quite illogical. "I had sex with Petra because I was consumed by longing for you, and I couldn't have you. I had to do something to take my mind off you."

James caressed Antonietta's exquisite breasts, imagining them being kissed and fondled by Petra Markovic. He felt a sharp pang of jealousy.

"Promise me you won't ever do that again,"

Antonietta looked down at James, her eyes shimmering with passion. "There will never, never be anyone else for me. I wish it were otherwise because you're married, but it's not."

James rolled her off him and kissed her. "You know you can be expelled for striking a professor."

Antonietta smiled prettily at him. "And you can be dismissed for sleeping with a student from your class."

James laughed. "*Touché*," he said, adding more seriously, "Which means that we must be very discreet, at least until the end of the year when I intend to marry you."

Antonietta gasped. "James, you can't marry me, you're already married."

"I'll get divorced. I don't want you as my mistress whom I have to hide, I want you as my wife. I want everyone to know you're mine."

"I am yours's, whether people know it or not." Antonietta's eyes misted over. "I can't marry you. I come from a very Catholic family, and I'm a practicing Catholic myself. I could never contemplate marrying outside the Church." Tears began to trickle down her cheeks.

"So you can envisage leaving me at some stage"? James's tone was almost savage.

"No, never."

"You can't seriously want to be my mistress all your life"?

"No."

"Well, you either have to marry me, be my mistress, or leave me. Which is it to be"? James was aware he was tormenting Antonietta, but the thought of losing her was too intolerable to bear.

"Please, James, let's just love each other. I'm here for two years. A lot can happen in two years."

James looked down at her intently. "I ask one thing. Don't do an Elena Muti on me."

"Elena Muti"? Antonietta asked, quite perplexed. "Who's she"?

"Shame on you! You have a degree in Italian literature, and you don't know who Elena Muti is"?

"That's your fault too. You put me in such a state that I can't think of anything else but you."

"You're a liar, but you're the loveliest liar I've ever known." James kissed her, and Elena Muti was forgotten as Antonietta returned his kiss and they made love again, this time more conventionally.

When their amorous frolics were over, Antonietta suddenly exclaimed, "Sperelli! She was Sperelli's mistress in *Il Piacere!*\*"

"That's right, and she almost destroyed him by leaving without an explanation. Never do that to me, or I don't know what I'd do."

"I promise."

✺

"He's bringing Antonietta," Bill remarked to Piotr and Danny, who had come that Saturday for supper.

"What do you expect"? said Piotr. "You got them together; now you have to put up with it."

"A little female sophistication will do us all the world of good, that it will," Danny added.

"I just hope she doesn't try to stop him drinking." Bill continued in the same morose tone. "When women fall in love with you, it's always the first thing they do."

⌘

"James, that's your third scotch."

James took Antonietta in his arms. "I adore you, I love you to distraction, I desire you with a violence that frightens me, but I'm not goddam giving up my scotch."

"Yes, you are." Antonietta took the glass from James's hand and placed it on the coffee table.

He sighed. "I fear I am about to lose my freedom."

Antonietta peeled off her sweater and bra. "Doesn't this make up for it"?

After they'd made love on the couch, James asked Antonietta to call Petra. "We're running out of time. The hearing is a week on Thursday, and I need to get some students on side."

Antonietta dialed Petra's cell. She prayed that her friend wouldn't say anything that would cause her more embarrassment.

"Petra"?

"Antonietta! Did our little plan work"? Are you two now an item"?

"Yes, he's here next to me in the cottage." At least Petra was forewarned.

"Did you get my message"?

"Yes. We both heard *all* of it." She heard Petra catch her breath.

"Oh, my God! I'm so sorry, Antonietta. I hope it didn't ruin everything."

Antonietta gave James a sidelong glance. "Actually, it all worked out for the best. He was even better at it than you."

There was a brief silence. "I'm jealous," was Petra's response. It was time to change the subject.

"James says you can meet him with Brett whenever you wish tomorrow."

"Oh, it's *James* now, is it"? Petra couldn't resist teasing Antonietta.

"It's a bit silly to call him Professor Markham when we've spent the last twenty-four hours making love."

"All the time"? Petra was impressed.

"Well, perhaps not *all* of it."

It was agreed that Petra and Brett would meet James in his office the next day at ten o'clock.

They left for James's house around six. The original plan had been for Antonietta to move in with James, but there was the problem of the neighbors. Antonietta's cottage was more secluded, and she didn't even know her neighbors. They decided that James would live at her place until Veronica came back. Once at the house, they cleaned up, throwing away most of the cheese and the wine left in half-finished bottles. They returned to the cottage, and Antonietta made *risotto al chianti*, which they ate with a bottle of Barolo while listening to Puccini.

"Will you take me to the opera in Montreal"?

"Yes, my darling. At the beginning of December they're playing *Tosca*. We'll stay the night. I normally do in the winter as I don't like driving back in the dark."

"Did you always stay alone"?

"Yes, but not this time."

Antonietta stood in front of James and brazenly stripped off her clothes. He took her on the couch in the same way as he'd taken her after Petra's revelations.

"Is it a sin to make love like that"? she asked as she lay with guilty contentment in James's arms.

"Why would it be a sin with me and not with Petra"? he asked, trying unsuccessfully to mask his jealousy.

Antonietta blushed deeply. "Of course it was a sin with Petra, but it won't ever happen again, and with you it will. I've never let any man do that to me before."

"I thought nothing was indecent between us."

"I said that as a good Catholic girl. I didn't know how dissolute you were."

"What a strange mixture you are," thought James. "Sensual, oversexed even, ready to arouse a man beyond endurance with the erotic perfection of your body, willing to commit adultery without any shame. Yet you won't marry outside the Church, and you worry whether some sex acts are sins." It wasn't logical, but it was part of her charm. And he was under its spell.

"I don't see what we do as sinful. Once you admit that sex is not just for the procreation of children but also for pleasure, the whole idea that only those acts that are open to procreation are permitted becomes untenable. If sodomy and anilingus give pleasure, as they do, why not? I have no time for all that silly puritanical nonsense dreamed up by a bunch of sexual perverts and ascetics sitting on rocks. I can't conceive that a God who created the whole universe is going to get all upset because I had anal intercourse with you."

Antonietta couldn't resist teasing James. "You're better at talking about sex than the European Union. At least I understood what you said. But," she added, "isn't that just a self-serving excuse for debauching me"?

""No, it's a self-serving rationalization." He looked down at Antonietta who had a skeptical smile on her face. "Anyway," he went on, "you don't seem to have any problem with cunnilingus and fellatio. You're very good at one of them." James paused but couldn't resist the temptation to take revenge for Antonietta's infidelity. "As for the other, I guess I'll have to ask Petra."

Antonietta's reaction was predictable, but even so James was hardly prepared for the violence of the attack.

"You're horrible, I hate you"! she shouted as she set about him with a cushion.

It took James quite a while to get hold of her and force her down on the sofa. When finally he had her under control, her eyes were still blazing.

"If you want to know, I asked Petra to go to bed with me another time, but she refused because of Brett." Immediately her anger had spoken, she regretted it for James winced and moved away from her. She threw herself at him and smothered him with kisses.

"Forgive me, James," she repeated over and over again.

"I forgive you. But swear it will never occur again."

"No, it won't. It happened on that day when I was in utter despair. Petra came and comforted me. We did Forget's paper together. I think it was out of gratitude more than lust."

James took Antonietta in his arms, kissed her, and led her into the bedroom. It was late and they were physically and sexually exhauster, but they made love a final time. "You're a satyr, but I must confess that's what I need. You're the only man who's ever completely satisfied me." James was about to remark that she owed that in part to Leonora's lesbian confidences but wisely desisted. He asked where she wanted to go for Mass the following morning.

"The Basilica in old Montreal."

"A good idea. Afterwards we'll have lunch at La Grille."

*Chapter 18*

# Sunday October 28, 2001

JAMES PARKED THE CAR in a side street near the Basilica. It was a cold day, but the sun was shining in a cloudless sky. They walked hand in hand to the Cathedral. Once they were inside, Antonietta put on the mantilla that James had found among her clothes in the cottage and insisted that she wear. She dipped a finger in the stoup, crossed herself with holy water, and offered some to James. They walked down the aisle, genuflected, and took their seats. It seemed unreal to be together in this same church where they had both spent one of the worst hours of their lives.

"Remember the last time we were here"? Antonietta whispered with a slight shudder at the recollection.

They may have been in church, but James couldn't resist kissing her. "It seems like a world ago," he replied.

Antonietta took a handkerchief out of her coat pocket and wiped the lipstick off James's face. "Behave yourself," she scolded.

The procession of the officiating priest and two deacons made its way past James and Antonietta to the sanctuary. One of the deacons picked up a thurible and lit the incense. He incensed the priest and the other deacon and turned to the congregation. They all stood up to be incensed by him. James glanced over at Antonietta. With her long, dark hair partially covered by the mantilla and her face serene and reverential, she was the epitome of a Catholic Madonna. It was difficult to believe this was the same woman whose moist and nude body had lain next to his only an hour or so ago. James, unlike the irritation he felt at Veronica's excessive devoutness, was moved by Antonietta's piety, and for once he followed the liturgy. After the consecration he stood up to go and take communion, but Antonietta tugged at his arm.

"We can't take communion. We're living in sin."

James had never seen her more beautiful or her eyes more lustrous. "How could any merciful God not pardon her"?

"Nonsense. It was a sin to try and live apart."

Antonietta rewarded him with a radiant smile. "You're right," she said, and they walked side by side to receive communion. At the end of Mass, Antonietta remained kneeling. James looked on as she prayed silently, her head bowed.

They left the Basilica and walked down St. Paul Street towards Jacques Cartier Square. Just before it on the left was La Grille. Unbeknownst to Antonietta, James had made a reservation. The owner recognized him and assumed that Antonietta was his wife. "*Par ici*, Madame Markham," he said, indicating a table in the corner of the small and quaint dining room. Antonietta felt a thrill run through her whole body. Madame Markham! Once they were seated, James grinned at her. "Well, Madame Markham, shall we order an apéritif"? Antonietta laughed, but there was sadness in her reply. "If only it were true," she sighed. James took her hand.

'What I don't understand, Antonietta, is how you can reconcile our relationship with your religious principles while at the same time refusing to marry me. It's not logical."

Antonietta's reply was cut off by the waiter, who had come to take their order. James asked for his habitual whisky and Antonietta, a Marsala.

"It is logical. I didn't choose to have this relationship. My passion for you burst upon me like a bolt of lightning. I did my best to resist it, but it was beyond my strength."

"Why don't we consummate it by getting married"?

Antonietta looked down so that James couldn't see the tears in her eyes, tears that would show her words for the hollow pretense she suspected them to be. "Because marriage to a divorced man would be a public and permanent act of disobedience to the Church."

"Our relationship is not permanent"?

The waiter arrived with their drinks, which gave Antonietta a brief respite in which to collect her thoughts. She sipped her Marsala and gazed into James's eyes. "Please, James, don't torment me like this. We're together at long last. Let's just enjoy that and let the future take care of itself." She couldn't stop her eyes misting over again. James noticed and smiled at her. He had the answer he wanted in those eyes, not in the words she'd uttered.

❧

They arrived back at the cottage. Antonietta disappeared into the bedroom. After a few moments James heard her call his name. She was lying on the bed, completely naked. He undressed hurriedly, and they made love as if it had been months since the last time.

They showered and dressed. While Antonietta was drying her hair, James inspected the small collection of books she'd brought over from Italy. He noticed three novels in Spanish, *La fiesta del chivo*, *Cien años de soledad* and Isabel Allende's *La casa de los espíritus*. He was surprised.

"Do you speak Spanish, Antonietta"? he asked as she emerged from the bedroom with her hair in a towel.

"My mother is half-Spanish," she replied without thinking, but before James could ask her any more awkward questions, she had one of her own. "Do you speak Spanish"?

"Yes."

Now it was Antonietta's turn to be surprised. Where had he learned it? He explained that he'd taken Spanish at school as his second foreign language and spent a year in Mérida when he was sixteen.

"I had a pen pal there," he explained, "His name was Rodrigo." James carefully avoided divulging his friend's very aristocratic family name.

"Where did you learn to speak such faultless French? It makes mine sound awful."

"My grandmother is French, and I've spent many holidays in France."

"That must be why I hit you. I must have felt you had French blood. I don't like them. They look down on us Italians."

James laughed. "The French look down on everyone, Antonietta, but I quite like them."

Antonietta disengaged herself from James and sat down crossly on the couch. "And Leonora? What language did you use with her"? She pronounced the "her" with vituperation.

"Mostly Spanish, some Italian." Antonietta's eyes blazed at him.

"I hate you for speaking Italian to her."

James was used by now to Antonietta's volatile moods and her quite irrational jealousy, and he'd already taken the precaution of sitting down and putting his arm around her. She turned towards him with an irresistible pout, and he kissed her passionately. He could feel her body tense up, and her nipples harden under the dress.

"You're insatiable," he told her.

"Yes. All my lovers have told me that."

James was seized by a fit of jealousy, which greatly amused Antonietta. "I thought 'the before' didn't count," she said.

Unwisely, James decided to get his own back. "No, it doesn't really, but it's difficult to forget certain nights of rapture, like mine in Buenos Aires." He realized immediately the words left his mouth that he'd gone too far.

Antonietta pummeled James on the chest with her fists. She was too upset even to shout at him, and it was some time before she was capable of listening to anything.

"I'm sorry, Antonietta. I was just being flippant. I didn't mean it."

Antonietta eventually calmed down enough to talk, but she was still overwrought. "*Giura! Giura!* she demanded.

"*Lo giuro,*" he swore, but Antonietta was still not satisfied. She went over to the bookcase and took out her old Roman missal. She opened it to a page on the gospel and put it down on James's lap. "Swear on the gospel." James put his hand on the missal and repeated "*Lo giuro*". "And swear you'll never say anything to me like that again."

James put the missal aside and made her sit on his lap. "I thought Tosca only existed in opera, but you're a real-life Tosca."

Antonietta stroked James's face. "*Ti tormento senza pausa*"?*

"*Sì.*"

"*Certa sono del perdono*"?

"*Sì*"

James laid her down on the couch, undressed her, and indulged her.

"What about you"? she asked afterwards, unzipping his pants.

"We're already late for the lads."

"They can wait."

⌒⋎⌒

"You see," Bill grumbled to his two friends. "Now Markham's with Antonietta, he's late. Almost a goddam hour late."

"Give them a break," said Piotr. "They're in love. It'll wear off."

"Don't be so cynical, Piotr, my boy." Danny filled Piotr's glass. "I think it's true love."

At that moment they saw the lights of James's Maserati pulling up outside Danny's house. All three were curious to see the new couple together, and they weren't disappointed. Antonietta entered the room first, having taken off her coat in the hall. She was wearing a tight-fitting green dress modestly buttoned up to the top, which gave just a hint of the attractions of the body beneath it. Her hair was swept to one side of her face and flowed down over her fulsome bosom. The earring on her exposed ear glittered with reflected light.

What struck all three of the men was not Antonietta's sheer elegance and beauty but the radiance she exuded. Particularly for Bill, who knew her better than the other two, the difference between this poised woman whose eyes shone with happiness and the anguished, distracted student in his class was startling. James came in and put his arm around her. The tense moroseness of the past weeks was gone. Looking at the pair, any misgivings Bill might have had about bringing them together evaporated before their obvious delight in each other. But he couldn't resist a provocative jibe.

"You're late. I suppose you were screwing"?

James was about to give a curt reply, but Antonietta forestalled him. "It's my fault, Professor Leaman. You see, I'm oversexed."

There was a brief silence. James was aghast at Antonietta's

candidness, and the others were completely taken aback. It was Danny who reacted first.

"She got you there, Bill"! he exclaimed, roaring with laughter, "That'll teach you to try and embarrass her."

"An excellent answer, Antonietta," Bill admitted. "Come and sit here." He pointed to the chair next to where James had taken a seat.

"No, I prefer it here," she replied, sitting down on the floor in front of James. She leaned her head against him, and he stroked her hair and kissed her head. They were gestures of such naturalness that none of the other three, even Bill, who hated public displays of affection, felt the temptation to mock. The passion uniting the two lovers was so palpable that it inspired respect.

Once the two newcomers had been accommodated with their drinks, a scotch for James and a glass of Chilean Sauvignon Blanc for Antonietta, Bill surveyed them with an air of great seriousness.

"Now, Antonietta, you can forget this professor nonsense. You're part of the gang now, and so it's Bill, Piotr and Danny." He pointed in turn to the two others. "By the way, your name has too many syllables."

"It does"? Antonietta looked at him in surprise.

"Yes, An, To, Ni, Et, Ta, that's five. Jimmy here has only two, so does Danny, Piotr has one and a half, and I have just one."

"What am I supposed to do about it"?

"Nothing, because I have the solution. From now on, you're Toni. Toni with an i."

"I don't want to be called Toni," Antonietta objected. "I like my name."

"Toni it is, and that's the end of the matter."

Antonietta looked up imploringly at James. "It's Bill's thing," he explained. "He hates using people's real names. Just be thankful it's Toni. He calls poor old Ilse Bromhoeffer the "She-Wolf"."

"Why"?

James stroked Antonietta's hair. "Because he once saw a film, which he considers the height of artistic achievement, called *Ilse the She-Wolf of the SS*. It made a great impression on him."

Bill ignored James's ironical tone. "It's about this lesbian concentration camp guard. As Bromhoeffer is both German and lesbian, the name fits nicely."

James could feel Antonietta tense up, "She's not a lesbian, Bill, any more than HB's gay."

"Arbuthnot's gay"! Antonietta exclaimed with a look of disgust on her face that had the others laughing raucously

"No, Antonietta, he isn't. It's another of Bill's wild imaginings, and the only reason he has a problem with Ilse is that he always hands his marks in late."

"I wouldn't have that problem if the Institute adopted my marking scheme," Bill said with a salacious grin.

James groaned. "Alright, Bill, I know you're bursting to tell Antonietta, so we might as well get it over with."

Bill needed no encouragement. "It's only for female students," he explained to a bemused Antonietta. 'D is for a student who doesn't perform at all. C is for a student who fucks. B is for a student who fucks *and* sucks and A…" Bill paused for effect, "is for a student who does sixty-four."

"What's sixty-four"? Antonietta asked, quite unperturbed by Bill's crudeness. He gave her a look of admiration and whispered in her ear. Antonietta wrinkled up her nose. "I think I'll make do with a B in your course," she said.

James was beside himself. "Antonietta"! Antonietta leaned up and kissed him. "Don't worry, James, I'll make sure to get Ds in all courses except yours's."

"I suppose you'll aim for an A in Jimmy's course," Bill insinuated with a prurient grin. Antonietta could sense James's irritation with the conversation, and she answered quickly that it was up to him.

"Who else knows about you two"? Piotr asked, wisely changing the subject.

"Apart from you three, the only person who knows for sure is Petra Markovic. Ilse Bromhoeffer knows we are attracted to each other, but no more."

"Talking of Dr. Bromhoeffer," Antonietta commented, "she told me that my time here was doing me absolutely no good." She hesitated and added slyly, "So I bought a ticket for Italy."

"You did *what*"! James was beginning to regret the evening. Antonietta's connivance with Bill's vulgarity had made him extremely jealous, and now he found out that she'd bought a ticket for Italy.

"Who's being irrationally jealous now"? she asked. "It's a return ticket for the Christmas holidays," she explained, "but you only have to say the word, and I won't go."

Immensely relieved, James was magnanimous. "No, you should be with your family over Christmas." He kissed her.

"When you two have quite finished with these outlandish displays of sappiness," Bill told them, "there's an important matter to de dealt with. Toni should call Petra right away and ask her not to tell Brett. He's a nice kid, but a gossip."

He handed Antonietta the telephone, and she dialed Petra's cell number. She put on the speakerphone.

"Antonietta! Where are you"?

"At Bill Leaman's."

"I'm envious. I'm studying, and Brett's busy with his jocks."

"Listen, Petra, have you told Brett about us"?

"Good Lord, no, he'd tell the whole Institute."

"Please don't tell him."

"I won't, don't worry," Petra promised. "Let's meet for lunch tomorrow. I want to hear all the gory details about you and James." Antonietta agreed and passed the phone to Bill.

"Markovic, why don't you come over"? he asked, but Petra demurred. There was an air of disappointment about Bill when he hung up the phone that Antonietta caught. It suggested that his real feelings for Petra went beyond mere camaraderie.

"Talking of Petra Markovic, I'm seeing her and Brett Taylor tomorrow morning at ten. Evidently Taylor's prepared to admit that he was put up to accusing Hunt by Doefman."

Bill whistled. "Good for Markovic. She's come up trumps."

"How are you going to handle it, James"? Danny enquired, "If Taylor admits he lied, he could get thrown out of the Institute. He might be prepared to admit it to you, but I doubt if he'll do it publicly."

"Yes, I know that. What I intend to do is to have him sign an affidavit saying that Doefman put him and the others up to accusing

Hunt wrongly. I'll promise not to make it public without his consent, but I'll use it to try and turn some of the others. If I can get at least two of them to sign similar affidavits, I'll go to HB and hopefully bluff him into dropping the case. My suspicion is that he's in cahoots with Doefman and will be afraid of the fall-out from the affidavits."

"That means you have to make the affidavits public," objected Piotr.

"No. All I need to do is make HB *think* I'm going to make them public. As I said, I must bluff him."

Antonietta, who'd been listening proudly to James outline his strategy, suddenly remembered something.

"Petra told me that he tried to threaten her into testifying against Hunt."

"Who"? James asked.

"That HB person."

Bill whooped with joy. "I think we've got him, Jimmy"! He patted Antonietta on the back "You're not just a pretty face, Toni."

James calmed Antonietta's indignation. "That confirms my suspicions," he said, "and it'll help in the game of bluff. I still need those other affidavits. I think I know which students may come over, but I'll check with Petra and Taylor tomorrow."

James got up and walked over to pour himself another scotch. He asked Antonietta if she wanted more wine, but her glass was still half full.

"I didn't know you were so sober," Bill complained. "Petra told me you drank like a fish."

"I don't drink like a fish," Antonietta protested. "Although I admit that recently I drank too much. It was because I was unhappy, but now I'm not." She gave James a luminous smile, and, much to Bill's disgust, he couldn't resist kissing her.

"Good Lord, are you two always going to be like this"? he groused, "This is a drinking party, not a goddam love-in."

James and Antonietta promised to mend their ways, and the evening passed off without further amorous incident. Bill trotted out his normal assortment of vulgar jokes, the whisky flowed freely, and by the end of the evening Antonietta and James's friends were completely at ease with each other. When they left Danny's house, James put his arm around

Antonietta. At the end of the driveway there was a streetlamp, and they turned to look at each other. Antonietta inveigled her hand into James's pocket and drew out the car keys before he could stop her. She held them up victoriously

"What are you doing with those"?

"I'm going to drive because you've had too much to drink." she replied and walked purposefully to the car. She stopped at the driver's door and looked back at James.

"In the first class I had with Bill, I daydreamed about coming with you to one of your get-togethers. I imagined leaving the house with your arm around me and driving back to our house. I can hardly believe that this dream has come true. But I'm still afraid that I'll wake up."

James put his hand under Antonietta's chin and lifted it up. Looking straight into her eyes where anxiety mingled with happiness, he said with a grin, "I have a scratch to prove this is not a dream."

Antonietta grinned back. "I didn't mean to do it the first time, but the second time you deserved it."

James took her into his arms, and it was not until they realized they were both freezing that they ended their embrace and got into the car.

Their three friends observed this whole scene from the living room window.

Danny looked wistfully at the couple. "What a lovely scene. I've never seen a couple more in love, that I haven't."

"Wait until they marry and have kids," Piotr opined.

"Don't be such a killjoy, Piotr," Danny admonished. "That's true love." He pointed airily in the direction of the disappearing Maserati.

Bill said nothing. He'd watched Antonietta steal James's keys and her almost childlike look of triumph as she held them aloft. He envied James this happiness with a woman who was clearly meant for him. The contrast with his own marital situation was painful. He also felt apprehension. Seeing James and Toni together tonight, he'd sensed for the first time the full depth of their passion for each other. "I just hope to God nothing goes wrong," he thought, "or there'll be hell to pay."

*Chapter 19*

# Monday October 29, 2001

ANTONIETTA FOUND IT STRANGE to be driving to the Institute without the usual foreboding and longing. She could still feel James's kisses on her lips and somewhat contritely his caresses on the most intimate parts of her body. He'd brought her an expresso in bed, and in their subsequent lovemaking they'd lost a sense of time. As a result, she was going to be late for Bill's class, but she couldn't care less. She smiled contentedly at the thought of James still in the cottage, *their* cottage.

She parked the car and started to walk to the Lecture Hall building so that she could take the internal passageways to the FEB building and escape the cold. As she was walking through the Administration building, she passed Dr. Bromhoeffer, and she couldn't stop herself smiling at her. Ilse watched Antonietta walk down the hall. The radiant smile and the spring in her step could only mean one thing. Contrary to what she would have expected of herself, Ilse felt a sense of relief. She had been much affected by the poor girl's torment, and her own premonition had forewarned her of this outcome. It was against all the rules, but unless someone brought her direct proof of their liaison, she would not take any action.

James arrived just before ten and took the same direction as Antonietta. As he walked through the FEB building, he passed the classroom where Bill was giving his lecture. Antonietta was sitting in the back row, and he could see from her expression that she was paying scant attention. James was tempted to stay there and gaze at her, imagining her naked in bed with him, but he controlled himself. It was easier now that he knew they would find each other again that afternoon in the cottage. He continued on his way to the LIR building.

Petra and Brett were waiting for him outside his office. Petra was clearly embarrassed, as well she might be in James's view, and Brett looked downright scared. "Sorry I'm late," he said and opened the office door. He ushered in the nervous couple.

"It's probably too early for this," he said, picking up the bottle of scotch on the side table, "but from the expression on your faces, you look as if you need some." He grinned at the two students and poured out three glasses. "I won't tell anyone about what's said in this room, if you promise not to tell anyone I plied you with liquor." The ice was broken. Petra gave him a broad smile, and Brett seemed a little more at ease.

James decided to come straight to the point. "This is an unpleasant business, and I appreciate your help." He smiled encouragingly at Brett. "What I want is to have the case closed without anyone, including you Brett, getting hurt. This is how I intend to do it." He outlined his plan with a confidence he didn't entirely feel, emphasizing what he knew was essential for Brett. "I won't make public either of your affidavits without your permission."

Brett continued to stare silently at his feet, but Petra looked unconcerned. "You can use mine however you please. It's the truth and just shows HB for the shit he is." She'd overcome her discomfiture at meeting the man whose girlfriend she'd bedded and was treating James more like a friend than one of her professors. James, on the other hand, couldn't suppress his jealousy of this beautiful young lady who'd enjoyed Antonietta.

Brett continued to stare at his feet. "I recommend you strongly to swear the affidavit if you want to live with yourself and keep respect." James didn't mention Petra, but the allusion was obvious.

Brett looked up at his girlfriend. She kissed him and whispered in a cajoling voice "Please, Brett, do it for us."

After some more reflection, Brett shook himself out of his torpor. "Yes, Professor Markham, I'll do it."

Petra rewarded him with a most delightful smile, but James had the impression that she was prouder of her victory than Brett's return to honesty.

James drove them both to his friend, François, who was a notary and had been told to stand by to take the affidavits before there was a change of mind. James had Brett recount how Doefman had put him up to lying about Annya and Hunt and insisted that he also mention HB's inducements aimed at encouraging him and the other students to give this testimony. Petra also swore her affidavit that HB had threatened her with not graduating if she didn't testify against Hunt. James read through the two affidavits.

"Excellent," he told them. "However, I need at least two other affidavits like Brett's. Who do you suggest I should try"?

Both Petra and Brett concurred that Ben Toll and Michèle Letellier were the least committed to Doefman. These were the same two students whom James had found more malleable.

James drove Petra and Brett back to the Institute. It was nearly twelve and in half an hour Antonietta would finish her class with Forget. James marched quickly to the Administration building and Ilse's office. She greeted him with an enigmatic smile.

"You seem in good spirits, James."

"I think I'm making progress in the Hunt case," he replied, but he could tell from Ilse's expression that she knew full well this not the main reason for his happy mien.

"That's good news," Ilse replied with the same enigmatic smile. "By the way, you're the second happy person I've seen today. Antonietta della Chiesa also seems to have found a new lease on life."

James shook his head. "No comment, Ilse."

"Very sensible." Ilse stood up and went to one of her many filing cabinets. "Which students do you want to see"?

James marveled at Ilse. She really was no one's fool. "Ben Toll and Michèle Letellier." Ilse noted down the telephone numbers on a piece of paper and handed them to James.

"They're both nice kids. I don't know what they're doing mixed up in this nasty business."

"That sounds promising," he commented, putting the piece of paper in his pocket. He turned to leave Ilse's office.

"Be careful, James," Ilse called after him.

He put his head round her office door. "I tried, Ilse, we both tried. I'm sorry to disappoint you."

Ilse just nodded. Strangely, she was not disappointed.

James returned to his office and called the two students on their cell phones. It was amazing how they could all afford these new-fangled gadgets, he reflected. They were useful, however, as students were rarely in their residences. He managed to contact them both, and somewhat nervously they agreed to meet him the next day at nine in the morning.

"I'm so very happy for you, Antonietta." Petra's eyes glowed with pleasure after Antonietta's somewhat truncated account of her first days with James.

"You can't believe, Petra, how changed I feel. My whole life up to last weekend now appears to me like a void, nothing but a waiting room for James."

"When are you getting married"?

"James wants to us to live together at the end of the academic year and marry once the divorce is finalized. I'm still resisting because it means a break with my family, and that prospect sickens me. But I can never leave him, so in the end I'll give in and do what he wants."

"That's a strange way of talking about marrying the love of your life."

Antonietta leaned over the table and took Petra's hand in her's. "If you really want to know, every moment of the day since he first kissed me, I dream of being his wife. But until I met you today, I've never admitted that it could actually happen."

Petra grinned mischievously. "I make you do all sorts of things, don't I"?

Antonietta blushed deeply. "Please, Petra, I don't want to think about that."

"Why not? You enjoyed it at the time."

Antonietta withdrew her hand. "I admit that, but I forbid you to mention it again."

Petra realized she was alienating Antonietta by her teasing and stopped. She changed the conversation and told Antonietta about the morning's meeting with James.

"Do you think he can pull it off"?

"Yes, he can do anything."

Petra laughed and stroked her friend's face. "That's his mistress talking, not an impartial observer."

"Just wait and see," was Antonietta's answer.

⁓

James was alone in the cottage. It felt strange to be in Antonietta's abode, waiting for her. Worse still, he had a terrible feeling of emptiness. "God, I hope it's not going to be like this from now on," he groaned inwardly, pouring himself a third whisky that he knew Antonietta would not approve of. "Adieu, freedom," he thought, quite aware that freedom without Antonietta was not worth having. With almost adolescent joy he heard her car pull up.

The door opened, and Antonietta threw herself into his arms. "I was afraid you wouldn't be here."

"I was afraid you'd never arrive."

"What are those pieces of string"? Antonietta asked, her eyes widening with surprise.

"I'm going to punish you for your lesbian infidelity with Petra," James explained. "I'm going to tie you to the four posts of the bed and submit you to sexual torment."

Antonietta looked at James with a mixture of alarm and curiosity. "Are you being serious"?

"Completely. Get undressed."

Antonietta opened her mouth to protest, but James shut it with a kiss. "It's not really punishment because at the end you will experience an orgasm of such unparalleled violence that you might even faint. It's called *la petite mort*."

Antonietta submitted to her punishment. Once he'd secured her legs and arms, James proceeded to stimulate her with a softness of touch that at first brought her little excitement. As he continued, her body began to react. It was never enough to bring her to a climax, but it constantly increased her sexual tension. She implored James to satisfy her, but he continued to arouse her until her whole body was consumed by lust. "It has to end soon," she told herself, but it went on and on. Eventually she lost consciousness of where she was, aware only of the burning desire between her thighs that infused her whole being. She didn't even hear her groans and incoherent pleas. With an expertise that surprised himself, James brought her slowly and inexorably to her culmination. Antonietta gave a deafening scream, ejaculated, and went limp. She'd fainted, but her body still reacted as James depleted the residue of her desire.

Antonietta regained consciousness with James looking down at her anxiously. "Are you alright"? he asked as he untied her.

Antonietta smiled. "As well as one can be after the *la petite mort*." Suddenly her eyes misted over, and she became serious. "Do you still love me even though I let you do all these things to me"?

James took Antonietta into his arms. "You know very well that I love you." He pointed to the sheets that were wet with Antonietta's ejaculation. "I want you to come like that. I want you to be totally satisfied."

Antonietta's reply was to turn James on his stomach and use her tongue to dally with him in a way that he hadn't even let Leonor. do. He was about to object, but when Antionetta's hand came from between his legs and began to caress his sex, his resistance crumbled. The combination of Antonietta's lascivious tongue and her manual expertise soon brought him to an explosive climax.

Antonietta surveyed the sheets with satisfaction. "Now you can't say that it's just me who messes them up."

Antonietta's wanton skill left James exhausted and speechless. Once he'd recovered, he poured out two glasses of whisky.

"Why do you have to leave so early for Italy"? he asked, sitting down next to Antonietta on the sofa. She explained that she had to be in Italy for her parents' wedding anniversary on the December 17.

"What's the point of me coming back any earlier? You'll be busy with your family over Christmas and the New Year." There was a trace of resentment in her voice.

"It's still a long time to be separated from you."

His obvious dismay at her long absence comforted Antonietta. "Will you meet me in Montreal on the fourth when I get back"?

"Yes, and I'll make sure we can spend the night together."

Antonietta's eyes glowed with delight.

Antonietta made them supper, after which James took another whisky. "That's your last one," Antonietta warned. He started to complain, but she ignored him and asked why on earth he'd taught Italian literature.

"In this strange place we all have to teach one course outside of our area. For me, as I speak Italian, it was Italian literature. Actually it was a pain in the neck as I don't particularly appreciate Italian literature. There's not much in it."

"James! How can you say such a preposterous thing about the country of Dante, Petrarca and Boccaccio, not to mention Ariosto, Leopardi, Goldoni, D'Annunzio, Moravia"? In her anger she couldn't think of any more names and picked up a cushion. Before she could set about him, James pulled her towards him. She struggled, but he managed to kiss her and take the cushion away.

"I exaggerated," he admitted, "but the problem is that the great figures of Italian literature are either too far removed in the past or they're poets, or both. I don't really like poetry, and I find early Italian difficult to read."

"That's not their fault." The look of reproach in Antonietta's eyes made James wish he'd never started this conversation.

"I know, but it means I can't appreciate them." He hoped Antonietta would let the topic drop, but she was too upset.

"We also have some great novelists," she insisted. "What about Boccaccio, Manzoni, D'Annunzio, Pirandello, Verga, Moravia, what about them"?

James sighed. He felt as if he were between a rock and a hard place. "They all wrote some splendid novels," he replied, keeping an eye on the cushion. "Nonetheless, except for Verga and Moravia, they were all primarily poets or playwrights. Boccaccio and Manzoni only wrote one important prose work each."

"What's wrong with that"?

"Nothing. It's just that I like novels and, apart perhaps from Moravia, there's no novelist in Italian literature to rank with the great French and Russian novelists, like Balzac and Zola or Dostoevsky and Tolstoy, or even Dickens and Trollope in England."

Antonietta glared at him. "I suppose you think Goldoni was a second-rate Molière."

"I like Goldoni," James replied, hoping that the lie was not obvious, "although I do prefer Molière."

"That's because you're half French," Antonietta retorted. "*I francesi disprezzano gli Italiani.*"

"My father's half French, I'm only a quarter French."

"That's still why you prefer the French to the Italians."

"That's not true."

"*Cazzo, sì*"!* Antonietta stamped her foot on the ground, but against her will she let James take her into his arms. "I don't prefer the French to the Italians," he told her." I find the modern French too prissy. Before they used to like wine, women and laughter, now they drink mineral water for lunch, they've become morose and they're more obsessed by political correctness than sex. They also tend to think of themselves as intellectuals, which is exceedingly tiresome. That's why there are so many left-wingers in France."

For the first time since they'd started arguing, Antonietta laughed. "What's the connection"? she asked, kissing James in a gesture of reconciliation.

"People who think they're intellectuals vote left, people who are intellectuals vote right," James replied with a grin. "Like me."

"And me," Antonietta added, dragging James to his feet. They returned to the bedroom, and their disagreement was forgotten amidst their immodest lovemaking.

Just as Antonietta was falling asleep, James leaned over and whispered in her ear. "I have a confession to make. Two of my favorite novels were written by Italians."

She turned over and gave him a happy smile. "Which ones"?

"Lampedusa's *Il Gattopardo** and D'Annunzio's *Il Piacere*."

"Then you're forgiven."

## Chapter 20

# Tuesday October 30, 2001 to Wednesday October 31, 2001

JAMES KISSED ANTONIETTA AND left the cottage to drive to the Institute. It was going to be another sunny day. Ever since Antonietta and he had come together, the gloomy overcast skies of the previous two weeks had dispersed. It was as if nature itself were rejoicing in their fulfillment. Some of the trees on either side of the highway still had their leaves, and the dramatic colors of red, yellow, and amber combined with the brilliant blue sky to create a picture of imposing beauty. Nevertheless, although the fall in Quebec had splendor, James was always saddened by its arrival as it heralded the winter. James hated the cold and the snow of Canadian winters. Today, however, the image of his exquisite mistress lying naked in bed drinking the coffee he'd prepared for her and the knowledge that he would soon see her in class and enjoy her afterwards banished all sadness.

Thinking of the institute brought James back to reality. The imminent meeting with Ben Toll and Michèle Letellier would decide Elliot Hunt's future. The affidavits from Brett Taylor and Petra might suffice, but he needed two more to clinch the matter. He arrived at his office. The two students arrived a few minutes later.

James decided on a different strategy from the one he'd employed with Taylor and Petra. Instead of putting the two at ease, he would play on their nervousness. He asked them stiffly to sit down and let them sit in tense silence while he slowly took Brett Taylor's affidavit out of his briefcase.

"Like you, Brett Taylor testified to seeing Annya Nowak in a compromising position with Professor Hunt before the end of term," he told them. "Unlike you, he has now seen the error of his ways."

He paused and watched the two students look at each other. They were certainly surprised, but they also seemed to take some comfort from Brett's defection. James suspected that they regretted their role in the duplicitous scheme hatched by Doefman and were looking for a way out. The resentment of receiving poor marks in Hunt's course had clearly worn off and with it their desire for revenge.

"Brett has admitted that he lied, that he was put up to it by Doefman and encouraged by Professor Arbuthnot." Now came the crucial moment when he would succeed or not in bringing the two onside.

"The effect of this affidavit is twofold. Firstly, I know it's the truth, as you do, and it casts considerable doubt on the testimonies against Professor Hunt, particularly coming from as respected a student as the captain of the football team."

James had not the slightest clue why being captain of a team playing such a weird game was so prestigious, but he had long since given up trying to understand North Americans. He knew it was the case, and he exploited the fact.

"Secondly," he went on, "it gives us a basis for appealing any decision against Professor Hunt by the Ethics Committee to a court of law." He looked searchingly at the two students, who were by now quite ashen. "Are you aware of the implications for you of an appeal to a court of law"?

The two shook their heads, both by now looking quite frightened. "It means that you will be called upon to give evidence. Unlike in the Ethics Committee, you'll have to do it under oath. If you lie, you commit perjury, which is an offence punishable by a mandatory prison term."

"We didn't really want to do it,' Michèle Letellier burst out. "Brett was very upset, and we were angry with Hunt. No one liked him, and he's a very hard marker. Professor Arbuthnot made it seem we were doing the right thing. So we thought it might be true. Ben knows Annya from Edmonton, and she's a flirt."

"I'm not blaming you." James handed Michèle a Kleenex. Now it was time for the carrot. "I want to help you both."

The two students looked expectantly at James.

"What I want is to have the matter closed before it even comes before the Ethics Committee. That way you don't have to lie, nor do you have to tell the truth, which could result in your being expelled from the Institute."

"But how"? Ben Toll asked, any pretense that they had told the truth now completely abandoned. James gave them the two affidavits to read.

"It's true Arbuthnot threatened Petra," Ben remarked. "I remember the icy stare she gave him. She's the only one of us who had any sense."

"There's still time for you. Will you swear a similar affidavit? I promise not to make it public without your consent, and I'm sure that this will not be necessary."

"What good are the affidavits if you don't use them"? asked Michèle.

James smiled. "I didn't say I wasn't going to use them, Miss Letellier, I merely said I wasn't going to make them public."

The two students looked at each other again. Michèle was still hesitant, but Ben suddenly sported a broad grin. He had a very good idea of exactly what purpose the affidavits would serve. He agreed readily for both.

"Perhaps Michèle should make up her own mind. You're not married, are you"?

Michèle laughed. James had won her over. He felt very proud of himself, though a little guilty at how he'd browbeaten the unfortunate couple.

They drove to François' office where everything went smoothly and quickly, and by a quarter to eleven James was back in his office. He called to see whether Antonietta had left the cottage. She was still there.

"I fell asleep," she explained, "so I'll be late for class."

"Don't bother coming."

"I wouldn't miss it for the world, James."

Before leaving for class James checked his emails. Much to his surprise, there was one from Professor van Wezel. To his horror, van Wezel had given Doefman's paper 60% and commented that, notwithstanding one or two inaccuracies, it presented a fair assessment of European labor law. James forwarded the email to Elliot Hunt with the cryptic remark "I don't think I'll be using this."

James entered the classroom with his old self-confidence. He caught Petra looking at him keenly, probably wondering where Antonietta was. He smiled at her and made a gesture to indicate that her friend had overslept. It was rather imprudent, but no one understood except Petra. After about ten minutes, Antonietta arrived. She sat down next to Brett Taylor rather than walk across the classroom to her normal seat next to Petra. As James had reprimanded a student only last class for being late, he felt obliged to do the same with Antonietta. Her answer took him by complete surprise.

"I'm sorry, Professor Markham. My boyfriend's over from Italy."

Petra put her hands over her mouth to stifle her laughter, James didn't know what to do with himself, and there was a general murmur that seemed to come mainly from the male students. Antonietta's sex life had, unbeknownst to her, been the subject of intense speculation among them. Their conclusions ranged from an affair with Professor Leaman, a lesbian relationship with Petra or, one student having seen her enter the church at Saint-Sauveur during the day, chastity born of excessive piety. Now they had their answer, or so they thought.

The class resumed. It was the first decent lecture James had delivered, but Antonietta found herself daydreaming about the marvelous days she'd just spent and took little in. They'd agreed she would go for lunch with her friends to alleviate any suspicions that might have arisen. James would use the time to do some work on his article. They would meet back at the cottage around two.

Lunch was enjoyable and highly amusing, particularly for Petra and Antonietta. Speculation was rife as to James's sudden resurrection as a good teacher. The consensus was very near the truth.

"He must be getting laid," Brett Taylor suggested, and all agreed with him.

"I wonder who it is"? Petra couldn't resist testing the waters.

"I know who it is," Simon replied without looking at anyone. Petra took fright and changed the subject quickly. As they were leaving, Simon took Antonietta aside.

"Be careful, old sport. You're never sure who you can trust in this place."

"Can I trust you"?

"I'm a Brit. Need I say more"?

*⁓*

James returned to his office after class. He was relieved to have given a decent lecture at long last, but he longed to be back in the cottage with Antonietta. He regretted her going for lunch with her friends. He thought of making an appointment to see HB, but it was lunchtime, and neither he nor his equally unpleasant secretary would be available. He turned without enthusiasm to the article on the Treaty of Nice. At first it was hard going, but just as the ideas were beginning to flow, there was a knock on the door. It was Annya Nowak.

"I hope I'm not disturbing you, Professor Markham," she said, turning the full force of her pretty smile on James. "There are two questions I wanted to ask you."

Annya intrigued James. It was true, as the other students had said, that she had class, but the way she was looking at him also gave credence to Ben's assessment of her as a flirt. Had she genuine questions, or were they just an excuse to come and see him? If so, why? Wasn't she happily shacked up with Elliot Hunt?

The first question concerned the hearing against Hunt.

"Annya," said James, unwisely using her first name, "You must know all I've told Elliot, and there's nothing more I can add."

James had decided not to inform Hunt about the affidavits and how he planned to use them. It was a delicate matter, and he neither wanted to give Hunt false hope nor divulge his plan before the time for its execution. Annya accepted his answer without demurring, which suggested to James that this question had little import for her. He waited for the second one.

"I'm in your international trade course next term, and I want to know whether you need any legal prerequisites to take the course. I'm worried about being out of my depth."

Annya might talk about her worry, but the smile that played about her lips and the sparkle in her clear blue eyes belied it. In any case, the prerequisites for every course were stated in the Institute's syllabus. James pointed this out and added that he was sure she wouldn't be out of her depth.

The phone rang. It was Antonietta, who was very upset. "James, what are you doing? It's twenty to three, and you're still in the office. You were supposed to be home at two."

James's heart sank. He'd been so fascinated by Annya's performance that he hadn't realized the time passing. How could he have done this to Antonietta?

"I'm sorry," he said, "I got tied up. I'm leaving immediately."

Antonietta hung up without replying. James turned round and saw Annya staring at him. The amused glint in her eyes had disappeared.

"I'm sorry I made you late. Thank you for your time." She left abruptly.

James drove to Ste. Anne des Lacs with foreboding. Not only was he late, but part of the reason for this was Annya Nowak. He knew Antonietta's capacity for violent and irrational jealousy, and he prepared himself for a difficult reception.

Antonietta met him at the door. She had obviously been crying, and she was overwrought. "Why, why"? she cried. With effort James got her into his arms and held her trembling body close to his. Once she'd calmed down, he ensconced her on the sofa and sat next to her. He took her face in his hands, drew it towards him, and kissed her tenderly.

"Antonietta, I hate myself for being late. I got caught up in my article. I'm sorry, I really am."

Antonietta looked at him with tear-filled eyes. "What's more, you were distant on the phone."

James had intended to tell Antonietta about Annya, but he realized it would be courting disaster in her present state. He let their kisses become more and more passionate amongst fervent declarations of his love for her. They moved to the bedroom.

"I want to make love, not have sex."

"Is there a difference"? James asked with an amused smile.

"Don't mock me," she replied indignantly, "You know what I mean. Screams and other things are fine, but I want to feel myself at one with you. I need reassurance, not ecstasy."

As they lay together afterwards, Antonietta made James promise he would never be late again. Remembering his own disarray waiting for her to arrive at the cottage, he readily agreed. However, something in the tone of his voice disturbed Antonietta.

"What's the matter, James"?

Knowing what she was probably thinking, he reassured her. "Antonietta, it's true that something is bugging me, but compared to my love for you, it's unimportant." He took her into his arms and kissed her all over her body until she begged him to take her again, which he did in thoroughly dissolute fashion.

"So, James." Antonietta propped herself up. "What's bugging you"?

James pushed her back down on the bed. This way he could better control any outbreak of jealousy.

"I'm telling you this because I don't want any lies or concealment between us, and also because it's part of what disturbs me." He drew a breath and plunged in, hoping for the best.

"I was about to leave at about two fifteen when Annya Nowak came to see me." Antonietta glared at James and tried to wriggle free. "Now listen to me. I wouldn't be telling you this if there was any need for you to be jealous. When will you understand that there is no one, *no one* who can ever mean anything to me but you."

Antonietta was only half convinced. "It doesn't change the fact that you were dallying with her in your office while I was waiting here in anguish for you.

"I wasn't dallying with her," he protested. "Now will you listen to what is bugging me or not"?

Antonietta cocked her head to one side. "Only if you promise to throw her out of your office the next time she appears." Relieved that the storm had passed, James promised.

"She came ostensibly to ask about progress in the case, which she knows anyway from Hunt, and then she asked a totally unnecessary question about prerequisites for my trade course next term. All this raises the inevitable question. If she flirts with me like this, she may have done the same with Hunt? What's more, one of the students I saw today knows her from Edmonton and says she is indeed a flirt."

"She is, and she'd better keep her hands off you." Thinking of Annya, she tried to stop James kissing her but surrendered quite quickly.

"There are other things that trouble me as well. I sent Doefman's paper to a professor in Holland, and he gave it 60% against 40% from Hunt. He intimated it wasn't a bad paper at all. There's also a strange thing, which may just be a coincidence." James paused, and Antonietta looked at him expectantly.

"When I asked Hunt how he and Annya got together, he replied that he'd wandered around the Institute until he bumped into her."

"Well, that seems quite logical."

"Yes, but when I asked Annya the same question, I got exactly the same reply. It's as if they'd rehearsed it together. At the time her reply made me uneasy, but it wasn't until today that I understood why."

"What does this all mean, James? That Annya and Hunt are lying, and the others are telling the truth"?

"I can't really believe that. We know Brett Taylor and the two today lied. They've even taken affidavits to that effect."

Antonietta glowed with pride. "You got them to sign affidavits"?

"Yes, I browbeat the poor couple, but I'll see they won't get into trouble." James let Antonietta kiss him passionately. "I have a funny feeling about this whole business, but not enough to give up on Hunt. I have no proof he's lying, and plenty of proof the others are."

"When are you seeing HB"? There was anxiety in Antonietta's voice.

"Probably Thursday or Friday." James stroked Antonietta's hair. "Don't worry, he won't eat me."

"No, but he'll want to get even."

James brushed aside Antonietta's suggestion that she do her term paper for him, which was due in his class on Thursday. "I want to meet that Italian godfather of your's," he told her.

They dressed and set off for Montreal. Within an hour they were seated in Luigi's café. He had no need to ask who James was.

Antonietta's happy serenity and the delight with which her eyes beheld her companion told the whole story.

❦

Antonietta was behind schedule again for her class with Bill Leaman, and her belated arrival was greeted with prurient smirks from some of the male students. The news of her boyfriend's arrival had by now done the rounds. James arrived a prudent half an hour after her and was working on his article when a worried Klaus Berger arrived at his office.

"What's the matter, Klaus," James asked, his mind more taken up with reminiscences of the early morning in bed with Antonietta than the upcoming battle at the Section meeting.

"Things are not looking good," Klaus replied. "FEB voted yesterday afternoon to go along with the proposal, and someone's got to the junior faculty in our Section. I've just talked to Susan Welland and Francois Vian. They've changed their minds and are going to support McGrath."

"Shit." James's mood darkened. "I guess we should have expected that. McGrath wasn't going to sit around and let us make the running."

"I think it's that young fellow, Goldberg, who's been talking to the juniors."

James looked aghast. "He must know I'm against the proposal, and he owes me for getting him that raise." He was angry now.

"He's a conniving, little asshole. He knows that most of his stuff is second-rate, and the only way for him to get on here is to suck up to the Section Head. McGrath must have played on that."

"What are we going to do? There's no time to go round the faculty again."

"Let's at least meet for lunch and plan strategy for the meeting this afternoon."

James agreed, but this created a problem as Antonietta would be waiting for him at the cottage. He called to tell her that he was having lunch with Klaus to discuss tactics. To his relief, Antonietta raised no objection.

The next phone call was to HB. As expected, it was his secretary

229

who answered. She seemed pleased to tell James that the earliest he could see the Senior Dean was Friday at eleven o'clock.

Ignoring her supercilious manner, James oozed charm. "That's perfect, Betty, thank you very much."

"Vicious bitch," he muttered after putting down the phone.

*Chapter 21*

# Wednesday October 23, 2001 to Friday November 2, 2001

ANTONIETTA FINISHED HER *FETTUCINE* *alfredo* with a glass of white wine and sat down to read Trollope's *Barchester Towers*. It reminded her a little of Jane Austen with its rich panoply of rather eccentric English characters. It also made her think of James. She was impatient for him to arrive back from the Institute, but it was not the same desperate longing that had possessed her the day before. She knew he was lunching with Klaus Berger, and very soon he would take her to bed and make love to her.

Antonietta felt an inner peace that had always eluded her. It was not just the fulfillment of the all-consuming passion that had wracked her ever since seeing James at Mass. Before James, she had constantly worried about her inability to establish a meaningful relationship with a man, even fearing that the affair with Dana at boarding school had sown the seeds of perversion within her. Until James she'd never experienced the same sexual fulfillment with men that she had with Dana or even with Petra. James was able to exorcise these demons. He satisfied her sexual needs beyond her wildest imaginings, combining seamlessly the conventional techniques of heterosexual lovemaking with the erotic and intrusive intimacies of sapphism. He alone understood that she required both.

James arrived, and after a passionate embrace they made their way into the bedroom. Suddenly, in the midst of undressing, Antonietta gasped. "James! I still haven't done your exam! You'll have to help me."

James looked at Antonietta in her skimpy underwear and shook his head. "If you think I have a mind for the European Union with your nearly naked body in front of me, you can think again."

Antonietta grinned at him coquettishly, slipped off her bra and string, and joined him in bed. After two hours of sexual indulgence the lovers separated, and James went off to his Section meeting.

Despite himself, James found the sight of Tom McGrath's lordly presence in what had been his chair for the past year extremely galling. The air of confidence he exuded also disconcerted him. McGrath was flanked by Ed Williams on his right and Nathan Goldberg on his left. Klaus was right, James thought bitterly, Goldberg had deserted the setting sun for the rising one. He was not the only one. Both Susan Welland and Mike Allen, whom he himself had hired, didn't even acknowledge his arrival in the room. François Vian, the francophone from Saskatchewan, for whose tenure and promotion to Associate Professor he had fought so tenaciously, barely returned his greeting. Klaus Berger, looking thoroughly despondent, came and sat next to James.

McGrath greeted everyone very graciously, telling them how proud he was to have been chosen as their Section Head. In a barely veiled reference to James's tussles with HB, he expressed the wish that the Section would henceforth play a more constructive role in the affairs of the Institute.

"The proposal before you today, which we shall discuss after dealing with some routine matters, should be seen from that perspective," he told the assembled professors.

James paid scant attention to the routine matters. He was shocked at the sudden change in his colleagues' attitude towards him. HB may have suffered two failures to impose his will, but his shadow was beginning to spread over the Institute. With Winstone, Khan and now McGrath on his side, it was clear to everyone that he was a force to be reckoned with. James's only remaining power base was the ephemeral area of international relations. He wondered too whether the disastrous series of lectures he'd given this term had contributed to his diminished standing.

The time came to discuss the proposal. Again McGrath made a veiled allusion to James.

"As you know," he said, "the Governing Council was unfortunately not able to agree on a uniform approach to evaluating professors. So, together with the Senior Dean, the Heads of the three Sections have agreed to an alternative plan that should ensure equity between the Sections."

He outlined the plan as Klaus had explained it to James. When he'd finished, he looked round expectantly.

Seeing his cue Nathan became the first speaker. He extolled the virtues of the Sections working together and believed it was fitting for the Senior Dean to be involved in a coordinating role.

"As Tom has said," he concluded, "this is a constructive proposal that enables our Section to play its proper role in the Institute."

James looked at Nathan with ill-disguised contempt. He was obviously cozying up not only to McGrath but also to HB. James wondered how many of the other juniors would agree with him. The answer was the three assistant professors and three of the four associate professors. The fourth associate professor, Kamila Zaworski, was the exception and the first member of the Section to speak against the proposal.

"I've been here seven years," she said, "and I have never had any problem with being evaluated solely by the Head of my Section."

McGrath was clearly irritated by Kamila's comments, and, suspecting that Klaus was of the same mind, he deliberately ignored his raised hand. Unfortunately for him the choice of Christine Desmoulins was unhelpful. Christine repeated Kamila's point and went on to ask two crucial questions.

"How does this proposal differ from the one that was rejected by the Governing Council, and do the Section Heads or even the Senior Dean have the authority to change the manner of evaluating professors"?

Sensing danger, McGrath gave the floor to his ally, Ed Williams.

"There are two major differences between the two proposals,"

Williams explained. "Firstly, it is the Section Heads who draw up the list of journals in coordination with the Senior Dean rather than the other way round. Secondly, there will be no additional report from the Senior Dean. As for the power to act, this is an informal arrangement. I really can't see any problem."

Williams smiled superciliously at Christine.

Not waiting to be called on by McGrath, Klaus Berger intervened.

"The essence of the proposal that was rejected by the Governing Council was the notion of a uniform approach and a coordinating role for the Senior Dean. These are exactly the hallmarks of this proposal. What it tries to do is bring in the rejected proposal by the back door, and that is unacceptable."

"Unacceptable to whom"? sneered Nathan Goldberg.

Klaus looked at the young professor with disdain. "To anyone who believes that the Institute should be run according to its Charter."

The tone of the meeting seemed to change. Once Christine and Klaus, who were both respected full professors, had opposed the proposal, two other full professors felt able to show their colors. André Boisseu and Miyako Nakamura now both criticized the proposal as unnecessary and unconstitutional.

"Only the Governing Council can decide on how professors are evaluated," Miyako stated.

James, who'd been listening to the litany of support for McGrath with growing resignation, now spoke. He left the constitutional issues aside as they had already been well aired and concentrated on the substance of the proposal. He reiterated the arguments he'd made before the Governing Council: the present system was more flexible, particularly for junior faculty, who find it more difficult to publish in top-tier journals. The uniform approach put the evaluation process into a straitjacket.

McGrath asked for one last speaker and with clear bias chose Nathan although he had already spoken. If James needed any further proof of his defection, it was in the openly contemptuous way the young professor refuted James's argument.

"Your view is alarmist and unfair on the Section Heads and the

Senior Dean. I am sure they will come up with a list that includes a fair sampling of journals."

McGrath asked for a vote, and the proposal was adopted by a 7 to 6 vote. It was a narrow majority, but it was still a defeat, and James was not used to that. He left the meeting quickly, but unless LAC rejected the proposal, he was determined to take the matter as far as the Board of Governors.

HB and his lackeys could not be allowed to ride roughshod over the Institute's Charter.

~

Antonietta was in the process of browning some sausage meat for a *risotto* when the doorbell rang. Intrigued, she opened the door and found Bill Leaman standing there with a sheaf of papers in his hand.

"I've come to talk to James about my tenure application, but I hope I'm early enough for supper," he said with a broad grin.

"I'm just making a *risotto*," Antonietta replied. "There should be enough for three."

"What's *risotto*"?

"It's arborio rice cooked in olive oil with some onion into which you pour a bouillon until it is all absorbed. It's a creamy rice dish. Today we're eating it with sausage meat and wild mushrooms."

"Where's James"?

"He has a Section meeting. Something to do with a uniform evaluation of the professors."

Bill remembered. "Our lot already voted in favor of it. Silly assholes."

"Cheer yourself up with some scotch, Bill," Antonietta suggested.

Bill poured himself a large scotch and eyed Antonietta suspiciously. "Do you ration poor old James"?

"Yes."

Bill sighed. "Why is it that women always try to stop men drinking"?

Antonietta scattered some parsley into the sausage meat and put it aside. She turned round and looked at Bill, her eyes twinkling with amusement.

"For two reasons. We don't want to become widows, and it's not very gratifying to have sex with a drunken man."

Bill grunted and sipped his scotch. He watched Antonietta pour some rice into a casserole. The sharp contrast between the Antonietta of a week ago and this carefree, happy woman cooking for James struck him again. It was strange too to be a guest in James's home, well, his temporary home. Bill had never been very welcome in Veronica's house.

"When are you two getting married"?

Antonietta finished pouring a small amount of bouillon into the rice and salted and peppered it. She lowered the flame and covered the casserole. She placed some butter in a small frying pan, waited for it to melt and put in wild mushrooms together with some salt, pepper and nutmeg. Only then did she turn to face Bill.

"I don't like to think about it, Bill," she told him, her eyes losing their lustrous shine. "It would mean a break with my family and my religion, and I'm terrified that James would hold it against me if he lost the children as a result of the divorce."

"You can't go on forever like this."

"We're in love, we're happy, and there's no rush."

"I just hope nothing untoward happens."

"Why should it"? Antonietta asked nervously, but before Bill could answer, James arrived.

Taking one look at his dispirited air, Antonietta flung herself into his arms and kissed him passionately.

"*Ti amo, ti amo, ti amo,*" she repeated. "*Solo il nostro amore ha importanza.*"

Bill didn't completely understand, but he sensed the burning passion behind Antonietta's words. He felt envy but also trepidation. He shuddered at the thought of what would become of James and Antonietta if ever they were forced to separate.

James caught sight of Bill.

"Those bloody idiots voted for the proposal. You should have seen them falling over themselves to suck up to McGrath. That shit Goldberg, whose salary I almost doubled, was openly contemptuous, and even François Vian hardly returned my greeting. Ungrateful bastards."

Bill sighed. "How did the vote go"?

"Seven to six."

"Well, Jimmy, you shouldn't complain too much. My lot voted six to five in favor, so at least it was a narrow victory in both cases."

James refused to be comforted "It's still a defeat. But I'm not letting go. If LAC don't can the proposal, I'll take the matter to the bloody Board. I'll not have HB and his lackeys take over the Institute."

James glared at Bill as if he were one of them. Antonietta looked anxiously at her lover, gave him another kiss, and rushed off into the kitchen. She managed to salvage the mushrooms before they burned and was now pouring the rest of the bouillon into the *risotto*.

"It'll be ready in fifteen minutes," she announced and started to prepare a Caesar salad. James had told her of Bill's addiction.

Meanwhile the men went over Bill's tenure materials. James remained skeptical, but Bill was certain he would have excellent references.

"I know I'm coming up early, but that shouldn't matter, and I have six papers in good journals. All of them are single-authored. That's much better than the average. Look at Flint."

"Flint was HB's protégé," James reminded him.

"Perhaps, but my referees are the best in their field."

"Who are they"?

"Dickens from Cornell, Yankovitch from Princeton, Khaladi from Brown and Broderick from Chicago. All but Broderick are from Ivy League universities, and no one can complain about Chicago University."

"Look, Bill, it's a very dickey scenario. Under the rules Hamid Khan, which means Arbuthnot, can substitute two referees of his own choice for two of yours's. Any two. And look at the make-up of FPC. You have McGrath, who is likely to be hostile, and HB, who's out to get at me through you. In addition HB will make sure that the Rector's appointee is from his camp. Your only safe bets are Forget, who's dumb but fair, and hopefully the representative elected by the faculty. We must hope that Hamid has the guts to defy HB and support you. That still leaves Winstone as chair of the committee with the casting vote. Traditionally he should support your Section Head, but will he"?

"They can't refuse me if my references are good, and the people I've chosen are the best in the field."

"In my opinion, if we don't get someone elected from the faculty who is not influenced by HB, you'll have three to two against you, and HB won't even need Winstone's casting vote."

"We must make sure the elected rep is on my side." Bill was beginning to sound less confident.

"Come and eat," Antonietta called, placing the Caesar salad in a bowl on the table. "James, open a bottle of wine."

Bill was amused at her imperious tone, but James didn't seem to mind. He went off and chose a bottle of Valpolicella.

They continued to discuss Bill's tenure, which he insisted on applying for despite James's misgivings, and the two votes in favor of the uniform evaluation approach.

"Let's hope LAC scuppers it," said James. "Ilse, Piotr and probably Claudio Pettroni are going to be against, and they're a funny Section. Bit artsy-fartsy. They may surprise us."

"Forget's in favor, remember," Bill pointed out.

"Yes, but he's a lightweight. Ilse has more influence."

"My God, things have come to a pretty pass when we have to rely on the She-Wolf."

The reference to Ilse reminded James.

"She's guessed about us, Antonietta, but she'll do nothing. She even seemed pleased."

Bill looked at Antonietta, who clearly didn't share James's optimism.

"She's always respected James," he told her. "You have nothing to fear."

Antonietta continued to look worried, so Bill changed the subject.

"Carol's coming on Wednesday for a few days," he informed them. "For me it's make or break. I don't want to go on like this."

James suspected it was his own idyll with Antonietta that had precipitated this decisiveness.

"Don't do anything rash, Bill."

"Rash! I've been waiting five years for her to come and live with me. I don't think I'm being rash."

They finished the meal, Bill and James had two scotches, and Bill, assuming his two friends wished to be alone, got up to leave.

"When are you seeing HB about Hunt"? he asked James as he put on his overcoat.

"Friday at eleven."

"Well, may the Force be with you."

"Thanks, I shall need it."

After Bill had left, Antonietta sat James down on the sofa. "Why is it always you who has to do the dirty work"?

"I was appointed by the Rector to defend Hunt. I have no choice," was James's reply. It didn't convince Antonietta.

"You've gone out of your way to do battle against HB, and I know you. If they deny Bill his tenure, you'll be at the forefront of the fight. Why, James, why do you put our love in danger? These are horrible people; they'll stop at nothing."

James took Antonietta in his arms and kissed her gently.

"Don't worry. They don't know about us, and as for my role I'm the only senior faculty member who seems to have the stomach to fight HB. Perhaps it's pride, perhaps a sense of justice, I don't know. I just hate his kind. Corrupt, hypocritical, ambitious to the point of megalomania, without humanity. A typical bloody Presbyterian."

Antonietta couldn't resist teasing James. "That's the Catholic in you talking," she told him with an indulgent smile. "I'm sure not all Presbyterians are like that."

"Leave me my prejudices," James retorted. "Anyone can be tolerant, but it takes character to be prejudiced."

Antonietta burst out laughing. She stood up and stripped off her clothes. "You talk too much. "How about some decadence"?

He took her on the sofa and let himself be pleasured by her. Many times. It was after midnight before they went to bed. Suddenly, Antonietta remembered her take-home exam.

"It's due tomorrow, James," she cried, "and if I don't hand it in, people will talk."

"Get the desktop, and we'll do it in bed."

Antonietta came back with the computer and took down James's dictation. She felt guilty. "You realize this is totally unethical."

"I don't give a damn. It's partly my fault if you didn't learn anything in my course, and no one will be disadvantaged by me helping you."

## Chapter 22

# Friday November 2, 2001 to
# Sunday November 4, 2001

R OY ARBUTHNOT WAS FRUSTRATED. He'd so nearly managed to salvage his plan to control research in the Institute. Sure, in order to get Forget on side, he'd pretended it was now the Section Heads who were deciding, but he'd intended to push through his own choices of journals, and, as for the pretense that only the Section Heads would write an evaluation, nothing prevented him from adding his own "informal" report. It had been a marvelous strategy. No one could argue that it was the same proposal the General Council had rejected, whatever Markham might say, and it would have given him the foot in the door he needed. Now all had failed because of that fool Forget, who couldn't even keep his own Section in line. One vote! LAC had voted 7 to 6 against the uniform evaluation. What upset him most was Ilse's stout opposition to the proposal. He'd thought of her as a possible ally, but she'd shown herself to be his enemy. He wouldn't forget it, but for the moment there was little he could do. "Who knows, perhaps Markham's seduced her!" The thought made Arbuthnot laugh mirthlessly.

Why did Markham want to see him? To grovel at his feet, asking for clemency for his client? He wished so much to have that arrogant English aristocrat at his feet. It would be a delight, better than all the women he secretly desired. In a few minutes he would be here in his office. Arbuthnot steeled himself. Despite all his bluster, HB feared

James Markham. Twice the Englishman had beaten him in the councils of the Institute, but now was the moment for the sweet taste of revenge. He had the testimony of the students on his side and the evaluation that showed Hunt for an unscrupulous fornicator. Nothing could now save that young whippersnapper who had dared rubbish his teaching and his research. Sometimes he believed it was true, that Hunt had indeed seduced the pretty little blond. If he hadn't, he should have!

"Professor Markham, Senior Dean," his secretary announced with fitting solemnity.

Arbuthnot stood up and frowned coldly at his colleague. "So, Markham," he hissed, "You've come to plead for your client, I see."

James said nothing. He just looked at HB, who winced at the hatred and contempt in his eyes.

"Well"? HB asked with a nervousness he couldn't quite master.

"Why don't you sit down? I have something for you to read."

Arbuthnot slumped into his chair. This was not the way he'd imagined the interview. He'd seen himself as the grand inquisitor receiving Markham as a supplicant humiliating his noble pride before his, Arbuthnot's, authority. Instead, it was he who was cringing before the implacable expression on James's face.

James threw the four affidavits on HB's desk.

"Read them. Read them very carefully." Arbuthnot made a dismissive gesture. "Read them, Arbuthnot," James repeated in the same icy tone of command, "Read and be damned. Or don't read them and be doubly damned."

Never for one second did James relax his stern demeanor as he watched HB read the affidavits. Once he'd finished reading, James made his play. Everything depended on this moment.

"You will see, Arbuthnot, that not only have the students lied, but you, a professor, you, the Chair of the Ethics Committee, have actually encouraged them to lie and even threatened the Vice-President of the Students' Association with reprisals if she didn't lie for you."

James eyed Arbuthnot, who was staring in disbelief at the affidavits. Suddenly, in a moment of fury, he ripped them up and grinned savagely at James. "Where are your precious affidavits now"? he asked with a maniacal laugh.

"You disappoint me, Arbuthnot. You're stupid enough to believe those were the originals"?

He held up the originals of the affidavits. Arbuthnot made a move to grab them, but James slapped him in the face with his hand. His signet ring left an ugly red mark on Arbuthnot's skin. James lifted his hand a second time, and Arbuthnot cowed before it. James dropped his hand and addressed Arbuthnot with brutal severity.

"These affidavits will destroy you and all those who've aided and abetted you. They will have you unseated and hauled before your own committee to be disciplined and dismissed for abuse of power, lying to your colleagues, and bringing the Institute into disrepute."

Arbuthnot stared at James, his mouth open, without saying a word. He appeared to be in a daze. For one moment James thought he was going to faint. It was time for the final bluff.

"I don't give a shit about you, Arbuthnot. I'd love to see you dismissed and discredited, but for the sake of the Institute's good name, I'm proposing a deal to you."

HB looked questioningly at James but still kept silent, as if he couldn't bring himself to utter the words that would signal yet another defeat at Markham's hands. James made his crucial pitch.

"You have the right as Chair of the Ethics Committee to drop the case against Hunt. Do that, and I won't make the affidavits public."

"But the members of the committee can appeal to the Governing Council against my decision to drop"! Arbuthnot cried.

James realized to his great relief that he had won. "Stop them. They're your creatures. Make them obey you." He turned to go but added before he left. "Next Friday, I will destroy you unless you do as I say. Drop the case."

Arbuthnot watched James leave, hatred rising to his throat.

"You English, Catholic bastard," he spat at his disappearing enemy.

James heard the words, and something gave way within him. The loathing he had for Arbuthnot and all those who'd made him feel like a second-class citizen in his own country suddenly overwhelmed him. He walked back into Arbuthnot's office and grasped him by the lapels, his eyes glowing with unspeakable fury.

"Yes, I'm English, Arbuthnot," he said from between clenched teeth, "but we English didn't sell our king to his executioners for pieces of silver like you Scots.* As for my religion, at least I don't believe in justification by faith alone, which permits all manner of baseness. And you are base, Arbuthnot, the basest creature I've ever come across. Your religion pardons you because you have faith, and good works are merely an epistle of straw.*"

James let go of Arbuthnot's lapels and looked deeply into his eyes, which were partly obscured by the bushy eyebrows that turned in upon them. "Your nation has no honor, Arbuthnot, and your religion mocks Christ." With a last venomous look at Arbuthnot, James left.

HB watched his nemesis leave. He sat staring at the door of his office, mesmerized by the scene that had just taken place. His secretary, Betty, who arrived with Bill Leaman's tenure application and a note from Hamid Khan, brought him out of his catalepsy. HB looked at the folder, and his crooked lips pursed into the simulacrum of a smile. Hamid was asking for his advice. He would give him advice that would rid the Institute of that philanderer, Leaman and rob Markham of a precious friend and ally.

Antonietta had the impression that Forget's class would never end. She was on tenterhooks, wondering what had transpired between James and HB. A dreadful foreboding gripped her that this day would sound the death knell of her happiness, and she longed to drown her worries in James's arms and feel the comfort of his kisses all over her body. Today, she vowed, she would surrender her body to whatever use he wished to make of it. Even sixty-four.

The class ended, and Antonietta rushed to the car park. She drove quickly through Saint-Sauveur, nearly killing an old woman who was crossing the road with maddening slowness at one of the crosswalks. Never had the short journey to Ste-Anne-des-Lacs seemed so long or the countryside so unwelcoming in its winter austerity. With a sigh of relief she saw James's Maserati parked in front of the cottage and skidded to a halt beside it. She raced to the door, flung it open, and threw herself at James, who had just risen at the sound of her coming. Without asking about Arbuthnot, she implored him to make love to her.

"Take me in any way you wish. Just make me forget my fears."

James led her into the bedroom. He made her undress and lie on her stomach. He undressed, and for over half an hour he used his tongue, lips and fingers to rouse her to intolerable excitement. When he ultimately brought her to orgasm, her screams were deafening. Once she was quieted, he took his pleasure of her anally. Antonietta turned round and looked at James, her face blushing bright red as she surveyed the soiled sheets.

"Why do I let you do these things to me"? James kissed her.

"Don't pretend it's my fault. You love it."

He took her in his arms, and they lay together. Comforted by her sexual odyssey, Antonietta questioned James about his meeting with HB.

"It was supreme bluff. I knew that those affidavits amounted to little. I couldn't use them, and if HB didn't panic, Hunt was finished. As it happened, the bluff worked but," he confessed, "I'm afraid I might have blown it. I had him beaten, and then I let him goad me into going too far." He explained how he'd exploded in fury. "I told him his country had no honor and his religion mocked God."

"James"! Antonietta cried in horror. "How could you say such things, even to HB"?

"It was stupid, I know. I don't pretend I didn't mean it, but I pushed him so far that he may feel now that he has no alternative but to brazen it out. If he does, I'm screwed, and I've only myself to blame."

Antonietta stroked James's face fondly. "You're such a contradiction, James. You're quite prepared to risk excommunication to marry me, yet you defend your religion like a ferocious beast against HB."

"It's not just religion," James replied cautiously. He was treading on dangerous ground. "My family has suffered ever since the Reformation for their religion. It's cost us money, land, standing. When I defend Rome, I defend all my family has stood for."

This was what should have been a defining moment. Instead, he replied to Antonietta's tentative enquiry about his father by telling her he was a sheep farmer. That was true, but he was also the major shareholder and one-time chairman of Britain's third largest bank as well as a former cabinet minister in the Heath Government*. Moreover, he was a marquis, a dignity to which the earls of Derwent had been elevated by Charles II as a reward for the family's loyalty to the Crown during the Republic*.

"And yours's"?

"He's a surgeon."

Satisfied by these answers, the two lovers let the topic drop.

"Have you told Hunt"?

"No. Until HB drops the case, I haven't won. After my outburst, who knows whether he will."

James reached over and grabbed the telephone. "Bill"?

Antonietta sighed. She'd hoped they would spend the evening alone together, perhaps even go to Montreal for a meal. This was their next-to-last evening together before Veronica came back on Sunday. But she understood that James needed the support and re-assurance of his friends, and she tried to look pleased when he arranged for them all to meet at Bill's house around seven-thirty.

"But no Hunt. I'm not spending an evening with Annya fluttering her eyes at you."

As compensation for her lost evening, Antonietta insisted that they stay in bed for the rest of the afternoon. After James had brought her to another climax, he kissed her and got out of bed. Antonietta dragged him back down. "You're not going anywhere. I haven't finished with you."

James attempted to point out that it was already seven o'clock, but his protest was drowned by a passionate kiss from Antonietta. His lips were still damp from her own wetness, and this excited her even more. She ran her tongue down his body and took him between her breasts. James was helpless before the sight of Antonietta's nakedness and the sensual feel of her nude breasts surrounding his sex.

"Turn over," she ordered, and James attempts to protest faltered as she pleasured his anus with her tongue and nipples while caressing his sex. After he'd come, she turned him over and moved down his body, drying her breasts on the hair of his chest. Her nipples betrayed her renascent desire, and James took hold of her and placed her perfunctorily on her stomach.

"This is the only way to keep you quiescent," he told her, running his hands over her perfectly rounded buttocks.

"Satyr," she whispered. There was no reproach in her voice, and she willingly let him service her in the way that always made her blush. When she'd stopped moaning in the afterglow of her pleasure, James cupped his hands around her breasts and brushed them along the still erect nipples.

"Can we leave now"? he asked, kissing her in the neck.

She turned round and gave him a beguiling smile. "Yes, I think you've finally satisfied me."

～

The tears didn't start on Saturday, but the lustrous shine in Antonietta's eyes was dimmed by sadness. When they made love, she clung to James as if he were about to disappear. He ran his lips down her body, but she pulled him back towards her.

"Kiss me," she said, and, from the tone of her voice, James could sense her distress. He kissed her, lay down next to her, and placed her head on his shoulder.

"It's not going to be as bad as you think. We'll be together every afternoon, and I'll try and get away in the evenings as often as possible."

"What about your research"?

"To hell with my research. Do you think I'd be able to concentrate on the bloody Treaty of Nice knowing you're alone and miserable in this cottage"?

"Promise me you won't make love to your wife"?

James nodded his acquiescence. He gazed into Antonietta's eyes. "Remember that this situation is your doing. You only have to say one word, and we can be together."

There was a silence while Antonietta fought with herself; she decided to tell the truth.

"I will marry you, James. Let me decide when and how. I prefer to suffer loneliness and misery than do anything that could endanger our love."

"I don't see how anything could."

"The divorce will be messy. There are children involved, there's your career, not to mention my religious scruples and your wife's.

Our families will not approve, your children will not approve, people here will suspect, rightfully, that we broke the rules. We've only been together a week, without doubt the most wonderful week in my life, but I don't want to face the trauma of your divorce before our relationship has stood the test of time."

"How can you be so reasonable? All I can think of is how much I love you, and how much I want to be with you."

Antonietta smiled. "James, I may be a volatile Latin, but I'm also a woman, and women are more patient and far-sighted than men. You see only the present and the desires that momentarily dominate you; we are more concerned with the future, with what is permanent. I want my future to be with you, and I'm not going to do anything rash that could prejudice that."

James rose from the bed and walked over to his jacket. He pulled out two tickets.

"On December 7 we're going to see *Tosca*," he told Antonietta. "I'll tell Veronica that I have a conference, and we'll stay in Montreal until Sunday." He cocked his head at Antonietta. "Do you think we can do that without putting our relationship in danger"?

Antonietta jumped out of bed and threw her arms around James. Ignoring the ironical look on his face, she kissed him passionately and dragged him back to the bed. The cares about the future were submerged in the joys of the present.

They were awakened by the telephone ringing. It was Bill, informing James that his wife had called late last night.

"I told her you'd gone to a concert in Montreal and stayed the night there."

"What did she say"? James asked.

"Nothing much, just to remind you that her plane arrives at five-thirty. Air Canada from Heathrow. I can't remember the flight number."

Suspecting that James would have his hands full with an emotional Antonietta, Bill didn't prolong the conversation.

The fateful Sunday arrived. To take their minds of their impending separation, they drove to Montreal and attended Mass at the Basilica.

Afterwards they went to Luigi's for an apéritif and then to the St. Amable, a chic restaurant in the old port that specialized in French cuisine.

"It'll make a change from Italian," James told an indignant Antonietta, who launched into her normal diatribe about the superiority of Italian food and Italian wines over their French rivals. However, she was graceful enough to admit that the escargots and the rack of lamb that followed them were delicious.

As they drove home, Antonietta thought about James's large house, his Maserati station wagon, which she was driving, his wife's BMW, his expensive clothes, the trips he was planning for her to South America and France, the nonchalance with which he paid for expensive meals. Where did all the money come from? It seemed unlikely to Antonietta that a professor's salary would suffice. He was hiding something from her, just as she was from him. One day they would have to be truthful with each other. Not now, not until their relationship was so well established that there could be no suspicion that he was courting her for her title.

James watched Antonietta as she drove the car. Her refusal to let him drive when he'd had more than one whisky always amused him. He marveled at the sheer perfection of her profile. He stroked her long, black hair, and she turned to give him a brief smile. Everything about her face seemed to fit together in perfect harmony, like the notes in a piece of music by Mozart. It was a blend of regularity and softness, of character and sensuality, of seriousness and fun. She bore herself with a nobility that bordered on but never became haughtiness. It was clear she was from a rich family, but was that all? One day he'd have to tell her who he was, and then he would learn her secret. If there was one.

Immediately they arrived at the cottage, Antonietta made for the bedroom. She whipped off her clothes and undressed James. She pressed her naked body against his. "Satisfy me as only you can. Make me forget this is our last full day together now that your wife will be back."

The mention of his wife summoned up for James the harsh reality of that day. In a few hours Veronica would be back. He looked across at Antonietta and saw that she was weeping silently.

"I'll bring you a coffee," he said kissing the tears that were rolling down her cheeks.

"I'm coming with you. I don't want to be separated from you for a second of these last hours."

They took their coffee on the sofa in the living room. James had a sick, empty feeling in his stomach. Antonietta couldn't stem her tears. James tried to soothe her by repeating that they would see one another as often as possible.

"But not tonight. Tonight you'll be with her, and I'll be here without you." Antonietta buried her face in her hands.

"*Vieni*," said James and led her back to the bedroom.

Inexorably, the time came for James to leave for the airport. As he was opening the door of the cottage, Antonietta appeared in the living room. She was wearing the same bra and string she'd worn on their first night together. Her lips gleamed sensuously with glossy lipstick. James gazed at her, quite captivated. Slowly she slid off her bra and string and walked towards James.

"Don't you want me"? It was too much for James.

"*Tentatrice*"! he exclaimed, taking his lubricious mistress into his arms.

It was nearly seven o' clock when James finally arrived at Dorval airport. As it happened, the plane was late, and the passengers were only just going through customs. It was strange to see his wife walking towards him, blissfully unaware of the tremendous change in his life. She kissed him perfunctorily on the cheek and apologized for their lateness.

"You know Air Canada, James. I sometimes think they're late on purpose to discourage people from traveling with them. I always have the impression the stewardesses think of us as nuisances."

James laughed. Their dislike of Canada's national airline was one of the few things they had in common.

He kissed his two children. Peter tensed up as normal. He found men kissing each other to be a silly and embarrassing French habit. Susanna, on the other hand, gave her father a big hug.

"Well, did you have a good time"? he asked his offspring. It was Veronica who answered.

"It was an excellent retreat. The priest who ran it was a Jesuit, very erudite and convincing. He said that Peter might have a vocation." Peter made a grimace.

"What's a vocation"? asked Susanna.

"It means you don't marry and wear silly clothes," was her brother's dry reply

Veronica looked predictably aghast, but James was highly amused.

"Really, James," his wife chided, "you're no support for me at all."

She stalked off towards the exit. James and the children followed, Susanna holding on to her father's hand and looking up at him in adoration.

"Nothing has changed in the Markham household, and yet everything has changed," James was thinking as he left the airport.

*Chapter 23*

# Monday, November 5, 2001 to Sunday November 11, 2001

JAMES HAD MISCALCULATED ARBUTHNOT'S reaction to their meeting. Once he'd overcome the panic caused by the affidavits, HB realized that, if Markham used them at the hearing of the Committee, the students involved would be expelled from the Institute. The only way he could have persuaded the students to do his bidding was by promising not to make the affidavits public. Markham was bluffing, Arbuthnot told himself with relief. There was nothing he could do.

Or was there? Arbuthnot recalled the pure hatred in Markham's eyes at the end of their encounter. That hatred surely made it impossible for Markham to let him win. He was capable of using the affidavits regardless of the consequences for the students. There was also the affidavit from that Markovic girl. She was a haughty bitch, but she had standing in the Institute because of her position, and she had nothing to fear from her affidavit being used. It wasn't enough to have the Senior Dean fired, but it would be very embarrassing. Arbuthnot wondered idly whether she was screwing Markham. Probably not. She seemed to be involved with that jock who was captain of the football team. More titillating were those rumors about her and that snotty Italian girl, della Chiesa. Arbuthnot's mouth twisted into the semblance of a prurient smirk. "Depraved sinners, the lot of them," he said aloud to himself.

Arbuthnot decided to play safe and hatched an alternative strategy.

He would gamble that Markham hadn't told Hunt about the affidavits. If he'd promised *not* to make them public, this probably included Hunt. He would also play on the antipathy that must exist, at least latently, between Hunt and Markham. He was sure that, as a good Baptist, Hunt didn't approve of Markham's drinking and the low company he kept, and HB had first-hand experience of Markham's Catholic prejudices. He'd play the hero with Hunt. He'd make it seem like his decision to drop the case, while intimating that Markham had not done a good job because he thought Hunt was guilty. It was possible that he could gain an unlikely ally out of this whole business.

Arbuthnot called a meeting of the Ethics Committee for Thursday morning.

Antonietta was desperate to see James. She paid little attention in her two classes and rushed home immediately after Forget's class where, to her immense joy, she found James already there. She collapsed in tears into his arms.

"I love you," he told her, wiping away the tears and kissing her tenderly.

"Tell me you didn't make love to her," she pleaded, incapable of masking the jealousy that was tormenting her. James shook his head. "Swear it," Antonietta insisted. James smiled at her indulgently. "I swear it, Antonietta." They kissed again, more passionately.

"Make love to me, James. Make love to me in every possible way." They made for the bedroom.

It was nearly four in the afternoon before they had satisfied their desire and longing. James looked down at the dark beauty nestled against him. She turned her face up towards him. Her features were softened by the contentment wrought by her pleasure, and her eyes were shining with delight.

"The problem, Antonietta, is that you look so lovely after we've made love that I always want to start all over again."

"Why don't you"?

"I have to pick up the kids in half an hour."

The mention of James's children brought Antonietta back to the harsh reality of their situation. Her eyes misted over, and she quickly changed the conversation.

"What's happening with HB"? Sensing her distress, James kissed her before answering.

"As yet, nothing. If he drops the case, we'll have to invite Hunt to the celebration."

Antonietta sat upright and glared at James. "*Without* Annya," she insisted.

"That's impossible."

"If you really loved me, it wouldn't be impossible," Antonietta got up from the bed. She put on a bathrobe and stalked off to the bathroom. James followed. She pushed away his hands as he tried to wind them around her breasts, but she couldn't avoid his kiss on her neck.

"I won't invite either of them," he murmured. Antonietta swiveled round and fixed James with a penetrating stare. "Promise." James didn't answer. He deftly slipped off Antonietta's bathrobe and held her naked body close to his. She refused the offer of his lips.

"Promise," she repeated.

"I promise."

Only then did she allow him to kiss her.

Arbuthnot was pleased with the meeting of the Ethics Committee. He had explained that the evidence against Hunt was severely tainted by the fact that all the students testifying against him had received poor marks in his course. Moreover, their evidence was contradictory as to when and where they had seen Hunt and Annya Nowak together. "So," he had concluded, "my suggestion is that we drop this case. I would rather see a guilty colleague get away with something like this than punish an innocent man." Ilse Bromhoeffer and Pettroni had been clearly impressed by his magnanimity, and Gowling and Williams, whom he had forewarned, had agreed readily.

Now, with the unanimous decision of the Committee in his possession, Arbuthnot called Hunt and invited him to come and see him. Hunt arrived, looking very apprehensive. Arbuthnot greeted him with collegial cordiality.

"Thank you for coming, Elliott. I've been reviewing the case against you, and I'm at a loss to understand why Professor Markham hasn't made a formal request for the complaint to be withdrawn. The testimony of the students is clearly tainted, and they can't even agree among themselves. There really is no case against you."

Hunt stared at Arbuthnot in disbelief. "Does this mean you're dropping it"?

"If Professor Markham agrees, yes."

Hunt's disbelief gave way to surprise tainted with a touch of annoyance. "Why wouldn't he agree? He's supposed to be defending me."

Hunt's tone told Arbuthnot that his insinuations about James's inaction had not fallen on deaf ears.

"That's true, but as he seems to have doubts about your case, I should consult him beforehand. A matter of professional courtesy, you know."

Arbuthnot paused, observing Hunt's reaction. He had succeeded in planting the seeds of suspicion; now it was time to play the religious card.

"I could be wrong. It may be that he just hasn't had enough time to deal with it thoroughly." He smiled knowingly at Hunt. "Too much drinking with that Catholic gang he hangs out with."

A hint of disgust flitted across Hunt's face.

"You're dropping it"? he asked again. Arbuthnot nodded. "Thank you, Roy. I'll not forget this."

Arbuthnot watched Hunt leave his office. His strategy had succeeded better than he'd dared hope. He'd awakened suspicion and disapproval in Hunt for Markham while placing the young upstart in his debt. It had been a good morning's work. Now it was time to deal with Leaman. Buoyed by his success, he walked lightly to Hamid Khan's office.

The meeting with Hamid was more difficult. Although, as Arbuthnot reminded him insistently, he had the right as Section Head to replace two of Leaman's choices with his own referees, he seemed disinclined to do so. HB had to resort to lying, at which he excelled. Smoothly he coaxed Hamid into believing that the two most influential referees, Broderick from Chicago and Yankovitch from Wharton, were friends of Leaman and couldn't be relied upon to give an objective judgment. As always, Arbuthnot was at his most reasonable and convincing when he was lying, and Hamid gave way. Arbuthnot suggested using Henry Keighley from Wickham College in Missouri and Kevin Mauser from Chicago. Both were his former classmates in the doctoral program at NUC.

"But Mauser's not a full professor, and Wickham College is hardly a first-rate school," Hamid objected.

Arbuthnot was dismissive. "Wickham has an excellent academic reputation even if it's not one of those snotty Ivy League places, and Mauser's coming up for full this year. With his record, he'll soon be at one of the top schools in the US."

Hamid said no more and replaced the two names on Bill's list.

"When you send the request for a reference, you should mention that this is a case of early tenure.".

"Is that really necessary"?

"Absolutely. Stricter criteria apply. You should point that out as well."

This was the first time Hamid had heard of such criteria, but Arbuthnot was the Senior Dean and presumably knew better. He submitted again.

⁓

On returning home on Tuesday after lunch with Petra and some other students, Antonietta had found James in the process of arranging his books and papers. She'd burst out laughing at the chaos he was creating.

"What are you doing"? she'd asked as James strode towards her and took her into his arms. The look he'd given her had been of such intensity that it'd made her tremble with emotion. "I can't work at the Institute, I have to be here," he'd told her. "You're like the air I breathe. Without you I suffocate."

However, on this Friday James was not at the cottage to greet her when she arrived. She sat down on the sofa feeling empty and downcast There must be some explanation for his absence, she told herself, but she had to struggle to hold back her tears.

James arrived around one thirty. Antonietta pushed him away when he came near her and heaped reproaches upon him for his lateness. He backed her up against the wall and forced her to kiss him. She surrendered grudgingly but soon broke away. "Where were you"? Always in the back of her mind was the image of the blond Annya.

James laughed. He knew exactly what Antonietta was thinking, and for a moment he was tempted to tease her. He abandoned the idea when he saw the anguish in her eyes.

"I was informed just before noon that the Ethics Committee has dropped the case against Elliott Hunt," he told her. Antonietta, forgetting her distress, cried out in triumph. "James, you did it, you did it! I'm so proud of you." She was about to embrace him with all her passion when she noticed the strange expression on his face. "What's the matter? Isn't this what you wanted"?

"It's Hunt." Antonietta could sense the perplexity in James's voice. "I went to see him, and he didn't even thank me. He was quite offish. Bloody ingrate"!

"Good. Now we don't have to invite him to the celebration." Antonietta kissed her petulant lover with such ardor that Hunt's lack of gratitude was forgotten. She made James sit on the sofa while she slowly stripped in front of him. Once she was completely naked, she undressed James and ran her breasts down his body before pleasuring him with her mouth. She made him follow her into the bedroom. She lay down on the bed in wanton abandon, her legs suggestively apart. "My turn," she told her lover without any shame.

They were, as always, late for the party at Bill's place. Carol was there, but the atmosphere between her and Bill seemed tense. Piotr, who hated dissension because he had so much of it at home, was looking glum. Danny was trying to enliven everybody, but he was already a little drunk.

"My God, what a gloomy lot you are"! James exclaimed as he entered the living room. "This is supposed to be a celebration for Christ's sake"

James's good cheer and Antonietta's habitual radiance succeeded where Danny's drunken efforts had failed. Piotr brightened up, Danny relaxed and seemed to become more sober, and Carol was too intrigued by James's new mistress to pursue her disagreement with Bill. She and Antonietta went off into the kitchen to make supper.

"My God, Itie and Chink food," groaned Bill, "Why don't we men go off to MacDonalds"?

"Don't be so crass, Bill," James scolded. "That's hardly the way to talk about your lovely wife's cooking."

Bill was about to make some quite inappropriate reply, but James cut him off by describing his strange meeting with Hunt.

"Perhaps that means he was lying," suggested Danny.

"I don't think so. If he'd been lying, he should be even more grateful," James replied. "I think he's just a shit."

The men continued to drink and complain about the Institute until Carol and Antonietta arrived with the food. Antonietta had cooked a traditional *bolonese* and Carol sautéed beef with vegetables and sweet and sour pork. The meal was served with pasta and rice cooked with chicken and eggs. Even Bill had to admit that the food was delicious. As they sat around afterwards sipping the Courvoisier cognac James had purchased for the occasion, Danny sprung his news on them.

"Ceara's coming for Christmas," he announced, his voice choking. He probably would have started to weep, were it not for the explosion of joy that followed his announcement. All of them knew how much he'd missed his daughter. He hadn't seen her for two years. Carol and Antonietta kissed him, and the men slapped him on the back. Danny filled his glass up and sat back in his chair, tearfully happy.

⁓

Bill dropped Carol off at the airport in Montreal. He fetched her bags from the trunk and deposited them in front of her. Without saying a word he got back into the car and drove off to Antonietta's cottage. It was Saturday afternoon, and he was certain he would find James there.

It was James who came to the door, which Bill found incautious.

"I could have been anybody. You really should be more discreet."

James just laughed, but Antonietta, who'd heard Bill's comment, was worried.

"He's right, James," she said with a shudder.

James ushered Bill nonchalantly into the living room. "Come on in, Bill." He noticed that his friend was pale and upset. "What's the matter"?

Bill sat down on the sofa, his head between his hands. "It's all over. We're getting divorced."

While James looked on, not knowing quite what to say, Antonietta sat down next to Bill and put her arm around him.

"I'm sorry, Bill, I really am." Bill glanced up gratefully at Antonietta's sympathetic face. "You know, it's not the end of the world. You couldn't continue as you were, and now you can get on with your life." Bill nodded miserably. "You can even start flirting openly with Petra," she told him with a mischievous smile. Bill smiled back.

"You're a lucky guy, Jimmy," he said with feeling. "She's not only beautiful. but adorable with it."

"There's only one way to deal with the blues, my friend." James handed Bill a glass of whisky. "That's to get thoroughly pissed."

After a few whiskies, Bill cheered up. "How do you manage to get away from home this often"? he asked James.

"It's my overdue paper. At least, that's what I tell Veronica."

"Veronica's going to smell a rat one of these days," Bill cautioned. "Either you two behave with more circumspection or, James, you leave Veronica and marry Toni. If you two go on like this, you're asking for trouble."

Bill's words made an impression on Antonietta. After he'd left, she summoned up the courage to tell James that they should see each other less. Reluctantly, James agreed.

"I suppose I'd better spend some evenings at home," he conceded.

When he left Antonietta around six, she had difficulty containing her emotions. As she heard him drive away, a feeling of emptiness and desolation descended upon her. She opened a bottle of Chianti and then another. It was a lonely, pitiless evening. She drank wine and listened interminably to Laura Pausini. Her song, *Come se non fosse stato mai amore*\*, held a morbid fascination for her. It would be her song if ever her terrible apprehensions came true.

It was not until after seven that James arrived at the cottage on Sunday evening. Antonietta was furious with him for being late, but once he was in the living room, her passion swamped her anger, and she demanded that he take her to bed. She was particularly demanding and insatiable, and it was nearly nine before they arrived at Bill's.

"You're even later than normal," he remarked, taking the bottle of wine from James. "Why do you always buy French wine"?

"Because I like French wine."

"Why can't you buy some decent California wine for a change"?

"Or Italian," interjected Antonietta.

James gave them both a scornful look. "Bloody xenophobes, that's what you are."

"There's nothing wrong with being xenophobic, or racist for that matter," Bill declared. "I hate all this pinko, politically correct crap about respecting other nations, even those that hate our guts, and bending over backwards to be lick the ass of every fucking colored person in the world. I love the US, and I think whites are superior. And I prefer American wine."

"Jesus, Mary and Joseph, Bill," objected Danny, "You can't say things like that."

Bill was about to give what promised to be a scathing reply, but James got in first. He knew he'd upset Antonietta and wanted to make amends.

"Bill, there's a difference between a love of one's country and a desire to preserve its culture and way of life and an unreasoning belief in its superiority over all other countries and cultures. It's the same with race. Being proud of being white doesn't have to mean you despise colored people. Unfortunately the pinkoes and the politically correct are too stupid to understand this."

He put his hand around Antonietta's shoulder, but she pushed it away.

Danny, who was aware of both the tiff between James and Antonietta and the real reason for Bill's bad mood and who in any case hated political discussions, decided it was time to put an end to this vexatious conversation.

"Why are we discussing wine when there's plenty of whisky? Piotr, you're nearest to the fountain of life. Do the honors."

James gratefully took his glass of whisky. "You see," he told Bill,

"There's an example of tolerance. I can't abide the Scots, but I drink their whisky."

It was not a particularly enjoyable evening. Neither the topic of Bill's divorce nor the possible problems he might have with his tenure application were destined to lighten the atmosphere. Normally, Antonietta's radiance would have helped, but she was upset with James and kept silent. She repulsed all his attempts to conciliate her.

At midnight everyone had had enough. James and Antonietta made their way silently to the Maserati.

"Give me the keys," she said when they reached the car.

"There's no point. I've got to drive from Ste. Anne to Prévost in any case."

"As you wish."

They drove in silence to the cottage. Antonietta got out of the car and without a word to James marched off to the front door. "Good Lord," James thought," I only called her a xenophobe." He drove off, but before he reached Highway 17, which led to Prévost, he turned back towards Ste. Anne.

On the way he crossed Antonietta in her Jetta. They both skidded to a halt on the snowy road. They met each other in the middle of the road, oblivious of any danger.

"I only called you a xenophobe," James protested after their long and fervent kiss.

"It was the way you looked at me. I would never have believed you could look at me like that."

James put his arms on her shoulders and fixed her with his eyes. "I was looking at Bill. You just happened to be next to him."

Antonietta looked down. "Do you know how much effort it took me not to talk to you, not to throw myself at you."

"I don't care how much effort it took." James put his hand under Antonietta's chin and lifted up her face. "Don't ever do that again. Hit me, walk out on me, but don't freeze me out like that."

It was early in the morning when James left Antonietta. She was too exhausted to complain when he got up from the bed and dressed.; her jaw ached, and her thighs were sore from their oral excesses. After a long and final kiss James went home. Veronica had been asleep for many hours.

*Chapter 24*

# Monday November 12, 2001 to
# Friday December 7, 2001

I T WAS A DIFFICULT week for Antonietta. Emotionally fragile because of the terrible dilemma facing her, she had difficulty putting the painful scene with James behind her. The panic and dread she'd felt hearing him drive off in exasperation pursued her all week, and there were more tears every time James left her to return home. Even worse, it was now Thursday, and he hadn't spent a single evening with her. She was still resolved not to surrender to the temptation of marriage, but the effort was noticeable. Petra remarked on her taut expression, and the luminescent shimmer of her beautiful eyes was dulled.

The pressure of work and the nascent suspicions of Veronica had finally persuaded James to work on his article at home. It was a hard decision. He missed the woman he loved with such boundless passion, and he was conscious of the grief his evening's absences caused her. His only consolation was the hope that Antonietta's distress would hasten her decision to marry him.

James entered the classroom, glanced quickly in Antonietta's direction, and began the lecture. He'd overcome the incoherence of the beginning of term, but his lectures still lacked their normal sparkle. Unfairly he held the students partly responsible for his predicament, and every class was an effort. Today was no exception, and it was without enthusiasm that he acknowledged Wrangel's hand. "Another self-opinionated question," he thought.

The question was interminable. James managed to control his impatience, but after a while he lost the thread of Wrangel's discourse, if indeed there was one. When the student finished, James hadn't the slightest idea what he'd been talking about. Without any intention of humiliating him, he asked Wrangel to repeat his question. The class thought James was deliberately putting him down and roared with laughter. Wrangel glowered angrily at James. "I'll get even with you, you arrogant bastard," he vowed.

That day James stayed with Antonietta until late in the evening. He was aware he'd humiliated Wrangel. It had been unintentional, but he hadn't been able to bring himself to apologize.

"You should have, James," Antonietta told him. "I don't like having enemies around us. We're at risk, and it only takes one person to see us."

"The Lord will protect us," James replied.

Antonietta rebuked him. "Don't blaspheme." She tried to repel his renewed advances but soon succumbed. However, she made him shave before giving her pleasure in the way she craved.

The next day Antonietta had lunch alone with Petra. They talked as always about their love lives. Petra was still madly in love with Brett, but she admitted he was a jock.

"He's got a great cock but a small brain," she told her friend, who, despite her discomfort with Petra's vulgarity, couldn't help laughing. "And you? When are you going to make *the* decision"?

"Not yet. I need to be sure our relationship can stand the strain of the divorce."

"Well, be careful. James has made an enemy of Wrangel, and he knows Annya, who's jealous of you. That's a dangerous combination."

Antonietta repeated Petra's warning to James, who didn't take it seriously. Bill also warned them at their Sunday get-together. "You two are so besotted with each other, even a blind man could see it! You're courting danger. For Christ's sake, get married."

Antonietta became very afraid. She made James leave early and spend the rest of the evening with her in the cottage. She made love to him with a frenzy that worried him. "What's the matter, Antonietta"?

Antonietta sat up, her eyes full of sorrow. "We mustn't see each again."

"Why ever not"?

"Because someone's bound to realize what's going on, and it'll ruin your career."

Antonietta collapsed sobbing on the bed. James drew her to him. He played for one moment with the idea of telling her that he didn't need his academic job, that he was a shareholder in the family bank, and that he wasn't going to let anyone come between him, Lord Markham, and the woman he loved. Instead, he just comforted Antonietta, and when she stopped weeping, declared forcibly that hell could freeze over before he would consent not to see her again. Antonietta came on top of him and devoured him with kisses.

"I couldn't leave you anyway. I couldn't live without you."

Although it was late, James made no effort to stop Antonietta descend his body with her lips. She excited him until he was able to penetrate her again. She sat on him so that he could fondle her taut breasts. They took their pleasure together. When it was over, James smiled slyly.

"You can't leave me," he told her, "We're going to *Tosca* on December 7, and the next day we leave for Mexico."

"Mexico"! Antonietta looked at James in joyful astonishment. "You're taking me to *Mexico*"?

"Yes. We leave the day after the opera. I have to go to Guadalajara, which is a beautiful city, and I'll take you as well to a resort in Manzanillo that's a paradise on earth. It's called Las Hadas."

"How long are we going for"? All sorrow was now banished, and Antonietta's eyes sparkled with happiness.

"*Una settimana corta.* Remember that you leave for Italy on the 14th."

Antonietta's eyes dimmed momentarily, but she chased away the specter of their separation. "All I want to think about is that we shall be together all day and all night for a whole week."

James was going over the notes for his class when the phone rang. It was Carlos Guarnieri from the University of Buenos Aires to tell him that the conference on the European Union, at which James had promised to give a paper, would be held from December 17th to 19th. James immediately realized the impossible situation he was in. He couldn't refuse without causing offence to Guarnieri and ruining the Institute's relationship with UBA. If he agreed to go, he risked incurring Antonietta's jealous wrath as he'd promised her never to go to Argentina without her. He tried to play for time.

"I must check with the Institute to make sure there's nothing on that week," he obfuscated.

Guarnieri was not to be put off. "James, we're counting on you. You've got to come."

Reluctantly and feeling slightly sick to his stomach, James agreed.

⁂

They'd been back in the cottage for over two hours before James summoned up the courage to tell Antonietta about the conference in Buenos Aires. Her reaction was worse than he'd feared. She jumped out of the bed, put on her dressing gown, and glared angrily at him.

"You promised *not* to go to Argentina without me," she cried, her voice quivering with jealous rage. "You promised me. If you break that promise, I never want to see you again. *Never*"!,

"Antonietta, I have no choice. I agreed to this before we knew each other. I can't go back on it without ruining the Institute's relationship with the University of Buenos Aires."

"I don't care *cazzo* about the University of Buenos Aires," Antonietta screamed, tears streaming down her face. "You tell me now that you're not going, or you leave and never come back."

"Postpone your flight to Italy and come with me."

"I can't. I must be in Italy for my parents' wedding anniversary. I promised, and *I keep my promises*."

Antonietta threw James his clothes. He was angered by her unreasonableness, so he dressed silently and walked out of the cottage. He made to get into the car but couldn't bring himself to leave. He walked back to the cottage, but Antonietta had locked the door. He called her name, but there was no answer. After a frustrating few minutes he drove off.

Inside the cottage Antonietta had thrown herself hysterically on to the sofa. It cost her an enormous effort not to respond to James. She knew she was being unreasonable, but the image of James with Carolina stoked a furious jealousy within her that she was unable to control. Torn between a desperate need for the man she loved and anger at his inconstancy, she drank herself into a stupor.

⁓

James dropped off the children for school and drove to Ste. Anne on the off chance that Antonietta had decided not to attend her class with Bill. The previous evening had been the worst he'd ever spent, followed by a sleepless night. He was desperate to see Antonietta and tell her that he wouldn't be going to Argentina.

He passed by Bill's class on the way to his office. He saw Antonietta in the back row. Her face was drawn, and he hoped it was because she too had spent a sleepless night. He reached his office and went morosely through the day's correspondence, which consisted uniquely of thoroughly uninteresting official notices. He was soon lost in thoughts of Antonietta when a knock on the door brought him out of his sad reverie. It was Annya Nowak. He stood up to greet her and sat on his desk. Annya remained standing.

"I just wanted to thank you for helping out Elliot." Her hair, which framed her oval face with perfect symmetry, seemed even blonder than usual and accentuated the deep blue of her eyes. She was wearing a sweater with a low-cut V-neck that afforded a glimpse of the cleavage between her breasts. James was drawn against his will by her seductive attire. He returned her smile.

"He told me it was Arbuthnot's decision to drop the case." She gave James a penetrating look. "Is that the whole story"?

James was in a quandary. He understood now why Hunt had seemed so ungrateful, and why Arbuthnot was in such high spirits. The only way to remedy the situation was to divulge the existence of the affidavits. He couldn't do that without putting the students at risk.

"I had a conversation with Professor Arbuthnot. I think he realized it would do him no good to pursue the matter."

"Really"? Annya's eyes danced flirtatiously, inviting James to dally with her. They were very close to each other.

James didn't have a chance to answer. The door of his office opened, and Antonietta walked in. She took one look at Annya and James together and stopped dead, her eyes blazing with rage. "*Spergiurato*"! she spat at James and marched out.

James was devastated. He couldn't have imagined a worse scenario for their first meeting since yesterday's row. He hurried Annya out of the office, muttered some excuse, and rushed off after Antonietta. Annya watched him go, her suspicions now confirmed. Her playful expression darkened.

"You'll not have him for long, della Chiesa. I promise you that."

James caught up with Antonietta in the parking lot. She was in tears and pushed him away.

"Go back to your blond Annya"! she shouted. "Leave me alone. I hate you, I hate you"!

Before James could get hold of her, she was in the car. He had to jump backwards as she reversed out of the parking space. She drove off quickly, much too quickly. James was gripped by despair and fear. Despair that he'd lost Antonietta, fear that she would have an accident. He walked to his car and went off after the woman he loved.

Unbeknownst to James and Antonietta, the scene between them had been witnessed by Ken Wrangel from a window in the Lecture Hall building. He'd been obsessed with Antonietta ever since her arrival and excited by the prurient rumors about her and Petra Markovic. He'd wanted them to be true so he could fantasize about the two of them. Now he saw with his own eyes what the truth was, and immediately the idea of revenge came to him. He ran to his locker, took out the digital camera he used mainly for taking furtive pictures of sexily dressed girls, and hurried to his car. He reached it just as James was driving off. Wrangel followed him.

James drove through Saint-Sauveur with a sickening feeling in his stomach. He would give anything, do anything to bring Antonietta back to him. Life without her would be unbearable. He felt his body tremble as he turned off the highway towards Ste. Anne. To his relief Antonietta's Jetta was in front of the cottage, She was still in it. He pulled up beside her. They both got out of their cars, and Antonietta threw herself, sobbing, into James's arms.

"*Perdonami, perdonami,*" she implored between their kisses.

"There's nothing to pardon," he told her, stroking her long dark hair, "I love you, and I'm not going to Argentina."

Antonietta laid her head on James's shoulder. "I love you, and you must go to Argentina." She glanced up at him, her eyes glistening with joy through her tears. "I'm glad you said you wouldn't go."

James stroked her cheek. "A promise is a promise, isn't it"?

He was answered by a kiss of such passion that it left him in a daze. Antonietta laughed at his stunned expression, put her arm in his, and walked him into the cottage.

~

Wrangel had parked on the road once James turned off down the driveway to the cottage. He made his way stealthily through the trees until he came close enough to take a photograph. His camera recorded in still pictures the whole scene between the two lovers. He made his way back to the car and went through the photographs he'd taken.

"I've got you, you bastard," he said out loud, savoring the compromising images that would ruin James Markham's career.

~

Blissfully unaware of the danger that menaced them, James and Antonietta were frantically making up for the torment they'd been through. Suddenly Antonietta broke off their lovemaking.

"What was she doing in your office"? James explained. "That's not why she came to see you. You know that." It was true, James admitted, feeling guilty for the attraction he'd felt for Annya. "I don't want you talking to her ever again." James didn't reply and began to play with her nipples. This always stimulated her libido, and thankfully for James she forgot about Annya.

It was after a late lunch that they discussed Argentina. "I promised not to go, and I'll keep that promise," James told Antonietta. She shook her head. "No, you have to go, I realize that, but you must promise not to see Carolina."

"I shall go through hell while you're there," she added.

"I shall go through hell the whole time you're away in Italy."

Antonietta put her arms around him. "Really? I'm looking forward to it."

James was horrified. "Do you mean that"?

Antonietta shook her head. "Of course not. I'll miss you beyond endurance. You know that. I said it just to punish you. After you left yesterday I spent the worst hours of my life. I wanted to die."

James was appalled "Promise me never to have thoughts like that again."

"Only if you promise never to leave me like that again."

"It was you who locked the door."

"You could have a broken a window or something. Or pleaded with me until I couldn't resist any longer." Antonietta's eyes were full reproach. "Instead, you just left me."

Realizing that he was on the losing end of the discussion, James pulled off the dressing gown that covered Antonietta's nakedness and began to caress her. She squirmed in delight. However, before surrendering completely she acquired her promise.

Despite their passionate reconciliation, both James and Antonietta remained unsettled. For all the promises that James made, Antonietta couldn't overcome her fear that one day he would leave her as he had after their quarrel. James himself was beset by guilt for having driven off, abandoning Antonietta to her almost suicidal despair. They sought comfort in unremitting bouts of frenzied lovemaking. James came to the cottage every afternoon and most evenings, ignoring Veronica's complaints. Her suspicions were still directed at James's supposed drinking, but the lovers both realized that sooner or later she would sense the truth.

The strain of their situation began to show. At their Sunday get-together at Danny's that weekend, Bill remarked that they both seemed pale and tense.

"You can't go on like this. Either you split up, or you get married."

Antonietta shot Bill a look of sheer horror. "How can you even think of us splitting up? It would kill me." She pressed herself against James.

Bill regretted the clumsiness of his remark. "I didn't mean it," he told an ashen Antonietta. "I'm just trying to make you two face up to reality."

Later in the car James tried again to persuade Antonietta to marry him.

"Wait until I come back from Italy. We'll talk about it then."

This eternal procrastination aggravated James, who began to wonder whether she would ever agree. He was in a somber mood when he arrived home. The house was in darkness, and he sat in the living room, sipping a scotch. "Perhaps we should indeed split up," he mused, but the very thought of it made him feel sick to his stomach.

⁓

Thankfully, their day of deliverance arrived. It was Friday, December 7. Term was over, and they were driving to Montreal. They had before them a whole week together. For the first time in what seemed an eternity, they would wake up in each other's arms. James glanced across at Antonietta, awed as always by the sheer perfection of her profile. She turned her head towards him. Her eyes were sparkling with happiness. He was so overcome by her resplendent beauty that he momentarily lost control of the car and swerved into the next lane. An irate Quebecois sounded his horn, and James quickly righted the car's trajectory.

"I nearly had us killed," he remarked.

Antonietta nestled up against him. "What would it have mattered? We would have died together."

James was troubled by Antonietta's words. Ever since the night he'd left her after their quarrel, the idea of death had seemed to obsess her. Just yesterday he'd found her reading a novel about Mayerling*.

"Why such sinister thoughts? Is it because you were reading about Rudolf and Vetsera"?

"Probably, but don't worry, James, a week alone with you will chase away all my chimeras."

They arrived at Le Reine Elizabeth about five and immediately went to their room. Within no time Antonietta was naked and lying on the bed, waiting impatiently for her lover.

"Men wear too many clothes," she complained.

For some reason the comment made James extremely jealous. "I don't like you talking about men in general."

Antonietta sat up and pulled him, half undressed, down on to the bed. She removed the rest of his clothes with an expertise that only served to increase James's jealousy. She came on top of him, dangling her succulent breasts provocatively before his eyes. He grasped them, turned Antonietta over on her back, and devoured their luscious softness. Antonietta squealed with delight and pushed James down her body.

"Don't you want me to shave first"?

"No, I want to feel your tongue right there, right now."

They made love with a dissolute abandon that had deserted them in the oppressive days leading up to their departure. All their problems dissipated in the silk sheets of their hotel bed. The Institute, Veronica, the constant need to hide and lie seemed to belong to another world far away from the splendor of their room overlooking the Place Ville Marie. Afterwards they took a shower together, which degenerated into another orgiastic bout of making love. Then Antonietta sent James down to the bar in his tuxedo while she prepared herself.

When Antonietta appeared about half an hour later, there seemed to emanate a collective gasp from the customers of the bar. Her new dress was long and cream-colored; it clung to her body and exhibited a low décolleté that was accentuated by the buttons on the bodice, which seemed to strain under her sumptuous bosom; it was supported by two thin shoulder straps that invited to be thrust aside, letting the dress fall and revealing the full splendor of her nudity. She was wearing her hair down, the dark cascade highlighting the clarity of her dress. Her eyes sparkled aside the tasteful mascara, and the soft, inviting contours of her lips glistened beneath the glossy pale-red lipstick. Instead of a necklace she wore a beige choker. In her ears she wore studs of emerald, one hidden by the flow of her hair. She was a picture of such sensuous perfection that James was speechless. Even the waiters seemed paralyzed, and James was vaguely aware of a strange silence descend upon the room as if no conversation could contend with Antonietta's matchless beauty.

All eyes were riveted on her as she sat down opposite James. She gave him a luminous smile in which there was also coquettishness. She knew the effect she was having on him, and she rejoiced at it.

"James, are you going to stare at me or order me a drink"?

"I'm going to stare at you. I know I always say this, but I've never seen you looking lovelier than at this moment. It's almost unearthly." James did, however, beckon the waiter.

"I'd like a gin martini," Antonietta told the waiter, who was staring at her in wonder. She had to repeat her order.

They took a taxi to the Place des Arts. It was a short ride, and normally taxi drivers react very grumpily, but this time the man was too busy gazing into the rearview mirror at Antonietta to complain. "Thank God, she's wearing a coat." James thought. "Otherwise we'd probably have an accident."

Once in the Opera House, James guided Antonietta to the cloakroom. This time it was the woman taking the coats who stared at her. "*Vous êtes ravissante, Madame,*" she said. Antonietta smiled at her and took James's arm in a proprietary gesture. Compliments from other women always troubled her. The woman came back for James's coat, and they walked away to the stairs leading to the hall. To Antonietta's surprise, James took the direction of the boxes.

"Unfortunately, we're not alone. But it's better than sitting in the hall."

There were two other couples already in the box. They were French Canadian and clearly from the upper strata of society. The women were very well dressed, their hair and make-up immaculate, and the men, like James, were wearing tuxedos. The men fell over themselves to greet Antonietta. The women were silent. All four eyed James with some animosity, suspecting that he was an English Canadian. They relaxed when he addressed them in perfect French.

"*Vous êtes français, Monsieur*"? asked one of the men.

"*Moitié,*" James replied.

Antonietta pinched him. "*Bugiardo,*" she whispered.

This was the extent of the conversation, and the opera soon started.

Tosca was Antonietta's favorite opera, but this time she felt an even greater intimacy with the two main characters. For her it could have been James singing Cavaradossi's lovely aria *Recondita harmonia*, comparing his dark-haired mistress with the blond Attavanti, and she found herself in the passionate jealousy of Floria Tosca. The music swept her away into a world of her and James, a world where no one else existed, a world that perished in the cruelty of the police chief, Baron Scarpia. She grasped James's arm as she listened to Scarpia's final aria, thinking of Arbuthnot. She was white when James led her to the bar in the interval.

"It's an opera, Antonietta. Scarpia is Scarpia and Arbuthnot is Arbuthnot."

"If I'm Tosca, as you keep telling me, then Scarpia can be Arbuthnot," Antonietta insisted, her eyes darkening with fear.

It took James some time to calm her down, but by the end of the interval she'd recovered her spirits. "Am I really as impossible as Tosca"?

"Absolutely."

She poked him in mock indignation, and he grasped hold of her and kissed her on the lips. "You're dreadful," she scolded, using her handkerchief to wipe James's face. "Now I've got to redo my lipstick"

The second act of *Tosca* contains the dramatic confrontation between Tosca and Scarpia as the heroine pleads for her lover's life. The exquisite beauty of Tosca's aria *Vissi d'arte* brought Antonietta near to tears, and she laid her head on James's shoulder. "*Ti amo*," she whispered. In the end Tosca knifes Scarpia and, refusing his pleas for help, condemns him to die a damned man. Antonietta shuddered at Tosca's terrible words "*Muori, muori dannato*," and the dripping contempt of her final comment as she contemplates Scarpia's corpse, "*E avanti a lui tremava tutta Roma*."

They decided to skip the third act. Both found the music far below the beauty and drama of the previous two acts. Besides, Antonietta was hungry. James teased her.

"All you ever think about is eating."

"That's untrue," she protested. "I think much more about sex."

The man handing back her coat was Italian. He understood the remark and looked enviously at James.

"Well, what's it to be? Sex or food"? Antonietta threw her arms around James, her eyes sparkling with delight. "Both, Food first, then sex."

It had been their intention to dine in a restaurant after the opera, but Antonietta wanted to be alone with James in their room. They ordered a bottle of Barolo and some sandwiches, which were left untouched while they lay on the bed, clasped together. Antonietta poured out all her fears. One day he would leave her; their relationship was sinful, and they would be separated as a punishment; he would succumb to Carolina's charms in Buenos Aires. James let her talk while holding her close to him, stroking her hair and occasionally wiping away the tears from her cheeks. He knew he was responsible for this crisis. He'd driven off in pique after their quarrel and waited for Antonietta to come to him. She'd done this, only to find him with Annya. It was an experience that had affected her deeply, and he was ashamed of his part in it.

"I know why you have all these thoughts. It's my fault, but I swear to you that I'll never drive off like that again. I swear it."

Antonietta opened the drawer of the night table and took out a Gideon's bible.

"I'm not swearing on that," James protested, "It's a Protestant bible."

Antonietta burst out laughing and threw her arms around him "You're impossible. You're so prejudiced." Her eyes had recovered their sparkle, and they were gleaming with amusement. James was about to reply, but Antonietta put her hand over his mouth. "Isn't it about time you made love to me"?

They had the Barolo and sandwiches in the early hours, and soon they would have to leave for the airport and their early morning flight to Guadalajara via Mexico City. After a short nap they started very sleepily to get dressed. Antonietta was wearing a pair of very tight jeans and a sweater that seemed to James to be at least two sizes too small for her. With her lovely face still softened by the afterglow of their night of love, she was a picture of blatant sensuality.

"How am I supposed to keep my hands off you"?

"You're not."

They nearly missed their plane.

*Chapter 25*

# Saturday, December 8, 2001 to Wednesday December 12, 2001

THEY ARRIVED IN GUADALAJARA a little after four in the afternoon on Saturday. They took a taxi and drove the fifteen minutes from the airport to the historic center of the city where their hotel was situated. The Hotel Morales Historico is a magnificent colonial-style building located near the Plaza de la Liberación, across from which arises the impressive Cathedral, which took a hundred years to build. The hotel rooms are arranged around a multi-story patio, whose vaulted arches and worked iron railings reminded Antonietta of southern Spain. James had reserved a junior suite, which was much grander than its name suggested. It was tastefully furnished in the same colonial style. Antonietta tipped the young Mexican Indian who had escorted them to the suite.

It was Antonietta's first experience of Mexico, and she was fascinated by the purity of the boy's Spanish. "I know it sounds awful," she commented, "but it's strange to hear such pure Castilian from an Indian."

James laughed. "At least the Spanish gave them something in return for all the gold they stole."

They showered and dressed. For once Antonietta didn't insist on James making love to her straightaway. She was too curious to see the city. James took her up to the panoramic terrace on the roof of the hotel.

She gazed in wonder at the architectural wonders of Guadalajara: the Cathedral, the Teatro Degollado, the Government Palace and the other buildings that clustered around the squares of the historic city. It was strange for Antonietta to hear Spanish spoken around her. It was ages since she'd last been in Spain. She liked the way Mexicans spoke the language, pronouncing "c" as an "s" and not a "th" and omitting the annoying Spanish lisp from the final "s". Some rather loud Americans at the next table enchanted her less.

"So, this is what it'll be like when we're married"?

"What do you mean"?

"Less sex and more sightseeing."

Antonietta downed the rest of her red wine, a Mexican one that was surprisingly good, and stood up. "I'll make you eat those words."

"Literally"? James enquired, and they both had a fit of giggles that greatly amused their American neighbors.

"Like to laugh, these Mexicanos, don't they"? one of them observed loudly.

"Ignorant people," Antonietta fumed. "They can't even tell the difference between Italian and Spanish."

After a bout of sex they showered and made their way down to the hotel's elegant dining room, El Ruedo. Happily, the Mexicans respect the Spanish tradition of late dining, and they were able to enjoy an entrée of tamales, a main course of steak tampiqueña and the ubiquitous flan for dessert.

"The Mexicans think they invented the flan. In reality, it's a legacy from the French."

Antonietta's hackles rose at this mention of the French, and she wrinkled up her nose in disgust. "That's the last one I'm eating" She looked so adorable that James couldn't resist kissing her in front of two very surprised Mexican waiters. Such public displays of affection were rare in El Ruedo.

As they passed the reception desk on their way up to their room, James asked about the times of Mass at the Cathedral.

"*A las nueve y las once*, the man replied, looking quite flustered.

"What was wrong with him"? Antonietta asked.

"I suspect he thought you were my mistress, so when I asked about

Mass times, he thought he'd made a mistake and felt embarrassed. Now he thinks you're my wife."

"Why"?

James laughed and took her into his arms. "Because, Antonietta, a man doesn't normally take his mistress to Mass."

"I'm not a normal mistress."

They arrived at their room and were soon in bed. James cuddled Antonietta's naked body. The touch of her skin aroused his desire for her, and he bent down for a kiss. She was already fast asleep, and he let her be. The weeks after their quarrel had been difficult for both, in particular for Antonietta. Tonight she'd seemed so content, and the peaceful look on her face as she slept touched James profoundly. He kissed her gently on the forehead and whispered "Goodnight, Lady Markham."

He had no idea why he addressed her in this way, but it made him feel ridiculously happy.

Sunday morning they woke up in each other's arms and made love lazily. They had time for a quick expresso before making their way across the Plaza de Armas to the Cathedral to hear Mass. James explained to Antonietta that the Plaza had originally been a garbage dump. The kiosk in the middle was built in Paris, and the four sculptures in the square represented the four seasons. To the right of the Plaza was the imposing Government Palace and right in front of them, the Cathedral.

Antonietta was impressed by the heterogeneity of the worshippers. There were Spanish-style duennas, elegantly dressed middle-class couples and their scrubbed children, young people in more casual clothes, and a large congregation of Indians. The Indian men wore spotless white shirts, the women colorful shawls, and some of the little girls had flowers in their hair. Everyone seemed to follow the Mass with a quiet devotion that was often missing in Canada, or Italy for that matter.

After Mass they strolled through the Plaza de la Liberación past the Teatro Degollado and along Morelos Street to an old-fashioned Mexican restaurant where they had a late breakfast. It seemed to Antonietta more like lunch. There was ham, eggs, steak, green and red chili sauce, salsa and guacamole. The waiter suggested coffee, but Antonietta balked at the insipid-looking *café Americano*. She plumped for red wine.

"It's more like lunch anyway," she explained defensively.

James agreed and changed his order, "*Olvide el café,*" he told the waiter. "*Tambien tomaré una copa de vino tinto.*"

Once lunch was finished, they had intended to return to their hotel room, but on the way they came across a horse-drawn carriage that provided a sightseeing tour of the historic city.

"James, please."

James looked distrustfully at the horse, but he couldn't refuse, particularly as Antonietta had already jumped with childlike enthusiasm into the carriage. The ride took them past a white marble building. James pointed to it.

"That's the Rectorate of the University of Guadalajara. That's where my meeting is tomorrow."

Antonietta stared in admiration at the neo-classical splendor of the building. "It looks too impressive for a university rectorate."

"It was originally intended to be the State Legislature."

The carriage wound its way through the wide streets past other imposing buildings and graceful residential areas. The brilliant blue of the sky and the warm sun on her arms chased away the lugubrious thoughts that had beset Antonietta in the gloom of the Canadian winter. She'd never felt so close to James and so completely happy. Their quarrel now seemed inconsequential and their predicament a minor irritant compared to the passion that united them. If James had suggested abandoning everything and staying in Mexico, she would have had difficulty denying him.

James was not particularly looking forward to his meeting at the Rectorate. He knew that the University of Guadalajara was keen to sign an undergraduate exchange agreement with the Institute, but there were already such agreements with ITESM* at the Monterrey campus, the University of Chile, and soon the University of Buenos Aires. The Institute had only a limited number of students who possessed the necessary Spanish language skills, and not all of these wanted to go on exchanges. All James would be able to offer the University of Guadalajara was a semester at the Institute for up to three students at the Guadalajara fee rate, accompanied by an engagement to promote exchanges with them if this did not encroach on the numbers going to the Institute's present Spanish-speaking partners.

He arrived at the Rectorate and presented himself at the reception desk. After a short wait, two men, one young and the other much older, approached him. The older man held out his hand.

"Good morning, Lord Markham. Welcome to the University of Guadalajara." His Spanish had a strong peninsular accent. "I am Dr. Manuel Ibañez, the Rector of the University. This," he added "is Licenciado Gerardo Blas, the director of our international program."

James was completely taken aback. Apart from the use of his noble title, he was surprised that the Rector himself would greet him. Mexican universities, like their counterparts throughout the Latin world, were extremely hierarchical, and it was very unusual for a Rector to even acknowledge the existence of an Assistant Dean like James, let alone go out of his way to welcome him. Clearly it had to do with his title, but how in hell's name did this Spaniard know about it?

The Rector was clearly pleased with the effect of his introduction on James. "We have a friend in common," he told James. "The Marqués de San Vincente."

James was irritated by the self-satisfied look on the Rector's face and couldn't resist correcting him. "The Marqués is not really my friend. My friend is his son, Don Rodrigo de Fuentes y Talavera," he explained with a hint of disdain in his voice that did not escape the Rector.

"Well," the latter said, "I'll leave you with Licenciado Blas to discuss business."

The clear insinuation was that a Rector had more important matters to attend to than mere student exchanges.

*cₘ*

James managed to escape from the Rectorate without meeting the overbearing Rector again. He walked back to the hotel and found Antonietta waiting for him in the lobby. She was wearing her tight jeans and an even tighter blouse that gave everyone a very clear idea of the shapely extent of her breasts. James was tempted to make a comment on her lack of modesty, but Antonietta forestalled him by a kiss.

"Now he's sure you're my mistress." James nodded in the direction of the receptionist.

It was one o'clock, and they retired to the bar for an apéritif. Antonietta recounted her visit to the market, which she hadn't found particularly interesting. "I can't get excited about vegetables. So I went and sat in the Plaza de los Mariachis and listened to some music." She turned her dark expressive eyes on James. "I started missing you terribly and came back to be here when you returned." Despite her hunger, she agreed to go up to the bedroom.

"If you dress like that, you must suffer the consequences."

They ate lunch around three, which is the normal time in Mexico. It was late afternoon when they arrived at Tlaquepaque, a pretty little town southwest of Guadalajara. It was well known for its pottery and the charm of its narrow streets and shaded squares. Antonietta bought a little figurine as a memento of their happiness together in Mexico, but they soon tired of looking at pottery and found a courtyard café where they sat sipping wine. It was another sunny day, and Antonietta soaked up the appeasing warmth. Here, faraway from everybody, it was easy to believe that there were just the two of them. Husband and wife or lover and mistress, it made no difference.

That evening James took her to La Destilería. It looked like a former Tequila factory, but James suspected that this was just the décor as it was part of a chain of restaurants. It served Mexican food and was stocked with over a hundred brands of Tequila. He persuaded Antonietta to try a light one as an aperitif, but she was not impressed. "It tastes like medicine," she complained and asked him to order her a glass of white wine. They had a traditional meal of Aztec soup, tacos and a *tres leches* cake for dessert. They drank a Mexican Cabernet Sauvignon from Lower California. James managed to persuade Antonietta to try another Tequila as a digestif. He chose a very old, heavy Tequila that tasted quite different from the astringent apéritif.

"It's almost as good as a cognac. It's a pity most people drink only the younger, lighter stuff."

"I prefer cognac," Antonietta replied.

James paid, and they left the restaurant. It was another late night.

The next day James picked up a rental car, and they drove to the coast. On the way they passed some eerie mud flats and crossed a long bridge that seemed to carve the mountains in two. They had lunch in the picturesque colonial city of Colima, which is dominated by a threatening volcano that occasionally belches black smoke. Between Colima and Manzanillo, where they were headed, they drove past a coconut forest. The tall trees with their rather obscene clusters of nuts swayed in the light breeze. Antonietta giggled at the sight and nestled up to James. "Wait till we get to the hotel," he said. "Otherwise we'll have an accident." Antonietta paid no attention and continued to excite him.

They arrived at Las Hadas. The beach of the resort stretches out to a cove that is sheltered from the turbulence of the Pacific Ocean. Behind it rise majestically the brilliant white buildings of the hotel and the surrounding apartments with their minarets and domes. They look down over marbled arcades of cobblestone paths interspersed with little *plazas*, fountains, and tropical flowers. "It's like something out of a thousand and one nights," Antonietta exclaimed. She slipped off her shoes and ran off over the hot sand to the sea. She dipped her feet into the calm and inviting water. James watched her, marveling at the difference between the blithe young woman playing in the sea and the tense and fearful Antonietta of a few days ago.

They checked in. Their room contained the same Moorish motifs with arches and a marble floor. It looked over the complex and beyond to the sea. Antonietta could hardly tear her eyes away from the exotic beauty of the scene: the dazzling white of the buildings, the pale yellow of the sand glistening in the heat, the turquoise of the sea, and the azure blue of the sky. James came up behind her and squeezed her in his arms.

"Happy"?

Antonietta sighed. "I could stay here all my life."

They decided to change into bathing suits and make straightaway for the beach. Antonietta disappeared into the bathroom and emerged topless wearing a tiny string that exposed her buttocks and barely covered her sex. She fluttered her eyes provocatively at James, whose jaw dropped.

"You can't wear *that*"!.

"Why not"?

"For three very good reasons. Firstly, I'm not having you exhibiting your body to every Tom, Dick and Harry on the beach. Secondly, this is Mexico, not France or Italy, and they'll probably lock you up for moral outrage. Thirdly, with the sight of you like that, I'll have to spend the day on the beach lying on my stomach."

Antonietta came up to James and made him sit on the bed. She took down his swimming trunks and began to fondle him. "What's the main reason? Jealousy, morality or an inability to control your sexual urges"? At these last words Antonietta used her mouth to pleasure James. When she'd finished, she looked up.

"Well"?

James drew her face up to his and kissed her. "Probably jealousy," he admitted. It was the answer Antonietta wanted to hear, and she lay down contentedly beside him. Once she'd been properly satisfied, she took a more decent two-piece bikini out of her case.

"Did you really intend to wear that string bikini"? There was still a hint of jealousy in James's voice.

Antonietta's eyes twinkled. "No, James. It's not a bikini, it's the string I wore our first night together."

The twenty-four hours they spent at Las Hadas passed like a dream for Antonietta. They lay on the sand, basking in the Mexican sun, they swam languidly in the warm sea, frequently they would return to the room to gratify their hot, lustful bodies, and when they were hungry, they would walk along the beach to the restaurant and eat deliciously fresh seafood to the sound of waves lapping gently against its façade. When they were forced to leave in order to return to Guadalajara, it was like Adam and Eve being turned out of the Garden of Eden. Antonietta made James promise to bring her back one day.

For James, it was another Antonietta that he experienced in Las Hadas. It was as if the sun and magic of Mexico had stripped away the veneer of fear and guilt and revealed her natural carefree high spirits.

Her beauty glowed in its natural setting, and her body responded like a pure-bred to the slightest touch. She had the intense sensuality of the dark women of the south. For James, the temptation to linger, to stay forever was strong, but he knew he had to resist. His children and Antonietta's religious scruples still stood in their way, however happy they might feel at this moment. It would be a long road before they could openly live together, somewhere on the Mediterranean, where the sea and the sand and the sun would complement and succor their love for each other.

*Chapter 26*

# Thursday, December 13, 2001 to
# Wednesday December 19, 2001

T HEY ARRIVED BACK IN Montreal on Thursday around six in the evening. They passed without a problem through customs and were about to make their dispirited way to the parking lot when they literally bumped into Danny. He was all smiles with his arm around a very pretty redhead.

"This is my daughter, Ceara," he told them. "This is my friend, James Markham," Danny informed Ceara. He wasn't quite sure how to introduce Antonietta, so he said nothing.

"I'm pleased to meet you, Mr. Markham," the girl said politely with a delightful Irish accent. Turning to Antonietta, she added, "And you too, Mrs. Markham."

Antonietta's Latin nature came to the fore, and she kissed Ceara warmly on both cheeks. "I'm not Mrs. Markham," she whispered, "I'm James's scarlet woman." The two of them laughed while James and Danny looked on awkwardly.

"She might as well know straightaway," Antonietta explained. "Isn't that so, Ceara"? The girl nodded, and the two of them burst out laughing again at the men's solemnity.

"You're right," James agreed, marveling at the ease and rapidity with which Antonietta had established a rapport with Danny's daughter.

After a few minutes' chatter, he and Antonietta resumed their doleful walk to the car.

Antonietta clung to James during the depressing drive from the airport. The weather didn't help. It was a typically cold, overcast and snowy winter's day in Quebec. Their spirits sank ever further as they neared Ste. Anne and the inevitable parting. The magic of Mexico was no more, and Antonietta had tears in her eyes as she implored James to spend time with her before returning to Prévost.

Once in the cottage Antonietta clutched James close to her and wept on his shoulder. "Make love to me," she murmured, trying desperately to control her sobs. He led her into the bedroom and undressed her. He gazed at her naked body, which bore the traces of the Mexican sun. He took off his clothes quickly, and they made love, not with the bold ardor of Mexico but with anguished frenzy. Twice James attempted to leave but couldn't. Around eleven he finally tore himself away from Antonietta's outstretched arms and dressed. Weary and sad, he kissed her goodbye. She followed him to the door of the cottage and held him back for one more impassioned embrace.

Veronica was waiting for James. "Why are you this late"?

"The plane was late. Air Canada, you know."

Veronica smiled. "You must be tired. Let's go to bed."

James followed her into the bedroom, hoping against hope that Veronica's pleasant manner didn't presage anything intimate. He needn't have worried. Within moments she was fast asleep, leaving him to reminisce with bitter nostalgia on the last week.

The day of Antonietta's departure for Italy inexorably arrived, and she awoke with a sick feeling in her stomach. It was only three weeks, but her need for James was so all-consuming that she was unable to conceive of life without him. On the rare days she didn't see him, she was reduced to misery. How would she cope with three weeks? She was tempted to cancel her flight, but she felt bound by the promise to attend her parents' anniversary. "It will be nice to see my friends again," she told herself without much conviction.

Antonietta put some clothes in the washing machine, made herself an expresso and started to pack. It was only seven o'clock, and the flight was not until five in the afternoon. James had promised to come to the cottage around ten, which left them four hours before they had to leave for the airport. By nine o'clock she couldn't stand waiting any longer and called James. She learned with a transport of joy that he was already on his way.

James had slept little, torn between sweet images of the blissful time in Mexico and dread of the separation from Antonietta. He had difficulty believing it could really happen. Now the fateful day had dawned, and soon he would be driving Antonietta to the airport.

James was used to Antonietta throwing herself into his arms on his arrival in the cottage, often in tears, but today she did it in complete despair.

"I can't go," she sobbed. "I can't live without you."

Without a word, James led her to the bedroom, laid her down on the bed, and lay next to her, holding her tightly. He waited for her to calm down.

"Antonietta, it's only three weeks, and when you come back, I'll meet you in Montreal. We'll spend the weekend together."

"You promise"?

"Absolutely."

They made love in a very traditional way. James knew why. Whenever Antonietta needed reassurance, she always wanted to feel him within her, to make love like a married couple as she'd put it once. "Not much of a recommendation for marriage," he'd teased her, "I think I'll keep you as my mistress." Today there was no place for facetiousness as they alternated between spasms of sexual pleasure and emotional distress.

As James caressed her face after one of these spasms, Antonietta's eyes suddenly became very serious, apprehensive even.

"Tell me honestly, James, if you'd known beforehand how much anguish our passion would bring us, would you have let me stay after that party"?

James smiled and kissed Antonietta softly on the lips. "How can you doubt it? From the first moment I saw you in church, I was your's. Once we were alone together for the first time after that party, there was only one possible outcome. Neither of us had any choice."

"Do you regret it"?

"Isn't the anguish worth the bliss when we're together"?

"Oh yes, a million times, But to be honest, I never thought my love for you would so alter me. I hardly recognize myself. I never used to cry, but with you I'm always in tears. You must get sick of it."

James laughed and played with Antonietta's disheveled hair. "*Cara*, when your eyes fill with tears, and they roll slowly down your cheeks, you look so adorably fragile that I can never resist taking you into my arms and drowning your distress in sexual pleasure."

"Between us it's not sex," Antonietta objected.

"It's a pretty good imitation."

"Don't make fun of me. Sex is when two people come together purely for pleasure. That's not the case with us. At least not with me." She gave James a meaningful look and went on. "Making love to you is the only way I can fully express the depth of my feelings for you. That's why I do anything you want, without reserve or shame. It's as if I'm offering you my soul each time in an amorous sacrifice. No, James, don't call it sex, it's making love in the real sense of the term." The last words were pronounced almost defiantly.

James saw from the clock that they were in danger of being late for Antonietta's plane, but he was moved by her words even if he didn't share her almost mystic view of their sexual union. He knew he had to find an adequate reply, particularly as they would be separated for three weeks.

"For me," he explained, "our passion for each other has an emotional and a physical side. They both need and feed off each other. When I feel your closeness, kiss you, hold you, talk with you, that satisfies my emotional need for you. When we make love, that fulfills my physical need for you."

"Another woman could fulfill that physical need."

"No, because my physical need for you comes from my emotional need for you, and both derive from the passion that binds me irrevocably to you."

"Make sure that you keep your physical need intact for my return from Italy. No Annya Nowak or Carolina."

The drive to the airport and the brief wait before Antonietta left to go through security was too painful for both of them. After a while they could stand it no longer. It would be better to get the parting over and done with. Antonietta stood up and fighting back tears made James promise again and again to think of her every moment of the day.

"Please, please, no Carolina or Annya."

He promised. "I shall be here on January 4 to take you to the hotel."

After one final passionate kiss, Antonietta tore herself away and hurried off, not daring to look back. James watched her go through security and disappear. A terrible feeling of emptiness came over him, and he walked slowly back to the parking lot. It was only then he realized that Antonietta hadn't given him her phone number in Florence.

❦

No member of Antonietta's family was there to greet her in Florence when she arrived promptly at ten past one in the afternoon. "What a fine beginning for my holiday," she thought grimly. She was making for the taxi stand when she encountered the family's faithful old retainer, Tonio. At least they hadn't completely forgotten about her.

"*Come va la nostra contessina,*" Tonio asked with a broad smile. All the servants were very fond of Antonietta. She kissed him affectionately on both cheeks.

"*Bene, grazie, Tonio,*" she replied. This was a lie as she'd spent the whole journey fighting a voracious jealousy. At times she'd persuaded herself that James would leave her for Carolina or at least take the Argentinean to his bed; at other times she'd managed to console herself that, if he loved her as much as he said, he would remain faithful to her. Even this consolation could not overcome her feeling of emptiness.

It was strange to be back in Florence. The sights were familiar, but Antonietta felt herself a foreigner. Her heart and her existence were elsewhere. Tonio, who was used to Antonietta's vivacious high spirits, interpreted her silence as disappointment that only a servant had come to meet her.

"The Countess della Chiesa and the Count Giovanni with his wife are in Rome with the Countess Carla," Tonio explained, "The Count della Chiesa is still in Perugia at a conference."

"I hope they'll be back tomorrow."

"They are coming back this evening, *contessa*. Anna is preparing dinner for you all."

Anna was Tonio's wife. They had met when she was a young chambermaid. Now, well into her seventies and like her husband without any real job in the household, she loved cooking. Antonietta's mother had insisted that they remain with the family instead of being pensioned off. It was the other, humane side of her aristocratic upbringing. "If only she were as kind to me as she is to the servants," Antonietta thought sadly.

Anna embraced her warmly, and Antonietta had to stop the old woman from carrying the suitcases up to her room. She was still a formidable person, but age deserved respect. Antonietta called for Silvio, the young servant her mother had hired just before she left for Canada. After he'd deposited the two suitcases in her room, Antonietta reflected guiltily on her self-indulgence. Whatever would James think of her behavior? Then she remembered Carolina. "I am a countess," she reminded herself defiantly. "Why shouldn't I behave like one"?

The defiance couldn't mask for long the emptiness and longing she felt. She wanted desperately to call James, but they'd forgotten to set a time when he would be available on the cell phone. Had it been deliberate on his part? "My God," she thought, "it's been less than twenty-four hours, and I'm already going out of my mind." She forced herself to unpack. She put on a disk of Umberto Tozzi, but it reminded her too much of the first night with James, so she changed to Laura Pausini. This reduced her to tears, and in the end she settled on Placido Domingo singing *Zarzuela* music*.

There was a knock on the door. It was Silvio. "A telephone call for you, *contessa*."

Antonietta's heart jumped for joy although it was unlikely to be James. She deliberately hadn't given him her telephone number for fear he might find out who she was. She raced downstairs and took the call in her father's study. It was her mother. Disappointed, she fought back tears as she assured her mother that she was well. "We shall be home around six, and your father is expected shortly afterwards." Her mother's tone was apologetic. Like Tonio, she interpreted Antonietta's reticence as disappointment at their absence on her arrival from Canada.

288

Antonietta couldn't stand it anymore. She left the house and drove her mother's car into the town of Fiesole. She went to the post office and dialed James's cell number. There was no answer. She made the same call about ten times before he answered. Antonietta heaped reproaches on him.

"Where were you? I was going out of my mind."

"Antonietta, how could I know when you were going to call"?

"You should have been waiting."

James ignored the rebuke "I love you, and I miss you. I didn't sleep all night."

"Well, I hope you didn't! To think of you sound asleep while I was tortured by fear and jealousy would be too much."

James didn't like the drift of the conversation. "Listen, Antonietta, it's bad enough being apart without letting our fears make us quarrel. I love you, and you have absolutely no reason to be jealous. No reason at all."

Antonietta was somewhat mollified. "Tell me that again."

James obeyed. "What about you? You haven't told me anything."

"Why do you think I'm being so unreasonable. I'm devoured by longing for you. I love you far too much."

"Well, don't try to love me less."

"You know I couldn't."

They talked for another half an hour in the same vein. Antonietta made James promise again and again not to see Carolina. He asked for her phone number in Florence. She demurred.

"It's better if you don't call me here. Otherwise, I'll have to answer a lot of questions I don't want to," she explained. She couldn't gauge James's reaction as it was cut off by a boy's voice asking for his father.

"I must go, I love you," he said, and the line went dead.

Antonietta felt depressed. Far from comforting her, the telephone call had brought home the distance separating them. Suddenly, their love seemed brittle and endangered. "Damn that university in Buenos Aires. Why did they have to pick a time when I was away in Italy to invite James"?

She started to drive home but remembered to her horror that she didn't have the telephone number of James's hotel in Buenos Aires. Why hadn't he given it to her? Was it to punish her for not giving him her number in Florence? Or was it…? Distraught, unable to bear her own thoughts, she raced back to the post office. All the cabins were taken. She waited for what seemed an eternity. When she finally made the call, there was no answer. She tried several more times with the same result.

Feeling sick and dejected, Antonietta drove home and remained in her room until her mother arrived with Giovanni and Renata. They were obviously pleased to see her, which brought her some solace. Then her father arrived. He embraced her warmly. Despite the dark thoughts that oppressed her, Antonietta enjoyed the meal and the excellent Italian wines her father served in her honor.

Antonietta's fears were quite unfounded. James had never felt more miserable in his whole life than on the drive back to Prévost from the airport. It had taken a superhuman effort to hide this misery from his family. As it was his last evening before leaving for Buenos Aires, he'd felt obliged to spend it with them rather than carousing with the gang. Fixated by Antonietta's absence, it was early morning before he fell asleep. He awoke late and immediately went to the car in the desperate hope that Antonietta would call him. He was immensely glad to hear her voice and felt slightly better after talking to her. He returned to the house to help Peter with his soccer equipment and started to pack for the journey.

He wasn't put out by Antonietta's demurrer over the phone number. He could see her point. If he, in turn, hadn't given her the number of the hotel in Buenos Aires, it was because he'd completely forgotten to book one. When he finished packing, he looked up the Melia. It was located on Reconquista, and the rooms had a view over the River Plate. It was near to the district of Puerto Madero and suitably far from the Plaza San Martín and the temptation of Carolina. As he wasn't sure whether Antonietta would have a chance to call him again before he left, he phoned Bill and gave him the telephone number of the hotel.

James caught the same plane for Toronto as Antonietta had done the day before. The flight from Toronto to Buenos Aires didn't leave until eleven fifteen that night. James was desperate to be alone with his thoughts of Antonietta, and he settled in the Air Canada lounge at Lester Pearson Airport to indulge himself with several whiskies. He had a few more on the flight and lapsed into unconsciousness. By the time he came to, it was only another half hour before they would land at Ezeiza airport.

It was a beautiful summer's afternoon in Buenos Aires. The streets were full of people walking around dressed for summer, and the city buzzed with effervescent life. The terraces of the innumerable cafes were full of people drinking wine, eating the delicious beef dishes for which Buenos Aires is famous, and talking and laughing. James loved Buenos Aires. It pulsated excitement and the sensual enjoyment of life. There was an air of old-world *douceur de vivre* about it. Yes, like all South American cities, it had its fair share of poverty, but walking along these streets one could almost believe one was in Paris.

James took a taxi to the Melia, put away his things, and took a shower. Refreshed, he went for a walk along the promenade at Puerto Madero. It was a district that had been redeveloped with international flair, drawing interest from businessmen, architects and designers from all over the world. One of the trendiest boroughs in Buenos Aires, it was the preferred address for growing numbers of young professionals and retirees alike. James inspected the menus at the various restaurants overlooking the docks and chose one where he could order a *Churrasco*. He returned to the hotel for a short nap. After a couple of aperitifs in the bar, he left for the restaurant. After his meal he went to listen to tango music at the Café Tortoni in the Avenida de Mayo before retiring for the night. The next day he had to be at the University of Buenos by eight o'clock.

It had been impossible for Antonietta to get away to call James again. She could hardly walk out on the family dinner without evoking the very questions she wanted to avoid. Now she was lying in bed thinking of him and wondering where he was. He was probably on his way to Buenos Aires. Her heart ached for him. As she'd drunk a lot of wine, she soon fell asleep. Next morning the ache returned.

The servants were already bustling around to prepare for the family celebration, which would take place after the family attended Sunday Mass. The actual anniversary was the following day, but it was usual to celebrate it on the nearest Sunday.

Paolo and Monica were due to arrive around ten o' clock, unfortunately with her grandmother, Maria Assunta. None of her uncles would be there, and Carla was still in the hospital after having given birth to her first child. Antonietta found it hard to share in the general festive air. "You look tired," her father remarked. It wasn't tiredness, it was the despair of knowing that James would arrive in Buenos Aires that day, and she had no way of contacting him. She felt utterly wretched.

There was a brief respite when Paolo and Monica arrived. They plied her with questions about Canada. Her grandmother was her normal austere self and insisted on speaking in Spanish. Weary and not wishing to add her grandmother's wrath to her present woes, Antonietta dutifully replied in the same language. Her mother beamed with satisfaction.

After Mass the family sat down to eat at two and were still at the table four hours later. Everyone was chatting and complementing Anna on the meal. Antonietta tried to keep up appearances, but her drawn mien did not escape Monica.

"Are you in love, Antonietta"? she whispered.

Antonietta nodded. "Don't tell anyone."

The two left the table and walked outside. Antonietta recounted the story of her passion for James, the fact he was married, and her despair at not being able to contact him in Buenos Aires. She didn't mention Carolina.

"Don't you know someone in Canada who might have the number of the hotel"? Monica asked.

Antonietta's face suddenly brightened. "Monica, you're a genius," she exclaimed. If only she could escape and call Bill straightaway, but that would arouse suspicion. It would have to wait for tomorrow.

The next day, Monday, Paolo and Monica left after breakfast for Rome, taking both Maria Assunta and Caterina with them. Shortly afterwards her father left for work. Antonietta was about to drive into Fiesole when she remembered that none of the servants spoke English.

There was nothing to prevent her phoning from home. It was nine-thirty, which meant it was three-thirty in the morning in Quebec. Hopefully Bill was not in too deep a stupor to hear the phone.

She let the phone ring several times and was on the point of hanging up when Bill answered.

"Who the hell is it"? he grumbled into the phone.

"It's me, Toni. I need James's number in Buenos Aires." Bill's mood changed.

"Toni! How are you? Enjoying yourself"?

"No, Bill, I miss James, and I want that number."

"What makes you think I have it"?

Antonietta's heart sank. If James hadn't even bothered to give it to Bill on the off chance she would call him, what did that mean? She had to grasp the counter on which the telephone was placed to steady herself. Then she heard Bill chuckle, and she exploded.

"Bill, don't play with me like this"! she shouted. "*Give me the number.*"

"Calm down, Toni, I'll get it for you."

There was a brief silence, and then Bill was back with the number. Antonietta thanked him contritely, adding an excuse for her outburst. "I'm going out of my mind, Bill. I never thought it would be this bad."

"The sooner you two get married, the better it'll be for all of us," Bill griped. "If it's any consolation, Jimmy was in poor shape too when he called me with the number."

It was indeed a consolation, and, after hearing this from Bill, Antonietta felt happier than at any moment since she and James had parted at Montreal airport. As the time in Buenos Aires was five hours behind Florence, she waited until eleven o' clock before calling James.

An attractive female voice answered at the hotel. Antonietta's happiness dissolved into suspicious jealousy. Was this Carolina? She waited with bated breath to be put through to James.

James answered the phone on the first ring. "Is it you, Antonietta"? he asked. Antonietta immediately demanded to know who the girl was at the reception desk. James laughed. "I haven't a clue. It's certainly not Carolina. I'm in the Melia, which is far away from the hotel where she works."

"How do you know she still works in the same hotel"?

"I don't." James replied and changed the subject. "You called Bill for the number"?

"Yes, but at first he said he didn't have it. I nearly died. Why didn't you give it to me before I left"?

James explained that he'd forgotten to book a hotel until Saturday morning.

"Do you miss me"? The anxiety in Antonietta's voice was palpable.

"Antonietta, I think of you constantly, and I've never known time go by so slowly. It's excruciating. I never want to be separated from you again. It's much worse than I thought it would be. I long for you. It's like a physical pain."

"I know. I feel the same. I'm never leaving you again."

They spoke for over an hour. The servants might not speak English, but it was clear to all of them that their young countess was head over heels in love. James told Antonietta very gently that he had to get ready. "It's a quarter past seven, and they've organized a damn breakfast for eight."

Antonietta made James stay on the line for another half hour and only let him go with great reluctance. They agreed she would call him again at six in the evening, Buenos Aires time.

"Make sure you're there," Antonietta admonished him.

*Chapter 27*

# Monday December 17, 2001 to Wednesday December 19, 2001

JAMES WAS GLAD TO get to the conference. Meeting colleagues, listening to tedious papers, and giving one himself would provide a welcome diversion from his yearning for Antonietta. Carlos greeted him at the Faculty of Law and took him to a smart café in the nearby Recoleta where James met some of the other professors who were speaking at the conference. Most were from Latin America, but there were two Americans. Consequently the conversation was in English.

After a continental breakfast, which the two Americans clearly found inadequate, they walked back to the Faculty. The conference was opened by a long speech from the Rector. James glanced idly at the program to pass the time. It was then he noticed that the banquet would take place at the Hotel Plaza San Martín. "Oh, my God," he thought, "couldn't they have chosen some other hotel"? It wasn't that he had any intention of being unfaithful to Antonietta, but, if Carolina were still working at the hotel, he could hardly miss seeing her, and that would be enough to trigger a major crisis with his temperamental mistress. It would be even worse if he actually had to talk to her. He could always lie, but little escaped Antonietta's perceptive jealousy.

It was an interesting conference. James gave his paper on the institutional failings of the European Union and the shortcomings of the Treaty of Nice. One of the American professors gave a windy discourse on the federal nature of the EU, with which James violently disagreed and said so quite forcibly. After a pleasant lunch of excellent Argentinean *bife* accompanied by a drinkable Malbec, the conference resumed on the topic of trade relations. A very serious Mexican professor gave a dry but discerning analysis of the economic agreement between Mexico and the EU, for which James acted as moderator.

The day ended at five. Carlos drove James back to the Melia and invited him to dinner that evening. He accepted with alacrity as the prospect of being on his own with only a frantic desire for Antonietta as company was not appealing. They agreed to meet at eight. In the meantime James showered and waited for Antonietta's call, which came at precisely six o'clock. She plied him with questions about his day, and then came the inevitable "Did you see her"?

James could tell that Antonietta was distraught. He told her that he hadn't seen Carolina. He promised--with fingers crossed--not to see her, and he repeated again and again all she meant to him and the infinite depth of his love for her.

"Try to see your friends. It'll occupy your mind and make the time go by faster," he suggested.

"Are you saying that you didn't think of me while you were at the conference"?

"No, I'm not saying that. I think of you all the time, but your absence is more bearable when there's something else going on. If I just sat and moped, I think I'd go mad."

There was silence at the other end of the line before Antonietta replied, "You're right. I've got to get through these three weeks somehow." She couldn't resist adding with a touch of malice, "Anyway, on the nineteenth I'm going to a party full of good-looking young men."

James felt a twinge of jealousy and nearly blurted out where tomorrow's banquet was taking place. Fortunately, he controlled himself. "Remember that I love you," was all he said.

They talked for another half hour, but the distance, their pent-up emotions and jealousies, and the impersonal nature of the communication left them both frustrated. After promising for the umpteenth time not to see Carolina, James rang off. He felt despondent. The carefree days in Mexico seemed far, far away. Not caring for the solitude of his own company, he went down to wait for Carlos in the bar. As he sat pointlessly stirring his whisky with a swizzle stick, he remembered that he hadn't set a time for Antonietta's next call. He'd also forgotten to tell her that he was going out for dinner with Carlos. He hoped to God she didn't call while he was out.

Antonietta felt equally despondent after their phone call. Hearing James so far away exacerbated her fears. She was obsessed by the idea of Carolina, and she didn't forgive James for occupying his thoughts otherwise than with her. She hadn't been planning to attend the Lescia's Christmas party, but now she decided to go. "What's sauce for the goose is sauce for the gander," she told herself. Possibly it would take her mind off James for a few hours.

Antonietta undressed and went to bed. Lying there naked, she yearned for the pleasure James was so adept at giving her. This led her to the realization that she hadn't set a time for their next phone call. She jumped out of bed and dialed the hotel Melia. The same silky female voice answered and put her through to James's room. There was no answer. Suspicious and still smarting from their previous conversation, Antonietta snapped. She left a message telling James that she wouldn't call him anymore. She'd see him on her return to Canada--perhaps.

James didn't enjoy his dinner with Carlos although he vainly tried to give the opposite impression. They were at the Cumaná in the Recoleta, and James had ordered a *churrasco*. He reflected on the last time he'd been there. It was with Bill, and he'd been looking forward to an uncomplicated night with Carolina. Now he was beset by the worry that Antonietta might have called. There was no greater contrast than that between his explosive Italian mistress and the calm, serene Carolina. Yet he couldn't bask in his passion for Antonietta without putting up with the jealousy and temperament that came with it.

"Is something bothering you, James," Carlos asked, noticing his colleague's preoccupation.

James smiled apologetically. "Excuse me for being so rude, Carlos. It's just that I forgot to tell my wife I was having dinner with you, and she'll be upset if she calls and I'm not in the room."

"How long have you been married"? James looked blankly at Carlos. "Well," he explained, "after a few years of marriage, wives normally stop being jealous. They seem to like us out of the way." There was a slight bitterness in Carlos' voice.

"Yes, you're right. I'm probably worrying about nothing."

He could hardly tell Carlos that his so-called wife was in fact his jealous mistress, who was now unlikely to believe he'd been invited by Carlos and was probably imagining him with Carolina.

Carlos dropped James off at the hotel around eleven. James took the elevator and walked apprehensively along the corridor to his room. As he'd dreaded, there was an angry message from Antonietta. He sat down on the bed with a long sigh and put his head in his hands. This separation was not working out very well

Antonietta was unable to sleep. She couldn't put the image of James with Carolina out of her mind. She tried to put a face to the image, but, apart from blond hair and blue eyes, Antonietta had no idea what Carolina looked like. Inevitably the image took on the features of Annya Nowak. How could James do this to her?

Incapable of bearing her torment any longer, the next day Antonietta called her friend Paulina. There was no answer. She called Alessa, who was overjoyed to hear her voice.

"Antonietta"! she cried, trying to make herself heard above the noise of the bar, "You're back"! Antonietta readily agreed to join her in the Bar Fiesco that evening.

Immediately Antonietta arrived at Fiasco's, she felt a tremor go through her body. This was the bar James had frequented as a student, and doubtless in the company of his Spanish girlfriend. She was tempted

to leave, but, seeing Alessa waving madly from across the room and the circle of students around her, she changed her mind.

"So you're the beautiful Countess della Chiesa," one of the students remarked with an admiring look at Antonietta. He smiled at her pleasantly. His Italian had a British accent. It was doubtless for this reason that Antonietta took an instant liking to him.

"I don't know about the beautiful," she replied, returning his smile, "and I'm plain Antonietta, not Countess della Chiesa."

"Fair enough," the student responded. "I'm David Smith-Bannerman, but you may call me just plain David."

The conversation turned to Antonietta's experiences in Canada. Alessa teased her. "Did you meet a handsome lumberjack"? The idea of James as a lumberjack caused Antonietta to burst out laughing. It was her first spontaneously happy reaction since leaving James at Montreal Airport.

They drank and talked into the early hours. Carried away by the infectious gaiety of the company and a rather too liberal indulgence in the bar's rather tart house wine, Antonietta flirted outrageously with David. He was not particularly tall, being, as he explained, Welsh, but he was very dark and quite handsome. "Why not"? she told herself. "It serves James right." Quite unreasonably, she was taken aback when David asked her out.

"David, it's better not. I have a boyfriend in Canada."

She felt rather silly referring to James as her boyfriend, but she could hardly say that he was her married lover. David was obviously disappointed and a little annoyed at having been led on by Antonietta. He left soon afterwards.

"Is it true"? Alessa clamored. "You've got a boyfriend in Canada"? Paulina, who had just joined the group, insisted on knowing all the details.

"Well, he's tall, dark, handsome, and British."

They all wanted more details, but Antonietta wasn't forthcoming. She wouldn't even tell them his name. The only additional information she gave away was that David reminded her of this boyfriend, which is why she'd flirted with him.

"Poor fellow," one of the men commented. "You certainly led him on."

⁓

At home in her room, Antonietta reflected guiltily on the evening. She was ashamed of herself, but James was right. The time passed more easily when you were in company. The thought of James reminded her of the angry message she'd left for him. It was eleven in the evening, which meant it was six in the afternoon in Buenos Aires. James had to be in his room. Frantically she dialed the number of the hotel and waited for the ingratiating voice of the receptionist. It was a man this time, and there was no answer in James's room. Antonietta panicked. If he'd heard her message, perhaps he'd gone down and invited the receptionist. That's why it was a man who answered. She left a new message pleading with James to forgive her.

"I love you, James. I'm out of my mind. *Please, please* be in the next time I call. Please."

She called back at twelve, and James answered. Despite her relief, she couldn't contain her jealousy. She demanded to know where he'd been. "Antonietta, I was bored, and so I went down to the bar to have a few whiskies."

"With whom"?

"No one."

"When are you leaving Buenos Aires"? I won't have any peace until you're back in Canada."

"The conference ends tomorrow, and I leave Thursday."

"Why not tomorrow"? Immediately Antonietta was suspicious again.

"Because there's a dinner on Wednesday evening, which I cannot miss without causing offence."

Antonietta was not pleased with the answer. She was glad to be going to the Lescia's party. "It'll serve him right," she told herself.

⁓

Antonietta looked round at the people attending the Lescia's party. It was such a pleasant change from Canada. Everyone was dressed very elegantly, the women almost all in long dresses and the men in tuxedos. It was so different from the depressing blue jeans, sneakers and formless ski jackets that were the ubiquitous uniform of many Canadians. Worst of all were those ridiculous baseball caps. Antonietta often had the impression that some people in Canada went out of their way to dress badly.

This night Antonietta was wearing a long, dark brown dress that showed off her shapely figure without being openly erotic. It was cut low enough to suggest a hint of cleavage but no more. She wore her hair down and had put on just sufficient make-up to accentuate the brilliance of her eyes and the soft curves of her mouth. Even her mother had congratulated her.

"You look extremely lovely," she told her.

The company was very elegant, but this could not overcome her regrets at coming to the party. She was stuck with Fabio, the Marquis' son, Rodolfo, Count Guardini's son, and their circle of aristocratic friends. They might constitute the cream of Florentine society for her mother, but she found them insufferably arrogant and boring. She was thinking of leaving to call James when a blond woman, who was probably in her mid-thirties, accosted her. Her classic beauty was only rivaled by the sensuality of her attire. Her slinky, white dress was slightly open down to her waist. It afforded a tantalizing glimpse of her shapely breasts and the golden bronzed skin of her stomach and belly. She wore a diamond in her navel. Two slits on each side of the dress exposed her thighs. The striking blond hair was done up in a chignon. She gazed languidly at Antonietta with hazel-colored eyes.

"*Contessa*," she purred, "I've been wanting to meet you. I am the Marquesa de Avila y de la Torre."

"I've just come back from Canada," Antonietta stammered, mesmerized by the Marquesa's raw sexuality.

The Marquesa smiled. It was a wanton, enticing smile. "Let's hope you're here to stay."

Antonietta tore herself out of her trance. "I can't place your accent, marchesa," she said, "You're not Spanish, are you"?

The Marquesa smiled again and moved her tongue suggestively along her upper lip. "I was born in Czechoslovakia, but my late husband was Spanish. That makes me Spanish too," she replied.

Antonietta's mother suddenly appeared. She didn't acknowledge the Marquesa, which surprised Antonietta.

"Come, Antonietta, your father wishes to talk to you." She hauled her daughter away. As soon as they'd rejoined her father and Giovanni with Renata, her mother lectured her.

"Don't talk to that woman. She has a very bad reputation."

"But she's a Spanish Marquesa. I thought you wanted me to mix with people of my class."

"She may be a Marquesa," her mother replied, "but only because she married a man forty years older than herself. People even say that he met her in a brothel."

"You should watch out," her brother added. "People also say she has a weakness for young women."

Caterina was horrified. "Giovanni, don't mention such things. Look how you've shocked Antonietta."

It was not shock that Antonietta was feeling. Giovanni's remark disturbed her for a quite different reason. She knew now why the Marquesa had sought her out, and she was horrified to have fallen under the woman's spell. It brought back all her old doubts. She wondered what would have happened if her mother hadn't rescued her. She resolved to give the seductive Marquesa a very wide berth. However, when she left the party, she couldn't resist a furtive glance in her direction.

It was a pleasant, warm summer evening in Buenos Aires, and James decided to walk to the Hotel Plaza San Martín. He went along Reconquista, up Córdoba and right at Maipú. There was a bustle about the city. Christmas was drawing near, and most of the terrace cafés were packed with people. He arrived at the hotel with some misgivings. Across the entrance hall he saw a pretty blond girl at the reception desk dealing with a client. It was Carolina. The view of Carolina gave James quite a jolt. She looked as serene as he remembered her. He felt a stab of jealousy watching her smile at the young man who was checking in.

He was tempted to walk across and interrupt them but stopped himself. "You faithless individual," he remonstrated with himself, "one look at Carolina and you forget all your promises to the woman you love." He waited until Carolina was occupied with her back to him and snuck past into the banquet room.

The meal was traditional Argentinean: empanadas, succulent beef and *arroz con leche*. The wine was a Pinot noir from Patagonia. James found himself next to the earnest Mexican professor, and the conversation was very serious. It was a relief when the speeches started for James was able to concentrate on his own thoughts. He asked himself how he could be so passionately in love with Antonietta, so completely incapable of envisaging life without her, and still be attracted to Carolina. Perhaps men were by nature bigamous just as women were apparently bisexual, at least in his experience. Mind you, the thought of Veronica having sex with anyone, man or woman, required a feat of imagination.

James may have felt remorse, but he couldn't resist another look towards the reception desk on his way out of the hotel after the banquet. Carolina was no longer there. He wondered what she was doing and was tempted to visit La Barra in the hope of meeting her there. Appalled with himself, he turned resolutely in the direction of the Melia. Thank goodness he was leaving Buenos Aires tomorrow.

## Chapter 28

# Wednesday December 19, 2001
# to Sunday January 13, 2002

**B**OTH JAMES AND ANTONIETTA arrived home, or at the hotel in James's case, at the same time. It was eleven-thirty at night in Buenos Aires and four-thirty in the morning in Florence. Both were feeling extremely guilty; Antonietta for the lure of the Marquesa and James for that of Carolina.

Antonietta immediately called the hotel and swamped James with declarations of love. James returned them, but he was suspicious. What was she doing up this late? Normally Antonietta's jealousy and fears were paramount, but this time she didn't even mention Carolina; she just asked about the banquet.

"The food and wine were excellent, but I was sat next to a very boring Mexican professor who insisted upon talking about law," James replied. "How about you? I hope you behaved yourself at that party with all those good-looking men."

"Of course I did"! Antonietta tried to sound indignant. "And you"?

"It was difficult to do otherwise in the company of a bunch of boring academics."

There was something inadequate about this reply, but Antonietta was anxious to end the topic of the last evening and didn't press the point.

"I love you, James. I hate this separation."

James reciprocated her feelings, and the call ended, leaving them both worried and suspicious.

Antonietta lay in bed playing over in her head the conversation with James. She became more and more convinced that he was hiding something, and it could only have to do with Carolina. He must have seen her; she could be in his bed at this very moment. A mixture of anger and despair possessed Antonietta. How could he? Stifling her sobs, she crept downstairs to find the telephone book. She would avenge herself for James's faithlessness. She leafed through the book and found the name she was looking for: *D'Avila y de la Torre, Eva.*

She returned to her bedroom. The Marquesa was probably back home by now. Antonietta began to dial the number and stopped. What on earth was she doing? Did she really mean to give herself to the Marquesa on a mere suspicion that James was cheating on her? She put the phone down. "This is madness." she realized. "I love James. No matter what he's done, I can't live without him." She lay down on the bed in a daze, feeling cold and miserable, tears streaming down her cheeks. She remembered James telling her how fragile she looked when she cried, and how it made him want to take her into his arms. "That's what I want, James's arms around me, not the perverse consolation of the Marquesa."

There was something wrong, James had convinced himself of this. Antonietta was guilty of some transgression. What it was, he didn't know. He couldn't bring himself to believe she'd been unfaithful to him, but she'd done something. His own transgression was forgotten in the welter of emotions that gripped him in the face of Antonietta's putative betrayal. He lay in bed, hoping that she would call, hoping that there was some obvious explanation for her awkwardness on the telephone. Why had he found her awkward? After all, she'd showered him with declarations of love. But she hadn't mentioned Carolina or displayed any signs of jealousy. The only explanation was that she felt too guilty about her own conduct.

There was no phone call, and James went off to the conference. He paid little attention at the final seminar to the extent of appearing discourteous. He excused himself from lunch. Carlos gave him a quizzical look. They shook hands, and James invited Carlos to Canada. "I'd very much like to come," the Argentinean replied as he escorted James to the taxi.

James passed by the hotel to fetch his suitcase and arrived in good time at Ezeiza airport. He checked in and ordered empanadas and a bottle of San Felipe at the airport restaurant. He ate and drank without much enjoyment.

It was a long flight, but, even with the whiskies, James couldn't find any sleep. The horrible, unbelievable thought that he might have lost Antonietta preyed on his mind. He'd hoped to find a message from her at the hotel, but there was none. It was as if she'd disappeared from his life, and he was consumed by an almost physical pain of loss. His thoughts became darker and darker. He couldn't live without her.

Although they continued to be mutually suspicious of each other's doings, the remaining time of their separation passed for Antonietta and James without undue incident, but with agonizing slowness. She spent time with her friends and even went for two days with her mother to Rome to visit her sister Carla. She found the baby Claudio quite adorable and walked him in his pram in the nearby park, accompanied by her mother and sister. Occasionally, her mother would try to talk her into staying in Italy and insisted on her attending as many aristocratic receptions as possible. It was always the same uninspiring crew, so Caterina's secret hope that the company of her peers would persuade her elder daughter to mend her errant ways was not fulfilled. The Marchesa was away in the Czech Republic visiting her family, and so Antonietta was spared any temptation. All this activity helped Antonietta deal with the absence of the man she loved, although there were nights when she was consumed by longing for him. Even in Rome she made sure that she was able to make the two daily phone calls. Without them James's absence was unbearable.

"*Tal dei profondi amori è la profonda miseria.**"* she reflected.

In the days before Antonietta's return, James managed to finish his eternal paper on the Treaty of Nice. It wasn't easy as he was fearful of what Antonietta was up to in Italy and found it difficult to concentrate on anything but her. He kept telling himself that nothing could possibly have happened, but he was so hopelessly in love with her that even the idea of her talking and laughing with other men made him ferociously jealous. He sought some respite from his torment in regular binges with his friends, but they offered him little sympathy. Danny was too immersed in the joy of having his daughter with him and his new relationship with Bernadette, whom he'd met just before Christmas, Piotr had never really approved of James's extramarital relationship, and Bill was downright impatient.

"Marry the goddam woman and be done with it"! was all he could say.

⌒ℳ⌒

Antonietta could hardly believe she was on the plane for Canada, and that in a little over ten hours she would be in bed with James. The last few nights had been very trying. "It won't be romantic when I get hold of him," she vowed, "it'll be sheer, naked lust."

Despite this lust and the enormous relief that their separation was ending, Antonietta was no nearer to making the crucial decision. There had been sporadic moments of friction, but her whole family without exception had been delighted to have her back. The time in Rome with Carla and Filiberto had been surprisingly enjoyable, perhaps due to the arrival of their new baby and the enlivening presence of Paolo and Monica. The religious ceremonies over Christmas had also played their part by strengthening her Catholic faith, in particular the solemn Latin High Mass celebrated by her uncle on Christmas Eve with its imposing ritual and transcendent music. So the idea of a breach with her family and her religion in order to marry a divorced man was even more difficult to envisage than before she returned home for the holidays. Yet it was impossible for her to renounce James. Her passion for him completely dominated her with overwhelming force. She longed to be reunited with him.

Apart from Monica, and to a lesser extent her student friends, she hadn't told anyone about James. Her tenseness and intermittent bouts of anguish had not, however, escaped her perceptive uncle, Giovanni.

"If I didn't know you better," he'd told her "I'd say you've taken the advice I gave you before you left for Canada."

She'd blushed but said nothing, and the Cardinal hadn't insisted.

~*~

James ran towards Antonietta as she emerged from customs. She dropped her suitcases and threw herself into his arms.

"It was horrible," Antoniette choked. "At times I thought I'd die."

James looked at her fixedly. "It was the worst time of my life. You're never going away again."

Antonietta's answer was another passionate kiss, and they made for the taxis. Within an hour they were in their room. Very quickly Antonietta was lying on the bed completely naked.

"James, get undressed. I've been longing for this for three weeks."

James did her bidding, his eyes riveted on the sensuous beauty of Antonietta's body stretched out waiting for him. Her lips were soft and yielding, her breasts tight with anticipation, and as he moved down her body, he was comforted by the scent of her excitement. Whatever she might have done in Italy, her avidity persuaded him that she hadn't been with any other man. He ran his lips along the smooth texture of her inner thighs and occasionally let his tongue stray into her intimacy, but never for long. He ignored her pleas until she was consumed by desire. She came quickly and with extreme violence.

"You sadist, it hurt."

"So much the better."

She took her revenge, using her breasts and the tip of her tongue to enrapture him. When she took him into her mouth, it was James's turn to experience the pain of intense pleasure.

"What happened in Florence"? James eventually plucked up the courage to ask.

"You tell me first about Buenos Aires," Antonietta countered, her hands tightening themselves around James's body.

"Nothing happened. It's just that the bloody people organizing the conference had the bright idea of having the banquet in the hotel where Carolina works."

"You saw her"? Antonietta buried her face against James. She didn't want to see the expression of guilt on his face that would plunge her into misery, but he made her look at him.

"It was inevitable," he said, looking directly at her and hoping that his face wouldn't divulge the whole truth. "I had to pass through the reception hall, and she was at the desk. I made sure she didn't see me. I had no contact with her. I swear that to you."

"Were you attracted to her"? Something in the tone of Antonietta's voice gave her away. The shock on James's face covered any hint that he was lying when he said no.

"Who were you attracted to"?

Antonietta had no escape. She recounted the episode with the Marquesa at the party. "It was a momentary fascination," she insisted, "I would never have done anything."

James was staring at her with a strange expression on his face. She didn't know whether he was angry or hurt or what.

"I love you, James," she went on, her voice breaking with emotion, "Please say you forgive me, please." Tears welled up in her eyes, and she was thankful for them. She hoped they would bring her James's forgiveness. Suddenly to her immense relief James smiled.

"Was Dana blond"?

Antonietta was taken aback by the question. "Yes. Why do you ask"?

"So is Petra and so is the Marquesa. It's not you who should be jealous of blue-eyed blonds, it's *me*. I'm going to have to keep you away from them." He expected Antonietta to be indignant, which always rendered her even more desirable, but she was looking at him slyly.

"So is Carolina. You should introduce her to me." She gave James the most promiscuous smile.

"Antonietta"! James was beside himself, and Antonietta burst out laughing.

"Serves you right for teasing me," she said, kissing him. "Really, you don't need to worry James. If I really were bisexual, I would've had more than one brief encounter since Dana."

James looked at Antonietta skeptically. He wasn't convinced. What Antonietta didn't know was that he'd met the Marquesa nearly ten years ago in Mérida at a reception in the home of the Marqués de San Vincente, his friend Rodrigo's father. He'd been awed by her enticing blond looks and the raw sexuality she exuded. Knowing Antonietta's rather dubious sexuality, he wasn't surprised that she'd been attracted to her and probably, despite her denials, tempted by the erotic delights offered by the Marquesa. He felt a sting of jealousy but comforted himself with the hope that Antonietta's passion for him was powerful enough to overcome the temptations of lesbian sex.

"James, I want you to take me to the most expensive restaurant in Toronto and spoil me."

He invited her to the St. Jacques, a new French restaurant on King Street. As usual, Antonietta teased James about his predilection for the cuisine of Italy's great culinary rival.

They ordered the most expensive champagne, chose the most expensive dishes, and drank the most expensive wines. "I've never spent a thousand dollars more happily," James told a rather inebriated Antonietta. The waiter arrived. "Do you want a dessert, Antonietta," James asked. "No" she replied. "I'll make do with you." The waiter was Italian and went away grinning.

Back in the hotel Antonietta was as good as her word.

The next day, Sunday, they attended Mass at the impressive St. Michael's Cathedral and had lunch at a trendy bistro on Yonge Street. They caught the three o'clock flight to Montreal. James stayed with Antonietta in the cottage for an hour. When he left, she felt sad and bereft, but at least, she consoled herself, she would see him the next day.

On Monday Winstone received Bill with his normal hollow solemnity and informed him that his tenure hearing would be on April 12, and that there would be an election for the faculty representative on February 6. All candidates for election would have to declare themselves by Friday, January 18.

Bill went off immediately to find James. He was on the phone to Antonietta, and, from the general drift of the conversation, Bill gathered that he was trying to calm her down.

"I can hardly throw her of my class," he was telling Antonietta. "Try to be reasonable."

The conversation seemed to end in a stalemate.

"Problems"?

"It's all very well for you to smirk. I love that woman, but she drives me crazy with her jealousy of Annya Nowak."

"Well, Toni has a point. That girl's always looking at you as if she'd jump into the sack at the first opportunity."

James grunted. "Maybe, but she's in my international trade class at eleven, and there's nothing I can do about it. Antonietta refuses to see that."

"Jimmy," Bill said, coming to the point of his visit. "Winstone's set my hearing for April 12 and the election of the faculty representative for February 6."

They agreed to a council of war Tuesday night at Bill's.

⁓⁘⁓

James made sure to leave immediately after his class. He saw Annya coming towards him but managed to avoid her. He arrived at the cottage before Antonietta. This mollified his volatile mistress somewhat, but she still demanded to know what Annya had been wearing, whether she'd smiled at him, whether she'd approached him at the end of the class.

James took Antonietta into his arms. "Listen, Antonietta. I don't want to go through this scene every Monday, Wednesday and Friday. Annya's in my class. If she wants to speak to me, I can't refuse, and if she wants to smile at me, I can hardly slap the smile off her face. You know how much I love you, you've had enough proof of that, so stop being jealous of Annya. She means *absolutely nothing to me.*" The last words were spoken with a raised voice.

"Promise to come back here *immediately* after the class." Antonietta insisted, turning dark, mournful eyes on to James. He couldn't resist kissing her but still held out.

"There's more than Annya in the class. I can't just rush off every time."

Antonietta pouted. She was using all her wiles, which were even more effective as her sweater had a plunging neckline that gave James more than a glimpse of the sexual pleasures awaiting him once this matter was settled. He surrendered.

"I'll tell them that I have an appointment at twelve-thirty and can't stay for their questions. They can email me or come and see me in my office."

Antonietta's eyes sparkled in triumph, but she wasn't finished. "Except Annya. She can limit herself to emails."

Despite the seriousness of the occasion, Bill couldn't resist teasing James when he arrived that evening at his place.

"What price was peace"? he asked, assuming from Antonietta's radiance that she'd been pacified.

"I'm not allowed to stay after class in case Annya talks to me."

"You're a weakling, Markham."

"Oh yes? You try and deal with Antonietta when she's in a jealous mood." He nodded in her direction where she was chatting with Bernadette and Ceara. "Particularly when she's wearing that sweater."

Bill laughed and slapped James on the back. "You have a point, asshole."

While the women talked among themselves, the lads discussed the election of the faculty representative. It was agreed that a candidacy of any one of them would be counterproductive. Because of their closeness to Bill, they were unlikely to be elected and, even if elected, not very credible on the tenure committee. What they needed was a full professor whom they could trust. But who?

James was categorical. "The most important factor is how they voted on the uniform evaluation proposal. Anyone who voted for it or abstained cannot be trusted."

He turned to Bill. "Who does that leave in your Section"?

"Apart from Danny and Wachowitz, who's too lightweight, that leaves Jason Levy, but he hates my guts since I told him I was sick of sucking up to Israel."

James groaned. "Why the hell did you tell him that? He's a New York Jew for Christ's sake."

"He fucking got on my nerves. He deserved it."

Danny frowned. He didn't approve of swearing in front of his daughter, although she probably hadn't heard. "Don't swear and face the truth," he told Bill. "It was a stupid thing to say." Bill wisely kept quiet.

"What about your Section, Piotr"? Danny asked.

"Of the seven who voted against, only Bromhoeffer and Bill Miles are full professors."

"Ilse can't stand as she's Dean of Students, which leaves Bill Miles." Danny turned to James. "He's British. What do you make of him"?

"He's a typically taciturn and stubborn northern Englishman. He'd do, but I have someone else in mind."

The others looked at him questioningly.

"In my Section five full professors voted against the proposal, Boisseu, Nakamura, Berger, Desmoulins and me. Of the other four, Berger is not forceful enough, and I'm not totally confident about Nakamura and Boisseu. They supported me over the evaluation plan, but only after Christine had spoken up. It's she who's our best bet. She has a better academic record than Bill Miles, she's a good speaker, and she won't let HB intimidate her."

It was agreed that James would ask Christine Desmoulins to stand.

"Why you"? Antonietta had joined the men.

"Because he speaks that froggy language, and that'll make her melt," explained Bill.

Antonietta's eyes blazed.

"Antonietta, she's forty-five and not particularly attractive, as well as being married with four kids," James made clear very quickly.

Antonietta nestled against him. "Good," she said and went off to rejoin Bernadette and Ceara.

Business done, the women joined the men, and the rest of the evening passed pleasantly enough. Around eleven James drove Antonietta back to the cottage. It was late, but she begged him to stay and make love to her. As they lay together afterwards, she asked him when they could next get away.

"I have a meeting in Montreal on Tuesday, February 5. You can come with me, and we'll spend the night there."

"What about your class"?

"To hell with my class," James retorted, covering Antonietta with kisses. She stopped him when he reached her belly.

"If you descend any further, you'll have to stay another hour."

It was already past one o'clock, and with regret James forswore the renewed enjoyment of Antonietta's enticing sex and drove home.

⁓

The next morning James went to see Christine Desmoulins before his class at eleven. At first she was unwilling to stand, using as a pretext the book that she was editing on international organizations.

"Christine, it won't take up hardly any time," James argued. "We need you. You have credibility, and you can be relied on to stand up to HB."

"You think he's out to get Bill Leaman"? Christine asked, showing some interest for the first time.

"Absolutely. He wants to get Bill as a means of avenging himself on me for his two defeats."

"Two"? Christine queried with a smile. "How about three"?

"What do you mean"?

"Come on, James, you're not having me believe that Arbuthnot dropped the case against Hunt out of the goodness of his heart. I don't know what you did, but you did something to make him drop it. I'm sure of that."

"Possibly." It was comforting to think that at least someone had seen through HB's apparent generosity of spirit even if that idiot Hunt was taken in. "That's another reason why we need you on that committee."

Christine gazed thoughtfully into space. "Alright, James, I'll do it. I don't particularly like Bill Leaman, but I like HB even less."

James thanked her effusively. "You haven't won yet, James" Christine warned him. "I might not get elected, and Arbuthnot will do his best to get the rest of the committee on his side. Remember that the Rector appoints a member of faculty to the committee, and Winstone will choose the person Arbuthnot wants."

"I know," James said grimly. He was well aware that what should normally be an open and shut case would probably end up in another tussle with the wily and unscrupulous Senior Dean. Despite Antonietta's pleas, he knew he'd be in the thick of it.

⁓

There were three candidates for the election as the faculty representative on Bill's tenure committee: Christine, Larry Flint, who'd obviously been put up to it by HB, and Brian Wilkins, a full professor from LAC who had voted for the evaluation proposal. James and Piotr talked of canvassing for Christine, but Danny dissuaded them.

"If you do that, she'll be seen as Bill's candidate, and that could hurt her."

Bill was indignant. "Shit, Danny, anyone would think I'm a pariah the way you talk."

"Bill, we here all know that you're just a lovable guy, but somehow that's not always the image you project. You know that." Danny filled up his friend's glass as a conciliatory gesture.

"I don't like assholes, and the Institute's full of them." Bill huffed.

"I think you're marvelous, Bill," Antonietta cooed, giving him a kiss on the cheek. She looked mischievously at James. "If I weren't so in love with James, I wouldn't be able to resist you."

Everyone laughed.

"It's not that funny," Bill complained, "Most women find me irresistible--except my wife of course." He turned towards James. "Talking of you and Toni, it's becoming more and more obvious what's going on between you. You've got to be more discreet."

As always, Bill's warning worried Antonietta. On the way home she was very quiet. James stayed with her in the cottage.

"We're going have to make a decision soon, Antonietta."

"It's not *a* decision, it's *the* decision. Unless you're planning on leaving me."

James didn't bother to answer and almost dragged Antonietta into the bedroom.

"I'll show you what I'm planning on doing." He undid her blouse.

She let him undress her completely. He caressed her breasts, her stomach, her belly, between her thighs. He made her turn over, stroked her buttocks and ran his hand between them. There was something peculiarly erotic about being touched so intimately by her fully dressed lover. Soon she couldn't bear it any longer. She rolled over and undid James's belt. Without undressing him any further she pleasured him with her mouth. He removed his clothes and did the same to her. Still dazed from her climax, Antonietta was too sleepy to react in her normal tearful way to his departure.

It was Sunday, and Antonietta was attending Mass at the Basilica in the *Vieux Montréal*. Eternally torn between her love for James and the demands of her religion and family, she felt the need to gather her thoughts. It was easier in the hallowed impersonality of the Basilica than in the more intimate setting of the church in Ste. Adèle, where she normally heard Mass to avoid the Markham family in St. Sauveur.

She wavered between two reactions to her present situation. As she knelt to pray on taking her seat, she felt guilt for her sinful relationship with James. This soon turned to defiance. She hadn't sought him out. The passion she felt for him had descended upon her like a thunderbolt from heaven. She'd resisted as best she could, but it had proven beyond her strength. It was now impossible for her to renounce this passion. When she knelt at the consecration, guilt gripped her anew. She forced herself to take communion, telling herself with more hypocrisy than conviction that she would moderate her sexual excesses with James. When she left the Basilica, she was no nearer to reconciling her unwillingness to marry a divorced man with the love for him that possessed her heart and soul.

She thought of having lunch at Luigi's. She hadn't seen him since she'd introduced him to James, and that was at the end of October. She felt guilty for her neglect, but she'd been too obsessed by her passion for James to think of anyone else. She drove up to Ste. Cathérine, but as she feared, the café was closed. She scribbled a note apologizing for her prolonged absence and pushed it under the door of the café. She returned to Ste. Anne.

Once back in the cottage, Antonietta tried to find solace in talking with James, but he didn't answer the cell phone. "He's probably having brunch with his family," she told herself forlornly. Feeling lonely and downhearted, she called Petra. To her surprise and joy, her friend answered. Brett was off playing basketball.

"It's a meaningless game," she explained to Antonietta. "It consists of running from one end to the other, plonking a big ball into a net and then running off to the other end and doing the same thing."

Antonietta laughed and began to feel better. They arranged to meet at St. Sauveur for a late lunch. Antonietta changed into more casual clothes. As she was leaving, she was beset by a wicked thought. After all, James was with his wife. Ashamed, Antonietta hurriedly put it aside and drove off.

*Chapter 29*

# Monday January 14, 2002 to
# Saturday, January 26,2002

T HE CAMPAIGN FOR FACULTY representative on Bill's tenure committee
started in earnest right away on the Monday morning. Tocheniuk,
Gowling, Williams, Goldberg and even McGrath, which was quite
irregular given his position, were seen canvassing for Larry Flint. This
alarmed Bill and Piotr, who insisted they should start campaigning for
Christine despite Danny's strictures. James was more sanguine.

"You can't turn a donkey into a purebred. No one except HB's
diehard cronies are going to vote for Flint in preference to Christine or
Wilkins."

It was agreed to hold a council of war at Danny's on Wednesday
evening.

"I can't understand what HB's up to," James was saying. "There's
three weeks to the election, and they're campaigning as if it's this week.
That goes against the elementary rule of campaigning. You start gently
and gain momentum, otherwise you peak too early."

"They must figure that they need time to convince people," Bill
suggested, "Flint's a weak candidate. God knows why they chose him."

"Yes, but, by being so aggressive, they're making sure that everyone
sees him as HB's candidate, which I can't understand either. At the

most, even counting those professors close to Winstone, he's only got around ten committed supporters in the faculty out of thirty-eight. A lot of other colleagues may fear Arbuthnot, but that doesn't mean they're going to vote for his candidate in a *secret* ballot."

There was silence. Suddenly Danny slapped James on the back. "You've put your finger on it, James"!

"I have"?

"HB knows that Christine is the strongest candidate. Flint is a nonentity, and Wilkins doesn't have the same standing in the faculty as she does. As it stands, Christine has a good chance of winning, and HB knows this. If she wins, it means that she and Forget will support tenure. Hamid will too if the references are as good as Bill says. Let's say HB, McGrath, and the faculty representative appointed by the Rector vote against. That leaves Winstone with the casting vote, and the custom is that he supports the candidate's Section Head. It's not a done deal as Winstone is under HB's thumb, but it gives Bill a good chance. However, if HB has the elected representative on his side, Bill's probably toast."

"So"? Bill was clearly nervous.

"What HB is doing is this." Danny went on. "By ostentatiously campaigning hard for Flint, he hopes to push us into doing the same for Christine. That way he and his supporters can paint Christine as our candidate, which of course she is. As James has pointed out, most of the faculty are neutral between them and us. I bet you that a week or so before the election, HB's lot will dump Flint and try to persuade our colleagues to vote for a neutral candidate as a compromise. That way they hope to get Brian Wilkins elected over Christine. Flint is just HB's stalking horse."

"That supposes HB can rely on Wilkins," Piotr objected.

"Not necessarily," James replied. "He knows he can't get anywhere with Christine; at least he must think he has a chance with Wilkins."

Antonietta had been listening intently to the discussion. She asked Bill if he had a copy of the survey of professors.

"Why"

"Just give it to me. You'll see." While the others continued to talk about the campaign, Antonietta looked through the survey.

"Eureka"! she cried, startling her male companions. "Tocheniuk and Wilkins both went to UBC, and Tocheniuk supports HB."

"So what"? Bill was skeptical. "They weren't there together. Wilkins is much older than Tocheniuk."

Antonietta gave Bill a look of triumph. "Agreed, but they were both in the *same* fraternity, Alpha, Beta, Zeta."

Danny, all smiles, congratulated Antonietta, who was very proud of herself.

"You're a genius, my lovely lady. That clinches it. Now we know that Wilkins is HB's real candidate." He pointed a finger at the others. "No canvassing for Christine, or we fall into HB's trap."

On Friday the inevitable happened. True to his promise, James had rushed from his class and was putting away his notes before leaving for the cottage when there was a knock on his office door. It was Annya Nowak. She was dressed in a tight blouse and short skirt. She was tanned from her skiing holiday. She had let her blond hair grow longer, and it cascaded down her shoulders. It was a most appetizing picture, which James could not fail to appreciate.

"What can I do for you, Annya"? Involuntarily, James again used the girl's first name, which obviously pleased her despite his very guarded tone. She gave him a smile in which seduction mingled with malice.

"Nothing, Professor Markham. On the contrary, I've come to promise you something."

Annya's answer added astonishment to James's discomfiture. "Promise? I don't understand."

Without being asked, Annya sat down and looked up at James who was standing awkwardly by his desk. Annya continued in her perfectly modulated voice, stroking her hair playfully as she spoke. "You don't have to rush off after every class. I promise not to accost you."

James struggled vainly to stop himself blushing, but the mocking smile on Annya's pretty face told him that he'd failed. He was furious with himself. "I have no problem with you accosting me, as you put it," he countered. The mocking smile remained.

"I'm sure you don't, but perhaps someone else does."

The sheer impudence of the girl saved James. Infuriated by it, he was able to look Annya straight in the eyes.

"I don't know what you're talking about, Miss Nowak. I have these meetings in St. Jérôme at 12.30 every Monday, Wednesday and Friday, but I'm going to change the times. It won't be necessary for me to rush off, as you put it, starting next week."

The force of James's reply disconcerted Annya, who lost her air of superiority. But she gave one last parting shot.

"That's good news," she told James, furrowing her brow. "You know how students like to complain." With that she left the office. James was too relieved at her departure to worry about the subtle menace in her last words.

He made for the parking lot and drove to the cottage, wondering the whole length of the journey how to tell Antonietta that Annya had come to see him. He decided the best strategy was to make love to her beforehand in the way that always brought her to the most violent climax. Sexual exhaustion might mitigate the violence of her reaction.

He arrived at the cottage and took a pliant Antonietta to bed. She reveled in the shameless intimacies with which he indulged her. As she lay cradled in his arms afterwards, James plucked up the courage to tell her of Annya's visit. To his astonishment, Antonietta just smiled up at him.

"I know she came to see you."

"How"?

"I had to hand in a paper for Professor Martinez that I forgot yesterday. Afterwards I met the two Brits, Simon and Malcolm, and we had coffee together. By the time we'd finished, it was nearly twelve, and I decided to see whether you were keeping your promise."

"You were spying on me"?

"Yes. I'm not going to apologize for it. It's your fault for making me lose all sense of dignity."

James laughed and kissed Antonietta. "She's always at her loveliest after making love," he thought, conveniently forgetting that he found her at her loveliest in many other situations. "Go on," he told her.

"I saw you rush out of class…" Antonietta began.

"Ah," James interrupted, "that must have made you feel very

proud." There was a hint of bitterness in his voice as he thought of the conversation with Annya that had followed his abrupt departure from class.

"No, James." Antonietta was contrite, "I felt guilty for making you do such a silly thing."

James began to have a sense of relief. This whole business was going to be much easier than he had feared.

"I saw Annya follow you," Antonietta went on. "She was all tarted up, short skirt, tight blouse. She's even grown her hair long like mine. I could have scratched her eyes out."

"Did she see you"?

"No. I followed her very discreetly and saw her enter your office." Antonietta glanced up at James, and he could see her eyes mist over. "I thought I was going to die. Knowing she was in there with you alone made me want to throw up. It was all I could do to stop myself from barging in on you."

"Thank God, you didn't. It was bad enough as it was."

"So I gathered. When she came out of your office, she looked like thunder. I was so relieved and so happy that I started to laugh. She was too preoccupied by her anger to notice. She stalked off, and I came home as quickly as possible to be here before you."

"Why"?

"I wanted to put you to the test. I didn't want you to know I'd been at the Institute. I wanted you to tell me about Annya and not because you feared I might possibly have seen her go to your office."

"And if I hadn't told you"?

"I wouldn't have trusted you completely anymore."

James sighed. "Why are you so jealous of Annya Nowak? You know how desperately I love you. It doesn't make any sense. You can't possibly doubt me."

"It's simple. The thought that there are moments when another woman shares your intimacy by smiling at you, talking to you, or just looking at you, those moments are torture for me. It makes no difference that you wouldn't cheat on me."

"*Tal dei profondi amori è la profonda miseria*" James commented, repeating Scarpia's words that Antonietta had recited to herself in Italy.

Antonietta gave James a wan smile. "I have to put up with the *profonda miseria* because I can't live without the *profondi amori*." She moaned softly as James's tongue played on her nipples, but she pushed him away. "Tell me what that girl wanted."

James recounted the incident. "It was disturbing, to say the least. She's guessed about us, she's jealous, and she's capable of anything. Why she can't make do with one professor, God alone knows."

"Because, James, she's wanted you ever since you were silly enough to offer her whisky. She is Polish."

"That's a little unfair on the Poles," James chided, but he was amused by Antonietta's resentful bitchiness. "Anyway, you must relieve me of my promise. Annya was quite right. If I continue to rush off like that, there'll be complaints from the students, and that won't help us."

Antonietta's reply was to throw her naked body on top of James and kiss him with such ardor that it took his breath away. "I should never have asked you for that promise, so I'll make amends by treating you to an afternoon of the most indecent, most immodest, most debauched sex." She drew back and paraded her erogenous breasts before James's eyes, placing his hand between her thighs as she did so.

Antonietta lived up to her engagement. "Did I shock you"? she asked James afterwards. He laughed. "A little, I must say." "Do you think I'm a whore"? "No, Antonietta, but we certainly went beyond the common decencies of regular folk."

"I don't care about common decencies. My whole body exists for your pleasure and the pleasure you give me. All of it. My lips, my tongue, my mouth, my breasts, my nipples, my hands and fingers, my sex, my buttocks, my...." Antonietta stopped and blushed.

"Go on, Antonietta," James said, highly amused by her embarrassment. "As you've admitted, you don't care about common decencies."

It was well after seven when James arrived home. He was late for supper.

"Where have you been"? Veronica's voice expressed suspicion for the first time. "You don't seem to have been drinking."

James blanched at Veronica's inquisitorial tone. "I apologize, Veronica. Bill's having problems with his tenure, and we met to discuss it."

"Perhaps in future you could do your discussing during one of your drinking sessions instead of making us all wait for supper."

Feeling rather like a scolded schoolboy, James agreed. He was relieved that Veronica had apparently believed him, but her compliance could no longer be taken for granted.

This worried him.

It was Saturday morning, but, instead of treating himself to his normal weekend breakfast of kippers and toast Roy Arbuthnot was meeting with Harold Winstone.

"They're not falling for it, Harold," he was telling the Rector. "I was convinced that if we went out with all guns blazing for Larry, they'd drop the mask and campaign for Desmoulins. But they haven't made a blasted move."

There was a silence.

"It's Markham," HB went on. "The others don't have the savvy to see through my plan."

"They may know about Ed Tocheniuk and Brian Wilkins," Winstone suggested.

"How could they"?

"Don't the students have a publication of some sort on the professors? They could have found it out there."

"I never thought of that. Do you have a copy"?

Winstone was rather pleased with himself. He needed Arbuthnot, but he disliked his superior airs and was glad for once to have the advantage over him. He handed HB the survey. Arbuthnot sought out the names of the two professors.

"Jesus wept"! he exclaimed. "It's right here. Alpha, Beta, Zeta. That's why they haven't reacted." He fixed Winstone. "Harold, this means you have to appoint Flint to the committee."

"Why not someone more credible"?

"There's nothing wrong with Larry, and I know we can count on him."

"Roy," Winstone objected, "even with Flint that probably means three to three, assuming Forget, Desmoulins and Hamid vote for tenure."

"Then you cast your vote against."

"It's not customary, Roy," Winstone objected again. "I should vote with the Section Head."

Arbuthnot decided not to pursue the matter. If his friends from NUC did their job properly, he'd be able to persuade Hamid to vote against tenure, and he wouldn't need Winstone's casting vote. It was more important to use his influence over the Rector to secure the appointments he wanted for the various faculty replacements and vacancies. Until now Winstone had proved unusually obdurate, so it would take a lot of persuading. However important it was to be rid of Leaman, it was even more crucial for him to increase the body of his supporters in the Institute. He was sure that Winstone's lack of direction and poor management of the Institute's finances would eventually catch up with him, and he had to be ready to step into his shoes.

When James arrived at his office on Monday morning to prepare for his lecture, there was a message asking him to call Ilse Bromhoeffer.

"Those bloody students," he thought. "They've complained already. Spoilt load of little brats." Dutifully he called Ilse.

"What's this about a meeting immediately after every class, James"? Ilse enquired.

"Yes, it's at St. Jérôme, Ilse. However, I've already had one complaint, and so I've changed the time."

"I'm glad to hear it. Be careful, James. I have a suspicion why you dreamed up that meeting. It's better that no one else does."

James returned to his office to prepare for his class. Once it started, he announced that he'd changed the time of his meeting.

"However, I doubt whether any of you suffered too much trauma from not being able to talk to me after class."

He couldn't help noticing Annya's sly grin. "You little bitch," he thought, "You're as dangerous as you're pretty."

The second week of campaigning saw a noticeable slackening in the promotion of Flint's candidacy. Despairing of tricking Bill's friends into an open effort on behalf of Christine Desmoulins, HB gave his men orders to gradually switch their efforts to Brian Wilkins. By the end of the week, Tocheniuk, Williams and McGrath were openly suggesting the LAC professor as a compromise choice, portraying Christine as too close to James and hence to Bill to be objective. The fact that the gang was not campaigning for her was ignored, and much was made of her belonging to the same Section as James.

By Friday Bill had become alarmed at the number of people who were being courted by HB's cronies. At the Saturday evening get-together he was nervous and ill-tempered. It took all of Danny's Irish charm and Antonietta's radiance to restore his spirits. Even so, he couldn't resist projecting his misgivings about his own future on to James and Antonietta.

"If that Annya knows what's going on, you can bet she's told others, particularly that Wrangel guy, who's probably never forgiven James for humiliating him in class." Usually James laughed off Bill's warnings, but since the episode with Annya he was worried himself although he kept his sinister thoughts hidden from the emotional Antonietta.

"What do you expect us to do? Break up"? There was a gasp from Antonietta. James quickly put his arm around her and drew her to him. She buried her face in his neck.

"Marry Toni. You should leave Veronica, she should leave the Institute, and the two of you should *get married*."

On their way back to the cottage, she reproached James bitterly for what he'd said.

"How could you imagine us breaking up?' she asked, her eyes brimming with tears. James, who was looking fixedly ahead to guide the car through the blinding snow, didn't reply at first.

"How? How? How"? Antonietta repeated.

James pulled into a lay-by and took his trembling mistress into his arms. He kissed her.

"I'm sorry, Antonietta. Bill irritated me, and I didn't measure my words. I should've known you'd be upset. Please forgive me." As he said the last words, he wiped away the tears that were beginning to glide down Antonietta's face.

"Only if you make love to me before going to Prévost." Antonietta always said Prévost, never "home". For her James's home was the cottage.

It was well after midnight before James had earned Antonietta's forgiveness. She waited apprehensively for him to prepare his departure. She hated late Saturday evenings as she didn't always see James on Sundays. To her surprise James made no move to leave. It was clear he had something to say to her, and this made her even more uneasy What's more, he seemed strangely embarrassed.

"Where were you this afternoon"? he asked finally. "I called, and you didn't answer. I came round to the cottage twice, and your car was gone."

Antonietta's fears evaporated. "You were spying on me"! she exulted. James protested. "Yes, you were," Antonietta insisted. "If I didn't answer the phone, there was no point in coming round unless you thought I was up to something." She looked at James with a triumphant look on her face.

"I admit it. But where were you"?

Antonietta kissed James. Gazing at her happy expression, James was struck again by her volatility. There was no resemblance with the distraught woman he'd comforted in the car and then in bed.

"I went with Petra to Montreal."

"Why didn't you tell me you were going"?

"Because of the reason I went."

"What was that"?

"James, you're very unobservant. It's almost insulting." Antonietta placed his hand between her thighs.

"You went to an esthetician"?

"Doesn't it feel like it"? Antonietta had an impish grin. "I think she likes me. Maybe next time I'll pay in kind."

James reacted as Antonietta hoped. He was furiously jealous and angry with her. She took no notice and nonchalantly descended his body with her tongue. She placed his sex between her breasts and stroked the shaft gently.

"You're a hypocrite, James Markham. It's not just my kisses that have made you this hard."

She proceeded to describe in intimate detail her visit to the esthetician, adding a few imagined details, until her breasts were wet with James's pleasure. She brushed them against his stomach and climbed up towards him. "You know what I want, and I want it very slowly." It was the early hours when James left for Prévost. Antonietta wrapped herself in the sheets. Their dampness recalled the satisfying violence of her last orgasm and mitigated the emptiness she always felt after James left.

Returning to Prévost, James found it difficult to fall asleep, his thoughts constantly obsessed with Antonietta. He could never live without her, he had to marry her, but whenever he reached this conclusion, as he did most days, the image of his two children, particularly his daughter, came to mind. He suspected that Antonietta went through the same vicious circle with her love for him forever at odds with her religious faith and her family ties. Since Christmas neither had mentioned marriage, but sooner or later they would have to face reality.

*Chapter 30*

# Wednesday February 6, 20002 to
# Tuesday February 26th, 2002

FEBRUARY 6 ARRIVED AND with it the election of the faculty representative for Bill's tenure committee. Not wishing to stay around waiting for the result, James took Antonietta after her class to Montreal for lunch at Luigi's. He didn't appear to resent Antonietta's long absence. Later that afternoon they set out for Bill's house to discover the result of the election. Bill's expression when they arrived told them the good news.

"She got 70% of the vote"! Bill was triumphant. "Wilkins got 22%, and that jerk Flint only got 8%"

Danny was already present with Bernadette, and Piotr soon joined them. James phoned Veronica to tell her the news and that he would be celebrating with the lads.

While Antonietta chatted with Bernadette, the men congratulated themselves on securing Christine Desmoulins's election. Bill was euphoric, but Danny dampened his optimism.

"It's not a done thing, Bill. You've still got HB and probably McGrath against you, and Hamid's decision will turn on your references. Christine will vote for you and hopefully Forget too. Assuming that Winstone picks one of Arbuthnot's pals as his appointee, at best that would mean three to three. You've got to hope that Winstone follows customary practice and casts his vote with the Section Head. That's by no means certain."

There was a silence, and Antonietta looked anxiously over at James. "What's the matter"? she asked.

"Danny's being a party pooper," Bill answered.

"You're right," said Danny, observing Bill's doleful expression. He poured him another scotch. "Let's look on the bright side. At least we've got Christine to keep them honest. That's worth a lot."

The wine and whisky flowed, and it was nearly midnight when James and Antonietta arrived at the cottage. She laid her head on his shoulder.

"Are you coming in"? she asked tremulously.

"It's late. I should go home. I'm afraid Veronica might be waiting up for me."

Antonietta tore herself away from James and got out of the car, slamming the door behind her. He did likewise and caught up with her as she was opening the door of the cottage. He forced her to turn round and kiss him. There was a little resistance, but it was soon over. When the kiss ended, Antonietta looked down to hide her tears.

"Forgive me, James. I know I'm being unreasonable, but I can't help it. Ever since I saw you in that church, I've lost all my self-control."

James put his hand under her chin and lifted up her face. He kissed the tearful eyes. "I don't want you to have any self-control. I want you just the way you are."

His words brought a smile to Antonietta's mournful face. "In that case, come in and make love to me."

It was nearly four in the morning before James arrived at Prévost. Veronica had long been asleep.

⁓

The euphoria of Christine's election did not last long. On Friday a circular came round from the Rector's office giving notice that Larry Flint had been appointed to Bill's tenure committee. The atmosphere that evening at Danny's was very different from Wednesday.

"I'm fucked," Bill wailed. "I'm fucked unless Winstone has the guts to vote with Hamid."

"We always knew Winstone would appoint a crony of HB's to the committee," Piotr pointed out. "All that's changed is that now we have confirmation."

"If the worst comes to the worst, I guess I can always appeal to the Board of Governors."

"That won't help much," Danny commented, rather unhelpfully in James's opinion. Bill was already depressed enough. "They have a record of supporting the decisions of FPC. Your best bet is the courts."

James was tempted to point out that the courts would only overturn the decision of FPC if it was clearly contrary to the evidence before it, and he had a suspicion that HB would doctor that evidence. For Bill's sake he kept silent.

"You know," Danny began, looking very thoughtful. "This appointment may turn out to be HB's biggest mistake."

"It seems like a fucking clever move to me," Bill retorted, "He wants me out, and with Flint on the committee, he goddam may get his way."

"Let's hope not, Bill," said James. He put his arms around Antonietta who was clearly upset by the tone of the conversation. She was very fond of Bill and hated the thought of losing him. "What are you getting at, Danny"?

"This appointment tells us three things, all of which are going to upset a lot of people who hitherto haven't paid much attention to what's going on in the Institute." Danny paused, leaving the others in anticipation of what he was going to say. "Firstly, it shows that Winstone cares nothing for the opinion of faculty. To appoint someone to a committee when he's just been soundly rejected by his colleagues is an insult. People will take it as such."

Danny paused again to take a sip of his scotch. "Secondly, it shows everyone that Winstone is completely dominated by HB. Otherwise he wouldn't have made such a stupid error. Thirdly, HB has just demonstrated to everyone that he's capable of riding roughshod over faculty opinion to get his way. He's shown his true colors."

"What's the overall effect of all this"? Piotr asked.

"Winstone has lost credibility and respect, and HB is seen for the ruthless bastard he is. In future years, when our champion here," Danny pointed at James. "is installed as Rector, we'll see that it was this moment when the uncommitted majority of our colleagues began to realize what was good for them."

"I don't want to be Rector." James sounded adamant. "I want to marry Antonietta and go and live on the Mediterranean somewhere."

Antonietta looked at James in amazement. "You'd leave the Institute? What will you do"?

James realized he was on dangerous ground. He toyed briefly with the idea of telling Antonietta the truth, that he didn't need to work, and that he would be much happier spending his days with her in the sunny climes of southern Europe than professing law. "I was just dreaming," was the answer he eventually gave her.

Whether it was disappointment at this answer or distress over Bill's predicament, Antonietta was overcome by despair when she and James arrived at the cottage. She sat on the sofa with her head in her hands.

"I can't go on like this, James. I see no solution." She picked up the book on Mayerling that she'd been reading. "This is our only solution."

James was shocked. He knelt in front of Antonietta and took her hands away from her face. "Antonietta, if you won't marry me because it's against your Catholic principles, you can hardly kill yourself. That's a mortal sin."

Antonietta fixed James with dark, sorrowful eyes. "I'm in hell anyway, so what's the difference"?

"Antonietta, please don't talk like that. We have these moments when everything seems to be against us. The business with Bill is depressing, but it doesn't change anything between us two. I love you, and I *am* going to marry you. Once term is over, we're going to do what we have to. You'll tell your family, and I will leave Veronica."

"What about your children"?

"'I'll make sure to see them often. I doubt whether Veronica will object to that."

James tried to sound optimistic, but he wasn't at all sure of Veronica's reaction. She was quite capable of trying to keep them away from the adulterous couple. Unaware of James's doubts, Antonietta threw her arms around his neck and drew him to her.

"Kiss me."

"I will, but first I have something to tell you. During reading week

I'm taking you to Chile and Argentina for a week. We leave on Friday, February 22."

Overjoyed, Antonietta put her anguish aside, and they made love with the frenzied abandon that often followed their difficult times. At one moment Antonietta's flailing arms knocked over the pot of flowers on the coffee table. Despite the proximity of her climax, she had a fit of giggles, and James had to start all over again. Afterwards he complained that his tongue was sore, which so infuriated Antonietta that she compelled him to make love to her until the early hours. Not that he minded. Antonietta exploited all her erotic expertise to stimulate and satisfy his lust with a brazen disregard of modesty.

Now it's my turn," she told him as he lay quite exhausted on the floor. "Make me blush. Make me feel utterly depraved."

James did her bidding despite his fatigue. He turned her over on her stomach and caressed the crack between her buttocks. He tantalized her by gently licking her anus and then pleasured her with his fingers in her sex and his tongue on her clitoris. After her orgasm he kissed her and prepared to leave. It was past three o'clock. Antonietta clung to him.

"I must go. Just remember that in two weeks' time we'll be on a plane for Santiago de Chile."

Reluctantly, Antonietta let her lover go.

Antonietta was too excited to pay much attention in Professor Forget's class. Once it ended, she was having lunch with Petra, and then she and James would be leaving for South America. Guilty over her irrational behavior after the depressing Friday get-together at Danny's, she'd tried hard over the last two weeks to control her explosive emotions. There had been no more scenes of despair and fewer tears than usual, but the effort had exhausted Antonietta.

She met Petra at a restaurant with the odd name of Le Chat Botté. Despite her happiness to be leaving with James, her face bore marks of fatigue that Petra noticed.

"The sooner you two get married, the better for you."

"That's what Bill is always saying, and James wants us to get together once term ends."

"And you"?

Antonietta sighed. "Sometimes I wish we could just go on like this for ever. Other times, I can't stand our situation and want to get married."

Petra sensed the turmoil within Antonietta and tactfully changed the subject to her own boyfriend. They were going skiing at Mont Tremblant for reading week, but she wasn't sure how it would turn out. "He thinks I boss him, and he's beginning to resent it."

Antonietta smiled. "The problem is, Petra, you do boss him."

"I can't help it. He's so infuriatingly indecisive."

The conversation moved on to their classes and Antonietta's trip to South America. Then it was time to go. As she watched Petra walk away to meet Brent with an air of sadness about her, Antonietta was convinced their relationship wouldn't last. She made a mental note to tell Bill.

⁂

Antonietta felt an enormous sense of relief once they were airborne. There was no one to see them, no Veronica for James to rush home to, no Institute to take away her precious time with him. She drank wine, attempted to eat the dismal Air Canada food, and fell asleep, her head on James's shoulders. Promptly at midday on what was now Saturday, they arrived at Arturo Merino Benitez airport in Santiago de Chile.

Antonietta was surprised by the cleanliness of Santiago. "Chileans are the Prussians of South America," James explained to her.

They arrived at the Hotel Bristol, and to James's relief their room was ready. "Sightseeing can wait," he told Antonietta, who happily accommodated him. Afterwards she demanded to see the city. They wandered up and down the Avenida O'Higgins. He waited for Antonietta to remark on the photo shops, but it was the absence of outdoor cafes that struck her. They were now at the Moneda Palace and too tired to walk all the way back to the café on Vicuña Mackenna. They took a taxi.

As they sat sipping their pisco sours, James informed Antonietta that they were having dinner with Eduardo. "Please don't mention the coup," he told her.

"Why not"?

"Because Eduardo will go into a long peroration on the merits of General Pinochet."

"You don't agree with him"?

"One could justify the coup itself, but not the terror that followed it."

Their nascent political discussion was interrupted by the arrival of Eduardo, who took them to Coco's.

It was a pleasant evening at Coco's, although James had been there so often that he would have preferred to try somewhere else. Antonietta, on the other hand, was thrilled with the food and the exotic atmosphere with its rushing waterfall and ponds of multi-colored water lilies. She felt as if she were by the sea. She adored the fresh oysters and the King klip with cream and finished her meal with fruit and meringue cake. James looked on indulgently. He found Antonietta's exuberant love of food endearing. It was so Italian and at the same time another expression of her sensuality.

Eduardo, quite overwhelmed by Antonietta's beauty, showered her with compliments. This pleased Antonietta, who had a vain streak. Unfortunately, the conversation turned inevitably to the coup, and Eduardo explained why it had happened. Antonietta didn't seem completely convinced.

"Don't tell me you're another leftie"?

"No. At home I vote Christian Democrat. In truth, I'm a Monarchist."

James looked at Antonietta in amazement. Until now they'd never talked politics, and he had no idea she was a Monarchist. He didn't realize there were any left in Italy, except among the black nobility. Could that mean…? James dismissed the idea as ridiculous. A daughter of the black nobility would be at far more prestigious school.

It was agreed that the next day, Sunday, they would all three go to Mass early at the Cathedral in the Plaza de Armas and spend the day in Valparaiso and the nearby seaside resort of Viña del Mar.

⁓

Eduardo drove very fast, and less than two hours after leaving the Cathedral they were in Valparaiso. 70 miles northwest of Santiago, it is Chile's main port and is known for its bohemian culture, brightly colored houses, and beautiful seaside views. It rises majestically from the sea up to the residential heights.

Eduardo took them up to the heights overlooking the magnificent Valparaiso Bay. The streets were narrow and rather shabby. They pulled up at a four-story house with a breathtaking view of the Bay called La Sebastiana. "It was Pablo Neruda's home*," Eduardo told them. "A great poet but a Communist."

Antonietta and James were intrigued by the house. They admired the little wooden horse on the first floor that Neruda had brought from Paris, and with which he would play even in old age. On the second floor there was an ornate bar.

"This is where Neruda would make his own concoction, which he called a *Coquetelon*," Eduardo recounted. "First, you pour in one measure of cognac, another of Cointreau, and two of orange juice. You mix well and then add Mumm's Champagne. A real working-class drink. That must be why he got the Stalin Prize."

James patted Eduardo on the back. "I think we get the picture, Eduardo.".

They proceeded up to the third floor and then the terrace overlooking the Valparaiso Bay." "It's glorious," moaned Antonietta, gazing out in awe. She missed the sea terribly in Quebec. She resolved at that moment to persuade James to move to Italy when they were married. When they were married? Antonietta quickly suppressed thoughts of their dilemma.

After Neruda's house, Eduardo tired of Valparaiso, a city he clearly thought inferior to Santiago, and he drove them to Viña del Mar. Antonietta was overjoyed to see the golden beaches and the sea stretching out into the distance. The elegant houses with their manicured lawns contrasted sharply with the back streets of Valparaiso. Eduardo suggested lunch.

After lunch, they went to sit on the beach. Antonietta regretted not bringing her bikini as she lay on the sand soaking up the sun. After a while she was too hot and ran towards the sea to paddle in it. When her feet hit the water, she gave a short cry. It was very cold. The two men burst out laughing. Antonietta came back up towards them, her beautiful dark eyes full of reproach for James. "I don't see what's so funny," she said.

"It's cold because of the Humboldt stream," Eduardo explained. "It flows along the west coast up to Ecuador. That's why so few people are swimming in the sea."

"Not much of a resort," Antonietta replied, shocking James by her rudeness.

They remained another hour on the beach and returned to Santiago. As she said goodbye to Eduardo, Antonietta apologized for her rudeness. Eduardo smiled broadly. "One forgives a beautiful woman anything. Even being rude about a famous Chilean resort."

James and Antonietta returned to their hotel room. They showered, made love, and supped in the elegant five-star dining room of the hotel. Antonietta was wearing the cream dress that had created such a stir in Montreal when they'd gone to see *Tosca*. This time she wore her hair in a chignon, showing off the sparkling emerald earrings that dangled from her ears. After dining they returned to the room.

Quickly undressed, Antonietta lay languidly on the bed.

"There's something unsettling about the rapidity with which you undress," James complained.

"It's just practice," she replied with a wanton grin.

Beside himself, James practically ripped off his remaining clothes. He had his revenge. Ignoring all her pleas and screams, he strung Antonietta along until the poor girl, bathed in perspiration and incoherent, could clearly take no more. After her climax she looked in dismay at the sheets.

"Whatever will the hotel staff think?'

"I don't give a fuck."

Antonietta giggled. "Nor do I." She descended James's body with her breasts and tongue. "Now I'm going to get my own back."

❧

They had breakfast at the hotel. James had arranged his meeting at the University of Chile for ten o'clock, and Antonietta was booked on a bus tour of the city and the surrounding area.

Antonietta's excursion started by a drive along the avenues of downtown Santiago. They were well kept and clean. The bus crossed the beautiful Forest Park and the prestigious Bela Vista district with its stately homes and started on its climb up the San Cristobal Hill. Antonietta admired the great variety of vegetation on their way to the top of the hill and the sparkling white statute of the Virgén de la Immaculada Concepción. Everyone descended from the bus to admire the panoramic view of Santiago stretched out beneath them. It was spoiled only by the patches of smog over the city.

It was when they re-entered the bus to drive along the mountain range that Antonietta found herself constantly looking at her watch. Although it was less than an hour since she'd left James and, although she knew that she would see him again at lunchtime, she couldn't suppress the feeling of emptiness and longing that was taking hold of her. Remonstrating with herself for the obsessive nature of her passion, she tried to concentrate on the journey. They were now driving along the canyon of the Mapocho River, surrounded by a beautiful landscape and the snow-capped peaks of the Andes. It was awesome, and for a few moments Antonietta managed to surmount her fixation on James. When they reached Las Condes, everyone descended again to visit the handicraft and clothing shops for which the district was famous. Antonietta wandered disconsolately around the shops. She was not interested in handicrafts and found the clothing shops vastly inferior to those in Florence, or Montreal for that matter. All she wanted was to be in James's arms.

The bus arrived back at the hotel at twelve thirty, and Antonietta found James waiting for her in the lobby. She threw herself at him as if they'd been separated for weeks. James kissed her lightly on the cheeks and more passionately on the mouth, disregarding some hotel guests who were staring at them.

They never managed to have lunch in the hotel. By the time James had restored Antonietta to a state of relative serenity, it was time to go to the airport. They checked in for the LAN flight to Buenos Aires and had a snack and some Chilean wine in the airport bar. James noticed that Antonietta was trembling slightly as she lifted up her wine glass. He asked her what the matter was.

"I'm nervous about Buenos Aires. I know I'm going to be jealous all the time, and I'm afraid you'll get tired of me."

James took Antonietta's hand. "Antonietta, I shall never in my whole life get tired of you. You have nothing to be jealous about. The *porteñas* are thought to be beautiful, but they don't appeal to me. They're too thin and diaphanous. Most of them seem to be suffering from anorexia."

Antonietta was not so easily comforted. "What was different about Carolina"?

James sighed. He'd foreseen this question and had the answer ready. "Listen, Antonietta. There are good reasons why I've brought you here. I wanted us to be together, night and day, and I wanted you to experience Buenos Aires. It's an exciting city with good food, and there's much to see. Above all, I could never have left you in Quebec to worry yourself silly about what I was up to. Don't spoil our time together by this unjustified jealousy of Carolina."

Antonietta had never heard James speak to her so severely, and she didn't know how to react. Her immediate impulse was anger. How dare he speak to her like that! The second was fear, fear that another display of jealous ire would exasperate him.

"I promise to behave," she murmured.

James was under no illusions. He knew that sooner or later Antonietta would wheedle an apology out of him for his stern words, and her jealousy of Carolina would undoubtedly surface again. However, for the moment all was well. The man at the reception desk in the Melia had recognized him, and there was no blue-eyed blond in sight. They'd made love with lazy ease and now were having dinner at the Cabaña Las Lilas in Puerto Madero. It was Antonietta's first taste of Argentinean beef, and she was obviously enjoying the experience. She was particularly content as the restaurant had even managed to provide her with a bottle of Barolo. Dressed in a light blue summer dress that clung to her body and showed off her bosom, her hair flowing casually down to her shoulders, tastefully made up, she was a picture of incandescent and overtly sensual beauty.

After dinner James took Antonietta to the Café Tortoni to listen to tango music. The men were wearing suits and ties, and the women were striking both for their looks and attire.

"I thought you said *porteñas* were thin and diaphanous," Antonietta remarked, her voice tinged with distrust. "Some of the women here are very voluptuous and far too beautiful."

James laughed and kissed Antonietta's lips, which were pursed in a jealous pout. The gesture evoked an exclamation from the man sitting opposite them, who thereupon embraced his own companion, a much younger woman who was obviously his mistress.

They listened and watched until the early hours, captivated by the sensuality of the dancers and the nostalgic, yearning sound of the bandoneon. When they made it back to the hotel, Antonietta flung herself into their lovemaking with zest and abandon. Without any shame she indulged herself in the most intimate indecencies and demanded the same from James. It was already light before they'd sated themselves. It seemed pointless to go to sleep, and so they showered and walked along the wharves of Puerto Madero until fatigue overcame them. They returned to the hotel, had a continental breakfast of croissants and expresso coffee and went back to bed. It was then that Antonietta struck. Cuddled against James, she looked up at him with dark mournful eyes

"How could you have talked to me so harshly," she asked in a tone that mixed amorous cajolery with sad reproach.

James knew he'd lost but gamely defended himself. "I wasn't harsh. I just don't want you torturing yourself unnecessarily."

"You were harsh," Antonietta insisted, her eyes glistening as if by design with tears. It was no use. James took her in his arms and apologized. "You have to make amends," she told him, the tears in her eyes miraculously disappearing.

"Amends"?

"Yes, when we're married, I want six children." James looked at Antonietta in horror. "Six"! Antonietta burst out laughing. "You little vixen." James grasped hold of her and forced her down on the bed. "You've been planning this ever since you made your promise, haven't you"? Antonietta nodded happily.

"And what about that promise to behave"?

"I don't have to keep it as it was given under duress."

James shook his head in disbelief. It was a complete defeat, but the expression of mischievous delight on Antonietta's face made up for it. It was quite a while before they fell asleep.

When they awoke, it was already late afternoon, but the Azorin restaurant in the hotel was still open. Antonietta, hungry as ever, docilely agreed to take only a light snack. Afterwards they set off for the Recoleta, which is located at the opposite end of the city in the Barrio Norte. James explained to Antonietta that it had initially been populated by rich citizens fleeing the 1871 yellow fever epidemic in the city. It had remained an affluent residential area ever since. Its many French-style palaces and villas and the verdant squares with their outdoor cafes and restaurants were one of the reasons why Buenos Aires was known as the Paris of the Americas.

They first toured the famous cemetery, which Antonietta found rather macabre. James pointed out that it was no different from visiting the various tombs in St. Paul's Cathedral. "Here you're surrounded just by death," she retorted. "At least in St. Paul's, there's the religious trappings, even if they are Protestant." She grinned at James as she said the last words. His religious intolerance always amused her. It was so out-of-character. Despite her qualms, Antonietta was soon intrigued by the procession of famous names on the tombstones.

They went on past the resting places of Fangio and Susan Barrantes* and then visited the Basilica of Nuestro Señora del Pilar, an impressive colonial-style building that was completed in 1732. After the Basilica they paid a short visit to the Recoleta Cultural Center, which is a major gallery for contemporary visual art. James had little appreciation of the plastic arts, and Antonietta's taste was for the more classical Italian art of the baroque and Renaissance. She quite liked the impressionists, but anything after that left her cold. She disliked Picasso. Besides, it was time for dinner, at least in Antonietta's view.

James took her to the Posadas. Antonietta let him order for her. They started with the inevitable *empanadas*, followed by the restaurant's specialty: fresh Patagonian deer with mushroom crust and fresh cuartilo cheese. The Susana Balbo they were served was a Riserva from 1999. At the table next to them was a family who were speaking both Spanish and Italian. Antonietta felt at home in this Latin environment, and the meal was superb, but still the jealousy gnawed at her. She couldn't resist the inevitable question.

"The answer is no. I never came here with Carolina."

They moved to the La Biela for dessert and coffee. After that, it was time to go. At ten next morning, Wednesday, James was seeing Carlos Guarnieri, and if he and Antonietta were going to indulge their sexual appetites in the usual fashion, it would be wiser to leave now. They stood up, and Antonietta planted a quick kiss on James lips. He led her by the hand out of the café. As they left, a young and very pretty, blond woman watched them leave. Her serene features briefly lost their composure.

"Is anything wrong, Carolina"? one of her friends asked.

"No," she replied, "It's nothing, absolutely nothing."

*Chapter 31*

# Wednesday February27th, 2002
# to Monday March 4th, 2002

ANTONIETTA INSISTED ON ACCOMPANYING James to see Carlos Guarnieri. "I don't want to be away from you for a single second." James was reluctant as Carlos would now realize that it hadn't been his wife for whom he'd wished to rush back to the hotel after their dinner. However, the idea of showing her off to Carlos appealed to him.

They arrived at the Law Faculty near the Recoleta and were shown to Carlos's office. They sat down, and Carlos ordered coffee. James was amused as normally the Argentinean was very businesslike with little small talk, but today he showed no haste and plied Antonietta with compliments. Reluctantly, he came to business. It was the same problem of course equivalencies and an additional problem with the bureaucracy of the Argentinean health service. Carlos gave Antonietta a university newsletter to read. "I'm sure our discussion would bore you," he told her.

Antonietta leafed absently through the newsletter. It didn't really interest her, and she was about to put it down when she came to a report on the conference that James had attended. There was fulsome praise for his contribution, which filled her with pride, and at the end of the report a brief description of the banquet at the Hotel Plaza San Martín. Antonietta remembered how James had told her that the banquet was held in the hotel where Carolina worked. Now she knew which one it was.

"What are you going to do for the rest of the day"? Carlos asked when his discussion with James ended.

It was Antonietta who answered. "I want to see the Plaza San Martín."

"Ah, you want to see the monument to the Fallen of the Malvinas."

Antonietta agreed, not knowing that the monument existed.

"You really want to see that monument," James asked when they were outside. Antonietta had never breathed a word about it before.

"Yes. Many who died were of Italian origin."

"There were many British dead as well, and we didn't start it." There was a hardness in James's tone.

Their conversation was cut short by the arrival of a taxi. Antonietta nestled against James. They had nearly quarreled, and it had been her fault. Also, she wanted to lull him into an amorous mood before springing upon him the suggestion of having lunch at the Hotel Plaza San Martín.

Although the monument to the Fallen of the Malvinas was not the real reason for her visit to the Plaza San Martín, Antonietta was much affected by it. It brought home to her the folly and waste of war. As she read through the names, many of them Italian in origin, she reflected on how they had died for nothing. After four years in a convent school in England, she knew the British well enough to understand they would never give up the Malvinas. Under their deceptive air of self-deprecation they were a proud and hard people. She respected but didn't like them very much, except for one, but even he shared some of this hardness for all the gentle charm that kept her in thrall. For the first time in her life she was glad of the French. At least a quarter of James was Latin, and she'd deal with other three quarters. Recalling her thoughts back to the Argentine dead, she murmured a quick prayer and crossed herself.

As James watched Antonietta, he thought of Carolina and her remark that war was not a game. This monument always caused him conflicting emotions. He had little time for the British Empire, which he regarded as a Protestant achievement, and he liked Argentineans. It saddened him to see all the names of those who had died in the mud and cold of the Falklands, or who had drowned in the dank waters of the Atlantic. However, Argentina's historic claim to the islands was spurious, and they were populated by people of British stock, who wanted to remain under the Crown. Britain had been justified in coming to their aid, he was convinced of that. He said nothing to Antonietta, and she, not wishing to provoke him, was also silent.

"Come. I'm sure you must be hungry."

James tried to lead Antonietta towards Suipacha street where there was a small restaurant he knew.

"No, James," she said, pointing in the opposite direction towards the Hotel Plaza San Martín, "I want you to spoil me. I want to eat in that elegant hotel."

James was momentarily horror-struck. The last thing he wanted was for Antonietta to come face to face with Carolina, but, if he demurred, she would guess the reason, and he would have no peace until he took her to the hotel. Quickly he decided that the lesser evil was to agree. Carolina had once told him that she hated early morning shifts. Normally she worked from three to eleven, and it was now twelve thirty.

"Come on, then."

Antonietta was surprised. She'd expected him to be at best evasive.

There was no Carolina in the hotel. Antonietta scrutinized the reception desk, but the only woman in sight was a slim brunette. She excused herself once during the meal, ostensibly to go to the washroom, and searched again for the elusive Carolina. In vain. She fell prey to a terrible suspicion that James had contacted Carolina to forewarn her that they were coming to Buenos Aires. That was why he'd so readily agreed to have lunch here. She returned to their table.

James commented on the rather dispirited way she was eating the very excellent grilled fish they had both ordered. Antonietta looked up at James, her dark eyes full of distrust. "Did you tell her that we were coming"?

James immediately understood why she'd wanted to come to the Plaza San Martín. It wasn't for the monument, which she probably didn't know about, it was to have lunch in this particular hotel.

"How did you know it was this hotel"?

"I read in that newsletter Carlos gave me that the banquet was here, and I remembered you told me that it was in the hotel where Carolina worked."

"So you're not enjoying your meal because you think I tipped her off that we were coming." Antonietta nodded miserably. "The answer is no. I've never had any contact with Carolina since that one time I was here with Bill. In any case, I had no need to tip her off as I never expected you to find out where she worked."

Antonietta was suddenly all smiles. James's explanation made sense. "Now, enjoy your meal."

"Only if you forgive me for tricking you into bringing me here."

James stood up and came round to Antonietta. He kissed her softly on the lips. "I love you," he said simply.

The meal was over, and James had no wish to linger over a digestif in case Carolina did arrive. "How do you feel about a long, sightseeing walk"? he asked. Antonietta, who was used to long walks around Florence, was enthusiastic. James led her safely away from the Plaza San Martín down the Avenida Santa Fe to the imposing Avenida 9 de Julio, which has a width of 140 meters and is the widest in the world. They crossed over and walked up to the Teatro Colón, an opera house built in the Italian style that was once famous throughout the world. They were able to go inside and admire the rich scarlet and gold décor and the cupola, which contained frescoes painted in 1966 by the renowned Argentinean artist, Raúl Soldí. "He was trained in Italy," Antonietta informed James.

They walked up to the Avenida de Mayo past the obelisk, which Antonietta found rather ridiculous, and then down to the Plaza de Mayo. The first building they came to was the Cabildo, which was the government building in the city of Buenos Aires at the time it was founded. It was now a museum housing a collection of old weapons as well as medals and garments from the time of independence in 1816. It was open, but neither James nor Antonietta was particularly interested.

They turned towards the magnificent domed neo-classical Cathedral with its imposing Corinthian columns at the entrance. They entered and viewed the mausoleum containing the remains of General José de San Martín, the founder of Argentinean independence. Three statues representing Liberty, Commerce and Labor, along with the seals of Argentina's neighbors that San Martín had helped liberate, flanked the mausoleum. The interior of the Cathedral also contained

Renaissance elements. The dome was tilted, and the architectural floor plan was that of a Latin cross, comprising three naves divided by pilasters and interconnected chapels. Antonietta was particularly taken by the paintings of European artists from the 18th century and the ornate Baroque altarpiece. All in all, however, she found the Cathedral contained too great a mixture of styles.

"I rather liked it," James commented, not knowing one architectural style from another. Antonietta threw him a look that was worthy of her mother. James tussled her hair and told her she was a cultural snob.

"Look what you've done to my hair," she complained.

Coming out of the Cathedral, they walked towards the government building known as the Casa Rosada. It was from the balcony of this building that Eva Peron used to give her impassioned speeches to ecstatic crowds gathered in the Plaza de Mayo. It was originally built in 1580, but the façade was-reconstructed and given an Italian-French look towards the end of the 19th century. "The architect was Francisco Tamburini, an Italian," Antonietta informed James.

"Was it he who chose that awful pink color"? James couldn't resist provoking Antonietta. Her pride in Italian culture was endearing, but at times rather overdone.

"No. During the presidency of Domingo Faustino Sarmiento, the building was painted pink to combine the colors of the two political parties of the time: red for the federals and white for the unitaries. The resulting color was pink."

After a quick walk around the Parque Colón, the pair returned hand-in-hand to the hotel. They showered, and the plan was to go out and sip wine on a café terrace. This changed immediately Antonietta emerged naked from the bathroom. It was early evening before they were eventually ensconced with a bottle of Susanna Balbo watching the *porteños* and *porteñas* stroll by

Early next morning James awoke Antonietta with a cup of coffee. She looked at him in surprise.

"It's only seven, James, and I'm still tired from last night's sex."

James sat on the bed and showed Antonietta two plane tickets. "Our plane for Punta del Este leaves at ten-thirty. I thought you might like to spend some time on a beach."

Antonietta's tiredness vanished. She pulled James down on to the bed and smothered him in kisses. "I'll have to buy a bikini," she informed him. "No you won't." James got up, walked over to his suitcase, and took out a bikini. "I packed this one for you." Antonietta gave it a disparaging look and pressed her naked body against James. "I'll still buy one," she murmured, going down on her knees to stifle any objection James might have to such extravagance. It was a quarter to nine before they checked out of the hotel, but the taxi driver was more than happy to rush them to the airport in return for a large tip.

The drive from Carrasco International Airport to the Hotel Las Dunas in Punta took them through pleasant, wooded countryside. The hotel itself was located right on the Playa Manantiales. Antonietta gazed at the large stretches of golden sand and the sea rolling gently in from the Atlantic Ocean.

They checked in, and Antonietta dragged James to one of the hotel's boutiques, where she bought a ludicrously expensive Brazilian-style bikini. "The less material there is, the more it seems to cost," James grumbled. "I'll make sure you earn it," he told her, shaking his head at the thought of his sexy mistress parading her nudity on the beach.

James had reserved a room with a magnificent view of the sea. He made up two gins and tonic from the provisions in the mini-bar, and the two of them sat and relaxed on the balcony. Her drink finished, Antonietta showered and put on the new bikini. She was the picture of erotic perfection. The top exhibited her shapely breasts more than it covered them, and if it hadn't been for the bikini intégral she'd endured before coming on holiday, the bottom would have exposed her pubic hair. She turned round to show off her nude, well-rounded buttocks. Without taking his eyes off her, James quickly undressed and hustled her onto the bed. Antonietta satisfied all his desires, but he still found her scanty attire disconcerting.

They spent the afternoon sunbathing, swimming in the pristine sea, sipping a variety of alcoholic drinks from the beach bar, and returning almost every hour to the bedroom. The sight of Antonietta's barely covered bosom, her bare buttocks, and the tantalizing strip of material that just covered her sex exacerbated James's lust, while the sea, sun and sand stimulated Antonietta's already strong sexual appetite.

"I don't know why you complained about my bikini. You've never enjoyed sex this much."

That was true, James reluctantly had to admit.

They stayed one more day in Punta del Este. They arose late and took a taxi to the peninsula that separates the River Plate from the Atlantic Ocean, and where the center of the town is located. They found a delightful little bistro in which they enjoyed an excellent expresso and croissants. "No wonder they call it the St. Tropez of the Americas," James remarked.

The next day, Saturday, they had lunch in the hotel after spending the morning on the beach. As the flight to Buenos Aires only took an hour; there was no hurry to leave Punta.

"I want us to live in Italy," Antonietta said. "I want to be near the sea."

"I'll try and get a job with the European University Institute."

Antonietta shuddered. The thought of living with a divorced man in Florence near to her parents brought home to her yet again the difficulty of her situation. James was too busy paying the waiter to notice.

They arrived in Buenos Aires with an hour to spare and went to the departure lounge for their flight to Toronto. Antonietta found it strange to hear Quebecois French and Canadian English again after being surrounded for almost three days by the sounds of Spanish and Italian. She began to feel the oppression that constantly afflicted her in Canada. James noticed the sadness creep into her eyes and put his arm round her.

"It's not for much longer, Antonietta."

They arrived in Montreal via Toronto around ten-thirty on Sunday. Antonietta had spent much of the flight nestled up to James. Once in Montreal, she was fearful that he would have to return to Prévost immediately. From her mournful expression James guessed what she was thinking, but said nothing. When, instead of continuing northwards to the Laurentians, he made for downtown Montreal, Antonietta let out a squeal of joy. They had lunch at a Greek restaurant on Ste. Cathérine.

Antonietta's mood became more somber as they traveled along Highway 15. The cold and snow contrasted sharply with the weather in Punta del Este, and this accentuated her melancholy. When they arrived at the cottage, she begged James to stay. Although he knew that Veronica would be wondering why he was so late, he couldn't resist Antonietta's imploring eyes. He called Bill and told him that he was supposed to be at his place discussing the tenure application. Bill was to call them if Veronica phoned him and should tell her that James had just left. Around six-thirty Bill duly called, and James had to leave an emotional Antonietta in tears. At home he was met by an irate Veronica.

"What were you up to at Bill's," she demanded.

"We were discussing his tenure application."

"You might think a little more about your family and less about that vulgar friend of your's. I had to look after the children and missed my none prayers."

James couldn't contain his exasperation. "Is that all you think about? Your bloody prayers"!

"Don't add blasphemy to neglect of your family," she shouted back at him.

James left the room in disgust and went off to find the children. Any guilt he might've felt disappeared. The sooner he put an end to this travesty of a marriage, the better.

The misery that gripped Antonietta after James's departure was more severe than ever previously when they had parted after spending time together. It was as if a vengeful God was punishing her for her adulterous happiness during the magic days they'd spent in Punta del Este. Her misery gave way to guilt and then to anger. She turned an accusing eye towards the crucifix she'd placed on the wall of the living room.

"Why did you send me this passion I cannot resist and then punish me for it"? she yelled at it.

To take her mind off the awful dilemma that weighed upon her, she listened to her messages in the hope of a cheery welcome home from Petra. She was not disappointed, but the message that followed plunged her into the depths of apprehension and despair. It was a crisp message from her mother, delivered in the best imperious Palmieri style, informing her daughter that she was arriving in Montreal at 2.15 on Saturday, March 16th for a whole week. She made it quite clear that the purpose of her journey was to check up on her daughter in the uncivilized country where she had perversely chosen to pursue her studies.

Antonietta's first thought was that this meant a week without James. In a lucid moment she might have comforted herself with the thought that a week was better than three weeks in Italy, and that she would see him in class and perhaps surreptitiously elsewhere. But the pain of her longing for him precluded such comfort, and she sat down on the sofa and wept. It was bad enough to play host to her suspicious and authoritarian mother in a country her mother despised without being deprived of the man she needed like the air she breathed. She opened one and then another bottle of wine and drank herself to sleep.

James drove the children to school earlier than normal on Monday morning and managed to arrive at the cottage a little after eight-thirty. He knew Antonietta would be in a very distraught mood, and this gave him two hours before his class to comfort her. It was always like this after they'd been together somewhere. He opened the door and was alarmed to find her stretched out on the sofa, fully dressed. He feared the worst, but, to his immense relief, he saw the two empty bottles of wine on the coffee table. He awoke Antonietta very gently, stroking her hair and kissing her on the cheek. At first she just murmured, but soon she opened her eyes and saw James.

"James, thank God you're here." She flung her arms around him and devoured him with kisses. "My mother's coming for a week," she told him between sobs. "That means I can't see you for a whole week."

James, who had come prepared with a large handkerchief, wiped away Antonietta's tears. "Nonsense. We'll take a room in a motel somewhere. We're both free on Tuesday and Thursday afternoons. You simply tell your mother you have a class, or you must study."

Antonietta's face lit up, and she smiled through her tears. "I never thought of that," she said. Suddenly she realized where she'd slept. "This is awful, James, I'm like an alcoholic."

James laughed. "Does your mother always have this effect on you"?

"No, only when she deprives me of the man I love." She got up, took James's hand, and led him into the bedroom. "Sex or lovemaking"? James enquired with a grin. Antonietta grinned back. "Lovemaking first and then sex."

After making love, they lay together for a while.

"You know, Antonietta, I had an almost irresistible desire to sodomize you when you were lying on the beach on your stomach with your buttocks completely bare."

Antonietta pretended to be shocked. "James, you're dreadful. You're totally dissolute. Anyway, you did it when we were back in the hotel room, so you can't complain." Antonietta cocked her head to one side. "You're the only man I've ever let do that or touch me there."

James gave her a quizzical look, which Antonietta immediately understood. She picked up a pillow and set about him. "I know what you're thinking," she cried. James didn't bother to defend himself. The sight of Antonietta, her opulent breasts swaying beguilingly and her mouth pursed in an indignant pout, was too seductive. Eventually she tired.

"Well, it's true, isn't it? You tacitly admitted it by saying that I was the only man." Antonietta blushed and looked away from James in embarrassment. "I don't care what happened before," he reassured her, "but I don't want to share you now with anyone, male or female."

Antonietta pressed her ample bosom against James's chest and kissed him torridly. "You know that you never will."

She began to slide her lips down his body.

*Chapter 32*

# Monday March 4, 2002 to
# Monday March 11, 2002

H AMID KHAN SIGHED. HE'D received the last reference in Professor Leaman's tenure case. It was from Henry Keighley and recommended strongly against granting tenure. "Taking into consideration that this is an application for early tenure, I do not find the supporting materials adequate to justify the grant of tenure," he'd written. Mauser from Chicago had written in the same vein. This left Dickens and Khaladi, both from Ivy League universities. They had recommended tenure, although Dickens considered that the application was premature. The two negative assessments together with Dickens's expression of reserve justified Hamid in not recommending tenure. Moreover, it was customary in the event of a 2-2 assessment from the referees that the Section Head would advise against tenure. This was certainly the view of Arbuthnot, who had pressed Hamid to oppose the tenure application.

"You have no choice," Arbuthnot had told him, very satisfied with the success of his strategy. "If only I could get rid of Markham that easily," he'd thought. Then he could work on Redfern and Leszek.

Hamid convoked Bill for a meeting on Tuesday afternoon. When the time came, he felt uneasy. Despite all Roy's assurances., he felt nervous about basing his decision on the view of two academics who were manifestly inferior in reputation to the two who had recommended tenure. He consoled himself with Dickens's comment about the tenure application being too early.

Bill arrived and knew immediately from Hamid's expression that something was up. Hamid handed him the four references.

"As you will see, two are against, one has a reservation, and only one is wholeheartedly in favor of granting your application." Hamid paused, before adding with some awkwardness. "I have decided to oppose your application for early tenure."

Bill was completely thunderstruck. He stared in disbelief at the four references. Once he came across the names of Keighley and Mauser, he exploded.

"What the fuck is going on! How dare you replace two experts in the field by two assholes. Wickham's a shitty school, and Mauser isn't even a fucking full professor."

"He doesn't need to be for a tenure application," Hamid replied, "and I would appreciate you moderating your language, Professor Leaman."

"Moderate my fucking language"! Bill raged. "I'm not moderating my language for a guy like you, Hamid. HB put you up to this, but it won't wash. I will not accept these substitutions."

"You have no choice," Hamid said as coldly as he could muster. He was beginning to regret his subservience to HB. Leaman was a friend of Markham's, and thus far the Englishman had always gotten the better of Roy Arbuthnot.

"We'll see," retorted Bill with a determination that accentuated Hamid's discomfiture.

Bill raced off to find James. He was not in his office. Bill drove immediately to Antonietta's cottage. James's car was parked in front. Bill rang the doorbell, and after a wait that strained his patience, Antonietta came to the door. She was in her dressing gown.

"James, it's Bill," she called. James appeared, likewise attired.

"Is that all you two ever do? God Almighty, it's three in the afternoon. Can't you think of anything else but fucking your brains out"?

James was about to give a very sharp answer but desisted on a nod from Antonietta. She'd realized immediately there was a good reason for Bill's irritability.

"Bill, what's the matter"? she asked, leading him into the living room. "May I pour you a large scotch"?

"Please." There was silence while he waited for the whisky. He took a large gulp. "Hamid and HB have fucked me. They've changed two referees for two mediocre assholes, who don't know shit from shinola, and these fucking nobodies have recommended against tenure. Into the bargain, that prick Dickens says that my application is 'premature'. I knew I shouldn't have taken a Brit."

"Which is why you've come to seek my help, I suppose."

"Point taken, Jimmy," Bill conceded. "I'm in deep shit. Hamid is going to recommend against, and you can be sure that Flint, McGrath and HB will follow suit. Even if Christine and Forget vote in favor, I'm fucked. Well and truly fucked."

⁓

James arrived at the cottage the following day, Wednesday, to pick up Antonietta for the crisis meeting at Danny's. She greeted him with dark, sorrowful eyes, but on this occasion it was not due to the eternal dilemma that faced them.

"Do you think he'll have to leave the Institute"? James drew her close to him. He knew she was very fond of Bill. "Not if I can help it," he replied. For once Antonietta did not object to his involvement in another battle at the Institute. "If anyone can do it, you can," she said.

The confidence that James tried to display for Antonietta's benefit matched in no way his real assessment of the situation. As Danny pointed out morosely when they were all together in his living room, the case was stacked heavily against Bill.

"Damn that Arbuthnot," said Danny angrily. He still hadn't digested the humiliation of being demoted from the position of Senior Dean by Arbuthnot.

"It's no good moaning and regretting what we can't change," James said with more than a trace of impatience. "We know that the changes were made by Hamid at HB's suggestion, which means he also chose the replacements. I bet you they're fellow students from NUC."

"Even if they are, it doesn't get us anywhere," Danny objected.

"I'm not sure. I don't want to be seen interfering in something that officially doesn't concern me, so I'm going to ask Christine to check up on these referees. If they were at NUC and if we can find some real connection between them and HB, Christine can ask to have them replaced on the ground of possible bias."

"The others on the committee won't agree," Danny objected again.

"Forget might, and although he's under HB's thumb, Hamid's fundamentally an honest guy."

Bill, who'd been listening intently to this conversation, suddenly brightened up. "That might work. I was mad with Hamid, but on reflection I don't think he was entirely happy with the situation."

"There's another possible irregularity that may help us," James said. "Bill said that Dickens commented that the application was 'premature'. Normal practice is to send the materials for assessment without any CV. So how did he know it was premature, and why is that important? The criteria are the same whether a person is coming up early or not."

It was agreed that James would talk to Christine Desmoulins. Although the atmosphere had lightened now that there seemed to be a ray of hope, no one was in a mood for alcoholic indulgence. James accompanied Antonietta to the cottage. Despite her admiration for James's initiative, she felt oppressed.

"It's as if we're in the lions' den, and they're waiting to pounce on us," she said, her eyes wide with apprehension. James tried to soothe her, but the prospect of her mother's visit was also depressing her, and she remained downcast.

"We'll see each other anyway. Take that mournful expression off that lovely face." Antonietta responded with a weak smile and rested her head against James's shoulder. "Don't forget that we're going to France for two weeks after term ends. We'll fly to Paris, spend a couple of days there, and then drive down to Bandol." Antonietta's smile broadened, but there was still doubt in her eyes.

"How are going to explain this to Veronica"?

"That's not a problem. She hates France, and it won't be the first time I've gone there on my own."

Antonietta drew away from James. "On you own, or with a woman"?

Unaware of the force of the jealousy building up in Antonietta, James replied nonchalantly that he'd once gone there with Leonora.

Antonietta stood up, her eyes blazing. "Then I *won't* go there," she cried, making for the bedroom. "You can go home to your wife."

She slammed the bedroom door shut. Instead of going to her, as he would normally do in such circumstances, James decided to teach his volatile mistress a lesson. He left the cottage, started his car and waited behind a bush by the door of the cottage. In no time Antonietta emerged in a panic.

"James, don't leave, please"! she was shouting. James came up and put his arms around her. She was standing in front of him, paralyzed by the fear that he would drive off as before.

"I love you," he whispered, but by now Antonietta was furious.

"How can you play such a horrible trick on me"? She tried to avoid James's kiss, but he was too strong for her. The kisses gained in intensity.

"Forgive me,".

"Now I know how to deal with you,"

Antonietta looked at him, her eyes full of reproach. "Promise never to do that again."

"Only if you promise not to be unreasonably jealous."

Antonietta promised, but with her fingers crossed behind her back. "It's time we made love," she declared, and they re-entered the cottage.

After James had left, Antonietta wondered about him. Money seemed to be no object. Goodness knows how much their South American trip had cost even if he'd charged some expenses to the Institute. And that villa in the south of France? Was James hiding something? After all, she was. They would have to divulge their secrets sooner or later.

⌒ℳ⌒

Next morning James called on Christine Desmoulins. He congratulated her on her election and hesitantly began to talk about Bill's references. He didn't want to appear to be lobbying a member of the tenure committee, which was highly irregular, but he knew that any revelations about the new referees would have more credibility if they came from Christine rather than him. In any case he couldn't bring them before the committee and would have to rely on Christine.

Christine smiled. "James, I know you want something because

you're talking to me in French, and Pierre Forget told me the other day that you always do that."

James grinned sheepishly. "Yes, I want something." He related the replacement of two referees by Hamid Khan with two others who had recommended against tenure.

"He has the right to do that. I've always found that unacceptable, but it's the rule in this strange place."

"I agree, but we both know that these replacements were suggested by Arbuthnot. You know how HB controls Hamid." Christine nodded. "I'm convinced that these two referees are buddies of HB's from NUC. There may be a case of bias."

"Which you want me to find out and bring up in the committee." This time it was James's turn to nod. Christine looked at him thoughtfully. "I will certainly find that out for you, but just because HB knows them doesn't necessarily constitute bias on their part. Academics are supposed to be honorable people." The last words were said with heavy irony.

"Thank you, Christine." Sensing that his colleague wished to return to her research, James turned to go. At the door he stopped. "One other thing, Christine. One of the referees mentioned about the application being 'premature'. I'd like to know what Hamid wrote in his letters requesting the references."

"If I'd known being on the committee would be this much trouble, I wouldn't have agreed to stand," Christine grumbled.

"I don't believe you," James said with the most charming of smiles. Christine grimaced and waved him out of her office.

Confident that Christine would cooperate fully, James returned to his office to prepare for his lecture at eleven. Despite the weeks that he and Antonietta had been together, he still had a hollow feeling in his stomach when he entered the classroom and saw her there sitting next to Petra. Sometimes, he would imagine them together, and a fierce jealousy would seize hold of him. By now, Antonietta knew when this was the case as James would momentarily lose track of what he was saying. It amused her, and the glint of satisfaction in her eyes would anger James. Inwardly he would resolve to be cold to her when he arrived at the cottage, but he never succeeded in the face of Antonietta's passion and lubricious beauty.

On this day he was more preoccupied by Bill's tenure case than Antonietta's past dalliance with Petra. Back at the cottage he made love distractedly, which aroused Antonietta's ire.

"What's the matter with you"?

"I'm thinking of Christine Desmoulins."

Antonietta rose. "You're thinking about *another woman* when making love to me"! she cried, quite beside herself. Realizing his blunder, James moved quickly to avoid another of Antonietta's crises. He pulled her towards him and forced his mouth against her's until she stopped struggling and returned his kiss.

"Antonietta, not even you can be jealous of Christine Desmoulins. It's just that this tenure business is obsessing me."

"Only *I* should obsess you," Antonietta riposted with a pout. That was enough to chase thoughts of Bill, tenure and Christine completely from James's mind. Antonietta had no more reason for complaint except to point out that James needed to shave twice a day.

"I'll grow a beard, so I won't scratch."

"Then you'll tickle, and that's worse." Antonietta replied. She turned over on to her stomach. James teased her.

"I thought your thighs were sore."

"Yes, but not my buttocks."

The Saturday evening get-together at Bill's house was a rather lugubrious affair. However much James insisted they had a chance to impugn the two referees chosen by HB, he had to agree with the others that it was at best a long shot. Bill clung to the idea that a court of law would overturn the decision of the tenure committee, and James chose not to disabuse him.

After about an hour, the atmosphere brightened a little. Danny, who tried not to appear too happy given the impending disaster facing Bill, told them proudly that his daughter had been accepted to study biology at McGill University. Piotr enquired whether he and Bernadette were going to get married. James couldn't help smiling. It was typical Piotr. If Ceara were to study at McGill, she would presumably live with her father, and in Piotr's conservative Polish mind it was unseemly that Bernadette should live there too without being married to Danny.

"Give us a chance, Piotr," Danny protested. "We've only known each other for a couple of months."

"But you two are now living together," Piotr stubbornly pointed out.

Danny put his arm around Piotr. "Let a man have a little sin in his life, Piotr."

"There's far too much in this group," his friend countered.

James could see that the conversation was embarrassing Bernadette and upsetting Antonietta. "Who wants another drink"? he asked, making his way to the drink's cabinet.

Antonietta demurred. "James, can we go? I'm tired." Without a word, James went out into the hallway and fetched their coats. They left quickly, relieved to be on their own.

"Don't take Piotr too seriously," James told Antonietta. "He's very conservative and not always the most tactful of people."

"He's right. What we're doing is sinful."

James stopped the car and took Antonietta into his arms. "I don't care a damn whether it's sinful. I love you, and I can't live without you. And I'm damn well not going to live without you." His vehemence comforted Antonietta, who drew him close to her for a lingering kiss.

They arrived at the cottage and made straight for the bedroom. After they'd made love, James looked down at Antonietta snuggled up to him. "You're feeling vulnerable"?

Antonietta looked up. "I wish you could stay."

"I'll try and see you tomorrow."

"Try! You *must* come. Promise me that."

For once James didn't surrender to her imploring eyes. "I will try, Antonietta, but on Sundays it's difficult."

"I need you, James," Antonietta insisted. "I feel demoralized." She kept him as long as possible, but eventually he had to leave.

"It doesn't help us to raise Veronica's suspicions," he explained, extricating himself from their embrace. "I must go."

Sorrowfully Antonietta acquiesced

Fortunately for James, Veronica was fast asleep when he arrived home. He also fell asleep immediately, and the next thing he knew was Veronica rousing him to prepare for Mass. He shaved, dressed, and went downstairs. His children looked at him wistfully. They were hungry and hoping that their father would come to their aid, but Veronica was keeping a watchful eye on the proceedings.

"I should go and do some work at the Institute this afternoon," James told his wife.

"You certainly will not. You hardly spend any time with your family except on Sundays, and you're not deserting us today."

"Mommy's right," Susanna put in, "We hardly ever see you."

The combination of his wife's intransigence and his daughter's reproach convinced James that he had no alternative but to spend the day with the family. Using the pretext of checking the tire pressure, he went to the car and with considerable trepidation called Antonietta on his cell with the news that he would not be seeing her that day. Predictably, she was angry and upset.

"Well, if you don't want me, I'll call Petra. She's tiring of Brett, and she might like to enjoy me even if you don't."

"Antonietta, don't even think of doing that." Although he didn't really believe her, James was seized by a ferocious jealousy.

"I will," Antonietta replied with a coolness that exacerbated James's jealousy. "Before that, I'll go to Mass at Saint-Sauveur so that you can see what you're missing."

Before James had a chance to reason with her, Antonietta hung up. James called back, but she didn't answer. Wearily he returned to the house, obsessed by a longing for his mistress and pursued by images of Antonietta and Petra together. It was going to be a horrible day.

The family arrived at Mass. To James's relief, there was no sign of Antonietta. They all knelt for the obligatory prayer. It was soon over for James and the children, but Veronica remained deep in religious fervor for a few more minutes. She didn't notice her husband turn white when a beautiful dark-haired young woman swept past them and took her place in a pew a little further down on the same side. "Oh, my God, did she have to do this to me?" James's stomach churned under the force of his jealous passion. Pitilessly Antonietta turned round, and their eyes met

361

briefly. James gripped the railing of the pew in a struggle to control his emotions.

Although she appeared calm, Antonietta was faring no better. It seemed to her that every second increased her yearning to throw herself at James. The beginning of Mass brought no relief, and fearful that she would soon no longer be able to control her feelings, she fled from the church. As she passed James, she couldn't resist a quick look at him. James could see that there was no anger in her eyes, only despair and contrition. In a way, this comforted him, but it also made it even harder to bear the separation from her.

Veronica had noticed Antonietta's precipitate departure, and for the first time she exhibited some suspicion.

"Who was that dark-haired girl who rushed out of Mass"? she asked James as they left the church. "She seemed to know you."

"She's in my European class," He replied, adding for no apparent reason. "She's Italian."

"She's very beautiful," Veronica remarked.

The family went to La Brûlerie for brunch with James feeling both uneasy and miserable. It was only by a supreme effort that he managed to hide his distress and take part in the family chatter. Peter informed them that the new Star Wars film was playing at the cinema in Le Carrefour du Nord at St. Jérôme. James was only too happy to offer to take him to see it. It would be a godsent distraction. Veronica didn't want to miss her none prayers, so James went alone with both the children.

As for Antonietta, she returned to the cottage. She regretted her irrational behavior and felt guilty at missing Mass. The thought of spending the day alone in longing and remorse was unbearable. She called Petra. Brett was off at training camp with the football team, and she was happy to meet Antonietta for lunch. Their conversation turned straightaway to the topic of their men. Antonietta asked about Petra's ski trip during reading week.

"The skiing was great, the fucking was great, but the conversation was zero," Petra replied. "How about you"?

"It was like being in paradise."

"So what's the problem"? Petra asked, surprised by her friend's dejected mien.

Antonietta recounted the morning's tribulations. "I knew I was being thoroughly unreasonable, but I couldn't help it."

"Well, if it'll make you feel any better, I don't mind enjoying you."

"No, Petra. I'm never doing anything like that again, and I'm not ever going to be unfaithful to James."

"Pity."

Petra continued to grin suggestively at Antonietta, who blushed and swiftly changed the topic. She'd intended to invite Petra to spend the rest of the afternoon with her at the cottage, but her sexual innuendoes were unsettling, and she went home alone to drink wine and masochistically fuel her sense of emptiness by listening to Laura Pausini. She fell asleep on the sofa, awoke sometime later with brutal suddenness, dragged herself into the bedroom, undressed, and slipped naked into bed. She tossed and turned for hours, tormented by sexual desire and emotional craving for the man she loved. As morning neared, she at last fell asleep.

With very bad grace, Veronica agreed to drive the children to school so that James could ostensibly have time to prepare for his eleven o'clock lecture and attend to some administrative matters.

"I shall be late for my terce prayers," she complained.

"No, you won't, if you drop the kids off at eight-thirty," he replied, barely concealing his irritation.

James arrived at the cottage a little before eight. He saw at once the telltale signs of Antonietta's distress: the empty bottles of wine and the CDs of Laura Pausini lying around without their jackets. He had a feeling of relief. It didn't seem she'd been with Petra. He turned on the coffee machine and made two cups of expresso. Gingerly he opened the bedroom, still half fearing to find Antonietta with her blond girlfriend. He spilled some of the coffee and swore loudly.

"James"! Antonietta was alone and overjoyed to see him. "Put the coffee down," she ordered and threw her naked body against him. After kissing James with great ardor, she gazed at him, her lovely eyes full of penitence.

"I behaved so badly. Please say that you forgive me."

James sat down on the bed. *"Non sei sempre certa del perdono"*?

*"Sì,"* she replied.

They drank the coffee quickly, and with growing impatience Antonietta helped James undress. Her desire for him was so overpowering that the mere caress of his hands on her breasts was sufficient to bring her close to orgasm. She pushed him down her body, and within seconds of his tongue touching her intimacy, she came to her climax. It didn't last much longer with James.

"It's always worse when we've been together somewhere," Antonietta sighed after their second and more protracted bout of sex. "What's more, I seem less and less able to deal with it. I knew I was being completely stupid yesterday, but I simply couldn't control myself. The thought of not seeing you drove me crazy." She gave James a rueful smile. "I was punished for it. I nearly broke down in church."

"So did I. We can't go on much longer like this."

"I know. Let me get my mother's visit over first, and then we'll decide what we're going to do."

"You mean we have a choice"?

"No, James, we have no choice."

## Chapter 33

# Wednesday March 13, 2002
# to Sunday March, 17th

TWO DAYS LATER JAMES was seated in his office at nine o'clock waiting to meet with Christine Desmoulins. For once Antonietta had renounced his morning visit without too much fuss. She was as concerned as James about Bill's future.

Christine arrived. Taking advantage of the *Freedom of Information Act*, she had obtained a copy of Hamid's letter to the referees.

"You were right, James," Christine said as she handed over the letter. "He mentions that it is a case of early tenure, and he tells the referees that the criteria are stricter."

James perused the letter. "This gives us some hope. It's a clear breach of procedure and can be construed as an attempt to influence the referees against Bill. The question is whether the committee will see it that way."

"I don't understand Hamid." Christine looked again at the letter. "Surely he knew this was irregular."

"Hamid's a nice guy, but he has no self-confidence. Presumably Arbuthnot told him to do this, and Hamid obeyed the Senior Dean."

"If McGrath will join Forget and me in impugning the references, Winstone can't possibly give his casting vote in favor of a breach of procedure."

James was doubtful. "McGrath is a buddy of HB's, Christine, and

Winstone is weak. We may need more than this letter if we're going to save Bill." He no longer made a secret of the fact that he considered Christine an ally.

"Well, there is something else." The normally placid Christine was almost bursting with animation "Keighley and Mauser did their doctorates at NUC at the same time as Arbuthnot. That's obviously why he picked them. There's no other reason. Keighley's from Wickham, which is a minor business school, and Mauser isn't even a full professor. The obvious choice from Chicago would have been Broderick."

"Who is the referee Bill chose and who was replaced by Hamid with Mauser."

"One more thing. Both Mauser and Keighley are general economists. They've never done any international work, and Bill's field is international finance and economics."

James noted everything Christine had to tell him and took a photocopy of Hamid's letter. He told Christine to keep everything to herself.

"What are you going to do"?

"I'm not sure." In fact, James had decided to go and see Tom Buchanan. Tom had contacts all over the place, and, before becoming Rector of the Institute in 1986, he'd been Chair of the Economics Department at Chicago. He saw no point in burdening Christine with this information. She'd played her role, and now it was up to him. *"Once more into the breach, dear friends*,*"* he said to himself.

It was past ten when Christine left. There was no time to go to the cottage, so James called Antonietta. She was disappointed, but the news of some hope for Bill consoled her.

"Try to come back immediately after your class, Annya or no Annya."

James laughed. "She doesn't pay any attention to me anymore."

"I'm not surprised. You made her so mad the last time she came to your office."

The satisfaction in Antonietta's voice was palpable.

The next morning before his class on Europe, James went to see Tom Buchanan. He explained the whole scenario that was taking place over Bill's tenure.

"Tom, they're out to get at me through Bill. HB sees me as an obstacle to taking over this place, and, if he manages to have Bill kicked out, our colleagues will understand their bread is buttered on his side."

Tom smiled. "You don't have a very high opinion of your colleagues, James."

"Most of them are vain, weak, and easily led, which is why it always ends in disaster if academics get political power. Look at that idiot Trudeau. He nearly bankrupted this country. Not to mention Wilson, who was the most useless Prime Minister Britain ever had."

"What about Lord North"? Tom enquired, his grin becoming broader.

"Excellent fellow. Ridded us of those troublesome Americans."

Tom guffawed loudly and slapped his knee in mirth. "Good comeback, James," he roared.

James was serious again. "It's not my comeback I'm worried about, Tom, it's Bill."

"What do you want from me"?

"Some advice. How strong a case do we have for rejecting the referees in toto because of Hamid's letter to them"?

Tom grimaced. "That's a difficult one. The rules don't provide for stricter criteria for early tenure, but neither do they prohibit them. The committee has wide discretion, and they are probably free to side with Hamid."

"Shit." Tom had just demolished James's one sure ace. "What about the substitutions. Both Keighley and Mauser are general economists."

'That doesn't matter. It's not unreasonable to have two general economists, particularly as the other two are internationalists."

James refused to let disappointment deter him. "Then what I want from you, Tom, is a little detective work. You know a lot of people in academia. See whether there is any way to disqualify Keighley and Mauser."

Tom reflected for a moment. "I promised myself that, once my Rectorship was over, I'd give academic shenanigans a wide berth."

"For Christ's sake, Tom. You're our only hope. If you don't help, a good academic has his career ruined, and a mediocre megalomaniac will run this place. He'll destroy the Institute you built up."

James had touched Tom's weak spot. He stood up and put his arm around James. "You're a good man, James, and Bill's lucky to have such a friend. Be patient. I'll do what I can."

"It's all very well to talk of patience. FPC meets in a little over four weeks."

Tom smiled enigmatically. "As your hero Wilson once said, a week is a long time in politics."

"This isn't politics; it's bloody academia."

"Same rascals."

Once James was gone, Tom picked up the phone and called his secretary on the interphone. "Will you get me Jim Reilly, Pat. He's the Chair of Economics at Chicago."

Back in his office, James called Danny. He'd been too involved with Antonietta to brief him before on the outcome of his talk with Christine, and now he recounted both that meeting and the one with Tom. Danny suggested they should all meet that evening at his place to take counsel on what was happening. James agreed and went off to his class.

Annya Nowak was sitting by herself in the students' bar drinking a beer. She 'd finished her two term papers and had nothing else to do. Elliot was at some meeting and wouldn't be home until later that afternoon. One of the papers was for Professor Markham. Annya grimaced at the thought of him. She was still smarting from his rejection of her in favor of that Italian girl. She wasn't quite sure why she wanted him so badly. Perhaps it was because she was no longer in love with Elliot and needed a romantic attachment to fill the void in her life. She wondered whether she'd ever loved Elliot. It had been more like a typical female student's crush on her professor, but at least it had ridded her of Brett Doefman. James Markham was a different matter. She was obsessed by him and would close her eyes when she had sex with Elliot and try to imagine he was her partner.

"Hi, Annya." It was Ken Wrangel. Annya returned his greeting frostily. She knew him from high school and thought him a pervert. He was always slinking around with his camera. She'd heard how Markham had put him down and wished she could have been there. He wasn't only a pervert; he was a jerk as well.

"What courses are you taking this term"? Wrangel sat down next to Annya with his beer, oblivious of her disdain.

"Global strategy from Professor Gowling, Slavic studies from Professor Tocheniuk and international trade law from James Markham." Unwittingly, Annya had betrayed her interest in James by the different way she referred to him. Wrangel didn't notice.

"Markham's a bastard. He's supposed to be a great teacher, but his first lectures were shitty as hell. Then he humiliated me in front of the whole class."

"You may have deserved it." Annya smiled sweetly at Wrangel as if she were complementing him.

"I damn well didn't! But I've got something on him, something that'll get me all the revenge I want."

Wrangel now had Annya's full attention. "Is it something to do with that Italian girl, della Chiesa"?

"Yes. I've got a picture of them making out," Wrangel replied. This was an exaggeration, but the picture was compromising enough to get Markham kicked out of the Institute.

"*Use it*"*!* Annya spat out venomously. "Della Chiesa is a stuck-up snob, and he's just a hypocrite. He goes to Mass like a saint with his whole family every Sunday and screws della Chiesa on the side."

Wrangel was taken aback by Annya's venom, not suspecting that it arose from jealousy. He was determined to have his revenge, but only if he failed the course, he told her. The humiliation still rankled, but Wrangel was aware that he'd helped make a fool of himself.

Annya was furious with him. Here was the perfect opportunity to break up James and della Chiesa. There was a good chance Markham would be more receptive to her charms when he needed some consolation in his disgrace.

"You're a fool, Ken. Even if you don't fail the course, you shouldn't let a prick like Markham treat you the way he did."

After Wrangel left, Annya was at least honest enough to admit to herself that, if James was a hypocrite, she wasn't much better.

The meeting at Danny's place in St. Jérôme was inconclusive. There was little they could do but wait and hope that Tom would come up with some dirt on the two replacements. This was hardly enough to lighten the morose atmosphere. Antonietta's absence didn't help. She and James seemed to radiate a happiness when they were together that was contagious. Without her, James was subdued and anxious to leave for the cottage. After a few unenthusiastic scotches, the friends went their separate ways.

Antonietta was thrilled to see James so soon. She deserted her term paper for his arms, and between kisses he related the mournful moments he'd just spent. She stood up and, taking hold of James's hand, made to lead him into the bedroom.

"No. This time you really must finish that term paper first."

Antonietta submitted with bad grace. James flipped through *La muerte de Artemio Cruz* while his impatient mistress hurriedly finished her essay on Simon Bolivar.

"There"! Antonietta announced triumphantly, printing off her epos. "Now I'm taking you to bed."

Once they were in bed, the feelings that Antonietta had controlled with much effort while writing her term paper boiled to the surface. Her kisses were febrile, her body tense, her eyes glistened with an array of conflicting emotions in which passion, despair, longing, anxiety all had their place. She pulled James on top of her and dug her fingers into his back. After their pleasure she kept him on her, and with her hands clasped behind his head, pulled him towards her voracious mouth and devoured him with kisses that burned on his lips.

"Come to me tomorrow evening."

"I will, but I can't stay too late. Veronica's getting suspicious ever since she saw you at Mass."

Antonietta pushed James away angrily. "You're going to have to deal with her because I want you here, *I need you here*." She turned away, ashamed of the tears that were beginning to flow. "If you loved me, it wouldn't matter if she's suspicious."

Overwrought by his worries about Bill and the interminable conflict of love, family and religion, James lost his patience.

"Fine," he snapped, "If you'll agree to marry me, Veronica can have all the suspicions she wants. But I'm not going to break up the family and put the kids through a divorce if you don't."

"So you're going to stay with Veronica"? Antonietta made to get up from the bed, but James stopped her.

"That's not what I said."

"Yes it is," Antonietta sobbed.

James took her in his arms and kissed the tears running down her cheeks. His anger evaporated into contrition and misery. "You are all I want, all I live for. You know that. I want to marry you, and I want you to agree."

Antonietta laid her head on James's chest and stroked his belly with her hand. "Sometimes I long to be the person I once was. Confident, in charge of myself, untouchable almost. Then I remember how empty life was. Sometimes, too, I feel unable to take a step that will separate from me from all I've always held dear: my family, my religion. Then I think of the alternative, of losing you, and I feel sick to my stomach. I live my life in a constant jumble of emotions and desires."

They lay a while in silence before Antonietta slid down James body. The pleasure was intense, and he returned it in full measure, but the prospect of the arrival of Antonietta's mother weighed on both and hindered their enjoyment of each other. Despite all James's assurances that they would meet in a motel each day, Antonietta remained despondent.

"You don't know my mother. I know I'm not going to be able to get away very often."

James reminded her of their plan to spend Friday night together in Montreal. "Think of that and take comfort from it."

James was very late home and found an irate Veronica waiting for him.

"What's going on, James"? she demanded to know. "Don't tell me that you've been working, and you don't seem to have been drinking either."

"I'm sorry, Veronica." James sought desperately for a plausible explanation for his tardiness. He'd used it before, but all he could think of was Bill's tenure case. This seemed to placate Veronica, and the storm passed. "It won't always pass," James thought as he lay in bed next to his wife. "Once term ends, we'll have to put an end to this situation. Antonietta must understand that."

⌒⁂⌒

Antonietta was traveling in driving snow towards Dorval airport. It was a complicated itinerary once you left Highway 15, and she lost her way. When she arrived at the airport, it was past the time for the arrival of her mother's flight, and her mother was waiting for her. She was not very pleased. "The least I expected was to find you here to welcome me," she complained.

Antonietta kissed her mother on both cheeks. "I'm sorry, *mamma*," she said contritely. "I got lost."

Caterina's expression suggested strongly that she didn't believe her daughter, but she said no more. Antonietta led her to the Jetta, put her luggage in the trunk, and started back to Ste. Anne. It was still snowing and seemed even colder.

"How can you survive in such a climate? In Florence it's already spring, and here you'd think you were in the Arctic Circle."

"This isn't going to be fun," Antonietta thought, observing her mother's pinched appearance. "It's not always like this," she replied. "The fall was beautiful." Caterina didn't seem impressed.

"Well, the climate doesn't seem to agree with you. I've never seen you looking this pale."

"It's not the climate that makes me pale," Antonietta thought. She was aware of her mother's penetrating stare and feared she might guess the truth.

"I hope you haven't thrown yourself at some man," her mother went on in a suspicious tone, confirming Antonietta's apprehension.

Antonietta felt the anger mount within her. For a brief moment she was tempted to fling the truth into her mother's disapproving face, but

372

she resisted the impulse and let her rage subside into indignation. "I never throw myself at men. Men throw themselves at me."

"Well, I hope none have here. I don't want a son-on-law who's not only a commoner but a North American as well."

Antonietta had to suppress a smile. She wondered how James would react to being stigmatized as a North American. "No, *mamma*, no North American has thrown himself at me."

They arrived at the cottage. "Where are you going to sleep"? her mother demanded to know. "There's only one bedroom."

"I'll sleep on the sofa."

Her mother's face froze in horror. "A Countess della Chiesa sleeping on a sofa"! she cried. "Now I've seen everything."

Matters improved a little when Antonietta took her mother to eat at Gio's. She was impressed by the food, and the intimate atmosphere of the restaurant calmed the tension between the two of them. This was until Caterina brought the subject around to Gina della Chiesa. Gina was Andrea della Chiesa's daughter and one of Antonietta's four cousins. The Palmieri cousins, Maria Giovanna and Clara were a decade older than Antonietta, and she'd never been close to them. Clara was a typical Palmieri, and Maria Giovanna had married a Spanish count, whose name Antonietta could never remember, and lived in Madrid.

The two della Chiesa cousins were much different. Alberto was charming and amusing, and Gina was sensitive and artistic. She'd just finished her doctorate in art history at the University of Rome. Antonietta had seen both when visiting her sister Carla at Christmas. She wondered what news her mother was bursting to tell her about Gina. From the look of disapproval on her mother's face, it wasn't good news.

"You'll never guess what she's done. She's married a *divorced* man, and outside the Church. Everyone's shocked, even Maria Luisa, who seems to accept almost anything. She won't even talk to her daughter now."

Antonietta could sense herself turning white. If her easy-going aunt, Maria Luisa, was prepared to cut her daughter off for marrying a divorced man, how much worse would she fare if she married James?

"I'm glad to see you don't approve," her mother commented, taking Antonietta's ashen expression for condemnation of her cousin.

Antonietta had no idea how to react. There was no point in contradicting her mother. She had to spend the next week with her, away from James, and the prospect of spending it arguing about marrying a divorced man was horrific. She might even betray herself.

"I'm surprised Aunt Maria Luisa reacted that way," she stammered.

"It's the first time I've known her behave correctly. It's inconceivable that a della Chiesa would marry a divorced man. *Inconceivable.*"

Caterina had raised her voice, and people were beginning to look at them askance. Antonietta noticed nothing. Her mother's words were the confirmation of all she feared. Her marriage to James would be at the expense of her family ties. She felt a misery descend upon her. Her dilemma, always terrible, was now like a knife in an open wound.

Desperately, Antonietta changed the conversation, asking about little Claudio. Mercifully, Caterina was only too happy to regale her errant daughter with an account of Carla's maternal bliss. Antonietta barely listened and sipped her wine in a daze of wretchedness. She longed to be alone, she longed for James's comforting presence, but all that awaited her was the loneliness of the sofa and her mother's ominous presence in the adjoining bedroom.

"You must be tired, *mamma.* Let's go back to the cottage, and you can have an early night."

Her mother agreed, and they drove to the cottage. Antonietta sat on the sofa reading listlessly while her mother prepared herself for bed. They kissed perfunctorily, and Antonietta was at last alone. She lay on the sofa in the dark turning over in her mind the hopelessness of her situation. Tears rolled silently down her cheeks. Exhausted by her misery, she fell into a troubled slumber. Suddenly, she heard her cell phone ring, and she answered it quickly so it wouldn't wake her mother.

"James"? she whispered in disbelief. It must be the early morning, and he never called at such an hour. "Where are you"?

"At the end of your driveway."

Antonietta threw the cell phone down on the sofa, and, dressed only in a flimsy nightdress she'd bought expressly for her mother's visit, she raced out into the cold and the snow. When she reached James, she threw herself hysterically into his arms. James interrupted her devouring kisses.

"Come into the car. You'll catch your death of cold out here dressed like that."

Once in the car, Antonietta continued to devour James with her kisses. He gently pushed her away to recover his breath.

"What made you come"?

James pulled her face up towards him. He gazed at her for a moment, taking full measure of her loveliness. "I had to see you, to make sure you were alright, to hold you in my arms."

Antonietta laid her head on James's shoulder. "I'm glad you're here. I've never needed you more."

She told him about Gina.

*Chapter 34*

# Monday March 18, 2002 to
# Thursday, April 4, 2002

THE WEEK OF CATERINA'S visit to Canada was very difficult for both Antonietta and James. Throughout the whole time of her visit, Caterina did little but criticize everything: the weather, the food (except for Gio's), the way people dressed and, most irritating of all given the level of her own French, the way the Quebecois spoke the language. The only moment of appreciation came with her attendance at Mass at the Basilica in old Montreal. But, although she admired the Basilica, she had little good to say about the rest of Montreal. When she wasn't complaining, she was trying to persuade her daughter to return to Italy. Although her patience was strained to the utmost, Antonietta bore all this with remarkable stoicism. She knew her mother and despite her exasperation kept her temper under control. From her earliest childhood she had been taught to respect her parents.

Worst of all, she was not able to seek much relief from her ordeal by seeing James. She spent the Monday tryst with James between tears and feverish lovemaking. Unfortunately, their presence evoked the motel owner's suspicions. When they left, he made a veiled allusion to professors and their female students. Regretfully, they decided to forego other such occasions. In any case, Antonietta's mother was so furious about being left alone until seven in the evening that another rendezvous would have been impossible. Antonietta was reduced to casting mournful eyes at James during their classes together and a few surreptitious meetings in his office. One of these nearly ended in disaster when Christine Desmoulins arrived unexpectedly. After this episode the lovers had no choice but to wait until Caterina's departure on Friday when they would finally be alone together for a night in Montreal. Consumed by longing for James, Antonietta counted the minutes as they passed with cruel slowness.

Initially, James had been more sanguine about the visit of Antonietta's mother, but the affair with Gina had shaken him. He feared it would fortify Antonietta's reticence to turn her back on her family and her religion. He was preoccupied and worried, and the false gaiety of Danny's party for St. Patrick's Day did little to improve his state of mind. He felt lost without Antonietta. Nor was Bill in the best of spirits. Only Danny's ebullience at the news that his daughter was coming for Easter and Bernadette's cheeriness saved the evening. The presence of her two sons from a previous marriage also helped. Aged fourteen and twelve, they were unusually happy boys. Their parents' divorce when they were youngsters had obviously not traumatized them. This was some comfort to James.

As the week progressed, James's mood became more and more somber. The Monday rendezvous with Antonietta had done more to upset than soothe him. Not only was Antonietta clearly under stress, and God alone knew what ideas her mother was putting into her head, but the motel owner's remarks were also unsettling. He was quite capable of contacting the Institute. The occasional phone calls that they managed normally ended with Antonietta in tears, and to top it all, there was still no news from Tom Buchanan.

The day of deliverance eventually arrived, and Antonietta drove her mother with barely suppressed excitement to the airport, her mind entirely absorbed by the prospect of meeting James at Le Reine Elisabeth. Although her snobbishness often clouded her judgment, Caterina was an acute observer, and her suspicions about her daughter's life in Quebec were strengthened by Antonietta's strange animation.

"Promise to come home soon," she told her daughter.

"When I've finished my master's degree," Antonietta replied.

Without exchanging any more words, Caterina kissed her daughter frostily and walked off through security. Antonietta watched her go with a mixture of relief and sadness. Her mother had many faults, but she was still her mother. She fought back tears as she watched her disappear without looking back again. She turned round and, to her inexpressible joy, saw James waiting for her. She ran towards him and threw herself into his arms.

"I didn't expect to see you here," she said, breaking off from their passionate embrace. "You told me you'd meet me at the hotel."

"I couldn't wait."

Once they were in the hotel room, Antonietta quickly stripped and pulling James onto the bed began to undress him. To James's surprise, she seemed calm, almost serene, more preoccupied by her sexual desires than the anguished week she must have spent. Or had it been so anguished? As she made to pull down his briefs, James stopped her.

"Do you know why I came to meet you at the airport"?

Antonietta shrugged. "At this moment I don't care. I want sex."

James surrendered to her concupiscence, and they made love. Antonietta was demanding and carefree, James, though transported to ecstasy by Antonietta's body and the various delights it offered, couldn't still his fears. He'd expected to find a distraught Antonietta desperate for emotional comfort; but his mistress seemed happily consumed by her sexual desire. As she lay exhausted in his arms, she asked why he'd met her at the airport.

"I was afraid you wouldn't come to the hotel."

Antonietta shot up and looked at James in amazement.

"Why ever not"?

"I feared your mother might have persuaded you to return to Italy."

Antonietta was silent for a few moments. She kissed James tenderly and looked into his eyes, her own intense and moist with emotion.

"Every night last week I spent alone on the sofa, turning over in my mind how to resolve what seemed to be an insoluble dilemma. Yes, I did imagine returning to Italy and giving you up, but when I did, my head began to spin, I was sick to my stomach, and I felt a pain, a physical pain, in my chest. It was as if I were suffocating. Last night I imagined the opposite scenario. I imagined being married to you, having our children, living every day with you. I felt an immense happiness tinged only by sadness that my parents and my Church would have disowned me, but even this sadness contained the hope that one day my family would understand, and that God would forgive me for surrendering to a passion I never sought but which it was beyond my strength to withstand."

Antonietta paused and gazed at James. "I have made my decision, and for me there is no longer a dilemma."

James felt a huge relief engulf him. "That's why you're so serene"?

Antonietta laughed. "Are you disappointed? Would you have preferred me to throw myself hysterically at you, weeping and sobbing"?

"I suppose not, but I'm not used to you being so calm, so sure of yourself. I feared the worst."

They made love one more time before discussing their immediate plans. It was agreed that, on their return from France, James would leave Veronica without telling her about Antonietta. He would take an apartment or move in with Bill. They would live together later in the summer, end of August perhaps, so that neither Veronica nor the Institute would know for certain that they'd already been lovers. Their marriage would have to wait until the divorce came through, which could take at least a year. Antonietta agreed that in the immediate future they must be discreet to avoid making Veronica suspicious.

"You should also spend more time with your children. That way it will be more difficult for Veronica to turn them against you."

"How are you going to react if we don't see each other so often"?

Antonietta sighed. "I won't like it, and I know I'll have a few crises, but if we want to marry in a way that causes the least problems, we have no choice." Antonietta looked forlornly at James. "If I'm difficult, just remind me of what I've just said."

Antonietta gave James a lingering kiss and went off to the bathroom to prepare herself for the restaurant.

"I'll wait for you in the bar," James called out to her. She poked her face round the bathroom door. "No you won't. After a week without you, I want you here."

When Antonietta emerged from the bathroom, James caught his breath.

"How can a woman be this lovely"? It was a rhetorical question and

Antonietta just smiled in reply. "Your eyes are so wonderfully expressive, and you nose is perfect. It's not too big and not too small. It fits your face perfectly."

Antonietta burst out laughing. "It would look silly elsewhere,' she said, her eyes dancing with amusement.

James ignored her ribaldry. "The soft contours of your lips are so seductive, particularly when they glisten."

"That's nothing to do with my lips," Antonietta pointed out. "It's the glossy lipstick I use, which my mother says makes me look like a whore."

James shook his head. "You're not appreciating my lyrical rhapsody on your beauty," he complained.

"Well, James, you're not exactly Shakespeare." Antonietta ducked to avoid James kissing her. "You'll ruin my make-up," she told him.

"Damn your make-up. I want you." Antonietta's resisted for a few seconds and then surrendered. An hour later she was re-doing her make-up. James had been banished to the bar.

⌒⁂⌒

On Sunday James accompanied his family to Mass at the Notre Dame Basilica in Montreal. To his surprise they came across Danny with Bernadette and her two boys. Danny and James greeted each other effusively, but Veronica rebuffed Bernadette's attempts at friendliness.

"They shouldn't be at Mass," she hissed at James as they walked down to their pews. "They're divorced and living in sin."

James couldn't hide his disgust. "How about a little Christian charity"?

"Christian charity doesn't extend to condoning sin," was Veronica's reply.

James shrugged. "Only a little while longer, and I'll be shut of this religious fanatic."

Antonietta attended Mass at the Cathedral in St. Jérôme and afterwards met Petra for lunch. She was on her own as Brett had gone to Ottawa to spend the weekend with his parents.

"He asked me to go, but they're too dull."

Antonietta gave her a searching look. "Do you really think there's

380

any future for you two? You find Brett indecisive and his parents dull. That's not much of a basis for marriage."

"At least he's not married," Petra retorted, but the bitterness of her tone was directed more against her own situation than Antonietta's.

Antonietta put her hand on Petra's. "I didn't mean to upset you, Petra, but I can see you're not happy, and that saddens me."

Petra smiled a little tearfully. "You're right, Antonietta. It's not going to work out." She gazed at her friend. "What about you? You seem uncommonly happy and composed. Does this mean you've taken the plunge"?

Antonietta recounted the visit of her mother and her resolution of the dilemma that had been plaguing her ever since she gave herself to James.

"We're going to live together later this summer, and we'll get married once the divorce is finalized."

"I doubt whether I'll move in with Brett," Petra declared sadly.

The next week was Holy Week, and the last classes were held on Tuesday, March 26. Antonietta and James spent the afternoon together, and in the evening, when she was on her own, Antonietta managed to do some studying. She still felt a dreadful emptiness without James's presence, but it was more bearable now she knew that before very long they would be living together. They saw each other every day, but only for short periods. Antonietta had a term paper to finish for Professor Martinez, and she needed to do a lot of preparation for Professor Wong's exam as she'd missed many of his classes. She and James arranged to do the take-home exam for the European course together on the Wednesday after Easter as it was due the next day.

They spent Thursday evening of Holy Week at Bill's with the others. It was not a particularly jovial occasion as the problem of Bill's tenure weighed heavily upon all of them. The only genuinely amusing moment was when Bernadette innocently asked Antonietta about her term paper for James. Despite his worries Bill couldn't resist such an opening.

"They do it in bed together, and they use my marking scheme."

"What's your marking scheme"? James put his face in his hands at Bernadette's question, Danny was grinning, Piotr had his bemused air, and Antonietta was looking beseechingly at Bill. To no avail.

'D is for a student who doesn't perform at all. C is for a student who sucks. B is for a student who sucks and fucks and A is for a student who does sixty-four," Bill explained, giving a chuckle of satisfaction.

"Please don't ask what sixty-four is, Bernadette," James put in quickly. As it was, poor Bernadette was red with embarrassment. But Bill hadn't finished.

"They used it last time, but she only got a B. This time she's hoping for an A."

Antonietta poured the remains of her white wine over Bill's head much to everyone's amusement, except Bill.

"Keep your woman under control, Markham," Bill growled, wiping himself dry.

"It serves you right," said James, still shaking with mirth.

This was the highlight of the evening. After that, the conversation turned inevitably to the topic of Bill's tenure.

"Nothing's happening," he complained. "Tom's come up with nothing."

"Be patient, Bill," James counseled. "I know he's working on it."

There was little else to be said, and all further attempts to cheer Bill up failed miserably. Antonietta and James took advantage of the morose ambiance to leave early. They wanted to spend what was left of the evening together as they were not going to see each other over Easter. When James wasn't accompanying the family to the Stations of the Cross on Friday, the Easter vigil on Saturday night, and Mass on Easter Sunday, he was looking after the children. Easter was a time of special devotion for Veronica, and she spent almost all her time in church.

James found the separation from Antonietta hard to bear. She dominated all his thoughts and desires. Unable to bear it any longer, he took advantage of Veronica's absence to seek refuge in the garage and call Antonietta on the cell phone. She was missing him, she said, but she sounded very reasonable and quite happy. James still found this newfound serenity unsettling, particularly in contrast to his own inner turmoil. "*Dimi che m'ami*," he implored just as Peter came into the garage in search of him. He gave his father a strange look and waited while James, trying desperately to hide his embarrassment, took his leave of Antonietta.

"My son's arrived," he explained.

"Who was that, Dad"?

"An Italian colleague from work."

Peter didn't believe his father. I knew it was Antonietta, he would affirm many years later, and "*dimi che m'ami*" was too near "*dis-moi que tu m'aimes*" for him not to have understood. As it was, he just asked his father to play video soccer with him.

By the time Easter Sunday Mass was over, even Veronica felt she had done her duty by the Lord and His Son and contrary to James's expectations raised no objection when he tentatively suggested that he should go to the Institute to finalize his exam questions. She merely pointed out that if he hadn't spent all that time drinking with his friends, he would've done this already. The exams had, of course, been prepared and handed in to Ilse long ago. It was to the cottage and not the Institute that James was headed.

Feeling strangely nervous, James made his way to Ste. Anne. He was relieved to see Antonietta's Jetta parked in front of the cottage and stopped the Maserati beside it. He knocked on the door as he'd forgotten his key. Puzzled but happy to be drawn away from her study of the Cultural Revolution, Antonietta answered. She stared at James in joyous disbelief. "James"! she cried and embraced him with boundless passion. Without waiting for an explanation for his unexpected apparition, she led him into the bedroom and demanded that he make love to her.

"What about your studies"?

Antonietta slid off her thong and lay down on the bed, naked, her legs apart. "Do you really care"? she asked, playing lasciviously with herself. She was a picture of such rampant sexuality that James tore a button off his shirt in the haste to undress.

～

Exams started in earnest for Antonietta the week after Easter. She handed in her take-home exam for Professor Martinez on Tuesday. It was a critique of Isabel Allende's *La Casa de los Espíritus* and a comparison of the events of September 1973 in Chile as they really happened with the way they were portrayed in the book. On Wednesday she and James worked on his term paper between bouts of sex and accompanied by much hilarity. He offered her an A but she preferred a B.

"I love fucking and sucking you, but I find "a to m" disgusting."

"You don't have to do it even if I give you an A." James replied, somewhat shocked by Antonietta's uncharacteristic crudeness.

"A 'B' raises less suspicion, anyway,"

She came on top of him, her luscious breasts swaying pruriently before his face. "Are you ready for my B"? she asked, beginning to descend his body with her tongue. What happened next provided ammunition for much bawdiness at that evening's get-together at Danny's. It was only when both Antonietta and Bernadette protested that the conversation was getting out of hand and James was threatening to leave that Bill and Danny relented. On the way home, James apologized for his friends.

Antonietta gave him a wanton smile. "It's true they began to go a bit too far, but, as I told you once before, allusions to our sex life don't upset me. My body exists for our pleasure together, and I don't care who knows it."

James glanced across at her, perplexed as ever by her unusual blend of unabashed sexuality and piety.

On Thursday morning James received the much-awaited phone call from Tom Buchanan asking him to come to his office.

"Is it good news"? he asked, unable to bear the suspense.

"Yes," Tom replied.

James walked through the quadrangle, pausing to throw a looney* into the fountain and make a wish. He was in a state of suppressed excitement.

Tom came immediately to the point. "You were right. Mauser and Keighley are indeed friends of Arbuthnot. They were in the same doctoral class together at NUC."

Tom paused. James was disappointed. He had hoped for something more, although he didn't really know what.

"This doesn't necessarily get us anywhere, particularly with the line-up of committee," he commented. Then he saw a wicked grin come over Tom's face and realized there was more to come. "Okay, Tom, you've had your fun. Now spill the beans before I throttle you."

Tom chuckled. "You never spoke to me like that when I was Rector."

"For Christ's sake, tell me what you know." James was almost out of his seat in frustrated expectation.

"Alright. Jim Reilly, the Chair of Economics at Chicago, was appointed Assistant Professor by me back when I was Chair. More than that, I helped him get tenure in what was a very difficult case. He owed me big time, and I called it in."

Tom paused again to light a cigarette. Smoking in the Institute buildings was now forbidden, but Tom paid no attention. Both of his successors had taken him to task but to no avail. "If they want to make silly rules, fine, but I'm not obeying them," he' d once told an irate Ilse Bromhoeffer, whose office was next to Tom's.

"I had Jim grill Kevin Mauser. He's up for a full professorship, and after a little badgering and some none too subtle hints about needing Jim's support for his promotion, Mauser cracked and confessed all. Both he and Keighley had been put up to writing negative references by Arbuthnot. In fact, it was Arbuthnot who wrote both references."

James beamed contentedly. This was better than he'd ever dared hope.

"Jim contacted Keighley and told him of Mauser's confession. He saw immediately the game was up and confirmed Mauser's account. In return for a promise not to make them known, the two signed statements outlining what had happened."

"What's the use of the statements if we can't produce them for the committee," James asked in alarm.

Tom gave a self-satisfied smile. "The statements were only intended as a guarantee that the two would go through with the other part of the bargain."

"What was that"? James fought to master his impatience. Tom pulled two letters out his desk drawer.

"These letters are addressed to Hamid Khan for you to give to him personally. They are from Keighley and Mauser announcing that they are withdrawing their references in deference to Broderick and

Yankovitch, who are senior to them and more qualified to judge Bill's work."

James heaved a sigh of relief, but he was bothered by Tom's approach.

"Wouldn't it have been better for them to send the letters directly to Hamid"?

"No. There is nothing to prevent Hamid ignoring them. Your job is to convince him that the statements will be made known if he doesn't replace Mauser and Keighley with Broderick and Yankovitch."

"If I don't have the statements, what's to make him believe they exist."

Tom shook his head. "James, you're normally sharper than this. Who is Hamid going to consult on this"?

"Arbuthnot."

"Exactly, and Arbuthnot will immediately contact his two friends and find out that the statements exist. He also knows they're true."

"What if Mauser or Keighley tell him that Jim promised not to make them known"?

Tom gave his wicked grin again. "They won't. Jim's promise only holds if they keep their little gobs shut."

James left Tom's office, elated but still anxious about the final outcome. He was in a better position than in the Hunt case, but he was loath to cry victory too soon and decided not to tell Bill until his reprieve was definite. He did, however, go to see Christine Desmoulins to give her the news. She was disgusted but not surprised at HB's perfidy.

"Is there anything I can do, James"?

"No, Christine. This is going to be brutal, but I've grown used to battling HB." His colleague looked immensely relieved.

James returned to his office and made an appointment to see Hamid the next afternoon at four. He went to the cottage to inform Antonietta of what had happened. She was thankful for Bill's sake, but she was upset that James was going to be the one to tackle Hamid and Arbuthnot. "Why is it always you who does the dirty work? Why can't Tom go, or Christine or Danny or…"

James took his worried mistress into his arms. "This is important. It's a question of Bill's whole career. I may be fooling myself, but I think I'm the best person to deal with Hamid and HB."

Antonietta's beautiful dark eyes were full of foreboding. "Promise me this will be the last time. We're near the end now, and I don't want anything to come between us and the happiness that awaits us."

"I promise, my love." James started to lead Antonietta into the bedroom, but she shook her head sadly.

"James, I've got Wong's exam on Monday, and I'm still far from ready for it."

To Antonietta's surprise, James lifted her up and carried her into the bedroom. "One hour won't make any difference," he said.

It was early afternoon before Antonietta returned to her studies. "If I fail this course," she pouted, "It'll be your fault." James tried to give her another kiss, but she waved him away. "James, you're impossible."

"And you, you're irresistible," he countered, kissing her in the neck from behind the chair.

"*Caro*, please let me study."

After one final touch of her breasts, James departed.

*Chapter 35*

# Friday April 5, 2002 to
# Friday April 12, 2002

HAMID KHAN WAS FEELING apprehensive. He suspected strongly that Markham's visit had to do with Leaman's tenure case, and he didn't feel totally at ease with the way Arbuthnot had persuaded him to handle it. He regretted too that he'd informed Arbuthnot of James's visit as he'd insisted on being present as well. Hamid would have preferred to talk with James alone. He feared that a meeting where both Arbuthnot and Markham were present would be an acrimonious affair. He also resented the fact that Arbuthnot clearly didn't trust him to deal with Markham on his own. After all, Roy hadn't exactly been very successful in his tussles with the Englishman. Markham had defeated him over the Flint case and the research proposal, and there was that funny business with Elliot Hunt. Hamid was sure that Arbuthnot hadn't withdrawn the charges out of the goodness of his heart. Markham must have been behind it somehow.

Arbuthnot arrived just before four. He was in a belligerent mood. "If that Markham thinks he can butt into Leaman's tenure case, he's got another think coming. He has no status whatsoever to get involved. We shall simply refuse to discuss the matter with him. Arrogant bastard."

These words were hardly out of HB's mouth when the arrogant bastard arrived. James greeted Hamid politely and nodded at Arbuthnot.

He'd expected to see HB there; indeed, his presence was a necessary element in James's strategy. He wasted no time in small talk.

"Hamid, I have two letters for you. They are from Kevin Mauser and Henry Keighley."

Hamid reacted with predictable surprise, but there was no hostility in his voice. "Why would you have them, James, and what do they say? We already have their refer…"

Arbuthnot cut Hamid off. "What game are you playing, Markham? You've no status in this matter. I suggest you leave the letters and bugger off."

James ignored Arbuthnot. "Let me answer your two questions in the opposite order, Hamid. The letters say that they both wish to withdraw their references and suggest that you use Borderick and Yankovitch as they are more senior and more competent to assess Professor Leaman's work."

Arbuthnot exploded in rage. "You interferring, arrogant son of a bitch," he roared at James. "Just because you're a damn aristocrat, you think you can poke your nose into everything." He glared at James, expecting an answer that didn't come. "Well, you can't" he finished rather lamely.

James continued to ignore Arbuthnot. "To answer your second question, Hamid, the reason why I am here to give them to you is that they come with an explanation."

Hamid was by now quite ashen. Even Arbuthnot was silent. It was obvious that James had information to impart that spelled trouble for them. Hamid had no idea what, but Arbuthnot harbored a horrible suspicion.

"Both Mauser and Keighley have signed statements that they were induced to submit negative references for Bill Leaman by Professor Arbuthnot, with whom they were fellow students at NUC." James turned towards HB. "Indeed, Professor Arbuthnot, they claim that you even wrote those references."

Hamid looked at Arbuthnot in horror. "Is this true, Roy"?

"No, it's not," HB snapped. "Markham has contrived all of this to save his friend and get rid of me." He made to snatch the letters from James, who fended him off.

"This matter concerns only FPC and the Head of FEB," HB shouted. "Not your bloody Lordship. You're not Head of this Section, or any Section. You're just a regular professor without any special status."

"It's a pity that I'm not Head of FEB," James replied tartly, "because I wouldn't have let myself be led into such dishonorable and illegal conduct."

"I had no knowledge of all this," Hamid wailed.

Arbuthnot looked at him contemptuously and shook a fist at James. "I shall report you to the Board of Governors for this disreputable attempt to subvert a committee by making outrageous allegations against the Senior Dean."

"You will be making no report to the Board of Governors, Arbuthnot. The Chair of Economics at Chicago has the two statements. You can check with Mauser and Keighley."

There was a silence. Hamid was slumped in his chair, and Arbuthnot was wiping the abundant perspiration from his forehead. He knew that he was beaten, beaten yet again by this insufferable, interfering Englishman.

"There are two possible outcomes to this unpleasant situation," James went on. "If you persist in using these references, the statements will be made public, and you, Arbuthnot, will lose your job, and you, Hamid, will lose all respect and credibility." He turned to Hamid. "I believe you knew nothing about Arbuthnot's machinations, but you will be perceived as weak and naïve. You'll have to resign."

"What is the other outcome"?

"You withdraw the references from Mauser and Keighley and replace them with references from Broderick and Yankovitch, and, if they are positive, you will support Professor Leaman's tenure application. You will as well, Arbuthnot."

"And the statements"?

"They won't be needed. Once Professor Leaman's tenure is confirmed, I shall instruct Jim Reilly to destroy them."

"There's no time to get new references," Arbuthnot growled in a final display of defiance.

"That's your problem--and Hamid's." James shrugged his shoulders in a gesture of disdainful indifference. "Either you get the two references from Broderick and Yankovitch, or you suffer the consequences."

Hamid nodded miserably, Arbuthnot just stared ahead into space, as if in a catatonic trance. The battle won, James left.

He went immediately back to his office and called Bill.

"Bill, I've got good news for you," he told his friend with a light heart. "They're going to replace the references from Mauser and Keighley with those from Broderick and Yankovitch. If they're positive, Hamid will support you for tenure."

There was a brief silence at the other end of the phone as Bill digested the news. "Jesus! How the hell did you pull that off, James"?

James recounted the whole scenario, dwelling with glee on Arbuthnot's raging discomfiture.

"I tried to be optimistic," Bill said, his voice breaking with emotion, "but I doubted that you and Tom could pull it off. I owe you guys. You've saved my neck."

"It should never have been in danger. Buy an extra-large bottle of J & B for tonight, and I'll call the others."

The next call was to Antonietta. He recited what had happened and promised to pick her up at seven to go to Bill's for the celebration.

"Oh, James," she cried, "I'm so proud of you, but I'm also cross with you."

"Why"?

"Because you're not coming to pick me up until seven."

"I thought you were going to be reasonable from now on."

"I haven't seen you all afternoon, so wanting you to come early is completely reasonable."

"You're right. I'll be there at six. That'll give us an hour, which should suffice."

"An hour's enough for you"?

"No, Antonietta. A lifetime wouldn't be enough for me."

It was a very contented mistress who put the phone down.

The evening at Bill's house was the first genuinely happy occasion since the problem with Bill's tenure had first arisen. Even so, there were still strains of anxiety. Bill was worried they wouldn't get the references in time from Broderick and Yankovitch. In that case, James told him, he would tell Hamid to have the meeting postponed. He was so scared at present that he would do anything James suggested, whatever Arbuthnot might say.

"I think HB's lost a lot of credit with Hamid," James told his friends. "This is the fourth time I've bested him."

"Be careful, James," Piotr warned. "HB must really hate you now, and you know what they say about a wounded animal. It can be even more dangerous."

"He's not an animal," Danny retorted. "He's an insect."

"Piotr's right," Antonietta said. "I'm afraid of what he might do."

"What can he do"? James answered, putting his arm around his fretful mistress.

Antonietta looked up at him, her eyes wide and bright with apprehension. "I don't know, but something."

"Are you sure Hamid will have the meeting postponed" Like Antonietta, Bill had a worried air.

"Yes," James responded. "He knows the mess HB's got him in, and he'll do anything to get out of it. He's not a bad guy."

"He's as guilty as that bastard Arbuthnot," was Danny's opinion.

"I disagree. True, he let himself be persuaded to substitute the referees and he wrote those letters about it being early tenure, but he had no idea that Arbuthnot was going to suborn Mauser and Keighley. His only fault was letting HB rule him, as always."

The wine and whiskey flowed, and none of the men were in a fit state to drive at the end of the evening. Contrary to her normal strictures, Antonietta had let James drink as much as he wanted. "He deserves it," she thought. Bernadette drove Danny and herself home and took Piotr as well. Antonietta would drive herself and James back to the cottage.

"How are you going to get to Prévost afterwards, Jimmy"? Bill asked. "You really shouldn't drive. The police are more active these days."

"By the time I've finished with him, he'll have sobered up," Antonietta said with a suggestive grin.

"You're a lucky guy, Jimmy." Bill came up to James and, most uncharacteristically, gave him a hug. "Thanks a million, buddy."

Somewhat embarrassed, James disentangled himself and went to fetch his coat. Antonietta kissed Bill on both cheeks. "I'm so relieved, Bill," she said with feeling.

Bill gave a short laugh. "Not as relieved as I am."

The following morning, Saturday, Hamid called James at home. He was upset and worried.

"I knew nothing about those references, and I've sent off requests by email and courier to Broderick and Yankovitch asking them to get their references to me by Friday morning. If they don't arrive, I'll have the meeting postponed."

"That's good, Hamid." James's tone was conciliatory. This was an opportunity to wean Hamid from Arbuthnot's sphere and perhaps make an ally of him. "I believe you didn't know about the references but take my advice and don't let yourself be used by Arbuthnot anymore. He's not a very ethical person."

"So I realize," Hamid replied.

James made his way back to the dining room where the children and Veronica were having breakfast.

"You were very late last night, James."

"Yes, I know, but we solved the tenure problem for Bill, and so we celebrated. Unfortunately a bit too much, and I stayed on at Bill's to sober up."

Veronica gave James a look of disgust and said no more. Failing to detect the note of suspicion in her voice, James unwisely told her that he planned to go to the Institute that afternoon to mark some exams.

"You seem to spend a lot of time at the Institute these days, James. I sometimes wonder why."

"There's been a lot going on recently," James replied as nonchalantly as he could. "Exams, seeing students, Bill's tenure case."

Veronica looked quizzically at James. "Is that dark-haired Italian girl among the students you see"?

James turned to fetch himself another coffee. He'd already had more than enough, but he could feel the blood drain from his face, and he was afraid this would betray him.

"No," he lied.

By the time he'd finished pouring out the coffee--very slowly--adding sugar, and stirring it, Veronica was already carrying out the children's plates. "Thank God, this will soon be over," he thought as he drank the coffee without any enjoyment.

He spent that afternoon with Antonietta. He told her about Veronica's suspicions.

"She even made an allusion to you."

"How does she know about me"?

"She saw you look at me when you came to Mass at Saint-Sauveur a few weeks ago to punish me for not seeing you that day."

Antonietta paled. "What an idiot I was."

They agreed James would have to be home in time for supper. As he was leaving, Antonietta held on to him.

"One last kiss, James."

He kissed her, long and passionately. "Remember that in a week's time we shall be on our way for two weeks in France together," he whispered.

Antonietta nodded but insisted on another kiss.

The references from Broderick and Yankovitch arrived on Thursday afternoon by fax. They were extremely positive, one calling Bill's work "original, incisive and considerably above average". Hamid immediately called James at home, but Veronica told him that her husband was at the Institute marking exams. Hamid called James's office, but there was no answer. James had finished his marking and was in bed with Antonietta.

Hamid made his way to Arbuthnot's office and showed him the references. The atmosphere between the two men was strained. Hamid had lost all confidence in Arbuthnot, and the latter was painfully aware of this.

"I am changing my recommendation to that of awarding tenure," Hamid told the Senior Dean. "I don't think you have any alternative but to support it too."

Arbuthnot waved Hamid out of his office without replying. All this was the fault of that bastard Markham, but there was nothing he could do for the moment. But his time would come, he was sure of that.

Hamid eventually got hold of James around seven and told him the good news.

"What did Arbuthnot say"?

"Nothing. He just glared and waved me out of his office."

"Don't worry, Hamid. I lied about the statements. I'm not going to tell Jim Reilly to destroy them. I don't trust Arbuthnot, and if he makes any moves against you, I'll threaten to make them public."

"Thank you, James." Hamid's relief was palpable. He would have been less relieved if he'd known that the statements were protected by Reilly's promise of confidentiality.

"How come he didn't tell you all this at the Institute," Veronica asked once James had told her the news. "I told him you were there when he called this afternoon."

James thought quickly. It was better to be scourged for drunkenness than adultery. "I finished marking at noon, so I had a liquid lunch with the lads."

"When will you grow up, James? You're thirty-two, and you still behave like a student."

"That's part of my charm," James replied flippantly. "Anyway, we deserved it. Bill's going to get tenure."

"A pity," Veronica remarked and marched off. James shook his head in abhorrence. "What an unpleasant woman." He picked up the phone again.

"Bill, the references have arrived, and you're home free."

There was a loud hoorah from the other end of the phone. "We have to celebrate that tonight."

"I'll be there at eight." Veronica could throw all the fits she wanted. This was one celebration he and Antonietta weren't going to miss. He went into the garage and called his mistress on the cell phone to tell her the news. Her reaction could not have been more different from his wife's. She wept for joy.

⌐ル⌐

The committee was waiting for the Rector to make his royal entry. Christine had been briefed by James and was curious to see how HB and Hamid were going to manage their volte-face. She noticed that Hamid was looking anxious, but Arbuthnot appeared more composed, although his mouth twitched nervously from time to time, and the red tufts of hair on his head seemed to stand out more than usual. Forget had his normal puzzled air as if not knowing why he was there at all. Flint also looked confused. McGrath was the only one of the men who exuded confidence.

Winstone arrived. "Good morning, ladies and gentlemen," he intoned pompously and then corrected himself with a mirthless smile. "Or should I say, lady and gentlemen." No one laughed, and Winstone quickly called on Hamid to make his presentation.

"There has been a change in the referees," he told the committee. "Two of the referees, Professors Mauser and Keighley, have withdrawn their references on the grounds that they do not feel competent to judge Professor Leaman's work. They suggested that we use Professors Broderick and Yankovitch, as they are more senior and experts in Professor Leaman's field."

There was a stir in the committee. Winstone forsook his normal air of lordly indifference, which he meant to be impartiality, and looked questioningly at HB. McGrath also seemed surprised, and poor Forget was even more confused. Flint was staring into space. Desmoulins couldn't suppress a smile.

"These two new referees have given extremely positive assessments of Professor Leaman's work," Hamid went on. "Together with Professor Khaladi, they recommend tenure without any reservations. Professor Dickens recommends tenure although he believes it to be too early. However," Hamid looked sternly at HB. "there is no precedent in this Institute for treating tenure cases differently just because they're brought early. This means there is a four to zero consensus among the referees in favor of tenure. So I am changing my recommendation and urge the committee to grant tenure to Professor Leaman."

Christine had to admire Hamid. He seemed to gain confidence as he spoke, and the words on early tenure were clearly directed at

Arbuthnot. The others, apart from Arbuthnot and Flint, whom HB had taken into his confidence, were perplexed at this sudden turn of events.

"It seems a little irregular to change the referees at this late stage," Forget objected.

"Perhaps," HB interjected quickly, "but what is surely important is to be completely fair, and it seems to me unfair to ruin someone's academic career on the basis of comments from referees who admit themselves that they are not competent to judge."

Forget nodded his agreement.

McGrath also had an objection. "There is still no top-tier journal," he pointed out. Christine looked expectantly at HB. How would he deal with this one?

"Professor Leaman has two articles in the *American Economic Review*," he countered. "That is a top-tier journal."

McGrath, who'd heard Arbuthnot claim just the opposite not too long ago, was clearly astonished but saw no point in opposing his ally. "If you say so, Roy," he said.

Winstone, who had listened to the whole discussion with growing amazement, asked if there were more comments. Desmoulins saw no reason to add to the consensus, Flint had been told by Arbuthnot to keep quiet, and Forget found the whole business far too complicated for another submission. Winstone called for the vote. He was sure that his friend, Arbuthnot, had engineered this change, and he assumed there were good reasons for it. The vote was unanimous in favor of granting tenure.

The meeting broke up. Winstone left first, as behooved the Rector. Arbuthnot also disappeared quickly with his acolyte, Flint. Christine left with Hamid, who was clearly very relieved at the outcome. She said nothing, although she knew the reason for his relief. McGrath and Forget exchanged bemused comments on the turn of events.

Hamid called James at home, where he was preparing for his trip to France the following day. James thanked him profusely and said that he would inform Bill. "He'll receive official confirmation next week," Hamid said. James in turn called Bill, who wanted to have another celebratory get-together. James demurred. "I'm leaving tomorrow for France. I must spend this evening with the family."

397

James went to the car and called Antonietta. He told her about the get-together and suggested that she go alone.

"No, James, I would feel lost without you." She made no attempt to persuade him to accompany her, which surprised James.

"I have you for two weeks starting tomorrow," she explained. "Tonight you must spend with the children." Significantly she didn't mention James's wife. James was again unsettled by Antonietta's newly found composure.

"Tell me you love me," he entreated.

"*Ti amo*," she replied, her voice redolent with emotion. "*Ti amo insensatamente.*"

*Chapter 36*

# Saturday April 13, 2002 to Sunday April 28, 2002

J AMES ARRIVED AT THE cottage on Saturday around three to pick up Antonietta. She was wearing a pale green jacket with a short skirt that showed off her shapely legs. As usual, the white blouse was at least one size too small and accentuated the fullness of her breasts. Her hair flowed untamed and voluminously over her shoulders. She flicked it back, and James caught sight of the emeralds in her gold earrings. Her make-up was tasteful and lightly applied.

"Why did you come so late? There's not time to make love."

"I had to take Peter to a friend's house," James replied. He gazed into Antonietta's dark, reproachful eyes. "I'll make up for it once we arrive in Paris."

"You'd better."

They left for Pierre Trudeau Airport. After checking in and delivering themselves of their suitcases, they went to the airport restaurant. The food was mediocre and the choice of wine limited. There was little point in lingering over their meal, so they bought some magazines and newspapers and made for the Air Canada lounge.

"Are we in first class"? Antonietta asked in surprise. "We normally fly economy."

"That's when the Institute pays," James replied. "They're too cheap to pay a first-class fare, and I'm damned if I'm going to pay anything out of my own pocket for those guys."

Antonietta gave James an enquiring look. "Where did all this money come from"? she speculated again as she walked over to the buffet and brought back some canapés and two half bottles of Valpolicella. James took his back and exchanged it for a 1998 Bordeaux. Antonietta pouted.

"You prefer the French to the Italians, don't you"?

James put his arm around her and went to kiss her, but she wriggled away. "Just because I prefer a 1998 Bordeaux to a Valpolicella doesn't mean I prefer the French over the Italians. 1998 was an excellent year for Bordeaux wine."

Antonietta continued to eat her canapé without replying.

"Anyway, I *am* a quarter French."

Antonietta put her plate down and turned towards James with a very determined expression on her face. "Well, you're going to have an Italian wife and Italian children, and you promised me we'd live in Italy. *That'll* cure you of your French xenophobia."

James burst out laughing. Antonietta had never forgotten how he'd called her a xenophobe, and this was her revenge.

Pleased with herself, Antonietta let James kiss her.

It was a pleasant flight, and unusually for Air Canada they arrived on time. They went quickly through immigration and were waved through customs. James picked up the rental car, and they were soon in the thick of Paris. James felt again that animation which Paris always conjured up in him. It was his favorite city, but he wasn't going to confess this to his Italian mistress.

It was six years since the one occasion on which Antonietta had visited Paris. As they traveled along the Seine, she was seized by a desire to dine on a *bateau-mouche* that evening. A friend of her's had once done so and told her that it was very romantic. The boat passed by some of the most impressive monuments in Paris as you dined. They were all illuminated, and it was a magical sight.

They crossed the Pont Neuf and arrived at the Hotel Esmeralda across from Notre Dame Cathedral. It was not among the finest hotels in Paris, but James had always stayed there. He was fond of the quaint old building, and it was well situated. The owner greeted James as an old friend and showed them immediately to their room. James went to the window and gazed in wonder at the lofty Gothic splendor of Notre Dame Cathedral. When he turned round, Antonietta was already stretched out on the bed, completely naked.

"I want sex," she declared, opening her legs provocatively.

"Shouldn't I shave first"?

"No, James, I want it *now, right now.*"

James needed no second bidding. He shed his clothes quickly and clasped Antonietta's hot body to himself. The humidity and odor of her sexuality wrought a frenzy in him. He mounted her, and they took their pleasure violently and together, inundating each other with the effluent of their gratified lust. Once was not enough, and they continued to indulge themselves without restraint or shame. It was nearly midday by the time they'd exhausted their pursuit of pleasure, just in time to catch the last Sunday Mass at the Cathedral. Afterwards they took a taxi--James wasn't going to drive in Paris more than necessary-- and were soon ensconced in Le Train Bleu, a magnificent brasserie in the Belle Epoque style located in the Gare de Lyon.

"Order for me, James. Something typically French."

James was surprised. Knowing Antonietta's antipathy towards the French, he'd expected some snide comment about the menu. Guessing his thoughts, Antonietta smiled sweetly at him. "After all, we *are* in France."

He ordered potted rabbit with rosemary for the hors d'oeuvre. It was served with mixed wild salad and toast and accompanied by a light, dry white wine from Vouvray. Her prejudices submerged by her appetite, Antonietta ate with evident relish. For the main course they had roast rib of veal, which was served with cannelloni stuffed with mashed mushrooms. The wine list contained a Barolo, which James was about to order when, again to his surprise, Antonietta stopped him.

"No, James, with French food we should have a French wine."

They had a bottle of 1994 Chateau Margaux. "It's a good thing my family has a bank," James reflected when he saw the price. The meal ended with a violet flamed cream, expresso coffee, cognac for Antonietta, and calvados for James. As they left the brasserie, Antonietta put her arm in James's and nestled her head against his shoulder.

"Thank you, James. I hate to admit it, but that was one of the best meals I've ever had."

James smiled down at her. "Wonders will never cease. We'll make a francophile out of you yet."

They spent the afternoon visiting the Louvre and Notre Dame Cathedral. Before entering the Cathedral, Antonietta noticed a little shop that sold religious articles.

"I lost my mantilla last summer," she explained, dragging a reluctant James into the store. "I want to buy another one."

"No one wears them any more in church," James objected, but when he saw Antonietta drape one over her head, he was touched by the perfect blend of beauty and piety.

"You look like an Italian Madonna," he told her.

Antonietta wore the mantilla as they toured the Cathedral. She lit a candle before the Virgin and prayed to her. Looking at his mistress kneeling demurely in prayer, her head covered in black lace, James had the impression of looking at a sacred painting from the Italian baroque or Renaissance period. It was difficult to imagine her as the wild, immodest lover of that morning.

After the Cathedral, Antonietta insisted on visiting the Conciergerie and the dark, dank cell where her namesake had languished before her execution. Gazing in horror at the squalid quarters that had housed the proud Queen of France, Antonietta shuddered.

"That's one reason I could never become a francophile," she told James. There was an unusual and bitter harshness to her normally soft-toned voice. "I can never forgive them for what they did to their royal family."

James looked at Antonietta in surprise. It was too dark to read the expression in her eyes, but her face betrayed all the repulsion this scene was calling up in her.

"That's an uncommonly royalist sentiment for an Italian," he remarked, forgetting that Antonietta was a Monarchist.

"I *am* a royalist. I come from a royalist family, and I hate republics."

Taken aback by Antonietta's vehemence, James was speechless.

"Aren't *you* a royalist"?

"Well, yes, but my country's a monarchy, yours's is a republic."

"More's the pity"!

This interchange left James perplexed. He was used to Antonietta's volatile nature. He had seen the ease with which his sensual mistress could transform herself into a pious Catholic on entering a church. But these royalist sentiments, and the forcefulness with which she'd expressed them, intrigued him. He himself preferred a constitutional monarchy to any republic, if only because any system that reduced the power of the people to decide their own destinies was welcome. He had an aristocratic distrust of democracy. However, his royalism was without Antonietta's fervor. "What sort of family did she come from"? he wondered anew. This was something he would have to ascertain before they married, although he didn't intend to disclose his own secret until the day of their marriage. He couldn't bring himself to believe that Antonietta would be swayed in her decision because of his title, but he was taking no chances. Her family was clearly upper class, and they were the worst when it came to adulating the aristocracy.

That evening they dined on a *bateau-mouche*. They boarded the boat at the national library, and it slowly made its way along the Seine past the town hall and the majestic Notre Dame Cathedral opposite, the Louvre, the Orsay museum, the Place de la Concorde in the distance, the Hôtel des Invalides, the last resting place of the great Napoleon as Antonietta called him to tease James, the Grand Palais and finally the Eiffel Tower, and on the other side of the river, the great spectacle of the Trocadéro. All these splendid buildings were illuminated in a way that added to their mystery and grandeur. For once in her life Antonietta paid little attention to what she was eating, so transported was she by the sights of Paris by night.

"It really is a beautiful city," she admitted.

⁓

As the car passed the city of Orange, the sky suddenly opened up into a brilliant blue. The northern clouds melted before the unseasonable warmth of the southern sun. Antonietta felt her body respond to the change in climate. She was more alive, more sensual, and a feeling of exhilaration gripped her as they neared the Mediterranean, *her* Mediterranean. All her negative feelings about the French dissolved when she beheld the bright colors of Provence. After all, as she told James, they were fellow Latins.

"They're not really Latins, you know," James told her. "The French are a mixture of Germanic Franks and Celts with a little Latin admixture in the south. Their racial mix is about the same as the English, but you'd probably get lynched if you told them that."

"They're culturally Latins, you must admit."

"Yes, if you mean unreasonable, bureaucratic, corrupt and thoroughly untrustworthy, yes, they're Latins."

"Antonietta"!

The car was swerving all over the road as James defended himself against Antonietta's blows. Realizing how irresponsible she'd been, Antonietta stopped her attack and apologized.

"I'm sorry, James, but it was your fault."

"Guilty, but truth is an absolute defense."

They reached Beaune around five o'clock, checked into the hotel, and wandered around the town. They visited the famous hospices where James bought some Burgundy wine for their stay in Bandol. They ate supper in a restaurant near the hotel. James insisted on ordering *boeuf bourguignon*, which Antonietta agreed was delicious.

"And the wine," asked James, pointing to the bottle of Gevrey-Chambertin.

"Almost as good as a vintage Barolo."

"Xenophobe."

"James, for love of you, I'll agree it was a very good wine." Antonietta smiled sweetly at her lover and finished her glass. James paid, they had another walk around the quaint Burgundian town and retired for the night. As if the approach of the Mediterranean had sharpened her sexuality, Antonietta was insatiable.

They made love a final time and fell asleep, only to be awakened around seven by the sound of the alarm.

"Oh my God"! James groaned. "You really are sexually profligate, Antonietta. I'm worn out, and I've got to drive to Bandol."

Antonietta jumped out of bed and made for the bathroom. "Serves you right for having a mistress in her sexual prime."

James followed her into the bathroom and caught her in his arms before she had a chance to turn on the shower.

"What about my sexual prime"?

"For men, it's the late teens, and for you that was quite a while ago."

"Is that so. Well, we'll see." He pinned Antonietta frontwards against the wall of the shower and turned the water on.

"James, please, not like that; you know it makes me scream."

She didn't resist when he took her anally, and her barely muffled cries were clearly audible downstairs in the hotel.

After a rather disapproving reception in the breakfast room, they set out for Bandol. After passing the tollbooth at Cassis, Antonietta clapped her hands with joy as the Mediterranean suddenly came into view.

"I've missed it so much," she lamented, tears streaming down her face.

To console her, James drove to Les Lecques for them to walk along the beach. They sat in a cafe at the end of the front and gazed out to sea. They watched children playing on the sand and paddling in the sea. One day soon their own children would be doing that in this same sea.

Antonietta put an arm around James and buried her face in his neck. "Thank you," she murmured.

It was late afternoon when they arrived at the villa in Bandol. It sat on a cliff overlooking the Bay of Bandol, which was dotted with countless sailing boats bobbing about on a calm sea.

"This is heaven," sighed Antonietta, sipping a glass of rosé wine.

The days the couple spent in Bandol were magical for both. The presence of the Mediterranean, the spring warmth, the blue and gold colors of Provence, the budding vines, the café terraces, the walks along the beach, the romantic dinners in the various restaurants scattered around *l'arrière pays*, all this infused them with a new vigor, and their love for each other blossomed as never before. They resolved to spend their life together in Italy, and to immerse themselves in the sensuous charms of southern Europe.

"Now I'm here, it's difficult to believe that Canada exists," Antonietta said as they took their breakfast of croissants and expresso coffee in the little restaurant on the beach at Les Lecques.

Imperceptibly, their moods began to change as the day of departure neared. Before them were difficult days, the prospect of which was only bearable because, at the end of their trials, they would be together, here on the Mediterranean. They traveled back to Paris, spending a night in Fontainebleau with a Scottish friend of James, who bore the same name.

As she sat in the plane traveling towards Montreal, Antonietta's emotions swirled between sadness at leaving the paradise of southern France, apprehension at what awaited them, and fragile anticipation of the joys to come. Once they arrived at Dorval, the dreary reality of their life in Quebec came as a shock after the two weeks they'd spent happily as man and wife. A despondent silence descended upon them as they drove towards Ste. Anne. It was a dull, overcast day. As they came further north into the Laurentians, snow still lay copiously on the ground despite the arrival of spring. The cottage where they had lived their illicit love seemed bleak and unwelcoming. An involuntary shiver of dread ran through Antonietta.

"Please stay with me," she pleaded. James took her in his arms.

"I can't. I don't want Veronica to be suspicious. I'm going to leave her next week, and she mustn't think that it's for another woman."

"Am I just another woman"? Antonietta's dark eyes glistened with sad reproach.

"You are the love of my life."

Without another word, he took hold of Antonietta, led her into the cottage, and placed her on the bed. "Which is why I can't leave you without this." He undid her blouse and extricated the enticing breasts from her bra. They made love with more tenderness than abandon, and Antonietta consented to let James leave.

Antonietta consoled herself that she would see James on Monday, and soon they would be together. Although this prospect filled her with joy, Antonietta couldn't suppress a nagging doubt, which intensified in the loneliness of the cottage. What she was planning to do was sinful, and her doubt was fed by her fear of divine retribution. Unable to bear it any longer, she went to six o'clock Mass at Saint-Sauveur. She prayed for forgiveness for what she was going to do and implored the Virgin to intercede for her. Slightly comforted, she returned home to find a message from James telling her that he must see her tomorrow and would call again later. The tone of his voice was urgent and worried.

A terrible foreboding gripped Antonietta. What had happened? Had Veronica found out about them? Were there some problems with his children, problems that would keep him in his marriage? The foreboding turned to panic, and Antonietta paced around the living room waiting in terror for James's call. When it came, Antonietta nearly tripped over in her race for the phone.

"I've been summoned to the Rector's office at three on Monday afternoon. Veronica says that Eleanor sounded very upset."

"Who's Eleanor"?

"The Rector's secretary."

A feeling of impending catastrophe came over Antonietta. She begged James to come round, but it was impossible. He tried to comfort her on the phone, but she was distraught when he rang off. Unable to sleep, she drank some wine and tortured herself by playing over and over again Laura Pausini's song of painful separation, *Come se non fosse stato mai amore.*

James's mood was somber as he attended Mass on Sunday with his family. He was preoccupied both by worry over the Rector's summons and dread at the difficult week that lay ahead. What on earth did Winstone want? He tried to downplay his anxiety by telling himself that it was doubtless another of HB's tricks, but he couldn't convince himself. Why would Eleanor have been upset if it was just that? He wished himself with fervor a year hence when all these troubles would be behind him, and he and Antonietta would hopefully be married.

Mistaking James's preoccupation for religious devotion, Veronica commented approvingly on his new attitude when they left the church. They made for the Brûlerie to have brunch. Petra was there with Brett.

James greeted her by her first name, as she did with him. This annoyed Veronica.

"You're getting very familiar with the students."

"She's a friend of Bill's."

"That's not a reason. He's hardly a person to emulate."

Brunch proceeded with agonizing slowness. Making some excuse about checking his mail and perhaps finding out what the Rector wanted, James escaped to visit Antonietta. She was in a terrible state. The Rector's summons had filled her with a menacing presentiment. They made love with a frenzy, desperate to drown their fears in erotic pleasure. When it came time for James to leave, Antonietta clung to him.

"I'm so afraid," she sobbed, trying to drag James back into the cottage.

With much effort he resisted. "The last thing we need at this very moment is a showdown with Veronica."

Antonietta nodded, her eyes moist with fear and sadness, and, after a final, long and passionate embrace, she let James go. She walked back to the cottage, beset by oppressive anxiety.

*Chapter 37*

# Monday April 29, 2002 to
# Tuesday April 30, 2002

J AMES'S APPREHENSIONS WERE CONFIRMED when he was ushered into Winstone's
office. Arbuthnot was there as well with a look of triumph on his
face.

"Please take a seat, Professor Markham," Winstone said with his
usual solemnity.

James did his bidding with a hollow feeling in his stomach. He
suspected what was coming, although he had no idea how the Rector
had found out about his liaison with Antonietta. He had his answer
when Winstone pulled out a collection of photos.

"Would you be good enough to explain these, Professor Markham"?

James looked at the photos. He realized immediately when they'd
been taken. It was the day Antonietta had burst into his office to find
him with Annya. It was the scene of their passionate reconciliation, and
their embrace left little doubt as to the nature of their relationship. He
remembered how Wrangel was always carrying his camera with him, so
it was probably he who had taken the photos to avenge himself for his
humiliation in class. There was an expectant silence as Winstone and
HB waited for James's answer. He didn't oblige them.

"Well, Professor Markham"? the Rector persisted.

"What explanation do you need? The photos would seem to be
self-evident."

"You admit to an intimate relationship with a student in your class"? Arbuthnot snarled. James nodded.

Arbuthnot looked as if he was about to launch into some vengeful diatribe when Winstone held up his hand to stop him. He addressed James in a friendly way that seemed completely out of place.

"James, you have rendered outstanding service to the Institute as a researcher, teacher, Assistant Dean for International Affairs, and in the short time you've been Chair of your Section. I want to spare you the indignity of a disciplinary hearing before the Ethics Committee."

HB tried to interject, but Winstone again stopped him.

"If you resign, there will be no hearing. This way, the matter does not become public knowledge. I advise you to agree. Think of your wife and children."

James was stunned by Winstone's apparent generosity. Perhaps he'd misjudged the man. The Rector's next words disabused him

"Think about it, James. We will take no action until after the Italian Ambassador has come on May 9 to open the new EU library. As you arranged it, he will expect you to be there."

So that was it! The last thing Winstone wanted was a scandal that would threaten his only achievement, which had been obtained solely because of James's reputation. It was a fair deal. James agreed to hand in his resignation after the visit of the Italian Ambassador, effective July 1, 2002.

After leaving the Rector's office, a very shaken James went to see Antonietta, who was waiting anxiously for him. He told her what had happened. "I'm to resign after the visit of the Italian Ambassador."

Antonietta was overwhelmed by worry and grief. "Your career will be ruined," she sobbed. "What will you do? How can you get another job? No one will hire you once this gets out." She laid her head on James's shoulder. "Arbuthnot will get his revenge even if you resign. I always knew he would."

It would have been easy for James to tell Antonietta who he was, that he had no need of his academic job, that he had enough money from his shares in the family bank and his investments to live without working. He didn't.

"I'll get an academic job elsewhere," he told his weeping mistress without conviction. "Somewhere in Europe. HB won't even know."

"Any place will contact the Institute," Antonietta wailed. "Winstone will tell HB, and he'll make sure you get a bad reference."

Antonietta clung to the man she loved. They moved to the bedroom, and as if they sensed it was the last time, they made love with desperate frenzy.

"I have to take Susanna to a concert tomorrow in Montreal," James told the distraught Antonietta. "I'll be back late. I'll see you on Wednesday, and I swear I'll make you forget all this."

Hiding her misery, Antonietta smiled wanly. James had enough problems without adding her anguish to them. Sadly she watched him drive off.

⁂

Left alone in the cottage, Antonietta was tortured by guilt. If only she hadn't stayed on at that party, all this would never have happened. She became convinced that she was the cause of James's ruin, and a single idea obsessed her. She had to save James's career, but how? Should she go to the Rector and tell him that it was she who'd seduced James? Or that she was not really a student in his class because she'd always been going to leave at Christmas? No, neither approach would work, Antonietta reluctantly concluded. Egged on by his rancorous Senior Dean, Winstone would be only too happy to have the chance of destroying James's career. Antonietta toyed for a moment with offering herself to him but set aside the idea with disgust.

Suddenly, she remembered the EU collection being donated by the Italian Ambassador on behalf of the European Union. Don Alfredo was her godfather. Was it possible to persuade him to make the donation contingent on James's continuing presence at the Institute? Antonietta felt an immense surge of hope. She rushed off to the church in Saint-Sauveur to pray for the success of her new plan.

As she prayed, she realized with growing horror that she could not have it both ways. She could not save James and at the same time continue her adulterous relationship with him. She knew Messina. Even her mother mocked his excessive piety and strait-laced Catholicism. He

411

would never agree to save James unless she renounced him. He took his duties as her godfather far too seriously for that. Antonietta felt giddy and sick to her stomach. Her whole being revolted against the idea of abandoning the man she loved, but it was the only way. She had gotten James into this mess, she had to get him out of it, even it meant never seeing or talking or making love to him again. Antonietta felt a storm of tears well up, but she suppressed them. She had to act quickly, like an automaton. If she once thought of what she was doing, she wouldn't have the strength to do it. She had to leave the cottage immediately and Canada as well once she'd seen Messina.

Antonietta returned to the cottage. No sooner had she arrived than the phone rang. Probably it was James, but with a superhuman effort that left her exhausted and grief-stricken, she didn't answer and sat down to write the most difficult letters of her life. One was to Dean Bromhoeffer withdrawing from the Institute and another to her landlady enclosing a check for the May rent and telling her to keep the damage deposit. She would leave the furniture she'd bought for the cottage.

The third letter was her greatest torment. She knew that Messina would require her to promise both to renounce James and to make sure he would not seek her out. She had to write a letter to the man she loved with an all-consuming intensity that would convince him that she didn't love him and never had. She started it many times, but every time she broke down into hysterical weeping. More out of emotional exhaustion than any rational ability to think, she penned the infamous lines.

*James, it's all over. It should never have started. I am returning to Italy. Please let me be. Antonietta.*

Then she added the cruelest line of all.

*Please drop the key in the mailbox. You won't need it anymore.*

She called Carlo and told him she had to leave Canada because of family problems. She would leave the Jetta at Luigi's. He could sell it and deposit the money in her account minus whatever commission he wanted to take. Then she called Alitalia. She knew how heartbroken she would be when she left Canada, and she preferred the Latin warmth of her own countrywomen to the cold efficiency of the Air Canada hostesses. She booked a flight from Toronto on Wednesday afternoon to Florence via Milan. She packed her clothes and some books and mementos between bouts of sobbing and throwing up. She couldn't bear to look at the cottage when she left. Two hours later, after stopping several times to fight back thoughts of James that caused her such physical pain that she was unable to drive, she arrived at the Hotel Versailles.

Antonietta spent a sleepless and wretched night. Her sense of loss gave her a physical pain as if her heart was really breaking. She felt nauseous, and her head throbbed. Constantly she had to fight the temptation to rush back to the cottage. At one stage she couldn't stand it anymore and started to call James. It was only with the greatest effort that she stopped herself. After that, her night was a trance of misery, alleviated only by the insidious consolations of the minibar. In the morning she ordered a double expresso in her room. Trembling, she called the Italian Embassy in Ottawa. At first, the receptionist was very uncooperative.

"The Ambassador doesn't take personal calls," she told Antonietta in heavily accented English.

"He will take one from me," Antonietta riposted in Italian. "I am the Countess Antonietta della Chiesa, and he is an old friend of my family and also my godfather."

The girl acquiesced. Antonietta wasn't half a Palmieri for nothing. Within seconds she heard the voice of Don Alfredo. "Antonietta! It's lovely to hear from you."

Without divulging the reason, Antonietta asked to see the Duke. He was only too happy to oblige, and it was agreed that they would meet at the Embassy at noon. Realizing that this offered her the opportunity to leave Canada a day earlier than planned, Antonietta called Alitalia to change her flight. She knew that the longer she stayed in Canada, the less capable she would be of fighting the longing for James that was eating at her. It was a painful, desolate longing for a paradise that she was about to exchange for hell.

Before leaving for the airport, Antonietta went to say goodbye to Luigi and leave her car for his son. She gave him the same family reason for her precipitate departure from Canada, but, from Antonietta's demeanor and her puffy eyes, Luigi guessed the reason was more likely a problem with her Englishman. He embraced Antonietta tearfully. He'd come to regard her almost as his own daughter and was very sad to see her go. He wished her well and asked her to keep in touch. Antonietta promised to do so but knew that she would not keep her word. She would have to put as much distance between herself and Canada as possible if she was going to keep the oath that Don Alfredo would surely require from her.

Antonietta took a taxi to the airport and boarded a plane for Ottawa. She arrived a little after eleven and took a taxi to the Italian Embassy. The Duke had clearly briefed the receptionist for she was all smiles and courtesy with Antonietta. Within minutes Don Alfredo himself came to fetch her. They went to his office.

Antonietta recounted the whole story of her love for James, their attempts to resist the passion that was consuming them, their surrender to it, the blissful six months they'd spent as lovers, the photos, and James's impending dismissal.

"Please save him, Don Alfredo," she begged. "The Rector desperately needs that European library. If you threaten to withhold it, he'll do whatever you say."

Antonietta looked imploringly at Messina, her eyes swimming with tears and her beautiful face etched by grief. He contemplated her with compassion, but there was also a severity in his mien. Antonietta knew what she was asking was quite irregular, and there was no reason for a man of Messina's strict morality to take pity on his adulterous goddaughter. She had to offer a sacrifice if she was to persuade him.

"If you help me, I will swear on the Holy Scriptures to renounce James." Now the self-control she had maintained with great effort gave way. She put her head in her hands and wept. Messina came round his desk and put his arm around Antonietta to comfort her. There was a short silence while the Duke reflected.

"I will help you," he said finally. "I don't particularly like that Rector. He's a weak individual and thoroughly untrustworthy. And James Markham *is* the reason we're putting the library there."

The Duke smiled down at the weeping Antonietta. "So no Markham, no library."

Antonietta felt a momentary stab of joy at Messina's words, but when he fetched the Bible for her to take the oath, the misery returned.

She had the impression that the pages of the Book were burning her hand as she laid it on them. Trembling, she swore to renounce James, never to seek to him out, and to refuse to have anything to do with him if he came to her. She was not to tell him that she had saved his career by this sacrifice.

Antonietta felt a dreadful hollowness in her stomach. It was as if she was forswearing all happiness in this world and condemning herself to perpetual sorrow and despair. Unable to maintain any further conversation, she quickly left the Embassy.

Once outside the Embassy, Antonietta began to realize the irrevocability of her decision. She would never see James again, never hold him, never feel his kisses, never again laugh and argue with him, never make love to him. He was banished from her life. It took all her strength of character to continue. As she sat in the departure lounge at Lester Pearson waiting for her flight to Milan, she was almost comatose with grief. At times she felt as if she couldn't breathe. Twice she had to rush to the washroom to throw up. She was desperately afraid of breaking down completely, and she fought to chase thoughts of James from her mind. The magazines she'd bought to divert herself couldn't shake the one terrible thought that obsessed her.

*James was lost to her forever.*

*Chapter 38*

# Tuesday April 30, 2002 to
# Friday June 7, 2002

AFTER AN HOUR AND a half of torment, Antonietta boarded the plan for Italy. She'd wanted a seat in business class, believing this would give her greater privacy, but they were all taken. She took her seat in economy class next to an older Italian lady. When the plane took off, it was if it was wrenching her heart with one part of it remaining with her love and the other, broken and useless, traveling with her to Italy. Tears streamed down her face.

The old lady touched her arm in a gesture of sympathy. "You are young and beautiful," she told her. "Time will heal your sorrow."

Antonietta thanked her, but she knew time would not help. Her passion for James was too infinite ever to fade away through the passage of time.

Once the captain had turned off the seatbelt sign, one of the airhostesses, who had noticed Antonietta's heartbroken demeanor, came to offer her a seat in an empty row at the back of the plane. Antonietta looked hesitantly at the old lady, not wishing to offend her.

"Go," she said with a smile. "A good cry will do you good."

Antonietta went to the back of the plane and wept as silently as she could. The airhostess discreetly brought her a little food and some wine. Antonietta drank the wine but couldn't bring herself to eat. She was too sick to her stomach. At times a feeling of utter despair and emptiness came over her, and she felt as if she were suffocating. The airhostess was concerned and asked whether she should enquire if there was a doctor on board. Antonietta assured her that she was alright. The airhostess looked unconvinced.

Antonietta was exhausted by the time she arrived in Milan on Wednesday morning, which was a help. She was too tired to think. She had a coffee and some Austrian buns with butter and jam before boarding her plane for Florence. Once there, she took a taxi to her parents' villa in Fiesole. She dreaded meeting her mother, but, to her relief, only Anna, the old maid who had practically brought her up, was at the home. Her mother was in Rome with Carla, who was expecting another baby, and her father was at a conference somewhere. Anne didn't expect them back for another two days.

Antonietta started to climb the stairs to her bedroom when she began to sway and would have lost her balance if Anna hadn't caught her. She turned round and threw herself into Anna's arms, sobbing violently.

"Come, little countess." Anna led Antonietta upstairs to her old bedroom. "Have a sleep, child. You look exhausted. We'll talk when you feel better."

Feel better? As she sank down on her bed, Antonietta doubted she would ever overcome her pain at the loss of the man she loved with all her being. Worn out by her convulsive sobbing, she fell asleep whispering James's name.

After dropping off the children at school on Wednesday, James made for the cottage. He was worried. He'd tried several times to call Antonietta, but there had never been an answer. His worry turned into foreboding when he saw that Antonietta's Jetta was not parked in front of the cottage. Whatever was going on? Apprehensively he opened the cottage door with his key and entered.

The first thing he noticed was that the crucifix, which normally hung on the wall of the living room, was missing. He began to feel sick to his stomach. He went to the bedroom and stared in horror at the empty closet.

"No, no"! he shouted. "No, no"!

He returned in a daze to the living room and saw an envelope on which was written his name. Trembling, already suspecting the worst, he opened the envelope and read the letter it contained.

James sank down on the sofa and stared at the letter. He read the brief, cruel message repeatedly as if hoping the words would change. His body felt cold, but his head was hot as if it were about to burst. He tried to stand up but couldn't move. He tried to collect his thoughts but couldn't think. His being was paralyzed by an overwhelming sensation of utter hopelessness. "It's unbelievable, it's impossible," he told himself, but the letter told him differently. The woman he loved with such boundless passion had left him. Antonietta was gone.

Unaware of time passing, James remained seated on the sofa, not moving, unable to comprehend. "Why? Why"? he asked himself repeatedly. The pain of losing Antonietta was unbearable, and he felt himself sinking into a stupor, as if neither his body nor his mind could cope with the disaster that had befallen him. He had to get away from this place of memories, where every item and every inch reminded him of his lost happiness.

He called Veronica and told her that something had come up, and he had to go to Montreal for some meetings. They should last a couple of days.

"That means I have to look after the children again," she complained. "You've only just come back from France."

There was a note of suspicion in Veronica's voice. "Now she's suspicious," James thought bitterly. "Just when there's no longer any need to be." He left the cottage, put the key in the mailbox, and made for Montreal. He booked into a hotel. This was where he would try to put his life back together and save his sanity.

❧

It was late evening when Antonietta awoke from a troubled sleep. With horror, she realized that the events of the last days were not a nightmare but brutal reality. She had left James. She pictured him reading her letter, and the pain was so unbearable that she desperately sought escape from the image. The most sensible thing would be to go downstairs and talk with Anna, even call some friends, but she couldn't master her tears long enough to leave the bedroom.

There was a knock on the door. It was Anna. She'd heard Antonietta crying and was bringing her hot soup.

"It'll give you strength," she told the pitiful young countess and sat on the bed to make sure that Antonietta drank it. Afterwards she had Antonietta tell her the whole story of her misery.

"Don't tell the family. I'm wretched enough without having to endure my mother's censure."

"Well, child, you're going to have to pull yourself together or your tears will give you away."

Anna was right, but how could she behave normally enough not to stir her family's curiosity? All she felt capable of was lying on the bed and weeping for her lost love. That alone provided some relief, scant though it was, from her torment. Nevertheless, she promised Anna to make an effort. She would allow herself one last night of lamentation before facing up to the wretchedness of life without James.

∽✳∾

After checking into the hotel, James remained seated on the bed for hours. He was numb from grief and shock, but gradually a conviction began to form within his mind that he'd been played for a fool; and the grief gave way to a simmering anger.

He dwelled on Antonietta's reluctance to commit herself to marrying him, her enigmatic remark in Santiago that perhaps they shouldn't get married, and her confession that she'd entertained the idea of leaving him during her mother's visit. Now it was clear to him what she'd meant when she'd told him that they had no choice. She'd never intended to marry him, and now he was about to be disgraced, she'd dropped him like a hot potato.

He fed on his anger, stoking it until he succeeded in perverting his image of Antonietta. Dismissing the innumerable proofs of her love for him, he told himself savagely that he shouldn't waste time regretting her. She had the morals of a whore and a bisexual one at that. She'd probably been screwing Petra as well as himself.

After a night spent between brief bouts of sleep and much weeping, Antonietta was woken at ten o'clock by a very determined Anna.

"I have prepared breakfast for you, child. Get dressed and come down to eat it."

"I can't" Antonietta buried her head in the pillow to stifle a new onset of sobbing.

"You must, Countess Antonietta," Anna persisted. "Think of who you are and stop behaving like a lovesick schoolgirl."

"But I *am* lovesick."

Anna was unyielding. "That may be, countess, but you must face your parents tonight, and you'd better start pulling yourself together. Crying like a baby isn't going to take you back to him."

Antonietta surrendered to Anna's implacable logic. She showered, made herself up, dressed, and went downstairs. She drank coffee and ate voraciously, suddenly realizing that she was very hungry. After breakfast Anna dispatched her into town to buy some groceries. The beauty of Florence lying below Fiesole and the warm Italian sun brought some comfort to the tortured young woman. By the time she returned to the villa, she'd come to accept that she would have to live with the pain and misery of her new reality.

James remained in Montreal until he felt able to face his family and life in general. By the time he arrived back in the Laurentians two days later, the passion he'd felt for Antonietta had been converted into loathing and contempt. He went to see Bill to inform him of the sorry state of his life.

"Oh. my God," Bill groaned on hearing of James's forced resignation. "What does Antonietta think about all this"?

"I don't want her name ever mentioned again in my presence," James declared and poured out all his venom. "For me the whore no longer exists," he concluded.

Bill eyed his friend sympathetically. "I knew there would be hell to pay if you two broke up. Now I wish I'd never got you together."

"So do I. On the other hand, she was a good fuck."

Bill shook his head in disbelief. "Vulgarity doesn't become you, James. Whatever she's done, Antonietta doesn't deserve it. There must be an explanation for her leaving."

"The explanation is only too obvious. She doesn't want to be with a loser. But don't fret. You'll never hear me mention the damn woman's name again."

Antonietta awoke to the now familiar pain of her loss. Her pillow was soaked with tears, and the bedclothes were in disarray from her frantic attempts to find relief from her suffering in sleep. Until today she'd seen little of her family, and with great effort had been able to hide from them the torment that was ravaging her. Her mother had remarked on her listlessness, and Antonietta's occasional and uncharacteristic bouts of irritability had angered her, but she'd put all this down to the nefarious influence of North America. A few weeks in Italy would cure her daughter.

Today the family would attend Mass together at the Basilica. Afterwards they were to lunch with the Cardinal, who was anxious to hear about his niece's experiences in Canada and, Antonietta feared, the reason for her precipitate return to Italy. All this would be an ordeal, and she felt ill with dread. She arose from her bed and made her way into the bathroom.

"Oh, my God"! she exclaimed, looking at her shattered appearance.

Her eyes were dull and puffy, her hair dank, and lifeless, and her features wore the imprint of her anguish. Fighting back another onset of sobbing, she took a shower and began to recapture some semblance of her beauty. Naturally gifted in the art of female contrivance, she had within minutes masked the damage, although a knowing eye would be able to discern the sad reality behind her outward splendor. As it was, her mother was too wrapped up in Carla's baby and Renata's pregnancy to notice, and her father was equally taken up by his new duties as President of the Association of Italian Hospital Surgeons. As for Giovanni and Renata, they were unlikely to take the trouble to penetrate the surface of her apparent normality. That just left her uncle.

⌒⁄ℓ⌒

James was not present when the Italian Ambassador arrived on Friday, May 17 at the Institute. Winstone, no doubt encouraged by HB, had obviously decided that, while James's presence was necessary, there was no need to flaunt it. He would attend the ceremony when the Institute formally took possession of the European collection, but that was all. So James was very surprised when he received a phone call from Eleanor inviting him to join the Rector, HB and the Duke of Messina for lunch after the ceremony.

The ceremony itself also reserved some surprises for James. The Duke greeted him with unusual warmth and referred in glowing terms to his contribution to European Union scholarship in his speech. Winstone was his usual pompous self, but he seemed ill at ease. Arbuthnot appeared to be simmering with rage. It was all very strange.

At the lunch that followed, the Duke spent most of the time discussing with James the institutional problems of the European Union. Unusually for an Italian, the Duke shared some of James's euroskepticism. Neither Winstone nor HB had anything to contribute and were left out of the conversation. Once lunch ended, the Duke immediately prepared to leave. He wished James well and thanked Winstone somewhat stiffly for the Institute's hospitality. Winstone replied with fulsome thanks for the collection. The Duke perfunctorily shook HB's hand and was gone. HB also left without a word to either of his two colleagues.

"James, I'd like to see you if you have time." The tone was friendly, almost sycophantic.

"Of course, Harold."

He was perplexed. What was going on? What was behind the Duke of Messina's privileged treatment of him, HB's bad humor, and now Winstone's unctuousness? They arrived at Winstone's office, and the Rector invited James to sit down. He offered him a brandy, which James accepted. If he was already mystified by the turn of events, the Rector's next words only increased his bewilderment.

"I understand from Dr. Bromhoeffer that the young lady with whom you were…" Winstone hesitated, searching for a convenient euphemism. "you were well acquainted has now left the Institute. Consequently, there is no reason to pursue the matter. Your resignation will not be needed."

James stared at the Rector in disbelief. This made no sense. The fact that his faithless mistress had left the Institute--James felt a sharp stab of pain at the thought--hardly excused his breach of the Institute's Ethics Code. Sensing that James was not convinced by his logic, Winstone quickly put an end to the discussion.

"I want you to remain on the faculty, James. The photos have been confiscated, and the matter is closed. No one is to know about it."

The obvious reaction was to thank Winstone for his unusual generosity, but James couldn't bring himself to do so. He was sure the Rector was acting from his own selfish motives, whatever they may be. He just nodded his acquiescence and made for his office to relay the news to the lads. Thank God, he hadn't told Veronica about his impending resignation.

There was no abatement to Antonietta's suffering. During the day she was consumed by a constant pain that sapped all her vitality. Unable to face her friends, she spent the days between crying alone in her room and the consoling presence of Anna in the kitchen. She would leave the house only to run errands for the maid, just as she had when she was a child. At night the pain became intolerable agony. She was tortured by images of James with Carolina or even worse Annya. The blond silhouette pursued her into her dreams, and she would awake, gasping for breath, her soul wracked by grief.

James arrived at Danny's on Friday evening with a magnum of champagne and a large bottle of scotch.

"I intend to get thoroughly pissed."

"A good idea," Bill agreed. "You certainly have something to celebrate."

James's only reply was a non-committal grunt.

"You know, James," said Danny, opening the bottle of champagne. The cork popped out with considerable velocity and nearly decapitated Piotr. Even James was forced to laugh. Encouraged by this change of mood, Danny unwisely continued. "I think there's a connection between Antonietta's departure and your reprieve. You should find her and ask her."

James exploded. "When are you assholes going to understand that I want nothing, absolutely nothing to do with that worthless whore"! he shouted. "She's not connected with my reprieve, as you call it. How the hell could she be"?

Somewhat pacified by his outburst, James downed his champagne and held out his glass to Danny for a refill. "She dropped me because it was all a game for her, and it wasn't fun anymore once the shit hit the fan."

There was a silence. Feeling ashamed of his outburst, James tried to make amends. "I can tell you one thing. This reprieve, as you call it, was Winstone's decision alone. You should've seen HB's face. He was furious."

"That's interesting, very interesting," mused Danny. "I bet you this signals the end of the HB-Winstone tandem. HB doesn't like to be crossed, and he won't forgive Winstone. We're in for fascinating times."

James left around midnight and arrived home to find the house in darkness. Veronica and the children were asleep. He poured himself a scotch and sat down, reluctant to go to bed where he knew he would be tortured by dreams of his lost happiness and images of Antonietta with other men, perhaps even the Marquesa. It was like this every night, and in the morning he had to force himself to despise and hate her before he could face the day.

〜

It was the end of May. The weather was glorious, but Antonietta was back in her bedroom trying to stem back persistent tears. She'd driven downtown in the vain hope of alleviating her anguish by a visit to the Uffizi gallery, but once she'd parked her car, she'd been beset by such despair that she'd returned in tears to her parents' villa. "Am I condemned to this misery for the rest of my life," she was asking herself despondently when there was a tap on her bedroom door. It was her uncle, the Cardinal.

"May I come in?" he asked, opening the door.

"Of course, uncle," Antonietta wiped away her tears as surreptitiously as possible.

The Cardinal sat down on a chair and surveyed the desolate spectacle of his niece sitting on the bed.

"Don't you think it would be better to talk about it"?

"About what"?

The Cardinal sighed. "About why a vivacious and fun-loving young woman has turned into a sad recluse."

Antonietta looked hard at her uncle and replied simply, "Passion."

"Ah"! The Cardinal was silent for a few moments. "I have difficulty believing that it's an unrequited passion. No man would be fool enough to refuse you."

"It was worse than that, uncle." Antonietta turned her tear-filled eyes upon the Cardinal. "It was an adulterous passion."

"Do you want to tell me about it"?

There was no censure, just sympathy in his voice, and between bouts of sobbing Antonietta recounted how she'd seen James at Mass, the passion he'd evoked in her, her frenetic attempts to combat it, her surrender, the few months of bliss she'd spent with her lover, and her sacrifice to save his career. When she'd finished, she collapsed on the bed and buried her face in a pillow.

The Cardinal put a hand on his niece's shoulder in a gesture of consolation.

"My dear Antonietta, I can feel your pain, but believe me, you have made the right decision. Such relationships can only bring great unhappiness, even worse than what you are now experiencing. Believe me."

Antonietta raised her head and turned round to face her uncle.

"Nothing could be worse than what I am now suffering. Nothing"!

she cried. "It eats at me, all the time. I don't have a second of peace. It overwhelms me, makes me sick with nausea." She clutched her breast. "Here where my heart is, there is a pain, a dreadful pain. It's constant." She paused to catch her breath. "*So don't tell me there is a greater unhappiness.*"

Putting her head in her hands, she exclaimed with an emotion that vibrated throughout the room. "James Markham, I wish to God I'd never set eyes on you"!

"James Markham"! her uncle exclaimed, emerging in his surprise from the shock produced by Antonietta's graphic description of her inner torment. "Did you say 'James Markham'"?

Antonietta stared at her uncle in disbelief. "You *know* him"?

"He's British"? Antonietta nodded.

"Catholic"? She nodded again. "Thirty-odd"?

Antonietta couldn't contain herself any longer. "Uncle, for the love of God, tell me. *Do you know him*"?

Giovanni contemplated his niece. What a terrible irony that it should be the son of his closest friend who was responsible for this devastation. The Cardinal felt a stab of guilt, remembering the oath that he and Philip had sworn in the Augustinerkeller. It was as if God, through Messina, had avenged their profanity on his innocent niece, as if she had been brought to swear an oath on the Holy Scriptures in order to thwart their pagan oath.

"Yes, I know him. He's the son of my friend, Philip Markham, the Marquis of Derwent."

Antonietta started as if galvanized by an electric shock. "James is the son of a *marquis*"?

"Well, he's the younger son, which means, if my knowledge of the English peerage is correct, that he has the courtesy title of Lord James Markham."

If the Cardinal had stopped there, Antonietta could perhaps have found a way to deal with her newfound knowledge. Unwisely, he added the information that would bring her close to death. "He's very wealthy. He has shares in the family bank."

Antonietta turned white. "His family owns a bank"?

"Yes. The Carlisle and District Bank. It's the third largest in the UK."

Antonietta stood up and kissed her uncle on both cheeks. "Please leave me," she requested.

Her uncle attempted to talk to her again, but she cut him off in best Palmieri style.

"I've heard enough, uncle. I wish to be alone."

Once her uncle had left the room, Antonietta abandoned herself to the bitterness building up within her. She had sacrificed her happiness, the passion that fed her like manna, for nothing, *nothing!* The pain, the suffering was all in vain. James didn't need his job. He wasn't an academic who had to work for his living, he was a wealthy aristocrat. Now she understood the expensive cars, the fabulous restaurants, the trips throughout Latin America. "Why, oh why hadn't he told her? Why hadn't I told him"?

All she wanted was to run back to James, to beg his forgiveness for leaving, to reclaim her happiness. But she was bound by that terrible oath, an oath she'd sworn in ignorance of her lover's real identity. Many other a woman would have used this as an excuse to renounce the oath and follow her heart, but Antonietta, despite her harsh disillusion, was too superstitious, too bound by the ancient ties of her religion, to do so. God had tricked her, and she was caught in the hell He'd created for her.

Antonietta reached up and tore down the crucifix that hung over her bed. A demented rage seized hold of her, and she threw the crucifix on the floor and stamped on it.

"*Porco Dio*"! she screamed, unaware of the crucifix biting deeply into her bare feet. Soon they were covered in blood, and Antonietta sank down, exhausted, on her bed. She lay there, barely conscious of the heat beginning to pervade her body.

That night, the fever started.

James arrived in Santiago on Sunday, June 2. After checking into the hotel, he walked down Avenida O'Higgins towards the Moneda Palace, but with every step he took recollections of his last trip to the city with Antonietta became more insistent. Before even reaching the presidential palace he fled back to the solitude of his hotel room. The evening was long and miserable. Even the food in the hotel's excellent restaurant had a bitter taste.

James spent two days in Santiago. During the day he was taken up by his discussions at the University of Santiago, and on Monday evening he dined with Eduardo at Coco's. It was a very enjoyable meal. They drank rather too much Carmenere, but at least this enabled James to fall asleep before he was troubled by images of Antonietta's unfaithful body.

Wednesday arrived, and James boarded a plane for Buenos Aires with enormous relief. He'd spent the previous evening on his own with a large bottle of scotch as solace for the emptiness that encompassed him. With a bit of luck, this evening would be spent in the company of Carolina.

The della Chiesa family was gathered around Antonietta's bed. Her brother Paolo had come from Rome to join the others in their vigil for the young woman, who was consumed by a fever that defied diagnosis. As he watched his daughter slip ever deeper into a coma, Paolo wept at his helplessness. His brother-in-law, the Cardinal, took him aside.

"I think I know the cause of this fever," he whispered, not wishing the others to hear. "Her heart is broken."

He told Paolo about Antonietta's passion for James Markham, and her decision to leave him because he was married. He didn't mention the circumstances under which she'd left or the oath to Messina.

Paolo was overcome by remorse. "I was too caught up in my work to notice her suffering," he moaned, looking over at his daughter. "I'd prefer her married to a divorced man a thousand times to watching her die before my eyes." He walked to the bed, took hold of Antonietta's burning hand, and covered it with his tears. Caterina put her arm around him.

"All we can do is pray," she murmured.

James entered the Hotel Plaza San Martín amidst a welter of emotions. Uppermost was his hope of finding a willing Carolina and a tentative anticipation of the sexual delights to come but lurking as always in the background was the vision of Antonietta. The last time he'd set foot in this hotel was with her.

He saw Carolina immediately. She was busy dealing with two irate Americans and didn't notice him. James marveled at her composure as she explained, politely but firmly, why their room was not yet ready. Won over by her charm, the couple agreed to take another room. Carolina turned towards James.

"Dr. Markham," she said with a slightly mocking smile. "What brings you back to Buenos Aires"? If she was surprised to see him, she gave no hint of it.

James had trouble collecting himself. He'd forgotten just how attractive Carolina was with her long blond hair, her serene blue eyes, her pretty mouth, and her inviting breasts beneath the tight blouse.

"I have some discussions with the University of Buenos Aires. I wanted to see you as well."

Carolina didn't react. She took James's Visa for an imprint and handed him a registration form to sign. She prepared a keypad for his room but pushed it to one side.

"It's the same room as last time," she told him. "505."

Ignoring his hand outstretched to take the keypad, Carolina motioned towards the elevators and turned to the couple behind James.

"May I help you"? she asked in her slightly accented English.

James walked slowly over to the elevators. It seemed clear what Carolina was up to, but he had difficulty believing it. It was many months since their brief affair, and it was unlikely that such a pretty girl had just twiddled her thumbs waiting for a man she hardly knew. Not knowing quite what to do, he stopped by the elevators, but the strange looks from other guests drove him off to study the dinner menu for the hotel's restaurant. Within seconds he heard Carolina's soft voice behind him.

"Here's your keypad, James. I finish at eleven. Be in your room."

She gave him a smile full of promise and returned to the reception desk. Startled by the rapidity of events, James made his way to his room, the vision of Antonietta now clouded by that of Carolina.

429

Whether it was the fervent prayers of her family or merely the natural course of events, Antonietta emerged from her coma. It had been nearly a week since she fell ill, and she was weak and pale. Soon the hearty Florentine fare cooked by Anna, the splendid wines her father fetched from the cellar, and the warmth of her family restored a semblance of her radiant beauty.

The doctors insisted she remain in bed for a few days. She lay there, thinking as always of James and longing for him, but there were no more tears. She must have used up her allotted amount. Sometimes she regretted surviving, at other times the idea of dying without seeing James again was too horrible to contemplate. But, as she reminded herself, she'd sworn to renounce him forever.

On the second day of her convalescence, the Cardinal came to see her. He was contrite.

"I feel responsible for what has happened," he told her, intending to disclose the oath he'd sworn with Philip Markham. At the last moment he thought better of it. "I should never have talked to you of passion. It was irresponsible and inappropriate."

Antonietta smiled at her uncle and shook her head. "No, uncle. It would have happened anyway." She cocked her head to one side. "On the other hand, it wasn't a good idea to tell me how rich James is. It made me realize that my sacrifice was meaningless, and I couldn't bear that thought. That's why I fell ill."

"Your sacrifice isn't meaningless, Antonietta. I know the measure of your pain, but it's better than a marriage that would have cut you off from your family and your religion and possibly, in the long run, lost you James Markham's love."

He took his niece's hand. "Time is a great healer."

"Not for me, uncle. Time may accustom me to the pain of my loss, but it will never heal my sorrow."

*Chapter 39*

# Monday June 10, 2002 to
# Friday August 2, 2002

I T WAS JUNE 10 and James's 33rd birthday. Carolina had taken the day off, and they had traveled by hydrofoil to Montevideo. It was warm for the southern hemisphere's midwinter, and they were able to sit on the beach.

"I prefer Montevideo," James declared. "At least it has a decent beach."

Carolina was put out. "How can you say that, James. Buenos Aires is much more exciting, and if you want a beach, you can always come here."

Carolina pouted, and James had a sudden flash of Antonietta. It had been like this all week. However much he enjoyed Carolina's easy company and the pleasures of her willing body, he had difficulty repressing images of his faithless mistress, particularly in the aftermath of sex. Antonietta had always been at her most gorgeous when she was newly sated.

They had dinner at the elegant Arcadia restaurant in the Plaza Independencia. The next day they returned to Buenos Aires where Carolina started work at three in the afternoon. James wandered aimlessly around the city, visiting a number of cafes before returning to his room to read and wait for Carolina. She arrived a little after eleven. She slipped off her clothes, removed James's dressing gown, and pressed her nude body against his. They kissed with James running his hands slowly down the smooth skin of Carolina's back. He laid her on

431

the bed, caressed and kissed her breasts, her stomach, the inside of her thighs, before exciting her sex. This time, instead of penetrating her, he turned her over and kneaded her buttocks. She protested weakly when he ran his fingers and tongue between them, but she let him have his way with her.

"I shall miss you," he told her after she'd turned over and was cuddled against him.

Carolina looked up, and for once her eyes lacked their normal serenity. "I wish I could believe you." She put her hand over James's mouth to silence his reply.

They slept until noon. James quickly packed, and Carolina accompanied him to the airport.

"The next time I'll meet you, and you can stay at my place," she told him. "That's if you bother to tell me you're coming."

She had the same mocking smile with which she'd greeted him a week ago. James promised to tell her. Carolina gave him a last kiss, and he passed through security.

*◈*

June was nearly over, but the passage of time had done nothing to alleviate Antonietta's sorrow. Although she no longer secluded herself in her room to weep for her lost love, the pain was not the less intense and at times unbearable. At night when she was beset by imaginings of James with another woman, Annya in particular, she was seared by jealousy.

So far she hadn't found the courage to take up her social life in Florence, and today was no exception. After helping Anna with the evening meal, she was at home reading some poems by Leopardi. The phone rang. It was her friend, Gino della Rovere. He invited her to a party at his apartment the following Saturday, July 6. Instinctively Antonietta refused.

"What's got into you, Netta"? Gino inquired. Antonietta hated her name being shortened, but for some reason she accepted it from Gino. "You've become a recluse."

"He's right," Antonietta thought. "Moping around my parents' villa is not achieving anything." The ache she still felt in her heart told her that.

"I've been ill," she said. "If I feel better next week, I'll come."
"You'd better."

⁓

James arrived in his office. He greeted his secretary, Sheila, who doted on him. She handed him the day's mail.

"There's a proposal from your friend, HB, for the July 15 meeting of the Governing Council," she informed him.

James studied the proposal. Arbuthnot was suggesting that all re-appointments to the positions of Section Head should be done by way of a committee in place of an assessment by the members of the Section concerned. It was a typical HB power grab. His proposal would take re-appointments out of the hands of the Section members and place them in a committee that he doubtless hoped to control.

James had no stomach for another fight with HB. The loss of Antonietta had drained away his energy, and his position was not threatened as he was no longer a Section Head. He went mechanically through the rest of the mail and was about to fetch Bill for a liquid lunch when Hamid arrived in his office. He looked pale and worried.

"Have you seen Roy's proposal"? he asked. James nodded and pointed to the document lying on his desk.

"This is aimed at me because of that Hunt business," Hamid went on. "I'm the only Section Head up for re-appointment next year. I'd get in on an assessment but not with a committee stacked by Arbuthnot. He'd see to that."

James sighed. He knew what was coming.

"I need your help, James. People listen to you. I want you to canvass against the proposal. I can't do it. It would seem too self-serving."

The Governing Council comprised the totality of the Institute's professors, and Hamid's request would entail going round all of them, except HB's buddies. It was not an attractive prospect, but at least it would prove a distraction from the constant battle to eliminate the bitter memories of Antonietta.

James agreed to do it.

⁓

Antonietta mingled with the guests at Gino's party, trying hard to avoid Rudolfo Guardini and his crowd. She didn't mix in the same artsy circles as Gino and found no one enjoyable to talk to. If she'd come to take her mind off James, the evening was a complete failure. With every person she met, her longing for him became even greater. To console herself, she drank liberally and was a little tipsy when she was accosted by the Marquesa de Avila y de la Torre.

"I heard you'd returned from Canada, countess." The smooth voice was like honey, and Antonietta fell immediately under its spell. She gazed at the Marquesa's provocative dress, which left little to the imagination.

"I've been back over two months, Marquesa." Her eyes fixed on the Marquesa's décolleté. The Marquesa noticed and smiled seductively.

"I think we have the most inviting décolletés at this party," she remarked, and before Antonietta could stop her, she ran a finger along the deep cut in Antonietta's dress, almost touching her nipples. "Don't you"?

Antonietta drew back from the Marquesa with a gasp, not because of shock at her gesture but at the spasm of pleasure that traversed her body under the Marquesa's touch. Unable to answer, she just stood there in confusion, intoxicated by the subtle scent of the Marquesa's perfume.

"Netta"! It was Gino, and he whisked her away from the seductive Marquesa. He led her over to the bar and poured her another glass of wine. "Be careful of the Marquesa. She's a lesbian, and you're her type."

Antonietta blushed deeply. Luckily, Gino misinterpreted her reaction. "Sorry. I didn't mean to shock you, but I thought you should be warned."

At that moment Gino's lover, Antonio, arrived, and the three of them were soon engaged in amusing chitchat. For the first time since her flight from Canada, Antonietta was doubled up with laughter as Gino described Antonio's attempts at renovating their apartment.

"We bought it for three hundred million lira," Gino recounted, "and now Antonio's renovated it, it's worth about a hundred million less."

Antonietta looked fondly at Gino's smiling face. An aristocrat like her, he had nothing of the empty snobbery of their class. "It's a pity he's gay," she thought.

"That's unfair, Gino," Antonio protested, sipping his expresso. "It's only worth fifty million less."

They continued to laugh together, but Antonietta found herself seeking out the Marquesa with her eyes. She was nowhere to be seen. Antonietta felt relief tinged with disappointment. After Gino and Antonio had wandered off to join other guests, she left the party.

When she arrived at her car, she was infuriated to find that two of her tires had been slashed. Now she would have to call a taxi and arrange to have the car towed to a garage. She was taking the cell phone out of her purse when a Maserati convertible with its roof down stopped beside the immobilized Alfa Romeo. It was the Marquesa.

"Countess," she called. Antonietta walked over to the Maserati. "I see you have a problem. Allow me to give you a ride."

The Marquesa lent over and opened the passenger door. As she did so, Antonietta caught a glimpse of her fulsome breasts, naked under the dress. She knew what the Marquesa wanted, and she suspected that her sudden appearance was linked to the fate of her car's tires. A little drunk and entrapped by the overpowering sensuality of the Marquesa, Antonietta felt the powerful stirring of sexual desire after two months of abstinence. She climbed into the Maserati.

They arrived at the Marquesa's villa. The door was opened by a very attractive blond girl dressed only in a skimpy nightdress.

"This is Irena, my Albanian maid," the Marquesa explained.

Antonietta was not fooled. The girl's attire and the wanton way she was leering at them made it very clear that her duties in the house had little to do with housework. To Antonietta's relief the maid left them to return to her bed. For one dreadful moment she thought that the Marquesa intended her to join them. Once she was gone, the Marquesa led Antonietta up the stairs to her bedroom.

She turned on the lights. They were dimmed and basked the room in a sensuous glow. Without further ado, she slipped off her clothes and stood opposite Antonietta, eyeing her with expectation. Her voluptuous breasts had lost some of the firmness of youth and dipped a little in a pear shape, but this rendered them even more inviting for Antonietta. They cried out to be fondled. Her sex was denuded, and the faint odor of her sexuality electrified Antonietta. The tautness of her small nipples betrayed the force of her desire. Her lithe and trim body was a golden color with no marks of modesty. Antonietta, in thrall to the sexual magnetism of the Marquesa, imagined her sunbathing in the nude, disrupted only by bouts of lesbian pleasure with her pretty Albanian maid. She could feel the arousal between her thighs and undressed, a little self-conscious at her nudity for she hadn't been waxed since returning to Italy. But the dark hair that partially hid her sex didn't seem to bother the Marquesa, who gazed lustfully at Antonietta's naked body, taking in the full splendor of her lubricious beauty and anticipating its enjoyment.

"Turn around," the Marquesa ordered.

She pressed herself against Antonietta's back and began to fondle her hardening breasts from behind. She rubbed the erect nipples between thumb and finger, and Antonietta's body shivered with excitement. The Marquesa kissed her in the neck and ran a finger down her spine, continuing on between her buttocks. She caressed her sex and her anus with the lightest of touches. Antonietta squirmed, wet and avid for gratification.

"You have to earn your pleasure," the Marquesa whispered and lay down on the bed, her legs opened.

Beside herself with lust, Antonietta devoured the Marquesa's voluptuous breasts and ran her tongue over her the golden skin of her belly before using it to savor and arouse her denuded sex. Soon the Marquesa was writhing and crying out in ecstasy. Antonietta made her turn over, and after teasing her with her nipples, brought her to a volcanic climax with her tongue in her anus and her fingers massaging her clitoris.

"Now it's your turn," the Marquesa told Antonietta, beginning to fondle the young woman's breasts and suck on her nipples.

Antonietta abandoned her body to the Marquesa's lascivious caresses with groans of sexual bliss, her longing for James temporarily stilled. She allowed the most indecent intimacies and reveled in the spasms of delight this gave her. Her desire mounted as the Marquesa caressed and serviced her sex before turning her over to enjoy her buttocks and anus. When the Marquesa penetrated her sex with her fingers and sucked on her clitoris, Antonietta couldn't contain herself any longer. A surge of pleasure ripped through her body that eclipsed all thoughts of her miserable plight and left her panting.

Physically sated, the two women lay together, naked, relishing the erogenous perfection of each other's body. When their lust was rekindled, the Marquesa introduced Antonietta to practices she'd never known before. They tribbed together and used a doubled-headed dildo in both their sex and anus. These practices revolted Antonietta, but the revulsion only served to arouse her libido all the more. Ultimately, both women were overcome by exhaustion and fell asleep.

Antonietta awoke first in the morning. She felt used and degraded. She looked across at the woman who'd seduced her so completely. The Marquesa was not to blame. Antonietta had known from the instant she stepped into the Marquesa's car what awaited her. She'd wanted to be in the Marquesa's bed, partly out of sexual desire and partly in order to drown her grief in carnal rapture. She'd succeeded, but, after the perversions of the night, she now felt not only the anguish of loss but also guilt. She no longer deserved James.

Resolving never to see the Marquesa again, Antonietta fled from the villa. Once she was well clear, she called for a taxi. She went straight to Mass, not at the Basilica but at Santa Maria Novella. She didn't want her family to see her face, which probably still bore the marks of perverse pleasure.

On Monday the Marquesa called Antonietta at her parents' house. Antonietta was petrified and begged the Marquesa not to call her there again. She would never see her again, she told the Marquesa. She was not a lesbian, and she'd been drunk on Saturday night.

The Marquesa continued to exercise a powerful attraction for Antonietta, and by Friday she was thinking with regret of the sexual joys she'd renounced. She decided that she needed a man, otherwise she would succumb anew to the erotic blandishments of the Marquesa. She called her old friends from university days, Alessa and Paulina, and arranged to meet them the next evening at Fiasco's.

James spent the week before the meeting of the Governing Council on July 15 discreetly canvassing against Arbuthnot's proposal. He had divided the faculty into three groups.

The first group was those professors who could be relied upon to follow James's lead and oppose HB. Apart from Bill, Piotr and Danny, this comprised James's new ally Hamid Khan, Christine Desmoulins and Klaus Berger from his own Section, and Anne-Marie Legrand and Claudio Pettroni from LAC. He also thought he could count on Saleema Nadjani. This made ten certain votes together with his own out of a total of thirty-nine.

The second group was made up of those professors allied to HB or Winstone. These were Len Flint, Ed Tocheniuk, Fred Gowling from FEB, McGrath, Ed Williams, Nathan Golberg and probably Mike Allen from James's Section, and Brian Wilkins, Georges Campeau and Emily Wright from LAC. Of these, McGrath, Gowling, Flint, Campeau and possibly Wilkins were sure allies of HB. The others were closer to Winstone. Counting HB, this group amounted to eleven professors.

The rest of the faculty could be considered neutral, although James hoped for a positive response from a number of them, including Ilse Bromhoeffer and perhaps Pierre Forget. Danny had volunteered to canvas these two.

After firming up the support of the first group, James turned his attention to the neutral members of the Council. It was a delicate business as he didn't want to appear vindictive against HB. This could prove counterproductive. He would stress the more democratic nature of the present approach, which gave all interested professors a say in the appointment. As it turned out, his task was much easier than he'd feared. Danny had been right. The appointment of Flint to Bill's tenure committee had shocked and angered the silent majority, and there was a groundswell of opposition to any measure that would increase HB's power. There was also a simmering dissatisfaction with Winstone, partly because of his association with HB and partly because of lack of direction and erratic hiring practices. James reacted noncommittally to these criticisms. He still had vague thoughts of the Rectorship, and it was not wise to be seen encouraging dissatisfaction with Winstone for his own ends.

By Thursday, James had secured enough votes to defeat HB's proposal handily, and Danny reported that both Ilse and Pierre Forget would also vote against it. On Friday Ed Williams, whom James had not even bothered to canvass, stopped him in the Administration Building.

"I don't think we should let HB get too big for his boots," he commented.

"Does that mean you're against his proposal"?

Williams nodded and walked on. James watched him go and smiled. If this defection meant that Winstone's group had broken with HB, the Senior Dean was set for a humiliation. "If only Antonietta were here to share in it," he couldn't help thinking before chasing away the thought.

*᙮*

Antonietta arrived at Fiasco's. As she entered the smoke-filled interior, a tremor went through her. Again she was beset by the thought that this was the bar James had probably frequented as a student with his Spanish girlfriend. Jealousy and longing overcame her, and she was tempted to leave. She forced herself to stay; she needed to find an antidote to the lesbian enticements of the Marquesa.

Alessa and Paulina greeted her with much affection and heaped reproaches on her for not contacting them before. She didn't have to answer, as immediately she sat down, a dark male student leaned over to her.

"We meet again, countess," he said with a Welsh lilt to his voice.

"So it seems." Antonietta smiled at the young man. "If I remember, your name is David."

"And your's is Antonietta."

They drank and talked into the early hours. The infectious gaiety of the company and a rather too liberal indulgence in the bar's rather tart house wine distracted Antonietta from her heartbreak, and she flirted outrageously with David. He had worked for an investment bank in London, and now he was studying for his doctorate in economics at the European University Institute. He had a typical British sense of humor, and, together with his rugged dark looks, he reminded her of James.

He took her back to his small studio in Fiesole. She let him kiss her, but she had to fight back memories of James, and she could feel herself trembling." It had to happen," she told herself, and almost in a trance she let him undress her. When he started to caress her breasts, she wanted to cry out for him to stop. He took off his clothes and led her to the bed. Her mind was full of the last time she and James had made love. She couldn't bring herself to take David into her mouth. She just caressed him until he was ready to take her. She feigned her climax.

It was so strange to sleep with a man other than James. She lay there, weighed down by nostalgia. Fortunately, David was already asleep. "If I'm with another man," she reflected, "James is probably with another woman." The vision of a triumphant Annya tortured her until, worn out by her suffering, she fell asleep in her turn.

The next morning David woke her with a cup of expresso. She contemplated the man who had now taken James's place, in bed if not in her heart. He was handsome enough, but Antonietta doubted he was a particularly good lover. If he didn't show any disappointment with her pitiful performance of last night, he didn't expect much. That was just as well. It would be a long time before she'd be able to abandon herself completely to a man again.

David wanted Antonietta to stay, but she had to meet her family for Mass and celebrate her 24th birthday with them afterwards. Her new lover wished her a happy birthday and kissed her before she left.

Once Winstone had effected his habitual royal entry, the Governing Council convened. The Rector called on Arbuthnot to present his proposal. The Senior Dean, who was unusually tense, went on about uniform standards and the good of the whole Institute. In his view, a faculty committee would better safeguard these essential factors in any re-appointment than an assessment by individual professors. It was not a particularly convincing performance, but his allies, Fred Gowling and Georges Campeau, jumped in to give the proposal their enthusiastic support without advancing any cogent arguments in favor of it. There was an ominous silence after they'd finished.

"Any other comments"? Winstone inquired and immediately gave the floor to Klaus Berger, whom he must have known was opposed to the proposal. Klaus demolished HB's arguments.

"It boils down to trusting an impersonal committee or trusting the judgment of those who actually serve under the Section Head in question," he concluded.

An avalanche of criticism of the proposal followed Berger. Brian Wilkins attempted in vain to defend it but was shot down by Ed Williams.

"HB's lost the Rector," Danny whispered to James.

He had indeed. When the vote was taken, only the seven professors close to Arbuthnot were in favor.

---

That evening at Danny's, the discussion centered on the rift between Winstone and HB.

"As I told you," James was saying, "it's because Winstone stopped the ethics proceeding against me. He deprived HB of his vengeance, and HB hasn't forgiven him"

"I still think Antonietta had something to do with that," Danny insisted. "There has to be some explanation for her leaving."

"Yes, there goddam well is"! James roared. "She's a faithless whore"!

"OK, James." Bill placed his hand on his friend's shoulder. "You're probably right, but there's no need to yell at Danny."

James glowered and took a large gulp of whisky. The conversation turned to the mid-term review of the Rector, which was due in January of next year.

"How does it work"? enquired Piotr.

"There's a committee consisting of a representative elected by each Section and one by the faculty at large," Danny replied. "They prepare a report."

They were interrupted by the arrival of Bernadette, who was bursting with her news.

"You know that football captain fellow," she told them. They all nodded, except James. "Well, I saw him kissing some dark-haired girl."

Bill whistled. "That must be Françoise. If so, it means he's dumped Petra and gone back to her."

Danny and Piotr smiled at each other. James looked into space.

---

On the Wednesday after the Saturday of their first night together, David invited Antonietta to the cinema. She agreed to go, more out of resignation tinged with nervousness than enthusiasm. She needed a man, and David was as good a choice as any other. She resolved to put James out of her mind when they made love that night and try to find some pleasure in it.

Once the film was over, and they were back in David's studio, Antonietta made him lie on the bed while she stripped in front of him. He drew her down onto the bed and began to caress her nude body. Trying desperately to suppress memories of James, Antonietta returned his kisses and began to undress him. Feeling like a whore, she took him into her mouth and willed herself to pleasure him. Afterwards he seemed at a loss what to do. Antonietta pushed his head down her body. she ached for James, but her sexual need was such that she came plentifully.

The next morning David suggested that Antonietta move in with him. She refused. The studio was too small for two, and she wished to keep her independence. David was disappointed but accepted her refusal with good grace. They agreed Antonietta would spend Friday and Saturday nights at the studio, and perhaps other nights if an evening at Fiasco's left her unfit to drive.

From now on, the two met frequently, and gradually Antonietta accustomed herself to sex with David. It was rather pedestrian, but this suited her. She had no desire to repeat with him the extravagances of her sex life with James. However, though David calmed Antonietta's sexual frustration, he couldn't heal the ache in her heart. The worst time was after their lovemaking when David was asleep. Then there was no rampart against the jealousy and pain that ravaged her.

*Chapter 40*

# Saturday August 3, 2003 to Saturday January 19, 2003

I T WAS A BEAUTIFUL August day when James arrived in Buenos Aires. There was not a cloud in the sky, and it was a pleasant fifteen degrees Celsius. He'd kept his word to Carolina, and she would be waiting for him. He felt a thrill of expectation but also a little guilt. He should have stopped over in Mexico City to settle some problems with ITAM*, but the pull of Carolina had been too strong. It wasn't only that he desired her. He found in her arms some way to fill the terrible void left by Antonietta's departure.

James passed through customs. As always, the Argentinean officials were charming, and he asked himself what evil genie had led their two countries into war. The question became even more pertinent when he glimpsed Carolina in the crowd greeting the flight. She was dressed in an elegant beige jacket and skirt, and she was smiling at him from a distance with that artless serenity that was so entrancing. She ran up and kissed him.

"I'm not working until Monday," she informed him.

They took a taxi to Carolina's apartment, which was situated in an upscale residential part of the Recoleta and decorated simply but with taste. Carolina had painted the walls a delicate shade of yellow, which, mellowed by the deep green drapes, gave the apartment a feeling of warmth and intimacy. The blue cushions on the cream sofa reflected the color of her eyes. Two watercolor paintings of Punta del Elste adorned one wall and the portrait of a beautiful blond woman the other.

"Who painted those pictures? And who is that beautiful woman"?

"My father painted them. The woman is my mother, Luisa Maria."

"You were close to your father"?

Tears welled up in Carolina's eyes, and, without waiting for a reply, James changed the subject.

"How do you afford this apartment"?

"It's difficult. I was brought up in a poor area of Buenos Aires, and I always swore that one day I would live in the Recoleta."

She grinned at James. "Also, it's near to work when I need some money at the end of the month."

James cringed and took Carolina into his arms. "Is that true, or are you just saying it to make me jealous"?

"Both," Carolina replied, laughing at the shocked expression on James's face. "I told you before that I do that."

"I didn't really believe you."

Carolina laughed again and opened a bottle of wine. "Don't worry, it's not the end of the month."

James shook his head. "What am I going to do with you"?

Carolina pulled him to her and gazed at him with her piercing blue eyes. "Drink some wine, and make love to me."

⁓

Antonietta was moving into her new apartment, which was near her old one in the Borgo Ognissanti. She liked the Santa Maria Novella district with its boutiques and the eponymous Dominican Basilica where she would go to hear Mass and occasionally to pray. The painters were still putting the final touches to the redecoration of the apartment.

It would be a relief to be on her own without having to make up stories to explain her nights with David. She'd taken the precaution of not installing a phone line. She would rely on her cell. This way, her mother wouldn't know where she spent her nights. David was helping, and she sensed that he wanted to move in with her. There was plenty of room for the two of them, but she was not prepared to commit herself. She enjoyed his company, but her heart still belonged to James.

Although she knew it was impossible, she still cherished deep down a frail hope that one day she might be reunited with him.

～

After a weekend walking around the Recoleta with Carolina, making love to her, spending tranquil moments in cafés under the charm of her radiant personality and demure beauty, James came rather brutally down to earth on Monday. So that they could spend the evenings together, Carolina had arranged to work from eight to four. This meant that James was left to his own devices for most of the day, and the black thoughts that Carolina was able to disperse came back with full force to haunt him. Try as he might to banish Antonietta from his mind, one thought kept pursuing him. "If I'm with Carolina, who's enjoying Antonietta's gorgeous but faithless body"?

If Carolina noticed James's bouts of introspection, she didn't allow them to disturb her. She had an inner serenity that fascinated but also frustrated James. She satisfied all his physical desires, and her company was like silk, soft and yielding, but there was nothing to latch on to. It was not that she lacked substance, it was finding it that was difficult. James had the strong impression she didn't want to reveal herself. Any time he became more serious, Carolina would divert the conversation with an enigmatic smile.

It was only when it came time to part that Carolina's façade--if that is what it was--slipped a little. She kissed James with unusual emotion.

"I'm spending the last two weeks of November in a cousin's apartment in Montevideo," she told him. "Do you want to join me"? Surprised by the invitation, James didn't answer at first, so Carolina added with a grin. "As you know, there's a beach in Montevideo."

James laughed, remembering her indignation at his preference for the Uruguayan capital. "Yes. I'm not teaching this term. I'd love to come."

～

Antonietta arrived at David's studio for her Friday sleepover around five. He greeted her with a kiss and a broad grin. Before she could ask the reason, he held up two tickets.

445

"We're going to a Laura Pausini concert tonight."

Antonietta felt her body tense up, and she returned David's kiss longer than usual to hide her distress.

"I thought you'd be pleased."

The concert was sheer agony for Antonietta. Every song reminded her of James, of the time she'd longed for him in the cottage, of their moments of bliss together. David noticed that she was flushed. She assured him it was just the heat of the concert hall. The interval came, and Antonietta restored her composure with a glass of wine. It didn't avail her as the next song was the one she'd always associated with the pain of losing James even before she'd renounced him. No sooner had Laura Pausini intoned the first words of *Come se non fosse stato mai amore* than Antonietta broke down. Bursting into tears, she rushed from the hall, followed by an anxious David.

"Just drive me home to my apartment," she implored.

Neither of them spoke on the way. Once they arrived at the apartment, Antonietta apologized and, although all she wanted was to be alone, asked David to come in. He was entitled to an explanation. But he'd already guessed.

"Who was he"?

"He was a man I met in Canada. I fell desperately in love with him, but he was married. So we broke up." It all sounded so banal that Antonietta cried out, "I love him still! I'll *always* love him"!

David put his arm around her. "You'll get over it in time."

Antonietta nodded, but she knew in her heart this was not true.

It was the beginning of term at NIIS. The students were milling around, and the professors were putting the finishing touches to their lecture notes. James was busying himself with the administrative details that accompany every new academic year, but it was a half-hearted effort. Try as he might to put them aside, he was dominated by memories of last year.

On Tuesday a notice came from the Rector's Office announcing that candidates for the Rector's midterm review committee had to be declared by Friday, September 27, and that the election would take place on Friday, October 18. James called Danny, and they agreed there should be a council of war at Danny's that evening. It was essential to prevent the committee falling under the control of faculty close to Winstone or HB.

James welcomed the distraction provided by the upcoming campaign. The first step was to secure suitable candidates. Bill wanted to stand, but Danny advised against it.

"Anyone would think I have the plague," Bill complained.

Danny gave him a pat on the back to console him. "None of us must stand. The committee must be seen as completely neutral. We're too associated with James, who is perceived as a possible replacement for Winstone."

Over the next two weeks, Danny and James discreetly sought out professors who could be relied upon to produce an honest report, which both were sure would be damning for Winstone. By the time September 27 came along, they'd found Claudio Pettroni to stand against the ubiquitous Brian Wilkins for LAC, Jason Levy against Ed Tocheniuk for FEB and Klaus Berger against Ed Williams for LIR. Christine Desmoulins had initially agreed to stand as candidate for the faculty at large but pulled out at the last moment. On Danny's prompting, Saleema Nadjani took Christine's place.

Each of the candidates held several meetings to feel the pulse of the faculty and explain their approach. All stressed the need for an objective and fair review, but Williams and Tocheniuk also argued against conducting a witch-hunt. This was a sign that the Rector was nervous about the review. James and Danny were confident that, given the prevailing feeling in the Institute, their candidates would be elected. This is what happened. A celebration was convened at Danny's for the Saturday after the election.

Antonietta started her doctorate in economics at the University of Florence on Monday, October 7. David had tried to persuade her to enroll at the European University, but the specter of James loomed too large. She continued to resist his none too subtle hints that he move in with her. She appreciated his sense of humor and his intelligence, but there was only room in her heart for James. David was a mediocre lover, and in her sexual frustration she now yearned for the carnal excesses of her time with James and was constantly tempted to return to the Marquesa's bed. There was a strong element of resignation in her relationship with David. He was not ideal, but what man apart from James would ever be?

~

"It's unlike Bill to be late," remarked Danny as they waited for him to celebrate their success at the elections. "He normally can't wait to get into the sauce."

Bill's car pulled up outside Danny's house. To everyone's surprise, Petra emerged from it with Bill. Once in the house, they were harassed by questions and admitted that they were, as the students put it, "an item". While the others were eloquent in their congratulations for this happy development, James had mixed feelings. He was glad for Bill, but the radiant Petra brought home both the emptiness of his own life without Antonietta and his jealousy of her sexual relations with his former mistress. Proceeding from an image of Antonietta in bed with Petra, he was pursued by the image of her luscious body being enjoyed by the Marquesa. He left early.

~

Inevitably, Antonietta's mother came to hear of her liaison with David. One of her women friends had seen the two walking around Florence holding hands.

"Who is he"? Caterina inquired of her daughter.

"He's doing his doctorate in economics at the European University. He's British."

"I suppose he's just another nobody."

It was unlike Antonietta to show anger towards her parents, but now she snapped, worn out by the constant pain of missing James and the effort to find some meaning to her relationship with David.

"He may be a nobody to you, *mamma*," she shouted, "but he's the man I love, and you will learn to mind your own business."

Outraged by Antonietta's defiance, Caterina slapped her. "How dare you speak to me like that"!

Her face burning, Antonietta gave her mother a look of such ferocity that Caterina cringed. She turned on her heels and stalked off without a further word.

Once she was back in her apartment, Antonietta was swamped by regret and shame. Why on earth had she behaved so badly? Was it worth provoking a rift with her mother for a man she didn't love, whatever she may have said in anger? Would this nightmare, this kaleidoscope of despair and longing never end? She thought of breaking up with David, but what would that achieve? She even felt guilty at the thought. He was considerate, and she enjoyed his company. It was not his fault that she couldn't put her passion for James behind her, and perhaps not his fault either that she was sexually frustrated. As James had once told her, only partly in jest, she was oversexed.

⌒⁓

James spent November 14 and 15 in Mexico City resolving the problems with ITAM. He arrived late afternoon on Saturday in Buenos Aires to be met by Carolina. The beginning of term with its reminiscences of last year and the anniversary of his first night with Antonietta had weighed upon him, and he was happy to find solace in Carolina's bed. She accommodated and often anticipated his desires and lent her body willingly to any immodest use he wished to make of it. Her conversation was light without being frivolous, her temper even without boring him, her disposition sunny but not without a concealed depth.

On Monday they traveled by boat to Montevideo. The apartment in which they stayed looked over the ocean, or more correctly the estuary of the River Plate. They relaxed on the beach, swam in the warm sea, ate too much and laughed a lot. They made love until the early hours. Carolina might lack the passion of Antonietta, but she knew how to satisfy a man

Despite the pleasures that Carolina procured him, James was not free of Antonietta. As he lay on the beach, he thought of Punta del Este and Antonietta's Brazilian bikini. At times he found himself aching for the sultry volatility of his raven-haired former mistress. Watching

Carolina twist and turn in bed as he serviced her, he was often beset by jealousy. To whose indecent touch was Antonietta now consigning her body?

November ended, and it was time to return to Buenos Aires. James spent one last night with Carolina and left on Sunday, December 1 for Montreal. He arrived to the habitual cool welcome from Veronica. He spent Monday catching up with administrative matters, apart from lunch with Bill.

"Well, did you roger her"?

"We enjoyed ourselves," James replied, not wishing to go into detail. He winced as Bill slapped him on the back. He really didn't go for this North American bonhomie.

"Let's hope she's cured you of Antonietta."

"Don't mention that goddam woman." James raised his voice, but his anger was directed at himself, not Bill. Two weeks with Carolina should have cured him, but it hadn't.

James returned home to find Veronica waiting for him with four boarding cards in her hands.

"Who is Carolina Sanchez? What were you doing spending two weeks in Montevideo with her"?

James was caught. Stupidly, he'd left all four boarding cards in his jacket, and it was impossible to deny that he'd traveled both to and from Montevideo with Carolina. He was tired and dispirited and incapable of dreaming up a story.

"I was having an affair with her." He was astonished by his own candor.

Veronica turned white with rage. She walked around the room in circles and then turned to face James.

"I will not live with a sinner"! she expostulated. "I am a Benedictine oblate, and I'm committed to living a Christian family life. How can I do that with a man who mocks the sacrament of marriage"?

James looked at his wife with repugnance. The pursed lips, the fanatic gleam in her eyes, the coldness of her whole bearing. How to God had he put up with her for so long? Without a word, he went upstairs and fetched his suitcases, which were still packed.

"I'm leaving," he told Veronica. "I expect to see the kids every other weekend. Any problems, and you'll hear from a lawyer."

He drove off to Bill's place.

David left Florence for Wales on Monday, December 16 to spend Christmas with his family. Depressed and vulnerable, Antonietta feared she would prove an easy victim for the Marquesa's erotic charms, so she decided to spend Christmas at her parents' villa in Fiesole. Despite the presence of Paolo and Monica for part of the time, it was a miserable experience. Her mother had not forgiven her for the episode over David, or indeed for her relationship with him, and she was distant and cold. Her father tried to make up for her mother and plied her with good Italian wine, but Antonietta's heart was not in it. She longed for James, and at times the pain was so unbearable that she considered taking a plane to Canada to see him. The oath held her back; it was not so much religious conviction as a superstitious fear of divine wrath if she broke it.

On the Wednesday after separating from Veronica, James came back to the house to pick up some things. Veronica greeted him with a look of cold disdain and didn't say a word, much to James's relief. Most of the time he was there she spent praying. James wondered idly what she was praying about. That he would convert from his wicked ways? More likely, that he would be struck down by lightning and consigned to hell for all eternity.

He established himself in one of the bedrooms in Bill's house. Bill was downright enthusiastic about his break with Veronica.

"You should've done it a long time ago," he told James.

He was more than willing to help James out, but Petra was now living with him, and James felt awkward with their *ménage à trois*. He also had a lingering jealousy of Petra; her presence recalled Antonietta's sexual promiscuity. "What a whore," he told himself. The contempt didn't resist the night when he was assailed by images of Antonietta in all her loveliness. The next week he started to look for his own apartment. He found one in Ste. Adèle, not far from Bill's. That would be convenient after an evening's over-indulgence.

The children spent the weekend of December 14 with him at Bill's. Susanna asked him when he was coming home and went very quiet when James gave an evasive reply. Peter said nothing. James wasn't sure what Veronica had told the children, and he was ill at ease with them. He felt relieved and at the same time guilty when the time came to drive them back to Prévost.

To take his mind off his unhappy personal situation, James spent much of the next week buying furniture and other paraphernalia for the apartment. He moved in on Friday, December 20 and left the next day to spend Christmas with his parents in England.

The Saturday after Christmas was the Lescia's party. Her parents were not going. Her mother was in Rome, and her father was attending a conference somewhere in Germany.

Antonietta was apprehensive about meeting the Marquesa at the party, but once she saw her, a thrill of excitement ran through her. The Marquesa was dressed, as always, in such a way as to exhibit all the enticements of her body, and Antonietta felt a sexual attraction towards her that she couldn't suppress. Noticing her stare, the Marquesa came over to her. "Do you want to come back to the villa after the party"? she asked, her eyes undressing Antonietta as she spoke.

A feeling of revolt, mixed with carnal desire, came over Antonietta. She'd renounced the man she loved, she suffered every day from this renunciation, and the present man in her life didn't satisfy her. The promise of perverted bliss that would momentarily blot out her misery seduced her. She nodded and walked away, not wanting people to notice her talking intimately with the Marquesa.

James was happy to be in England. Here at least was somewhere that didn't remind him of Antonietta, and the hurly-burly of sisters and their offspring and the joys of English country pubs provided ample distraction during the day. The night was a different matter, but by now James was becoming resigned to the torment of his nocturnal reminiscences. He went for walks with his father, and they discussed sheep rearing, which was his father's new hobby. It was far from the life of high finance and politics in which he had spent his whole adult life. James envied him the calm and peace he'd found through his involvement with the family farm

His mother was a less restful experience. She was horrified at his separation and urged him constantly to reconcile with Veronica.

"Think of your children," she kept telling him.

It was difficult to explain to his mother that, if reconciliation with Veronica meant living up to his marriage vows, he wanted none of it. He just promised to think about it in the vain hope that his mother would drop the topic. She didn't, and James decided to take up his brother's invitation to spend New Year's Eve with him and his family in London.

Antonietta followed the Marquesa to her villa. There was, thankfully, no sign of the maid. Without even waiting until they were in the bedroom, the Marquesa pulled down Antonietta's dress, detached her bra and began to fondle her breasts. Antonietta abandoned herself, and soon she was naked on the sofa, luxuriating in the expert ministrations of the Marquesa's fingers, tongue and nipples on her sex and anus. She let herself be turned over and satisfied in a way that obliterated all else but her sexual enjoyment. Still possessed by lust, she stripped the Marquesa in her turn and enjoyed and pleasured her. Afterwards they mounted the stairs to continue their unbridled sexual activity in bed.

The next morning Antonietta felt the usual pangs of guilt and disgust at the unnatural delights in which she'd reveled, but she let herself be persuaded to stay for breakfast before leaving for Sunday Mass. She never went to Mass. She arrived back at her apartment in the early evening and showered, as if to purify herself. She looked at her naked body in the mirror and was ashamed of the use to which she'd put it. "What am I becoming"? she asked herself in alarm and resolved again to resist the tempting pleasures offered with such dissolute skill by the Marquesa. It was better to suffer pain and longing than allow herself to be perverted. "What would James say if he knew"? This dreadful thought gave her a feeling of strength, and she went to Santa Maria Novella to pray that it would not desert her.

Antonietta met David at the airport on December 31 and drove him back to her apartment. They made love very conventionally, but she was glad to feel a man's body next to her. It made her seem more normal. She got ready for the evening's celebration and drove David to his studio for him to prepare himself. They met Alessa and Paulina and other friends at Fiasco's and drank and danced until the early hours. For once, Antonietta enjoyed herself, exhilarated by the festive atmosphere.

The sense of exhilaration did not last. Within a few days the suffering returned and her sense of sexual frustration. For all his excellent qualities, David neither fulfilled the yearning in her heart nor her physical needs. She longed for James and was tempted again by the Marquesa. It didn't help that she kept calling.

Antonietta met David at the airport on December 31 and drove him back to her apartment. They made love very conventionally, but she was glad to feel a man's body next to her. It made her seem more normal. She got ready for the evening's celebration and drove David to his studio for him to prepare himself. They met Alessa and Paulina and other friends at Fiasco's and drank and danced until the early hours. For once, Antonietta enjoyed herself, exhilarated by the festive atmosphere.

On January 14 the midterm review of the Rector was released. It was very critical, citing in particular poor financial management and dubious appointments of friends with poor qualifications. The Rector was also criticized for lack of direction and a poor working relationship with the Section Heads. The appointment of a Senior Dean, which had not been necessary, had contributed greatly to this poor working relationship. As he read the report, James felt a great sense of satisfaction. If he'd written it himself, he couldn't have done a better job. Winstone was finished.

Two days later a group of professors came to see him. Winstone had to go, they told him. James reacted cautiously. He couldn't afford to be seen as a prime mover in getting rid of Winstone if he wanted to replace him. He told the group that he was not prepared to act without consulting the Deans and Section Heads. Once his colleagues had left, he called Danny, who agreed to play the role of front man.

Over the next few days Danny canvassed opinion in the faculty. With the obvious exception of Winstone's cronies, there was a strong feeling that the Rector should resign. At no time did Danny mention James as a possible replacement.

"One thing at a time," he told an impatient Bill Leaman.

It was not clear how HB would react, but it seemed probable that he would support Winstone in order to protect his own position. Strangely, Winstone himself seemed to be doing nothing to save his skin.

The Deans and Section Heads met, at Danny's invitation, on Tuesday, January 21. All except HB agreed that Winstone should go. HB argued that he should be given a second chance but on very strict terms. He doubtless wanted the strict terms to include more power for the Senior Dean. The others, including Forget, who was normally inclined to compromise, were having none of it.

"Enough is enough," Forget declared with uncharacteristic firmness.

All but HB signed a letter to Winstone inviting him to resign for the good of the Institute. When the meeting broke up, HB couldn't resist a last show of defiance.

"Your letter will mean nothing without the Senior Dean's signature."

Immediately after the meeting HB made his way to the Rector's Office. Giving Eleanor short shrift, he barged it. He might despise Winstone, but HB knew that his influence would disappear if Winstone resigned. He told Winstone what had transpired at the meeting. Winstone didn't' t react. He just stared into space as if Arbuthnot was not there.

"I hope you're not going to cave in." Arbuthnot was dismayed at the Rector's demeanor.

At that moment Eleanor announced Danny.

"We'll talk later," Winstone told Arbuthnot and waved him out of the office. Reluctantly, Arbuthnot departed. As he passed Danny, he didn't even look at him. He knew the game was up.

Danny gave the letter to the Rector and informed him that all but Arbuthnot had signed it. Winstone took the letter without comment. Knowing that HB had already seen the Rector, Danny feared this last-minute attempt to stiffen Winstone's resolve. No longer so confident that the letter would have the desired result, Danny joined the lads for a drink at James's apartment. The atmosphere was morose.

It needn't have been. Winstone had already made his decision, and, by morning of the next day, a letter was circulating to the Deans and Section Heads to the effect that the Rector was resigning as from July 1, 2003. Very soon a number of professors, including Hamid, Ilse and Forget, were urging James to stand for election as Rector.

〰

That Friday there was an excited evening at Danny's. Victory now seemed near.

"It depends to some extent on whether it's an internal or external process," Danny pointed out. "If it's internal, James should be shoo-in."

There were many presumptuous toasts to the new Rector, and James was quite drunk when he arrived at his apartment. He fell asleep immediately and was spared his usual nocturnal torments. When he woke up the next morning, he remonstrated with himself. You won't get to be Rector if you're picked up for drunk driving, he told himself. He resolved to restrict his nights of excess to those occasions when he was at home or could walk from Bill's. It was stupid to blow it now that he was so near. Near what? Not happiness, that was certain, but at least power.

Chapter 41

# Friday February 14, 2003 to
# Saturday April 26, 2003

T HE SECOND WEEK IN February is a time when there are no classes at the European University. Many of the students take advantage of this respite to go skiing, and David was no exception. Antonietta didn't accompany him. She hated skiing, and she'd committed herself to attending Gino della Rovere's Valentine's Day party on the Friday of that week. She knew the Marquesa would be there, and, sexually frustrated and emotionally distraught, she welcomed the prospect of the unnatural pleasures of her bed.

The Marquesa was involved with other guests when Antonietta arrived. Deliberately, she drank a lot to drown any qualms about what she was planning. By the time the Marquesa noticed her, she was quite drunk, and with a provocative smile the Marquesa offered her a ride. Antonietta was about to accept when she heard a familiar voice.

"Antonietta, how lovely to see you"! It was Philippe de Pothiers.

"Philippe! What are you doing here"?

In her surprise and pleasure at this unexpected reunion, Antonietta completely forgot about the Marquesa.

"I'm spending some time at the Careggi clinic," he explained. "I'm studying some new techniques your father has introduced."

"Antonietta, come on," the Marquesa interjected. "We have to go."

Philippe put his arm around Antonietta in a protective gesture.

"The countess and I are old friends," he told the Marquesa. "Please allow us the privilege of talking a little together."

With a heinous look at Philippe, the Marquesa stalked off. Antonietta watched her go. The spell was broken, and she realized with horror what she'd been about to do.

"I'm drunk, Philippe. Please take me home." She turned the full force of her beautiful eyes on her one-time lover. "Or anywhere else you wish."

Philippe drove to Antonietta's apartment. She asked him in and slipped off her dress.

"I want you to make love to me."

Philippe removed the rest of Antonietta's clothing and caressed her nude body. She cried out in surprise when he picked her up and carried her into the bedroom. She lay on the bed, naked, watching him undress. What happened next both astonished and enchanted her. It was no longer the rather pedestrian lover of the Chateau Frontenac but a dissolute rake who wrang from her screams of ecstasy.

Panting and bathed in perspiration, Antonietta broke off their last embrace. "How you've changed, Philippe," she gasped.

Philippe laughed. "After our last bout I realized my inadequacy, so I found a young mistress in Paris to give me some further education."

Antonietta was highly amused. "She was a good teacher. I'm very impressed."

Philippe gazed into Antonietta's eyes, and behind the amusement he detected her deep sadness.

"Do you want to tell me about it"? he asked. "And why you were about to abandon yourself to that lesbian slut"?

Fighting back her tears Antonietta recounted the whole sad story, including her brief encounters with the Marquesa.

"You need to find another man. One who is not married."

"I have," Antonietta wailed, "but I feel no passion for him. At times it's worse than having no one. It just makes me long for James even more."

They spent the next day walking around Florence. Antonietta found comfort in Philippe's presence, just as she had in Quebec City. She was sorry when the day ended, and they parted.

On Monday, February 17, the Board of Governors of the Institute announced that there would be an internal choice for Rector. Their experience with Harold Winstone had obviously made them wary of outsiders. There would be an election by the faculty for Rector on May 1, but the Board reserved the right to appoint a person of its choice in place of the person winning the election. Candidates were to declare themselves by Friday, February 28. At their Wednesday evening get-together, the lads decided to keep James's candidacy under wraps until that date. There was no point in giving the opposition time to talk him down before campaigning began in earnest.

The breach between Winstone and HB was confirmed the following Friday when the Rector appointed Bill Leaman as one of the members of the internal Section committee to conduct the assessment of Hamid Khan for re-appointment as Head of FEB. Bill was proud like a child of his appointment, and Petra was particularly happy.

"You see, Bill, I'm changing your life."

Over the next two weeks after David's return from his skiing weekend, Antonietta arranged several trysts with Philippe. She felt a little guilty when she made love to David after being with Philippe, but she needed him. Philippe satisfied her sexually, and, as she'd met him before James, she was more able to disassociate him from the man she still loved to distraction. With David, James was an unknown menace hovering over their relationship; with Philippe she could talk openly about him. This brought her a measure of comfort.

Three candidates declared themselves by the deadline of February 28, Brian Wilkins, Bill Wachowitz and James. The following Sunday there was a council of war at James's apartment. Much to James's surprise, Elliot Hunt had also asked to be there. Bill argued strenuously against including him. He thought him unreliable.

"He was taken in by HB over that Annya business," he reminded James.

Piotr was at best lukewarm. Being Polish, he had an ingrained distrust of men who didn't drink. Danny, however, supported James.

"We're too much of a clique. Hunt will bring a different perspective. I think we need that."

Hunt was included.

First, they discussed the two other candidates. Wilkins had only managed 22% in the vote for a faculty member on Bill's tenure committee and might suffer from a perceived closeness to HB. Wachowitz worried James more.

"He's honest, pleasant, unlikely to rock the boat. He'd make a good compromise choice. He could come up the middle."

Next, they turned to the substance of the campaign. It was essential to keep a momentum going and not peak too early. They agreed that there would be a couple of new proposals each week, and each week would have a different focus. The first week would be devoted to finance. It was an important issue but a little arcane. It was ideally suited to the first week of campaigning when interest was still relatively low. The two proposals were the formation of an elected finance committee to assist the Rector and the provision for monthly financial disclosure statements. The committee would have the right to refer matters on which it disagreed with the Rector to the Governing Council, which would have the last word. This would end the Rector's discretionary control over the Institute's finances, which had proved so disastrous under Winstone.

On Monday afternoon, as James was preparing to announce the first proposal to a meeting of professors, Bill burst into his office.

"Wilkins has pipped you to the post. He's suggested setting up a finance committee at a lunch meeting with some professors from FEB just like the one you're planning."

James was shocked and dismayed. "Are you sure it's the same proposal"?

Bill nodded. "Right down to giving the last word to the Governing Council."

James put his head in his hands. What was he going to do? He couldn't substitute the disclosure proposal as it was quite detailed, and he didn't have it with him. Elliot had taken it to solve some accounting problems that James didn't understand. But he couldn't now make the committee proposal. He would appear to be just aping Wilkins. The result was an inconsequential meeting at which James promised a more open administration in touch with the problems of professors. It didn't impress many people.

The presentation of the disclosure proposal was scheduled for Wednesday afternoon. Just before lunch, Elliot Hunt came to see James. He was furious.

"What's going on"? he bellowed at James. "Your apartment must be bugged. Wilkins has just told a meeting of LAC that he favors a monthly reporting system on the Institute's finances. It's not as detailed as our proposal, but it's very close."

"My God"! James was horrified. "What indeed is going on"?

He was pressing Elliot for more details when Bill arrived in the office. He glared at Hunt.

"Are you the snitch? It has to be you." He grasped Hunt by the collar and began to shake him.

James intervened. "Calm yourself, Bill. It's not Elliot. He's as upset as we are."

Bill was unconvinced but said no more.

Danny and Piotr joined them, and it was agreed that James would present his proposal as a supplement to Wilkins. It was no use trying to convince people that it had been drawn up before Wilkins talked to LAC. This was better than another empty meeting like Monday's. Or was it? Both Campeau and Gowling were at the meeting, and they took a gleeful delight in making hay out of James apparently following Wilkins' lead. Three days into the campaign, James was floundering. It was a good thing it was only the first week.

The next campaign meeting had been set for the following Saturday, but Elliott was in Toronto, and it was postponed to Sunday. Left with nothing to do on Saturday evening, James accompanied Bill and Petra to the student bar. He didn't like fraternizing with students, particularly as he was running for Rector, but he felt depressed and needed a distraction both from thoughts of Antonietta and the problems with his campaign.

He was seated with Petra and Bill and a couple of Bill's colleagues from FEB when Annya joined them. She was looking particularly attractive, wearing a tight blue sweater that emphasized the curve of her breasts and the brilliant color of her eyes. Disregarding Petra's disapproving glances, James let himself be sequestered by this Polish beauty. They both drank too much.

"We're leaving," Petra informed James.

He waved airily at her and Bill and continued his conversation with Annya. After a few minutes she asked him to drive her home.

"Elliot doesn't like me driving when I drink," she explained.

"I never drink and drive," James assured her. "I drink first and drive afterwards."

Annya went into peals of laughter and pressed herself against James. The scent of her perfume was intoxicating.

If he'd been a little less under the influence, James probably wouldn't have accepted Annya's invitation to take a last drink in her apartment. He did, without weighing the consequences. Once in the apartment Annya disappeared, and when she returned, she was wearing a very scanty bikini.

"Do you like it? I bought it for my next trip to Mexico."

The sight of Annya parading her well-proportioned and alluring body brought James quickly back to his senses. Elliot was a colleague and a valuable member of his election team. It was hardly a good idea to bed his girlfriend, however appetizing she was. When Annya came and knelt in front of him, he pushed her hands away from his belt.

"No, Annya, I can't do this to Elliot."

Annya threw back her head and laughed. "Really"? Her voice was full of irony. "James, you're a fool, a blind fool."

She undid her bra and put her hands under her perfectly rounded breasts, offering them up to James.

"You won't touch them because of Elliot"? she asked in the same bantering tone.

"For Christ's sake, Annya, get dressed." James looked away, remembering Oscar Wilde's line about being able to resist anything except temptation.

"Do you know why Wilkins made those proposals"? Annya asked. James shook his head. "Because Elliot gave them to him."

Annya stood up and removed the bottom part of her bikini. James stared at her, taken aback as much by her promiscuous nudity as Elliot's betrayal.

"Why"?

Annya began to undo James's belt, and he no longer stopped her. "Do you remember the appraisal of Doefman's paper from that Dutch professor"?

The belt was now off, and Annya was undoing the zipper on James's pants. All he could manage was a nod.

"Well, you sent it to Elliot with a caustic comment that made him think you knew he was lying."

James again pushed Annya's hand away. A few moments more, and he would be incapable of rational thought.

"Lying about what"?

"About him and me.".

"You mean, you and he were together *before* the end of term"?

"Yes." Annya smiled up at him. "He's terrified that if you became Rector, you'll re-open the process. Arbuthnot told him you would. That's why he's helping Wilkins."

James was torn between shame at his own lack of discernment, disgust at Hunt's duplicity, and desire. Annya had extricated his sex and was caressing it.

"Why would I have him on my election team if that were the case? It doesn't make..."

At that moment Annya took him into her mouth. She aroused him and then stopped. She straightened herself and placed James's hand on her pert breasts.

"Why don't you take your revenge"? she asked, her lips pursed in a promiscuous pout. She was irresistible. She led James into the bedroom and lay on the bed. "I've wanted you to fuck me for a long time."

Her voice was hoarse with lust. James undressed. He caressed the soft inviting breasts, the smooth, sunburned skin of her body and enjoyed her trim and avid sex.

"Come in me," she ordered, and fighting back thoughts of his first night with Antonietta, James penetrated her.

"Why did you tell me all this"? James asked as they lay together afterwards.

Annya gave him an enigmatic smile. "It was a way to get you to fuck me. I also want you to win. HB's a shit, Wilkins is an asshole and Wachowitz is a wanker."

James burst out laughing, and they took their pleasure with each other again. This time more adventurously, much to Annya's delight.

In addition to her two lovers, Antonietta was also pestered by the Marquesa's phone calls. She refused to meet her, but the Marquesa persisted time and again.

"I know you want me," she insisted. "I know you want the pleasure I alone can give you."

Antonietta lost her patience. "You're a perverted and immoral woman who's taken advantage of my vulnerability," she fumed. "I'm not a lesbian, and I want nothing more to do with you."

The following Sunday Antonietta and David were woken up by a phone call from Gino della Rovere, informing them that the Marquesa had committed suicide. Antonietta felt at once saddened and relieved. There was also some guilt. Was it because of her that the Marquesa had killed herself? Had she really needed to be so harsh? The Marquesa hadn't forced her. She'd been a willing participant in their lesbian escapades. But surely that didn't mean she'd been obliged to become the Marquesa's mistress?

It was past midday before James tore himself away from the carnal pleasures at which Annya proved herself so adept.

"Do you make love like this with Elliot"?

Annya's sexual licentiousness sat ill with Hunt's austere Protestantism. Annya just smiled, and James didn't press the point. He dressed and returned to his apartment to wash and shave before picking up the children from Prévost. He drove them to Bill's, who was giving a party. Everyone was there, including Ela and her two girls, Izabella aged eight and Natalya aged five. The children went off to play, although Peter's expression told of his reluctance to spend the afternoon with younger children who were, into the bargain, girls. The women chatted among themselves, and the men sat down to decide how to deal with Hunt's treachery.

"I told you not to trust him," Bill said. "Now we're up shit creek."

James was about to give a sharp retort, but Danny got in first. "I don't agree. We could use this to James's advantage."

Bill was skeptical. "I'd like to know how."

Danny gave one of his crafty smiles. "We dream up some stupid proposal, let Hunt think that we're going to use it and wait for Wilkins to make a fool of himself."

"He won't fall for that," James objected. "Wilkins is not that stupid."

"No, you're right," Danny admitted. "In that case, we take a controversial proposal. Let's say, we propose the abolition of the Sections. No one wants that, but I think Hunt and Wilkins may just buy it."

James shook his head in admiration. "Are you sure you weren't brought up by Jesuits, Danny"?

"No, my good man, by pedophiles."

Once the hilarity had subsided, Danny continued. "If, perhaps that's a big if, but if Wilkins falls for it, James can confront him and threaten to expose his underhand tactics unless he withdraws."

"What about Hunt"? Bill asked.

"I can't do anything about Hunt unless Wilkins uses the proposal. Otherwise he might suspect Annya."

Bill looked at James with suspicion. "I hope you're not getting yourself too involved with that vicious bitch"?

"She may be a bitch and she may be vicious, but she's a real bombshell and damn good in bed."

As he said these words, James felt a pinch of remorse. What on earth would Antonietta say if she heard him? Then came his immediate reaction; what the hell did it matter? On the contrary, it served her right for her falseness and infidelity.

That evening Hunt arrived, and they decided on the proposal for abolishing the Sections. He didn't show any surprise. He pointed out that many places were now de-departmentalizing. After he left, the group decided on the real proposal, which was the creation of an executive committee consisting of the Section Heads and the Deans to advise the Rector. This would ensure better communication between the Sections, the administration and the Rectorate.

James deliberately delayed his presentation of the real proposal until Tuesday afternoon. This gave Wilkins enough time to present the fake proposal, which he did on Tuesday morning to a breakfast meeting of professors. It was greeted with derision.

"After all the problems we've had with Winstone, nobody wants a Rector calling all the shots," an irate member of FEB told the hapless Wilkins.

Piotr attended the meeting and reported back to James and the others. They were immensely pleased and relieved that their stratagem had worked.

"You've got him now," Danny told James.

James delivered his own proposal later on Tuesday, and it was enthusiastically received. Hunt was there, and from his somber mien it was clear that he understood he'd been found out and tricked. He left before the end of the meeting, but James caught up with him in the quadrangle.

"I don't know what game you're playing, Hunt," he told him, taking care not to incriminate Annya. "I don't want to see you again at any of our meetings, and if I'm appointed Rector, you'd be advised to find another place to work."

James carried on towards the LAC Building. Wilkins was surprised to see him and obviously nervous. James didn't waste time or words. He informed his rival candidate that he'd discovered his underhand tactics and would expose them if he didn't withdraw from the election.

"No one will believe you," Wilkins blustered.

"I faxed myself a copy of the proposal you were stupid enough to present. The fax has Monday's date."

This was false, but it was a good ploy. "It's a pity I didn't," James's thought as he left Wilkins' office without exchanging any more words with him.

The next afternoon Wilkins withdrew from the election, and James received Annya in his apartment. She made frenetic love to him. It seemed to excite her that she'd betrayed the man whom she was supposed to love. She offered her body without any modesty to all the exigencies of James's lust. It made him feel uneasy.

"I don't understand you," he told her.

"I don't want you to understand me. I just want you to fuck me."

James surveyed the naked young woman lying next to him. Her self-assurance reminded him of Carolina as did her blue eyes and long, blond hair. But beneath Carolina's poise there was lightness and an elusive warmth. Annya was darkness. Even when she made love, you could feel the malice below. Nonetheless, James was entrapped by her promiscuous sexuality and the delights of her wanton body.

Once she left, he ached for the wholesome passion of his lost love.

⁓

Once Wilkins had withdrawn from the election for Rector, it was plain sailing for James. Wachowitz's only chance had been to appear as a compromise candidate, but now he was being compared directly with James, his pleasant geniality was not sufficient to garner much support. This allowed James to slow down the rhythm of his campaign and spend more time with his children.

This time was necessary because Veronica was becoming ever more obsessed by her religious devotions. The children complained that sometimes she was so taken up with her prayers that she forgot to prepare their supper or their sandwiches for school lunch. On the weekends when they stayed with her, they were left very much to their own devices.

"She doesn't seem to care about us anymore," Susanna told her father sadly.

Peter was more direct. "She's becoming really weird."

James decided to take the children every weekend. Veronica didn't object; she seemed relieved.

Antonietta spent Thursday night and all of Good Friday with Philippe. His easy-going charm soothed her troubled spirit, and his new sexual prowess satisfied her lustful sexuality. They had just finished making love on the floor of the living room when Philippe turned to Antonietta with a sad look on his face.

"I'm returning to France tomorrow. My time here is finished, and I must spend Easter Sunday with the family."

"I shall miss you," Antonietta replied. "You're my only consolation."

They spent one more night together before Philippe departed for Paris on Saturday morning. As he was leaving, he turned to Antonietta. "Why don't you go to Canada and talk to James? Why do you let an oath that was sworn in ignorance, one can even say under false pretenses, prevent you from going back to the man you love with all your being? If you don't, your passion for him will destroy you."

"I can't," Antonietta replied, her voice redolent with despair and sorrowful resignation. "If I break that oath, no good can come of it."

Philippe sighed, kissed Antonietta gently on the mouth, and left. Once in his car he called an old friend on the cell phone. It was André Pointet, who happened to be the President of the European University Institute in Florence. It was a long shot but worth a try for Antonietta's sake.

With Philippe gone, Antonietta was left alone to the emptiness of her life. Unable to face the day before her, she drank a bottle of scotch and slept. It was a good thing she'd arranged to go to the cinema with Alessa and Paulina that evening; otherwise she would have been consumed by her misery.

David arrived back on Tuesday. Antonietta was glad to see him, and she let him spend the next few nights in her apartment. She was afraid of being on her own, but his presence didn't cure her. She was plagued by longing for James and regret at Philippe's departure. Still sexually underserved by her boyfriend, she even found herself wishing that the Marquesa were still alive. "This cannot go on," she would tell herself, but life just continued in the same tormented way.

*Chapter 42*

# Thursday May 1, 2003 to Monday September 29, 2003

T HE RESULTS OF THE election for Rector were known by late afternoon on May 1. It was a clear victory for James with 76% of the votes to 24% for Wachowitz. Even James was surprised, and that night was one of great celebration. Only Danny sounded a note of caution.

"It's not over till the fat lady sings. The Board still has the last word. They could even appoint HB."

The others refused to let him dampen their spirits, and they were all very much the worse for wear when the evening ended in the early hours. This included Danny, who called Bernadette to tell her that he was spending the night at James's apartment. Bill and Petra were able to walk to their house, and only Piotr drove home. He was more wary of Ela than the police.

Notwithstanding their brave words, the next week was nerve-wracking for all of them. The Board members consulted the Deans, including HB, the Section Heads and even Winstone himself. Danny hadn't been able to discern their thinking from his meeting with them. Finally, on Thursday, a week after the election, James was summoned to meet the Board. They offered him the post of Rector.

"Congratulations, Dr. Markham." The Chairman of the Board shook James's hand. "We can discuss salary in due course, but are there any particular requests or conditions you wish to raise"?

There were none, and, after shaking hands with all the Board members, James left to join his friends. He informed them of the appointments he was going to make. The position of Senior Dean would be abolished, and Wachowitz would replace Arbuthnot as Chair of the Ethics Committee. Danny as Dean of Administration would regain both his position as the senior Dean and his office, and Bill would become Assistant Dean of International Affairs in James's place.

"Does that mean I get to travel all over South America"?

Bill received a black look from Petra. "You're not going anywhere."

Once the excitement over James's appointment died down, Bill piped up. "I've got two pieces of news myself," he announced.

"First, the assessment committee will recommend re-appointment for Hamid."

Bill paused to let this news sink in. They all raised their glasses in a toast to the absent Hamid, and then everyone except Petra looked expectantly at Bill. He took a large gulp of whisky to keep them on tenterhooks and announced that he and Petra were getting married in Edmonton on August 16.

"You're all invited, and James is going to be best man." Bill turned to James with a broad grin. "That means you have to look after the bridesmaids, including Petra's hot sister, Mila."

There was a second round of toasts to the prospective bride and bridegroom. James was as happy as anyone at the news, but he felt a jolt at the thought of his own forlorn plans to marry Antonietta. For her they had meant nothing. He turned away so the others couldn't see the tears in his eyes.

After this exhausting week, James was relieved to spend a quiet weekend with his children. Their wide-eyed admiration touched him, and he entertained briefly the idea of seeking a reconciliation with Veronica for their sakes before realizing that it was out of the question. At the end of the month, he was spending two weeks with Carolina at Puerta Vallarta in Mexico.

He drove the children to school on Monday morning and arrived in his office just as a phone call came through for him. It was his old friend from Spain, Rodrigo de Fuentes y Talavera, with news that the Marquesa de Avila y de la Torre had committed suicide.

"They say it's because she was deserted by her beautiful young mistress."

James was assailed by a twinge of jealousy. Was that beautiful young mistress Antonietta?

⚜

Sunday May 18 dawned bright and sunny. Antonietta had spent the previous night at David's. She was preparing to join her family at the Basilica when David sat her down. His manner was unusually serious.

"Antonietta, I love you. I know you still think of that man in Canada, but it's over now. Forget him and marry me."

Antonietta had no idea what to say. She still longed for James and could never quite abandon the dream that they might somehow, through a miracle, come together again. She knew it was a dream, and miracles rarely happened. She was bound by her oath and too afraid of divine retribution to break it. She and David had been together now for almost a year. If she couldn't have James, why not David? She promised him that she would think about his proposal and went off to meet her family.

Antonietta paid little attention to the service in the Basilica. Her mind was dominated by the question of her answer to David. She didn't pray for guidance because the considerations that moved her were of a very secular nature. The truth was that David didn't satisfy her either sexually or emotionally. Rather than marrying him, it would be make more sense to end the relationship, but she shied away from this decision. She preferred the comfort of his company to the bleakness of her own solitude. "Certainly I could find someone else, but would he be any better"?

Antonietta made an excuse not to have lunch with the family. Her mother was still distant with her, and she didn't feel like fencing with Giovanni and his insipid wife. She drove back to David's studio and told him that she needed more time. Relieved not to receive a blunt refusal, David was only too happy to oblige her.

⚜

The following Thursday, Annya came to James's apartment. They made love even more indecently than usual. Annya was desperate to be

472

taken in every possible way and to give pleasure using all the considerable expertise she possessed. After three hours of indulgence, James found out the reason. While still playing with his sex, Annya told him that this was their last time.

"I'm getting too attached to you, and I hate that," she explained. "I can't control you, and I want my freedom. I can do what I like with Elliott, and he's going to Florida now you're Rector. I don't want to miss out on the Florida sun, and perhaps I'll find a rich, older man whom I can milk."

Although shocked by Annya's amorality, James had to admit that at least she was honest. She wasn't playing a game like Antonietta. There was no tenderness between them, but their last kiss before Annya left was not devoid of emotion.

"I have a horrible feeling that I won't be able to forget you, but I'll damn well try," were her last words.

James watched her leave with a mixture of regret and relief.

⁘

The next day James was in his office when his secretary popped her head around the door

"James. There's a phone call from some foreigner."

James picked up the phone.

"Dr. Markham"? a voice enquired.

"Yes."

"André Pointet, President of the European University Institute in Florence."

The President's Italian had such a heavy French accent that James continued the conversation in that language. The President appeared relieved. He came to the reason for his call.

"We would like you to be the invitee of the Students' Visiting Speakers Committee on November 21. We want you to give a talk on the future of the European Union."

The European University Institute! Florence! Antonietta's hometown! James's stomach churned under the avalanche of emotions that gripped him. Was she in Florence? How would he manage to be in the same city? Instinctively he prevaricated.

473

"We're counting on you, Dr. Markham," the President insisted. "We want to hear a British perspective."

James let himself be persuaded to give the lecture. The President was very pleased.

"Excellent. The Secretary of the Visiting Speakers' Committee will send you the tickets and inform you of all the arrangements. His name is David Bannerman-Smith."

As usual, James took the children for the weekend of May 24 to 26 as he would be with Carolina in a week's time. It was a long weekend as Monday was the Queen's official birthday. Peter informed him that his mother had cut herself badly on a piece of glass underneath the fridge. He seemed concerned that she hadn't sought medical attention.

James reassured him. "I'm sure she'd see a doctor if it were really serious."

⌁

Antonietta and David left Florence for a touring holiday on Monday, May 26. Antonietta loved Verona with its grandiose plaza and remarkably preserved arena, but she was disappointed with Milan. The Cathedral was impressive from the outside, but the interior was drab and uninteresting. The La Scala opera house was swathed in scaffolding. Monte Carlo didn't impress her either. It had come to resemble a concrete jungle. She enjoyed Nice but was happy to be on their way to Avignon. She'd never visited the papal palace there. Unexpectedly, David took the motorway to Marseilles.

"I've always wanted to see that city," he told Antonietta.

The motorway took them through Toulon and on to Marseilles. On the way Antonietta noticed the exit to Les Lecques. It was too much. Memories of her idyllic days there with James descended upon her, and she dissolved in tears. David stopped at the next aire*.

"I'm sorry, Antonietta. I had no idea." He wiped away the tears.

"It's not your fault. I have to deal with it, and I will."

David took heart and smiled. They continued towards Marseilles. He seemed to believe her, but Antonietta knew better. She was no further getting over James than the day she'd boarded the Alitalia flight in Toronto for Italy, half demented with grief.

⌐⌐⌐

James met Carolina at the airport in Mexico City. It was the end of May. They spent an enjoyable night in the airport hotel and left the next day for Puerto Vallarta. It was the hottest season of the year, and they spent most of their time either in the swimming pool or making love in the air-conditioned hotel room. On June 10, James's 34ᵗʰ birthday, they had dinner in one of the finest restaurants in Puerto Vallarta, Le Café des Artistes. It was then that James learned that Carolina would be 22 exactly a week later.

"We're both Gemini's," she said with a grin.

James grinned back, but it was a little forced. He was thinking of Antonietta, who would be 26 on July 14.

Carolina's cell phone rang. She excused herself and took the call. While she was talking, James scrutinized her face to find some indication of her feelings. The clear blue eyes betrayed nothing. For over a week they'd made love, laughed together, had long conversations, but unlike Antonietta, whom James had felt he knew intimately after just one night together--a dreadful miscalculation, it now appeared-- Carolina remained an impervious mystery.

"Why were you looking at me so intently"? Carolina asked, putting away her cell phone.

"I was trying to decipher what you're really thinking."

"What you mean is whether I've fallen in love with you like most of the other women you've taken to your bed."

James reddened with embarrassment. That was exactly what he'd been thinking, but put so bluntly it sounded unforgivably arrogant and egotistical. He hastened to redeem himself.

"Let's drop it Carolina, I've no right to pry like that."

"No, James, it's a fair question. The answer is that I won't allow myself to fall in love with you because there are at least three good reasons why our relationship can't go anywhere."

"Tell me." James was intrigued by Carolina's sudden openness.

"In the first place, you're married with two young children, you're

Catholic, and I can't see you divorcing." Carolina stopped and looked questioningly at James.

"Perhaps not," he replied, not wishing to disclose his separation from Veronica. "Go on."

"Secondly, I can't see a man like you marrying a hooker like me."

"You're not a hooker. You may occasionally have sex for money to round off the month, but that doesn't make you a hooker. At one time it was quite common for respectable French women to do the same, and no one would've dreamed of calling them hookers."

Carolina put on a delightful smile. "I'd better move to Paris, then" she said. "Still, I can't see myself as the wife of a British lord."

James stared at her in amazement. "How on earth do you know I'm a lord"?

"I looked you up on the internet and saw you went to a school called Ampleforth. I went to the school's website, and they have a short biography of some former pupils. I couldn't find your name, but I clicked on Charles Markham. When I found out he was a viscount, I looked up his family in Debret's Peerage, and lo and behold I found Lord James Markham."

James's amazement turned to admiration. "That's quite some detective work. But you're wrong. I don't give a damn about your month ends. It certainly wouldn't stop me marrying you."

"Perhaps not, as you would say." Carolina smiled sweetly at James before delivering the *coup de grace*.

"However, there is the third and main reason. You would never marry me because you're not in love with me, and you're not in love with me because you're in love with someone else."

James was stunned "That's not true."

"Yes, it is." Carolina paused for a moment and continued. "You told me that you hadn't contacted me because you weren't ever in Buenos Aires. I appreciate you wanting to spare my feelings, but it was a lie nonetheless. I saw you in the Recoleta with a very beautiful, dark-haired woman who was clearly not your wife. It was in La Biela."

"Yes, I lied," James admitted. "I was in La Biela with a woman, and I was in love with her. She proved to be a faithless hussy, and I've almost forgotten her."

"I wish it were true, but it isn't."

The clear blue eyes seemed less serene. James took Carolina's hand in his. This short conversation had turned his image of her upside down. She wasn't a good time girl intent only on indulging her senses without any commitment. She had feelings but was sensible enough to control them when they couldn't lead her anywhere. And she was extraordinarily perceptive.

"Let's go to a night club. I'm a lousy dancer, but it's time we had a little romance."

James paid the bill, and they went to El Gato Tonto, a new and very expensive nightclub. They found seats in the corner and ordered some wine. They listened to the music without speaking. James was trying to come to terms with a young woman who suddenly meant more to him than just a fling far from home. The band started to play "Feelings", and a woman sang it in Portuguese.

"Whenever I hear Portuguese sung, I've the impression of being in a bordello," James remarked.

Carolina burst out laughing, and the tension between them eased. They got up to dance. James held Carolina very close.

"*Claro que te quiero,*\*" she whispered.

James was about to reply, but Carolina put her hand over his mouth. "Don't lie, James."

Without a word, he led her out of the nightclub. She made no protest, and they were soon back at the hotel in bed. This night there was passion in their lovemaking. Afterwards James gazed at Carolina as she lay next to him. She might not have Antonietta's stunning beauty, but she was exceptionally pretty, and her body yielded nothing in sexual attractiveness to that of his perfidious Italian mistress. He had no desire to patch up his marriage with Veronica, so why not marry Carolina? He asked her whether she would consider marrying him despite her three reasons.

"I'll think about it," she replied.

The phone rang. It was Bill Leaman. James was about to ask, rather irritably, what on earth he was doing phoning him in the middle of the night but stopped himself. There was an urgency about Bill's voice that silenced him.

"Veronica's been taken to hospital. She's unconscious and suffering from acute septicemia."

James was stunned. "Good God! Is it serious"?

There was a short silence. "She may die, James."

In a daze James told Bill he would come home immediately. He felt a dreadful sense of guilt. Here he was frolicking with his Argentinean mistress while his wife perhaps lay dying in hospital. He told a shaken Carolina what was happening, and they made plans for the next morning. She would return to Buenos Aires, and he would return to Montreal.

There was no more talk of marriage.

⁓

James arrived in Montreal late afternoon on Wednesday, June 11th. Bill and his children met him at the airport. They were crying, and James took them in his arms and tried to comfort them.

"I'm sure everything will be alright," he said without conviction. The expression on Bill's face told him that the truth was otherwise. He held them tightly against him in the back of the car while Bill drove to the hospital.

"Did she go by herself to the hospital"? James asked of no one in particular.

"I called an ambulance," Peter replied. "Then I called Dr. Leaman."

James looked at his son and closed his eyes. Never had he felt himself so insignificant, so worthless. It had been up to his ten-year-old son to succor his wife while he was gallivanting in Mexico.

"I'm sorry, Peter."

In a gesture that took James quite by surprise and brought him close to tears, Peter kissed him on the cheek. "It's okay, Dad. You weren't to know."

They arrived at the hospital and made their way immediately to the intensive care unit. They met Petra, who was in tears. She was with a doctor, and the expression on his face portended the worst. He took James aside.

"I'm sorry, Lord Markham," he said with a British accent. "Lady Markham died an hour ago. There was nothing we could do. She left it too late."

James had a sense of the unreal. Just a few days ago, June 7, was his eleventh wedding anniversary. Now his wife, the mother of his children, was dead, and all he could think of was how strange it was to be called by his title in a Canadian hospital.

"Can I see her"? he asked, wishing to make amends for his insensitivity. The doctor led him to the room where Veronica still lay.

James gazed at the woman he'd once cared for. He knelt by the bed with his head bowed.

"Forgive me, Veronica, if it's because of me that this happened."

He looked up and noticed the serenity of his dead wife's features. "Now you're where you've always wanted to be," he thought. He kissed her lifeless cheeks and stood up. With one last glimpse at the woman who was supposed to have been his life's companion, he crossed himself and left the room.

*⁓*

Despairing of ever overcoming her obsessive love of James, Antonietta let David move in with her.

"Let's see how it works," she told him. "I'm not rushing into anything, but I want to give us a chance. Keep your studio, though, just in case."

Overjoyed, David agreed to her terms. Over the next two weeks, he gradually moved his things.

On the next visit to her parents, Antonietta plucked up the courage to tell them. Her mother was about to make an unpleasant scene, but her father, still mindful of the pain of nearly losing Antonietta, put his wife firmly in her place. "It's Antonietta's decision. She's old enough to make it, and we must respect it."

Her mother acquiesced, but her manner towards Antonietta became even colder.

This contributed to Antonietta's pervasive sadness.

*⁓*

July 1 arrived and with it James's installation as Rector. He made a speech promising reforms to make the administration more efficient and transparent and to recapture the drive of the Buchanan years. It was well received, although HB and his cronies didn't join in the applause.

All this activity since his return from Mexico had taken James's mind off Antonietta to some extent without eradicating the jealousy and emptiness that plagued him. He awoke on July 14 realizing that it was her 26th birthday. He wondered who she was celebrating it with. He wandered downstairs to make himself a coffee and collected the mail from the outdoor mailbox. There was a letter from Carolina. He opened and read it.

*Mi querido James. No puedo pretender que no me he enamorado de ti, pero no puedo casarme contigo. Mi vida está aquí en Buenos Aires. No es quizás la vida perfecta o incluso la más respetable, pero es con la que me siento cómodo. Por favor, déjeme vivirla. No sería lo suficientemente fuerte para resistir si vinieras a verme, pero nuestro matrimonio sería una catástrofe para ambos. Nunca te olvidaré. Carolina.\**

It was the hottest summer for years, and Antonietta decided to spend mid-July to mid-August at her family's villa on the Versilia Riviera, a beautiful stretch of coast comprising several seaside resorts on the Ligurian Sea, an arm of the Mediterranean. It nestles beneath the imposing peaks of the Apuan Alps. All along the several miles-long beaches is the seafront of Viareggio--called by the locals *la passeggiata* because it's where people go for their late afternoon walk. It is an uninterrupted promenade of trendy boutiques, fashionable shops, ice-cream parlors, cinemas, pizzerias, art galleries, discos, stylish patisseries, lively bars, elegant cafes, and restaurants with pavement tables to watch the world go by.

Her mother allowed her to invite Alessa and Paulina but no men, particularly not David. This didn't bother Antonietta. David was taken up with his thesis, and she didn't care for Alessa's and Paulina's boyfriends. She was glad to be on her own. There was a discotheque near the villa and plenty of men with whom to indulge her dissatisfied lust. To allay David's suspicions and assuage a little her conscience, she agreed that he would spend two weekends at the villa. Alessa and Paulina also arranged for their boyfriends to visit them.

The girls spent the first three days sunbathing, swimming in the sea, cooking, and dancing away the evenings in the discotheque. They all flirted outrageously, but it went no further. Alessa's and Paulina's boyfriends came for the weekend, and on the Saturday evening Antonietta was left to her own devices. The sun and the skimpy bikini she'd been wearing all day served to stir her libido, and, after about an hour in the discotheque, she left with a man whose name she didn't even know. They made love on a deserted beach. The man was younger than Antonietta and very virile. She was exhausted when she arrived back at the villa. The sex hadn't been particularly exciting, but there had been plenty of it.

The next week Antonietta brushed off the young man's renewed advances in favor of an older man. He had an apartment on the Riviera and took Antonietta back there. This time Antonietta couldn't complain, and both her thighs and buttocks were sore from their excesses. It was nearly midday when she returned to the villa. Both her friends were outraged at her infidelity.

"Whatever would David say"? Paulina asked, quite beside herself at Antonietta's behavior.

"I don't know, and I don't care. I'm not in love with him, and that man at least knew how to satisfy me."

"If you're not in love with David, why don't you leave him"? Alessa asked.

Antonietta didn't reply, but her friends pressed her. Both liked David and were confounded by Antonietta's attitude. Eventually, she told them about James.

"He's the only man I love, the only man I'll ever love." Her eyes were brimming with tears. "Neither David nor any other man can ever mean anything to me."

After this confession, her friends left Antonietta in peace. She spent two more nights with her new lover. At the end of the week, she told him that her boyfriend was coming for the weekend. He shrugged and wished her good luck. She never saw him again.

The weekend with David passed pleasantly enough, but after his departure Antonietta returned to her promiscuous ways. What she wanted was anonymous sex, and she managed to find a different man for almost every night of the week. She continued the week afterwards, albeit at a slightly lesser pace. By the time David arrived on August 9 for the last weekend at the villa, Antonietta's surfeit of carnal pleasure meant that she had little enthusiasm for more sex with David. He noticed her apathy and tackled her. Never a very good liar, Antonietta was forced to confess her infidelities. David was very upset, but he was too deeply in love with her to make the break. He pleaded with her not to cheat on him again. The sight of his distress moved Antonietta, and she promised. After he left, she didn't accompany Paulina and Alessa to the discotheque for the final three nights of their stay on the Riviera.

༺

On Wednesday August 13 James left for Edmonton with Danny, Bernadette and Piotr, who had just returned from Poland the evening before. Ela was staying behind to look after the girls.

James was unimpressed by Edmonton. It was a typical modern North American city, lots of concrete and little charm. He went for a walk with the others along the riverbank, and they had lunch in an English-style pub downtown. In the afternoon Bernadette wanted to see West Edmonton Mall, reputed to be the largest shopping mall in North America, but James stayed back at the hotel. Bored, he watched a couple of films.

The wedding rehearsal was that evening. One of the bridesmaids was a school friend of Petra's, a pleasant looking brunette of no particular distinction. The other was Petra's eighteen-year-old sister, Mila. She was blond like her sister but had none of Petra's poise. From the way she looked at him, James suspected immediately what was afoot. She was pretty in a teenage way, but she inspired resignation more than desire in James. Here was another meaningless encounter, like Annya and, in a way, Carolina. He was relieved when the rehearsal ended, and he could spend a boozy evening with his friends.

The next day was the wedding, and both Bill and James were in poor shape.

"I can't get married like this," Bill groaned.

James hauled him off for a brisk walk around a park that rejoiced in the rather ugly name of Hawrelak Park. As they walked, it began to snow.

"Good God"! James exclaimed. "It even snows in August in this Godforsaken hole.*"

Despite their ire at the Edmonton climate, the cold air did them good. By the time they were back at the hotel, they'd both recovered.

The wedding went off without a hitch. Petra was extremely beautiful, and James had never seen Bill looking so elegant, decked out as he was in a rented tuxedo. After the ceremony in an Orthodox Church, which went on far too long in James's view, there was afternoon tea at the Hotel MacDonald, where everyone from Quebec was staying. Mila flirted with James, which made him feel awkward. She was Petra's sister, and he wasn't at all sure she'd approve of him bedding her.

The reception was held at the Faculty Club of the University of Alberta in a large dining room that overlooked the Saskatchewan River. In the distance was the Edmonton skyline. The snow had stopped, and it was now a warm sunny evening. James danced with both bridesmaids, but gradually Mila came to monopolize him. Almost against his own volition he found himself dancing very closely with her as the evening ended.

"Take me back to your hotel," she whispered once Petra and Bill had left.

Mila may have been young, but she was an expert in the sexual arts. She reminded James of Annya with her complete lack of inhibition and dispassionate pursuit of pleasure. James found her somewhat over-demanding. He was still exhausted when he awoke to find her, fresh as a daisy, wandering around in the nude, gathering up her clothes.

"Hi," she called over to him and began to dress. She went into the bathroom. "Have you money for a taxi"? she asked upon re-appearing.

"There's my wallet in the jacket," James replied, taken aback by the young woman's cavalier attitude.

Mila took two $20 notes out of the wallet. "This should do," she said, adding nonchalantly. "It was a great night. Thanks." She departed, leaving James completely flummoxed. He shook his head. "Today's youth," he muttered to himself.

Around midday James, Danny, Bernadette and Piotr caught a plane for Montreal. Petra and Bill were off on their short honeymoon in

Hawaii. "I want to go somewhere where they speak a normal language," Bill had told Petra when she suggested Costa Rica.

"How did you find Petra's sister"? Danny asked James. Her flirting had escaped no one's notice. James was non-committal. For some reason he was ashamed to admit that he'd slept with her. Danny didn't pursue the matter, but the sly grin on Bernadette's face told James that she'd guessed the truth.

⌇

The relationship between David and Antonietta remained strained. Antonietta was outwardly contrite for her infidelities but inwardly defiant. She wasn't engaged to David and didn't owe him anything. If he were a better lover, perhaps she'd be more faithful. She regretted asking him to move in with her. While trying her best to convince him that it was not the end of their relationship, she persuaded him to return to his studio in Fiesole. It would be more convenient, she argued, as he needed to be near the library to finish his thesis. With great reluctance, David agreed.

She did feel guilt, but it was towards James not David, and it was not because of Philippe or the men from the discotheque but because of the Marquesa. She comforted herself with the excuse that her lesbian diversions, like all her sexual flings, were just an attempt to escape from her obsessive longing for James. She came to repent of her sacrifice. How could she have believed that she could live without him? Why had she thought that his career was so important that it was worth sacrificing her love for it? What would it have mattered if he were disgraced as long as they were together? It was worse now that she knew who he was. She contemplated the sterility and misery of her life and played with the idea of suicide. There was nothing to live for, but suicide was a mortal sin, and she was afraid of the act.

⌇

kkk

August melted into September, and on the first day of that month David moved back to Fiesole. Absorbed by his thesis, he spent most of his time in the library. He and Antonietta saw each other much less, which suited Antonietta even though she feared solitude. Out of the blue Philippe called her on Wednesday, September 24.

"Philippe"! She was overjoyed to hear his voice. "Where are you"?

"In Paris," he replied, "but I shall be in Florence tomorrow, and I plan to stay until the following Monday. Can you get away"?

"Yes. I have a party with David on Thursday evening, but I'll tell him I have to go somewhere after that. I'll be free Friday and all weekend."

❦

Antonietta spent a comforting weekend with Philippe. He satisfied her sexually while acting as the confidant of her love for James. He asked her whether she'd seen him.

"No," she replied, mystified by the question. "How could I have seen him"?

Philippe said nothing but just hoped that his friend André had done his bidding. Before leaving Antonietta on Monday morning, he made her sit down and listen to him.

"If you won't go back to James, make something of your relationship with David or find someone else."

"Why? No man can mean anything to me but James. David's considerate and intelligent, but he's a lousy lover. I can't force myself to love him, or any man other than James."

Philippe sighed and left. He called André Pointet and was thankful to know that James would soon be coming to Florence.

*Chapter 43*

# Wednesday October 1, 2003 to Saturday November 22, 2003

A T FIRST ALL WENT well for James at the Institute. His proposed reforms were well received at the October 1ˢᵗ meeting of the Governing Council. The candidates announced themselves for the election to the Finance Committee. Saleema Nadjani and André Boisseu were unopposed in FEB and LIR, respectively. In LAC, James's friend Claudio Pettroni was opposed by the ubiquitous Wilkins, but James was not concerned. He was confident Claudio would be elected.

The first meeting of the Executive Committee took place on October 3ʳᵈ. The initial discussions were collegial, but then Ilse Bromhoeffer came up with her perennial idea of replacing the nine-point grading system with A to D. Forget objected mildly to the idea, but McGrath raged against it, and the discussion degenerated into a slanging match. Much to Ilse's disgust, James had little choice but to adjourn the matter to a later, unspecified date.

Following closely on this unfortunate meeting was the report from the accountants on the Institute's finances. It declared that the Institute was badly in need of funds, so James charged Danny with spearheading a fundraising drive. This provoked murmurs within the faculty that Danny was being given too much power. A consequence of this disaffection was the surprise election of Brian Wilkins as the

LAC representative on the Finance Committee. James was dismayed. Running the Institute was not going to be as easy as he'd thought.

James's dismay was justified by Wilkins' performance at the first meeting of the Finance Committee. He tore into the financial report and practically accused James of conniving with the accountants to undervalue the Institute's assets. Unfortunately the accountants had failed to include land owned by the Institute in Montreal, where it was originally to have been located. James protested that he hadn't known about it, to which Wilkins replied that his ignorance was no excuse. Happily for James, Saleema intervened and offered to prepare the next report. This offer seemed to placate Wilkins, who said no more. Relieved, James agreed.

It is said that bad luck comes in threes. This was certainly the case for James when he received Nathan Goldberg's file from McGrath with a note that he was going to propose him for early tenure. James was flabbergasted. Goldberg had only been in the Institute for three years and had published little of any note. He immediately went to see McGrath, who remained adamant.

"He's got good references. Check the file, and you'll see."

James did just that and saw to his disgust that the referees were from NUC. It was clear that this was a clever ploy by the Arbuthnot gang. The worst scenario was a split vote, which would leave James with the impossible choice of supporting McGrath or defying convention and voting against a Section Head's proposal for tenure. If Goldberg was awarded tenure, McGrath and Arbuthnot would win an important victory, and the Institute would be saddled with a mediocrity. If James opposed tenure, he could be accused of abusing his power. He was the loser whatever happened. His only hope was that the committee would vote against.

By Wednesday, October 25 Saleema had finished preparing the next month's financial report, and she and James arranged to meet at the Institute the following evening to go over it. She arrived, wearing as always the Islamic scarf that irritated James. The report was quite complicated, and James was no accountant. It was well past eleven when Saleema finished taking him through it. She looked at her watch and groaned.

"I've missed the last bus. I'll have to take a taxi."

"Nonsense. I'll drive you home."

Saleema shook her head. "I'm not supposed to be alone in a car with a man."

James laughed. "You will anyway if you take a taxi." As Saleema didn't react, he added with a smile. "At least you know you can trust me."

Saleema gave James a strange look. "Can I"?

There was something in the tone of her voice that puzzled James. "Of course," he replied, and they departed the building together.

Saleema lived in Ste. Adèle, quite near to James. He stopped the car, expecting her to rush off. Instead, she hesitated and looked up at James, treating him to the full force of her dark eyes. They reminded him of Antonietta, and involuntarily he bent to kiss Saleema but checked himself in time. He was shocked by his own behavior and half expected Saleema to slap his face. Her reaction was quite different and completely unexpected.

"You could always convert."

"Convert to what"?

"Islam."

James could hardly believe what he was hearing. Was this an oblique admission of attraction, even something more? Not knowing how to react, he took refuge in facetiousness.

"I've enough problems with Christianity without taking on a religion that would deprive me of one of my few remaining pleasures in life."

"Which is"?

"Drinking. To excess."

"That's a pity." Saleema got out of the car and whipped off the scarf covering her head, releasing her long dark hair. She was the nearest any woman could come to Antonietta's beauty, and James stared at her, open-mouthed.

"Enjoy your whisky," she called out and walked towards her apartment building.

⌀

The next day James recounted the scene to Bill. "I don't know what to make of it," he confessed.

Bill roared with laughter. "You really are naïve, Jimmy. It would seem to me quite obvious. You convert, and you can have her. I've always said she had the hots for you."

James sighed. "I don't know what it is about me, but women either dump me, leave me because they love me., or want me to convert to Islam."

"Stick to teenage girls." The illusion to Mila Markovic was obvious.

"Damn girl. I told her not to tell anyone. What the hell does Petra think of it"?

"She was amused. Mila's a scalp hunter, and she was hardly going to keep quiet about getting yours's. It was quite a coup for her."

"My God," James groaned. "Once I was married with a mistress on the side, and now I'm just a scalp."

"Don't complain. She must have been a good lay. She's had enough practice according to Petra."

James sighed. "Yes. They're all good lays. But that's all. It's depressing."

Bill leaned forward to James. "Now, I don't want you shouting at me, but I'm going to tell you something. You'll never get over Antonietta. You'd better go and find her and discover why she left and persuade her to come back. I've never believed she dumped you. She was head over heels in love. There has to be an explanation."

Bill paused, expecting a violent reaction from James, but the answer was quite unexpected.

"I'm going to Florence late next month. Perhaps I'll see her."

This was the nearest James had come to admitting to his friends that he was still in love with Antonietta.

Antonietta was pleased when the university term started on October 6. She had some courses to take, and the work would occupy her mind. It also gave her an excuse to delay starting on her thesis. She hadn't even submitted the topic to her supervisor. David was still working hard on his thesis and hoped to finish it by Christmas. Antonietta wondered whether he would return to Britain. They hadn't talked about it.

Time passed. Sooner or later Antonietta knew that she would have to give David a definite answer to his proposal for marriage. As she was thinking about him, he called her on the cell phone. They agreed to meet at Fiasco's that Friday evening, and Antonietta would spend the night in the studio. David was not in a good mood when he joined her. He'd been planning a skiing weekend in November. Now he was saddled with babysitting some law professor who was coming to give a talk at the Institute.

"I thought you were pleased to be elected Secretary of the Visiting Speakers Committee."

"Not when it interferes with my skiing."

They went to the studio and made love. David was unusually active, hoping to soothe Antonietta's irritation with his inordinate love of skiing. He fell asleep afterwards, and Antonietta, more assuaged than usual, did likewise, but not before wondering idly who that law professor was.

After all, James was a law professor.

The election for the faculty member on Goldberg's tenure committee on November 3 was between Jason Levy and Ed Williams. James was due for another shock, for it was Williams who was elected. That evening he gave vent to his bitterness.

"I don't understand people. They elected me in opposition to HB's and Winstone's crew, and now they're busy electing them back on to committees. I always thought academics were assholes, and now I know."

Danny tried to placate James. "It's irritating, I know, but they probably see it as a way of counter-balancing my and Bill's influence. They don't want to exchange one clique for another."

"Whom do you think I should appoint to the committee? I can't pick someone who's obviously on my side. Those idiots are likely to see it as the same trick Winstone pulled with Larry Flint on Bill's committee."

"I played tennis once this summer with David Wong," Piotr told them. "He's a nice guy and not connected to any of us."

Bill wanted to know whether he was trustworthy.

"I think so," James answered. "He voted against the Arbuthnot proposal."

Wong was duly appointed, and the committee met on Tuesday, November 18. James was confident it would vote against awarding Goldberg his tenure, but he was to suffer another disappointment. When the vote was taken, Forget unexpectedly voted for tenure, together with McGrath and Williams. Danny, Hamid and Wong voted against. It was the worst possible outcome. Feeling trapped and bitter, James used his casting vote in favor of tenure.

That evening Bill hosted a get-together. Still furious with what had transpired, James was soon well into his cups.

"Bloody people," he kept repeating. "Thank God I'm off to Florence tomorrow."

"Well, don't get too drunk," Bill told him. "You know Antonietta doesn't like you drinking too much."

Piotr and Danny cringed, fearing an explosion from James.

He just smiled wistfully.

Antonietta had spent Thursday night at David's studio. It was now the morning of Friday, November 21· It had been a very late night, and they were sleeping in.

"Christ"! exclaimed David. "It's already eleven, and I've got to meet that law professor at the Hotel Imperial at twelve."

He quickly shaved and washed and dressed in a rush.

"I've got to drive him back to the hotel for seven. Do you want to meet at Fiasco's later on"?

Antonietta shook her head. "After last night I want to go to bed early. I'll come over tomorrow afternoon."

Disappointed, David said no more and left. Antonietta prepared herself leisurely and drove back to her apartment. She tried to do some reading for her courses but found it difficult to concentrate. She was beset by a terrible longing for James and for once permitted herself to daydream about meeting him again. It was on a beach in France.

James was waiting for David in the hotel lobby. He felt queasy about being in Florence. He couldn't stop himself wondering whether Antonietta was in the city, and what she was doing. He'd been tempted last night to look for her telephone number on the off chance that she was in Florence, but the memory of her letter stopped him. Whatever the others wanted to believe, she'd dumped him. What was the point of seeking her out?

David arrived and drove them to the European University Institute. It was strange for James to be back after so many years. Nothing had changed much. They arrived at the building where lunch was to be served. James was greeted by André Pointet. It was an excellent meal accompanied by a vintage Amarone, but it didn't quieten James's nervousness. He half expected to see Antonietta any second. It was most unsettling.

After lunch David took James to the lecture theater where he was to give his talk. As they entered the building, James heard David swear.

"What's the matter"?

"I've forgotten my wallet," David replied. "I'll have to phone my girlfriend and get her to bring it to me."

As he had no change to make the call, James lent him his VISA. David went off and came back looking rather crestfallen.

"Problems"?

"She wasn't very pleased. She has to go over to my place to pick it up. I thought she was still there."

"That's a woman for you," James commented.

Not suspecting that David's phone call was being made with James's visa, Antonietta was not very pleased to be hauled out of her sweet daydreams. She agreed reluctantly to fetch David's wallet and bring it to him after the lecture. He told her to come around 4.30. This didn't leave much time, so she went immediately to the studio in Fiesole and arrived at the EUI promptly at 4.30.

Antonietta entered the lecture theater. The talk was already over, and David was talking to a tall man who had his back to her. She gasped and felt her heart constrict. From the back the man looked exactly like

James. She hesitated, but David had already seen her and was waving her over. He said something to the man while pointing in her direction. The man turned round. It was James.

Antonietta felt dizzy and grasped at a table to steady herself. Engulfed by an indescribable emotion, she slowly walked, trembling, towards the man she loved with all her being. Mechanically she handed David his wallet, not daring to look at James. She was forced to when David introduced them.

"Hello," she stammered.

James merely nodded in reply. Antonietta was transfixed by the coldness of his manner and the disdain in his eyes.

David was quite ignorant of the drama being played out before him. Someone had nabbed him, and he was deeply engaged in conversation with that person. James started to walk away. Antonietta stared at his disappearing back in panic. He couldn't go away like that, he couldn't! She strived for something to say that would retain him and uttered the first thing that came into her mind.

"How is your wife, Lord Markham"? she asked, immediately cursing herself for having said something so stupid.

"I cannot see how that's any business of yours's, Miss della Chiesa," he replied and walked off.

Antonietta was mortified. "James, wait, please"!

James turned round with a look of undisguised contempt. "When I was just a university professor, you dumped me. Now you've found out I'm a lord, you're trying to creep back. You disgust me."

He stalked off.

Antonietta collapsed into a chair to collect herself, submerged by complex feelings of grief and hurt pride. His contempt wounded her dreadfully, but how dare he speak to her like that! She left in a rush without a word to David. She drove back to her apartment and threw herself on to the bed, convulsed by sobbing. She had a dreadful pain in her heart, and her head felt as if it were going to explode. Her whole being revolted at the appalling idea that James disdained her. Her dream that one day they could be together again was shattered. Life no longer had any meaning, any purpose.

Antonietta rose unsteadily and made for the bathroom She would end it all now. The knowledge that James hated her, added to the dreadful price she was already paying, was too much. She couldn't bear it. She remembered reading about the Roman custom of committing suicide by cutting your wrists in a hot bath. It was painless, and you quietly slipped into oblivion.

Before turning on the taps in the bathtub, Antonietta looked around for a razor blade or something sharp. Her eyes fell upon the unopened bottle of whisky that David had bought and forgotten about. "Why not enjoy one last drink"? she told herself. I'll give me the necessary courage to go through with it."

She filled one glass and another and another. Then she dozed off in an armchair.

A deluge of emotions gripped James as he walked away from Antonietta. Meeting her with another man had stirred in him a raging jealousy. She was faithless, a whore, an unfeeling bitch who merely wanted him for his title. That mocking comment about his wife! How he hated her!

He couldn't stop himself looking back. He watched Antonietta leave the lecture theater with a sinking feeling in his stomach. He had the impression that his heart was leaping out of its enclosure. Seeing his former love in all her radiant beauty had brought back how much she'd meant to him, and he wanted to run after her. Remembering the letter, he stopped himself. Antonietta's eyes may have shimmered with passion, but it was for that twit David Bannerman-Smith, not for him. Any hopes he may have secretly entertained about his trip to Florence dissolved into bitter resignation and recrimination.

When Antonietta awoke from her drunken stupor, it was already day. She looked at the empty whisky bottle on the coffee table and thanked Bacchus for saving her from the ultimate folly--and the ultimate sin.

Why should she kill herself for this man? She was beautiful, she was rich, she was a countess. He was just some younger son, a mere lord. Her pride revolted at the contemptuous way he'd treated her. It also hurt, deeply. Did the love they'd shared mean nothing to him anymore? Obviously not.

Antonietta was also a Palmieri, and it was her pride that won the day over her grief. She would never forgive the disdain James had showed her, a countess in her own right.

She would shut James Markham out of her mind. She would put an end to her bohemian existence as a student and live as the rich aristocrat she was. She would leave the university and her pointless doctorate. She would abandon David and Florence and move to Rome where she would indulge her senses without restraint and above all without regret for her past love of a man who despised her and who was not worthy of her. She could have any man she wanted--and any woman. She would have both, and she would be proud and treat people below her as befitting her rank.

As Antonietta was nursing her hurt pride, James boarded his flight for Montreal. The journey back to Canada gave James much time for reflection. He thought angrily of Antonietta's ironical and callous question about his wife. She must have known that she'd died. What a bitch! Yet James was honest enough to admit that, despite Antonietta's treachery and heartlessness, he was still desperately in love with her and had, in his innermost being, hoped his visit to Florence would bring them back together. These hopes had been cruelly dashed. Antonietta may not belong to that brash young student, but she'd certainly made clear that she no longer had any feelings for him--if she had ever had any.

James now realized that the indifference he'd assumed before his friends about her departure was a mere posture. It still hurt, both emotionally and physically, but now he'd heard the truth from Antonietta's own lips. It was partly fear of hearing this, as well as his pride, that had prevented him from following Antonietta to Florence immediately after she'd left him. "Perhaps I should have done so. It would have been better to know for certain that she was an opportunistic whore, and that I had no alternative but to get on with life without her."

He thought briefly of Carolina, so decent and wholesome, and then Annya, who was anything but, and the ephemeral Mila, and then Saleema throwing off her veil and revealing her lustrous black hair. "*Une de perdue, deux de retrouvées*," he thought, remembering the French adage.

*Chapter 44*

# Monday November 24, 2003 to
# Wednesday December 17, 2003

O N THE MONDAY FOLLOWING his return from Florence, a much-subdued James drove to work. The return to the Institute brought little relief. The first person he crossed on his way to the Rectorate was Nathan Goldberg. The insolent way in which the newly tenured professor greeted James told of his triumph at James's expense, and it bode ill for the future. James's opponents were gathering strength, and he seemed incapable of checking them. The job as Rector that he'd been so ambitious to obtain was turning out to be a bed of thorns rather than roses.

Antonietta arrived in Rome on Wednesday, December 3. It had taken her just over a week to break with David, complete the formalities for her withdrawal from the Ph.D. program, and shop and pack for her move to Rome. Both her father and her uncle, the Cardinal, had been surprised and not altogether supportive of her decision. Her mother was overjoyed that she was moving to Rome. Now she would find a suitable husband.

On leaving Fiumicino Airport, Antonietta hailed a taxi to take her to her parents' Roman residence, the Villa Peruzzi, where she would stay until she found her own apartment. This would give her the privacy she needed for her new life, away from Giuseppina and Tomaso, the two domestics who looked after the Villa Peruzzi. They were on hand to greet her, but she hardly acknowledged them.

"Our *contesina* has changed," Tomaso remarked sadly.

While she was still unpacking, Carla called and invited her to a reception that she and her husband, Filiberto, were giving that evening.

"The Spanish Ambassador's son will be here," Carla told her sister.

Antonietta changed, took a shower, and made herself up with great care. She chose a dress that was short enough to show off her legs and a bra that lifted up her breasts. The dress was cut low enough to afford a glimpse of them without exposing too much flesh. She did her hair in a chignon, which she felt made her look more aristocratic. Long flowing hair was fine for student life but not for Roman high society. As she descended the stairs, Giuseppina asked whether she wanted to eat or drink something.

"Why would I? I'm going out to eat and drink."

The reception was already underway when Antonietta arrived at her sister's villa. They had never been close, although they'd spent a pleasant time together last Christmas. But Antonietta no longer despised Carla's *mondain*, aristocratic lifestyle. Indeed, she intended to emulate it.

"I'm so glad you could come." Carla seemed genuinely pleased to see her sister, and their embrace even held some warmth. "Let me introduce you around."

Antonietta's entrance had already caused quite a stir. Her sensual beauty contrasted sharply with Carla's more austere Spanish looks, and the eyes, and not only of the men, were riveted on the voluptuous promise of her décolleté. But her eyes were cold and her manner distant when she was introduced. Few of the guests found conversation comfortable with her. Her sister introduced her to a tall, slim young man, who was twiddling a champagne glass awkwardly in his hands.

"May I present to you my sister, Don Federico," Carla purred.

So this was the Ambassador's son, the future Duke of Pontevedra. Don Federico de Talavera y Muñoz seemed everything but a swashbuckling *hidalgo*. Antonietta eyed him with barely concealed condescension and graced him only with a slight nod of her head.

"I will leave you two to make acquaintance," said Carla, walking away before Antonietta could object.

"I understand you have recently come to Rome, *contessa*."

"Today," Antonietta replied.

"Are you intending to stay in Rome"?

"Probably."

"Have you found somewhere to live"?

Antonietta noticed how Federico would look furtively at her and then turn away, blushing. At first this irritated her, but then she realized that it was her décolleté. Poor Federico was not used to a glimpse of a lady's bosom. Greatly amused, Antonietta took pity on the poor man and deserted her monosyllabic replies.

"I'm living in my parents' villa in the viale di valle Giulia until I find my own place."

"That's a very nice area." Federico was clearly impressed.

"Of course. We're black nobility."

Her mother would have been proud of her.

Classes at the Institute ended on Friday, December 5, and James and Danny were closeted together to review James's first term as Dean. The next two weeks were dedicated to exams, but for all intents and purposes the term was over. It was not a happy review.

In the two elections that had taken place since James became Rector, one had been won by Wilkins, a supporter of Arbuthnot, and the other by Williams, one of the former Winstone gang. What's more, Williams had voted for Goldberg's tenure, knowing that James opposed it. That, together with Goldberg's arrogance, suggested that his hopes that Winstone's gang would now come over to his side were to be disappointed. Then there was the Finance Committee, which James had instituted and where Wilkins was making life difficult for him, the breach with Bromhoeffer over her marking system, and the disaffection in the faculty at large over Danny's appointment to head the fundraising campaign.

"What did they expect"? James expostulated. "You're the senior Dean. It's only logical you would head the campaign."

"It may be logical," Danny replied, "but that hasn't stopped the opposition stirring up shit about it."

James sighed. "I don't understand. They voted for me as Rector, and now they seem to be against me."

"They aren't all against you, but, unlike Winstone, who only had us against him, and we behaved decently, you have a determined and unscrupulous group against you. There's Arbuthnot's gang and, despite your best efforts at reconciling them, Winstone's lot. They can do a lot of damage because academics are generally a lily-livered bunch of assholes who don't know which side their bread is buttered on. It's easy to bully them or make them think you're trying to take over."

"But I *have* taken over. I'm the *fucking* Rector."

Danny made a gesture of impotence.

⌇

The same Friday Antonietta was invited to dinner by her older brother, Paolo. He'd always been the sibling to whom she was the closest, and she had appreciated his American girlfriend, Monica. Now she found their casual lifestyle and left-wing views irritating. She felt more at home with Carla. Her sister's haughty snobbism was more suited to her new attitude towards life. When Monica suggested that they could have lunch together on Sunday at a new restaurant she and Paolo had discovered, Antonietta was non-committal.

On arriving back at her parents' villa, Antonietta was surprised to find a bouquet of roses awaiting her.

"Look and see who sent them," she ordered Giuseppina, who ferreted among the flowers and found a note.

"What does it say"? Antonietta's tone suggested a distinct lack of interest.

"It says: *May I invite you to dinner tomorrow at the Convivio di Troianai? Federico de Talavera y Muñoz*"

Antonietta was bewildered. Her sparse and somewhat chilly conversation with Federico hardly warranted an invitation to one of Rome's best restaurants, even though, on her last visit to Rome,

Antonietta had found the menu too modern. It must have been the décolleté. It was a good start to her life in Roman high society, even if she could have wished for a more exciting dining partner.

"Reply yes for me," she told Giuseppina, who looked at her with incomprehension.

"How, *contessa*"?

"Well, he must have given a telephone number on the card. How else was I supposed to reply at such short notice? Phone."

Giuseppina followed her impatient mistress's instructions and telephoned the acceptance to Federico's major-domo.

It was not until Saturday, December 6 that the gang met at Bill's place. James's two children accompanied him. Petra, who was very fond them, insisted they sleep over.

"Make sure they don't disturb us," James growled as Petra escorted Peter and Susanna into the family room where they could watch the television. Petra said nothing but gave James a black look.

Once the children were taken care of, James began the recital of his visit to Florence. He recounted Antonietta's callous behavior with a certain degree of satisfaction.

"She doesn't give a tuppence for me. It's quite clear why she left me. I was right about her all the time."

No one raised an objection, but a strange silence descended upon the company. Everyone seemed to be keeping their thoughts to themselves. Petra gave Bill a knowing look. Danny picked up a bottle of scotch.

"Is this a wake or what? If we're all going to be mournful, we might as well do it drunk."

Everyone laughed, and the atmosphere lightened. James expostulated on the ingratitude of his colleagues; Danny waxed lyrical about his daughter Ceara, who was in her second year of biology at McGill; and Piotr complained about his wife. It turned out to be a very normal evening, except that Petra was cross with James.

"They are really lovely kids," she told him as he was leaving. "You were mean to them."

"I'm sorry, Petra. It's just that I have to look after them every day, and I'm not cut out for fathering."

"You should learn."

James left feeling suitably chastened. "To think she was once my student," he muttered to himself as he got into his car. "How does Bill deal with her"?

⚓

Antonietta was in two minds how to dress. It was her first date with a stiff-necked Spaniard, as her uncle would have called him, and she wasn't sure she wanted to spend the dinner with him leering at her breasts. The problem was that she didn't really possess anything that was both suitable for dinner in an upscale restaurant and demur at the same time. She tried on several long dresses until she found one that passed muster. Federico would really have to peer into the dress to satisfy his voyeurism.

She reached the restaurant at the agreed hour of nine o'clock, cursing the Spaniards for their habit of eating late as she was very hungry. Federico was there to greet her with a small and ridiculous bow and a *handkuss*. He seemed taller, and Antonietta had to admit that he was good-looking. He still seemed very unsure of himself as he led her to a table in a corner.

Federico was polite and attentive. He was also courteous to the waiters, which was surprising in a Spanish aristocrat. He made Antonietta feel ashamed of her brusqueness towards them.

"How do you like Rome"? As an opening gambit it lacked originality, but Antonietta forced herself to reply civilly.

"I know Rome quite well. We used to live here, and my sister lives here now, as you know."

There followed an awkward silence as Federico searched for another subject of conversation. Unable to stand the suspense, Antonietta asked him the same question.

"I feel a little lost. It's a far cry from Extremadura."

Another silence ensued, which was mercifully broken by the arrival of the waiter to take their orders. As the waiter began to enumerate the dishes he would recommend, Antonietta stopped him abruptly.

502

"Perhaps we could have something to drink first"? If she was going to spend an evening in silence with Federico, at least she would do it with wine.

The waiter apologized, and Federico stumbled over his apologies for not thinking of it first. He ordered a white Soave Bolla, which Antonietta felt lacked imagination, but it was better than nothing. While waiting for their libations, they perused the menu in silence.

"I'll have the scampi as an antipasto, the risotto alla parmigiana for the primo piatto and the lamb for the main course," Antonietta told Federico, who seemed aghast at her appetite. Unable to understand the menu with his rudimentary Italian, he chose the same dishes.

The rest of the evening passed off with a few conversations about the cultural differences between Spain and Italy, interspersed with silences that were mercifully filled by eating the meal. Federico made a valiant effort to finish his lamb but eventually abandoned half of it.

"Do you want a dessert"? he asked Antonietta when at last she laid down her knife and fork. There was a note of resignation in his voice.

"No, thank you, but I would like a cognac."

After two cognacs, in which Federico did not join her, Antonietta declared herself satisfied. The bill was paid, and the two left the restaurant. By now, Antonietta had had enough of Federico and asked him to find her a taxi.

"Where should I ask him to take you"? he asked with his normal politeness.

"Don't worry about that," was the only reply he received. The taxi arrived, and Antonietta got in after shaking Federico's hand and thanking him for dinner. As the taxi drove off, she heaved a sigh of relief.

"Take me to the Via di Monte Testaccio." That was where the best discos were to be found, and Antonietta intended to find someone more exciting than Federico for the rest of the night.

The taxi dropped her off at Squadri, which was more a place for finding uncomplicated sex than dancing. Antonietta soon found a man to her taste, and, after some rudimentary banter, she asked him to take her back to his place. He was only too happy to oblige; the prospect of sex with this sultry and beautiful woman was most enticing. Antonietta stayed until the early hours, refused to give her name or say where she lived, and after several bouts of oral, anal and more traditional sex, she left. She wanted anonymous sex, not a relationship.

❦

Petra brought Susanna and Peter back to James's house in time for Mass. While the children were upstairs readying themselves for church, she apologized to James for her sharpness of the previous evening.

"James, it's not their fault that Antonietta left you."

"That woman has nothing to do with it," James retorted. "She's just a callous bitch, and I don't want to hear about her anymore."

Petra was not to be put off. "James, be reasonable. How could she have known that your wife had died? It's not like her to be callous. I know her."

"I'm aware you know her. A little too well."

The allusion was obvious. Petra blushed but resolved to exculpate Antonietta. "That was my fault. She was totally unhinged because of her passion for you, and I seduced her." She didn't mention that Antonietta had once propositioned her to do it again, and that she had refused.

James was unconvinced. "You weren't the first and I doubt whether you will be the last."

Quite unexpectedly, Petra burst out laughing. "That's what I told Bill."

"You told Bill *what*"?

"That Antonietta wasn't the first and may not be the last."

"Whatever did Bill say"?

"Not much, but we had great sex that night."

James shook his head in disbelief. "Petra, you are an impossible, immoral, domineering woman." He placed a hand affectionately on her shoulder. "Just what Bill needs."

Petra was almost through the door when she turned round and looked back at James.

"James, you'll have to get used to the fact that I'm no longer your student, but the wife of one of your best friends.

"I know, Petra." He kissed her on the cheek.

After Petra's departure, James reflected on what she'd said. It was true that Antonietta may not have known that Veronica had died. It was probable, he had to admit.

James and the children set off for Mass.

~*~

For a few days after their dinner engagement, Antonietta heard nothing from Federico. Then, on the following Saturday he called and invited her to a Christmas reception at the Portuguese Embassy the following week on Wednesday. This surprised Antonietta as she hadn't been exactly an accommodating dinner date, but obviously this had not put him off. "He must be a sucker for punishment," she thought.

Antonietta arrived a little late for the reception. She climbed up the stairs past the oak panels, on which were hung what she presumed were portraits of eminent Portuguese statesmen, to where Federico was standing. He greeted her with a rather perfunctory *handkuss* and led her into the ballroom. It was packed with diplomats from various countries. Antonietta could make out some French, something guttural, which was either German or Dutch, quite of lot of Italian, and even some Spanish. She had difficulty making out the other language that many people were speaking until she realized it was Portuguese. Despite its affinity to Spanish, Antonietta could understand very little. It sounded more Slavic than Latin.

A man about Federico's age came up, and he and Federico started an animated conversation in Portuguese. Antonietta was astonished at Federico's obvious fluency in the language and forgot she was being ignored. It was Federico who realized this and very apologetically introduced Antonietta to his friend.

"Please don't interrupt your conversation on my account," Antonietta told them. Federico thought at first that she was being ironical until she gave him, for the first time since they'd met, a pleasing smile.

After a few more minutes of conversation, Federico led Antonietta towards the buffet.

"I'm sure you must want to eat something."

Antonietta blushed, remembering her rather indelicate performance at their dinner engagement. For once it was she, and not Federico, who seemed unsure of herself.

"How come you speak such good Portuguese"? she asked to mask her embarrassment.

"Extremadura borders on Portugal, and our family has a summer home in the Algarve. I spent most of my summer holidays there when I was young."

"Do you like the Portuguese"? Antonietta had always had the impression that the Spanish looked down on the Portuguese.

"Yes. I like them a lot. They have a very rich culture and an interesting history, and I love fado music."

Federico seemed a different person when waxing eloquent about Portuguese history. Antonietta's astonishment grew when he demonstrated a wide knowledge of Portuguese literature, about which Antonietta was woefully ignorant.

"The only bad time in their history was when they were ruled by Spain, poor bastards," Federico concluded. It was a remark that could not fail to endear him to Antonietta with her visceral dislike of the Spanish involvement in Italy.

She was almost beginning to like Don Federico de Talavera y Muñoz

*Chapter 45*

# Friday December 19, 2003 to Friday January 2, 2004

I T WAS LATE AFTERNOON on Friday, December 19, and the term had ended except for a last meeting of the Finance Committee to discuss the progress of Danny's fundraising efforts. There was as yet little to report, and Wilkins lost no time in criticizing Danny's strategy. Even André Boisseu was mildly critical.

Danny was furious and about to lose his temper when Saleema Nadjani came to his aid.

"Listen, Bill," she told Wilkins. "Danny has only just set out the strategy for the campaign. You can hardly expect money to be flowing in already."

"Why not"? Wilkins retorted, looking to Boisseu for support. But Boisseu had seen the logic of Saleema's comment.

"I think we should wait before being too critical."

Wilkins gave him an unfriendly look and said no more. It was agreed to review progress in the fundraising at the next meeting, which was scheduled for some time in February. The meeting passed on to other less controversial matters and then broke up.

"Are you coming, James"? Danny asked as he prepared to rush off for a boozy evening with Bernadette and lads.

"Later," James replied. "I'll drive Saleema home first." He expected an objection from Saleema, but none came.

Danny gave them both a quizzical look and departed. Saleema collected her coat and waited for James.

"I expected you to object."

"Why? You've already driven me home without molesting me."

They walked in a self-conscious silence down to the car park, and James opened the passenger door for Saleema to get in.

"Thank you, James. Very gentlemanly of you." Saleema could see James thought she was being sarcastic. "I mean it. I like being treated like a lady."

At a loss for a reply, James walked round to his side of the car. The journey continued in the same silence. They arrived at Saleema's apartment.

"Don't take your veil off this time."

"It's not a veil but a scarf--you know the thing your Queen wears sometimes. I don't know why you westerners always call it a veil. Why shouldn't I take it off"?

"Because you look dangerously attractive without it, and I don't want to have to convert to Islam."

Saleema laughed and took off her scarf.

"Get out of the car before I'm hauled before the ethics committee for sexual harassment"!

"I won't tell if you don't." Saleema kissed James quickly on the lips and got out of the car.

He watched her go, wondering whether she would turn round. She did.

"Enjoy your whisky," she called, giving James a smile that was anything but innocent.

"Women", James muttered to himself, quite bewildered by Saleema's behavior. "How the hell is one to understand them"?

As was customary, Antonietta returned to her parents' villa in Fiesole for Christmas, but she felt ill at ease. The Roman accent that she'd acquired might please her mother, but the other members of the family found her distant. Even Giovanni, who had not always approved of his sister's blithe ways, complained it was not "the old Antonietta."

Her father was perplexed by her seeming hardness, but it was her uncle, the Cardinal, who was the most upset with her. He noted her lack of attention at the Christmas Eve Mass that the family attended and her apparent indifference to the religious side of Christmas.

"I hope you still go to Mass regularly."

"Sometimes," she replied. In fact, she hadn't once been to Mass since her arrival in Rome, but despite her haughty airs she was afraid to admit this to her uncle.

The Cardinal also noticed how Antonietta, who had before been happy to confide in him, seemed to avoid any situation of intimacy between them. It happened only once, and the Cardinal had taken advantage of it to tell Antonietta that James was now a widower. "At least this piece of news should break the ice," he'd thought. Antonietta's reaction was quite the opposite of what he expected.

"Well, he never liked his wife. He must be happy she's dead," she replied with an indifference and insensitivity that both astonished and horrified her uncle.

The news of James's widowhood had not left Antonietta as cold as she pretended. Later that evening, in the solitude of her bedroom, she was beset by images of her time with James, and she couldn't suppress a longing for him. Then she remembered his disdainful attitude towards her, and her Palmieri pride reasserted itself. "James is the past, "she told herself firmly, "and good riddance to it. There are plenty of other men to fuck. Even Federico."

Once Christmas was over, Antonietta was eager to return to Rome. Braving the disappointment of her family, she left on the Monday after Christmas. That evening she dressed provocatively in a tight sweater with a low V-neck and clinging jeans and went to Squadri to show off her wares. She soon found someone and went home with him. He was a good lover, and Antonietta left his apartment in the early hours, quite sated with sex.

She spent the last day of December shopping for the dress she would wear for the New Year's celebration at the Spanish Embassy. It was an important occasion as she would be introduced for the first time to Federico's parents, the Duke and Duchess of Pontevedra, and she needed something elegant and demure to impress the austere Spanish couple. She finally found the exact dress: long and black with a suitably high décolleté but cut tightly enough to show off her opulent figure.

So attired, she arrived at the Embassy. Federico was waiting for her at the top of the spiral staircase beneath a large portrait of King Juan Carlos. For the first time, he kissed her on the cheek instead of the hand and led her into the ballroom where his parents awaited them. For all her outward aristocratic haughtiness, Antonietta was nervous. She hadn't made up her mind whether she was serious about Federico--she was sure he was serious about her--but she wanted to make a good impression on the Duke and Duchess.

Federico led her up to his parents. The Duke was a large man with a rubicund face. He was adorned in a uniform with a row of medals at his breast, which made him look like someone out of Ruritania. His wife was dressed as if she were about to go to Mass. Only the mantilla was missing.

"*Permitan Uds que les presenta la condesa della Chiesa.*"

Federico bowed slightly to his parents and indicated Antonietta. "My God," she thought, "he actually addresses his parents with the formal 'you'." It was a habit that had long since died out among the Italian aristocracy.

"*Ci fa molto piacere conoscerla.*" The Duke's Italian was heavily accented, but Antonietta was gratified by the gesture. After all, they were in Italy.

"*Il piacere é tutto mío,*" Antonietta replied as the Duke bent to kiss her hand. She turned towards the Duchess, who kissed her on the cheek but said nothing. She clearly was not overly pleased at the prospect of an Italian daughter-in-law.

After this perfunctory introduction, Antonietta joined Federico and the younger crowd. They were mostly Spanish and predictably stiff. Antonietta drank little and behaved with becoming snootiness to the waiters. Her real test came when the Duchess of Pontevedra joined them. Antonietta made every effort to be charming, but it was hard going. Sensing the delicacy of the situation, Federico asked Antonietta about Cardinal Palmieri. He knew his mother wouldn't be able to resist the niece of a cardinal.

"You are acquainted with His Eminence, *condesa*"? The Duchess was already impressed.

"He's my uncle," Antonietta replied.

This piece of news galvanized the Duchess into newfound warmth for her son's girlfriend. She was won over. A little later in the evening, Antonietta saw her talking animatedly to the Duke while gesturing towards Antonietta. His face reddened even more at the wondrous news. At least, the parents were onside, but did she really want to marry Federico? That was the question.

Soon the band started up, and Federico asked her to dance. To her surprise, he was a skillful dancer. Antonietta was more used to disco music than foxtrots and waltzes, so she let Federico lead her.

"You dance well."

"That, Federico," she replied with a smile, "is a lie. And you know it." Federico laughed. "I'm sure you'll learn."

After the champagne and the obligatory kisses that attended the coming of the New Year, Antonietta asked Federico to call a taxi. He pressed her to stay, but she pretexted tiredness. On arriving at her apartment, she found a message from Philippe announcing that he would be in Rome for a month starting the next weekend.

James's New Year's Eve party was considerably more raucous and laid back than Antonietta's. Everyone was in a good mood and resolved to forget the problems at the Institute. Only Danny was a little morose as his daughter was back in Ireland visiting her mother, but Bernadette's good spirits and the good-natured banter of her two sons soon cheered him up. Much alcohol was consumed, and James became quite tipsy.

"I'm leaving the Institute to become a banker," he suddenly announced, somewhat unsteadily.

A furor ensued. Everyone was aghast that he would leave the Rectorship, and no one could fathom why he would turn to banking, about which, on his own admission, he knew little to nothing. The evening threatened to become serious, but Bill saved the show.

"You can't leave, or you'll never get to bang Saleema."

"You know, Bill, you have a point there." James proceeded to recount his last bout with Saleema. "She said she wouldn't tell if I didn't."

"Tell what"? enquired Piotr.

"That he'd banged her, you twit." Bill looked at Piotr with a mixture of amusement and exasperation. Petra was not amused, and Bernadette quickly changed the subject.

Saleema was forgotten, and as the clock chimed midnight, there was a general kissing and clinking of champagne glasses. Perhaps it was advancing years or a vague unease that things were not quite as rosy as the champagne would have them believe, but after an hour or so of further sybaritic indulgence everyone was ready to call it quits. Mindful of Petra's meaningful looks James went upstairs to wake Susanna and Peter and take them home with him.

⌐⫟⌐

Antonietta knew that Federico would expect to spend some time with her over the weekend following New Year's Eve, but she was determined to spend it in bed with Philippe. It was a long time since she'd enjoyed such a skillful lover. When Federico called the day after the New Year's party, she told him that she was going to Florence to see her parents for the weekend. For Federico, with his quaint conservatism, this was reason enough.

Philippe arrived on Friday night, and Antonietta picked him up at Fiumicino airport. On arriving at the hotel, Philippe disappeared into the bathroom to freshen up. When he emerged, he found Antonietta lying naked on the bed, her breasts taut with desire, her legs opened wide enough to expose her sex glistening with expectant pleasure.

"Get undressed," she ordered Philippe.

He obeyed willingly, and they were soon locked in a frenetic embrace. Philippe played with Antonietta's nipples, which aroused her even more, so much so that she demanded that he penetrate her immediately without any foreplay. Just as she seemed to be moving aggressively towards her climax, she asked Philippe to stop and turned over on to her stomach. Philippe caressed her perfectly rounded buttocks before acceding to her imperious command for anal penetration. After their climaxes he turned Antonietta over again and used his mouth to drain the remnants of her lust. Then he returned to the bathroom.

"You don't have to wash, you know."

Philippe looked at her in surprise. "Since when have you indulged in a to m"?

"Since I decided that the only real pleasure in life is sex."

Antonietta was not telling the truth. She had never indulged in what Bill called sixty-four and had no intention of doing so. She was playing an act, and she was fortunate that Philippe didn't take her at her word.

"What about love"? Philippe was clearly perplexed by Antonietta's attitude.

"Love doesn't exist."

"Even for James Markham"?

"James is the past, Philippe. He impressed me when I was a young student, but that's all."

Philippe had never experienced such coldness in Antonietta's voice, and he hesitated before pursuing the conversation. He was sure she wasn't telling the truth.

"I don't believe you."

Antonietta rose from the bed and looked at him with a sardonic smile. "It's the truth, and what's more I'm going to marry Don Federico de Talavera y Muñoz."

"Who the hell is he"?

"The son and heir of the Duke of Pontevedra."

Philippe was aghast. What had happened to Antonietta? Why on earth would she of all people be marrying the son of a Spanish grandee?

"What happened between you and James"?

Antonietta laughed and avoided a straight answer. "Why should I marry the younger son of a marquis when I can marry the heir to a dukedom"?

"I can't believe you love him."

Antonietta laughed again, but it was not the sensual and warm laugh Philippe had known; it was cold and cheerless.

"Of course not. As I told you, love doesn't exist. Only sex, and if he can't satisfy me, there should be plenty of men and women in Extremadura who can. It's worth a try."

Philippe looked at Antonietta, quite speechless. This nihilistic hedonist was not the woman he'd once known, but before he could remonstrate with her, she pushed him down on the bed.

"Philippe, we haven't come to this hotel to talk nonsense. We came for sex. At least I did."

She placed his sex between her breasts, caressed it, and took it into her mouth. For the next while Philippe forgot about James and Federico.

*Chapter 46*

# Monday January 5, 2004 to
# Friday March 19, 2004

O N THE MONDAY FOLLOWING the weekend with Philippe, Antonietta moved
into her new apartment. It was situated in a narrow, cobbled street
in the Trastevere district across the river from Campo de' Fiori. From
her bedroom window Antonietta could glimpse the steeple of the
Church of Santa Maria. There were plenty of bars and restaurants in the
neighborhood, and it was not far from Squadri and two other discoes.
In short, there was everything to satisfy Antonietta's sundry appetites.

She spent the next week buying furniture and other necessities for
her abode during the day and romping with various men at night. She
only saw Federico once when she met him for lunch on Wednesday, but
she agreed to accompany him to Mass on the following Sunday as his
family had places at St. Peter's. They would all go for lunch afterwards,
which was a somewhat daunting prospect for Antonietta. Although,
contrary to what she'd told Philippe, she hadn't decided whether to
marry Federico, she wanted to keep the option open.

Antonietta didn't pay much attention to Mass, spending her time
ruminating on the prospect of a future union with Federico. He was
certainly good looking, but, forgetting her own former piety, she feared
that the devotion with which he paid attention to the liturgy of the
Mass boded ill for their sexual relationship. On the other hand, he was
likeable, courteous, and at times amusing. She didn't love him, that was

certain, but love, as she knew to her cost, could easily turn to contempt and hatred. If she was discreet about her extramarital affairs, they could perhaps have a pleasant life together.

The lunch following Mass was a laborious affair. Antonietta had to drink with uncommon moderation, make polite and thoroughly vacuous conversation, and constantly watch her manners. This was the price she had to pay if she wished to become Federico's wife, and she consoled herself with the prospect of a relaxed meal that evening at her local restaurant, washed down with plentiful glasses of wine, and the night of abandon that would doubtless follow it. In a way, she was rehearsing for her life to come without admitting to herself its appalling and amoral aridity.

Over the next month Antonietta divided her time between sedate evenings with Federico among Roman high society and frequent visits to the lower life discoes near her neighborhood. She found a perverse pleasure in this dichotomy of her social life. She didn't dance much in the discoes as she was there for sex. She never invited the partners in her nightly promiscuity to her apartment or told them her name. She wanted to shroud the encounters in anonymity. Men existed purely to satisfy her sexual needs, and that was all, but, much to her displeasure, they were not always up to the task. After one particularly frustrating experience, she began to tell herself that lesbian sex would be more rewarding. The news that her mother was arriving in Rome early February for a weekend put these wayward plans to one side.

She met her mother at Carla's, who was pregnant again. After the reception where she had met Federico, Antonietta had seen little of her sister, and she didn't know she was expecting. Her mother was shocked by this lack of interest, but any discontent with her daughter was soon squelched by the news that she was seeing Federico. She was all smiles.

"At last you're going with someone I approve of. If you play your cards right, you could end up a duchess."

Antonietta smiled. Some people never changed, and her mother was one of them.

"We'll see, *mamma.*"

The Finance Committee met on February 11, and the main item on the agenda was the progress of the fundraising campaign. Little progress had been made, which Danny was obliged to admit. James waited on tenterhooks for Wilkins' onslaught, but to his chagrin it was André Boisseu who led the attack.

"It's been almost six months since you started, Danny, and so far there have been no results. That is, to say the least, disappointing."

Danny managed to control his Irish temper and pointed out with admirable calm that until now the campaign had been limited to preparing and sending out the fundraising literature to potential donors. Some had already replied positively-- Danny reeled off some rather insignificant corporate names--but the problem was that most donors had already fixed their expenditures for the coming financial year.

"So you're telling us we can't expect any progress until next year," Wilkins sneered.

"That's not what I said," Danny replied.

"It was what you implied," Wilkins retorted. He turned to face James. "You see what happens, Markham, when you favor your friends."

James was about to reply angrily when Saleema intervened.

"I don't think it's a question of favoring friends, Wilkins." Saleema deliberately used his surname as Wilkins had done with James. "It seems quite normal that fundraising should be entrusted to the senior Dean."

"We all know why *you* are supporting the Rector, Dr. Nadjani."

The allusion was all too crude, and it was a mistake. Until that moment Boisseu, who was also critical of Danny's efforts, was on Wilkins' side, but this indelicate hint of a liaison between James and Saleema shocked him. For the faculty at large, Saleema with her Muslim headscarf was regarded as untouchable. Realizing his error, Wilkins softened his tone.

"I suggest we set up a committee to assist Danny in his fundraising efforts," he suggested.

Anxious to end the fractious discussion, James agreed. It was put to a vote, and Wilkins' suggestion was accepted unanimously.

On the way to Saleema's apartment, James mused disconsolately on his problems at the Institute.

"I'm tempted to throw in the towel and go into banking."

"You can't"! Saleema almost shouted.

"Why not"?

The car had by now come to a halt outside Saleema's apartment. She took off her headscarf and shook free her long dark hair.

"Because I don't want you to leave."

Before James could react, he found himself kissing Saleema, at first tentatively and then with more passion. No words were spoken, and James followed Saleema into her apartment. She led him to her bedroom and proceeded to take off her dress, revealing a tiny string and a bra that provocatively offered up her barely covered breasts.

James was in a daze, hovering between amazement and desire. "But, Saleema....," he stuttered.

"But what"? She slid off her bra. "Do you want to make love to me or not"?

James's answer was to take Saleema in his arms. The scent of her perfume and the smooth feel of her skin as his hands slipped down her back and fondled her denuded buttocks fueled his lust. They kissed again, and Saleema with unexpected expertise removed James's shirt and pants. She pulled him down on the bed and rubbed her breasts against his bare chest.

"I hope you don't have any Christian hang-ups."

"I don't think so," James replied, not knowing quite what she meant. Once they started to make love, it became clear. James was quite taken aback by Saleema's total lack of modesty as she made available all her body and enjoyed all of his.

"Muslims are very strict about feminine modesty in public," she explained afterwards, "but, in matters of sex, we don't have to cope with all that nonsense about every sex act being open to the transmission of life."

"I don't think Christians are that hung up," James protested. "Certainly he wasn't," he thought.

Saleema looked at him skeptically. "Perhaps not, but I'm sure your Church doesn't approve of fellatio or sodomy or mutual masturbation."

James was stunned by Saleema's bluntness. It was some time before he could reply.

"You're right," he managed eventually, "but then I thought all

Muslim girls had to remain virgins until marriage or get stoned or something equally distressing."

"They do what they want in marriage."

"You're not married, and you're certainly no longer a virgin."

"True. If I ever marry, it will have to be a non-practicing or atheist Muslim."

"Not a Christian"?

Saleema's mood became somber. "No. If I married a Christian, I would be cut off from my family. I'm not religious, but being a Muslim is a sort of family tradition. It's dumb, I know, but there it is. I can't change it."

"You don't believe in Allah"?

"I believe there is a God, but I'm not sure it's Allah." Saleema stroked James's face. "Do you believe in your God"?

"I'm a Catholic in the same way you're a Muslim. It's a family tradition that I am loyal to. I *do* believe in my God in the sense that Christianity is one way of trying to define what God is. It is not the only way. All religions are true to the extent that they seek to define the indefinable, and each one has some element of the divine truth that we human beings are incapable of fully comprehending."

James smiled at Saleema, who was nestled against him. "Does that make any sense"?

Saleema sat up and kissed him. "Yes, but I never thought you were such a relativist."

"It's not relativism, it's logic. How can any religion, whether it's Christian, Muslim, Jewish, Hindu or whatever, claim to be the one true religion when at least half if not more of the world doesn't share it and may not even know of it. You'd think that if there is one true revelation of the divine truth, we'd all have the same religion. As it is, we all follow the religions we are born into and then claim, for some inexplicable reason, that our religion is truer than the one other people are born into."

"Do you think some religions are better than others"?

"All religions are imperfect, fragmentary conceptions of the divinity based on local cultural attributes. That's why converting from one imperfect, fragmentary conception to another equally imperfect and fragmentary conception makes no sense. What's more, they all have silly rules that have nothing to do with divine truth. My religion has dumb rules about sex and can't even tell the difference between contraception and abortion. Your lot and the Jews don't eat pork because a few centuries ago there was no refrigeration. The Hindus won't each beef because they worship cows. Why they chose cows is beyond me. They could at least have chosen horses. They're a lot nobler than a stupid cow. Buddhists can't eat anything in case they're devouring one of their ancestors. Islam won't let you drink alcohol although it's quite happy to let you kill yourself with cigarettes."

James paused, afraid that he'd gone too far, but Saleema was clearly amused by his tirade.

"The worst are Mormons," he continued in the same vein. "If you're a Mormon, you can't even have a bloody cup of tea. Do they really think that the creator of the universe is going to get his nickers in a twist just because some poor sod has a cup of tea? It's ludicrous."

Once she'd recovered from her laughter, Saleema pushed James down on the bed and kissed him.

"You Christians talk too much. It's time for some more sex."

James devoured her body with kisses. As his lips pleasured her intimacies, Saleema moaned in delight. They made love again in the Muslim fashion.

Monday, February 16 was Presidents Day in the United States, and Federico and Antonietta were attending a reception at the American Embassy. It was a rather bombastic affair with lots of accolades for the great American Revolution and the noble cause of anti-slavery, pioneered, according to the speaker, by the United States under Abraham Lincoln.

"The silly idiot must think we still have slaves in Spain," Federico complained.

"Probably. Let's get out of here before it gets worse."

They left as surreptitiously as possible but couldn't avoid a look of displeasure from the Duchess of Pontevedra. Federico took no notice, which surprised Antonietta as he'd always deferred to his parents.

They found a small restaurant not far from the Embassy and ordered *vitello alla marsala.*

"A bottle of Verdicchio dei Castelli di Jesi," Federico added. This was an excellent white wine and one of her father's favorites. Antonietta looked at Federico with new respect.

They ate in silence. Antonietta was now used to this habit of Federico's. He'd explained to her that his parents hated people talking and eating at the same time, and this had become engrained in him. At the time Antonietta had taken it as another example of his weak character, but it no longer bothered her.

The meal was over and with it a second bottle of Verdicchio dei Castelli di Jesi. To Antonietta's surprise, Federico ordered another one. She'd never seen him drink so much. She feared it might give him the courage to pop the question. She wasn't wrong. Federico stretched his hand over the table and placed it on Antonietta's.

"Antonietta," he said with a solemnity a little tinged by alcohol. "I want to ask you to be my wife."

So, the moment had come. Antonietta had known it would, but she was nonetheless quite unprepared. Federico was a pleasant companion, courteous, kind and not devoid of intelligence, but very Spanish, very correct and, given that he was asking to marry her without having bedded her, clearly lacking in libido. Mind you, as she told Philippe, she could always find sexual fulfillment outside of her marriage. Federico was not at all the man of her dreams, but she had no more dreams, except perhaps that of becoming a duchess. Nevertheless, she prevaricated.

"Give me some time to think, Federico. It's a big step."

Federico had obviously anticipated this reserve. "Of course," he replied. "Let's finish this last bottle."

"The way to a man's heart is through his stomach," Antonietta thought. "Federico must think the way to mine is through a bottle of wine."

This didn't stop her drinking the lion's share.

⁓

In the month following Federico's proposal, Antonietta carried on with her dual life, dividing her time between sedate receptions and the occasional Mass with Federico and his family and her disco nights of sexual promiscuity. She still hadn't given Federico any indication of her response to his proposal. This evening she would be dining with Philippe and doubtless having sex with him afterwards. It would be a pleasant change from the tenseness of the previous evening with Paolo and Monica. She was still smarting from her brother's evident disapproval of her new persona.

The dinner with Philippe passed off pleasantly enough, and the sex that followed was satisfying. But once her libido was satiated, Antonietta had the bad idea of asking Philippe for advice regarding Federico's proposal.

"I think it would be pure folly to marry him."

"Why," Antonietta was indignant. 'You don't think I'm good enough for the son of a duke"? She moved away and glared at Philippe.

"That's nothing to do with it, and you know it." Philippe gave Antonietta a look in which concern mingled with censure. "What game are you playing, Antonietta? This new persona is a travesty of your real self, a sort of self-induced character assassination."

"I am what I am. I'm a rich aristocrat, and I have every right to behave as one, and no one, not even you, Philippe, has a right to criticize me."

"As you wish." Philippe rose from the bed and dressed. Antonietta made no attempt to stop him leaving, and they parted without any exchanging another word.

Angered by her brother's and her lover's attitudes and dissatisfied with most of her male partners, Antonietta decided that she'd had enough of men. Tonight she would go to a gay bar and find a woman for her sexual pleasure. She looked up an address on the internet and took a taxi.

The bar was dimly lit and quite crowded. Most of the women were very masculine looking, and Antonietta was not looking for a dyke. She was about to leave when an attractive woman whom Antonietta took to be an Asian came up to her. She was slim, but a tightly fitting dress accentuated a curvaceous body. Her jet-black hair fell loosely around her shoulders. She exuded a wanton sensuality, and Antonietta felt an immediate sexual attraction to her. This attraction was clearly mutual for without any preliminaries the woman, who was in fact Eurasian, asked "Your place or mine"? Normally Antonietta preferred not to use her own apartment for her sexual encounters. but without thinking she answered "Mine." They drove off in the woman's car.

Once they arrived at Antonietta's apartment, they made for the bedroom. The woman whipped off her dress. She was naked underneath, and Antonietta gazed with mounting desire at her duskily erotic body. Excitement began to moisten her thighs, and she undressed in such a hurry that she broke the clasp on her bra. Soon their naked bodies were intertwined on the bed. They kissed with passion, caressed, licked and sucked other's breasts and played with each other's sex until Antonietta could contain herself no longer. She devoured her partner and turned her over to enjoy the feel of her taut, round buttocks. She fingered and licked her anus and penetrated it with her nipples, but desirous of watching the woman take her pleasure, she turned her back over and brought her to a climax with her fingers. Afterwards she gently drew the woman's swollen clitoris into her mouth and, caressing her breasts as she did so, drained it of any remaining lust. Trembling with a voracious desire for the same sexual delights, she lay down beside the woman and had her minister to her most dissolute needs. With her anus and sex wet from these ministrations, she let the woman expertly finish her.

For a while the two women lay together, sensually stroking each other's bodies. Then, the Eurasian woman, whose name was Naomi, got up.

"I must go. My husband is due back at two in the morning."

"Your husband"!

"Yes, he's a pilot."

"Does he know what you get up to when he's away"?

"That's not a problem. He screws the stewardesses, and I enjoy myself like this."

Antonietta was intrigued. "And your marriage"?

"We're happily married, but neither of us can keep our hands off other women."

Antonietta looked at Naomi with a mixture of admiration, envy and renewed lust. But Naomi was already on the way out.

"Give me your name and phone number," Antonietta asked. At that moment the delights of Naomi's dusky body were far more appealing than those of any man. Except perhaps…

Naomi obliged and disappeared into the night. Antonietta stretched out her naked body on the bed. "A happy marriage and lesbian indulgence on the side," she thought. "Not a bad solution". She could certainly have the latter but was not sure about the former.

⌒⁄⌒

The last month had seen no let-up in James's problems at the Institute. Shortly after the fractious finance meeting and despite the compromise that had been reached there, Wilkins brought a motion of censure against James in the Governing Council. Emily Wright seconded it. Although the motion was roundly defeated, the whole episode had left James even more bitter.

On the Friday when Antonietta was cavorting with Philippe, more bad news arrived in the shape of an application from Emily Wright for promotion to full professor. James considered that nothing in Emily's record supported such a promotion. When the gang met at Bill's the following Saturday evening, James gave full vent to his exasperation.

"I'm sure she was put up to it by Wilkins and the opposition. She seconded that motion of censure just to suck up to them."

"Come on, James." Danny put his hand on his irate friend's shoulder. "You're getting paranoid. I can't see why seconding that motion is going to help her get promotion. It's true Emily's publishing record isn't that great, but she's a good teacher."

"Good teaching doesn't count for promotion."

The discussion turned to tactics. Rumor had it that Goldberg was a candidate for being the faculty representative, and James intended to ask Claudio Petttroni to run against him. He would appoint either Anne-Marie Legrand or Klaus Berger as the Rector's choice. The others agreed, and James started to leave.

"What's the rush," Bill asked, surprised by James's early departure. "We haven't even finished the first bottle of scotch."

"I smell a rat," Danny said with a malicious grin at James. "You didn't show up after the finance meeting, and now you're rushing off.

You wouldn't be having a little hooky with our favorite Muslim, would you, James"?

"I knew it! I knew it"! Bill shouted. "Own up, you horny bastard"!

James had no choice but to own up, as Bill put it. Once the initial surprise passed, the lads passed a severe judgment on James's latest adventure. Danny thought it was another dead end, and Piotr was aghast at a good Catholic bedding a Muslim. Only Bill sort of approved.

"If she's a good fuck, why not? But, as Danny said, it *is* a dead end."

"I agree. All my affairs are dead ends. What's the difference with Saleema"?

✳

On Monday after her sexual extravaganza with Naomi, Antonietta phoned Federico and suggested that they meet for dinner. It was the first time she'd taken such an initiative, but, after a weekend of soul searching driven by fright at the attractions of lesbian sex, and inspired by Naomi's arrangement with her husband, she'd decided to marry him. Now she wanted to commit herself before she changed her mind. They arranged to meet the following evening at La Pergola in the elegant Cavalieri hotel.

✳

Federico was waiting for Antonietta in the reception hall of the Cavalieri Hotel. He seemed more boyish and flushed than usual. Clearly he suspected that this was the moment of truth, and he was between hope and despair. In one way, it seemed natural to him that Antonietta would wish to marry the heir to the dukedom of Pontevedra, but there was something indecipherable about this Italian beauty that surpassed his limited understanding of women.

Antonietta smiled at him, and he kissed her on the cheek. "A great beginning for our first night as fiancés," she thought, but she banished an upsurge of aversion to the marriage that awaited her. Federico led her to a table in a corner where their conversation would not be overheard. "Was it delicacy or a desire not to be humiliated in public by a refusal," she wondered.

525

Once they were seated, Federico ordered drinks. A white wine for himself and, somewhat to his disapproval, a double martini gin for Antonietta.

"Shaken, not stirred," she told the waiter, who laughed uproariously.

"What was the matter with him"?

"You haven't seen a James Bond film"?

"Good Lord, no. I don't like the British."

"You'd like them even less if you knew whose bed I would like to be in now." Antonietta thought and immediately chastised herself for such misplaced nostalgia.

"Federico," she began and then stopped. "Stop twisting that serviette, for God's sake."

Federico obeyed and put the serviette down. He looked at Antonietta as if he were about to hear his sentence of death.

"Federico, I accept your proposal of marriage."

⁓

Neither Antonietta nor Federico ate much of their meal. Federico didn't seem able to wipe the smile off his face long enough to down a morsel, and Antonietta had little appetite now she'd committed herself to what would doubtless be an arid marriage. She might have renounced the whole idea and fled from the restaurant, were it not for her resolve to break completely with her former life.

Just as Federico was finally managing to deal with a large piece of cheese, Antonietta dropped her bombshell.

"I want you to come back to my apartment and make love to me."

Federico choked on his cheese. "But we're not married"!

"Federico, we are in twenty-first century Italy, and couples make love before marriage."

"*Not* in Spain," Federico countered.

"Oh, Federico, grow up. Perhaps not under Franco, but thank God he's dead."

"I admire Franco," Federico retorted. "He saved us from Communism."

"That's as maybe, Federico, but under him Spain lived in the nineteenth century with nineteenth century morals. Things have changed in Spain. Look at your king. He's not exactly a model of conjugal fidelity."

"Don't insult the King." Antonietta had never seen Federico angry, and she regretted her tactlessness.

"I admire Juan Carlos. For your information, I'm a Monarchist. But I still want you in my bed." This was not the exact truth, but Antonietta was anxious to find out just how arid her marriage would be.

Dismayed that his bride-to-be was obviously not a virgin and apprehensive at the prospect before him, Federico reluctantly followed Antonietta to her apartment.

Antonietta arrived first and waited for Federico to find a parking place. Together they climbed the stairs to Antonietta's apartment in silence. Once inside, Antonietta wasted no time. She led Federico into her bedroom and slipped off her dress. Her skimpy underwear hid little of her physical charms. Federico stared at her as if in a trance. He made no move to undress. Irritated by his passivity, Antonietta undid her bra and let it fall to the floor. Her breasts now quite uncovered, she walked up to Federico, took his hands, and placed them on her breasts. By now, Federico was quite flushed.

"Caress me," she ordered, and Federico hesitantly obeyed. Gradually the erotic feel of Antonietta's firm and rounded breasts and the sight of her nudity overcame his conservative, Catholic scruples, and when Antonietta kissed him, he returned the kiss with some passion. Antonietta disengaged herself and, taking off her string, laid down completely nude on the bed.

"Get undressed, Federico, and come to me." Again Federico obeyed, but this time with a little more alacrity.

What ensued was better than Antonietta had feared. Federico caressed and kissed her breasts, her belly, her thighs and caressed her sex. When she was sufficiently aroused, he penetrated her but held off his own pleasure until she was herself satisfied. But that was all. Afterwards, he just lay next to her for a while and then got up and dressed. He seemed ashamed of what had happened.

"You don't appear to enjoy sex."

"Yes, I do," he replied, without looking at her, "but I think we should now wait until we are married."

"As you wish," Antonietta replied. It mattered little to her as she would be seeking her sexual satisfaction elsewhere in any case. At least now she knew what her conjugal relationship would be like. Not completely arid but not very exciting, unless she could train Federico to be a more enterprising mate. "It's possible," she thought.

After Federico left, Antonietta felt sexually frustrated. One modest orgasm was not her idea of a night of sex. Unfortunately the other men she went with were not always much better than Federico. The image of Naomi's duskily erotic body came to her mind. She decided to call in case she was available. She was, and still moist and naked after her disappointing sexual experience with Federico, Antonietta lay on the bed awaiting her lesbian paramour.

Friday, the nineteenth of March, was another black day for James with the news that Nathan Goldberg had been elected in preference to Claudio Pettroni as the faculty representative for the committee on Emily Wright's application for a full professorship. James was furious.

"He's not even a bloody full professor himself"! he expostulated to his friends that evening. "Well, I'll show them. I'll appoint Pettroni anyway as my choice."

"That's not very smart, James," Danny cautioned. "Remember the furor it caused when Winstone appointed Flint to Bill's tenure committee after he'd been defeated as faculty representative. You'd be seen as doing the same thing."

Bill and Piotr agreed with Danny, but James remained obdurate. "I don't care what the bastards think, I *am* going to appoint Pettroni."

Seeing that they were getting nowhere with James, the others dropped the subject. After some serious drinking the evening ended, and James made it home. There was a message from his father telling him that his mother was hospitalized with angina but that she was making good progress. There was no need for worry. Nevertheless, the next morning James phoned home for further reassurance.

Antonietta took a taxi for lunch at the residence of the Spanish Ambassador with her fiancé and her future parents-in-law. "Funny type of fiancé who doesn't come to pick me up," she thought, but it rather amused her. He must be afraid that I'd seduce him again. He met her on the steps of the residence with a very proper kiss on the cheeks. It seemed very incongruous to Antonietta. The last time they'd been together, they'd had sex. Obviously Federico wanted to put their relationship back on a virtuous path. "He can't have much of a libido. Most men find me irresistible. It must be the Spanish, Catholic way."

A beaming Duke of Pontevedra met the two in the hall of the residence. He bowed low as he kissed Antonietta's hand. The Duchess, whose reservations had been overcome by the revelation that Antonietta was the niece of a cardinal, kissed her on each cheek.

"We are so pleased to welcome you into our family," she purred. The Duke nodded in enthusiastic agreement.

At a loss for words as she didn't quite share this pleasure at being part of the Pontevedra family, Antonietta merely smiled. A servant appeared to summon them to the table, so she was spared the need for a more communicative answer.

The lunch was a trial for Antonietta. The conversation consisted mainly of the Duke and Duchess singing their son's praises and making it clear to Antonietta that she was very lucky to have made such a good match. They did admit that Federico was also fortunate to have found such a beautiful and well-born girl with good Catholic morals. Antonietta had some difficulty keeping a straight face at this totally erroneous assessment of her qualities. She glanced briefly at Federico and could see that he was as embarrassed as she was amused. It was the only entertaining moment of the whole meal.

After lunch, the plans were laid for the future of the engaged pair, plans in which the pair had little say. Their engagement would be announced publicly at a reception to be given at the Spanish Embassy on Saturday, April 10, two days prior to Federico's 29th birthday. Antonietta was at a loss to understand the connection between the two events, but it seemed important to the Duke and Duchess. The actual wedding would take place later in the year, either in Mérida, where the Pontevedra's had their main residence, or in Florence. It went without saying that either the Archbishop of Mérida or the Cardinal Archbishop of Florence would officiate.

Once her future had been decided by her future parents-in-law, Antonietta made an excuse and left. Federico accompanied her down the steps of the residence but seemed relieved not to be invited to spend the rest of the afternoon with her. "He must be afraid of another romp," Antonietta thought with amusement. She was equally relieved to be on her own.

Upon her arrival in the apartment, she called her mother. She hadn't told her of the engagement earlier as she hadn't been sure whether Federico would go through with it once he'd found out that she wasn't a pious Catholic virgin. Her mother was predictably ecstatic at the news.

"I must tell Giovanni immediately. He'll be so happy."

Antonietta was quite sure her uncle would not be happy at all, given his dislike of Spanish *hidalgos*, but she decided not to spoil her mother's joy. Her uncle could be trusted to do that.

She was quite right. To her mother's disappointment, the Cardinal's reaction to the engagement was far from positive. He most certainly was not happy about it.

"This is a tragedy," he told his sister. "Antonietta is throwing her life away on a pampered, sycophantic nincompoop. God knows why."

"Giovanni, he's the heir to a dukedom."

The Cardinal lost his temper. "Caterina, if you could for once snap out of your outdated snobbism, you'd go to Rome immediately and talk some sense into that daughter of your's instead of exulting like a petty bourgeois on her marrying the heir to a dukedom."

Livid at being called a petty bourgeois, Caterina hung up.

*Chapter 47*

# Friday March 19, 2004 to
# Saturday April 10, 2004

L EFT TO HIS OWN devices, the Cardinal reflected sadly on his niece's decision. It was a travesty of all that she'd stood for, but it was in keeping with the new haughty persona she'd adopted since moving to Rome. Whatever had happened to her? What was preventing her and James getting together now that he was a widower? Despite her apparent indifference to the news of his widowhood, Giovanni could not believe that Antonietta was no longer in love with him. A passion that had almost caused her to die of grief could not just melt away like snow on warm spring day. No, she was marrying a man she couldn't possibly love instead of the man she loved. It didn't make any sense, and it had to be stopped. But how?

For a while Giovanni was lost in thought. Then he suddenly got out of his chair and went over to the telephone. He dialed Philip Markham's number.

"Hello, Giovanni. How goes your flock"? The marquis could never resist the temptation to tease his friend about his transformation from rake to priest. This time, Giovanni didn't react with the normal bonhomie.

"It's not my flock, as you put it, that worries me, it's my niece, Antonietta," he replied. His voice was unusually grave.

"What's the matter with her"?

"She's marrying a man she doesn't love instead of the man she loves."

"Giovanni, stop being so enigmatic. Whom is she marrying, and whom does she love"?

"She's marrying a Spanish *hidalgo*. The son of the Duke of Pontevedra, that overblown Spanish Ambassador to Italy."

Philip smiled to himself. This was vintage Giovanni. Despite his ancestry, his dislike of Spaniards was notorious. "And the man she loves"?

"Your son, James."

"*What*"! Philip's equally notorious English phlegm quite deserted him. "How in Heaven's name did she manage to fall in love with James? To my knowledge the only time they met, she was a child."

Philip's assertion startled Giovanni. He'd completely forgotten that years ago when he was Bishop of Bolzano-Bressanone, James and his father had visited him. His sister Caterina had also been visiting at the time with her two girls, and he now recalled that Antonietta had come to retrieve a book from the room where he was entertaining James and Philip. She must have been about ten years old.

"She met him again in Canada. She was his student." Giovanni deliberately omitted the date. He didn't particularly want Philip to know that it was an adulterous relationship.

"Good Lord"! Philip was too astonished to ask any embarrassing questions. He came right to the point. "How can I help"?

Giovanni explained what he wanted Philip to do.

⌒⅋⌐

James's *série noire* continued on the Friday following Goldberg's unexpected success in the election for Faculty representative with the promotion of Emily Wright by the committee. Only Pettroni and James had voted against. Goldberg, McGrath, Forget and even Hamid Khan had voted for promotion. James was in a dark mood when he arrived at Saleema's apartment.

"This time, I really *am* going to resign," he told her.

"No, you're not. If you do, Allah alone knows what idiot will take over as Rector."

Saleema's words might not have convinced James, but the pleasures of her curvaceous body put him in a much more positive frame of mind. Unfortunately this euphoria did not last long.

"James." Saleema sat up and kissed James passionately. "I have something to tell you."

"What"? James sensed this was not going to be good news.

"I've taken a job at Chicago U starting on July 1. I'm leaving once term is over, and I don't think we should see each other again."

"Why? Why are you doing this"? James was more upset that Saleema had expected. She kissed him again.

"I'm in love with you, and I cannot marry you. It would be better for both of us."

Before James could answer, Saleema came on top of him, and they made love. Once their passion had subsided, James got up, dressed and with a last kiss left without a further word.

As he drove home, he ruminated on his recent calamitous love life: Antonietta, who had played him for a fool, and Annya, Carolina and now Saleema who'd left him although they were in love with him. It didn't make sense. Nothing in his life made sense. It was a meaningless life.

⁓

The next day, a Saturday, Antonietta arrived at the Archiepiscopal Palace in Florence. Her uncle had insisted that she come for dinner, which caused her much apprehension. Her relationship with Uncle Giovanni had deteriorated greatly since her move to Rome. He made no secret of his disapproval of her new persona.

A rather scruffy looking priest opened the door of the palace. From his accent Antonietta took him to be Austrian. She looked at him with disdain.

"I am the Countess Antonietta della Chiesa. I have come to see my uncle, the Cardinal."

"This way, countess." The priest ushered her reverently into the palace. Antonietta took no further notice of him and marched up the stairs to the reception room. She entered and stopped dead in her tracks. The man standing next to her uncle was the image, albeit with more advanced age, of James. Antonietta looked at him, unable to speak, so great was her disarray.

"My dear Antonietta, I'm so glad you could come." Giovanni kissed his niece and led her towards the man. "May I introduce you to my old friend, the Marquis of Derwent."

With a poisonous look at her uncle, Antonietta shook Philip's outstretched hand. So this was why she'd been invited to dinner. Well, so be it.

"It's a pleasure, my lord," she managed. Summoning up all her courage, she added, "I believe I met your son James in Canada."

Philip felt sorry for the young woman. He suspected what she was going through. However, he just smiled and played his assigned role.

"Yes. Actually, it was not the first time you'd met him."

Antonietta looked at Philip in amazement, at a loss for words.

"Many years ago, sixteen I think, James and I were visiting your uncle at the same time as you and your mother were there. I remember James saying how pretty you were."

Antonietta paled, and for a moment Philip feared she would faint. "This is beginning to look like death by a thousand cuts, but it has to be done." he thought as he led a shaken Antonietta gently to the table.

Giovanni, who was deliberately ignoring Antonietta's distress, started an animated conversation with Philip, leaving his poor niece to her own thoughts. The timbre of Philip's voice, his laugh, his wayward hair, his smile, everything reminded her of James and memories of their time together came flooding back. She had to fight back her tears.

"You now live in Rome, Antonietta"? Philip asked. Deep in her own bittersweet reflections, Antonietta was startled by the sound of her name. Unable to recall the question, she apologized. Her uncle came to the rescue but only to plunge the dagger more deeply into the wound.

"She's been there since the New Year. Tell me, Philip, talking of the younger generation, what is James up to? I heard some rumor about a remarriage."

"A remarriage"! Antonietta cried involuntarily, now looking quite sick. Despite his sympathy for the young woman, Philip gave the required answer.

"Yes, it's true. She's Argentinean. Apparently, she's a very pretty blond called Carolina."

Neither Philip nor Giovanni was aware that Antonietta knew of Carolina's existence, and that she had always been fiercely jealous of her. All they had hoped was that the prospect of losing James forever would provoke Antonietta into admitting her love for him and acting on it before it was too late. As it was, the news that James was to marry her hated rival had a terrible effect on her. Without a word she got up from the table and rushed into the bathroom, where she threw up and broke down in a fit of weeping. Desperately she tried to pull herself together, but she needed all the remnants of her pride to return to the table. The two men acted as if nothing were amiss and made no comment on her temporary absence.

The rest of the dinner was a torment for Antonietta. The two men were content to talk together, aware that Antonietta was not in a fit state to take part in the conversation. All her false pride, her haughtiness, the denial of her love for James, indeed the whole façade of her present existence lay shattered, and she was submerged by a feeling of immeasurable loss, of utter misery. She sat there in a daze, oblivious of the tears running down her cheeks.

Only vaguely mindful of the passing time, Antonietta was shaken out of her torpor by Philip's departure.

"It was a pleasure to meet you again," he told her. Antonietta was unable to reply.

Philip left, and Antonietta was alone with her uncle.

"How could you be so cruel"? she cried.

"Sometimes you have to be cruel to be kind."

"You call that…that charade *kind*"?

"Yes, Antonietta." The Cardinal put his arm around his weeping niece. "Now look me in the face and tell me that you're not still desperately in love with James Markham."

Antonietta lifted up her tear-stained face. Her grief lent a touch of fragility to her beauty, and the assumed hardness of her eyes had surrendered to the candid truth of her heart's desires.

"Yes, uncle, I will never love anyone else, but…" Antonietta stopped, unable to continue through her sobs.

"But what"?

"James doesn't love me anymore. He's always loved this Carolina. It's over, uncle, completely over."

"You know about Carolina"?

"Yes. James met her before me."

"Listen, Antonietta, we were not entirely honest with you. It's true that James mentioned her name to his father, but as far as we know there are no marriage plans."

Antonietta looked sadly at her uncle. "Perhaps not and perhaps not ever, but I met James in Florence in November, and he made it quite clear that he has no time for me."

So this was the reason for Rome and the new persona. Now Giovanni understood. He took Antonietta's hands into his and tried to convince her that she was wrong about James. Antonietta was obdurate. Partly through conviction, partly also through pride, she refused to give their love another chance.

"I've given my word to Federico, and I'm going to keep it."

After Antonietta left, Philip, who'd been waiting in the next room, came back to hear about the outcome of their little scenario.

"It's no good. She's convinced James doesn't love her, and she's got a bee in her bonnet about her word to Federico. As far as I'm concerned, it's her damn Palmieri pride."

⌘

It was Monday, March 29, and the last week of classes was about to begin. James was in the office preparing his own final lecture on the European Union when his secretary informed him that there was a call for him "from some sort of foreigner." Intrigued, James picked up the phone.

"James, *mi amigo, qué tal*"? It was Rodrigo de Fuentes y Talavera.

"Rodrigo"! A call from his old friend was just the tonic James needed. "To what do I owe the pleasure"?

"Apart from the pleasure of talking with me, I want a favor from you."

"Any favor you like, Rodrigo."

"My idiot cousin, Federico--you know the prissy one we used to make fun of--is marrying some Italian countess."

"My God, she must be uncommonly ugly," James commented with unwitting irony.

"Apparently not, which is surprising," Rodrigo replied. "Anyhow, I've been invited to the engagement party at the Spanish Embassy in Rome on Saturday April 10. I don't speak Italian, so would you come as my interpreter? It would also give us a chance to spend some time together."

*Italy! Antonietta!* was James's first thought. But the party was in Rome, and there was no reason for her to be there. Moreover, she hated Spaniards.

"I'd be delighted to come."

Once his conversation with Rodrigo was over, James called his father. The trip to Italy would give him an opportunity to visit his mother.

"Why are you going to Italy"? his father asked.

"Rodrigo's cousin Federico is marrying some Italian countess. I'm accompanying him to the engagement party at the Spanish Embassy."

Philip hid his excitement, but following the call from his son he phoned Giovanni and told him the news. The Cardinal was overjoyed.

"That's excellent! Messina will doubtless be there, and I'll have him tell James why Antonietta left him. That should soften him up. It's a long shot, but with a little help from above perhaps a miracle may happen."

After the phone call from Philip, Giovanni went into his private chapel and prayed.

The Cardinal's charade may not have attained its objective of bringing Antonietta and James back together, but it had opened Antonietta's eyes to the travesty of a life she was leading in Rome. She remembered Philippe's words that her passion for James would destroy her and his description of her new persona as self-willed character assassination. On arriving back in Rome, she went to the nearby Church of Santa Maria and prayed to the Virgin. Lifting her eyes to the statue of the Mother of God, she felt deep shame for the promiscuity and uncaring arrogance of her recent life. "It was madness, sheer madness," she told herself and made a solemn promise to mend her ways.

Antonietta acted immediately to implement her good resolution. She bought his favorite cigars for Tomaso and a pretty shawl for Giuseppina. She asked them to forgive her for treating them so cavalierly. The humiliation of seeking forgiveness from two domestics brought her a sense of unaccustomed serenity. She repeated her *mea culpa* with Paolo and Monica, who were overjoyed to welcome back the old Antonietta.

She didn't know quite how to deal with Federico. Apart from cheating on him in serial fashion-- and she could hardly confess that to him if she still wanted to marry him--she'd behaved towards him as he'd expected and no doubt wanted. Yes, she realized now, this is how he wanted her to be. Aristocratic, arrogant, unfeeling. He was no more in love with her than she was with him. What was important for him was her aristocratic lineage and, for purely esthetic reasons, her beauty. Nothing else mattered, certainly not character or love or passion. She was destined to be nothing more than the anodyne wife of the future Duke of Pontevedra, a beautiful, wellborn but essentially irrelevant appendage. Now that she'd cast off her false persona, could she really put up with such a marriage? But she was trapped. The engagement reception was tomorrow. How could she get out of it without causing a great scandal? She couldn't. She'd made her bed, and now she had to lie in it.

James and Rodrigo arrived at the reception. It was a very formal affair. They entered the hall where it was being held by a short ladder leading up to a platform, which was closed off in front by a low balustrade. To the right were steps down into the mingling crowd of guests. They gave their invitations to a man whose attire reminded James of a medieval town crier. So did his robust voice as he announced portentously "Don Rodrigo de Fuentes y Talavera and Lord James Markham". No one seemed to take much notice, but once they had descended from their pedestal, a tall man, immaculately dressed, came forward to greet James.

"Lord Markham," he said, holding out his hand. "It's a pleasure to meet you again."

James stared at the man, and it was a few moments before he recognized the Duke of Messina. He apologized profusely, but the Duke waived away his apology. He turned to Rodrigo.

"Don Rodrigo, we haven't met. I am the Duke of Messina." Before Rodrigo could react, the Duke carried on. "May I steal your friend James for a little chat"?

"Of course, Your Grace," Rodrigo replied, although it was clear that he found the Duke's behavior somewhat odd and not entirely to his liking.

James followed Messina to the bar, where the Duke had them served two glasses of white wine.

"I'm glad you kept your job at the Institute,' he told James, who looked at the Duke in astonishment. Did this mean Messina had known about his impending resignation? A suspicion began to form in James's mind that the Duke was no stranger to his unexpected reprieve. But why? Why would Messina have interceded to save him? He was about to find out.

"Actually, you don't owe your good fortune to me alone," the Duke went on, as if reading James's thoughts. "A young lady, a very beautiful young lady, persuaded me to make that fellow Win-something understand that it was no Markham, no European library."

James gasped at the enormity of Messina's revelation. Although dreading the answer, he nevertheless put the question.

"What did she agree to in return"?

Messina put down his glass of wine. "You know the price she paid, Lord Markham. I am a devout Catholic, and I was unable to help Antonietta if it meant her continuing an adulterous relationship. I'm sorry, but for me there was no alternative."

Stupefied by Messina's revelations, James walked away from the Duke in a complete daze of self-contempt. The lads had been right all along, and he had been wrong, hideously wrong. How could he have so misjudged Antonietta? How could he have believed all the horrible things he'd thought of her--and said to her. He thought of their conversation in Florence and felt sick to his stomach.

"What the hell did Messina say to you"? Rodrigo asked, putting an arm around his wretched friend. "You look as if someone has just assassinated your whole family."

"Rodrigo, I've been a fool, a complete, irredeemable fool. An asshole of the first order."

James recounted the whole tale of his passion for a beautiful Italian girl, their tumultuous affair, her sacrifice to save his career, and his venomous reaction to her departure.

"Who was she"? Rodrigo asked, beginning to feel uneasy.

"Her name was Antonietta della Chiesa."

Rodrigo blanched. He'd found out only a few moments before the identity of Federico's fiancée. James's answer confirmed his worst fears.

"You'd better prepare yourself for another shock, old friend."

Immersed in his own dark thoughts, James paid no attention to Rodrigo's forewarning. He continued to stare blankly into space until the appearance of the Duke of Pontevedra on the platform heralded the arrival of the *promessi sposi*.

"My lords, ladies, and gentlemen," the Duke intoned with great solemnity. "I am very happy to introduce to you our engaged couple: my son, Don Federico de Talavera y Muñoz, and my future daughter-in-law, the Countess Antonietta della Chiesa."

Federico and Antonietta appeared on the platform. James stared at them in stunned disbelief. Seeing Antonietta in all her incandescent beauty and knowing he had lost her, realizing now for the first time who she was, and remembering how he had thrown his own modest title in her face, it was too much. How could he have been so blind, so arrogant, so utterly stupid? There was no answer, nothing but a feeling of incommensurate loss, of unfathomable emptiness, an overwhelming desire to flee the misery of witnessing the loss of his love, his happiness.

Unable to prevent himself, James turned his eyes one last time on Antonietta. Their eyes met, and James turned and fled out of a side door. He wandered aimlessly among a series of corridors before finding an exit. Slowly, stricken by unbearable grief and self-loathing, he descended the steps of the embassy towards a taxi that was waiting for a customer.

It was a very confused and apprehensive Antonietta who awoke on the day of the reception. She realized now that Federico didn't love her any more than she loved him. It was a marriage of convenience for him. What was it for her? A flight from the passion for James that still burned within her? Was it true he hated her? Or did he still love her despite the horrid words he'd spat at her? It was possible, as her uncle maintained, that they were just words born of jealousy at seeing her with another man. Would she have reacted any differently in a similar situation, finding him with another woman and believing he wanted to come back just because she was a countess?

Antonietta put her head in her hands, engrossed in confusion and indecision. She dressed and did her make-up like an automaton. Wisely, she'd prepared her clothes before going to bed: a long black dress, cut low enough to give an idea of her opulent bosom without offending the Pontevedra's Spanish sense of propriety, with the diamond necklace and matching earrings that Federico had given her as an engagement present. She felt a little guilty putting them on as she was not at all sure she would marry him. She'd go along with the engagement reception as it was too late to back out, and she didn't want to cause a scandal. With a feeling of revolt, she chose a minute string and bra as her undergarments, but, given Federico's attitude to pre-marital sex, he was unlikely to be shocked by them.

For the first time in their relationship, Federico came to pick her up. He was using the Embassy car, complete with uniformed chauffeur. "Typically Federico," Antonietta thought. "All very formal and correct." He kissed her lightly on the cheek and complemented her on her attire.

"You look every inch a future Duchess of Pontevedra," he told her.

There was some pride but little warmth in his voice. Antonietta said nothing and merely smiled at this confirmation of Federico's real feelings about her.

They arrived at the embassy and made their way up the stairs leading to the reception hall. Federico looked solemn and said little except to comment on the new portrait of King Juan Carlos hanging over the entrance to the hall. Antonietta was quite silent, absorbed by her inner conflict. Did James still love her? Could she really marry

Federico? She looked over at his handsome, expressionless face and found little comfort.

Antonietta ascended the steps to the platform with hesitation. In an unhabitual gesture of impatience, Federico pulled her after him, which left her even more determined to escape her impending destiny. She caught a glimpse of her parents and thought how a scandal would humiliate them. She felt trapped. She took the glass of champagne offered by her future father-in-law as if in a dream. Everything seemed unreal, she felt as if she wasn't there on that platform between her solemn husband-to-be and his beaming, self-satisfied father.

*Then she saw him!* James's face was a picture of misery and despair. As their eyes met, Antonietta's doubts were swept away. With a shiver of exhilaration, she realized the truth: *James still loved her!* When he turned away and began to walk towards a side door, Antonietta felt that it was as if all hope of love and happiness was vanishing through that door. In a frenzy, she thrust her glass of champagne into the hand of a startled Duke of Pontevedra and, mindless of the scandal, mindless of all those around her, she bolted from the hall and raced down the stairs of the embassy. On the way, without recognizing him, she jostled a tall man dressed in a vivid red cassock.

She reached the entrance, and, as she emerged from the Embassy, she saw James below about to enter a taxi.

"James, stay, stay! she cried in desperation. "Don't leave, please, don't"! In her disarray, Antonietta called out in Spanish.

James stopped, perplexed at being implored in Spanish. He turned round and for a moment stared blankly at Antonietta. Her presence seemed unreal to him, a phantom of his squandered past. What could she possibly want? He shook his head sadly.

"Why...To do what"?

"To marry me"!

For a second or two James looked at Antonietta in disbelief. Then, with one bound he was up the stairs and holding her body close to his for the first time in two years. Their mouths came together, and they kissed with growing passion until James caught a glimpse of an irate Duke of Pontevedra emerging from the embassy followed by his son. He drew away from Antonietta, who looked at him with reproach.

"Come quickly, Antonietta," he told her, smiling at her offended reaction, which was so typical of her. "We have visitors."

Antonietta glanced back. "Oh, my God"!

James took her hand and led her to the waiting taxi. He bundled her inside and jumped in after, narrowly evading the Duke's outstretched hand.

"What's going on, father"? Federico asked his enraged genitor.

"What's going on"? the Duke roared. "What's going on, you cretin, is that your bride has done a bunk"!

The Duke continued to glare after the taxi, which was fast disappearing. A red-robed man came up quietly beside him and, turning away, allowed himself a smile of satisfaction.

Cardinal Palmieri was a happy man.

# EPILOGUE

I T SEEMED STRANGE TO wake up in the bedroom she'd occupied as a child. It was not only pleasant childhood memories that came to mind. This was also the room where she had suffered the first torments of her break with James. Antonietta winced at the thought of the days and months and years of misery and longing she had gone through. Impatiently, she chased away these black recollections. Today was no time for such morbidity. In a few hours she would be marrying the man she loved.

Antonietta focused her mind on the momentous events of the last three months. Her scandalous behavior at the Spanish Embassy, which her mother had only been brought to forgive on hearing that James was the son of a marquis; the ineffable joy of the first kiss since their estrangement and the days and nights of boundless passion that followed; introducing James to her family, and her relief that his aristocratic charm and faultless Spanish had quite seduced her mother; the return to Quebec and reunion with the gang, now supplemented by her friend Petra and Danny's new wife, Bernadette; the amusement at seeing Arbuthnot's reaction when they crossed him on their way to Bill's office; the first meeting with James's children, which went off quite splendidly despite Antonietta's apprehensions. Susanna was enraptured by her stepmother's beauty. Peter was more prosaic. "I hope that's the end of Dad's cooking," was his only comment, but James, who knew his son well, had interpreted this remark as approval of Antonietta.

Other events of the past were less pleasant to recall. Last night she'd been to confession in preparation for the nuptial Mass. She was ashamed of her rampant promiscuity, her lesbian episodes, her lapse from piety, and the travesty of a life she had led in Rome, and it had caused her no little embarrassment to confess these sins to her uncle. They came as no surprise to the Cardinal, which is why she'd chosen him as her confessor, He merely admonished her to put the past behind her and concentrate on the future. He didn't give her a penance, believing that the suffering she had endured over the last two years was sufficient atonement. Nonetheless, she had prayed five decades of the rosary before leaving the Cathedral.

The whole Institute had been shocked by James's decision to resign and leave the Institute. Even James's opponents seemed dismayed. Except for Arbuthnot, who hoped no doubt that this was his golden opportunity, and a few of his friends on the faculty, the others seemed to take the view that the devil you know is better than the devil you don't know. The other members of the gang were horrified and had made strenuous efforts to change James's mind. Even Ilse Bromhoeffer had appealed to him to stay. She was very happy to see James and Antonietta together. "I don't know why," she told Antonietta when they had lunch together, "I had a premonition about you two."

The move to Italy had gone off without a hitch, although Peter and Susanna were clearly nervous about their life in a new country where they didn't even speak the language. Antonietta had taken this matter immediately in hand, and within a few days of arriving in Florence she had hired a tutor to teach them Italian. Susanna was making rapid progress.

On their arrival in Florence, they'd taken over the family's apartment in the city. Their first days were taken up with finding a villa and for James with organizing the investment bank, of which he was to be the CEO. They had found the villa they wanted in Fiesole not far from Antonietta's parents. The bank was proving more of a problem, and James had decided to hire a prominent banker away from HSBC's office in Rome as CEO in his stead, He would act as chairman of the board of directors to keep an eye on affairs on behalf of their two families, who owned the bank.

Antonietta's reminiscences were interrupted by a knock on the bedroom door. It was her mother.

"It's time to get up, Antonietta. It's past nine o'clock, and the wedding's at one."

Antonietta rose and let her mother into the room. She began the laborious process of preparing herself for the wedding: the make-up, the dress, the hairdo, the appropriate jewelry, and the tiara that her mother had worn at her own wedding. It was past twelve when she was ready. The result was worth the time it had taken.

The dress was made of natural silk woven with silver thread continuously from shoulder to floor, creating a gown that was slim in front and flowed out into a large round train in the back. It was tightened at the bust Empire-style, which accentuated Antonietta's generous bosom, and was cut low enough to give a hint of cleavage. Silver and gold threads were embroidered in the dress in shapes of fleur de lys (a symbol of the city of Florence) with fleur de lys flowers and Savoy stars (a symbol of the Italian monarchy) around the sleeves and the base of the dress and train. A tiara glittering with diamonds crowned her long dark hair, which she wore unfettered. Earrings of diamonds and rubies sparkled from her ears, and above her décolleté a simple crucifix hung from an exquisitely worked gold chain. So attired, Antonietta was a vision of lustrous beauty and discrete sensuality.

"James's a lucky man," her father said as he gazed at his daughter in admiration. "He's outdone even Paris. Helen was a mediocrity in comparison with you, Antonietta.

"Quite a complement," her brother Paolo remarked. "After all, Helen's was "the face that launched a thousand ships and burnt the topless towers of Ilium."*

The wedding took place in the Cathedral before a great crowd of well-wishers. The whole della Chiesa and Palmieri families were there, including Antonietta's maternal grandmother, who was ninety-four. All of James's family were also present. Bill was acting as James's best man and Petra as matron of honor. Susanna was one of the bridesmaids, and Peter had been persuaded to be the ringbearer. Among the other attendees were the Duke of Messina and James's friend Rodrigo, who had by now overcome his indignation at Antonietta's humiliation of his cousin. Her uncle, the Cardinal Archbishop, officiated. Once the nuptial Mass ended, Antonietta lit a candle in the Lady Chapel and recited before her effigy the traditional Neapolitan prayer that her mother had recited many years before, and in deference to her mother she did it in Spanish as her mother had done: *"Conceda, O Santa Madre de Díos, que viva mi vida en la pureza, el honor y la fidelidad. En el Nombre del Padre, del Hijo y del Espíritu Santo.*\**"*

After crossing herself, Antonietta returned to James's side, and they walked together down the aisle past the rows of family, friends and distinguished guests.

The wedding reception took place at *Il Salviatino.* James and Antonietta stood at the entrance of the luxurious banqueting hall to receive the invited guests. Just as they thought the chore was over, a tall, elegant, silver-haired man approached James and shook his hand.

"Congratulations, James," he said with a very upper-class British accent.

"Thank you, my lord," James replied, recognizing Her Britannic Majesty's ambassador to the Holy See and a friend of his father's.

Lord Allern turned to Antonietta. "I wish you every happiness, Lady Markham."

Antonietta gave a little start. It was the first time anyone had addressed her by her new title. James looked at her quizzically.

"You won't miss being a countess?'

Antonietta looked deeply into his eyes, her own misty with tears of emotion.

"I am now what I have wanted to be ever since I first cast my eyes upon you."

"In that case, may I be permitted to escort the Lady Antonietta Markham to the banquet"?

Antonietta acquiesced with a radiant smile. They walked hand-in-hand to the head of the main table and took their places between Bill and Petra Leaman. It had been a long and often painful road, but they had finally reached their destination. Perhaps it had been their destiny ever since that fall day in Vienna.

# ENDNOTES

p.iv. The black nobility (Italian: *nobiltà nera*) are those Roman aristocratic families who sided with the Papacy under Pope Pius IX after the Savoy army of the Kingdom of Italy entered Rome on 20 September 1870, overthrew the Pope and the Papal States, and took over the Quirinal Palace, as well as any nobles subsequently ennobled by the Pope prior to the 1929 Lateran Treaty.

p.2. Calcio is an early form of football that originated during the Middle Ages in Italy. Interest in Calcio waned in the early 17th century. However, in 1930 it was reorganized as a game in the Kingdom of Italy. It was widely played by amateurs in streets and squares using handmade balls of cloth or animal skin. Today, three matches are played each year in Piazza Santa Croce in Florence in the third week of June. A team from each quarter of the city is represented. After playing each other in two opening games, the two overall winners go into the yearly final on June 24, the feast of San Giovanni (St. John), the Patron Saint of Florence.

p.3 Pope Leo X reigned from 1513 to 1521.

p.4. The *Accademia della Crusca* is a Florence-based society of scholars of Italian linguistics and philology. It is one of the most important research institutions of the Italian language, as well as the oldest linguistic academy in the world. It was founded in Florence in 1583, and has since been characterized by its efforts to maintain the purity of the Italian language. *Crusca,* which means "bran" in Italian, helps convey the metaphor that its work is similar to winnowing, as also does its emblem depicting a sifter for straining out corrupt words and structures (as bran is separated from wheat). The academy motto is *"Il più bel fior ne coglie"* ('She gathers the fairest flower'), a famous line by the Italian poet Francesco Petrarca. In 1612 the Academy published the first edition of its dictionary, the *Vocabolario degli Accademici della Crusca*, which has served as the model for similar works in French, Spanish, German and English.

p.4. Giacomo Leopardi (1798-1837) is one of the greatest lyric poets in Italian literature. His collection of poems, *I Conti*, are full of introspection and longing.

p.7. Oblates are individuals, either laypersons or clergy, who normally live in general society and who, while not professed monks or nuns, have individually affiliated themselves with a monastic community of their choice. They make a formal, private promise (annually renewable or for life, depending on the monastery with which they are affiliated) to follow the Rule of the Order in their private lives as closely as their individual circumstances and prior commitments permit. Such oblates are considered an extended part of the monastic community.

p.8. The Quiet Revolution was a period of intense socio-political and socio-cultural change in the Canadian province of Quebec that started after the election of 1960. A primary change was an effort by the provincial government to take more direct control over the fields of healthcare and education, which had previously been in the hands of the Roman Catholic Church. It created ministries of Health and Education, expanded the public service, and made massive investments in the public education system and provincial infrastructure.

p.9. DEFAIT is the Canadian Department of Foreign Affairs and International Trade.

p.30. This traditional Catholic prayer reads: REMEMBER, O most gracious Virgin Mary, that never was it known that anyone who fled to thy protection, implored thy help, or sought thy intercession was left unaided. Inspired with this confidence, I fly to thee, O Virgin of virgins, my Mother; to thee do I come; before thee I stand, sinful and sorrowful. O Mother of the Word Incarnate, despise not my petitions, but in thy mercy hear and answer me. Amen.

p.40. The rosary mysteries are the joyful, light, sorrowful and glorious mysteries. The glorious mysteries comprise the Resurrection of Jesus, the Ascension of Jesus, the Descent of Holy Spirit, the Assumption of the Virgin Mary and the Coronation of the Virgin Mary

p.48. The *Estate Fiesolana* is a festival that takes place between June and August and proposes a calendar of musical and theatre events including classical and not so classical concerts as well as comedy shows and classical theatre.\

p.57. Louis XVIII, a very much an underrated monarch, once remarked: "La ponctualité est la politesse des rois." (Punctuality is the politeness of kings)

p.63. Wellington was referring to his victory over Napoleon in the Battle of Waterloo.

p.70. The Carmenere grape variety was once very popular in Bordeaux but was wiped out during the phylloxera plague in 1867. Fortunately, it had been imported into Chile in 1850 and has survived there. It is similar to Merlot but richer and sturdier.

p.72. A pisco sour is an alcoholic cocktail of Peruvian origin that is typical of the cuisines from Peru and Chile. The drink's name comes from pisco, which is its base liquor, and the cocktail term sour, in reference to sour citrus juice and sweetener components. The Peruvian pisco sour uses Peruvian pisco as the base liquor and adds freshly squeezed lime juice, simple syrup, ice, egg white, and Angostura bitters. The Chilean version is similar, but uses Chilean pisco and Pica lime and excludes the bitters and egg white.

p.76. In Argentina and some other countries in South America, Spanish is referred to as Castilian (*castellano* in Spanish).

p.76. The inhabitants of Buenos Aires are called *porteños* or *porteñas*.

p.76. The girl is telling the truth. The British invaded what is now Argentina twice in 1806 and 1807. They were beaten back on both occasions.

p.77. *Churrasco* is a boneless cut of beef that is sliced slightly thin as a steak and grilled over hot coals or on a very hot skillet. It is a prominent feature in the cuisine of Brazil, Uruguay, and Argentina.

p.81. A French expression, which means here "knowing what you are doing."

p.97. There are many versions of the tale of Tristan and Isolde. Perhaps the most well-known is that told in Wagner's eponymous opera. Attempting to poison Tristan for killing her fiancé and then to kill herself, Isolde is fooled by her maid into offering him instead a love potion from which she also drinks. The overwhelming passion for each other than ensues leads the pair to become lovers despite Isolde's marriage to Tristan's uncle, King Mark. Banished and wounded, Tristan dies just as Isolde arrives to heal him and she herself dies from passion after singing one of Wagner's greatest arias, *Isoldes Liebestod*.

p.102. The princely House of Grimaldi is known for the apparent ease with which it obtains annulments from the Catholic Church.

p.102. A whore's sauce. The name comes from the fact that this is supposed to be the favorite dish of Rome's ladies of the night.

p.157. England won, but the winning goal was disputed by Germany.

p.159. Laura Pausini is not well known in North America, but she was once the most popular Latin singer in Europe and Latin America.

p.181. "This love of mine is indelible. I could never any more live without you."

p.181. "I love you with a wild passion. The moment that I saw you the first time in church, like Isolde, I lost myself in you."

p.182. "I have never seen a woman like this one." These are the words of Des Grieux in Puccini's opera *Manon Lescaut*.

p.187. "As I have already told you, I can no longer liver without you."

p.188. Floria Tosca is the heroine of the opera *Tosca* by Giacomo Puccini (1858-1924). It is thought by many to be his best work on account of its emotional intensity and the sheer beauty of the music.

p.188. "What eyes in the world can compare with your black and glowing eyes? It is in them that my whole being fastens, eyes soft with love and rich with anger. Where in the whole world are eyes to compare with your black eyes"?

p.188. "How well you know the art of making yourself loved."

p.198. *Il Piacere* (Pleasure) is a novel by Gabriele d'Annunzio (1863-1938) that tells of a passionate love affair between Count Andres Sperelli-Fieschi d'Ugenta and Elena Muti, the Duchess of Scerni. When Elena suddenly and without explanation deserts Sperelli, he reacts with self-destructive bitterness and vilifies his former mistress in his own mind by perverting his recollections of the affair.

p.206. "I torment you without a pause." These words are addressed by Tosca to her lover, Cavaradossi

p.220. *"Shit, yes"!* In her annoyance, Antonietta is uncharacteristically vulgar.

p.220. *Il Gattopardo* (The Leopard) is a novel that chronicles the changes in Sicilian life and society during the Risorgimento. Published posthumously in 1958, it became the top-selling novel in Italian history and is considered one of the most important novels in modern Italian literature. The novel was also made into an award-winning 1963 film of the same name, directed by Luchino Visconti and starring Burt Lancaster, Claudia Cardinale and Alain Delon.

p.243. In January 1647, the Scots handed over Charles I of England to the English, precipitating a series of events that would lead to the king's execution two years later.

p.243. The epistle of St. James stresses the need for good works. Luther, who believed in justification by faith alone, dismissed it as an "epistle of straw."

p.244. Edward Heath was Prime Minister of the United Kingdom from 1970 to 1974.

p.245. Non-Britons are often surprised to learn that staunchly monarchist England was a republic from the execution of the king, Charles I, in 1649 to 1660 when his son, Charles II, was recalled to the throne.

p.258. "As if there hasn't ever been love."

p.269. Mayerling was the hunting lodge where Archduke Rudolf, the heir to the Austro-Hungarian Crown, committed suicide with his mistress.

p.277. *The Instituto Tecnológico y de Estudios Superiores de Monterrey* (The Monterrey Institute of Technology and Higher Studies) is a secular and coeducational private university based in Monterrey, Mexico, which has grown to include 35 campuses throughout Mexico It is widely recognized as one of the most prestigious universities in Larin America.

p.288. *Zarzuela* is a Spanish lyric-dramatic genre that alternates between spoken and sung scenes, the latter incorporating operatic and popular song, as well as dance. The name derives from the Zarzuela Palace, where this type of entertainment was first presented to the Spanish King Philip IV in 1657.

p.307. "Such is the profound misery of profound love." These words are spoken by Scarpia in Puccini's opera *Tosca*.

p.336. Pablo Neruda (1904-1973) became known as a poet when he was 13 years old, and wrote in a variety of styles, including surrealist poems, historical epics, overtly political manifestos, a prose autobiography, and passionate love poems such as the ones in his collection *Twenty Love Poems and a Song of Despair* (1924). He was awarded the Nobel Prize for Literature in 1971.

p.341. Fangio (1911—1995) was an Argentine racing car driver. He dominated the first decade of Formula One racing, winning the World Drivers' Championship five times. He was one of the world's most successful racing drivers. Susan Barrantes (1937 1998) was the mother of Sarah, Duchess of York, and the maternal grandmother of princesses Beatrice and Eugenie. Her elopement with an Argentinian polo player caused a stir in social circles. After his death, she became a film producer in Buenos Aires, but was killed in a road accident.

p.366. These words are uttered by Henry V in Shakespeare's eponymous play.

p.384. A looney is a one-dollar Canadian coin.

p.443. ITAM (*Instituto Tecnológico Autónomo de México*) is a leading Mexican business school based in Mexico City.

p.474. French motorways are expensive, but they are studded with pleasant stopovers, replete with restaurants that even serve wine! They are called *aires*.

p.477. "Of course, I love you."

p.480. My dear James. I cannot pretend to you or myself that I have not fallen in love with you, but I cannot marry you. My life is here in Buenos Aires. It is not perhaps the perfect or even the most respectable life, but it is the one I am comfortable with. Please leave me to live it. I would not be strong enough to resist if you came to see me, but our marriage would be a catastrophe for both of us. I shall never forget you. Carolina.

p.483. It is said of the Edmonton climate that the only month it does not snow is July, and you can't be certain of that!

p.547. The lines spoken by Dr. Faustus of Helen of Troy in Marlowe's eponymous play.

p.548. "Grant, Holy Mother of God, that I may live my life in purity, honor and fidelity. In the Name of the Father, the Son and the Holy Spirit."